The chances tha ... ... *hit earth head-o* ... *a million.*
Then one in a thousand.
Then one in a hundred.
And then . . .

LUCIFER'S HAMMER

LUCIFER'S HAMMER

Larry Niven
and
Jerry Pournelle

FAWCETT CREST • NEW YORK

LUCIFER'S HAMMER

THIS BOOK CONTAINS THE COMPLETE TEXT OF
THE ORIGINAL HARDCOVER EDITION.

Published by Fawcett Crest Books, a unit of CBS Publi-
cations, the Consumer Publishing Division of CBS Inc., by
arrangement with Playboy Press.

ISBN: 0-449-23599-8

Printed in the United States of America

20   19   18   17   16   15   14   13   12   11

To Neil Armstrong and Buz Aldrin, the first men to walk on another world; to Michael Collins, who waited; and to those who died trying, Gus Grissom, Roger Chaffee, Ed White, Georgi Dobrovolsky, Viktor Patsayev, Nikolai Volkov, and all the others.

ACKNOWLEDGMENTS

Excerpts from GIFFORD LECTURES, 1948 by Emil Brunner.

Excerpt from a private speech by Robert Heinlein. Reprinted by permission.

From "Pure, Sweet, Culture" by Frank Garparik. Copyright © 1977 by Frank Garparik. Used with permission of the author.

From How The World Will End by Daniel Cohen. Copyright © 1973, McGraw-Hill. Used with permission of McGraw-Hill Book Co.

From The Naked Ape by Desmond Morris. Copyright © McGraw-Hill 1967. Used with permission of McGraw-Hill Book Company.

Excerpt from The Cosmic Connection by Carl Sagan. Copyright © 1973 by Carl Sagan and Jerome Agel. Reprinted by permission of Doubleday & Company, Inc.

Excerpts from The Coming Dark Age by Roberto Vacca, translated from the Italian by Dr. J. S. Whale. Translation Copyright © 1973 by Doubleday & Company, Inc. Reprinted by permission of Doubleday & Company, Inc.

From Moons and Planets: An Introduction to Planetary Science by William Hartman. Copyright © 1972, Wadsworth Publishing Co., Inc. Used with permission of Wadsworth Publishing Co., Inc.

Excerpts from Sovereignty by Bertrand de Jouvenal. Copyright © 1957 by University of Chicago Press. Used with permission of University of Chicago Press.

From The Elements Rage by Frank W. Lane. Copyright © 1965 by Chilton Book Co. Used with permission of Chilton Book Co.

Song "The Friggin Falcon" © 1966 by Theodore R. Cogswell. All rights reserved, including the right of public performance for profit. Used by permission of the author and the author's agent, Kirby McCauley.

DRAMATIS PERSONAE

TIMOTHY HAMNER, amateur astronomer

ARTHUR CLAY JELLISON, United States Senator from California

MAUREEN JELLISON, his daughter

HARVEY RANDALL, Producer-Director for NBS Television

MRS. LORETTA STEWART RANDALL

BARRY PRICE, Supervising Engineer, San Joaquin Nuclear Project

DOLORES MUNSON, Executive Secretary to Barry Price

EILEEN SUSAN HANCOCK, Assistant Manager for Corrigan's Plumbing Supplies of Burbank

LEONILLA ALEXANDROVNA MALIK, M.D., physician and *kosmonaut*

MARK CZESCU, biker

GORDON VANCE, Bank President and neighbor to Harvey Randall

ANDY RANDALL, Harvey Randall's son

CHARLIE BASCOMB, cameraman

MANUEL ARGUILEZ, sound technician

DR. CHARLES SHARPS, Planetary Scientist and Project Director, California Institute of Technology's Jet Propulsion Laboratories

PENELOPE JOYCE WILSON, fashion designer

FRED LAUREN, convicted sex offender

COL. JOHN BAKER, USAF, astronaut

HARRY NEWCOMBE, letter carrier, US Postal Service

MRS. DORA COX, Housekeeper and wife of the foreman of Senator Jellison's ranch

GEORGE CHRISTOPHER, rancher, neighbor to Senator Jellison

ALICE COX, schoolgirl and horsewoman

JOE CORRIGAN, owner of Corrigan's Plumbing Supplies

ALIM NASSOR, formerly George Washington Carver Davis, one-time political leader

HAROLD DAVIS, Alim Nassor's natural brother

THE REVEREND HENRY ARMITAGE

DR. DAN FORRESTER, Member of technical staff, JPL

LT. COL. RICK DELANTY, USAF, astronaut

MRS. GLORIA DELANTY

BRIGADIER PIETER JAKOV, *kosmonaut*

FRANK STONER, biker

JOANNA MACPHERSON, Mark Czescu's roommate

COLLEEN DARCY, bank teller

GENERAL THOMAS BAMBRIDGE, USAF, Commander in Chief, Strategic Air Command

JOHN KIM, Press Secretary to the Mayor of Los Angeles

THE HONORABLE BENTLEY ALLEN, Mayor of Los Angeles

ERIC LARSEN, Patrolman, Burbank PD

JOE HARRIS, Investigator, Burbank PD

COMET WARDENS, a Southern California religious group

MAJOR BENNET ROSTEN, USAF, Minuteman Squadron Commander

MRS. MARIE VANCE, wife of Gordon Vance

HARRY STIMMS, automobile dealer in Tujunga, California

CORPORAL ROGER GILLINGS, Army

SERGEANT THOMAS HOOKER, Army

MARTY ROBBINS, Tim Hamner's assistant and caretaker

JASON GILLCUDDY, writer

HUGO BECK, owner of a commune in the foothills of the High Sierra

Prologue

Before the sun burned, before the planets formed, there were chaos and the comets.

Chaos was a local thickening in the interstellar medium. Its mass was great enough to attract itself, to hold itself, and it thickened further. Eddies formed. Particles of dust and frozen gas drifted together, and touched, and clung. Flakes formed, and then loose snowballs of frozen gases. Over the ages a whirlpool pattern developed, a fifth of a light-year across. The center contracted further. Local eddies, whirling frantically near the center of the storm, collapsed to form planets.

It formed as a cloud of snow, far from the whirlpool's axis. Ices joined the swarm, but slowly, slowly, a few molecules at a time. Methane, ammonia, carbon dioxide; and sometimes denser objects struck it and embedded themselves, so that it held rocks, and iron. Now it was a single stable mass. Other ices formed, chemicals that could only be stable in the interstellar cold.

It was four miles across when the disaster came.

The end was sudden. In no more than fifty years, the wink of an eye in its lifetime, the whirlpool's center collapsed. A new sun burned fearfully bright.

Myriads of comets flashed to vapor in that hellish flame. Planets lost their atmospheres. A great wind of light pressure stripped all the loose gas and dust from the inner system and hurled it at the stars.

It hardly noticed. It was two hundred times as far from the sun as the newly formed planet Neptune. The new sun was no more than an uncommonly bright star, gradually dimming now.

Down in the maelstrom there was frantic activity. Gases boiled out of the rocks of the inner system. Complex chemicals developed in the seas of the third planet. Endless hurricanes boiled across and within the gas-giant worlds. The inner worlds would never know calm.

The only real calm was at the edge of interstellar space, in the halo, where millions of thinly spread comets, each as far from its nearest brother as Earth is from Mars, cruise forever through the cold black vacuum. Here its endless quiet sleep could last for billions of years . . . but not forever. Nothing lasts forever.

1

THE ANVIL

Against boredom, even the gods themselves struggle in vain.
Nietzsche

January: The Portent

The bay-trees in our country are all wither'd
And meteors fright the fixed stars of heaven;
The pale-faced moon looks bloody on the earth
And lean-look'd prophets whisper fearful change.
These signs forerun the death or fall of kings.

William Shakespeare, *Richard II*

The blue Mercedes turned into the big circular drive of the Beverly Hills mansion at precisely five after six. Julia Sutter was understandably startled. "Good God, George, it's Tim! And dead on time."

George Sutter joined her at the window. That was Tim's car, yup. He grunted and turned back to the bar. His wife's parties were always important events, so why, after weeks of careful engineering and orchestration, was she terrified that no one would show up? The psychosis was so common there ought to be a name for it.

Tim Hamner, though, and on time. That was strange. Tim's money was third-generation. Old money, by Los Angeles standards, and Tim had a lot of it. He only came to parties when he wanted to.

The Sutters' architect had been in love with concrete. There were square walls and square angles for the house, and softly curving free-form pools in the gardens outside; not unusual for Beverly Hills, but startling to easterners. To their right was a traditional Monterey villa of white stucco and red tile roofs, to the left a Norman château magically transplanted to California. The Sutter place was set well back from the street so that it seemed divorced from the tall palms

12

the city fathers had decreed for this part of Beverly Hills. A great loop of drive ran up to the house itself. On the porch stood eight parking attendants, agile young men in red jackets.

Hamner left the motor running and got out of the car. The "key left" reminder screamed at him. Ordinarily Tim would have snarled a powerful curse upon Ralph Nader's hemorrhoids, but tonight he never noticed. His eyes were dreamy; his hand patted at his coat pocket, then stole inside. The parking attendant hesitated. People didn't usually tip until they were leaving. Hamner kept walking, dreamy-eyed, and the attendant drove away.

Hamner glanced back at the red-coated young men, wondering if one or another might be interested in astronomy. They were almost always from UCLA or Loyola University. Could be . . . Reluctantly he decided against it and went inside, his hand straying from time to time to feel the telegram crackle under his fingers.

The big double doors opened onto an enormous area that extended right through the house. Large arches, rimmed by red brick, separated the entry from the living areas: a mere suggestion of walls between rooms. The floor was continuous throughout: brown tile laid with bright mosaic patterns. Of the two hundred and more guests expected, fewer than a dozen were clustered near the bar. Their talk was bright and cheery, louder than necessary. They looked isolated in all that empty space, all that expanse of tables with candles and patterned tablecloths. There were nearly as many uniformed attendants as guests. Hamner noticed none of this. He'd grown up with it.

Julia Sutter broke from the tiny group of guests and hurried to meet him. There was a tight look around her eyes: Her face had been lifted, and was younger than her hands. She made a kissing motion a fraction of an inch from Tim's cheek and said, "Timmy, I'm glad to see you!" Then she noticed his radiant smile.

She drew back a little and her eyes narrowed. The note of mock concern in her voice covered real worry. "My God, Timmy! What have you been smoking?"

Tim Hamner was tall and bony, with just a touch of paunch to break the smooth lines. His long face was built for melancholy. His mother's family had owned a highly successful cemetery-mortuary, and it showed. Tonight, though, his face was cracked wide apart in a blazing smile, and there was a

13

strange light in his eyes. He said, "The Hamner-Brown Comet!"

"Oh!" Julia stared. "What?" That didn't make sense. You don't smoke a comet. She tried to puzzle it out while her eyes roved to her husband—was he having a second drink already?—to the door—when were the others coming? The invitations had been explicit. The important guests were coming early—weren't they?—and couldn't stay late, and—

She heard the low purr of a big car outside, and through the narrow windows framing the door saw half a dozen people spilling out of a dark limousine. Tim would have to take care of himself. She patted his arm and said, "That's nice, Timmy. Excuse me, please?" A hasty intimate smile and she was gone.

If it bothered Hamner it didn't show. He ambled toward the bar. Behind him Julia went to welcome her most important guest, Senator Jellison, with his entourage. He always brought everyone, administrative assistants as well as family. Tim Hamner's smile was blazing when he reached the bar.

"Good evening, Mr. Hamner."

"Good it is. Tonight I'm walking on pink clouds. Congratulate me, Rodrigo, they're going to name a comet after me!"

Michael Rodriguez, laying out glasses behind the bar, missed a beat. "A comet?"

"Right. Hamner-Brown Comet. It's coming, Rodrigo, you can see it, oh, around June, give or take a few weeks." Hamner took out the telegram and opened it with a snap.

"We will not see it from Los Angeles," Rodriguez laughed. "What may I serve you tonight?"

"Scotch rocks. You *could* see it. It could be as big as Halley's Comet." Hamner took the drink and looked about. There was a group around George Sutter. The knot of people drew Tim like a magnet. He clutched the telegram in one hand and his drink in another, as Julia brought the new guests over and introduced them.

Senator Arthur Clay Jellison was built something like a brick, muscular rather than overweight. He was bulky, jovial and blessed with thick white hair. He was photogenic as hell, and half the people in the country would have recognized him. His voice sounded exactly as it did on TV: resonant, enveloping, so that everything he said took on a mysterious importance.

Maureen Jellison, the Senator's daughter, had long, dark red hair and pale clear skin and a beauty that would have

14

made Tim Hamner shy on any other night; but when Julia Sutter turned to him and (finally!) said, "What was that about a—"

"Hamner-Brown Comet!" Tim waved the telegram. "Kitt Peak Observatory had confirmed my sighting! It's a real comet, it's *my* comet, they're naming it after me!"

Maureen Jellison's eyebrows went up slightly. George Sutter drained his glass before asking the obvious question. "Who's Brown?"

Hamner shrugged; his untasted drink slopped a little onto the carpet, and Julia frowned. "Nobody's ever heard of him," Tim said. "But the International Astronomical Union says it was a simultaneous sighting."

"So what you own is half a comet," said George Sutter.

Tim laughed, quite genuinely. "The day you own half a comet, George, I'll buy all those bonds you keep trying to sell me. And buy your drinks all night." He downed his scotch rocks in two swallows.

When he looked up he'd lost his audience. George was headed back to the bar. Julia had Senator Jellison's arm and was steering him toward new arrivals. The Senator's administrative assistants followed in her wake.

"Half a comet is quite a lot," Maureen said. Tim Hamner turned to find her still there. "Tell me, how do you see anything through the smog?"

She sounded interested. She looked interested. And she could have gone with her father. The scotch was a warm trace in his throat and stomach. Tim began telling her about his mountain observatory, not too many miles past Mount Wilson but far enough into the Angeles Mountains that the lights from Pasadena didn't ruin the seeing. He kept food supplies there, and an assistant, and he'd spent months of nights watching the sky, tracking known asteroids and the outer moons, letting his eye and brain learn the territory, and forever watching for the dot of light that shouldn't be there, the anomaly that would . . .

Maureen Jellison had a familiar glazed look in her eyes. He asked, "Hey, am I boring you?"

She was instantly apologetic. "No, I'm sorry, it was just a stray thought."

"I know I sometimes get carried away."

She smiled and shook her head; a wealth of deep red hair rippled and danced. "No, really. Dad's on the Finance Subcommittee for Science and Astronautics. He loves pure

15

science, and I caught the bug from him. I was just . . . You're a man who knows what he wants, and you've found it. Not many can say that." She was suddenly very serious.

Tim laughed, embarrassed; he was only just getting used to the fact. "What can I do for an encore?"

"Yes, exactly. What do you do when you've walked on the moon, and then they cancel the space program?"

"Why . . . I don't know. I've heard they sometimes have troubles. . . ."

"Don't worry about it," Maureen said. "You're on the moon now. Enjoy it."

∎

The hot dry wind known as the Santa Ana blew across the Los Angeles hills, clearing the city of smog. Lights glittered and danced in the early darkness. Harvey Randall, his wife, Loretta, beside him, drove his green Toronado with the windows open, relishing the summer weather in January. When they arrived at the Sutter place he turned the car over to the red-jacketed attendant, and paused while Loretta adjusted her smile before moving through the big front doors.

They found the usual mob scene for a Beverly Hills party. A hundred people were scattered among the little tables, and another hundred in clumps; a mariachi group in one corner played gay background music and the singer, deprived of his microphone, was still doing pretty well telling everyone about the state of his *corazon*. They greeted their hostess and parted: Loretta found a conversation, and Harvey located the bar by searching out the thickest cluster of people. He collected two gin and tonics.

Bits of conversation ricocheted around him. "We didn't let him on the white rug, you see. So the dog had the cat 'treed' in the middle of the rug and was pacing sentry duty around the perimeter. . . ."

". . . was this beautiful young chick one seat ahead of me on the plane. A real knockout, even if all I could see was her hair and the back of her head. I was thinking of a way to meet her when she looked back and said, 'Uncle Pete! What are *you* doing here?' "

". . . man, it's helped a lot! When I call and say it's *Commissioner* Robbins, I get right through. Haven't had a customer miss a good option since the Mayor appointed me."

They stuck in his mind, these bits and pieces of story. For

Harvey Randall it was an occupational hazard of the TV documentary business; he couldn't help listening. He didn't want to, really. People fascinated him. He would have liked to follow up some of these glimpses into other minds.

He looked around for Loretta, but she was too short to stand out in this crowd. Instead he picked out high-piled hair of unconvincing orange-red: Brenda Tey, who'd been talking to Loretta before Harvey went to the bar. He made for that point, easing past shoals of elbows attached to drinks.

"Twenty billion bucks, and all we got was rocks! Those damn big rockets, billions of dollars dropped into the drink. Why spend all that money out there when we could be—"

"Bullshit," said Harvey.

George Sutter turned in surprise. "Oh. Hello, Harv. . . . It'll be the same with the Shuttle. Just the same. It's all money thrown down the drain—"

"That turns out not to be the case." The voice was clear, sweet and penetrating. It cut right through George's manifesto, and it couldn't be ignored. George stopped in mid-sentence.

Harvey found a spectacular redhead in a green one-shoulder party gown. Her eyes met his when he looked at her, and he looked away first. He smiled and said, "Is that the same as bullshit?"

"Yes. But more tactful." She grinned at him, and Harvey let his own smile stay in place instead of fading away. She turned to the attack. "Mr. Sutter, NASA didn't spend the Apollo money on hardware. We bought research on how to build the hardware, and we've still got it. Knowledge can't go into the drink. As for the Shuttle, that's the price to get out there where we can really learn things, and not much of a price at that. . . ."

A woman's breast and shoulder rubbed playfully against Harvey's arm. That had to be Loretta, and it was. He handed her her drink. His own was half gone. When Loretta started to speak he gestured her silent, a little more rudely than he usually did, and ignored her look of protest.

The redhead knew her stuff. If careful reason and logic could win arguments, she won. But she had a lot more: She had every male's eye, and a slow southern drawl that made every word count, and a voice so pure and musical that any interruption seemed stuttered or mumbled.

The unequal contest ended when George discovered that his drink was empty and, with visible relief, broke for the bar.

Smiling triumph, the girl turned toward Harvey, and he nodded his congratulations.

"I'm Harvey Randall. My wife, Loretta."

"Maureen Jellison. Most pleased." She frowned for half a second. "I remember now. You were the last U.S. newsman in Cambodia." She shook hands, formally, with Harvey and Loretta. "And wasn't your newscopter shot down over there?"

"Twice," Loretta said proudly. "Harvey brought his Air Force pilot out. Fifty miles of enemy lines."

Maureen nodded gravely. She was fifteen years younger than the Randalls, and seemed very self-possessed. "So now you're here. Are you natives?"

"I am," Harvey said. "Loretta's from Detroit—"

"Grosse Pointe," Loretta said automatically.

"—but I was born in L.A." Harvey could never quite bring himself to tell Loretta's half-truth for her. "We're scarce, we natives."

"And what do they have you doing now?" Maureen asked.

"Documentaries. News features, mostly," Harvey said.

"I know who you are," Loretta said in some awe. "I just met your father. Senator Jellison."

"That's right." Maureen looked thoughtful, then grinned broadly. "Say, if you do news features there's somebody you ought to meet. Tim Hamner."

Harvey frowned. The name seemed familiar, but he couldn't place it. "Why?"

Loretta said, "Hamner? A young man with a frightening grin?" She giggled. "He's a teensy bit drunk. He wouldn't let anyone else talk. At all. He owns half a comet."

"That's him," Maureen said. Her smile made Loretta feel part of a conspiracy.

"He also owns a lot of soap," Harvey said.

It was Maureen's turn to look blank.

"I just remembered," Harvey said. "He inherited the Kalva Soap Company."

"May be, but he's prouder of the comet," Maureen said. "I don't blame him. Dear old Dad could have been President once, but he's never come close to discovering a comet." She scanned the room until she spotted her target. "The tall man in the suit with white and maroon in it. You'll know him by his smile. Get anywhere near him and he'll tell you all about it."

Harvey felt Loretta tugging at his arm, and reluctantly looked away from Maureen. When he looked back someone else had snared her. He went to fetch another pair of drinks.

As always, Harvey Randall drank too much and wondered why he came to these parties. But he knew; Loretta saw them as a way to participate in his life. She didn't enjoy his field trips. The one attempt to take her on a hike with their son had been a disaster. When she went with him on location she wanted to stay in the best hotels, and if she dutifully came to the small bars and gathering places Harvey preferred, it was obvious that she was working hard to hide her unhappiness.

But she was very much at home at parties like this one, and tonight's had been especially good. She even managed a private conversation with Senator Jellison. Harvey left her with the Senator and went to find more drinks. "Light on the gin, Rodriguez. Please."

The bartender smiled and mixed the drink without comment. Harvey stood with it. Tim Hamner was alone at one of the little tables. He was looking at Harvey, but the eyes were dreamy; they saw nothing. And that smile. Harvey made his way across the room and dropped into the other chair at the table. "Mr. Hamner? Harvey Randall. Maureen Jellison said I should say 'Comet.'"

Hamner's face came alight. The grin broadened, if that were possible. He took a telegram out of his pocket and waved it. "Right! The sighting was confirmed this afternoon. Hamner-Brown Comet."

"You skipped a step."

"She didn't tell you *anything*? Well! I'm Tim Hamner. Astronomer. Well, not professional, but my equipment's professional. And I work at it—anyway. I'm an amateur astronomer. A week ago I found a smear of light not far from Neptune. A dim smear. It didn't belong there. I kept looking at it, and it moved. I studied it long enough to be sure, and then I reported it. It's a new comet. Kitt Peak just confirmed it. The IAU is naming it after me—and Brown."

For just that moment, envy flashed through Harvey Randall like a lightning strike. It was gone as quickly; he made it go, shoving it into the bottom of his mind where he could pull it up and look at it later. He was ashamed of it. But without that flash he would have asked a more tactful first question. "Who's Brown?"

Hamner's face didn't change. "Gavin Brown is a kid in Centerville, Iowa. Ground his own mirror to build his tele-

19

scope. He reported the comet at the same time I did. The IAU rules it a simultaneous sighting. If I hadn't waited to be certain . . ." Hamner shrugged and continued, "I called Brown this afternoon. Sent him a plane ticket, because I want to meet him. He didn't even want to come until I promised to show him around the solar observatory at Mount Wilson. That's all he really cares about! Sunspots! He found the comet by accident!"

"When will we see this comet? That is," Harvey backtracked, "will it be visible at all?"

"Much too early to ask. Wait a month. Watch the news."

"I'm not supposed to watch the news. I'm supposed to report the news," said Harvey. "And this could be news. Tell me more."

Hamner was eager to do that. He rattled on, while Harvey nodded with a broadening grin. Beautiful! You didn't have to know what all the words meant to know the equipment was expensive, and probably photogenic to boot. Expensive and elaborate equipment, and the kid with a bent pin for a hook and a willow stick for a rod had caught just as big a fish as the millionaire!

Millionaire. "Mr. Hamner, if this comet turns out to be worth a documentary—"

"Well, it might. And the discovery would be. How amateur astronomers can be important . . ."

Hooked, by God! "What I was going to ask was, if we can make a documentary on the comet, would Kalva Soap be interested in sponsoring it?"

The change in Hamner was subtle, but it was there. Harvey instantly revised his opinion of the man. Hamner had a lot of experience with people after his money. He was an enthusiast, but hardly a fool.

"Tell me, Mr. Randall, didn't you do that thing on the Alaskan glacier?"

"Harvey. Yes."

"It stunk."

"Sure did," Harvey agreed. "The sponsor insisted on control. And got it. And used it. I didn't inherit control of a big company." And to hell with you, too, Mr. Timothy Comet Hamner.

"But I did. And this would be worth doing. You did the Hell's Gate Dam story too, didn't you?"

"Yes."

"I liked that one."

"So did I."

"Good." Hamner nodded several times. "Look, this could be worth sponsoring. Even if the comet never becomes visible, and I think it will. Lord knows they spend enough of the advertising budget sponsoring crap that nobody wants to watch. Might as well tell a story worth telling. Harvey, you need a refill."

They went to the bar. The party was thinning out fast. The Jellisons were just leaving, but Loretta had found another conversation. Harvey recognized a city councilman who'd been after Harvey's station to do a show on a park that was his current goal. He probably thought Loretta would influence Harvey—which was correct—and that Harvey had influence over what the network and its Los Angeles station did—which was a laugh.

Rodriguez was busy for the moment and they stood at the bar. "There's all kinds of excellent new equipment for studying comets," Hamner said. "Including a big orbital telescope only used once, for Kahoutek. Scientists all over the world will want to know how comets differ, how Kahoutek was different from Hamner-Brown. Lot of scientists right here. Cal Tech, and the planetary astronomers at JPL. They'll all want to know more about Hamner-Brown."

Hamner-Brown resonated in his mouth, and Tim Hamner obviously loved the taste. "You see, comets aren't just something pretty up in the sky. They're left over from the big gas cloud that formed the solar system. If we could really learn something about comets—maybe send up a space probe— we'd know more about what the original cloud of gas and dust was like before it fell in on itself and made the Sun and the planets and moons and things like that."

"You're sober," Harvey said in wonder.

Hamner was startled. Then he laughed. "I meant to get drunk just to celebrate, but I guess I've been talking instead of drinking." Rodriguez came over and put drinks in front of them. Hamner lifted his scotch rocks in a salute.

"The way your eyes glow," Harvey said, "I thought you must be drunk. But what you say makes a lot of sense. I doubt we could get a space probe launched, but what the hell, we could try. Only you're talking about more than a single documentary for something like that. Listen, is there a chance? I mean, could we send a probe *into* the comet? Because I know some people in the aerospace industry, and . . ."

And, thought Harvey, that *would* be a story. Who can I get for editor? he wondered. And Charlie Bascomb's available to do camera. . . .

"Jellison, too," Hamner said. "He'd be for it. But look, Harv, I know a lot about comets, but not *that* much. It's all guesswork right now. Be a few months before Hamner-Brown gets to perihelion." He added quickly, "Closest point to the Sun. Which isn't the same as the closest point to the Earth. . . ."

"How close will that be?" Harvey asked.

Hamner shrugged. "Haven't analyzed the orbit yet. Maybe close. Anyway, Hamner-Brown will be moving *fast* when it rounds the Sun. It will have fallen all the way from the halo, out there beyond Pluto, a *long* way. You understand, I won't really be computing the orbit. I'll have to wait for the professionals, just like you."

Harvey nodded. They lifted their glasses and drank.

"But I like the idea," Hamner said. "There's going to be a lot of *scientific* pressure for studies of Hamner-Brown, and it wouldn't hurt to push the idea with the general public. I like it."

"Of course," Harvey said carefully, "I'd have to have a firm commitment on sponsorship before I could do much work on this. Are you sure Kalva Soap would be interested? The show might pull a good audience—but it might not."

Hamner nodded. "Kahoutek," he said. "They were burned on that one before. Nobody wants to be disappointed again."

"Yeah."

"So you can count on Kalva Soap. Let's get across why it's important to study comets even if you can't see them. Because I can promise the sponsorship, but I can't promise the comet will deliver. It might not be visible at all. Don't tell people anything more than that."

"I have a reuptation for getting my facts straight."

"When your sponsor doesn't interfere," Hamner said.

"Even then, *I* have my facts straight."

"Good. But right now there aren't any facts. Hamner-Brown is pretty big. It has to be, or I couldn't have seen it out that far. And it looks to get pretty close to the Sun. It has a chance of being spectacular, but really, it's impossible to tell. The tail could stretch way-y-y out, or it could just blow away. It depends on the comet."

"Yeah. Look," Harvey said, "can you name one newsman who lost his reputation because of Kahoutek?" He nodded at the puzzled look that got. "Right. None. No chance. The public blamed the astronomers for blowing it all out of proportion. Nobody blamed the news people."

"Why should they? You were quoting the astronomers."

"Half the time," Harvey agreed. "But we quoted the ones who said exciting things. Two interviews. One man says Kahoutek is going to be the Big Christmas Comet. Another says, well, it's going to be a comet, but you might not see it without field glasses. Guess which tape gets shown on the six o'clock news?"

Hamner laughed. He was draining his glass when Julia Sutter came over.

"Busy, Tim?" she asked, but didn't wait for an answer. "Your cousin Barry is making a fool of himself out in the kitchen. Can you get him to go home?" She spoke low and urgently.

Harvey hated her. *Was* Hamner sober? Would he remember any of this in the morning? Damn.

"Be right with you, Julia," Hamner said. He broke free and made his way back to Harvey. "Just remember, our series on Hamner-Brown is going to be honest. Even if it costs ratings. Kalva Soap can afford it. When do you want to start?"

Maybe there was some justice in the world after all. "Right away, Tim. I want some footage of you and Gavin Brown up at Mount Wilson. And his comments when you show him your setup."

Hamner grinned. He liked that. "Right. Call you tomorrow."

Loretta slept quietly in the other bed.

Harvey had been staring at the ceiling long enough. He knew this feeling. He would have to get up.

He got up. He made cocoa in a big mug and carried it into his study. Kipling greeted him with tail-thumping joy, and he rubbed the German shepherd's ears absently as he opened the drapes. Los Angeles was semidark below. The Santa Ana had blown away the smog. Freeways were rivers of moving light even at this late hour. Other major streets were marked by a grid of lights whose yellow-orange brilliance Harvey noticed for the first time. Hamner had said they played hell with the seeing at Mount Wilson Observatory.

The city stretched away endlessly. High-rise apartments in shadowed darkness. Blue squares of still-lit swimming pools. Cars. Bright flashing light winking at intervals, the police helicopter on patrol. He left the window and went to the

23

desk, picked up a book, set it down; scratched the dog's ears once more; and very gently, because he didn't trust himself to move rapidly, put the cocoa on the desk.

He'd never had any trouble getting to sleep in the mountains on camping trips. He'd get into his sleeping bag just after dark and sleep all night. It was only in the city that he had insomnia. For years he'd tried to fight it by lying rigid on his back. These nights he got up and stayed up until he was sleepy. Only he didn't usually have trouble on Wednesdays.

Wednesdays, he and Loretta made love.

He'd tried to fight that habit once, but that was years ago; and yes, Loretta would come to his bed on a Monday night; but not always, and never in the afternoon when it was light; and it was never as good on a Tuesday or a Saturday because on Wednesdays they knew it was coming, they were *ready*. By now the habit had set like concrete.

He shook away those thoughts and concentrated on his good fortune. Hamner had meant it. The documentary would be made. He thought about problems. They'd need an expert on low-light photography; probably time-lapse for the comet itself. This would be fun. Have to thank Maureen Jellison for putting me onto Hamner, he thought. Nice girl. Vivid. More real than most of the women I meet. Too bad Loretta was standing right there. . . .

He submerged that thought so quickly that he was barely aware of it. It was a habit he'd developed long ago. He knew too many men who talked themselves into hating their wives when they didn't really dislike them at all. The grass *wasn't* always greener on the other side of the fence; a lesson that he'd learned from his father and never forgotten. His father had been an architect and builder, always close to the Hollywood set but never quite catching the big contracts that would make him rich; but he'd gone to plenty of Hollywood parties.

He'd also had time to take Harvey up into the mountains, and on those long camping hikes he would tell Harvey about producers and stars and writers who spent more than they earned and built themselves images that could never be satisfied. "Can't be happy," Bert Randall would say. "Keep thinking somebody else's wife is better in bed, or just prettier at parties, and talk to themselves enough that they believe it. This whole damn town's got itself believing its own press agents, and nobody can live up to those dreams."

And it was all true. Dreams could be dangerous. Better to concentrate on what you had. And, Harvey thought, I have a lot. A good job, a big house, a swimming pool . . .

None of it paid for, and you can't do what you want on the job, a malicious voice said inside his head.

Harvey ignored it.

■

The comets were not alone in the halo.

Local eddies near the center of the maelstrom—that whirling pool of gas which finally collapsed to form the Sun—had condensed into planets. The furious heat of the newly formed star had stripped the gas envelopes from the nearest, leaving nuggets of molten rock and iron. Worlds further out had remained as great balls of gas which men would, in a billion years, name for their gods. There had also been eddies very distant from the whirlpool's axis.

One had formed a planet the size of Saturn, and it was still gathering mass. Its rings were broad and beautiful in starlight. Its surface churned with storms, for its center was furiously hot with the energy of its collapse. Its enormous orbit was tilted almost vertically to the plane of the inner system, and its stately path through the cometary halo took hundreds of thousands of years to complete.

Sometimes a comet would stray too near the black giant and be swept into its ring, or into the thousands of miles of atmosphere. Sometimes that tremendous mass would pluck a comet from its orbit and swing it out into interstellar space, to be lost forever. And sometimes the black planet would send a comet plunging into the maelstrom and hellfire of the inner system.

They moved in slow, stable orbits, these myriads of comets that had survived the ignition of the Sun. But when the black giant passed, orbits became chaos. Comets that fell into the maelstrom might return partially vaporized, and fall back, again and again, until nothing was left but a cloud of stones. But many never returned at all.

January: Interlude

On a clear day the view stretched out forever. From his vantage point on the top floor of the San Joaquin Nuclear Project,
Site Supervisor Barry Price had an excellent view of the vast
lozenge-shaped saucer that had once been an inland sea, and
was now the center of California's agricultural industry. The
San Joaquin Valley ran two hundred miles to his north, fifty
to the south. The uncompleted nuclear-power complex stood
on a low ridge twenty feet above the totally flat valley—the
highest hill in sight.

Even at this early hour there was a bustle of industrial
activity. His construction crews worked a full three shifts,
through the night, on Saturdays and Sundays, and if Barry

Price had had his way they'd have worked Christmas and New Year's too. In their latest flurry of activity they'd finished Number One reactor and had a good start on Number Two; others had begun excavation for Three and Four; and none of it did any good. Number One was finished, but the courts and lawyers wouldn't let him turn it on.

His desk was buried in paper. His hair was cut very short, his mustache was neatly trimmed and thin as a razor's edge. He wore what his ex-wife had called his engineering uniform: khaki trousers, khaki shirt with epaulets, khaki bush jacket with more epaulets; pocket calculator swinging from his belt (when his hair was all brown it had been a slide rule), pencils in his breast pockets, notebook in its own pocket sewed to the jacket. When forced to—as he increasingly was by court appearances, command performances before the Mayor of Los Angeles and its Commissioners of Water and Power, testimony before Congress and the Nuclear Regulatory Commission or the State Legislature—he reluctantly put on a gray flannel suit and tie; but on his home turf he gratefully changed back to field clothing, and he was damned if he'd dress up for visitors.

His coffee cup was empty, dead empty, and there went his last excuse. He keyed the intercom. "Dolores, I'm ready for our visiting firemen."

"Not here yet," she said.

Reprieved. For a little while. He went back to his papers, hating what he was doing. As he worked he muttered to himself. "I'm an engineer, dammit. If I'd wanted to spend all my time with legal briefs or sitting in a courtroom, I'd have been a lawyer. Or a mass murderer."

Increasingly he regretted taking the job. He was a power-systems man, and a damned good one; he'd proved that by becoming Pennsylvania Edison's youngest plant supervisor and keeping the Milford nuclear plant operating with the highest efficiency factor and best safety record in the country. And he'd wanted this position, to be in charge of San Joaquin and get the plant on line, four thousand megawatts of clean electric power when the project was completed. But his job was to build, to operate, not to explain. He was at home with machinery; more than that, with construction people, power operators, linemen and switchyard workers; his enthusiasm for nuclear power was infectious and spread through all those who worked for him—and so what? he thought sourly. Nowadays he spent all his time on paper work.

Dolores came in with more urgent memos that had to be answered. Every one of them was a job for a public-relations type, and every one of them came from people important enough to demand the time of the supervising engineer. He hefted the stack of memoranda and documents she dropped into his IN basket. "Look at this crap," he said. "And every bit of it from politicians."

She winked. "Illegitimi non carborundum," she said.

Barry winked back. "It ain't easy. Dinner?"

"Sure."

He felt the anticipation from the bright promise in her quick smile. *Barry Price sleeps with his secretary! I suppose,* he thought, *I suppose the Department would get upset if they knew. And to hell with them.*

He felt the quiet: The building should be humming with the faint vibrations of turbines, the feel and sound of megawatts pouring into the grid, feeding Los Angeles and its industries; but there was nothing. Below him was the rectangular building that contained the turbines, beautiful machines, a paean to man's ingenuity, weighing hundreds of tons and balanced to micrograms, able to spin at fantastic speeds and not vibrate at all. . . . *Why couldn't people understand? Why didn't everyone appreciate the beauty of fine machinery, the magnificence?*

"Cheer up," Dolores said, reading his thoughts. "The crews are working. Maybe this time they'll let us finish."

"Wouldn't that make the news?" Barry asked. "Actually, I'd rather it didn't. The less publicity we have, the better off we are. And that's crazy."

Dolores nodded and went to the windows. She stared across the San Joaquin Valley toward the Temblor Range thirty miles away. "Haze out there," she said. "One of these days . . ."

"Yes." That was a cheerful thought. Southern California *had* to have power, and with natural-gas shortages the only ways were coal and nuclear—and there was no way at all to burn coal and not get *some* haze and smog. "We've got the only clean way to go," Barry said. "And we've won every time the public got to vote. You'd think even lawyers and politicians would get the message." He knew he was preaching to the converted, but it helped to talk to someone, anyone, who would be sympathetic, who understood.

A light went on at his desk and Dolores flashed a parting smile before hastening out to greet the visiting delegation

29

from the State Assembly. Barry prepared for another long day.

■

Morning rush hour in Los Angeles: streams of cars, all moving; thin smell of smog and exhaust fumes despite last night's Santa Ana wind; patches of morning mist from the coast dying as warmer winds from inland swept them away. There was this about the morning rush hour: The freeways were jammed, but not necessarily with idiots. Most drove the same route at the same time every morning. They knew the ropes. You could see it at the off ramps, where nobody had to swerve across lanes; and at the on ramps, where the cars seemed to take turns.

Eileen had noticed it more than once. Despite the stand-up comics who had made California drivers the joke of the world, they were much better on freeways than any people she had seen anywhere else—which meant that she could drive with half her attention. She knew the ropes, too.

Her routine seldom varied now. Five minutes to finish a last cup of coffee before she got to the freeway. Stow the cup in the little rack she'd got from J. C. Whitney, and use the hairbrush for another five minutes. By then she was awake enough to do some real work. It would take another half-hour to get to Corrigan's Plumbing Supplies in Burbank, and she could get a lot done with the dictaphone in that time. It improved her driving, too. Without the dictaphone she would be tense and nervous, pounding the dash in helpless frustration at every minor traffic jam.

"Tuesday. Get on Corrigan's back about the water filters," her voice said back to her. "We've had two customers install the damned things without knowing there were parts missing." Eileen nodded. She'd taken care of that already, and smoothed out the rage of a guy who'd looked like a barge tender and turned out to be related to one of the biggest developers in the valley. It just went to show, you could never kiss off a deal just because it looked like a one-item sale. She hit the rewind, then recorded: "Thursday. Have the warehouse people check every one of those filters in stock. Look for missing Leed nuts. And send a letter to the manufacturer." She returned to PLAYBACK.

Eileen Susan Hancock was thirty-four years old. She was

30

on the thin side of very pretty, and the reason showed in her hands, which were always in motion, and in her smile, which was nice, but which flashed always too suddenly, as if she'd turned on a light bulb, and in her walk. She had a tendency to leave people behind.

Somebody had once told her that was symbolic: She left people behind both physically and emotionally. He hadn't said "intellectually," and if he had she wouldn't have believed him, but it was largely true. She'd been determined to be something more than a secretary long before there was anything like a women's rights movement; and she'd managed that despite the responsibilities of a younger brother to raise.

If she ever talked about it, she laughed at how trite the situation was: Older sister puts younger brother through college but can't go herself; helps younger brother get married, but never marries herself; and none of it was really true. She'd hated college. Maybe, she sometimes thought (but never said to anyone), a very *good* college, a place where they make you think, maybe that would have worked out. But to sit in a classroom while a timeserver lectured from a book that she'd already read, to teach her nothing she didn't already know— it had been sheer hell, and when she dropped out the reasons weren't financial.

And as to marriage, there wasn't anybody she could live with. She'd tried that once, with a police lieutenant (and watched how nervous he was to have her living there without benefit of City Hall license), and what had been a good relationship came apart inside a month. There had been another man, but he had a wife he wasn't going to leave; and a third, who'd gone east for a three-month assignment that hadn't ended after four years; and . . .

And I'm doing all right, she told herself when she thought about such things.

Men called her "hyperthyroid" or "the nervous type," depending on education and vocabulary; and most didn't try to keep up with her. She had an acid wit that she used too much. She hated dull talk. She talked much too fast; otherwise her voice was pleasant with a touch of throatiness derived from too many cigarettes.

She'd been driving this route for eight years. She took the curve of the four-level interchange without noticing; but once, years before, she had swept her car down that curve, then pulled off at the next ramp and parked her car and strolled back to stare at that maze of concrete spaghetti.

She'd been laughing at her own picture of herself as a gawking tourist, but she'd stared anyway.

"Wednesday," the recorder told her. "Robin's going to come through on the Marina deal. If he does, I stand to be Assistant General Manager. If he doesn't, no chance. Problem . . ."

Eileen's ears and throat were red in advance, and her hands shifted too often on the steering wheel. But she heard it through. Her Wednesday voice said, "He wants to sleep with me, it's clear it wasn't just repartee and games. If I cool him, do I blow the sale? Do I go to the mat with him to clinch the deal? Or am I missing something good because of the implications?"

"Shit-oh-dear," Eileen said under her breath. She ran the tape back and recorded over that segment. "I still haven't decided whether to accept Robin Geston's dinner invitation. Memo: I should keep this tape cleaner. If anyone ever stole the recorder, I wouldn't want to burn his ears off. Anyone remember Nixon?" She switched the recorder off, hard.

But she still had the problem, and she still felt burning resentment at living in a world where she had that kind of problem. She thought of how she'd word the letter to the goddam manufacturer who'd sent out the filters without checking to see that all the parts were enclosed, and that made her feel a little better.

It was late evening in Siberia. Dr. Leonilla Alexandrovna Malik was finished for the day. Her last patient had been a four-year-old girl, child of one of the engineers at the space-development center here in the Soviet northern wastes.

It was midwinter, and the wind blew cold from the north. There was snow piled outside the infirmary, and even inside she could feel the cold. Leonilla hated it. She had been born in Leningrad, so she was no stranger to severe winters; but she kept hoping for a transfer to Baikunyar, or even Kapustin Yar on the Black Sea. She resented being required to treat dependents, although of course there was little she could do about it; there weren't many with pediatric training up here. Still, it was a waste. She had also been trained as a *kosmonaut,* and she kept hoping she'd get an assignment in space.

Perhaps soon. The Americans were said to be training women astronauts. If the Americans looked likely to send a woman into space, the Soviet Union would do it also, and quickly. The last Soviet experiment with a woman *kosmonaut* had been a disaster. (Was it really her fault? Leonilla wondered. She knew both Valentina Tereskovna and the *kosmo-*

naut she'd married, and they never talked about why her spacecraft had tumbled, ruining the chance for the Soviet Union to make the first space docking in history.) Of course, Valentina was much older, Leonilla thought. That had been in primitive times. Things were different now. The *kosmo-nauts* had little to do anyway; ground control made all the important decisions. A silly design philosophy, Leonilla thought, and her *kosmonaut* colleagues (all male, of course) shared this view, but not loudly.

She put the last of her used instruments into the autoclave and packed her bag. *Kosmonaut* or not, she was also a physician, and she carried the tools of the trade most places she went, just in case she might be needed. She put on the fur cap and heavy leather coat, shuddering a little at the sound of the wind outside. A radio in the next office had a news program, and Leonilla paused to listen when she heard a key word.

Comet. A new comet.

She wondered if there would be plans to explore it. Then she sighed. If there was a space mission to study the comet, it wouldn't include her. She had no skills for that. Pilot, physician, life-support-systems engineer; those she could do. But not astronomy. That would be for Pieter or Basil or Sergei.

Too bad, really. But it was interesting. A new comet.

On Earth there was plague. Three billion years after the planet's formation there came a virulent mutation, a form of life that used sunlight directly. The more efficient energy source gave the green mutant a hyperactive, murderous vigor; and as it spread forth to conquer the world, it poured out a flood of oxygen to poison the air. Raw oxygen seared the tissues of Earth's dominant life and left it as fertilizer for the mutant.

That was a time of disaster for the comet, too. The black giant crossed its path for the first time.

Enormous heat had been trapped in the planet's formation; it would be pouring out to the stars for a billion years to come.

A flood of infrared light boiled hydrogen and helium from the comet's tissues. Then the intruder passed, and calm returned. The comet cruised on through the cold black silence, a little lighter now, moving in a slightly changed orbit.

February: One

*On the other hand, it is necessary to shape the social
structure of the worker's world in such a way as to
take away his fear of being a mere cog in an impersonal machine. A true solution can come only
through the conception that work, whatever it must
be, is the service of God and of the community and
therefore the expression of man's dignity.*
Emil Brunner, Gifford Lectures, 1948

Westwood Boulevard was not even remotely on the way between the offices of the National Broadcasting System and the
Randall home near Beverly Glen, which was the main reason
Harvey Randall liked the bars there. He wasn't likely to run
into any of the network officials and he wasn't likely to find
any of Loretta's friends.

Students wandered along the wide street. They came in
assortments: bearded and wearing jeans; clean-cut with expensive jeans; deliberately weird, and young-fogey conservative,
and everything between. Harvey strolled with them. He passed
specialty bookstores. One was devoted to gay lib. Another
called itself the Macho Adult Bookstore and meant it. And
another catered to the science-fiction crowd. Harvey made a
mental note to go in there. They'd probably have a lot of stuff
about comets and astronomy geared to a general readership;
after he read that he could go to the UCLA campus store and
get the really technical material.

Past the sisterhood place was a plate-glass window. Letters
in Gothic script said SECURITY FIRST FEDERAL BAR.
Inside were stools, three small tables, four booths, a pinball
machine and a jukebox. The walls were decorated with whatever the customers preferred; a supply of marking pens lay

on the bar, and the walls were whitewashed at intervals. Paint peeled away in places to reveal comments made years before, a kind of pop-culture archeology.

Harvey moved into the dimness like a tired old man. As his eyes adjusted he spotted Mark Czescu on a stool. He pulled himself up next to Czescu and propped elbows on bar.

Czescu was thirty-odd, almost ageless, a perpetual young man about to launch himself on his career. Harvey knew Mark had been in the Navy for four years, and had tried several colleges, starting at UCLA and working down through community junior colleges. He sometimes called himself a student even yet, but no one believed he'd ever finish. He wore biker's boots, old jeans, a T-shirt and a crumpled Aussie digger hat. He wore his black hair long and his black beard full. There was ground-in dirt under his nails and fresh streaks of grease on the jeans, but his hands and clothes had been freshly washed for all of that; he just didn't have any pathological need to be scrubbed pink.

When Mark wasn't smiling he had a dangerous look, despite the respectable beer belly. He smiled at lot; but he could take some things very seriously, and he sometimes moved with a tough crowd. They were part of his image: Mark Czescu could run with the real bikers if he wanted to, but he didn't want to. Just now he looked concerned. "You don't look good," he said.

"I feel like killing somebody," said Harvey.

"You feel that way, I could maybe find somebody," Mark said. He let it trail off.

"No. They're my bosses. They're all of them my bosses, damn their innumerable souls." Harvey ordered a pitcher and two glasses, and ignored Mark's suggestion. He knew Mark couldn't arrange a real murder. It was part of the Czescu image, to know more than you did about whatever subject came up. It usually amused Harvey, but just now he wasn't in the mood for games.

"I want something from them," Harvey said. "And they *know* they're going to give it to me. How the hell can they *not* know? I've even got the sponsor wired! But the sons of bitches have to play games. If one of them fell off a balcony tomorrow, I'd be in for an extra month breaking in a new one, and I can't afford the time." It didn't hurt to humor Czescu; the guy could be useful, and a lot of fun—and maybe he *could* arrange a murder. You never really knew.

"So what are they going to give you?" Mark asked.

"A comet. I'm going to make a whole series of documentaries about a new comet. The guy who discovered it chances to own seventy percent of the company that will sponsor the documentaries."

Czescu chortled. Harvey nodded agreement. "It's a beautiful setup. Chance to make the kind of films I really want to do. And to learn a lot. Not like that last shit, interviewing doomsters, everybody with his own private vision of the end of the world. I wanted to cut my throat and get it over with before that one was finished."

"So what's wrong?"

Harvey sighed, and drank more beer, and said, "Look. There are about four guys who could really tell me to go take a flying frig and make it stick. But that'd be a mistake, right? The New York people won't put up with blowing a sponsored series. They're going to buy the show. But how will anyone know they've got the power to say no if they don't hesitate and demand I write up treatments and do budget estimates and all that crap? None of that shit gets used, but they've got to have a 'sound basis for decisions.' Four fucking prima donnas who actually have the power.

"Okay, I could live with them. But then there are a couple of *dozen* who couldn't stop a *Time for Beany* revival, but they want to show how important they are, too. So to show each other they could really stop the show if they wanted to, they raise as many objections as they can. Got the best interests of the sponsors in mind, right? Don't want to get Kalva Soap mad, right? Bullshit. But I've got to put up with it." Harvey was suddenly aware of what he sounded like, "Look, let's change the subject."

"Right. You've noticed the name of this place?"

"Security First Federal Bar. Cute. Stolen from George Carlin. About time, too."

"Right! Now maybe some others will pick up the idea. Can you see Crazy Eddie's Insurance?"

"Why not? They bought cars from Madman Muntz. How about Fat Jack's Cancer Clinic?"

"Fat Jack's Cancer Clinic and Mortuary," Czescu said.

The tightness in Harvey's neck and shoulders was going away. He drank more beer, then went to a booth where he could lean against something. Mark followed and took the opposite seat.

"Hey, Harv, when we making another run? Your bike still work?"

"Yeah." A year ago—no, dammit, two years and more—he'd said the hell with it and let Mark Czescu lead him on a ride up the coast, drinking in little bars, talking to other drifters, camping where they felt like it. Czescu took care of the bikes, and Harvey paid the bills, not that they amounted to much. It had been a time of no worries. "The bike works, but I won't get a chance to use it. When this series gets going it'll take full time."

"Anything I can get in on?" Mark asked.

Harvey shrugged. "Why not?" Mark often worked on Harvey's shows. He carried cameras or clipboards and did maintenance or just plain acted as gofer. "If you'll shut up once in awhile."

"I'm hip."

The bar was filling up. The jukebox ran out of sound, and Mark got up. "Something just for you," he said. He retrieved his twelve-string guitar from behind the bar and took a chair at the end of the room. This, too, was part of his routine: Czescu sang for drinks and meals in bars. On their run up the coast Mark had got them free steaks in half the places between L.A. and Carmel. He was good enough to be professional, but he wouldn't discipline himself; whenever he got a regular gig it didn't last a week. To Mark, those who made steady money were magicians with a secret that he couldn't quite learn.

Mark strummed an experimental chord, then began a prologue. The tune was the old cowboy number, "Cool Clear Water."

All day I face the TV waste, without a trace of culture,
Pure culture.
With soapbox operas all day long, and giveaway shows that run too long,
And lead you on,
From culture.
Pure . . . sweet . . . culture.

Harvey laughed approval. A fat man at the bar sent over a pitcher of beer and Mark acknowledged with a toss of his head.

The sun goes down, and through the town you hear the cry for culture,
Sweet culture.

While lawyers grin, and cops will win, to stop the sin of culture.
Culture. Pure . . . culture.

There was a short break as Mark picked at the guitar. The chords jangled, obviously wrong, but obviously right too, as if Mark were searching for something he could never find.

Keep a tunin', friend, it'll set you in a trend,
And your mind it's goin' to bend,
And hook you in the end,
With culture. Culture. Pure culture.
Friend, can't you see, for you and me, and a mind that's free,
It's pay TV for you and me,
And culture. Culture. Pure . . . sweet . . . culture.

The guitar stopped and Mark said in a plonking voice, "Almost as much as you get from an old Bogart movie."

PURE, SWEET, CULTURE.

"Leonard Bernstein conducts the London Symphony Orchestra and the Rolling Stones in a *dazzling* display of

"CULTURE. Pure, sweet, culture.

"Folks, tonight we have a debate between the president of the United Farm Workers versus twenty-two hunger-maddened housewives armed with butcher knives. It's

CULTURE. P*U*R*E, S*W*E*E*T, C*U*L*T*U*R*E."

Jesus, thought Harvey. Jesus, I'd like to play a recording of that in a goddam executive council meeting at the network. Harvey leaned back to enjoy his moment. It wouldn't be long before he had to go home to dinner, and Loretta, and Andy, and Kipling, and the home he loved but whose price was just so damned high.

The Santa Ana still blew, hot and dry across the Los Angeles basin. Harvey drove with open windows, his coat thrown onto the seat beside him, tie atop the pile. Headlights picked up green hillsides among bare trees, palm trees at intervals. He drove in the full summery darkness of a California February and he noticed nothing unusual about it.

He hummed Mark's song as he drove. One day, he thought. One day I'll slip a tape of that onto the Muzak system so three-quarters of the business people in Los Angeles and Beverly Hills will have to listen to it. Half concentrating, he daydreamed in fragments that shattered when some car ahead slowed and the flare of brake lights surged like a wave.

At the top of the hill he turned right onto Mulholland, right again onto Benedict Canyon, downhill slightly, then right onto Fox. Fox Lane was one of a cluster of short curved streets lined with fifteen-year-old houses. One of them belonged to Harvey, courtesy of Pasadena Savings and Loan. Further down Benedict Canyon was the turn onto Cielo Drive, where Charlie Manson had proved to the world that civilization was neither eternal nor safe. After that Sunday morning of horror in 1969 there was not a gun or a guard dog to be had in Beverly Hills. Back orders for shotguns stretched delivery time to weeks. And ever since, despite Harvey's pistol and shotgun and dog, Loretta wanted to move. She was searching for safety.

Home. A big white house with green roof, trimmed front lawn, a big tree and small porch. It had a good resale value, because it was the least expensive house on the block; but least expensive is a relative thing, as Harvey well knew.

His house had a conventional driveway, not a big circular entry like the house across the street. He took the corner at a good clip, slowed in the drive, and zapped the garage door with the radio-beam widget. The door swung up before he could reach it; perfect timing, and Harvey scored a mental point with himself. The garage door closed behind him and he sat for a moment in darkness. Harvey didn't like driving in rush hours, and he drove the rush hour twice nearly every day of his life. Time for a shower, he thought. He got out of the car and walked back down the drive toward the kitchen door.

"Hey, Harv?" a baritone voice bellowed.

"Yo," Harvey answered. Gordie Vance, Randall's neighbor on the left, was coming across his lawn with a rake trailing behind him. He leaned on the fence, and Harvey did the same, thinking as he did of cartoons of housewives chatting this way; only Loretta didn't like Marie Vance, and would never be seen leaning on a back fence anyway. "So, Gordie. How are things at the bank?"

Gordie's smile wavered. "They'll keep. Anyway you're not

ready for a lecture on inflation. Listen, can you get away on the weekend? Thought we'd take the scouts up for a snow hike."

"Boy, that sounds good." Clean snow. It was hard to believe that no more than an hour away, in the Angeles Forest Mountains, was deep snow and wild, whistling wind in the evergreens, while they stood here in their shirt sleeves in the dark. "Probably not, Gordie. There's a job coming up." Christ, I hope there's a job coming up. "You better not count on me."

"What about Andy? Thought I'd use him as patrol leader this trip."

"He's a little young for that. . . ."

"Not really. And he's got experience. I'm taking some new kids on a first hike. Could use Andy."

"Sure, he's up on his schoolwork. Where are you going?"

"Cloudburst Summit."

Harvey laughed. Tim Hamner's observatory wasn't far from there, although Harvey had never seen it. He must have hiked past it a dozen times.

They discussed details. With the Santa Ana blowing there'd be melt-off on all but the top elevations, but there would certainly be snow on the north slopes. A dozen scouts and Gordie. It sounded like fun. It *was* fun. Harvey shook his head ruefully. "You know, Gordo, when I was a kid it was a good week's hike to Cloudburst. No road. Now we drive it in an hour. Progress."

"Yeah. But it is progress, isn't it? I mean, now we can get there and still keep a job."

"Sure. Damn, I wish I could go." By the time they'd driven up—an hour—and hiked in and got the gear out of their backpacks and set up camp, and got damp wood burning and their backpack stoves going, the freeze-dried mountain food always tasted like ambrosia. And coffee, at midnight, standing in a shelter out of the wind and listening to it whistle above . . . But it wasn't worth a comet. "Sorry."

"Right. Okay, I'll check with Andy. Go over his gear for me, will you?"

"Sure." What Gordie meant was, "Don't let Loretta pack for your son. It's hard enough hiking at that altitude without all the crap she'd make him carry. Hot-water bottles. Extra blankets. Once even an alarm clock."

Harvey had to go back for his jacket and tie. When he came out of the garage he went another way, into the backyard. He'd thought of asking Gordie, "How do you feel

41

about calling it 'Gordo's Bank and Kaffeeklatsch'?" From the look on Gordie's face when the bank was mentioned, it wouldn't go over. Some kind of trouble there. Private trouble.

Andy was in the backyard, across the pool, playing basketball solitaire. Randall stood quietly watching him. In zero time, in what must have been a year but felt like a week, Andy had changed from a boy into a . . . into a stick figure, all arms and legs and hands, long bones poised behind a basketball. He launched it with exquisite care, danced to catch the rebound, dribbled, and fired again for a perfect score. Andy didn't smile; he nodded in somber satisfaction.

Kid's not bad, Harvey thought.

His pants were new, but they didn't reach his ankles. He'd be fifteen next September, ready for high school; and there was nothing for it but to send him to Harvard School for Boys, certainly the best in Los Angeles; only the school wanted a fortune just to hold a place, and the orthodontist wanted thousands now and more later. And there was the funny noise from the pool pump, and the electronics club Andy was involved in, it wouldn't be long before the boy wanted a micro-computer for himself and who could blame him? . . . And . . . Randall went inside, quietly, glad that Andy hadn't noticed him.

A teen-age boy used to be an asset. He could work in the fields—drive a team, or even a tractor. The pressure could be shared, shifted to younger shoulders. A man could ease off.

There was wrapping paper in the kitchen wastebasket. Loretta had been shopping again. Christmas had been on charge accounts, and those bills would be coming to roost on his desk. He'd already heard the stock-market report on the radio. The market was down.

Loretta was nowhere around. Harvey went into the big dressing room off the bathroom and stripped, got into the shower. Hot water beat down on his neck, draining away tension. His mind was turned off; he imagined himself as meat being massaged by hydraulic pressure. Only. If only his mind would *really* turn off.

Andy has a conscience. God knows I never tried to make him feel guilty. Discipline, sure. Punishment, standing in a corner, even a formal spanking, but when it's over it's over, no lingering guilt . . . but he knows guilt anyway. If Andy knew what he's costing me in dollars and cents—and in the years of my life. If he ever knew what it does to the way I have to live, the shit I put up with to keep that goddam job and win the bonuses that keep us afloat . . . What would

42

Andy do if he knew? Run away? Get a job as a street sweeper in San Francisco to try to pay me back? He damned well is not going to know.

A voice in the roar of water. *Huh?* Randall came out of the internal world and found Loretta smiling through the glass shower door. She mouthed, "Hi. How'd it go?"

He waved. Loretta took it as an invitation. Randall watched her undress slowly, lasciviously, and slide through the glass door quick so the water wouldn't splash out . . . and it wasn't Wednesday. Harvey folded her in his arms. The water beat down on them, and they kissed. And it wasn't Wednesday.

She asked, "How'd it go?"

He had read her lips the first time, but she couldn't guess that. Now he had to answer. "I think they'll do it."

"I don't see why not. It doesn't make sense. If they wait, CBS will take it."

"Right." The magic went out of the shower/orgy scene, *poof.*

"Isn't there any way to tell them how silly they're being?"

"No." Harvey fiddled with the shower head. The water expanded to a fine spray.

"Why not?"

"Because they know. Because they're not playing the same game we are."

"It all depends on you. If you insist on doing it *your* way, just once. . . ." Loretta's hair darkened and dampened under the shower. She held him in her arms and looked up into his face, looked for the strengthening of purpose that would mean she'd convinced him: that he would stand by his principles and force his superiors to face the consequences of their mistakes.

"Yeah. It all depends on me. Which makes me the obvious target if anything goes wrong. Turn around and I'll do your back."

She turned her back. Harvey reached for the soap. His will loosed its hold on the muscles of his face. His soapy hands made patterns in the slippery contours of Loretta's back . . . slowly, every move a caress . . . but he was thinking, *Don't you know what they'd do to me? They'd never fire me, but one day my office is an inside broom closet, the next day the rug is gone. Then my phone doesn't work. By the time I quit, everyone in the industry has forgotten I exist. And we're still spending every cent I make.*

43

He had always loved Loretta's back. He searched his mind for growing lust . . . but he felt nothing.

She was in on this from the beginning. It's her life too. Not fair to lock her out. But she just won't understand. I can get Mark off a subject! He'll drink my beer and talk about something else, if I make it plain enough. But I can't talk to Loretta like that. . . . What I need is a drink.

Loretta washed his back for him, and then they dried each other with the big towels. She was still trying to tell him how to handle the situation at the studio. She knew something was wrong, and as usual she probed at it, trying to understand, trying to help.

Myriads of orbits later, when true humans were spreading through a world held fast in the grip of an ice age, the black planet came again.

The comet was larger now. It had grown, snowflake by isolated snowflake, over a thousand million years, until it was four and a half miles across. But now its surface warmed in a bath of infrared heat. Within the comet's tissues, pockets of hydrogen and helium vaporized and seeped through the crust. The tiny sun was eclipsed. The ringed black disk covered a third of the sky, leaking the heat of its birth.

Then it had passed, and calm returned.

The comet had healed from a previous pass. Centuries, millennia, what are they in the cometary halo? But time had come at last to this comet. The black giant's passing had stopped it cold in its orbit.

Slowly, urged by the faint tugging of the Sun's gravity, it began to drop toward the maelstrom.

February: Two

It appears that the inner planets have ceaselessly been bombarded since their formation. Mars, Mercury, and Earth's Moon have undergone repeated strikes by objects ranging in size from micrometeorites to whatever cracked the Moon and created the large lava basin called Oceanus Procellarum.

Although it was originally thought that Mars, because it was at the edge of the asteroid belt, experienced a higher rate of meteoric bombardment, examination of Mercury indicates that Mars is not exceptional, and the inner planets have approximately equal probabilities of being struck. . . .

Mariner Preliminary Report

The TravelAll was crammed with equipment: cameras, tape recorders, lights and reflectors, battery belts; the myriad paraphernalia of the roving TV interview. Charlie Bascomb, cameraman, was in the back with the sound man, Manuel Arguilez; everything normal, except that Mark Czescu was in the front seat when Harvey came out of the NBS offices.

Harvey beckoned to Mark. They walked across the studio lot toward Mercedes Row, where the executives parked. "Look," Harvey said, "your job title is Production Assistant. That theoretically makes you management. It has to be that way because of union rules."

"Yeah—" Mark said.

"But you aren't management. You're a gofer."

"I'm hip." Mark sounded hurt.

"Don't get upset and don't get huffy. Just understand. My crew has been with me a long time. They know the game. You don't."

"I know that, too."

"Fine. You can be a big help. Just remember, what we don't need is—"

"Is me telling everybody how to do their job." He flashed a big grin. "I like working for you. I won't blow it."

"Good." Harvey detected no signs of irony in Mark's

voice. It made him feel better. He had been worried about this interview—it had to be said, but that didn't make it easier. One of his associates had once remarked that Mark was like a jungle, all right but you had to chop him back every now and then or he'd grow all over you.

The TravelAll started instantly. It had been through a lot with Harvey Randall: from the Alaska pipeline to the lower tip of Baja, even into Central America. They were old friends, the TravelAll and Harvey: a big three-seat International Harvester four-wheel drive, truck motor, ugly as sin, and utterly reliable. He drove in silence to the Ventura Freeway and turned toward Pasadena. Traffic was light.

"You know," Harvey said, "we're always complaining how nothing works, but here we are going fifty miles for this interview, and we count on being there in less than an hour. When I was a kid a fifty-mile trip was something you packed lunches for and hoped you'd make it by dark."

"What'd you have, a horse?" Charlie asked.

"No, just L.A. without the freeways."

"Yuk."

They drove through Glendale and turned north on Linda Vista to go past the Rose Bowl. Charlie and Manuel talked about bets they'd lost a few weeks before.

"I thought Cal Tech owned JPL," Charlie said.

"They do," Mark told him.

"Sure put it way the hell far from Pasadena."

"Used to test jet engines there," Mark said. "JPL. Jet Propulsion Laboratories, right? Everybody thought they'd blow up, so they made Cal Tech put the labs out in the Arroyo." He waved to indicate the houses outside. "Then they built the _ost expensive suburb in this end of L.A. just around it."

The guard was expecting them. He waved them into a lot near one of the large buildings. JPL nestled into its arroyo and filled it with office buildings. A big central steel-and-glass tower looked strangely out of place among the older Air-Force standard "temporary" structures erected twenty years before.

There was a PR flack waiting for them. She led them through the routine: Sign in, wear badges. Inside, it looked like any other office building, but not quite: There were stacks of IBM cards in the corridors, and almost no one wore coats or ties. They passed a ten-foot color globe of Mars gathering dust in a corner. No one paid any attention to Harvey and his people; it wasn't unusual to see TV crews.

JPL had built the Pioneer and Mariner space probes, had set Viking down on Mars.

"Here we are," the PR flack said.

The office looked good. Books on the wall. Incomprehensible equations on the blackboards. Books on every flat surface in view, IBM print-outs all over the expensive teak desk.

"Dr. Sharps, Harvey Randall," the flack said. She hovered near the door.

Charles Sharps wore glasses that curved around to cover his whole field of view; very modernistic, vaguely insectile against his long pale face. His hair was black and straight, worn short. His fingers played with a felt-tip pen, or fished into his pockets, always moving. He looked to be about thirty, but might have been older, and he wore a sport jacket and tie.

"Now let's get this straight," Sharps said. "You want a lecture on comets. For yourself or for the public?"

"Both. Simple for the camera, as much as I can understand for me. If it's not too much trouble."

"Too much trouble?" Sharps laughed. "How could it be too much trouble? Your network tells NASA you want to do a documentary on space, and NASA sends up red rockets. Right, Charlene?"

The PR flack nodded. "They asked us to cooperate—"

"Cooperate." Sharps laughed again. "I'd jump through hoops if I thought it would help get a budget. When do we start?"

"Now, please," Harvey said. "The crew will set up while we chat. Just ignore them. I take it you're the resident expert on comets."

"I suppose so," Sharps said. "Actually I like asteroids, but somebody has to study comets. I gather you're interested mainly in Hamner-Brown."

"Right."

Charlie caught Harvey's eye. They were ready. Harvey gave them the nod. Manuel listened and watched the indicator, and said, "Speed."

Mark stepped in front of the camera. "Sharps interview, take one." The chalkboard came together with a loud *clack!* Sharps jumped. They always did, first time. Charlie busied himself with the camera. He kept it aimed at Sharps; they'd film Harvey asking the questions later, when Sharps wasn't around.

"Tell me, Dr. Sharps, will Hamner-Brown be visible to the naked eye?"

"Don't know," Sharps said. He sketched something unlikely on the IBM print-out in front of him. The sketch might have been of a pair of mating Loch Ness monsters. "A month from now we'll know much better. We already know it's going to get as close to the Sun as Venus, but—" He broke off and looked at the camera. "What level do you want this at?"

"Anything you like," Harvey said. "Make me understand, then we can decide how to tell the public."

Sharps shrugged. "All right. So there's the solar system out there." He waved toward one wall. A big chart of the planets and their orbits hung next to the blackboard. "Planets and moons, always where they should be. They do a great complicated dance around each other. Every planet, every moon, every little rock in the asteroid belt, all dancing to Newton's song of gravity. Mercury got a little out of step and we had to revise the universe to make it fit."

"How's that?" Harvey asked. And I'd have preferred to do the poetry myself, but what the hell . . .

"Mercury. Orbit changes just a little every year. Not much, but more than Newton says it should. So a man named Einstein found a good explanation, and incidentally managed to make the universe a stranger place than it was before."

"Oh. I hope we don't need relativity to understand comets—"

"No, no. But there's more than gravity to a comet's orbit. That's surprising, isn't it?"

"Yes. Are we going to have to revise the universe again?"

"What? No, it's simpler than that. Look . . ." Sharps jumped to his feet and was at the blackboard. He looked for chalk and muttered.

"Here you go." Mark took chalk from his pocket and handed it.

"Thanks." Sharps sketched a white blob, then a parabolic curve. "That's the comet. Now let's put in planets." He drew two circles. "Earth and Venus."

"I thought planets moved in eliptical orbits," Harvey said.

"So they do, but on any scale you could draw you can't see the difference. Now look at the comet's orbit. Both arms of the curve look just the same, coming in and going out. Textbook parabola, right?"

"Right."

"But here's what the comet really looks like when it falls away from the Sun. A dense nucleus, a coma of fine dust and gas"—he was drawing again—"and a plume of dusty gas streaming away from the Sun. Ahead of the comet, going out. The tail. A *big* tail, a hundred million miles long, sometimes. But it's nearly a vacuum. It has to be—if it were thick, there wouldn't be enough matter in the comet to fill that much space."

"Sure."

"Okay, and again like the textbooks. Material boils out of the head of the comet into the coma. It's a thin gas, tiny particles, so tiny that sunlight can push them around. Light pressure from the Sun makes them stream away, so the tail always faces away from the Sun. Okay? Tail follows the comet going in, leads it coming out. But—

"The stuff boils out unevenly. When the comet first falls into the system, it's a solid mass. We think. Nobody really *knows*. We have several models that fit the observations. Me, I like the dirty-snowball model. The comet's made of rocks and dust, the dirt, balled up with ices and frozen gases. Some water ice. Methane. Carbon dioxide—dry ice. Cyanogen and nitrogen, all kinds of stuff. Pockets of these gases thaw and blast out to one side or the other. Like jet propulsion, and it changes the orbit." Sharps was at work with the chalk, holding it sideways. When he finished, the incoming arm had jogs and jiggle in it, and the outgoing arm was blurred into a wide sweep not unlike the comet's tail. "So we don't know how close to Earth it's coming."

"I see. And you don't know how big the tail will be."

"Right. But this seems to be a new comet. Maybe it's never made the trip down close to the Sun before. Not like Halley's Comet, which comes every seventy years and gets smaller each time. Comets die a little every time they pass near the Sun. They lose all that tail material forever. So each time the tail's smaller, until eventually there's nothing left but the nucleus, and that comes as a handful of rocks. Meteor showers. Some of our best shooting stars are pieces of old comets falling onto Earth."

"But this one's new—"

"That's right. So it ought to have a spectacular tail."

"I seem to remember people said that about Kahoutek."

"And I seem to remember they were wrong. Wasn't there an outfit selling commemorative medals that would show Kahoutek exactly as it appeared? You see there's no way to know. But my guess is that Hamner-Brown will be quite a sight. And it ought to pass fairly close to Earth."

Sharps drew a dot within the blur of the comet's outgoing course. "There's where we'll be. Of course we won't see a lot until the comet passes the Earth, because until it gets by we'll be looking straight into the Sun to see it. Hard to observe then. But when it's passed us, it should be quite a sight. There have been comets with tails across half the sky. See them in daytime. We're overdue for a big comet this century."

"Hey, doc," Mark said. "You've got Earth right in that thing's path. Could it *hit* us?"

Harvey turned to look daggers at Mark.

Sharps was laughing. "Chances are zillions to one against it. You see the Earth as a dot on the blackboard. Actually, if I drew this to scale you wouldn't be able to *see* the Earth in the drawing. Or the comet nucleus either. So what's the chance that a couple of pinpoints will come together?" He frowned at the board. "Of course, the *tail* is likely to go where we do. We might be in it for weeks."

"What does that do?" Harvey asked.

"We went through the tail of Halley's Comet," Mark said. "Didn't hurt a thing. Pretty lights, and—"

This time Harvey's look was enough.

"Your friend's right," Sharps said.

I knew that. "Dr. Sharps, why do all the astronomers get so excited about Hamner-Brown?" Harvey asked.

"Man, we can learn a *lot* from comets. Things like the origins of the solar system. They're older than Earth. Made out of primordial matter. This comet may have been out there way past Pluto for billions of years. Present theory says the solar system condensed from a cloud of dust and gas, an eddy in the interstellar medium. Most of that blew away when the Sun started to burn, but some is still in the comet. We can analyze the tail. The way we did with Kahoutek. Kahoutek was no disappointment to astronomers. We used tools we'd never had before. Skylab. Lots of things."

"And that was useful?" Harvey prompted.

"Useful? It was magnificent! We should do it again!" Sharps's hands waved around in dramatic gestures. Harvey glanced quickly at his crew. The camera was rolling, and Manuel had that contented look a sound man has when things are going well in his phones.

"Could we get something like Skylab up there in time?" Harvey asked.

"Skylab? No. But Rockwell's got an Apollo capsule we could use. And we've got the equipment here at the labs. There are big military boosters around, things the Pentagon doesn't need anymore. We could do it, if we started now, and we weren't chicken about it." Sharps's face fell. "But we won't. Too damn bad, too. We could really learn something from Hamner-Brown that way."

The cameras and sound equipment were packed away and the crew went out with the PR lady. Harvey was saying his farewells to Sharps.

"Want some coffee, Harvey? You're in no hurry, are you?" Sharps asked.

"Guess not."

Sharps punched a button on the phone console. "Larry. Get us some coffee, please." He turned back to Harvey. "Damnedest thing," he said. "Whole nation depends on technology. Stop the wheels for two days and you'd have riots. No place is more than two meals from a revolution. Think of Los Angeles or New York with no electricity. Or a longer view, fertilizer plants stop. Or a longer view yet, no new technology for ten years. What happens to our standard of living?"

"Sure, we're a high-technology civiliz—"

"Yet . . ." Sharps said. His voice was firm. He intended to finish. "Yet the damned fools won't pay ten minutes' attention a day to science and technology. How many people know what they're doing? Where do these carpets come from? The clothes you're wearing? What do carburetors do? Where do sesame seeds come from? Do *you* know? Does one voter out of thirty? They won't spend ten minutes a day thinking about the technology that keeps them alive. No wonder the research budget has been cut to nothing. We'll pay for that. One day we'll need something that could have been developed years before but wasn't—" He stopped himself. "Tell me, Harv, will this TV thing of yours be big or will it get usual billing for a science program?"

"Prime time," Harvey said. "A series, on the value of Hamner-Brown, and incidentally on the value of science. Of course, I can't guarantee people won't turn to reruns of 'I Love Lucy.'"

"Yeah. Oh—thank you, Larry. Put the coffee right here."

Harvey had expected styrofoam cups and machine coffee. Instead, Sharps's assistant brought in a gleaming Thermos pitcher, silver spoons and sugar-and-cream service on an inlaid teak tray.

"Help yourself, Harvey. It's good coffee. Mocha-Java?"

"Right," the assistant said.

"Good." He waved dismissal. "Harv, why this sudden change of heart by the networks?"

Harvey shrugged. "Sponsor insists on it. The sponsor happens to be Kalva Soap. Which happens to be controlled by Timothy Hamner. Who happens—"

Harvey was cut off by shrieks of laughter. Sharps's thin face contorted in glee. "Beautiful!" Then he looked thoughtful. "A series. Tell me, Harv, if a politician helped us with the study—helped a *lot*—could he be worked into the series? Get some favorable publicity?"

"Sure. Hamner would insist on it. Not that I'd object—"

"Marvelous." Sharps lifted his coffee cup. "Cheers. Thanks, Harv. Thanks a lot. I think we'll be seeing more of each other."

Sharps waited until Harvey Randall had left the building. He sat very still, something unusual for him, and he felt excitement in the pit of his stomach. It might work. It just might. Finally he punched the intercom. "Larry, get me Senator Arthur Jellison in Washington. Thanks."

Then he waited impatiently until the phone buzzed. "He'll talk to you," his assistant said.

Sharps lifted the phone. "Sharps here." Another wait while the secretary got the Senator.

"Charlie?"

"Right," Sharps said. "Art, I've got a proposition for you. Know about the comet?"

"Comet? Oh. Comet. Funny you mention that. I met the guy who discovered it. Turns out he was a heavy contributor, but I never met him before."

"Well, it's important," Sharps said. "Opportunity of the century—"

"That's what they said about Kahoutek—"

"God damn Kahoutek! Look, Art, what's the chance we could get funding for a probe?"

"How much?"

"Well, take two cases. Second best is anything we can get. The lab can cobble up an unmanned black box, something that goes on a Thor-Delta—"

"No problem. I can get you that," Jellison said.

"But that's second best. What we *need* is a manned probe. Say two men in an Apollo with some equipment instead of the third man. Art, that comet's going to be *close*. From up there we could get good pictures, not just the tail, not just the coma, there's a fair chance we could get pix of the *head!* Know what that means?"

"Not really, but you just told me it's important." Jellison was silent for a moment. "Sorry. I really am, but there's no chance. Not one chance. Anyway, we couldn't put up an Apollo if we had the budget—"

"Yes we can. I just checked with Rockwell. Higher-risk mission than NASA likes, but we could do it. We've got the hardware—"

"Doesn't matter. I can't get you a budget for that."

Sharps frowned at the phone. The sick excitement rose in his stomach. Arthur Jellison was an old friend, and Charlie Sharps did not like blackmail. But . . . "Not even if the Russkis are putting up a *Soyuz?*"

"What? But they're not—"

"Oh, yes, they are," Sharps said. *And it's not a lie, not really. Just an anticipation—*

"You can prove that?"

"In a few days. Rely on it, they're going up to look at Hamner-Brown."

"I will be dipped in shit."

"I beg your pardon, Senator?"

"I will be dipped in shit."

"Oh."

"You're playing games with me, aren't you, Charlie?" Jellison demanded.

"Not really. Look, Art, it's important. And we need another manned mission anyway, just to keep up interest in space. You've been after a manned flight—"

"Yeah, but I had no chance of getting one." There was more silence. Then Jellison said, more to himself than Sharps, "So the Russkis are going. And no doubt they'll make a big deal of it."

"I'm sure they will."

Another silence. Charlie Sharps almost held his breath. "Okay," Jellison said. "I'll nose around the Hill and see what kind of reactions I get. But you better be giving it to me straight."

"Senator, in a week you'll have unmistakable evidence."

"All right. I'll give it a try. Anything else?"

"Not just now."

"Okay. Thanks for the tip, Charlie." The phone went dead. Abrupt he is, Sharps thought. He smiled thinly to himself,

53

then punched the intercom button again. "Larry. I want Dr. Sergei Fadayev in Moscow, and yes, I know what time it is over there. Just get him on for me."

The legend of Gilgamesh was a handful of unconnected tales spreading through the Earth's Fertile Crescent in Asia . . . and the comet was nearly unchanged. It was still far outside the maelstrom. The orbit of the runaway moon called Pluto would have looked like a quarter held nearly on edge, at arm's length. The Sun, an uncomfortably bright pinpoint, still poured far less heat across the comet's crust than had the black giant at its worst. The crust was mostly water ice now; it reflected most of the heat back to the stars.

Yet time passed.

Mars swallowed its water in another turn of its long, vicious weather cycle. Men spread across the Earth, laughing and scratching. And the comet continued to fall. A breath of the solar wind, high-velocity protons, flayed its crust. Much of the hydrogen and helium in its tissues had seeped away. The maelstrom came near.

March: One

And the Lord hung a rainbow as a sign,
Won't be water but fire next time.

Traditional spiritual

Mark Czescu looked up at the house and whistled. It was California Tudor, off-white stucco with massive wood beams inset at angles. They'd be real wood. Some places, like Glendale, had the same style of house with plywood strips to fake it, but not Bel Air.

The house was large on a large lot. Mark rang the front door bell. Presently it was opened by a young man with long hair and pencil-thin mustache. He looked at Mark's Rough-rider trousers and boots and at the large brown cases Mark had set on the porch. "We don't need any," he said.

"I'm not selling any. I'm Mark Czescu, from NBS."

"Oh. Sorry. You'd be surprised how many peddlers we get. Come on in. My name's George, I'm the houseboy." He lifted one of the cases. "Heavy."

"Yeah." Mark was busy looking around. Paintings. A telescope. Globes of Earth, Mars and the Moon. Glass statuary. Steuben crystal. Trip toys. The front room had been set up as for a theater party, couches facing the TV. "Must have been a bitch moving that stuff," Mark said.

"Sure was. Here, put that in here. Anything tricky about it?"

"Not if you know video recorders."

"I ought to," George said. "I'm a drama student. UCLA. But we haven't had that course yet. You better show me."

"Will you be running it tonight?"

"Nah. I've got a rehearsal. *Wild Duck*. Good part. Mr. Hamner will do it."

"Then I'll show him."

"You'll have to wait, then. He's not home yet. Want a beer?"

"That'd go nice." Mark followed George to the kitchen. A big room, gleaming chrome and Formica everywhere; two double sinks, two gas ovens, two ranges. A large counter held trays of canapés covered with Saran Wrap. There was a desk and bookshelves which held cookbooks, the latest Travis McGee thrillers and Stanislavski's *An Actor Prepares*. Only the thrillers and Stanislavski showed any signs of use. "I'd have thought Hamner would find himself an astronomy student—"

"Last guy here was," George said. He got out beer. "They fought a lot."

"So Hamner fired him."

"No, he sent him up to his place in the mountains. Hamner likes to fight, but not when he's at home. He's easy to work for. And there's color TV in my room, and I get to use the pool and sauna."

"Hard to take." Mark sipped at the beer. "This must be one swinging party pad."

George laughed. "Like hell. The only parties are when I bring in a show cast. Or like tonight, relatives."

Mark eyed George carefully. Pencil mustache. Actor's fine features. What the hell, he thought. "Hamner gay or something?"

"Christ, no," George said. "No, he just doesn't go out much. I fixed him up with the second lead in our last show. Nice girl, from Seattle. Hamner took her out a couple of times, then nothing. Irene said he was polite and a perfect gentleman until they were alone, then he leaped at her."

"She should have leaped back."

"That's what I said, but she didn't." George cocked his head to one side. "That's Mr. Hamner coming now. I recognize the engine."

Tim Hamner went to the side door and into the small suite

that he thought of as his home. It was the part of the house he felt most comfortable in although he used the whole place. Hamner didn't like his house. It had been chosen by the family money managers for resale value, and it had that; it gave him plenty of space to display the things he'd collected; but it didn't seem like a home.

He poured himself a short scotch and sank into an Eames chair. He put his feet up on the matching footstool. It felt good. He'd done his duty. He'd gone to a directors' meeting and listened to all the reports and congratulated the company president on the quarterly earnings. Tim's natural inclination was to let those who liked playing with money do it, but he'd had a cousin who lost everything that way; it never hurt to let money managers know you were looking over their shoulders.

Thinking of the meeting reminded him of the secretary at the office. She'd chatted pleasantly with Tim before the meeting, but she'd pleaded a date when he asked her for dinner for tomorrow. Maybe she did have a date. She was polite enough. But she'd turned him down. Maybe, he thought, maybe I should have asked her for next Friday. Or next week. But then if she said no there'd have been no doubt about why.

He heard George talking with someone out in the living room and wondered idly who it might be. George wouldn't disturb him until he came out; that was one nice thing about this house, he could have this suite to himself. But then Tim remembered. That would be the man from NBS! With the cut scenes, the ones Tim had liked but hadn't got into the documentary. He got up in enthusiasm and began changing clothes.

◆

Penelope Wilson arrived about six. She had never answered to Penny; her mother had insisted. Tim Hamner, looking at her through the spy-eye in the door, suddenly remembered that she had given up Penelope too. She'd taken to using her middle name, and Tim couldn't remember it.

Be brave. He threw the door wide and, letting his agony show, cried, "Quick! What's your middle name?"

"Joyce. Hello, Tim. Am I the first?"

"Yes. You look elegant." He took her coat. He had known her forever: since grade school, anyway. Penelope Joyce had gone to the same girls' prep school as Tim's sister and half a dozen girl cousins. She had been the homely one, with her wide mouth and too-square jaw and a figure best described as sturdy. In college she had begun to bloom.

She was indeed elegant tonight. Her hair was long and wavy and complexly arranged. Her dress was clean of line and of a color and texture soft to the eye. Tim wanted to touch it. He'd lived with his sister long enough to know how long it must have taken to get that effect, even if he had no hint as to how it was done.

Wanting her approval was automatic. He waited as she inspected his living room, wondering to himself why he'd never invited her before. Finally she looked up with an expression Tim hadn't seen her use since high school, when she'd decided she was judge of all morals. "Nice room," she said approvingly. Then she giggled, ruining the pose.

"Glad you like it. Damned glad, in fact."

"Really? Is my opinion so important?" She was still teasing him with facial expressions from their childhood.

"Yes. In a few minutes the whole damned family's going to be here, and most of them haven't seen this place. You think like they do, so if you like it, they will."

"Hmm. I guess I deserved that."

"Hey, I didn't mean . . ." She was laughing at him again. He got her a drink and they sat.

"I've been wondering," she mused. "We haven't seen each other for two years at least. Why did you ask me here tonight?"

Tim was partly prepared for that. She had always been direct. He decided to be truthful. "I was thinking about who I wanted here tonight. A big ego thing, right? The show about my comet. And I thought of Gil Waters, the top of my class at Cate, and my family, and you. Then I realized I was thinking of all the people I wanted to impress most."

"Me?"

"Right. We used to talk, remember? And I never could tell you what I wanted to do with my life. The rest of my family, everyone we grew up with, they make money, or collect art, or race cars, or do *something*. Me, I only wanted to watch the sky."

She smiled. "I'm really flattered, Tim."

"You really do look elegant. Your own creation?"

"Yes. Thank you."

She was still easy to talk to. Tim was finding that a

58

pleasant rediscovery when the doorbell rang. The others had come.

It was a pleasant evening. The caterers had done their job well, so there was no trouble with the food, even without George to help. Tim relaxed and found he was having fun.

They listened.

They never had before. They listened as Tim told them how it had been: the cold, dark hours of watching, of studying star patterns, of keeping the log; of endless hours poring over photographs; all with no result except the joy of knowing the universe. And they listened. Even Greg, who usually made no secret of how he felt about rich men who didn't pay proper attention to their money.

It was only a family gathering in Tim's living room, but he was elated, and nervous, and quiveringly alert. He saw Barry's smile and headshake and read Barry's mind from that: What a way to spend a life! He's actually envying me, Tim thought, and it was delicious. Tim glanced up to catch his sister watching with wry amusement. Jill had always been able to tell what Tim was thinking. He'd been closer to her than either had been to their brother Pat.

But it was Pat who trapped him behind the bar and wanted to talk.

"Like your place," Pat said. "Mom doesn't know what to make of it." He tilted his head to indicate where their mother was wandering around the room, looking at gadgets. At the moment she was fascinated by the Kalliroscope's random and strange patterns. "Bet I know what she's thinking. Do you?"

"Do I what?"

"Bring girls here. Have wild parties."

"None of your goddam business."

Pat shrugged. "Too bad. Man, there are times when I wish I . . . to hell with it. But you really ought to take advantage. You won't have forever. Mom will have her way."

"Sure," Tim said. Why the hell did Pat have to bring that up? His mother would, before the night was over. Timmy, why aren't you married yet?

One day I'll answer, Tim told himself. One day I'll say it. "Because every time I find a girl I think I could live with, you scare her spitless and she runs away, that's why."

"I'm still hungry," Penelope Joyce announced.

"Good Lord." Jill patted her stomach. "Where do you

put it? I want your secret. Only don't tell me it's your clothes. Greg says we can't afford your creations."

Penelope took Tim's hand. "Come on, show me where the popcorn is. I'll shake. You get the bowls."

"But—"

"They'll find their own drinks." She led him to the kitchen. "Let them talk about you while you're out here. They'll admire you even more. After all, you're the star tonight."

"Think so?" He looked into her eyes. "I can never tell when you're putting me on."

"There's luck. Where's the butter?"

The show was great. Tim knew that when he saw his family watching it, watching *him* on television.

Randall had gone all over the world, showing amateur astronomers staring at the sky. "Most comets are discovered by amateurs," Randall said. "The public rarely appreciates how much these skywatchers aid the big observatories. Of course, some amateurs aren't amateur at all." The scene cut to Tim Hamner showing off his mountain observatory, and his assistant, Marty, demonstrating equipment. Tim had thought the sequence would be too short, but when he watched his family watching him and it ended with them eager for more he realized that Harv Randall had been right. Always leave them wanting a little more. . . .

"And," Randall's voice said, "some are more amateur than others." The camera zoomed in on a smiling teen-age boy with a telescope. The instrument looked competent, but it was obviously home-built. "Gavin Brown, of Centerville, Iowa. Gavin, how did you happen to be looking for comets at the right time and place?"

"I wasn't." Brown's voice was not pleasant. He was young, and shy, and he talked too loud. "I made some adjustments to the setting circles because I wanted to look at Mercury in the daytime, only you have to have everything adjusted right to find Mercury because it's so close to the Sun, and—"

"So you found Hamner-Brown by accident," Harvey Randall said.

Greg McCleve laughed. Jill gave her husband a sharp look.

"Tell me, Gavin," Randall said. "Since you didn't see the comet until well after Mr. Hamner did, but you reported it almost at the same instant—how did you know it was a new comet?"

"It was something that didn't belong there."

"You mean you know everything that does belong there?" Randall said. The screen showed a photograph of the sky around Hamner-Brown. It was full of stars.

"Sure. Doesn't everybody?"

"He does, too," Tim said. "He stayed here a week, and I swear, he can draw star maps from memory."

"He stayed here?" Tim's mother asked.

"Sure. In the spare room."

"Oh." Tim's mother stared very hard at the set.

"Where's George tonight?" Jill asked. "Another date? Mother, did you know that Tim's houseboy has been dating Linda Gillray?"

"Pass the popcorn," Penelope Joyce said. "Where is Brown now, Tim?"

"Back in Iowa."

"Those commercials sell much soap?" Greg asked. He pointed at the set.

"Kalva does all right," Tim said. "Twenty-six point four percent of the market last year—"

"Jeez, they must be better than I thought," Greg said. "Who's your advertising man?"

Then the program was on again. There wasn't much more about Tim Hamner. Once discovered, Hamner-Brown Comet was the world's. Now the star was Charles Sharps, who talked about comets and the importance of knowing the Sun and planets and stars. Tim wasn't disappointed, but he thought the others were. Except for Pat, who watched Sharps and kept nodding. Once, Pat looked up and said, "If I'd had a science professor like him in my freshman year, I might have discovered a comet myself. Do you know him very well?"

"Sharps? Never met him. But I've got more of him on the video recordings," Tim said. "There's more of me, too."

Greg pointedly glanced at his watch. "Got to be in the office at five A.M.," he said. "The market's going crazy. And after that show, it will be worse."

"Huh?" Tim frowned. "Why?"

"Comets," Greg said. "Signs in the sky. Portents of evil change. You'd be surprised how many investors take things like that seriously. Not to mention that diagram the professor drew. The one that showed the comet hitting Earth."

"But it didn't," Pat protested.

"Tim! Could it?" his mother demanded.

"Of course not! Didn't you listen? Sharps said it was billions to one," Tim said.

"I saw it," Greg said. "And he said comets did hit the Earth, sometimes. And this one will be close."

"But he didn't mean it that way," Tim protested.

Greg shrugged. "I know the market. I'm going to be in the office when the big board opens—"

The phone rang. Tim looked puzzled. Before he could get up, Jill answered it. She listened for a moment, then looked puzzled as well. "It's your answering service. They want to know whether they should put through a call from New York."

"Eh?" Tim got up to take the phone. He listened. On the TV a NASA official was explaining how they might, just might, be able to get up a probe to study the comet. Tim put the phone down.

"You look dazed," Penelope Joyce said.

"I am dazed. That was one of the producers. They want me to be a guest on the 'Tonight Show.' With Dr. Sharps, Pat, so I'll meet him after all."

"I watch Johnny every night," Tim's mother said. She said it admiringly. People who got on the "Tonight Show" were important.

Randall's documentary ended in a blaze of glory, with photographs of the Sun and stars taken by Skylab, and a strong plea for a manned probe to explore Hamner-Brown Comet. Then came the last commercial, and Tim's audience was leaving. Tim realized, not for the first time, just how far apart they'd grown. He really didn't have much to say to the head of a stockbroker firm, or to a man who built town houses, even if they were his brother-in-law and his brother. He found himself mixing drinks for himself and Penelope (Joyce!) alone.

"It felt like opening night in a bad play," Tim said.

"In Boston with an allegory and the Shriners are in town," Joyce teased.

He laughed. "Hah. Haven't seen *Light Up the Sky* since . . . by golly, since you were in that summer drama thing. And you're right. That's what it was like."

"Poo."

"Poo?"

"Poo. You always did think like that, and there never was

any reason to, and there isn't one now. You can be *proud*, Tim. What's next? Another comet?"

"No, I don't think so." He squeezed lime into her gin and tonic and handed it to her. "I don't know. I'm not strong enough on theory to do what I really want."

"So learn the theory."

"Maybe." He came around and sat next to her. "But anyway, I made the history books. *Skoal.*"

She lifted her drink in salute. She wasn't mocking him. *"Skoal."*

He sipped at his drink. "I'll follow it as far as it goes, whatever else I do. Randall wants another documentary, and we'll do it, if the ratings aren't *too* bad."

"Ratings? You worry about ratings?"

"You're teasing me again."

"Not this time."

"Hmm. All right. I'll back another documentary. Because *I* want it. We'll go heavy on the space probe. With enough publicity we might get the probe up, and somebody like Sharps really will understand comets. Thanks."

She put a hand on his arm. "You're welcome. Run with it, Tim. Nobody else here tonight has done half of what they want to do. You've already got three-quarters, and a shot at the rest."

He looked at her and thought, If I married her, Mom would heave a great sigh of relief. She was in that limited class of women. They all seemed to know his sister Jill; they'd gone east to college, and to New York during vacations; they'd broken the same rules; they were not afraid of their mothers; they were beautiful and frightening. The sex urge in a teen-age boy was too powerful, too easily twisted and repressed. It made the beauty of a young woman into a flame, and when that flame was coupled to total self-confidence . . . a girl like any of Jill's friends could be a fearsome thing, to a boy who had never believed in himself.

Joyce wasn't fearsome. She wasn't pretty enough.

She frowned. "What are you thinking?"

God, no! He couldn't answer that one! "I was remembering a lot." Had he been deliberately left alone with Joyce? Certainly she had stayed after the others had left. If he made a pass now . . .

But he didn't have the courage. Or, he told himself, the kindness. She was elegant, yes, but you don't go to bed with a Steuben crystal vase. He got up and went to the video recorder. "Want to watch some of the other clips?"

For a moment she hesitated. She looked at him carefully, then just as carefully drained her glass and set it on the coffee table. "Thanks, Tim, but I'd better get some sleep. There's a buyer coming in tomorrow."

She was still smiling when she left. Tim thought it a bit forced. Or, he wondered, am I just flattering myself?

■

The maelstrom was intolerably crowded. Masses of all sizes whirled past each other, warping space into a complex topology that changed endlessly. The inner moons and planets were all scar tissue, worn craters beneath the atmospheres of Earth and Venus, naked ring walls and frozen lakes of magma spread across the faces of Mars, Mercury, Earth's Moon.

Here was even the chance of escape. The gravity fields around Saturn and Jupiter could fling a comet back out into the cold and the dark. But Saturn and Jupiter were wrongly placed, and the comet continued to fall, accelerating, boiling.

Boiling! Pockets of volatile chemicals burst and spurted away in puffs of dust and ice crystals. Now the comet moved in a cloud of glowing fog that might have shielded it from the heat, but didn't. Instead the fog caught the sunlight across thousands of cubic miles and reflected it back to the comet head from every direction.

Heat at the surface of the nucleus seeped inward. More pockets of gas ruptured and fired like attitude jets on a spacecraft, tossing the comet head this way and that. Masses tugged at it as it passed. Lost and blind and falling. The dying comet dropped past Mars, invisible within a cloud of dust and ice crystals the size of Mars itself.

A telescope on Earth found it as a blurred point near Neptune.

March: Interludes

None of the astronauts ever walked on solid lunar rock, because everywhere they have gone there was "soil" underfoot. This powdery layer is present because the Moon has been bombarded by meteorites throughout geologic time. The unceasing barrage has so pulverized the surface that it has created a residual layer of rocky debris several meters thick.

Dr. John A. Wood, Smithsonian Institution

Fred Lauren made delicate adjustments to the telescope. It was a big instrument, a four-inch refractor on a heavy tripod. The apartment cost him too much money, but he had to have it for the location. His only furniture was a cheap couch, a few cushions on the floor, and the big telescope.

Fred watched a darkened window a quarter-mile away. She had to come home soon. She always did. What could she be doing? She'd left alone. No one had come for her. The thought frightened him, then made him sick. Suppose she had met a man somewhere? Had they gone for dinner, and then to his apartment? Even now he might be putting his filthy hands on her breasts. He would have hairy hands, rough, like a mechanic's, and they would be sliding downward, caressingly down across the flat curve of her belly.

No! She wasn't that kind. She wouldn't let anyone do that to her. She wouldn't.

But all women did. Even his mother. Fred Lauren shuddered. Unwanted, the memory came back, when he was just nine, when he'd gone in to ask his mother to say his prayers, and she'd been lying on the bed with the man he called Uncle Jack on top of her. She was moaning and writhing, and Uncle Jack had leaped from the bed.

"You little bastard, I'll cut your goddam balls off! You

65

want to watch? You'll sure to God watch? Stand there and if you say one word, I'll cut your prick off!"

He'd watched. And his mother had let that man—

The window came alight. She was home! Fred held his breath. Was she alone? Was she?

She was carrying a big bag of groceries, which she took to the kitchen. Now she'll have her drink, Fred thought. I wish she wouldn't drink so much. She looks tired. He watched as the girl mixed a martini. She carried the pitcher with her to the kitchen. Fred didn't follow with the telescope, although he could have. Instead he teased himself, waiting.

Her face was triangular, with high cheekbones and a small mouth and big dark eyes. Her long, flowing blond hair was tinted; her pubic hair was very dark. Fred had forgiven her that small deception, but he'd been shocked.

She came back with the pitcher and a glass spoon. There was a silver-handled martini spoon in the gift shop down the street, and Fred had often stared at it, trying to get up the nerve to buy it for her. Maybe she'd invite him to her apartment. Only she wouldn't until he'd given her gifts, and he couldn't do that because he knew what she liked and she'd want to know how he knew that. Fred Lauren reached out to touch her through the magic mirror of his telescope . . . but only in his mind, only in his hopeless yearning.

Now. Now she'd do it. She didn't have many dresses good enough to wear to work. She worked in a bank, and although the banks let the girls wear trousers and all the ugly things girls were wearing lately, she didn't. Not Colleen. He knew her name. He wanted to keep his money in her bank, but he didn't dare. She dressed well to win promotions, and she'd been promoted to New Accounts, and Fred couldn't talk to her there. He was proud of her promotion, but he wished she'd stayed a teller, because then he could come in and go to her window and . . .

She took off the blue frock and carefully hung it in the only closet. Her apartment was very small, only one room with a bathroom and kitchen alcove. She slept on the couch.

Her slip was frayed. He'd watched her mending the straps at night. Under the slip she wore lacy black underpants. He could see the color through the slip. Sometimes she wore pink ones with black stripes.

Soon she'd be taking her bath. Colleen took long baths; Fred could be knocking at her door before she finished. She'd open the door. She trusted people. Once she'd opened the door wearing nothing but a towel, and the man outside had been a telephone man, and another time it was the building superintendent, and Fred knew he could imitate the super's voice. He'd followed the super to a bar and listened to him. She would open the door. . . .

But he couldn't do it. He knew what he'd do if she opened her door to him. He knew what would happen afterward. This would be his third time. Third sex offense. They'd lock him up with those men, those *animals*. Fred remembered what the caged men had called him and how they had used him; he whimpered, throttling the sound as if she might hear.

She put on her robe. Her dinner was in the oven, and she sat in the robe and turned on the TV set. Fred scurried across the room to turn on his own set and tune it to the same channel, then moved quickly back to the telescope. Now he could watch over her shoulder, watch her own TV, and hear the sound, and it was as if Fred and his girl were watching TV together.

It was a program about a comet.

The stocky man's hands were large and smooth, slender, stronger than they looked. They moved over Maureen, knowingly, cunningly. "Purr," said Maureen. She pulled him suddenly against her, and arched sideways, wrapping him in her long legs.

He gently pushed her away and continued to stroke her, playing her like . . . the attitude jets on a Lunar Lander. The bizarre image stuck in her mind, jarring. His lips moved against her breast, his tongue darting. Then it was time, and she could lose herself in him. She had no thought of technique now. But he had; he was always in control. He wouldn't be finished until she was, and she could depend on it, and now there was no time for thought, only the waves of shuddering feeling. . . .

She came home from a long way away.

They lay together, breathing each other's breath. Finally he stirred against her. She caught a handful of curly hair and tilted his face up. Standing, he was just her height; astronauts are generally short. Lying above her, his head reached her throat. She lifted herself to kiss him, and sighed contentment.

But now her mind was turned on again. I wish I loved him, she said to herself. Why don't I? Because he's too invulnerable? "Johnny? Does your mind ever turn off?"

He thought it through before answering. "There's a story they tell about John Glenn . . ." He rolled onto an elbow. "The space medicine boys were trying to find out what we could go through and still function. They had John Glenn wired with widgets so they could watch his heartbeat and perspiration while he went through a program on the Gemini flight simulator. Right in the middle of it they dropped a shitload of scrap iron onto a tilted iron plate, right behind him. The whole room rang with it, and it went on and on. Glenn's heartbeat went *blip!*" Johnny's finger sketched a tepee shape. "He never even twitched. He went through the whole sequence, and then he said, 'You sons of bitches. . . .'"

He watched her laugh, and then he said a bit sadly, "We can't get distracted." He sat up. "If we're going to watch your program we ought to be getting up."

"Yes. I suppose. You first."

"Right." He bent to kiss her again, then left the bed. She heard the shower running and thought of joining him. But he wouldn't be interested now. She'd said the wrong thing, and now he'd be remembering his ruined career; ruined not by any mistake of his, but by America's retreat from space.

She found his robe where he'd left it for her. Forethought. *We can't get distracted.* One thing at a time, and do that perfectly. Whether it was crawling along a ruined Skylab and repairing it in orbit, or conducting a love affair, he did it *right.* And he was never in a hurry.

When they met, Baker had been in the Astronaut Office in Houston and was assigned as liaison to Senator Jellison and party. Johnny Baker had a wife and two teen-age kids, and had been a perfect gentleman, taking Maureen to dinner when the Senator was called away, keeping her company for the week the Senator was in Washington, taking her to the launch in Florida. . . .

A perfect gentleman up to the time they'd had to go back to her motel room for her purse—and she still wasn't sure who had seduced whom. She didn't sleep with married men. She didn't like sleeping with men she didn't love, for that matter. But, love aside, he had something, and Maureen had no defense against it. He had a single goal and the ability to go after it no matter what.

And she was young and had been married once and had taken no vow of chastity and the hell with what you're thinking, girl! Maureen rolled off the bed fast and switched on the TV with a vicious *click*. Just to break the chain of thought.

But I am not a tramp.

His divorce is final next week, and I had nothing to do with that. Ann never knew. Ann doesn't know now. But maybe he wouldn't have let her go? If that's my fault, all right, but Ann never knew. We're still good friends.

"He's not the same anymore," Ann had told her. "Not since he flew the mission. Before that it was always tough here, he was on training missions all the time, and I had only a little part of him—but I had something. And then he got his chance, and everything worked fine, and my husband's a hero—and I don't have a husband anymore."

Ann couldn't understand it. I can, Maureen thought. It wasn't flying the mission, it was that there aren't any more missions, and if you're Johnny Baker and all your life you've worked and trained to do one thing, and nobody's ever going to do that again . . .

One goal in life. Tim Hamner had a touch of that. Johnny had it, and maybe she had tried to borrow a piece of it. And now look: Johnny had used up his one goal, and the most important thing in Maureen Jellison's life was a fight with a silly Washington hostess.

It still bothered her every time she thought of it.

Annabelle Cole was liberated. Six months ago it had been the threatened extinction of the snail skimmer; in six months more it might be the decline of artistic tradition among Australian blackfellahs. At the moment there was nothing for it but to blame men for everything bad that had ever happened. Nobody really minded. They didn't dare. No mean amount of the world's business was conducted at Annabelle's parties.

Maureen must have been edgy the night Annabelle braced her for her father's support. Annabelle wanted Congress to fund studies on artificial wombs, to free women from months of slavery to their suddenly altered bodies.

And I told her, Maureen thought. I told her that having babies was part of the sex act, and if she was willing to give up being pregnant she could give up fucking too. *I* said that! And I never had a baby in my life!

Dad might miss some important contacts through his daughter's exercise in tact, but Maureen could handle that. In six months, when Annabelle found a new cause, Maureen would host a party and invite someone Annabelle *had* to meet. She had it all worked out. *That* was the problem: As if a fight with Annabelle Cole was the most important event in her life!

"I'll fix some drinks," Johnny called. "Best get your shower, the program's on in a minute."

"Yo," she answered, and she thought: Him? Marry the man. Promote him a new career. Get him to run for office, or write his memoirs. He'd be good at anything he tried . . . but why couldn't she find goals of her own?

The room was definitely a man's room, with books, and models of the fighter planes Johnny Baker had flown, and a Skylab, with broken wings; and a large framed picture of a bulky-suited man crawling in space along one of those wings, a faceless, alien shape, disconnected from the spacecraft, risking the loneliest death ever if he let go for even an instant. The NASA medal hung below the picture.

Mementos of times past. But only the past. There were no pictures of the Shuttle, delayed once more; no reminders of the Pentagon, Johnny's present assignment. Two pictures of the children, one with Ann in the background, short, browned, competent Ann, who already had a look of puzzled unhappiness in the photo.

His hand was wrapped around the glass, but he had forgotten glass and hand. Maureen could watch his face without his knowing it. Johnny Baker saw only the screen.

Parabolic orbits diagramed against the concentric circular paths of the planets. Old photos of Halley's Comet and Brooks's Comet and Cunningham's Comet and others, culminating in a blurred pinpoint that was Hamner-Brown. A man with large insectile glasses lectured with fierce intensity:

"Oh, we'll get hit someday. It probably won't be an asteroid, either. The orbits are too nearly fixed. There must have been asteroids whose orbits intersected Earth's, but those have had four billion years to hit us, and most of them eventually did," said the lecturer. "They hit so long ago that even the craters are gone, weathered away, except for the biggest and the newest. But look at the Moon!

"The comets are different."

The lecturer's pointer traced a parabola drawn in chalk. "Some mass way out there beyond Pluto, maybe an undiscovered planet . . . we even have a name for it. Persephone.

Some mass disturbs the orbits of these great snowballs, and they come down on our heads in a wake of boiling chemicals. None of them have ever had a chance to hit the Earth until they get thrown down into the inner system. One day we'll be hit. We'd have about a year's warning. Maybe more, if we can learn enough about Hamner-Brown."

Then an antiseptic young woman proclaimed that she wasn't married to her house, and was told that that was why Kalva Soap had invented a new disinfectant for her toilet bowl . . . and Johnny Baker came smiling back into the world. "He really makes his points, doesn't he?"

"It is well done. Did I tell you I met the man who put it together? I met Tim Hamner, too. At the same party with Harvey Randall. Hamner's a case. Manic. He'd just discovered his comet, and he couldn't wait to tell everyone."

Johnny Baker sipped his drink. Then, after a long pause, he said, "Some funny rumors in the Pentagon."

"Oh?"

"Gus called. From Downey. Seems Rockwell's refurbishing an Apollo. And there's some mutters about diverting one of the Titan boosters from a Big Bird to something else. Know anything?"

She sipped her drink and felt a wave of sadness. Now she knew why Johnny Baker had called yesterday. After six weeks in the Pentogon, six weeks in Washington with no attempt to see her, and then . . .

And I was going to surprise him. Some surprise.

"Dad's trying to get Congress to fund a comet-study mission," Maureen said.

"This for real?" Johnny demanded.

"It's for real."

"But . . ." His hands were shaking. His hands never shook. John Baker had flown fighters over Hanoi, and his maneuvers were always perfect. The MIGs never had a chance. And once he'd taken splinters out of his crew chief when there wasn't time to get the medics. There was a splinter in the chief's chest and Baker had removed it and sliced deftly to expose the artery, clamped it together with steady fingers while the chief screamed and the Cong mortars thudded onto the field, and his hands had never shaken.

But they were shaking now. "Congress won't put up the money."

"They might. The Russians are planning a mission. Can't

let them outdo us," Maureen said. "Peace depends on showing them we're still willing to compete if that's the way they
want it. And if we compete, we win."

"I don't care if it's Martians we're competing with. I've
got to go. I've got to." He drained his scotch. His hands
were suddenly steady.

Maureen watched in fascination. He's stopped shaking because he's got a mission. And I know what it is. Me. To get
me to get him on that ship. A minute ago he might really
have been in love with me. Not now.

"I'm sorry," he said abruptly. "We don't have all that
much time together, and I'm laying *this* on you. But . . . you
had me dead to rights. My mind doesn't turn off." He drank
deeply of his ice-diluted scotch. His attention went back to
the screen, and left Maureen wondering if she'd been
imagining things. Just how clever *was* John Baker?

The commercial mercifully ended and the cameras
zoomed in on the Jet Propulsion Laboratories.

Harry Newcombe hastily chewed the last of his sandwich
while he drove the mail truck with one hand. The regulations
gave him time off for lunch, but Harry never took it. He used
the time for better purposes.

It was long past noon when he got to Silver Valley Ranch.
As usual he stopped at the gate. There was a spot where he
could look through a pass in the foothills to the majesty of
the High Sierra to the east. Snow gleamed off their tops. To
the west were more foothills, the sun not too far above them.
Finally he got out to open the gate, drove through, and
carefully closed the gate behind him. He ignored the large
mailbox on its post beside the gate.

He stopped along the drive to pick a pomegranate from
the grove that had started as one tree and was still, untended,
propagating itself downhill toward the stream. Harry had
seen it grow in the half-year he'd been on the route, and
was guessing when the pomegranates would roll all the way
downhill into the cocklebur patch. Would they choke out
the burrs? He had no idea, really. Harry was a city boy.

Harry was an ex–city boy. Hah! And if he never saw a
city again he'd be happy.

He was grinning as he shouldered his load and walked
lopsided to the door. Rang. Set the bag down.

The dimly heard hurricane of a vacuum cleaner calmed. Mrs. Cox opened the door and smiled at the bulging bag beside Harry. "That day again? Hello, Harry."

"Hi. Happy Trash Day, Mrs. Cox!"

"And a Happy Trash Day to you too, Harry. Coffee?"

"Don't stay me. It's against guv'mint regulations."

"Fresh coffee. And new-baked rolls."

"Well. . . . I can't resist that." He reached into the smaller pouch that still hung at his side. "Letter from your sister in Idaho. And something from the Senator." He handed her the letters, then shouldered the bag and wobbled in. "Anyplace special?"

"The dining table's big enough."

Harry spilled the contents of the larger bag across a polished table of lovely grain. It seemed to have been carved out of a slice of a single tree, and must have been fifty years old. They didn't make tables like that anymore. If there was furniture like that in the caretaker's home, what must it be like in the big house up the hill?

The wood grain was hidden under a deluge: begging letters from charities, from several political parties, from colleges. Offers to join lotteries by buying records, clothing, books, subscriptions to magazines. "YOU MAY ALREADY HAVE WON $100 A WEEK FOR LIFE!" Religious tracts. Political lessons. Single-tax literature. Free samples of soap, mouthwash, detergent, deodorant.

Alice Cox brought in the coffee. She was only eleven, but she was already beautiful. Long blonde hair. Blue eyes. A trusting girl, as Harry knew from seeing her when he was off duty. But she could be trusting here; nobody was going to bother her. Most of the men in Silver Valley kept rifles slung on racks in their pickups, and they damned well knew what to do with anybody who'd bother an eleven-year-old girl.

It was one of the things Harry liked about the valley. Not the threat of violence, because Harry hated violence; but that it was *only* a threat. The rifles came off their racks only for deer (in season or out, if the ranchers were hungry or the deer got into the crops).

Mrs. Cox brought in rolls. Half the people on Harry's route offered him coffee and eats, on days when he ignored regulations and brought the mail up to their houses. Mrs. Cox didn't make the best coffee on the route, but the cup was definitely the finest in the valley: thin bone china, much too good for a half-hippie mailman. The first time

73

Harry had been to the house he'd drunk water from a tin cup and stood at the door. Now he sat at the fine table and drank coffee from bone china. Another reason to stay out of cities.

He sipped hurriedly. There was another blonde girl, this one over eighteen and legal, and it would be Trash Day for her house, too. She'd be home. Donna Adams was always home for Harry. "Lot here for the Senator," Harry said.

"Yes. He's back in Washington," Mrs. Cox answered.

"But he's coming soon," Alice piped.

"Wish he'd hurry," Mrs. Cox said. "It's nice here when the Senator's in residence. People coming and going. Important people. The President stayed at the big house one night. Secret Service made a big fuss. Men wandering all over the ranch." She laughed, and Alice giggled. Harry looked puzzled. "As if anybody in this valley would harm the President of the United States," Mrs. Cox said.

"I still think your Senator Jellison's a myth," Harry said. "I've been on this route eight months, and I haven't seen him yet."

Mrs. Cox looked him up and down. He seemed a nice enough boy, although Mrs. Adams said her daughter paid him entirely too much attention. Harry's long, flowing, curly brown hair would have looked good on a girl. His beard was beautiful. The real masterpiece was the mustache. It came to long points which, on formal occasions, Harry could curl and wax into circles like small spectacles.

He can grow hair, Mrs. Cox thought, but he's little and skinny, not as big as I am. She wondered again what Donna Adams saw in him. Car, maybe. Harry had a sports car, and all the local boys drove pickups like their fathers.

"You'll likely meet the Senator soon enough," Mrs. Cox said. It was a sign of ultimate approval, although Harry didn't know that. Mrs. Cox was very careful about who the Senator met.

Alice had been sifting through the mound of multicolored paper on the table. "Lot of it this time. How much is this?"

"Two weeks," Harry said.

"Well, we do thank you, Harry," Mrs. Cox said.

"So do I," Alice added. "If you didn't bring it up to the house, I'd have to carry all of it."

Back in the truck, and down the long drive, with another stop to look at the High Sierra. Then on to the next ranch, a good half-mile away. The Senator kept a big spread, although a lot of it was dry pasture, shot through with ground-squirrel holes. It was good land, but there wasn't enough water to irrigate it.

At the next gate George Christopher was doing something incomprehensible in the orange groves. Probably setting up to smudge, Harry decided. Christopher came plodding up as Harry opened the gate. He was a bull of a man, Harry's height and two or three times Harry's width, with a thick neck. His head was bald and tanned, but Christopher couldn't be a lot over thirty. He wore a checkered flannel shirt and dark trousers, muddy boots.

Harry set the bag down and got out beside it. Christopher frowned. "Trash Day again, Harry?" He studied the long hair and extravagantly trimmed beard and the frown deepened.

Harry grinned in return. "Yup, Happy Trash Day, every two weeks, like clockwork. I'll take it up to the house for you."

"You don't have to."

"I like to." There wasn't a Mrs. Christopher, but George had a sister about Alice Cox's age, and she liked to talk to Harry. A very bright little girl, pleasant to talk to and full of news about Harry's valley.

"All right. Mind the dog."

"Sure will." Harry never worried about dogs.

"Ever wonder what the advertising industry would give for your head?" Christopher asked.

"I'll trade 'em question for question," Harry said. "Why does the government give them a lower rate so they can waste more of our time? And your taxes?"

Christopher's frown faded and he almost smiled. "Have at 'em, Harry. Lost causes are the only ones worth fighting for. And the taxpayer's cause is about as lost as they come. I'll close the gate behind you."

Day's end. Clockout time. Harry went into the sorting rooms behind the Post Office. There was a note pinned to his station.

"Hairy: the Wolf wants to see you. Gina XXX"

Gina—tall, black, erect of posture and large of bone, the only black in the valley as far as Harry knew—was at the counter. Harry winked at her, then knocked at the supervisor's door.

When he entered, Mr. Wolfe regarded him coldly. "Harry. Happy Trash Day," Wolfe said.

Oops! But Harry smiled. "Thank you, and a Happy Trash Day to you, sir."

"Not funny, Harry. Why do you do it? Why do you separate out the commercial mail and reserve it for one day every two weeks?"

Harry shrugged. He could have explained: Sorting junk mail took so much of his time that he didn't have a chance to chat with his customers, so he'd started letting it pile up. It had begun that way, but it had become popular with his people. "Everybody's happy with it," Harry said defensively. "People can go through the stuff or just drop it in the fireplace."

"It is illegal to withhold a citizen's mail," Wolfe said.

"If someone has complained, I'll take him off the list," Harry said. "I like to keep my customers happy."

"Mrs. Adams," Wolfe said.

"Oh." Too bad. Without Trash Day he wouldn't have an excuse to go up to the Adams house and talk to Donna.

"You will deliver the commercial mail according to regulations," Wolfe was saying. "As it comes in. Not in batches. Trash Day will cease."

"Yes, sir. Any other way I can be obliging?"

"Shave your beard. Cut your hair."

Harry shook his head. That part of the regulations he knew.

Wolfe sighed. "Harry, you just don't have the right attitude to be a mailman."

Eileen Susan Hancock's office was small and cramped, but it was an office; she had worked for years to get an office of her own, away from the area behind the counter. It proved that she was more than a secretary.

She was poking at the buttons on her calculator, frowning, when a sudden thought made her burst into rippling laughter. A moment later she realized that Joe Corrigan was standing in her doorway.

Corrigan came into the office. He had unbuttoned the top button of his trousers again, and it showed. His wife wouldn't let him buy larger sizes. She hadn't given up hope that he would reduce. He put his thumbs into the waistband and regarded her quizzically.

Eileen's laughter cut off. She went back to the calculator, and now she wasn't even smiling.

"Okay," Corrigan said. "What's the punch line?"

Eileen looked up with wide eyes. "What? Oh, no. I couldn't possibly tell you."

"If you drive me nuts, you think you can gain control of the company, right? Because it won't work. I've covered that." Corrigan liked to see her like this. Eileen was all-or-nothing: very serious and hard at work, or enjoying herself to the full. "Okay," Corrigan sighed. "I'll give away my secret for yours. I've had the decorators in. You see, Robin Geston signed up for the Marina deal."

"Oh? That's good."

"Yup. Means we'll need more help. As of the first, you're Assistant General Manager, if you want the job."

"Oh, I want it. Thank you." She smiled flickeringly (like a flashbulb, on and off almost before you saw it) and turned back to the desk calculator.

"I knew you would. That's why I had the decorators in. They're turning that room next to mine into a new office for you. I've told them to consult you after they do the preliminaries." Corrigan lowered his weight onto the corner of her desk. "There. I was keeping it for a surprise. Now what's your secret?"

"I've forgotten," Eileen said. "And I do have to get these estimates done so you can take them to Bakersfield with you."

"Okay," Corrigan said. He went back to his office, defeated.

If he knew, Eileen thought. She had an urge to giggle, but she held it back. She wasn't really trying to tease Corrigan. She had been thinking: Well, I did it. And Robin was nice. Not the world's greatest lover, but he didn't pretend to be, either. The way he'd suggested a rematch: "Lovers need practice," he'd said. "The second time is always better than the first."

They'd left it vague. Maybe, just maybe, she'd take him up on it sometime; but probably not. He'd also told her definitely that he was married; she'd only suspected it before.

Never had there been any suggestion that business had anything to do with their private lives. But he'd signed up with Corrigan's Plumbing Supplies for a very large deal—and she felt funny about that, and wondered if she'd have been as careless about finding out Robin's marital status if the deal hadn't been pending. But he'd signed up.

So here she was, adding up numbers, pushing papers around, and suddenly she'd asked herself: What does this have to do with plumbing? I don't make pipe. I don't lay pipe. I don't ream it out, or tell people where to put it. What I do is push paper around.

It was an important job. Measure it by the chaos she could create with one random mistake or one malicious error: Thousands of tons of supplies might be sent to the ends of the Earth by a slip of her pen. But what she did had no more to do with creation, with making the things that held a civilization together, than income tax, or being the fireman on a diesel train.

Mr. Corrigan would probably spend the whole day wondering why she'd suddenly burst into sparkling laughter, and there was no way she could tell him. It had just come to her, unexpected and irresistible: What she had done with Robin Geston on the night before last was the closest she had ever come to any activity actually connected with plumbing.

The car wouldn't be reported stolen for hours. Alim Nassor was pretty sure of that, sure enough that he would sit in it for another ten minutes. Alim Nassor had been a great man. When he had made himself great again, he would have to hide what he was doing now.

Before he was great he had been George Washington Carver Davis. His mother had been proud of that name. She'd said the family was named for Jefferson Davis. That honky had been a tough dude, but it was a loser's name, no power in it. He'd had a lot of street names since. His mother hadn't liked those. When she threw him out he took his own.

Alim Nassor meant wise conqueror in both Arabic and Swahili. Not many knew what it meant, and so what? The name had power. Alim Nassor had a hell of a lot more power than George Washington Carver ever did. You could read about Alim Nassor in the newspapers. And he could still walk into City Hall and get in to see people. He'd been able to do that ever since he broke up a riot with his switchblade and the razor blades in his shoes and the chain he carried around his waist. There was all that Federal money around for a tough dude. The honkies shoveled out money. Anything for quiet in the black ghetto. It had been a damn good game, and too bad it was over.

He cursed quietly. Mayor Bentley Allen. Los Angeles had itself another black mayor and this goddam Tom had cut off the pipeline. New people in city council. And that stupid son of a bitch of a black congressman who couldn't be satisfied with the take, no, that asshole had to put *all* his relatives on the community payroll and the fucking TV reporters found out. A black man in politics needed a snow-white rep these days. . . .

Well, the game was over, and he'd started another. Eleven jobs, each one worked fine. They'd taken . . . what? A quarter of a million dollars in loot in four years? Less than a hundred thousand after the fences went through it. Twenty thousand each for four men in four years. That wasn't even wages! Easy to say, now, that some of it should have been stashed for lawyers' fees, but at five thousand a year?

This would be the thirteenth. It wouldn't be long now. The store did a lot of business. Alim waited, always aware of the time. Two customers left, and nobody was coming down the street.

He wasn't happy about this job. He didn't like ripping off blood. Honkies were fair game, but you ought to leave brothers alone. He'd hammered that into his followers' heads, and what were they thinking of him now? But he was boxed in, he had to act fast.

The place was ripe, and he'd been saving it for an emergency, and this was one shitpot motherfucker of an emergency. His honky lawyer would probably beat this for him, but lawyers and bondsmen wanted bread, and *now*. It was crazy, robbing a store to pay a lawyer to get him off for robbing a store. Someday things would be different. Alim Nassor would *make* them different.

Almost time. Two minutes ago one of his brothers had got himself stopped for a traffic violation fourteen blocks away, and that took one pigmobile off patrol. Twenty minutes ago another brother had a "family argument" and the sister called the station house, and there went the other fuzzwagon. There'd be only the two. Black areas didn't get patrolled the way honky business districts did. Blacks didn't have big insurance policies, or know how to kiss ass down at City Hall.

Sometimes he used as many as four diversions, with traffic jams thrown in; they only took spreading some bread among the kids to get them playing in the streets. Alim Nassor was a natural leader. He hadn't been busted since juvenile days, except for that last one where an off-duty cop had come out of a laundromat. Who'd have thought that brother was a pig? He still wondered if he should have shot it out. Anyway, he hadn't. He'd run into an alley and ditched the gun and the mask and the bag. Lawyers could take care of those. The only other evidence was the honky storekeeper's identification, and there were ways to talk him out of testifying. . . .

Time. Alim got out of the car. The mask looked like a face; from ten feet away you wouldn't know it was a mask at all. The gun was under his windbreaker. Windbreaker and mask would be gone five minutes after the job. Alim's mind closed down, shutting out past and future. He walked across at an intersection. No jaywalking, nothing to attract attention. The store was empty.

It went down nice. No problems. He had the money and was on the way out when the brother came in.

A man Alim had known for years. What was that bastard doing over in this part of town? Nobody from Boyle Heights ought to be here below Watts! *Aw*, shit. But that brother *knew*. Maybe from his walk, maybe anything, shit, he *knew*.

It took him a second to make up his mind. Then Alim turned, aimed and fired. A second shot to be certain. The man went down, and the old storekeeper's eyes were big with horror, and Alim fired three times more. One more robbery wouldn't have upset anyone, but the pigs worked hard on murder. Best leave no witnesses. Too bad, though.

He came out fast, and didn't go to the stolen car across the street. Instead he walked a fast half-block, went through an alleyway and came out on another street. His arm still tingled with that unique, atavistic thrill. Man was made to use a club. and a gun is the ultimate in clubs. Point and make a fist, and if the enemy is close enough to see his face, one blow will knock him over dead. Power! Alim knew people who had got hooked on that sensation.

His brother (mother's son, not just blood) waited for him in a car that wasn't hot. They drove off just at the speed limit, fast enough not to attract attention, slow enough not to get busted.

"Had to waste two," Alim said.

Harold winced, but his voice was cool. "Too bad. Who were they?"

"Nobody. Nobody important."

March: Two

Most astronomers envisage comets as forming a vast cloud surrounding the solar system and stretching perhaps halfway to the nearest star; the Dutch astronomer J. H. Oort, after whom the cloud is usually named, has estimated that the cloud contains perhaps 100 billion comets.

        Brian Marsden, Smithsonian Institution

They loaded them up well in the Green Room. Two ushers and an astonishingly pretty hostess poured their glasses full as soon as they were half empty, so that Tim Hamner had drunk more than he liked. At that, he thought, I'm well off compared to Arnold. Arnold was a best-selling writer, and Arnold never talked about anything that wasn't in his books. When Tim told him Hamner-Brown was now visible to the naked eye, Arnold didn't know what Tim was talking about; when Tim told him, Arnold wanted to meet Brown.

One of the ushers signaled and Tim got unsteadily to his feet. The stairs hadn't seemed so steep when he came down them. He arrived onstage to hear the last of Johnny's smoothly professional monologue and to bask in the audience applause.

Johnny was in full form, joking with the other guests. Tim remembered from the monitor downstairs that Sharps of JPL had been giving a lecture on comets, and that Johnny seemed to know a great deal about astronomy. The other guest, a dowager whose breast equipment had, twenty years ago, given a new word to the English language, kept interrupting with off-color jokes. The dowager was quite drunk. Tim remembered that her name was Mary Jane, and that no one ever called her by her stage name anymore. At her age and weight it would have been ridiculous.

The opening chatter got Tim through a terrible moment of stage fright. Then Johnny turned to him and asked, "How do you discover a comet? I wish I'd done that." He seemed quite serious.

"You wouldn't have time," Tim said. "It takes years. Decades sometimes, and no guarantees, ever. You pick a telescope and you memorize the sky through it, and then you spend every night looking at nothing and freezing your can off. It gets cold in that mountain observatory."

Mary Jane said something. Johnny was alarmed but didn't show it. The sound man with his earphones gave Johnny a high sign. "Do you like owning a comet?" Johnny asked.

"Half a comet," Tim said automatically. "I love it."

"He won't own it long," Dr. Sharps said.

"Eh? How's that?" Tim demanded.

"It'll be the Russians who own it," Sharps said. "They're sending up a *Soyuz* to have a close look from space. When they get through, it will be their comet."

That was appalling. Tim asked, "But can't we do something?"

"Sure. We can put up an Apollo or something bigger. We've got the equipment sitting around getting rusty. We even did the preliminary work. But the money has run out."

"But you could put something up," Johnny asked, "if you had the money?"

"We could be up there watching Earth go through the tail. It's a shame the American people don't care more about technology. Nobody cares a hang as long as their electric carving knives work. You ever stop to think just how dependent we are on things that none of us understand?" Sharps gestured dramatically around the TV studio.

Johnny started to say something—about the housewife who ran a home computer as a hobby—and changed his mind. The studio audience was listening. There was a careful silence that Johnny had long since learned to respect. They wanted to hear Sharps. Maybe this would be one of the good nights, one of the shows that ran over and over, Sundays, anniversaries. . . .

"Not just the TV," Sharps was saying. "Your desk. Formica top. What is Formica? Anyone know how it's made? Or how to make a pencil? Much less penicillin. Our lives depend on these things, and none of us knows much about them. Not even me."

"I always wondered what makes bra straps snappy," Mary Jane said.

Johnny jumped in to give the show back to Sharps. "But tell me, Charlie, what good will it do to study that comet? How will that change our lives?"

Sharps shrugged. "It may not. You're asking what good new research does. And all I can answer is that it *always has* paid off. Not the way you thought it would, maybe. Who'd have thought we'd get a whole new medical technology out of the space program? But we did. Thousands are alive right now because the human-factors boys had to develop new instruments for the astronauts. Johnny, did you ever hear of the Club of Rome?"

Johnny had, but the audience would need reminding. "They were the people who did computer simulations to find out how long we could get along on our natural resources. Even with zero population growth—"

"They tell us we're finished," Sharps broke in. "And that's *stupid.* We're only finished because they won't let us really *use* technology. They say we're running out of metals. There's more metal in one little asteroid than was mined all over the world in the last five years! And there are *hundreds of thousands* of asteroids. All we have to do is go get 'em."

"Can we?"

"You bet! Even with the technology we already have, we could do it. Johnny, out there in space it's raining soup, and we don't even know about soup bowls."

The studio audience applauded. They hadn't been cued by the production assistants, but they applauded. Johnny gave Sharps an approving smile and decided how the program would go for the rest of the night. But first there was a frantic signal: time for a Kalva Soap commercial.

There was more after the commercial. When Sharps got going he was really dynamic. His thin, bony hands waved around like windmills. He talked about windmills, too, and about how much power the Sun put out every day. About the solar flare Skylab's crew had observed. "Johnny, there was enough power in that one little flare to run our whole civilization for hundreds of years! And those idiots talk about doom!"

But they were neglecting Tim Hamner, and Johnny had to bring him into the conversation. Hamner was sitting there nodding, obviously enjoying Sharps. Johnny carefully maneuvered the scientist back onto the comet, then saw his chance. "Charlie, you said the Russians would get a close look at Hamner-Brown. How close?"

"Pretty close. We'll definitely pass through the tail of the comet. I showed you why we can't tell how close the head will come—but it's going to be *very* close. If we're lucky, maybe as close as the Moon."

"I wouldn't call that luck," Mary Jane said.

"Tim, it's your comet," Johnny said. "Could Hammer-Brown actually *hit* us?"

"That's Hamner-Brown," Tim said.

"Oh." Johnny laughed. "What did I say? Hammer? It would be a hammer if it hit, wouldn't it?"

"You know it," Charlie Sharps said.

"Just what would it do?" Johnny asked.

"Well, we've got some pretty big holes left from meteor strikes," Tim said. "Meteor Crater in Arizona is nearly a mile wide. Vreedevort in South Africa is so big you can't see it except from the air."

"And those were the *little* ones," Sharps said. They all turned to look at him. Sharps grinned. "Ever notice how circular Hudson's Bay looks? Or the Sea of Japan?"

"Were those meteors?" Johnny asked. The thought was horrifying.

"A lot of us think so. And something pretty big cracked the Moon wide open—a quarter of its surface is covered by that so-called ocean, which was once a sea of lava welling up from where a big asteroid hit."

"Of course, we don't know what Hamner-Brown is made of," Tim said.

"Maybe it's time we found these things out," Mary Jane said. "Before one of them does hit us. Like this one."

"It's only a matter of time," Sharps said. "Give it long enough and the probability of a comet hitting us approaches certainty. But I don't think we have to worry about Hamner-Brown."

■

Henry Armitage was a TV preacher. He'd been a radio preacher until one of his converts left him ten million dollars; now he had his own slick-paper magazine, TV shows in a hundred cities, and an elaborate complex of buildings in Pasadena, complete with editorial staff.

For all that, Henry wrote much of the magazine himself, and he always did the editorials. There were too few hours in the day for Henry. He gloried in the troubles of the world. He knew what they meant. They were the signs of a greater joy to come.

For the disciples had asked the Master, " 'Tell us, when shall these things be? And what shall be the sign of thy coming, and of the end of the world?'

"And Jesus answered and said unto them, 'Take heed that no man shall deceive you. For many shall come in my name, saying "I am Christ"; and shall deceive many.' " Henry had seen the entry on the Inyo County, California, police blotter: "Charles Manson, also known as Jesus Christ; God."

"And you shall hear of wars and rumours of wars: see that ye be not troubled: for all these things must come to pass, but the end is not yet. For nation shall rise against nation, and kingdom against kingdom; and there shall be famines, and pestilences, and earthquakes, in divers places."

Matthew was Henry's favorite Gospel; and of all the Bible, that was his favorite text. Were these not the times Christ spoke of? The signs were all present in the world.

He sat at his expensive desk. The TV was concealed behind a panel that opened when Henry touched a button. It was a long way from the wood-frame, whitewashed one-room church in Idaho where Henry had started in the Thirties. The ostentatious wealth sometimes disturbed Henry, but his supporters insisted on it, even if Henry and his wife would have been as happy in plainer surroundings.

Henry toyed with his editorial, but he didn't feel inspired. As a lesson in humility he had the TV turned to an interview show; the lesson was to watch that shallow frivolity without hating those who took part in it; and that was hard, hard. . . .

Something caught his attention. A thin tall man in a herringbone sport jacket, arms waving about. Henry admired his technique. The man would make an impressive preacher. He focused all attention on himself, and his words washed across the listener.

The man was talking about a comet. A comet. A sign in the heavens? Henry knew what comets were, but because comets were natural did not mean that their timing was not miraculous. Henry had seen many healed by prayer and the doctors later "explain" the miracle.

A comet. And it would pass very close to Earth. Could this be the final sign of all? He drew a yellow lined tablet toward him and began writing in sloppy block print, using a dozen pencils. He was through three sheets before he knew his headline, and he turned back to the first page.

In two weeks his magazine would be in half a million homes around the world; and across the cover in blazing red twenty-point type would be his headline:

It would make a good text for his TV shows, too. Henry began writing frantically, feeling the way he had felt nearly forty years before, when he'd really begun to understand Matthew 24 and had carried the message to a world that didn't care.

The Hammer of God was coming to punish the decadent and the willful. Henry wrote eagerly.

April: One

From the fury of the Norsemen,
Spare us, good Lord.
From the great comet,
Good Lord deliver us.
                              Medieval litany

Tim Hamner arrived in a taxi just as Harvey's TravelAll reached JPL. As Tim handed the driver a twenty and waved him away, Harvey swore; then he put on his best face as Tim came over to join him.

Hamner looked sheepish. "Look, Harvey, I said I wouldn't interfere—and I won't. But I met Sharps on that interview show."

"Yeah, I saw that," Harvey said. "Sharps was great."

"He sure was," Hamner said. "I want to meet him again. I called JPL and they said you were coming here for an interview. Harvey, I want to come along."

Inwardly Harvey felt anger, but it was a reasonable request from a sponsor. "Sure."

Charlene, the PR lady, was waiting, and she didn't make any fuss about Tim Hamner's unexpected appearance with the crew. Sharps's office hadn't changed. There were different books scattered across the expensive desk, and instead of an IBM print-out there was a large diagram. The cast changes, Harvey thought, but the play's the same.

"What ho," Sharps said. He lifted a brow at Hamner. "Sponsor coming along to check on you? Harvey, I hope this won't take long. I'm due in the labs shortly."

Harvey waved to the crew. Charlie was already setting up,

and Mark moved around with the light meter. Mark had become pretty good at this job, and he'd stayed around longer then Harvey could remember him keeping a job before. If he left, Harvey would miss him.

"We're interested in the probe," Harvey said. "Does it look as if it will really go?"

Sharps smiled broadly. "Looks good, looks good. Thanks to Senator Arthur Jellison. Remember our conversation about that?"

"Right."

"Well, he's the man. I'd appreciate any good publicity you can give him."

Harvey nodded. He signaled to the crew. "Let's run it."

"Speed," Manuel said. Charlie was behind the camera. Mark stepped out with the board. "Sharps interview, take one." *Clack*.

"Dr. Sharps," Harvey said, "there's been some criticism of the proposed Apollo mission to study the comet. It's said it will be too dangerous."

Sharps made a gesture of dismissal. "Dangerous? We've done it all before. A tried-and-true booster and a proven capsule. Not so many months of planning as NASA likes, but ask the men who'll fly it. Ask the astronauts if they think it's too dangerous."

"Has the crew been chosen yet?"

"No—but there are forty volunteers!" Sharps grinned at the camera.

Harvey went on with his questions. They talked about the instruments the Apollo would carry. Many of them were being put together at JPL, and at Cal Tech. "Students and technicians working overtime without pay," Sharps said. "Just to help out."

"Without pay?" Harvey asked.

"Right. They get their regular work done, the things we have contracts for, and then put in overtime on comet packages. Without pay."

That ought to go well, Harvey thought. He made a note to interview some of the technicians. Maybe he could find a janitor who worked overtime to help.

"It sounds like you can't carry enough gear," Harvey said.

"Well, we really can't," Sharps agreed. "Not all we'd like to carry. But what's enough? We can take up enough to learn a *lot*."

"Right. Dr. Sharps, I understand you've done a new plot of Hamner-Brown's orbit. And you've got new photos of it."

"Hale Observatories has the photos. We did the orbit. We're safe in saying it will be a big comet. It's got the largest coma ever recorded for this distance from the Sun. That means there's a lot of ice left in the snowball. And it's going to come quite close. First it will pass at a reasonable distance, and we'll see a spectacular tail. Then it goes inside the orbit of Venus and most of it will vanish, although some of the tail may be visible for a while. Naked-eye visible, I might add. After that it will be too close to the Sun for us to see from here, but of course the Apollo crew will be able to get good observations from space. We won't see it again until it gets very near Earth on its way back out. By then the sky should be filled with the tail. I'm willing to bet that tail will be visible in daytime."

Mark Czescu whistled. Manuel didn't glitch, so Harvey knew it hadn't got onto the tape. Harvey felt like whistling himself.

The office door opened. In came a short, rounded, vague man, about thirty years old. He had a trimmed dark beard and thick glasses. He wore a green Pendleton wool shirt, and both pockets bristled with pens and pencils of every imaginable color and nib. A pocket computer hung at his belt. "Oh—sorry, I thought you were alone." His voice was apologetic. He began to back out.

"No, no, stay and hear this," Sharps said. "Let me introduce Dr. Dan Forrester. His job title is computer programmer. His degrees say Ph.D. in astronomy; around here we usually call him our sane genius."

Mark was muttering behind Harvey. "If they call him a genius in *this* outfit . . ."

Harvey nodded. He'd thought of that too.

"Dan's been doing more recasts of Hamner-Brown's orbit. He's also working on the optimum launch date for our Apollo, given the limited amount of equipment we can take, and the limited amount of consumables—"

"Consumables?" Harvey asked.

"Food. Water. Air. They take mass. We can only put up so much mass, and so we trade consumables for instruments. But consumables mean *time* in orbit. So Dan's working on the problem: Is it better to launch earlier, with less equipment, so they can stay longer but get less information—"

"Not information," Forrester said. His voice was apologetic. "Sorry to interrupt—"

"No, tell us what you mean," Harvey said.

"We're trying to maximize *information*," Forester said. "So the problem is, do we get more information by having more data about a shorter time, or less data about a longer time."

"Oh." Harvey nodded. "So what have you got on Hamner-Brown? How far away at its closest point?"

"Zero," Forrester said. He didn't crack a smile.

"Uh—you mean it's coming down our throats?"

"I doubt it." Now he smiled. "Zero within the limits of prediction. Which is a good half-million miles error."

Harvey relaxed. So, he noticed, did everyone in the room, including Charlene. They took Forrester seriously here. He turned to Sharps. "Tell us, what would happen if the comet did hit us? Suppose we got unlucky."

"You mean the head? The nucleus? Because it looks as if we might actually pass through the outer coma. Which is nothing more than gas."

"No, I mean the head. What happens? The end of the world?"

"Oh, no. Nothing like that. Probably the end of civilization."

There was silence in the room for a moment. Then for another. "But," Harvey said, his voice puzzled, "Dr. Sharps, you told me that a comet, even the head, is largely foamy ice with rocks in it. And even the ice is frozen gases. That doesn't sound dangerous." In fact, Harvey thought, I asked to get it on the record.

"Several heads," Dan Forrester said. "At least it looks that way. I think it's beginning to calve already. And if it does it now, it will do it later. Probably. Maybe."

"So it's even less dangerous," Harvey said.

Sharps wasn't listening to Harvey. He rolled his eyes toward the ceiling. "Calving already?"

Forrester's grin widened. "Ook ook."

Then he noticed Harvey Randall again. "You asked about danger," he said. "Let's look at it. We have several masses, largely the same material that boils off to form the coma and the tail: fine dust, foamy frozen gases, with pockets where the really volatile stuff has been long gone, and maybe a few rocks embedded in there. Hey—" Randall looked up at Forrester.

Forrester was grinning his cherubic smile. "That's probably why it's so bright already. Some of the gases are interacting. Think what we'll see when they *really* get to boiling near the Sun! Ook ook."

Sharps was getting that thoughtful, lost look again. Harvey said quickly, "Dr. Sharps—"

"Oh. Yes, certainly. What happens if it hits? Which it won't.

Well, what makes the nucleus dangerous is that it's big, and it's coming fast. Enormous energies."

"Because of the rocks?" Harvey asked. Rocks he could understand. "How big are those rocks?"

"Not very," Forrester said. "But that's theory—"

"Right." Sharp's was aware of the camera again. "That's why we need the probe. We don't *know*. But I'd guess the rocks are small, from the size of a baseball to the size of a small hill."

Harvey felt relief. That couldn't be dangerous. A small hill?

"But of course that doesn't matter," Sharps said. "They'll be embedded in the frozen gases and water ice. It would all hit as several solid masses. Not as a lot of little chunks."

Harvey paused to think that over. This film would take careful editing. "It still doesn't sound dangerous. Even nickel-iron meteors usually burn out long before they hit the ground. In fact, in all history there's only been one recorded case of anyone being harmed by a meteor."

"Sure, that lady in Alabama," Forrester said. "It got her picture in *Life*. Wow, that was the biggest bruise I ever saw. Wasn't there a lawsuit? Her landlady said it was *her* meteor because it ended up in her basement."

Harvey said, "Look. Hamner-Brown will hit atmosphere a lot harder than any normal meteorite, and it's mostly ice. The masses will burn faster, won't they?"

He saw two shaking heads: a thin face wearing insectile glasses, and a thick bushy beard above thick glasses. And over against the wall Mark was shaking his head too. Sharps said, "They'd bore through quicker. When the mass is above a certain size, it stops being important whether Earth has an atmosphere or not."

"Except to us," Forrester said, deadpan.

Sharps paused a second, then laughed. Politely, Harvey thought, but it was done carefully. Sharps took pains to avoid offending Forrester. "What we need is a good analogy. Um . . ." Sharps's brow furrowed.

"Hot fudge sundae," said Forrester.

"Hah?"

Forrester's grin was wide through his beard. "A cubic mile of hot fudge sundae. Cometary speeds."

Sharps's eyes lit up. "I like it! Let's hit Earth with a cubic mile of hot fudge sundae."

Lord God, they've gone bonkers, Harvey thought. The two men raced each other to the blackboard. Sharps began to draw. "Okay. Hot fudge sundae. Let's see: We'll put the vanilla ice cream in the center with a layer of fudge over it. . . ."

He ignored the strangled sound behind him. Tim Hamner hadn't said a word during the whole interview. Now he was doubled over, holding himself, trying to hold in the laughter. He looked up, choked, got his face straight, said, "I can't stand it!" and brayed like a jackass. "My comet! A cubic mile of hot . . . fudge . . . sun . . . dae . . ."

"With the fudge as the outer shell," Forrester amplified, "so the fudge will heat up when the Hammer rounds the Sun."

"That's Hamner-Brown," Tim said, straight-faced.

"No, my child, that's a cubic mile of hot fudge sundae. And the ice cream will still be frozen inside the shell," said Sharps.

Harvey said, "But you forgot the—"

"We put the cherry at one pole and say that pole was in shadow at perihelion." Sharps sketched to show that when the comet rounded the Sun, the cherry at the oblate spheroid's axis would be on the side away from Sol. "We don't want it scorched. And we'll put crushed nuts all through it, to represent rocks. Say a two-hundred-foot cherry?"

"Carried by the Royal Canadian Air Force," Mark said.

"Stan Freberg! Right!" Forrester whooped. "Shhhh . . . plop! Let's see you do *that* on television!"

"And now, as the comet rounds the Sun, trailing a luminous froth of fake whipped cream, and aims itself down our throats . . . Dan, what's the density of vanilla ice cream?"

Forrester shrugged. "It floats. Say two-thirds."

"Right. Point six six six it is." Sharps seized a pocket calculator from the desk and punched frantically. "I *love* these things. Used to use slide rules. Never could figure out where the decimal point went.

"A cubic mile to play with. Five thousand two hundred and eighty feet, times twelve for inches, times two point five four for centimeters, cube that . . . We have two point seven seven six times ten to the fifteenth cubic centimeters of vanilla ice cream. It would take a while to eat it all. Times the density, and lo, we have about two times ten to the fifteenth grams. Couple of billion tons. Now for the fudge . . ." Sharps punched away.

Happy as a clam, Harvey thought. A very voluble clam equipped with Texas Instruments' latest pocket marvel.

"What do you like for the density of hot fudge?" Sharps asked.

"Call it point nine," Forrester said.

"Haven't any of you made fudge?" Charlene demanded. "It doesn't float. You test it by dripping it into a cup of cold water. Or at least my mother did."

"Say one point two, then," Forrester said.

"Another billion and a half tons of hot fudge," Sharps said. Behind him Hamner made more strangled noises.

"I think we can ignore the rocks," Sharps said. "Do you see why, now?"

"Lord God, yes," Harvey said. He looked at the camera with a start. "Uh, yes, Dr. Sharps, it certainly makes sense to ignore the rocks."

"You're not going to *show* this, are you?" Tim Hamner sounded indignant.

"You're saying no?" Harvey asked.

"No . . . no . . . ." Hamner doubled over and giggled.

"Now, she's coming at cometary speeds. *Fast*. Let's see, parabolic speed at Earth orbit is what, Dan?"

"Twenty-nine point seven kilometers per second. Times square root of two."

"Forty-two kilometers a second," Sharps announced. "And we've got Earth's orbital velocity to add. Depends on the geometry of the strike. Shall we say fifty kilometers a second as a reasonable closing velocity?"

"Sounds good," Forrester said. "Meteors go from twenty to maybe seventy. It's reasonable."

"Right. Call it fifty. Square that, times a half. Times mass in grams. Bit over two times ten to the twenty-eight ergs. That's for the vanilla ice cream. Now we can figure that most of the hot fudge boiled away, but understand, Harvey, at those speeds we're just not in the atmosphere very long. If we come in straight it's two seconds flat! Anyway, whatever mass you burn up, a lot of the energy just gets transferred to the earth's heat balance. That's a spectacular explosion all by itself. We'll figure twenty percent of the hot-fudge energy transfers to Earth, and"—more buttons pressed, and dramatic rise in voice—"our grand total is two point seven times ten to the twenty-eighth ergs. Okay, that's your strike."

"Doesn't mean much to me," Harvey said. "It sounds like a big number. . . ."

"One followed by twenty-eight zeros," Mark muttered.

"Six hundred and forty thousand megatons, near enough," Dan Forrester said gently. "It *is* a big number."

"Good God, pasteurized planet," Mark said.

"Not quite." Forrester had his own calculator out of the belt case. "About three thousand Krakatoas. Or three hundred Thera explosions, if they're right about Thera."

"Thera?" Harvey asked.

"Volcano in the Mediterranean," Mark said. "Bronze Age. Where the Atlantis legend comes from."

"Your friend's right," Sharps said. "I'm not sure about the energy, though. Look at it this way. All of mankind uses about ten to the twenty-ninth ergs in a year. That's everything: electric power, coal, nuclear energy, burning buffalo chips, cars—you name it. So our hot fudge sundae pops in with about thirty percent of the world's annual energy budget."

"Um. Not so bad, then," Harvey said.

"Not so bad. Not so bad as what? A year's energy in one minute," Sharps said. "It probably hits water. If it hits land, it's tough for anyone under it, but most of the energy radiates back out to space fairly quickly. But if it hits water, it vaporizes it. Let's see, ergs to calories . . . damn. I don't have that on my gadget."

"I do," Forrester said. "The strike would vaporize about sixty million cubic kilometers of water. Or fifty billion acre-feet, if you like that. Enough to cover the entire U.S.A. with two hundred and twelve feet of water."

"All right," Sharps said. "So sixty million cubic kilometers of water go into the atmosphere. Harvey, it's going to rain. A lot of that water is moving across polar areas. It freezes, falls as snow. Glaciers form fast . . . slide south . . . yeah. Harvey, the historians believe the Thera explosion changed the world's climate. We *know* that Tamboura, about as powerful as Krakatoa, caused what historians of the last century called 'the year without a summer.' Famine. Crop failure. Our hot fudge sundae will probably trigger an ice age. All those clouds. Clouds reflect heat. Less sunlight gets to Earth. Snow reflects heat too. Still less sunlight. It gets colder. More snow falls. Glaciers move south because they don't melt as fast. Positive feedback."

It had all turned dead serious. Harvey asked, "But what *stops* ice ages?"

Forrester and Sharps shrugged in unison.

"So," Hamner said, "my comet's going to bring about an ice age?" Now you could see the long lugubrious face of his grandfather, who could look bereaved at a $60,000 funeral.

Forrester said, "No, that was hot fudge sundae we were talking about. Um—the Hammer is bigger."

"Hamner-Brown. How much bigger?"

Forrester made an uncertain gesture. "Ten times?"

"Yes," said Harvey. There were pictures in his mind. Glaciers marched south across fields and forests, across vegetation already killed by snow. Down across North America into California, across Europe to the Alps and Pyrenees. Winter after winter, each colder, each colder than the Great Freeze of '76–'77. And hell, they hadn't even *mentioned* the tidal waves. "But a comet won't be as dense as a cubic mile of h-h-h—"

It was just one of those things. Harvey leaned back in his chair and belly-laughed, because there was just no way he could say it.

Later he made his own tape, alone, in a studio approximation of an office—fake books on the shelves, worn carpet on the floor. Here he could talk.

"Sorry about that." (This would run just after one of Harvey's breakups. He'd done that several times in the Sharps interview.) "The points to remember are these. First, the odds against any solid part of Hamner-Brown hitting us are literally astronomical. Over these distances even the Devil himself couldn't hit a target as small as Earth. Second, if it did hit, it would probably be as several large masses. Some of those would hit ocean. Others would hit land, where the damage would be local. But if Hamner-Brown did strike the Earth, it would be as if the Devil had struck with an enormous hammer, repeatedly."

April: Interludes

Fifty thousand years ago in Arizona:

> *Friction with the air makes the surface incandescent*
> *as the oxygen in the atmosphere blowtorches the iron.*
> *From this great flying mass, sputtering chunks as large*
> *as houses fly off as the meteoroid, travelling at a low*
> *angle, nears the ground. A huge cylinder of super-*
> *heated air is forced along by the meteoroid and, as it*
> *strikes, this air is forced across the surrounding*
> *countryside in a fiery blast that instantaneously*
> *scorches every living thing for a hundred miles in*
> *every direction.*
>
> Frank W. Lane, *The Elements Rage*
> (Chilton, 1965)

Leonilla Malik scribbled a prescription and handed it to her patient. He was the last for the morning, and when the man had left her examining room, Leonilla took the bottle of Grand Marnier from her lower desk drawer and poured a small, precious glass. The expensive liqueur was a present from one of her fellow *kosmonauts*, and drinking it gave her a delicious feeling of decadence. Her friend also brought her silk hose and a slip from Paris.

And I've never been outside Russia, she thought. She let the sweet fluid roll over her tongue. No matter how I try, they will never let me go.

She wondered what her status was. Her father had been a physician with a fairly good reputation among the Kremlin elite. Then had come the "Doctors' Plot," an insane Stalinist delusion that the Kremlin physicians were trying to poison The Revolutionary Leader of Our Times, Hero of the People, Teacher and Inspired Leader of the World Proletariat, Comrade Josef Vissarionovich Stalin. Her father and forty other doctors had vanished into the Lubianka.

One of her father's legacies was a 1950 copy of *Pravda*. He had carefully underlined every mention of Stalin's name:

ninety-one times on the front page alone, ten times as Great Leader, and six as Great Stalin.

He *should* have poisoned the bastard, Leonilla thought. It wasn't a pleasant concept; there was a long tradition about that. The Oath of Hippocrates wasn't taught in Soviet medical schools, but she had read it.

As the daughter of an enemy of the people, Leonilla's future hadn't seemed very bright; but then had come a new era, and Dr. Malik was rehabilitated. By way of reparations, Leonilla had been rescued from secretarial work in an obscure Ukrainian town and sent to the university. A liaison with an Air Force colonel had resulted in her learning to fly, and from that, weirdly, to her ambiguous status in the *kosmonaut* corps. The colonel was now a general and long since married, but he continued to help her.

She had never been in space. She had been trained for it, but she had never been chosen. Instead, she treated flyers and their dependents, and got in flying time when she could, and hoped for a lucky break.

There was a tap at the door. Sergeant Breslov, a young man of no more than nineteen years, proud to be a sergeant in the Red Army; only, of course, it wasn't the Red Army anymore and hadn't been since Stalin had been forced to rename it during what he had to call The Great Patriotic War. Breslov would have preferred the Red Army. He often talked of carrying freedom across the world on the point of his bayonet.

"There is a long message for you, Comrade Captain. You have been transferred to Baikunyar." He frowned at the bottle which Leonilla had forgotten to put away.

"Back to work," Leonilla said. "That is worth celebration. Will you join me?" She poured a glass for Breslov.

He drank standing at stiff attention. It was one way of showing disapproval of officers who drank before lunch. Of course, many of them did, which to Breslov was another indication of how things had gone downhill since the Red Army days his father boasted of.

In three hours she was flying toward the spaceport. She could hardly believe it: urgency orders, authorizing her to fly a jet trainer, her belongings to be sent after her. What could be so important? She pushed the question from her mind and reveled in the joy of flying. Alone, in the clear skies, no one looking over her shoulder, no other pilots eager for their chance at the stick: ecstasy. Only one thing could be better.

Could that be why they'd sent for her? She knew of no space missions. But perhaps. I've been lucky for a long time. Why not more luck? She imagined being in a real *Soyuz*, waiting for the big boosters to roar and fling the spacecraft up into clean space, and for the hell of it she flipped the jet trainer into a series of aerobatics that would have got her grounded if anyone had been watching.

A sudden gust across the San Joaquin Valley shook the trailer slightly, bringing Barry Price to instant wakefulness. He lay still, listening for the reassuring sound of the bulldozers; his crews were still at work on the nuclear power plant. There was light outside. He sat up carefully to avoid waking Dolores, but she stirred and opened one eye. "What time is it?" she asked, her voice heavy with sleep.

"About six."

"Oh, my God. Come back to bed." She reached for him. The covers fell away, revealing her tanned breasts.

He moved away, avoiding her, then caught her hands in one of his and held them while he bent to kiss her. "Woman, you're insatiable."

"I haven't had any complaints yet. Are you really getting up?"

"Yes. I've got engineering work to do, and we've got visitors later, and I've *got* to read that memo McCleve sent over yesterday. Should have got to it last night."

She grinned muzzily. "Bet what we did was more fun. Sure you won't come back to bed?"

"No." He went to the sink and ran water until it was hot.

"You wake up faster than any man I've ever known," Dolores said. *"I'm* not getting up at the crack of dawn." She pulled the pillow over her head, but she continued to move slightly under the covers, letting him know she was awake.

Still available, Barry thought. Yo ho! Then why am I putting on my pants?

When he was dressed he pretended to think she was asleep and quickly left the trailer. Outside he stretched in the morning sunshine, breathing deeply. His trailer was at the edge of the camp that housed much of the San Joaquin Nuclear Project work force. Dolores had one far away, but she didn't use it often these days. Barry walked toward the plant with a grin that faded as he thought about Dolores.

She was wonderful. And what they did in their copious free time hadn't affected their work at all. She was more administrative assistant than secretary, and he knew damned well he couldn't get along without her; she was at least as important to his work as the operations manager, and that terrified Barry Price. He kept waiting for the posessiveness, the not unreasonable demands for his time and attention that had made life with Grace so unpleasant. He couldn't believe that Dolores would remain satisfied simply to be his . . . what? he wondered. Mistress wasn't right. He didn't support her. The idea was funny: Dolores wasn't about to let any man have that kind of control over her life. Make it lover, he thought. And enjoy it and be glad.

He stopped to get coffee from the big urn at the construction supervisor's shack. They always had excellent coffee. He carried a cup up to his office and took out McCleve's memo.

A minute later he was screaming in anger.

He hadn't calmed down when Dolores arrived about eight-thirty. She came in with more coffee to find him pacing the office. "What's the matter?" she asked.

Another thing I love about her, Barry thought. She never demands anything personal at the office. "This." He lifted the memo. "Do you know what those idiots want?"

"Obviously not."

"They want me to *hide* the plant! They want us to bulldoze up a fifty-foot earth embankment around the whole complex!"

"Would that make the plant safer?" Dolores asked.

"No! Cosmetics, that's all. Not even cosmetics. Dammit, San Joaquin is *pretty*. It's a beautiful plant. We should be proud of it, not try to hide it behind a lot of dirt."

She put the coffee down and smiled uncertainly. "You have to do it?"

"I hope not, but McCleve says the Commissioners like the idea. So does the Mayor. I'll probably have to, and dammit, it messes *hell* out of the schedule! We'll have to pull men off the excavations for Number Four, and—"

"And meanwhile, your PTA ladies are due in fifteen minutes."

"Lord God. Thanks, Dee. I'll compose myself."

"Yes, you'd better do that. You sound like a bear. Be nice, these ladies are on our side."

"I'm glad somebody is." Barry went back to his desk and his coffee and looked at the piles of work he still had to do, and hoped the ladies wouldn't take long. Maybe he'd get a chance to call the Mayor, and just maybe the Mayor would be reasonable, and then he could get to work again. . . .

The plant yard buzzed with activity. Bulldozers, forklifts, concrete trucks moved in an intricate, seemingly random pattern. Workmen carried materials for concrete forms. Barry Price led the group through this maelstrom almost without noticing it.

The ladies had seen the PR films, and they'd dressed sensibly in slacks and low shoes. They hadn't made any fuss about wearing the hard hats Dolores got for them. So far they hadn't had many questions, either.

Barry took them to the site of Number Three. It was a maze of steel girders and plywood forms, the dome-shaped containment only partially finished; it would be a good place to show them the safety features. Barry hoped they'd listen. Dolores said they'd seemed very reasonable to her, and he was hopeful, but past experience kept him on his guard. They reached a quieter area where there weren't any construction workers at the moment; there was still noise from the bulldozers and the carpenters putting up forms, boilermakers welding pipes . . .

"I know we're taking a lot of your time," Mrs. Gunderson said. "But we do think it's important. A lot of parents ask about the plant. The school's only a few miles away. . . ."

Barry smiled agreement and tried to show her that it was all right, that he knew their visit was important. His heart wasn't in it. He was still thinking about McCleve's memo.

"Do all those people really work for you?" one of the other ladies asked.

"Well, they're employed by Bechtel," Barry said. "Bechtel Engineering builds the plants. The Department of Water and Power can't keep all those construction crews on permanent payroll."

Mrs. Gunderson wasn't interested in administrative details. She reminded Barry of himself: She wanted to get to the point, and quickly. An ample woman, well dressed. Her husband owned a big farm somewhere nearby. "You were going to show us the safety equipment," she said.

"Right." Barry pointed to the rising dome. "First there's the containment itself. Several feet of concrete. So that if anything does happen inside, the problem *stays* inside. But this is what I wanted you to see." He indicated a large pipe that ran into the uncompleted dome. "That's our primary cooling line," he said. "Stainless steel. Two feet in diameter. The wall thickness of this pipe is one inch. There's a cut piece over there and I'll bet you can't pick it up."

Mrs. Gunderson went over to try. She hefted at the four-foot piece of pipe but was unable to move it.

"Now, for us to lose coolant, that would have to break completely," Barry said. "I'm not sure how that could happen, but suppose it did. Inside the containment the men are putting in the emergency cooling tanks now. Yes, those big things. If the water pressure from the primary cooling lines ever falls, those dump water at high pressure directly into the reactor core."

He led them through the structure, making them look at everything. He showed them the pumps which would keep the reactor vessel filled with water, and the 30,000-gallon tank that would contain makeup water for the turbines. "All of that is available for emergency cooling," Barry said.

"How much does it take?" Mrs. Gunderson asked.

"One hundred gallons a minute. About what six garden hoses can put out."

"That doesn't seem like very much. And it's all you need?"

"All we need. Believe me, Mrs. Gunderson, there's nobody more concerned about your children's safety than we are. Most of these so-called accidents we prepare for have never happened. We have people whose job it is to think up strange accidents, silly things that we're sure will never happen, just so that we can prepare for them." He let them wander through, knowing they'd be impressed by the massive size of everything. So was he. He loved these power plants; he'd spent most of his life preparing for this job.

Finally they had seen everything, and he led them back to the visitors' center, where the PR people could take over. Hope I did it right, he thought. They can help us a lot, if they want to. They can hurt us, too. . . .

"One thing still concerns me," Mrs. Gunderson said. "Sabotage. I know you've done all you can to prevent accidents, but suppose somebody deliberately tried to . . . to make it blow up. After all, you won't have that many guards here, and there are a lot of crazy people in this world."

"Yeah. Well, we've thought of ways people can try," Barry said. He smiled. "You'll excuse me if I don't tell you about them."

They smiled back, uncertainly. Finally Mrs. Gunderson said, "Then you're satisfied that some bunch of nuts can't harm the plant?"

Barry shook his head. "No, ma'am. We're satisfied that they can't harm *you* by anything they can do to us. But nobody can protect the plant itself. Look at the turbines. They turn thirty-six hundred revolutions a minute. Those blades are spinning so fast that if drops of *water* got in the steam lines, the turbines would break apart. The switchyard is vulnerable to any idiot with dynamite. No, we can't stop them from wrecking the plant, but then we can't stop them from setting fire to the oil tanks at a fossil plant. What we can do is see that nobody outside the power plant site gets hurt."

"And your own people?"

Barry shrugged. "You know, nobody thinks it's remarkable that police and firemen are dedicated to their work," he said. "They don't hear so much about power workers. They'd think different if they ever saw one of our apprentices standing up to his waist in oil to turn a valve, or a lineman up on a pole in the middle of an electrical storm. We'll be on the job, Mrs. Gunderson. If they'll just let us."

The wind was warm and the skies clear in the Houston suburb of El Lago. The rainy season had ended, and a hundred families had come out into their backyards. The local Safeway was almost sold out of Coors beer.

Busy, hungry, and happy to be home for a whole weekend, Rick Delanty scooped hamburgers off the grill and slid them between buns. His fenced backyard was warm and smoky and noisy with a dozen friends and their wives. From the distance they could hear the children shouting as they played some new game. Children get used to glory, even if they don't see it very often, Rick thought. Having Daddy home wasn't such a big deal to them.

". . . nothing new about the idea," his wife was saying. "Science fiction writers have been talking about big space colonies for decades." She was tall and very black, and she wore her hair in the tiny braids called corn rolls. Delanty could remember when she straightened her hair.

"For that matter, Heinlein wrote about them," Gloria Delanty said. She looked to Rick for confirmation, but he was busy at the grill, and remembering his wife when they were both students in Chicago.

"It *is* new," said a member of a very exclusive club. Evan

had been to the Moon—almost. He'd been the man who stayed in the Apollo capsule. "O'Neill has worked out the *economics* of building these giant space colonies. He's proved we can *do* it, not just tell stories."

"I like it," Gloria said. "A family astronaut project. How do we sign up?"

"You already did," Jane Ritchie said. "When you married the test pilot there."

"Oh, are we married?" Gloria asked. "I wonder. Evan, can't you people in the training office *ever* manage to keep a schedule?"

John Baker came out of the house. "Hey, Rickie! I thought I had the wrong house. There wasn't any sign of action from out front."

There was a chorus of greetings, warm from the men who hadn't seen Colonel John Baker since he went off to Washington, not so warm from the women. Baker had done it: got divorced after his mission. It happened to a lot of the astronauts, and having him back in Houston set the others to wondering.

Baker gave them all a wave, then sniffed. "Do I get one of those?"

"I'll take your order, sir, but unless there's a cancellation . . ."

"Why is it you never serve fried chicken?"

"I'm afraid of being stereotyped. Because I'm—"

"Black," Johnny Baker said helpfully.

"Eh?" Rick looked at his hands in apparent dismay. "No, that's just hamburger grease."

"So who are they picking for the big comet-watching flight?" Evan demanded.

"Damned if I know," Baker said. "Nobody in Washington's talking."

"Hell, they're sending me," Rick Delanty said. "I have it on good authority."

Baker froze with his beer half opened. Three other men nearby stopped talking, and the wives held their breath.

"I went to a fortune-teller in Texarkana, and she—"

"Jesus, give me her name and address, quick!" said Johnny. The others smiled as if hurt and went back to talking. Johnny whispered, "That was a terrible thing to do," and giggled.

"Yeah," Rick said without shame. He began turning the hamburgers with a long-handled spatula. "Why won't they tell us earlier? They've had a dozen of us training for weeks, and still no word. And this'll be the last flight for anyone until they finish the Shuttle. Six years I've been on the list, and never been up. Sometimes I wonder if it's worth it."

He set the spatula down. "I wonder, and then I remember Deke Slayton."

Baker nodded. Deke Slayton was one of the original Seven, one of the first astronauts to be chosen, and he never went up until the Apollo-*Soyuz* handshake in space. Thirteen years before a space mission. He was as good an astronaut as anyone, but he was better in ground jobs. Training, mission control; too good on the ground. "I wonder how he stood it," Johnny Baker said.

Rick nodded. "Me too. But I am the world's only black astronaut. I keep thinking that's got to be worth something."

Gloria came over to the grill. "Hi, Johnny. What are you two talking about?"

"What," Jane shouted from near the beer cooler, "do astronauts *always* talk about when there's a mission planned?"

"Maybe they're waiting for the right moment," Johnny Baker said. "Race riots. Then they can send up a black man to prove we're all equal."

"Not funny," Gloria said.

"But as good a theory as any," Rick told her. "If I knew how NASA picks one man over another, I'd be on every mission. What the hell brings you back from the five-sided funny farm, anyway?"

"Orders. Start training again. I'm in the pool for Hammerwatch."

"Hmm." Rick poked at one of the burgers. Almost done. "And wouldn't *that* do it," he said. "Two in a row. You'd have a first."

Baker shrugged. "I don't know how it works either. Never have understood how I got on the Skylab—"

"You'd be a good one," Rick said. "Experience in space repair work. And this thing's being cobbled up fast, no time for all the tests. It makes sense."

Gloria nodded, and so did the others, who weren't quite listening to them. Then they went back to their conversations. Johnny Baker hid his expression of relief by draining the Coors. If it made sense to them, it probably made sense to the Astronaut Office at Houston. "I do bring some word from Washington, though. Not official, but the straight stuff. The Russians are sending up a woman."

Odd, how the silence spread in a growing circle.

"Leonilla Malik. An M.D., so we don't have to take a doc." Johnny Baker raised his voice for a wider audience. "It's

105

definite, the Russians are sending her up, and we'll dock with their *Soyuz*. My source is confidential, but reliable as hell."

"Maybe," said Drew Wellen, and he was the only one talking, "maybe they think they have something to prove."

"Maybe we do too," someone said.

Rick felt it like a soft explosion in his belly. Nobody had promised him anything at all, but he *knew*. He said, "Why is everybody suddenly staring at me?"

"You're burning the hamburgers," said Johnny.

Rick looked down at the smoking meat. "Burn, baby. Burn," he said.

■

At three in the morning Loretta Randall followed strange sounds into the kitchen.

Yesterday's newspaper was spread across the middle of the kitchen floor. Her largest rectangular cake pan was in the middle, and was filled with a layer of flour. Flour had sprayed across the newspaper and beyond its edges. Harvey was throwing things into the cake pan. He looked tired, and sad.

Loretta said, "My God, Harvey! What are you doing?"

"Hi. The maid's coming tomorrow, isn't she?"

"Yes, of course, it's Friday, but what will she *think?*"

"Dr. Sharps says that all craters are circular." Harvey posed above the cake pan with a lug nut in his fingers; he let it drop. Flour sprayed. "Whatever the velocity or the mass or the angle of flight of a meteor, it leaves a circle. I think he's right."

The flour was scattered with shelled peas and bits of gravel. A paperweight had left a dinner-plate-size circle now nearly obliterated by smaller craters. Harvey backed away, crouched, and hurled a bottle cap at a low angle. Flour sprayed across the paper. The new crater was a circle.

Loretta sighed with the knowledge that her husband was mad. "But, Harvey, why *this?* Do you know what time it is?"

"But if he's right, then . . ." Harvey glanced at the globe he had brought from his office. He had outlined circles in Magic Marker: the Sea of Japan, the Bay of Bengal, the arc of islands that mark the Indies Sea, a double circle within the Gulf of Mexico. If an asteroid strike had made any one of those, the oceans would have boiled, all life would have been cremated. How often had life begun on Earth, and been scalded from its face, and formed again?

If he could explain succinctly enough, Loretta would lie

awake in terror until dawn. "Never mind," he said. "It's for the documentary."

"Come to bed. We'll clean this up in the morning, before Maria gets here."

"No, don't touch it. Don't let her move it. I want photographs . . . from a lot of angles. . . ." He leaned groggily against her, their hips bumping as they returned to bed.

April: Two

*No one knows how many objects ranging in size from
a few miles in diameter downward may pass near the
Earth each year without being noticed.*

> Dr. Robert S. Richardson,
> Hale Observatory, Mount Wilson

Tim Hamner was waiting by the TravelAll when Harvey came
out of the studio building. Harvey frowned. "Hello, Tim.
What are you doing out here?"

"If I go inside, it's a sponsor calling, and that's a big deal,
right? I don't want a big deal. I want a favor."

"Favor?"

"Buy me a drink and I'll tell you about it."

Harvey eyed Tim's expensive suit and tie. Not really appropriate for the Security First. He drove to the Brown Derby.
The parking attendant recognized Tim Hamner, and so did
the hostess; she led them in immediately.

"Okay, what's it about?" Harvey asked when they had a
booth.

"I liked being out at JPL with you," Hamner said. "I've
sort of lost control of my comet. Nothing I can do the experts
can't do better, and the same with the TV series. And it *is*
your series. But . . ." Tim paused to sip his drink. He wasn't
used to asking for favors, especially from people who worked
for him. "Harvey, I'd like to come along on more interviews.
Unpaid, of course."

Oh, shit. What happens if I tell him it can't be done? Will
he talk to his agency? I sure as hell don't need a test of

strength just now. "It's not always so exciting, you know. Right now we're doing man-in-the-street interviews."

"Aren't those pretty dull?"

"They can be. But sometimes you get pure gold. And it doesn't hurt to check in with the viewers now and then." And I work *my* way, goddammit!

"What are you looking for? Can you use much of it?"

Harvey shrugged. "I won't throw away good film—but that's not the point. I want attitudes. I want the unexpected. If I knew what I was after, I could have someone else do it. And . . ."

"Yeah?" Tim's eyes narrowed in the dim light. He'd seen a funny expression on Randall's face.

"Well, there are strange reactions I don't understand. They started after Johnny called it the Hammer—"

"Damn him!"

"And they'll probably get stronger after we air the Great Hot Fudge Sundae strike. Tim, it's almost as if a lot of people *wanted* the end of the world."

"But that's ridiculous."

"Maybe. But we're getting it." Ridiculous to you, Harvey thought. Not so ridiculous to a man trapped in a job he hates, or a woman forced to sleep with a slob of a boss to keep her job. . . . "Look, you're the sponsor. I can't stop you, but I insist on making the rules. Also, we start early in the mornings—"

"Yeah." Tim drained his glass. "I'll get used to it. They say you can get used to hanging if you hang long enough."

The TravelAll was crammed full of gear and people. Cameras, tape equipment, a portable field desk for paper work. Mark Czescu had trouble finding a place to sit. Now there were three in back, since Hamner claimed the front seat. Mark was reminded of trips out to the desert with the dedicated bike racers: motorcycles and mechanic's equipment braced with care, riders shoved in as afterthought. As he waited for the others to come out of the studio building, Mark turned on the radio.

An authoritative voice spoke with the compelling quality of the professional orator. "And this Gospel of the kingdom shall be preached in all the world for a witness unto all nations; and then shall the end come. When ye therefore see

110

the abomination of desolation spoken of by Daniel the prophet stand in the holy place: then let them which be in Judea flee into the mountains." The voice quality changed, from reader to preacher. "My people, have you not seen what is now done in the churches? Is this not that abomination? 'Whoso readeth, let him understand.' And the Hammer approaches! It comes to punish the wicked.

" 'For then shall be great tribulation, such as was not since the beginning of the world unto this time, no, nor ever shall be. And except those days be shortened, there should be no flesh saved.' "

"Really lays it on," a voice said behind Mark. Charlie Bascomb got into the TravelAll.

"The Gospel has been brought to you by the Reverend Henry Armitage," the radio announcer said. "The Voice of God is broadcast in every language throughout the world in obedience to the commandment. Your contributions make these broadcasts possible."

"Sure hear him a lot nowadays," Mark said. "He must have a lot of new contributors."

They drove out into Burbank and parked near the Warner Brothers Studios. It was a good street: lots of shops, from hole-in-the-wall camera stores to expensive restaurants. People flowed along the wide avenue. Starlets and production people from the studios mingled with straight business types from insurance offices. Middle-class housewives parked station wagons and took to the streets. A famous TV personality who lived in nearby Toluca Lake strolled past. Mark recognized the ski-shaped nose.

While the crew set up camera and sound equipment, Harvey took Tim Hamner into a restaurant for coffee. When everything was ready, Mark went inside. As he neared the booth he heard Randall speaking. Harvey's voice had an edge that Mark recognized.

". . . whole purpose is to find out what *they* think. What I think, I hide in neutral questions and a neutral voice. What you think, you hide in silence. Clear?"

"Absolutely," Hamner drawled. He looked more awake than he had on the drive out. "So what do I do?"

"You can look useful. You can help Mark with the release forms. And you can stay out of the way."

"I've got a good tape machine," Hamner said. "I could—"

"We couldn't use anything you've got," Randall said. "You're not in the union." He looked up and saw Mark, got the nod and left.

Mark walked out with Hamner. "He gave me that same routine," Mark said. "Really ate me out."

"I believe you. I think if I blew an interview for him he'd abandon me on the spot. And cabs home from here cost a *lot*."

"You know," Mark said, "somehow I got the idea you were the sponsor."

"Yup. That Harv Randall is one tough mother," Hamner said. "Have you been in this business very long?"

Mark shook his head. "Just temporary, just working for Harv. Maybe one day I'll do it permanently, but you know how the TV business is. It'd cut into my freedom."

There was smog in Burbank. "I see Hertz has reclaimed the mountains," Hamner said.

Mark looked up in surprise. "How's that?"

Hamner pointed northward where the San Fernando Valley horizon faded into a brown smear. "Sometimes we keep mountains up there. I even have an observatory on one of them. But I guess Hertz Rent-A-Mountain has taken them back today." They reached the TravelAll. The cameras were set up, ready to zoom in for close-ups or pan out for a wide view. Harvey Randall had already stopped a muscular man in hard hat and work clothes; he looked out of place among the shoppers and business types.

". . . Rich Gollantz. We're putting up the Avery Building over there."

Harvey Randall's voice and manner were intended to get the subjects talking; his questions could be filmed again if they were needed on camera. "Have you heard much about the Hamner-Brown Comet?"

Gollantz laughed. "I don't spend as much time thinking about comets as you might expect." Harvey smiled. "But I did see the 'Tonight Show' where they said it could hit the Earth."

"And what did you think about that?" Harvey asked.

"Buncha . . . crap." Gollantz eyed the camera. "Same kind of thing people are always saying. Ozone's gone, we'll all die. And remember 'sixty-eight, when all the fortune-tellers said California was going to slide off into the sea, and the crazies took to the hills?"

"Yes, but the astronomers say that if the head of the comet hit, it would cause—"

"Ice age," Gollantz interrupted. "I know about it. I saw that thing in *Astronomy* magazine." He grinned and scratched under the yellow metal helmet. "Now that'd really be something. Think about all the new construction projects we'd need. And the Welfare boys could pass out polar bear furs instead of checks. Only, somebody'd have to shoot bears for them. Maybe I could get that job." Gollantz grinned widely. "Yep, it might be fun. I wouldn't mind trying life as a mighty hunter."

Harvey dug for more. The interview wasn't likely to produce usable film, but that wasn't its purpose. Harvey was fishing, with the camera as bait. The network didn't approve of this method of research. Too expensive, too crude, and unreliable, they said. They got that opinion straight from the motivational-research outfits that wanted NBS to hire them.

A few more questions. Science and technology. Gollantz was enjoying being on camera. Had he heard about the Apollo shot to study the comet, and what did he think of that?

"Love it. Be a good show. Lots of good pictures, and it'll cost me less than I paid for Rose Bowl tickets, I guarantee you that. Hey, I hope they let Johnny Baker go up again."

"Do you know Colonel Baker?"

"No. Wish I did. Love to meet him. But I saw the pictures of him fixing Skylab. Now *that* was construction work. And when he got back down, he sure gave those NASA bastards hell, didn't he? Hey, I got to be moving. We got work to do." He waved and moved off. Mark chased him with a release form.

"Sir? Moment of your time?"

The young man walked with his head down, lost in thought. He was not bad-looking, but his face was curiously wooden. He showed a flash of anger when Randall interrupted his thoughts. "Yes?"

"We're talking with people about Hamner-Brown Comet. May I have your name?"

"Fred Lauren."

"Have you any thoughts on the comet?"

"No." Almost reluctantly he added, "I watched your program." Muscles knotted at Fred Lauren's jaws, in a manner that Harvey recognized. Some men go through life perpetually angry. The muscles that clamp their jaws and grind their teeth are very prominent.

Harvey wondered if he had found a mental patient. Still . . . "Have you heard there's a chance the head of the comet might hit the Earth?"

"Hit the Earth?" The man seemed stunned. Abruptly he

turned and walked away striding rapidly, much faster than he'd approached.

"What was that all about?" Tim Hamner asked.

"Don't know," Harvey said. Man on his way to do murder? The violently insane are constantly released back to the public. Not enough hospitals. Was Lauren one of those, or just a man who'd had a nonfight with his boss? "We'll never know. If you can't stand not knowing, you're in the wrong game."

Fred had not been watching Randall's previous program. He had been watching Colleen watch a program about a comet . . . but some of what he had heard began to surface. The Earth was in the comet's path. If the comet hit, civilization would end in fire.

The end of the world. I'll be dead. We'll *all* be dead. He gave up all thought of going back to work. There was a magazine stand down the street and he walked rapidly toward it.

There were other interviews. Housewives who'd never heard of the comet. A starlet who recognized Tim Hamner from the "Tonight Show" and wanted to be filmed kissing him. Housewives who knew as much about the comet as Harvey Randall did. A Boy Scout taking a merit badge in astronomy.

There were few trends that Harvey could spot. One wasn't surprising: There was a lot of space industry in Burbank, and people there overwhelmingly approved of the coming Apollo shot. Still, the near unanimity was unusual, even for this area. People, Harvey suspected, wanted another manned shot and more looks at their heroes, the astronauts, and the comet was a good excuse. There were mutters about costs, but, like Rich Gollantz, most thought they paid more for worse entertainment every month.

They were about to pack it in when Harvey spotted a remarkably pretty girl. Never hurts to have a few feet of beauty, Harvey thought. She seemed preoccupied, and scurried along the sidewalk, her face abstracted with weighty matters and lean with efficiency.

Her smile was sudden and very nice. "I don't watch much

television," she said. "And I'm afraid I never heard of your comet. Things have been hectic at the office—"

"It will be a very big comet," Harvey said. "Look for it this summer. There's also a space mission to study it. Would you approve?"

She didn't answer immediately. "Will we learn a lot from it?" When Harvey nodded, she said, "Then I'm for it. If it doesn't cost too much. And if the government can pay for it. Which seems doubtful."

Harvey said something about the comet study costing less than football tickets.

"Sure. But the government doesn't *have* the money. And they won't cut back on anything. So they'll have to print the money. Bigger deficit. More inflation. Of course we'll get more inflation no matter what, so we might as well learn about comets for our money."

Harvey made encouraging noises. The girl had turned very serious. Her smile faded into a pensive look that turned to anger. "What difference does it make what I think, anyway? Nobody in government listens. Nobody cares. Sure, I hope they do send up an Apollo. At least something *happens*. It's not just pushing papers from one basket to another."

Then that smile was back again, a sunburst on her face. "And why am I telling you about the political sorrows of the world? I've got to go." She scurried off before Harvey could ask her name.

There was a conservatively dressed black man standing patiently, obviously waiting to get on camera. Muslim? Harvey wondered. They dressed that way. But he turned out to be a member of the Mayor's staff who wanted to tell everyone that the Mayor *did* care, and if the voters would approve the Mayor's new smog-control bond issue, people would be able to see the stars from the San Fernando Valley.

"You might be on for all of five seconds. A flash of that lovely smile," Tim Hamner was saying. "And 'Hamner-Brown? What's that?' Then cut to someone who's sure it's going to blast Culver City to smithereens."

She laughed. "All right. I'll sign your form."

"Good. Name?"

"Eileen Susan Hancock."

Hamner wrote it carefully. "Address? Phone number?"

She frowned. She looked at the TravelAll, and all the

camera gear. She looked at Hamner's expensive leisure suit, and the thin Pulsar watch. "I don't see—"

"We like to check with people before we use them on camera," Tim said. "Blast. I didn't mean it that way. I'm not really a professional at this. Just unpaid labor. Also the sponsor. And the man who discovered the comet."

Eileen made a face: mock astonishment. "How . . . incestuous!" They both laughed. "How did you get to be all that?"

"Picked the right grandfather. Inherited a lot of money and a company called Kalva Soap. Spent some of the money on an observatory. Found a comet. Got the company to sponsor a documentary on the comet so I could brag about it. See, it all makes perfect sense."

"Of course, it's all so simple now that you've explained it."

"Listen, if you don't want to give me your address—"

"Oh, I do." She lived in a high-rise in West Los Angeles. She gave him her phone number, too. She shook his hand briskly, and said, "I have to run, but I'm really glad I met you. You've made my day." And she was gone, leaving Hamner with a dazed and happy smile.

"Ragnarok," the man said. "Armageddon." His voice was strong, persuasive. He had a *great* beard, a full black beard with two tufts of pure white at the chin, and mild, kindly eyes. "The prophets of all lands saw this day coming. The Day of Judgment. The war of fire and ice is foretold by the ancients. The Hammer is ice, and it will come in fire."

"And what do you advise?" Harvey Randall asked.

The man hesitated; he may have feared that Randall was mocking him. "Join a church. Join any church you can believe in. 'In my father's house are many mansions.' The truly religious will not be turned away."

"What would you do if Hamner-Brown happens to miss?"

"It won't."

Harvey turned him over to Mark and the release form, and gave Charlie the signal to pack it in. It had not been a bad day; they had a few minutes he could use, and Harvey had learned something about the mood of his viewers.

Mark came up with the form. "Went well, didn't it. You will notice that I kept my mouth shut."

"So you did. Nice going."

Hamner came grinning at some private pleasure. He stowed

116

his recording equipment in the truck and climbed aboard. "Did I miss anything?"

"Ragnarok is coming. Earth will die in fire and ice. He had the best beard I've ever seen. Where the hell were you?"

"Getting a release form," said Tim. He wore that sappy smile all the way back to the lot.

From the NBS lot Tim Hamner drove to Bullocks. He knew what he was after. From there to a florist, and then to a drugstore. At the drugstore he bought sleeping pills. He was going to be keeping strange hours.

He flopped on the bed, fully dressed. He was deeply asleep when the phone rang around six-thirty. He rolled over and felt around for the receiver. "Hello?"

"Hello, I'd like to speak to Mr. Hamner, please."

"This is me. Eileen? Sorry, I was asleep. I was going to call you."

"Well, I beat you to it. Tim, you really know how to get a girl's attention. The flowers are beautiful, but the vase—I mean, we'd only just met!"

He laughed. "I take it you're a Steuben crystal fan, then. I've got a nice collection myself."

"Oh?"

"I go ape over the animals." Tim shifted to a sitting position. "I've got . . . let's see, a blue whale, a unicorn, a giraffe I got from my grandmother, it's in an older style. And the Frog Prince. Have you seen the Frog Prince?"

"I've seen pictures of His Majesty. Hey, Tim, let me take you to dinner. There's an unusual place called Dar Magrib."

A man would usually pause when Eileen asked *him* to dinner. With Tim the pause was barely noticeable. "Mr. Hamner accepts, with thanks. Dar Magrib's unusual, all right. Have you been there?"

"Yes. It's very good."

"And you were going to let me go without warning? Without telling me I'd be eating with my fingers?"

Eileen laughed. "Test your flexibility."

"Uh-huh. Why don't you come over here for cocktails first? I'll introduce you to His Majesty and the other crystal." Tim told her how to get there.

Fred Lauren came home with a stack of magazines. He dropped them beside the easy chair, sank into the sagging springs and began reading the *National Enquirer*.

The article confirmed his worst fears. The comet was certain to hit, and nobody had any idea where. But it was going to hit in summer, and therefore (the sketch made clear) it would hit in the Northern Hemisphere. Nobody knew how massive the comet head would be, but the *Enquirer* said it might mean the end of the world.

And he had heard that radio preacher, that fool who was on all the stations. The end of the world was coming. His jaw tightened, and he picked up the copy of *Astronomy*. According to *Astronomy* it was a hundred thousand to one against any part of the head striking the Earth, but Fred barely noticed that. What drew him were the artist's conceptions, infinitely vivid, of an asteroid strike sending up jets of molten magma; of an "average" asteroid poised above Los Angeles for comparison; of a comet head striking ocean, the sea bed laid bare.

The pages had grown too dark to see, but Fred didn't think of turning on the light. Many men never believe they are going to die, but Fred believed, now. He sat in the dark until it occurred to him that Colleen must have come home, and then he went to the telescope.

The girl wasn't in view, but the lights were on. An empty room. Fred's eye suddenly painted it with flame. The stucco wall around the window flashed blinding light, which died slowly to reveal curtains flaming, bedclothes, couch, tablecloth and table, everything afire. Windows shattered, splinters flying. Bathroom door—opened.

The girl came out struggling into a robe. She was naked. To Fred she glowed like a saint, with a beauty almost impossible to see directly. An eternity passed before she closed the robe . . . and in that eternity Fred saw her bathed in the light of Hammerfall. Colleen glowed like a star, eyelids clenched futilely shut, face speckled with glass splinters, robe charring, long blonde hair crisping, blackening, flaming . . . and she was gone before they had met. Fred turned away from the telescope.

We can't meet, the voice of reason told him. *I know what I'd do. I can't face prison again.*

Prison? When the comet was coming to end the world? Trials took time. He'd never reach prison. He'd be dead first. Fred Lauren smiled very strangely; the muscles at the corners of his jaw were knotted tight. *He'd be dead first!*

May

By the 1790's, philosophers and scientists were aware of many allegations that stones had fallen from the sky, but the most eminent scientists were skeptical. The first great advance came in 1794, when a German lawyer, E.F.F. Chladni, published a study of some alleged meteorites, one of which had been found after a fireball had been sighted. Chladni accepted the evidence that these meteorites had fallen from the sky and correctly inferred that they were extraterrestrial objects that were heated from falling through the earth's atmosphere. Chladni even postulated that they might be fragments of a broken planet—an idea that set the stage for early theories about asteroids, the first of which was discovered seven years later. Chladni's ideas were widely rejected, not because they were ill conceived, for he had been able to collect good evidence, but because his contemporaries simply were loath to accept the idea that extraterrestrial stones could fall from the sky.

William K. Hartmann, *Moons and Planets: An Introduction to Planetary Science*

The young man walked with a decided limp. He almost tripped on the thick rug in the big office, and Carrie, Senator Jellison's receptionist, took his arm for a moment. He shrugged her angrily away. "Mr. Colin Saunders," Carrie announced.

"What can I do for you?" Senator Jellison asked.

"I need a new leg."

Jellison tried not to look surprised, but he wasn't successful. And I thought I'd heard 'em all, he thought. "Have a seat." Jellison glanced at his watch. "It's after six. . . ."

"I know I'm taking up your valuable time." Saunders's voice was belligerent.

"Wasn't thinking about my time," Arthur Jellison said. "Being it's after six, we can have a drink. Want something?"

"Well . . . yes, please, sir."

"Fine." Jellison got up from the ornate wooden desk and went to the ancient cabinet on the wall. The building wasn't *that* old, but the cabinets looked as if they might have been used by Daniel Webster, who was reputed not to wait until six. Senator Jellison opened the cabinets to reveal a huge stock of liquor. Nearly every bottle had the same label.

"Old Fedcal?" the visitor asked.

"Sure. Don't let the labels fool you. That's Jack Daniels bourbon in the black bottle. The rest of 'em are top brands, too. Why pay brand prices when I can get it from home a lot cheaper? What'll you have?"

"Scotch."

"Right here. I'm a bourbon man myself." Jellison poured two drinks. "Now tell me what this is all about."

"It's the VA." Saunders poured out his story. This would be his fourth artificial leg. The first one the Veterans Administration gave him had fit fine, but it had been stolen, and the next three didn't fit at all, they hurt, and now the VA wasn't going to do anything about it.

"Sounds like a problem for your representative," Jellison said gently.

"I tried to see the Honorable Jim Braden." The young man's voice was bitter again. "I couldn't even get an appointment."

"Yeah," Jellison said. "Excuse me a second." He took a small bound book from a desk drawer. "HAVE AL LOOK INTO PRIMARY OPPOSITION FOR THAT SON OF A BITCH," he wrote. "THE PARTY DON'T NEED CREEPS LIKE THAT, AND THIS AIN'T THE FIRST TIME." Then he drew a memo pad toward him. "Better give me the names of the doctors you've been dealing with," he said.

"You mean you'll really help?"

"I'll have somebody look into it." Jellison wrote the details on the memo pad. "Where'd you get hit?"

"Khe Sanh."

"Medals? It helps to know."

The visitor shrugged. "Silver Star."

"And Purple Heart, of course," Jellison said. "Want another drink?"

The visitor smiled and shook his head. He looked around the big room. The walls were decorated with photographs: Senator Jellison at an Indian reservation; Jellison at the controls of an Air Force bomber; Jellison's children, and staff, and friends. "I don't want to take any more of your time. You must be busy." He got up carefully.

Jellison saw the visitor to the door. Carrie had to unlock it. "That's the last," she said.

"Fine. I'll stick around awhile. Send Alvin in, and you can go home—oh, one thing. See if you can get me Dr. Sharps at JPL first, will you? And call Maureen to tell her I'll be a little late."

"Sure." Carrie grinned to herself as the Senator went back into his office. Before she finally left he'd have nine other last-minute items. She was used to it. She looked into the staff rooms on the other side of her office. Everyone was gone except Alvin Hardy. He always waited, just in case. "He wants you," Carrie said.

"So what else is new?" Al went into the big office. Jellison was sprawled out in his judge's chair, his jacket and narrow-striped tie laid across the desk, his shirt unbuttoned halfway down. A big glass of bourbon sat next to the bottle. "Yes, sir?" Al said.

"Couple of things." He handed Al the memo. "Check this story out. If it's true, I want a medium-size fire built under those people. Let 'em save money on their goddam salaries, not cheating a Silver Star vet out of a leg that fits."

"Yes, sir."

"And then you can take a look at Braden's district. Seems to me the Party ought to have a bright young chap in there. I mind a city councilman—"

"Ben Tyson," Al said helpfully.

"That's his name. Tyson. Think he could beat Braden?"

"He might. With your help."

"Look into it. I've about had it with Mr. Braden being so goddam busy saving the world he hasn't got time to look after his constituents." Senator Jellison wasn't smiling at all.

Al nodded. Braden, he thought, you're dead. When the boss gets in that mood—

The intercom buzzed. "Dr. Sharps," Carrie said.

"Right. Don't go, Al. I want you to hear this. Charlie?"

"Yes, Senator?" Dr. Sharps said.

"How's the launch going?" Jellison asked.

"Everything's fine. It would be even better if I didn't have every VIP in Washington calling me to ask about it."

"Goddammit, Charlie, I went out on a long limb for you. If anybody's got a right to know, it's me."

"Yes. Sorry," Sharps said. "Actually, things are better than we expected. The Russians are helping a lot. They've got a big booster, and they're taking up a lot of consumables they'll share with our team. Lets us take up more science packages. For once we've got a division of labor that makes sense."

"Good. You won't ever know how many favors I used up getting that launch for you. Now tell me again how valuable all this is."

"Senator, it's about as valuable as we can get—given what we're doing. It's not going to cure cancer, but we'll sure learn a lot about planets and asteroids and comets. Also, that TV fellow, Harvey Randall, wants you in his next documentary. He seems to think the network ought to thank you for getting this launch."

Jellison looked up at Al Hardy. Hardy grinned and nodded vigorously. "They'll love us in L.A.," Al said.

"Tell him I like it," Jellison said. "Any time. Have him check with my assistant. Al Hardy. You got that?"

"Right. Is that all, Art?" Sharps asked.

"Nooo." Jellison drained the whiskey glass. "Charlie, I keep getting people in here who think that comet's going to hit us. Not crazies. Good people. Some of 'em with as many degrees as you have."

"I know most of them," Sharps admitted.

"Well?"

"What can I say, Art?" Sharps was quiet for a moment. "Our best projected orbit puts that comet right on top of us—"

"Jesus," Senator Jellison said.

"But there's several thousand miles' error in those projections. And a miss by a thousand miles is still a miss. It can't reach out and grab us."

"But it *could* hit."

"Well . . . this isn't for publication, Art."

"Didn't ask for it for publication."

"All right. Yes. It *could* hit us. But the odds are against it."

"What kind of odds?"

"Thousands to one."

"I recall you said billions to one—"

"So the odds have narrowed," Sharps said.

"Enough so we ought to be doing something about it?"

"How could you? I've spoken with the President," Sharps said.

"So have I."

"And he doesn't want to panic anybody. I agree. It's still thousands to one against anything happening at all," Sharps insisted. "And a complete certainty that a *lot* of people will get killed if we start making preparations. We're already getting crazy things. Rape artists. Nut groups. People who see the end of the world as an opportunity—"

"Tell me about it," Jellison said dryly. "I told you, I saw the President too, and he's got your opinion. Or you've got his. I'm not talking about warning the public, Charlie, I'm talking about *me*. Where will this thing hit, if it does?"

There was another pause.

"You've studied it, haven't you?" Jellison demanded. "Or that crazy genius you keep around, uh, Forrester, he's studied it. Right?"

"Yes." The reluctance was plain in Sharps's voice. "The Hammer has calved. If it does hit, it's likely to be in a series of strikes. Unless the central head whams us. If that happens, don't worry about preparations. There aren't any."

"Wow."

"Yeah," Sharps said. "That bad."

"But if only part hits—"

"Atlantic Ocean, for sure," Sharps said.

"Which means Washington. . . ." Jellison let his voice trail off.

"Washington will be under water. The entire East Coast up to the mountains," Sharps said. "Tidal waves. But it's long odds, Art. Very long. Best guess is still that we get a spectacular light show and nothing more."

"Sure. Sure. Okay, Charlie, I'll let you get back to work. By the way, where'll you be on That Day?"

"At JPL."

"Elevation?"

"About a thousand feet, Senator. About a thousand feet. Goodbye."

The connection went before Jellison could switch off the phone. Jellison and Hardy looked at the dead instrument for a moment. "Al, I think we want to be at the ranch. Good place to watch comets from," Jellison said.

"Yes, sir—"

"But we want to be careful. No panic. If this gets a big play the whole country could go up in flames. I expect Congress will find a good reason for a recess that week, we won't have to do anything about that, but I want my family out at the ranch, too. I'll take care of Maureen. You see that Jack and Charlotte get there."

Al Hardy winced. Senator Jellison had no use for his son-in-law. Neither did Al. It wouldn't be pleasant, persuading

Jack Turner to take his wife and children out to the Jellison ranch in California.

"May as well be hung for a sheep," Jellison said. "You're coming out with us, of course. We'll need equipment. End-of-the-world equipment. Couple of four-wheel-drive vehicles—"

"Land Rovers," Al said.

"Hell no, not Land Rovers," Jellison said. He poured another two-finger drink. "Buy American, dammit. That comet probably *won't* hit, and we sure as hell don't want to be owning foreign cars after it goes by. Jeeps, maybe, or something from GMC."

"I'll look into it," Al said.

"And the rest of it. Camping gear. Batteries. Razor blades. Pocket computers. Rifles. Sleeping bags. All the crap you can't buy if—"

"It's going to be expensive, Senator."

"So what? I'm not broke. Get it wholesale, but be quiet about it. Anybody asks, you're . . . what? You're going along on a junket to Africa. There must be *some* National Science Foundation project in Africa—"

"Yes, sir—"

"Good. That's what all this is for, if anybody asks. You can let Rasmussen in on the plot. Nobody else on the staff. Got a girl you want to take along?"

He really doesn't know, Al thought. He really doesn't know how I feel about Maureen. "No, sir."

"Okay. I'll leave it to you, then. You realize this is damn foolishness and we're goin' to feel awful silly when that thing has passed by."

"Yes, sir." I hope we are. Sharps called it the Hammer!

"There is absolutely no danger. The asteroid Apollo came within two million miles, very close as cosmic distances go, back in 1932. No damage. Adonis passed within a million miles in 1936. So what? Remember the panic in 1968? People, especially in California, took to the hills. Everyone forgot about it a day later—that is, everyone who hadn't gone broke buying survival equipment that wasn't needed.

"Hamner-Brown Comet is a marvelous opportunity to study a new kind of extraterrestrial body at comparatively—and I emphasize comparatively—close range, and that's all it is."

"Thank you, Dr. Treece. You have heard an interview with Dr. Henry Treece of the United States Geological Survey. Now back to our regularly scheduled program."

The road ran north through groves of oranges and almond trees, skirting the eastern edge of the San Joaquin Valley. Sometimes it climbed over low hills or wound among them, but for most of the way the view to the left was of a vast flatland, dotted with farm buildings and croplands, crossed by canals, and stretching all the way to the horizon. The only large buildings visible were the uncompleted San Joaquin Nuclear Plant.

Harvey Randall turned right at Porterville and wound eastward up into the foothills. Once the road turned sharply and for a moment he had a view of the magnificent High Sierra to the east, the mountaintops still covered with snow. Eventually he found the turnoff onto the side road, and further down that was the unmarked gate. A U.S. Mail truck had already gone through, and the driver was coming back to close the gate. He was long-haired and elegantly bearded.

"Lost?" the mailman asked.

"Don't think so. This Senator Jellison's ranch?" Harvey asked.

The mailman shrugged. "They say so. I've never seen him. You'll close the gate?"

"Sure."

"See you." The mailman went back to his truck. Harvey drove through the gate, got out and closed it, then followed the truck up the dusty path to the top of the hill. There was a white frame house there. The drive forked, the right-hand branch leading down toward a barn and a chain of connected small lakes. Granite cliffs reared high above the lakes. There were several orange groves, and lots of empty pastureland. Pieces of the cliff, weathered boulders larger than a California suburban house, had tumbled down into the pastures.

An ample woman came out of the house. She waved to the mailman. "Coffee's hot, Harry!"

"Thanks. Happy Trash Day."

"Oh, that again? So soon? All right, you know where to put it." She advanced on the TravelAll. "Can I help you?"

"I'm looking for Senator Jellison. Harvey Randall, NBS."

Mrs. Cox nodded. "They're expecting you, up to the big

house." She pointed down the left-hand branch of the drive. "Mind where you park, and look out for the cats."

"What's Trash Day?" Harvey asked.

Mrs. Cox's face already wore a suspicious look. Now it changed to deadpan. "Nothing important," she said. She went back onto the porch. The mailman had already vanished inside the house.

Harvey shrugged and started the TravelAll. The drive ran between barbed-wire fences, orange groves to the right, more pasture to the left. He rounded a bend and saw the house. It was large, stone walls and slate roof, a rambling, massive place that didn't look very appropriate for this remote area. It was framed against more cliffs, and had a view through a canyon to the High Sierra miles beyond.

He parked near the back door. As he started around to the big front porch, the kitchen door opened. "Hi," Maureen Jellison called. "Save some walking and come in this way."

"Right. Thanks." She was as lovely as Harvey had remembered her. She wore tan slacks, not very highly tailored, and high-top shoes, not real trail shoes but good for walking. "Waffle-stompers," Mark Czescu would have called them. Her red hair looked recently brushed. It hung down just to her shoulders, in waves with slight curls at the ends. The sun glinted off in pleasing highlights.

"Did you have an easy drive?" she asked.

"Pleasant enough—"

"I always like the drive up here from L.A.," Maureen said. "But I expect you can use a drink right about now. What'll you have?"

"Scotch. And thanks."

"Sure." She led him through a service porch into a very modern kitchen. There was a cabinet full of liquor, and she took out a bottle of Old Fedcal scotch, then fought with the ice tray. "It's always all over frost when we first come up," she said. "This is a working ranch, and the Coxes don't have time to come up and fuss with the place much. Here, it will be nicer in the other room."

Again she led the way, going through a hall to the front room of the house. The wide veranda was just beyond it. A pleasant room, Harvey decided. It was paneled in light-colored wood, with ranch-style furniture, not really very appropriate for such a massive house as this. There were photographs of dogs and horses on most of the walls, and a case of ribbons and trophies, mostly for horses, but some for cattle. "Where is everybody?" Harvey asked.

"I'm the only one here just now," Maureen said.

Harvey pushed the thought firmly down into his unconscious, and tried to laugh at himself.

"The Senator got caught by a vote," Maureen was saying. "He'll catch the red-eye out of Washington tonight and get here in the morning. Dad says I'm to show you around. Want another drink?"

"No, thank you. One's enough." He put the glass down, then picked it up again when he realized he'd set it on a highly polished wood lamp-table. He wiped the water ring off with his hand. "Good thing the crew didn't come up with me. Actually they've got some work to finish up, and I'd hoped we could get the footage on Senator Jellison tomorrow morning, but if he couldn't be available tomorrow I've got the gear in the car. I used to be a fair cameraman. They'll be here in the morning, and I thought I would use the evening to get acquainted with the Senator, find out what he'd like to talk about for the camera. . . ." And I'm chattering, Harvey thought. Which is stupid.

"Care for the grand tour?" Maureen asked. She glanced at Harvey's Roughrider trousers and walking shoes. "You won't need to change. If you're up to a tough walk, I'll show you the best view in the valley."

"Sure. Let's go."

They went out through the kitchen and cut across the orange groves. A stream bubbled off to their left.

"That's good swimming down there," Maureen said. "Maybe we'll have a dip if we get back early enough."

They went through a fence. She parted the barbed wire and climbed through effortlessly, then turned to watch Harvey. She grinned when he came through just behind her, obviously pleased at his competence.

The other side of the fence was weeds and shrubs, never plowed or grazed. The way was steep here. There were small trails, made by rabbits or goats. They weren't really suited for humans at all. They climbed several hundred feet until they got to the base of a great granite cliff. It rose sheer at least two hundred feet above them. "We have to go around to the left here," Maureen said. "It gets tough from here on."

Much tougher and I won't make it, Harvey thought. But I will be damned if I'll have a Washington socialite show me up. I'm supposed to be an outdoorsman.

He hadn't been hiking with a girl since Maggie Thompkins blew herself up on a land mine in Vietnam. Maggie had been a go-get-'em reporter, always out looking for a story. She had no interest in sitting around in the Caravelle Bar and getting her material third- or fourth-hand. Harvey had gone with her to the front, and once they'd had to walk out from behind Cong lines together. If she hadn't been killed . . . Harvey put that thought away, too. It was a long time ago.

They scrambled up through a cleft in the rocks. "Do you come up here often?" Harvey asked. He tried to keep the strain out of his voice.

"Only once before," Maureen said. "Dad told me not to do it alone."

Eventually they reached the top. They were not, Harvey saw, on a peak at all. They were at one end of a ridge that stretched southeastward into the High Sierra. A narrow path led up into the rock cliff itself; they'd come all the way behind it, so that when they got to its top they faced the ranch.

"You're right," Harvey said. "The view's worth it." He stood on a monolith several stories high, feeling the pleasant breeze blowing across the valley. Everywhere he looked there were more of the huge white rocks. A glacier must have passed through here and scattered the land with these monoliths.

The Senator's ranch was laid out below. The small valley carved by the stream ran for several miles to the west; then there were more hills, still dotted with bungalow-size white stones. Far beyond the hills, and far below the level of the ranch, was the broad expanse of the San Joaquin. It was hazy out there, but Harvey thought he could make out the dark shape of the Temblor Range on the western edge of California's central valley.

"Silver Valley," Maureen announced. "That's our place there, and beyond is George Christopher's ranch. I almost married him, once—" She broke off, laughing.

Now why do I feel a twinge of jealousy? Harvey wondered. "Why is it so funny?"

"We were all of fourteen at the time he proposed," Maureen said. "Almost sixteen years ago. Dad had just been elected, and we were going to Washington, and George and I schemed to find a way so I could stay."

"But you didn't."

"No. Sometimes I wish I had," she said. "Especially when I'm standing here." She waved expressively.

Harvey turned, and there were more hills, rising higher and higher until they blended into the Sierra Nevada range. The big mountains looked untouched, never climbed by human. Harvey knew that was an illusion. If you stooped to tie your bootlaces on the John Muir Trail, you were likely to be trampled by backpackers.

The great rock they stood on was cloven toward the edge of the cliff. The cleft was no more than a yard wide, but deep, so deep that Harvey couldn't see the bottom. The top of the rock slanted toward the cleft, and toward the edge beyond it, so that Harvey wasn't even tempted to go near it.

Maureen strolled over there, and without a thought stepped across the cleft. She stood on a narrow strip of rock two feet wide, a three-hundred-foot drop in front of her, the unknown depth of the cleft behind. She looked out in satisfaction, then turned.

She saw Harvey Randall standing grimly, trying to move forward and not able to do it. She gave him a puzzled look; then her face showed concern. She stepped back onto the main rock. "I'm sorry. Do heights bother you?"

"Some," Harvey admitted.

"I should never have done that—what were you thinking of, anyway?"

"How I could get out there if something happened. If I could make myself crawl across that crack—"

"That wasn't nice of me at all," she said. "Anyway, let me show you the ranch. You can see most of it from here."

Afterward, Harvey couldn't remember what they'd talked about. It was nothing important, but it had been a pleasant hour. He couldn't remember a nicer one.

"We ought to be getting back down," Maureen said.

"Yeah. Is there an easier way than the one we came up?"

"Don't know. We can look," she said. She led the way off to their left, around the opposite side of the rock face. They picked their way through scrub brush and along narrow goat trails. There were piles of goat and sheep droppings. Deer too, Harvey thought, although he couldn't be sure. The ground was too hard for tracks.

"It's like nobody was ever here before," Harvey said, but he said it under his breath, and Maureen didn't hear. They were in a narrow gully, nothing more than a gash in the side of the steep hill, and the ranch had vanished.

There was a sound behind them. Harvey turned, startled. A horse was coming down the draw.

Not just a horse. The rider was a little blonde girl, a child not more than twelve. She rode without a saddle, and she looked like a part of the huge animal, fitted so well onto him that it might have been an undergrown centaur. "Hi," she called.

"Hi yourself," Maureen said. "Harvey, this is Alice Cox. The Coxes work the ranch. Alice, what are you doing up here?"

"Saw you going up," she said. Her voice was small and high-pitched, but well modulated, not shrill.

Maureen caught up to Harvey and winked. He nodded, pleased. "And we thought we were the intrepid explorers," Maureen said.

"Yeah. I had enough trouble getting up by myself, without taking a damn big horse." He looked ahead. The way was steep, and it was absolutely impossible for a horse to get down there. He turned to say so.

Alice had dismounted and was calmly leading the horse down the draw. It slipped and scrambled, and she pointed out places for it to step. The horse seemed to understand her perfectly. "Senator coming soon?" she asked.

"Yes, tomorrow morning," Maureen said.

"I sure like talkin' to him," Alice said. "All the kids at school want to meet him. He's on TV a lot."

"Harvey—Mr. Randall makes television programs," Maureen said.

Alice looked to Harvey with new respect. She didn't say anything for a moment. Then, "Do you like 'Star Trek'?"

"Yes, but I didn't have anything to do with that one." Harvey scrambled down another steep place. Surely that horse couldn't get down that?

"It's my favorite program," Alice said. "Whoa, Tommy. Come on, it's all right, right here—I wrote a story for television. It's about a flying saucer, and how we ran from it and hid in a cave. It's pretty good, too."

"I'll bet it is," Harvey said. He glanced at Maureen, and saw she was grinning again. "I'll bet there's nothing she can't do," Harvey muttered. Maureen nodded. They scrambled up the sides of their dry wash when it ended in a thicket of chaparral. The ranch was visible again, still a long way down, and the hillside was steep enough that if you fell, you'd roll a long way and probably break something. Harvey looked back and watched Alice for a second, then stopped worrying about her and the horse. He concentrated on getting himself down.

"You ride alone up here a lot?" Maureen asked.

"Sure," Alice said.

"Doesn't anybody worry about you?" Harvey asked.

"Oh, I know the way pretty good," Alice told him. "Got lost a couple of times, but Tommy knows how to get home."

"Pretty good horse," Maureen said.

"Sure. He's mine."

Harvey looked to be sure. A stallion, not a gelding. He waited for Maureen to catch up to him. Masculine pride had kept him trying to lead the way, although it was obvious that they ought to leave that to Alice. "Must be nice to live where the only thing to worry about is getting lost—and the horse takes care of that," he told Maureen. "She doesn't even know what I'm talking about. And last week a girl her age, about eleven, was raped in the Hollywood Hills not more than half a mile from my house."

"One of Dad's secretaries was raped in the Capitol last year," Maureen said. "Isn't civilization wonderful?"

"I wish my boy could grow up out here," Harvey said. "Only, what would I do? Farm?" He laughed at himself. Then the way was too steep for talking.

There was a dirt road at the bottom of the steep hillside. They were still a long way from the ranch, but it was easier now. Alice somehow got onto the horse; Harvey was watching the whole time, but he didn't see how she managed it. One second she was standing next to the animal, her head lower than its back, and the next moment she was astride. She clucked and they galloped off. The illusion that she was somehow a part of the beast was even stronger: She moved in perfect rhythm with it, her long blonde hair flowing behind.

"She's going to be one real beauty when she grows up," Harvey said. "Is it the air here? This whole valley's magic."

"I feel that way sometimes too," Maureen told him.

The sun was low when they got back to the stone ranch house. "Little late, but want to catch a swim?" Maureen asked.

"Sure. Why not? Only I didn't bring a suit."

"Oh, there's something around." Maureen vanished into the house and came back with trunks. "You can change in there." She pointed to a bathroom.

Harvey got into the trunks. When he came out, she was already changed. Her one-piece suit was a shiny white material. She had a robe over one arm. She winked at him and dashed off, leaving Harvey to follow. The path led by a pomegranate grove and down to a sandy beach by a bubbling stream. Maureen grinned at him, then plunged quickly into the water. Harvey followed.

131

"Ye gods!" he shouted. "That's ice water!"

She splashed water onto his dry chest and hair. "Come on, it won't hurt you."

He waded grimly out into the stream. The water was swift, out away from the banks, and the bottom was rocky. He had trouble keeping his feet, but he followed her upstream to a narrow gap between two boulders. The water plunged out swiftly there, threatening to dump both of them. It was just chest-deep for Harvey. "That cools you off fast," he said.

They paddled around in the pool, watching small trout dart near the surface. Harvey looked for larger fish, but they were keeping out of sight. The stream looked perfect for trout, deep pools below small rushing falls. The banks were overhung with trees except for two places where they'd been cleared, obviously by someone who liked fly fishing and had opened the banks out for his back cast.

"I think I'm turning blue," Maureen shouted finally. "You finished?"

"Tell the truth, I was done ten minutes ago."

They climbed out onto another of the enormous white boulders, the contours smoothed by floodwaters. The sun, low as it was, felt good on Harvey's chilled body, and the rock was still hot from old sunlight. "I've been needing this," he said.

Maureen turned over on belly and elbows to look at him. "Which? The freezing water, or the acrophobia, or the climbing your legs off?"

"All of the above. And not interviewing anyone today, I needed that, too. I'm glad your father didn't make it. Tomorrow—shazam! I'm Harvey Randall again."

She had changed back into the tan slacks. Harvey came out to find she'd also made drinks.

"Stay for dinner?" she asked.

"Well . . . Sure, but can I take you out somewhere?"

She grinned. "You haven't sampled the wild night life of Springfield and Porterville. You'll do better here. Besides, I like to cook. If you want, you can help clean up."

"Sure—"

"Not that there's much cooking involved," Maureen said. She took steaks out of the freezer. "Microwave ovens and frozen food. The civilized way to gourmet meals."

"That thing's got more controls than an Apollo."

"Not really. I've been in an Apollo. Hey, you have too, haven't you?"

"I saw the mock-up," Harvey said, "not the real thing. Lord, I'd like to do that. Watch the comet from orbit. No atmosphere to block it out."

Maureen didn't answer. Randall sipped at his scotch. There was an edge on his hunger. He searched the freezer and found frozen Chinese vegetables to add to the meal.

After dinner they sipped coffee on the porch, in wide chairs with wide, flat arms to hold the mugs. It was chilly; they needed jackets. They talked slowly, dreamily: of the astronauts Maureen knew; of the mathematics in Lewis Carroll; of social politics in Washington. Presently Maureen went into the house, turned off all the lights and came back out feeling her way.

It was incredibly dark. Randall asked, "Why did you do that?"

A disembodied voice answered, "You'll see in a few minutes." He heard her take her chair.

There was no moon, and the stars lit only themselves. But gradually he saw what she meant. When the Pleiades came over the mountains he didn't recognize them; the cluster was fiercely bright. The Milky Way blazed, yet he couldn't see his own coffee cup!

"There are city people who never see this," Maureen said.

"Yeah. Thanks."

She laughed. "It could have been clouded over. My powers are limited."

"If we could . . . No, I'm wrong. I was thinking, if we could show them all what it looks like—all the voters. But you see star scenes on the newsstands all the time, paintings of star clusters and black holes and multiple systems and anything you could find out there. You'd have to take the voters up here, a dozen at a time, and *show* them. Then they'd know. It's all out there. Real. All we have to do is reach out."

She reached out (her night vision had improved that much) and took his hand. He was a bit startled. She said, "Won't work. Otherwise the main support for NASA would come from the farming community."

"But if you'd *never* seen it like this . . . Ahh, you're probably right." He was very aware that they were still holding hands. But it would stop there. "Hey, do you like interstellar empires?" Harmless subject.

133

"I don't know. Tell me about interstellar empires."

Harv pointed, and leaned close so she could sight down his arm. Where the Milky Way thickened and brightened, in Sagittarius, that was the galactic axis. "That's where the action is, in most of the older empires. The stars are a lot closer together. You find Trantor in there, and the Hub worlds. It's risky building in there, though. Sometimes you find that the core suns have all exploded. The radiation wave hasn't reached us yet."

"Isn't Earth ever in control?"

"Sure, but mostly you find Earth had one big atomic war."

"Oh. Maybe I shouldn't ask, but just where are you getting your information?"

"I used to read the science fiction magazines. Then around age twenty I got too busy. Let's see, the Earth-centered empires tend to be small, but . . . a small fraction of a hundred billion suns. You get enormous empires without even covering one galactic arm." He stopped. The sky was so incredibly vivid! He could almost see the Mule's warships sweeping out from Sagittarius. "Maureen, it looks so *real*."

She laughed. He could see her face now, pale, without detail.

He slid onto the broad arm of her chair and kissed her. She moved aside, and he slid in beside her. The chair held two, barely.

There is no harmless subject.

There was a point at which he might have disengaged. The thought that stopped him was: tomorrow, *shazam!* I'm Harvey Randall again.

Inside the house it was utterly black. She led him by the hand, by touch and memory, to one of the bedrooms. They undressed each other. Their clothes, falling, might as well have fallen out of the universe. Her skin was warm, almost hot. For a moment he wished he could see her face, but only for a moment.

There was gray light when he woke. His back was cold. They lay tangled together on a made bed. Maureen slept calmly, deeply, wearing a slight smile.

He was freezing. She must be too. Should he wake her up? His slow brain found a better answer. He disentangled himself, gently. She didn't wake. He went to the other of the twin beds, pulled off the bedclothes, took them back and spread them over her. Then—with the full conviction that he was about to climb under the covers with her—he stood without moving for almost a minute.

She wasn't his wife.

"Shazam," Harvey said softly. He scooped up an armload of his clothes, careful to miss nothing. He padded out into the living room. He was starting to shiver. The first door he tried was another bedroom. He dumped the clothes on a chair and went to bed.

Not dead, but transmuted! The comet is glorious in its agony. The streamer of its torn flesh reaches millions of miles, a wake of strange chemicals blowing back toward the cometary halo on a wind of reflected light. Perhaps a few molecules will plate themselves across the icy surfaces of other comets.

Earth's telescopes find the comet blocked by the blazing sun itself. Its exact orbit is still uncertain.

The glory of the tail is reflected sunlight, but more than sunlight glows in the coma. Some chemicals can lie intimately mixed at near absolute zero, but heat them and they burn. The coma seethes in change.

The head grows smaller every day. Here, ammonia boils from the surface of an ice-and-dust mixture; the hydrogen has long since boiled out. The mass contracts, and its density increases. Soon there will be little but rock dust cemented together by water ice. There, a stone monolith the size of a hill blocks the path of a gas pocket that grows hourly warmer, until something gives. Gas blasts away into the coma. The stony mass pulls slowly away, tumbling. The orbit of Hamner-Brown has been changed minutely.

June: One

The Lord Himself will descend from heaven with a cry of command, with the archangeal's call, and with the sound of the trumpet of God. The dead in Christ will rise first; then we who remain alive shall be caught up together with them in the clouds to meet the Lord in the air; and so we shall always be with the Lord.

Paul of Tarsus, First Thessalonians

There at the top of the great disintegrating totem pole, there in that tiny space at the tip, Rick Delanty lay on his back with his smile blinking on and off. His carefully enunciated voice gave no hint of that. It sounded just like Johnny's; and Johnny Baker wore the slight frown of a man doing delicate work.

"Switch to internal power."

"Internal power check. In the green."

"T minus fifteen minutes, and counting."

Whenever he glanced over at Rick, at that wavering smile, *then* Johnny's lips twitched at the corners. But Johnny Baker had been up before; he could afford to be supercilious. Fifteen minutes, and no glitches. It would take a man his whole life to write down all the glitches that could stop an Apollo launch.

Delanty kept smiling. They'd picked him! He'd gone through the training, and the simulators, and then off to Florida. Two days ago he's been doing barrel rolls and loops and Immelmanns and dives above Florida and the Bahamas. That final loosening-up flight two days before a launch was just too firm a tradition to get rid of. It worked the tension out of the chosen astronauts and laid it on the ground crew, who could go nuts wondering if their crew would smear themselves in a jet trainer, after all that careful planning. . . .

"T minus one minute, and counting."

Those final, hurried, crammed hours ended when Wally Hoskins led him up the elevator and arranged him, clumsy in his pressure suit, within the Apollo capsule. After that he could lie on his back with his knees above his head, waiting for the glitch. But the glitch hadn't come yet, and it looked like they were going, it really—

"Five. Four. Three. Two. One. Ignition. First motion . . ." Going!

"We have lift-off. . . ."

The Saturn rose in thunder and hellfire. A hundred thousand official visitors and more, newsmen, science fiction writers with scrounged press passes, dependents of astronauts, VIPs and friends . . .

"There he goes," Maureen Jellison said.

Her father looked at her curiously. "We mostly call those ships 'she.' "

"Yes. I suppose so," Maureen said. Why do I think I'll never see him again?

Behind her the Vice-President was muttering, just loud enough to hear. "Go, go, you bird—" He looked up with a start, realized others were listening, and shrugged. "GO, BABY!" he shouted.

It did something to the watchers. The power of the thundering rocket, the knowledge that had gone into it; to the older watchers it was something impossible, a comic-book incident from their childhood. To the younger ones it was inevitable and to be expected, and they couldn't understand why the older people were so excited. Space ships were real and of course they worked. . . .

Inside the Apollo the astronauts smiled: the rictus smile of a cadaver, as several gravities pulled their facial muscles back onto their cheeks. Eventually the first stage shut down and fell away, and the second stage did the same, and the third stage gave them a final push . . . and Rick Delanty, in free fall, was still smiling.

"Apollo, this is Houston. You're looking good," the voice said.

"Roger, Houston." Delanty turned to Baker. "Now what, General?"

Baker grinned self-consciously. He'd been promoted, just before the launch, so that he'd be the same rank as the Soviet *kosmonaut*.

"On one condition," the President had said when he handed Baker his stars.

"Yes, sir?" Baker asked.

"You don't tease your Russian counterpart about his name. Resist the temptation."

"Yes, Mr. President."

But it was going to be hard. Pieter Jakov didn't have a double meaning in Russian—but Comrade General Jakov spoke very good English, as Baker knew from their orientation meeting at Houston. He'd also met the other one, a dish—but only in Russia. She'd been officially too busy to come to the U.S.

"Now we find that bloody garbage can, Lieutenant Colonel Delanty," Baker said. "Great up here, isn't it?"

"You know it." Delanty peered out, eyes wide in wonder. They had showed it all to him, many times, in simulators. There were movies, and the other astronauts talked incessantly of space; they put him in wet suits underwater to simulate no-gravity. But none of that mattered. This was real.

There was the absolute black of space ahead, stars shining brightly, although the Sun lit the Earth below. There were Atlantic islands, and coming up ahead was the coastline of Africa, looking just like a map with bits of cotton stuck on it for clouds. Later, to the north, was Spain, and the Mediterranean Sea, and after a while the dark green slash across the wastelands of Egypt, the Nile with all its bends and crooks.

And then they were in sunset, and the lights of the fabled cities of India lay below.

They were above the darkness covering Sumatra when Delanty got the blip on his radar screen. "There it is," he said. "Hammerlab."

"Rojj," Baker acknowledged. He looked at the Doppler; they were slowly drawing up to the capsule. They'd catch up to it in dawn over the Pacific, just as Houston's computer had predicted. They waited. Finally Baker said, "Unlimber the cage. We've got to catch our house." He thumbed the downlink set on. "Goldstone, this is Apollo. Hammerlab is in visual range, we are beginning final rendezvous maneuver."

"Apollo, this is Houston, what did you say was in visual range, interrogative?"

"Hammerlab," Baker said. He looked over at Delanty and grinned. Officially it was *Spacelab Two;* but who called it that?

They approached rapidly: slowly to the astronauts, who were themselves moving at 25,000 feet each second. Then it was time. Delanty flew the Apollo. Jets edged their craft closer to their target: a big steel garbage can, forty feet long and ten in diameter, with viewports along the sides, one airlock, and docking hatches at each end.

"The economy-price spacelab," Baker muttered. "It's tumbling. I make that one rotation in four minutes, eight seconds."

First to match completely with Hammerlab: Fire the Apollo's attitude jets in just the precise pattern, so that it would tumble with the target. Then move closer to the thing, waiting for the chance, until the big docking probe on Apollo could enter the matching hole in the end of Hammerlab . . . and they were in darkness again. Rick was amazed at how long it had taken him to fly what looked like far less than a mile. Of course they'd also come 14,000 miles in the same fifty minutes. . . .

When dawn came Rick was ready, and made one pass, and a second, and cursed, and eased forward and felt the slight contact of the two ships, and the instruments showed contact at center, and Rick drove forward, hard . . .

"Virgin no more!" he shouted.

"Houston, this is Apollo. We have docking. I say again, we have docking," Baker said.

"We know," a dry voice said from below. "Colonel Delanty's mike was live."

"Woops," Rick said.

"Apollo, this is Houston, your partners are approaching, *Soyuz* has you in visual. I say again, *Soyuz* has visual contact."

"Roger, Houston." Baker turned to Rick. "So now you stabilize this mother, while I talk to friendly Asian brother—and sister. *Soyuz, Soyuz*, this is Apollo. Over."

"Apollo, this is *Soyuz*," a male voice said. Jakov's English was grammatically perfect, and almost without accent. He'd studied with American-speaking teachers, not Britishers. "Apollo, we copy you five by five. Is your docking maneuver completed, interrogative? Over."

"We are docked with Hammerlab. It is safe to approach. Over."

"Apollo, this is *Soyuz*. By 'Hammerlab' do you mean Spacelab Two, interrogative? Over."

Baker said, "Affirmative."

Delanty was aware that he was using too much fuel. No

one but a perfectionist would have noticed that; the maneuver was well within the error program devised by Houston. But Rick Delanty cared.

Eventually they were stable: Apollo, its nose buried in the docking port in one end of the garbage can that was Hammerlab, both now stable in space, not wobbling and not tumbling. The Apollo led, at 25,000 feet per second: Baker and Delanty, ass-backward around the Earth each ninety minutes.

"Done," Rick said. "Now let's watch them try."

"Rojj," Baker said. He activated a camera system. There was a cable connector in the docking mechanism, and the picture came through perfectly: a view of *Soyuz*, massive and closer than they'd expected, approaching Hammerlab from the far side. The *Soyuz* grew, nose on. It wobbled slightly in its orbit, showing its massive bulk: *Soyuz* was considerably larger than the Apollo. The Soviets had always had their big military boosters to assist their space program, while NASA designed and built special equipment.

"That big mother better not have forgotten the lunch," Delanty said. "Or it will get *hungry* up here."

"Yep." Baker continued to watch.

The *Soyuz* was vital to the Hammerlab mission. It had brought up most of the consumables. Hammerlab was packed with instruments and film and experiments; but there was food and water and air for only a few days. They needed *Soyuz* to stay for Hamner-Brown's approach.

"Maybe it will anyway," Johnny Baker said. He looked grimly at the screen, and at the maneuvering Soviet vehicle.

Watching was painful.

Soyuz floundered like a dead whale in the tide. It nosed violently toward the camera and shied as violently back. It edged sideways, stopped—almost; tried again and drifted away.

"And that's their best pilot," Baker muttered.

"I didn't look too good myself—"

"Bullshit. You had a tumbling target. We're as stable as a streetcar." Baker watched a few moments more and shook his head. "Not their fault, of course. Control systems. We've got the onboard computers. They don't. But it's a bloody damned shame."

Rick Delanty's mahogany face wrinkled. "Don't know I can take much more of this, Johnny."

It was excruciating for both of them. It made the fingers

flex, itching to take over. Back-seat drivers are formed by such tensions.

"And he's got the lunch," Baker said. "When's he going to give up?"

They entered darkness. Communications with *Soyuz* were limited to official messages. When they came into the light again, the Soviet craft approached once more.

"It's going to get hungry up here," Delanty said.

"Shut up."

"Yes, *sir*."

"Fuck you."

"Not possible in a full pressure suit."

They watched again. Eventually Jakov called: "We are wasting needed fuel. Request Plan B."

"*Soyuz*, roger, stand by to implement Plan B," Baker said with visible relief. He winked at Delanty. "Now show the commies what a real American can do."

Plan B was officially an emergency measure, but all the American mission planners had predicted privately that it would be needed. In the U.S. they'd trained as if Plan B would be the normal mode of operation. Across the Atlantic it was hoped it wouldn't be needed—but they'd planned on it too. Plan B was simple: The *Soyuz* stabilized itself, and the Apollo-Hammerlab monstrosity maneuvered to it.

Delanty was flying a spacecraft and a big, clumsy, massive tin can. (Now picture an aircraft carrier trying to maneuver under a descending airplane.) But he also had the world's most sophisticated computer system, attitude controls painstakingly turned out by master machinists with thousands of hours' experience, instruments developed in a dozen laboratories accustomed to making precision instruments.

"Houston, Houston, Plan B under way," Baker reported.

And now the whole damned world's watching me. Or listening, Rick Delanty thought. And if I blow it . . .

That was unthinkable.

"Relax," Baker said.

He didn't offer to do it himself, Delanty thought. Well. Here goes. Just like on the simulator.

It was. One straight thrust; check just before contact, and a tiny pulse of the jets to move the two crafts together. Again the mechanical feel of contact, and simultaneously the flare of green lights on the board.

"Latch it," Rick said.

142

"*Soyuz*, we are docked, latch the docking probe," Baker called.

"Apollo, affirmative. We are locked on."

"Last one inside's a rotten egg," Baker said.

They shook hands, formally, all around, as they floated inside the big tin can. A historic occasion, the commentators were saying below; but Baker couldn't think of any historic words to say.

There was just too damned much to do. This wasn't a spectacular, a handshake in space like Apollo-*Soyuz*. This was a working mission, with a hairy schedule that they probably couldn't keep up with, even with luck.

And yet . . . Baker had the urge to laugh. He might have if it wouldn't have needed so many explanations. He would have laughed at how good they all looked.

God bless us, there's none like us. Leonilla Alexandrovna Malik was darkly beautiful. With her imperious self-confidence she could have played a czarina, but her smooth, hard muscles would better have fitted her for the prima ballerina's role. A cold and lovely woman.

Heartbreaker, Johnny Baker thought. But secretly vulnerable, like Moira Shearer in *The Red Shoes*. I wonder if she's as coldly polite with everyone as she is with Brigadier Jakov?

Brigadier Pieter Ivanovitch Jakov, Hero of the People (which class? Baker wondered); the perfect man to illustrate an enlistment poster. Handsome, well muscled, cold eyes: He looked a lot like Johnny Baker himself, and this wasn't really more surprising than Rick Delanty's superficial resemblance to Muhammad Ali.

Four of us, fully mature specimens in the prime of athletic good health—and photogenic as hell to boot. Pity that Randall fellow from NBS isn't here to take a group picture. But he'll get one. Eventually.

They floated at strange angles to each other, and shifted as in vagrant breezes, smiling at nothing. Even for Baker and Jakov it was exhilarating, and they'd been up before. For Rick and Leonilla it was sheer heaven. They tended to drift toward the viewports and stare at the stars and Earth.

"Did you bring the lunch?" Delanty asked.

Leonilla smiled. The smile was cold. "Of course. I think you will enjoy it. But I will not harm Comrade Jakov's surprise."

"First we have to find a place to eat it," Baker said. He looked around the crowded capsule.

It was crammed with gear. Electronics bolted to the bulkheads. Styrofoam packing around amorphous lumps suspended on yellow nylon strapping. Plastic boxes, racks of equipment, canisters of film, microscopes, a disassembled telescope, tool kits and soldering irons. There were multiple copies of diagrams that showed where everything was stowed, and Baker and Delanty had drilled until they could literally lay their hands on any item in total darkness; but it made for crowding and gave no sense of order.

"We can eat in the *Soyuz*," Leonilla suggested. "It is packed, but . . ." She waved helplessly.

"It is not what we have been given to expect," Jakov said. "I have spoken to Baikunyar, and we are now on our own for a few hours until we can deploy the solar wings. But I suggest we eat first."

"What's not what you've been given to expect?" Delanty asked.

"This." Jakov waved expressively.

John Baker laughed. "There wasn't time to do any real planning. Just pile the stuff aboard. Otherwise, everything here would have been designed especially for comet watching, at half the weight—"

"And nine times the cost," Delanty said.

"And then there would have been no need of us," Leonilla Malik said.

Jakov looked at her coldly. He started to say something, but decided not to. It was true enough, and they all knew it.

"Jesus, they sure packed it in," Delanty said. "Let's eat."

"You feel no effect? From the free fall?" Leonilla asked.

"Him? Old Iron Ear?" John Baker laughed. "Hell, he eats lunch on roller coasters. Now me, I feel it a bit, and I've been here before. It goes away."

"We should eat now. We are entering darkness, and we will want to deploy the solar wings in light," Jakov said. "I, too, suggest the *Soyuz*, where there is more room. And we have a surprise. Caviar. It should be eaten in bowls, but doubtless we can make do from tubes."

"Caviar?" Baker said.

"It is high in food value," Leonilla said. "And soon the new canal will be finished and there will be plenty of water in the Caspian and the Volga for our sturgeon. I hope you like caviar—"

"Sure," Baker said.

"Shall we get to it?" Jakov led the way into the *Soyuz*.

No one noticed that Rick Delanty held back, as if reluctant to begin lunch after all.

Delanty and Baker were outside. Thin lines connected them to Hammerlab; around them was the vacuum of space, brightly lit in sunshine, dark as the darkest cave in shadow.

Skylab had wings covered with solar cells. They were supposed to deploy automatically, but they hadn't.

Hammerlab had a different design. The wings were folded against the body, and were designed to be deployed by human musclepower. Baker and Delanty supplied that.

The solar-cell power was all needed. Without it they couldn't operate the laboratory—or even keep it cool enough to live in. Space is not cold. It has no temperature at all: There is no air to give it a temperature. Objects in sunlight absorb heat, which must be pumped out. Human beings generate even more heat: No man can live long in an insulated environment, whether a pressure suit or a space capsule. A man generates more heat inside each cubic inch of his body than the Sun does in each cubic inch of its surface. Of course, there are a great many cubic inches of Sun. . . .

So they needed the solar cells, and that took work. They moved large masses—in space there is no weight, but the mass remains—against friction. Their pressure suits resisted every motion, but eventually it was done. Nothing was broken, nothing was jammed. The system had been designed for simplicity—and to use the talents of intelligent men in orbit.

"At last," Johnny Baker said. "And we've got a few minutes' oxygen left. Rick, take a moment to enjoy the view."

"Good," Rick huffed into his mike.

Baker didn't like the way he said it. Delanty was breathing too hard, and too irregularly. But he said nothing.

"I thought that last one would never come loose," Delanty puffed.

"But it did come loose. And if it hadn't, we'd have fixed it," Baker said. "Those goddam bastards with their perfect black boxes. Well, this time they gave me the tools for the job. There's nothing a man can't do with the right tools."

"Sure, it's all a piece of cake now."

"Right. No worries. Barring a few international tensions, a possible Cuban hijacker, and several masses of dirty ice moving at fifty miles a second—our way."

"That's a relief." Huff! "Hey, John, I see South Africa. Only—you can't tell where the international boundaries leave off. No national borders. Johnny, I'm on the verge of a philosophical breakthrough."

"You can't see the lines of latitude and longitude, either, but that doesn't make them unimportant."

"Um."

"So you can't see international borders from space, and everyone tries to make a big point of it. If we keep that up, you know what'll happen?"

Rick laughed. "Yeah. Everybody's gonna start painting their borders in neon orange a mile wide. Then all the college kids will scream about damage to the environment—"

"And blame you for starting it. Let's go in."

June: Interludes

But what about a direct head-on collision with a comet? How big and massive are the heads of comets? The head of a comet consists of two parts. The solid nucleus and the glowing coma. We only have to worry about the nucleus. Of course, comets vary a good deal in size. One estimate is that the nucleus of an average comet is 1.2 miles in diameter. But a really huge comet may have a nucleus thousands of miles in diameter. Any comet that hits the earth directly is going to pack quite a wallop.

Daniel Cohen, *How the World Will End*

"Woe to you, my people! For have you not raised the abomination of desolation across the earth? Have you not seen the wickedness of the cities, and smelt the very stench of the air itself? Have you not defiled the earth, which is the very temple of the Lord?

"Hear the words of the Prophet Malachi: 'For, behold, the day cometh, that shall burn as an oven; and all the proud, yea, and all that do wickedly, shall be stubble; and the day that cometh shall burn them up, saith the Lord of Hosts, that it shall leave them neither root nor branch.

" 'But unto you that fear my name shall the Son of righteousness arise with healing in his wings.'

"My people, the Hammer of God comes to smite the wicked and the proud; but the humble shall be exalted. Repent, while there is yet time; for no man can escape the mighty Hammer that even now blots out the stars. Repent, before it is too late. There is yet time."

"Thank you, Reverend Armitage. You have heard the Reverend Henry Armitage and 'The Coming Hour.' "

Mark Czescu had the saki heating in a reagent bottle with a ground-glass stopper. He poured refills into tiny cups, then poured more saki into the bottle and set it back in water simmering on the stove.

"I had two plants sitting on my desk," he said. "One was a rubber marijuana plant, with 'cannabis sativa' stamped under the leaves. The other was an *Aralia elegantissima*. If you don't know, it looks a lot like marijuana." He handed a cup to Joanna, another to Lilith. "One day my boss came in with a bigwig from the central office. They didn't say anything that day, but the next day my boss was saying, 'Get rid of it.' " He handed Frank Stoner the third cup, and settled in the armchair with his own. "I said, 'What?' He said, 'I'm not completely ignorant, you know. I know what that is.' Carol Miller went into hysterics. She called the other guys in and we made him repeat it. *They* all knew what it was."

Frank Stoner sprawled in sinful comfort on the couch, with Joanna MacPherson under one arm and the other around Lilith Hathaway's waist. Lilith was his own height, five nine, but tiny Joanna's shoulders just fit beneath Frank's thick arm. He asked, "How long ago was that?"

"Couple of years. They had to lay me off two months later."

Frank grinned. "By one of those interesting statistical flukes?"

"Huh? No, it had nothing to do with the rubber marijuana. They just had to lay off some people. Since then . . . Well, the steadiest work has been with Harv Randall." Mark leaned forward, eyes sparkling. "Those man-in-the-street gigs are fun. We met this army colonel who was afraid to open his mouth, afraid something would get out. There was a guy at a wrestling match who couldn't *wait* for Hammerfall. That's when the real he-men will rule the world, right?" He smiled at Lilith, who was a pale blonde with a lovely heart-shaped face and big boobs. He'd met Lilith at the Interchange, the topless bar where she danced.

Frank Stoner was sipping just enough saki to be polite. Mark hadn't noticed. He emptied his cup in one swallow— you had to drink it fast or it would get cold—and said, "We even interviewed some bikers. The Unholy Rollers were in that night. I don't think they took it seriously, though."

Joanna laughed. "End of the world. No cars on the road. No fuzz. Your biker friends would think that was fat city."

"But they couldn't say that."

"It's maybe true," said Frank Stoner. He and Mark had

met on the dirt tracks, fighting it out for prize money across the country. "We can go places cars can't. We don't use as much gas. We stick together. We don't mind a fight. If we had some gas cached somewhere . . . Hey. What are the chances?"

Mark waved a hand and almost hit his cup. "Almost zilch, unless you believe the astrology columns. Sharps says we might go through the tail, though. Man, won't that be a kick!"

Joanna explained, "Sharps is one of the astronomers they interviewed." She got up to refill saki cups.

"Yeah, and he was stranger than any of them! You'll see it on TV. Hey, did you know that Hot Fudge Sundae falls on a Tuesdae this month?" He gave it a good dramatic pause —during which Joanna got the giggles—before he went on.

An hour later, and Lilith had had to go to work. The saki was dwindling fast. Mark was feeling good. Joanna was feather-light in his lap, while he and Frank talked around her.

Mark had been living with Joanna for almost two years now. Sometimes it struck him as strange, that he had gotten himself involved with a total monogamist. It had changed his life-style, sure—and he liked it. Granted he didn't dare sleep with anyone else; but he didn't get into as many fights either. And he still met interesting people. He'd been afraid that would end. . . .

"You'd have a hell of a time getting back in shape," said Frank.

"Huh?" Mark tried to remember what they'd been talking about. Oh, yeah: the duels they'd fought on the racing circuit years ago. For Mark the dirt tracks were a spectator sport these days. He still had the muscles, but he had grown a great soft pillow of a beer belly. He glanced down and said, "Right. Well, Joanna's making me have the baby."

"Fair's fair," Joanna said. "You lost the toss."

"I'm gettin' too old for fooling around. I should sign up permanently with Randall." He picked up Joanna and set her on her feet (yes, the muscles were still there) and went to the kitchen for the last of the saki. He called, "What do we do if the Hammer hits?"

"Don't be there," Stoner answered. A few seconds later, "Don't be at the beach either. Don't be near a coastline. Three out of four it'd be an ocean strike. Bring me a beer."

"Yeah."

"You got a map of the fault lines in California, don't you?"

Mark was sure he did. He began hunting for it.

Frank said, "I think I'd want the same bike I took to Mexico. The big single, the Honda four-stroke. Not so much problem getting spare parts." Frank let his mind track possibilities, taking its time. He and Joanna and Mark, they'd known each other a long time. They didn't have to talk just to fill in silences, though Mark did have a touch of that. "You'd have to think about riots and rip-offs. The rain and the tidal waves and earthquakes, they'd wipe out all the services, cops included. I guess I'd want gas and bike parts hidden outside the city, some place where nobody could steal them."

"Guns?"

"I brought a souvenir back from 'Nam. Registered lost."

"So did I." Mark gave up on the map. "We'd want a siphon. For awhile you'd find abandoned cars—"

"I always carry a siphon."

"Hey. Why don't we get together about the time the head's supposed to pass?"

Frank didn't answer immediately. Joanna said, "Even if nothing happens, it'd be a great comet-watching party. Maybe we could get Lilith in."

Frank Stoner thought it over for a few seconds longer than was tactful. He did not make promises lightly, and the comet was becoming real to him. Mark was a good man in a fight, but he couldn't always do what he said he could do, and he tended to drop things, and there was that brand-new beer belly. To Frank, that belly was a piece of personal sloppiness. Still . . . "Yeah. Okay. Not here, though. Say we take some sleeping bags up onto Mulholland the night before."

Mark raised his saki cup in salute. "Good. It'd take a bitch of a tsunami to reach that high. And we could go off the road if we had to." He would have been displeased if he could have followed Frank's reasoning.

Frank was concerned for Joanna. He didn't think Mark could protect her. And Joanna, with her kung fu training and Women's Lib self-confidence, probably thought she could protect herself.

It took Eileen almost half a minute to realize that Mr. Corrigan was sitting on the edge of her desk, studying her.

Bolt upright at her desk, she sat with her fingers motionless on the keyboard. Her eyes seemed to study a blank wall . . . and then, somehow, they found Corrigan in the foreground. She said, "Yah!"

"Hi. It's me," said Corrigan. "Care to talk about it?"

"I don't know, Boss."

"About a month ago I would have sworn you were in love. You'd come in with that sappy look, and sometimes you'd be dead tired and grinning all over. I thought your efficiency would go down, but it didn't."

"It was love," she said, and smiled. "His name's Tim Hamner. He's indecently rich. He wants me to marry him. He said so last night."

"Um," said Corrigan, not liking that. "The crucial question, of course, is whether the business will collapse without you."

"Naturally that was the first thing I thought of," said Eileen, but with a pensive look that Corrigan didn't quite know how to take.

"Occupational hazard," he said briskly. "Do you love him?"

"Oh . . . yes. But . . . nuts. I've already made up my mind," she said, "but I don't have to like it." And she attacked her typewriter with a ferocity that drove Corrigan back to his own desk.

She called Tim three times before she found him home. Her first words were, "Tim? I'm sorry, but the answer's no."

Long pause. Then, "Okay. Can you tell me why?"

"I'll try. It's . . . it'd make what I've been doing look silly."

"I don't see that."

"Just before we met I made Assistant General Manager at Corrigan Plumbing Supplies."

"You told me. Listen, if you're afraid of losing your independence, I'll settle, say, a hundred thousand dollars on your cringing head and you'll be as independent as anyone."

"I don't know how I knew you'd say that, but . . . that isn't it. It's me. I'd change more than I'd like. I made myself what I am, and I want to stay proud of the result."

"You want to keep your job?" Tim had trouble getting the word out; he must have thought the idea was silly. But—"Okay."

Eileen pictured herself arriving at Corrigan's every morning in a chauffeured limousine—and she laughed. After that, things went all to hell.

Colleen was reading a paperback novel. Her hair was in curlers. She'd switched on the stereo, and sometimes her fingers tapped in rhythm on the table beside her easy chair.

Fred wondered wistfully what she was hearing. He knew what she was reading; he couldn't see the title, but the cover bore a woman in long, flowing garments in the foreground and a castle in the background, with one lighted window. Gothics were all alike, outside and in.

And he didn't mind the curlers. She looked cute in them.

Half the joy was in the anticipation. Soon, soon, they would meet.

Sometimes the guilt was overwhelming. Then the mad temptation would come on Fred Lauren: to destroy his telescope, to destroy himself, before he could hurt Colleen. But that really was insane. A month and a week from now he would be dead anyway, and so would she. Any hurt he did her would be a passing thing, and done for love.

For love. Fred yearned for the girl in his telescope. His hands were tender on the little wheels that controlled the image, and the fingers trembled. It was too soon, much too soon.

June: Two

General, you don't have a war plan! All you have is
a kind of horrible spasm!
        Secretary of Defense Robert S. McNamara, 1961

The policy of the United States remains unchanged.
Upon confirmation of actual nuclear attack on this
nation, our strategic forces will inflict unacceptable
damage on the enemy.
        Pentagon spokesman, 1975

Sergeant Mason Jefferson Lawton was SAC and proud of it.
He was proud of the sharply creased coveralls, and the blue
scarf at his throat, and the white gloves. He was proud of
the .38 on his hip.

It was late afternoon in Omaha. The day had been hot.
Mason glanced at his watch again, and just as he did, the
KC-135 swept out of the sky and down the runway. It taxied
over to the unloading area where Mason waited. The first
man out was a colonel permanently stationed at Offutt.
Mason recognized him. The next man fit the photograph
Security had furnished. They came over to the jeep.

"ID, please?" Mason asked.

The colonel took his out without a word. Senator Jellison
frowned. "I just came in on the General's plane, with your
own colonel—"

"Yes, sir," Mason said. "But I need to see your ID."

Jellison nodded, amused. He took a leather folder from
an inside pocket, then grinned as the sergeant came to an
even more rigid position of attention. The card was Jellison's
Air Force Reserve Officer ID, and showed him to be a
lieutenant general. And that, Jellison thought, ought to shake
the kid up.

If it did, Mason showed no other signs. He waited while

another officer brought Jellison's bag and put it in the jeep. They drove down the runway past the specially equipped Looking Glass ship. There were three of those ships, and one was in the air at all times. They carried a Strategic Air Command general officer and staff.

Back at the end of World War II, SAC Headquarters was put in Omaha, at the center of the U.S. The command center itself was built four stories belowground, and reinforced with concrete and steel. The Hole was supposed to withstand anything—but that was before ICBMs and H-bombs. Now there were no illusions. If the Big One came off, the Hole was doomed. That wouldn't keep SAC from controlling its forces, because Looking Glass couldn't be brought down. No one except its pilots ever knew where it was.

Mason ushered the Senator into the big brick building and up the stairs to General Bambridge's office. The office had an old-fashioned air about it. The wooden furniture, most with leather upholstery, was ancient. So was the huge desk. The walls were lined with shelves, each holding USAF models: WWII fighters, a huge B-36 with its improbable pusher props and jet pods, a B-52, missiles of every description. These were the only modern features except the telephones.

There were three on the desk: black, red and gold. A portable unit containing a red and a gold phone stood on a table near the desk. Those phones went with General Bambridge: in his car, to his home, in his bedroom, in the latrines; he was never more than four rings from the gold phone and never would be during his tour of duty as Commander in Chief, Strategic Air Command. The gold phone reached the President. The red one went downhill, from Bambridge to SAC, and it could launch more firepower than all the armies in history had ever employed.

General Thomas Bambridge waved Senator Jellison to a seat, and joined him in the conversation group near the big window overlooking the runway. Bambridge didn't sit behind his desk to talk to people unless there was something wrong. It was said that a major once fainted dead away after five minutes standing in front of Bambridge's desk.

"What the hell brings you out here like this?" Bambridge asked. "What couldn't we settle on the phones?"

"How secure are your phones?" Jellison asked.

Bambridge shrugged. "As good as we can make them—"

"Maybe yours are all right," Jellison said. "You've got your own people to check them. I'm damned sure mine aren't safe. Officially, it's what I told you, I need some help understanding budget requests."

"Sure. You want a drink?"

"Whiskey, if you've got it here."

"Sure." Bambridge took a bottle and glasses from the cabinet behind his desk. "Cigar? Here, you'll like 'em."

"Havana?" Jellison said.

Bambridge shrugged. "The boys get 'em in Canada. Never have got used to U.S. cigars. Cubans may be bastards, but they sure can roll cigars." He brought the whiskey to the coffee table and poured. "Okay, just what is this all about?"

"The Hammer," Arthur Jellison said.

General Bambridge's face went blank. "What about it?"

"It's coming pretty close."

Bambridge nodded. "We've got some fair mathematicians and computers ourselves, you know."

"So what are you doing about it?"

"Nothing. By order of the President." He pointed to the gold phone. "Nothing is going to happen, and we mustn't alarm the Russians." Bambridge grimaced. "Mustn't alarm the bastards. They're killing our friends in Africa, but we shouldn't upset them because it might mess up our friendship."

"It's a hard world," Jellison said.

"Sure it is. Now what is it you want?"

"Tom, that thing's coming close. Really close. I don't think the President understands what that means."

Bambridge took the cigar out of his mouth and inspected the chewed end. "The President doesn't take much interest in us," he said. "That's good, because he leaves SAC pretty much to run itself. But good or bad, he's President, which makes him my Commander in Chief, and I've got funny notions. Like I ought to obey orders."

"Your oath's to the Constitution," Jellison said. "And weren't you a Pointer? Duty, Honor, Country. In that order."

"So?"

"Tom, that comet's coming really close. Really. They tell me it'll knock out all your early-warning radars—"

"They tell me that, too," Bambridge said. "Art, I don't want to be a smart-ass, but aren't you trying to teach your grandmother to suck eggs?" He went to the desk and brought back a red-covered report. "We'll see what looks like an attack that isn't really there, and we won't be able to see a real one—if there is one. Sure, the day they think they can win clean, they'll hit us, but Air Intelligence tells me things are pretty quiet over there right now." Bambridge thumbed

155

through the document again, and his voice fell. "Of course, if we can't see them coming, they couldn't see us—"

"Get that look off your face!"

"Well, I can't be court-martialed just for thinking."

"This is serious, Tom. I don't think the Russians will start anything—so long as it's only a near miss. But . . ."

Bambridge cocked his head to one side. "Jesus! My people didn't tell me it would *hit* us!"

"Nor did mine," Jellison said. "But the odds are now hundreds to one against. Used to be billions. Then thousands. Now it's only hundreds. That's a little scary."

"It is that. So what am I supposed to do? The President ordered me not to go on alert—"

"He can't give you that order. Your charter says you have authority to take any measure needed to protect your forces. Anything short of launching."

"Christ." Bambridge looked out the window. The Looking Glass KC-135 was taking off, which meant that the airborne ship would be coming in after its replacement was safely airborne and lost. "You're asking me to defy a Presidential direct order."

"I'm telling you that if you do, you've got friends in Congress. You might lose your job, but that'll be the worst." Jellison's voice was very low and urgent. "Tom, do you think I *like* this? I doubt that goddam comet will hit Earth, but if it does and we're not ready . . . God knows what will happen."

"That's for sure." Bambridge tried to imagine it. An asteroid strike in some remote part of the Soviet Union—would they believe it wasn't a U.S. sneak attack? Or why remote? Moscow! "But if we've gone to alert status, they'll know it, and it'll give 'em that much more reason to think we did it," Bambridge said.

"Sure. And if we haven't gone to alert, and they see this as a golden opportunity? If the Hammer hits, Washington may be gone, Tom. Washington, New York, most of the eastern seacoast."

"Shit. All we'd need would be a war on top of that," Bambridge said. "If the Hammer really does hit, the world is going to be in a big enough mess without starting the Big One to go with it. But if it hits us and not them, they'll want to finish the job. It's what I'd do, if I was them."

"But you wouldn't—"

"Not from this office," Bambridge said. "Not even if I got orders that I'll never, thank God, get." The General stared at the missile models on the far wall. "Look, what I can do is see that my best people are on duty. Put my top men in the holes, and I'll be up in Looking Glass myself. But how do I tell a meteor hit from a missile attack?"

"I think you'll know," Jellison said.

■

Outside was night and glory. In the Apollo capsule Rick Delanty was moored to his couch. His eyes were tightly closed and he lay rigid, fists clenched. "All right, dammit. I've been sick ever since we came up. But don't tell Houston. There's nothing they could do anyway."

"You damn fool, you'll starve," Baker told him. "Hell, it's no disgrace. Everybody gets space sickness."

"Not for a whole week."

"You know better. MacAlliard was sick the whole mission. Not as bad as you, but he had help. And I'm getting Dr. Malik."

"No!"

"Yes. We haven't got time for macho pride."

"That's not it and you know it." Delanty's voice was pinched. "She'll report it. And—"

"And nothing," Baker said. "We're not going to scrub this mission just because you keep puking up your guts."

"You're sure of that?"

"Yeah. They can't abort unless I say so. And I won't. Unless—"

"Unless nothing," Delanty said. "That's the whole point. Good God, Johnny, if this flops because of me . . . Hell, I wish they'd picked somebody else. Then it wouldn't matter so much. But I've *got* to keep going."

"Why?" Baker demanded.

"Because I'm—"

"A gentleman of color?"

"Black. Try to remember." He tried to grin. "All right, get the lady doc. Something's got to help. Mothersills, maybe?"

"Best thing is to keep your eyes closed."

"Which I'm doing, and a fat lot of help I am," Delanty said. His voice was bitter. "Me, old Iron Ear, space-sick. It's insane." He realized Baker had left, and nervously began buttoning up his fly.

The official name was "sustained duty clothing." Everyone else would have called them long johns. Or a union suit. What the well-dressed spaceman will wear. It's a very practical costume, but Rick Delanty couldn't quite hide his nervousness: He wasn't used to having women see him in his underwear. Especially not white women.

"Man, will the old boys in the back towns in Texas go nuts over this," he muttered. ..

"What is this you have not reported?" Her voice was sharp, totally professional, and blew away any residual thoughts Rick Delanty might have had. She came into the capsule and unclipped a lead from Rick's union suit. She plugged it into a thermometer readout. The other end of the lead went inside the long johns and up inside Rick Delanty. All astronauts became gun-shy about their anuses—not that it did them any good.

Leonilla said, "Have you eaten anything at all?" She read the thermometer and made a note.

"Nothing that stays down."

"So you are dehydrated. We will try these, first. Chew this capsule. No—do not swallow it whole. Chew it."

Rick chewed. "Jesus Christ, what is this stuff? That's the nastiest—"

"Swallow, please. In two minutes we will try a nutrient drink. You need hydration and nourishment. Do you often fail to report illnesses?"

"No. I thought I could make it."

"In every space mission approximately one-third of the personnel involved have experienced from mild to extreme forms of space sickness. The probability that one of us would have the difficulty was very high. Now drink this. Slowly."

He drank. It was thick and tasted of oranges. "Not bad."

"It is based on American Tang," Leonilla said. "I have added fruit sugars and a vitamin solution. How do you feel? No, do not look at me. It is important that this stay down. Keep your eyes closed."

"It's not too bad, this way."

"Good."

"But I'm no damned use with my eyes closed! And I've got to—"

"You've got to rehydrate and stay alive so the rest of us can stay here," Leonilla said.

Delanty felt something cold on his forearm. "What—"

"A sleeping injection. Relax. There. You will sleep for several hours. During that time I will give you an intravenous. Then when you are awake we can try other drugs. Good-night."

She went back into the main Hammerlab compartment. There was room in the center of it now; the equipment had been stowed in proper places, and much of the styrofoam packing had been ejected out into space.

"Well?" John Baker demanded. Pieter Jakov asked the same thing, in Russian.

"Bad," she said. "I think he has not kept water in his system for at least twenty-four hours. Possibly longer. His temperature is thirty-eight point eight. Badly dehydrated."

"So what do we do?" Baker asked.

"I think the drugs I have given him will keep the drink down. I gave him nearly a liter, and he showed no signs of distress. Why did he not tell us before?"

"Hell, he's the first black man in space. He doesn't want to be the last one," Baker said.

"Does he think he is the only one under pressure to succeed?" Leonilla demanded. "He is the first black man in space, but the physiological differences between races are small compared to those between sexes. I am the second woman in space, and the first failed. . . ."

"It is time for more observations," Pieter Jakov said. "Leonilla, assist me. Or must you attend to your patient?"

With the gear properly stowed, there was still very little room to spare in Hammerlab. They had found ways to achieve some privacy: Delanty in the Apollo, Leonilla Malik in the *Soyuz*. Baker and Jakov traded off watchkeeping and slept in Hammerlab when they slept at all. With three to cover the work of four, there wasn't a lot of time for sleep.

And Hamner-Brown was approaching. Tail-first it came, directly toward them, the tenuous gas that streamed from it already engulfing Earth and Moon and Hammerlab. They took hourly observations, visual, and daily went outside to gather samples of nothing: the thin vacuum of space, bottled to take back to Earth, where sensitive instruments could find a few molecules of a comet's tail.

At first there was little to see. Only in the direction of the comet was it obvious that the tail was streaming across space to cover hundreds of millions of miles; but later, as it came closer, they could see it in any direction they looked.

When they weren't watching the comet they could take observations of the Sun. There were another dozen experiments, in crystallography, in thin-film research, to occupy any spare time left from that.

It made for a busy day.

They hadn't much privacy, but they had some. By mutual agreement and ship design, the personal facilities were in the spacecraft, not the lab capsule. For Baker and Delanty the system was simple enough: a tube to fit over their male members, with a tank to pee in. It flushed.

This time when Baker used the system he felt Delanty's eyes on him.

"You're supposed to be asleep. Not watching me piss."

"You I'm not interested in. Johnny . . . how does Leonilla manage it? In space."

"Yeah. I managed to forget I don't know. I'll ask her, huh?"

"Sure. Do that. It's a cinch *I'm* not gonna."

"Me neither." Johnny opened a valve. Urine jetted from the Apollo into space. Frozen droplets formed a cloud around the craft, like a new constellation of stars, and gradually dissipated. "Why the hell did you get me worrying about that again?"

"I should be the only one with trouble?"

"How're you getting along?"

"Pretty good."

Two days later, Delanty was much better—but Baker didn't have an answer.

He had just returned from taking a vacuum sample, and was alone with Jakov when Baker said, "I can't stand it."

"I beg your pardon?" the Russian said.

"Something bothering me. How does Leonilla take a leak in free fall?"

"This concerns you?"

"Sure. It's not even idle curiosity. One reason we never sent women into space, the design boys couldn't come up with proper sanitary facilities. Somebody suggested a catheter, but that *hurts*." Jakov said nothing. "So how does she do it?" Johnny demanded.

"That is a state secret. I'm sorry," Pieter Jakov said. Could he be joking? It didn't show. "It is time for a new series of solar observations. Will you help me with the telescope, please."

"Sure." I'll ask Leonilla, Johnny thought. Before we get

160

down, anyway. He glanced sideways at the Russian. Maybe Jakov didn't know either.

"How you doing?" Baker asked.

"Fine," Delanty said. "Does Houston know?"

"Not from me," Baker said. "Maybe from Baikunyar. I don't guess Jakov keeps much from his people. But why should they tell Houston?"

"I hate it," Rick said.

"Sure you do. So what? You've proved whatever you needed to. You're here, and we got the wings opened out. Christ, man, if you can do that kind of work while you're sick, they ought to call you Ironman. You'll be working tomorrow."

"Yeah. You solve that problem that was bothering you?"

Baker shrugged. "No. I asked Pieter. 'State secret,' he said. State secret my ass."

"Well, maybe we can find out. We've sure got enough cameras. . . ."

"Sure. That'll look good in the report. Two U.S. Air Force officers sneaking into the lady's powder room with cameras. Well, I've got the watch. I'll go wake up Comrade Brigadier. See you." Johnny Baker floated out of the Apollo capsule and across Hammerlab. It was quiet out there; Leonilla was asleep in *Soyuz*, Delanty strapped down in Apollo, and Jakov supposedly catching a nap before going on watch.

Baker swam toward the Russian's bunk. In the maze of telescopes and cameras and growing crystals and x-ray detectors Jakov floated, lightly strapped to a nylon web. He was grinning at the bulkhead. When Johnny reached him, the grin blinked out.

Like he just gave somebody a hotfoot, Johnny Baker thought. And was caught in the act.

State secret my ass.

June: Three

The outer receptionist was new, and she didn't send Harvey Randall on into the big executive suite on the third floor of Los Angeles City Hall. Harvey didn't mind. There were others waiting out there, and his crew wouldn't be up with the cameras for a few minutes anyway. He was early for his appointment.

Harvey took a seat and indulged in his favorite game: people-watching. Most of the visitors were obvious. Vendors, political types, all there to see one of the deputy mayors or an executive assistant. One was different. She was in her twenties, and Harvey couldn't tell if early or late twenties. She wore jeans and a flowered blouse, but they'd come from an expensive shop, not from The Gap. She stared frankly, and when Harvey looked at her she didn't let her eyes drop in embarrassment. Harvey shrugged and crossed the room to sit next to her. "What's so interesting about me?" he asked.

"I recognized you. You do TV documentaries. I'll remember your name in a minute."

"Fine," Harvey said.

That did make her look away; but she turned back to him with half a smile. "All right. What is it?"

"You first."

"Mabe Bishop." Her accent was definitely native.

Harvey fished into his memories. "Aha. People's Lobby."

"Right." She didn't change expressions, which was curious; most people would be pleased to have a national documentary reporter recognize their name. Harvey was still finding that surprising when she said, "You still haven't told me."

"Harvey Randall."

"Now it's my turn to say 'aha.' You're doing the comet shows."

"Right. How did you like them?"

"Terrible. Dangerous. Stupid."

"You don't mince words. Mind telling me why?" Harvey asked.

"Not at all. First, you've scared the wits out of fifty million halfwits—"

"I did not—"

"And they should be scared, but not of a damned comet! Comets! Signs in the heavens! Evil portents! Medieval crap, when there's plenty to worry about right here on Earth." Her tones were full and bitter.

"And what should they be scared of?" Harvey prompted. He didn't really want to know, and cursed himself the instant he said it. It was a reporter's automatic question, but the trouble was, she'd sure as hell tell him.

She did. "Spray cans ruining the atmosphere, destroying ozone, causing cancer. A new atomic power plant in the San Joaquin Valley making radioactive wastes that will be around for half a million years! The big Cadillacs and Lincolns are burning m-megatons of gasoline. All these things that we've got to *do* something about, things we *should* be scared of, and instead everyone's hiding in the root cellar afraid of a comet!"

"You've got a point," Randall said. "Even if I don't think all of those are good causes—"

"Oh, don't you? And which ones aren't?" she demanded. Her voice was full of hate, and readiness for attack.

My, my, Harvey thought. There were times when he wanted to take his reportorial objectivity, roll it tightly and stuff it in an anatomically uncomfortable place about the person of a pompous professor of journalism.

"I'll tell you," he said. "The reason people are still burning gas in those big comfortable cars is that they can't get enough electricity to run electric cars. They can't get electricity because the air's already full of crap from fossil fuel plants and we're running out of fossil fuels, and damned fools keep delaying the nuclear plants that might get us out of that particular box." Harvey stood up. "And if I ever hear the words 'spray can' and 'ozone' again, I'll track you down wherever you hide and throw up in your lap."

"Huh?"

Harvey went back to the receptionist. "Tell Johnny Kim that Harvey Randall is out here, please," he said. His voice was commanding. The new receptionist looked at him in alarm, then turned to her intercom.

Behind him Harvey could hear Mabe Bishop spluttering. It gave Harvey great satisfaction. He went over to the door that led into the executive suite and waited. In a second it buzzed. "Go right in, Mr. Randall," the receptionist said. "I'm sorry I kept you waiting—"

" 'Sall right," Harvey mumbled. The door let him into a long hall. There were offices on both sides of it. An Oriental of indeterminate age, over thirty and under fifty, came out of one of them.

"Ho, Harv. How long did that quim keep you waiting?"

"Not long. How are you, Johnny?"

"Pretty good. The Mayor's got a conference running over-time. Community-development thing. Mind waiting a sec?"

"Not really—the crew should be up pretty soon."

"They're coming up now," John Kim said. He was Mayor Bentley Allen's press secretary, speechwriter and sometimes political manager, and Harvey knew that Kim could be in Sacramento or Washington if he wanted to be; probably would be anyway, if he stayed on with Bentley Allen. "I sent down to have them come up the private elevator."

"Thanks," Harvey said. "They'll appreciate that—"

"Hah. The conference is breaking up. Let's go in and see Hizzoner until the crew gets up." Kim led Harvey down the hall.

There were two offices. One was large, with expensive furniture and thick rugs. Flags hung on the walls, and there were trophies and plaques and framed certificates everywhere. Past the ornate formal outer office was a much smaller room, with an even larger desk. This desk was piled high with papers, reports, books, IBM print-outs, and memos. Some of the memos held large red stars. A few held two red stars, and one had three. The Mayor was just picking that one up when Kim and Harvey Randall came in.

He looks good, Randall thought as the Mayor read the memo. Los Angeles' second black mayor. He'd kept to a winning game: He was tall and fit and dressed like a wealthy professional man, which he'd been before getting into politics.

His mixed blood showed, and his education showed because he let it. Bentley Allen was not going to talk down to people. He didn't *need* the political jobs; he was technically on leave from a tenure appointment on the faculty of a wealthy private university.

"Documentary, Mr. Randall?" Bentley Allen asked. He initialed the memo and put it in an OUT tray.

"No, sir," Johnny Kim answered. "Evening news this time."

"So what's newsworthy about me tonight?" the Mayor asked.

"Fallout from the documentaries," Harvey Randall said. "Network news, all networks. What are public officials on the day Hamner-Brown doesn't hit Earth."

"All networks?" Johnny Kim asked.

"Yes."

"Wouldn't have been a bit of pressure on that, would there?" Kim asked. "Like from an off-white house on Pennsylvania Avenue?"

"Might have been," Harvey admitted.

"And what The Man wants is good vibes," the mayor said. "Keep calm, cool and collected on Hot Fudge Sundae."

"Which falls on a Tuesdae next week," Harvey responded automatically. "Yes, sir—"

"So what if I screamed panic?" Mayor Allen asked. There was a gleam of amusement in his eye. "Or said, 'Here's your chance, brothers! Burn whitey out! Get yours, you'll never get a better time'?"

"Aw, bullshit," Harvey said. "I thought everybody wanted to be on the evening national news."

"You ever get impulses like that?" Bentley Allen asked. "You know. Irresistible impulses to do the one thing that would put you in a new line of work? Such as spilling a martini down the dean's wife's dress? Which, I may add, I did once. Purely accidental, I assure you, but look where it got me."

Now Harvey really did look worried, and Mayor Allen let the grin play across his face. "Needn't worry, Mr. Randall. I like this job. Or another one, in a somewhat larger office back east. . . ." He let his voice trail off. It was no secret that Bentley Allen would like to be the first black President; there were serious political managers who thought he could do it in another dozen years or so.

"I'll be a good boy," Mayor Allen said. "I'll tell the people how we expect full attendance in all city offices, and I'll be right here—well, literally here, but I'll tell them there," he added, pointing to the ornate office. "And I expect all my top people to set the same example. I may or may not say that I'll have a color TV going, because I'm damned if I'm going to miss a show like that."

"Business as usual with time off for a light show," Harvey said.

The Mayor nodded. "Of course." His face took on a serious look. "Privately, I'm a bit worried. Too many people taking off. Do you know that almost every U-Haul trailer in the city has been rented? By the week. And we've even had a big surge of requests for time off from my police and fire-fighters. Not granted, of course. All leaves canceled on Hot Fudge Sundae."

"Worried about looting?" Harvey asked.

"Not enough to say so in public. But yes," Mayor Allen said. "Looting and burglaries with all the homes that have been or will be abandoned. But we'll handle it. If your crew is set up out there, we'd better get to it. I've a meeting with the director of Civil Defense in half an hour."

They stood and went into the outer office.

The traffic on Beverly Glen was nice. Very light for a Thursday evening. Harvey drove with a wide grin. I've got a hell of a story, he thought. Even if I never get another foot in the can, I've got a story. Not only do millions think the world's going to end, but millions more *hope* so. It shows in their attitudes. They hate what they're doing, and keep looking nostalgically at the "simple" life. Of course they won't voluntarily choose to be farmers or live in communes, but if *everybody* has to . . .

It didn't really make sense, but people's attitudes often didn't. That didn't bother Harvey Randall at all.

And there'd be another great story in follow-up. The day after the world didn't end. That's a good title for a book, Harvey thought. Of course there'll be a thousand novelists scrambling to beat each other into print. Books with titles like *Chicken Little*, and *The Day the World Didn't End* (not as good as his title) and *Rock, Won't You Hide Me?* Come to that, some of the radio stations were playing disaster-religious songs twenty-four hours a day, and end-of-the-world preachers were doing a land-office business.

There were also the Comet Wardens, a Southern California sect who were putting on white robes and praying the comet away. They'd staged a couple of stunts to get publicity, and about half their leaders were out on bail for blocking traffic or getting into the outfield during televised baseball games. That had stopped; a judge had ordered that no more be released on bail until next Wednesday. . . .

Hell, I could write a book, Harvey thought. I ought to. I never wanted to before, but I'm literate, and I've done the research. I'm *way* ahead of the flock. *The Day After the World Didn't End.* No. No good. Too long, for one thing. I can call mine *Hammer Fever.* And of course there'll be plenty of publicity, we'll have a show on the air just afterward.

I could even make some money on this. A *lot* of money. Enough to pay off the bills and take care of the tuition at Harvard School for Boys and . . .

Hammer Fever. I like it.

Only one problem. It's real. Like a war scare.

He'd found that everywhere. Coffee, tea, flour, sugar, any staple capable of being hoarded, was in short supply. Freeze-dried foods were *gone.* Clothing stores reported runs on rain gear (in southern California, with the next rains due in November!). You couldn't find outdoorsman's clothing anywhere, no surplus hiking boots in the stores. And nobody was buying suits, white shirts, or neckties.

They were buying guns, though. There wasn't a firearm to be bought in Beverly Hills or the San Fernando Valley. There wasn't any ammunition, either.

Backpacking stores were sold out of everything from hiking boots to trail food to fishing equipment (more hooks than flies; you could still get dry flies, but only the expensive American-made ones, not the cheap ones from India). There weren't any tents to be had, nor sleeping bags. There was even a run on life jackets! Harvey grinned when he heard that one. He'd never seen a tsunami himself, but he'd read about them. After Krakatoa a great wave had deposited a Dutch gunboat miles inland at an elevation of two hundred feet.

Then there were the mail-order "survival packages" that had been sold for the past few weeks. They'd not be getting any more orders, of course, not this close to Hammerfall. Maybe—just maybe—they weren't intending to deliver? Have to look into that. There were four companies selling them. For from fifty to sixteen thousand dollars you could get anything from just a food supply to the whole thing in one lump. The foods were nonperishable and constituted a more-

or-less-balanced diet. (Which religious sect was it that required all its members to keep a year's supply of food? They'd been doing that since the Sixties, too. Harvey made another mental note. They'd be worth interviewing, *after* That Day had passed.)

The cheap outfits were food only. There was progressively more, up to the sixteen-grand package, which included a Land Cruiser, clothing from thermal underwear out, machete, sleeping bag, butane stove and tank, inflatable raft, almost anything you could name. One included membership in a survival club: You were guaranteed a place if you could get there, somewhere in the Rockies. The different companies didn't sell identical items, and none of the four included guns (courtesy of Lee Harvey Oswald; and how many people has the ban on mail-order guns saved or killed, depending on whether or not the Hammer falls?).

But all four companies sold you the same outfit whether you lived on a mountain or a seashore or the High Plains. Harvey grinned. *Caveat emptor*. The stuff was all overpriced, too. Lord, what fools these mortals be. . . .

The traffic was very light. He'd reached Mulholland already. The San Fernando Valley spread out below him. The wind had been strong today and there was no smog.

The valley stretched on for miles. Row after row of California suburban houses, rich areas and poor areas, stucco subdevelopments and old wooden frame homes, here and there a magnificent Monterey style, ancient, the only remnants of the time when the valley had been orange groves—and every one of them built in a flood basin. The neat squares of the valley were cut through by freeways—and there weren't many cars out there.

All over the basin, on four successive midmornings, the outbound freeways were more crowded than the inbound. Cars, trucks and rented trailers loaded with a lifetime of clutter, all moving out of the basin toward the hills beyond, or over the passes into the San Joaquin. All over the L.A. basin, stores had closed for the week, or for the month, or forever; and the remaining businesses were suffering badly from absenteeism. Hammer Fever.

There was almost no traffic on Benedict Canyon. Harvey chuckled. Here were the people coming home from work . . . but the ones with Hammer Fever were elsewhere. Hammer Fever had sent the mountain resort business to an all-time high, all across the country. The Treasury Department was worried: Consumer credit levels had broken all records; people were buying survival gear on credit cards. Employment up, economy up, inflation up, all because of the comet.

It's going to make one hell of a story.

Unless the damned thing does fall. It hit him, just then: If the Hammer fell, nobody was going to give a damn about the story. There'd be no programs. No TV. Nothing.

Harvey shook his head. His smile faded as he glanced at the package in the passenger seat. His compromise with Hammer Fever: an Olympic target pistol, .22 caliber, with a sculpted wooden grip that wrapped fully around the hand, steadying and bracing the wrist. It would be inhumanly accurate, but it was nothing anyone could point to while bellowing, "Look, Old Harv's got Hammer Fever!"

Only maybe I wasn't so damned smart after all, Harvey thought. He began to take inventory in his head.

He had a shotgun. Backpacking gear too, but only for himself. The idea of Loretta carrying a backpack was ludicrous. He had taken her on a hike, just once. Did she still have the shoes? Probably not. She couldn't exist at distances greater than five miles from a beauty shop.

And I love her, he reminded himself firmly. I can play rugged outdoorsman whenever I want to, and have elegance to come back to. Unwanted there came to him the memory of Maureen Jellison standing high on a split rock, her long red hair blowing in the wind. He pushed the memory very firmly back down into his mind and left it there.

So what can I do to prepare? Harvey wondered. Not a lot of time left. Supplies. Well, I can compromise. Canned goods. Good hedge against inflation anyway. They'll get us through a disaster, if any, and we can still eat them when the damned thing's gone past. And bottled water . . . No. Neither one. There's been a run on both. I'd be lucky to find much this week, and I'll pay a premium.

He turned into the driveway and braked sharply. Loretta had stopped the station wagon in the drive and was carrying packages into the house. He got out and started helping her, automatically, and only gradually realized that he was carrying bag after bag of frozen food. He asked, "What is this?"

Puffing slightly, Loretta set her load on the kitchen table. "Don't be angry, Harv. I couldn't help it. Everyone says— well, says that comet may hit us. So I got some food, just in case."

"Frozen food."

"Yes. They were nearly out of cans. I hope we can get it

all in the freezer." She surveyed the bags doubtfully. "I don't know. We may have to eat Stouffer stuff for a couple of days."

"Uh-huh." Frozen food. Good God. Did she expect power lines to survive Hammerfall? But of course she did. He said nothing. She meant well; and while Loretta had been out getting useless supplies, Harvey Randall had been dithering and doing nothing; it came down to the same thing, except for the money, and she'd probably saved them money if the Hammer didn't fall. Which it wouldn't. And if it did— why, money wouldn't be important anyway. "You done good," Harvey said. He kissed her and went out for another load.

"Hey, Harvey."

"Yo, Gordie," Harvey said. He went over to the fence.

Gordie Vance held out a beer. "Brought you one," he said. "Saw you drive up."

"Thanks. You want to talk about something?" He hoped Gordie did. Vance hadn't been himself the last few weeks. There was something bothering him. Harvey could sense it without knowing what it was, and without Gordie knowing that Harvey knew.

"Where you going to be next Tuesday?" Gordie asked.

Harvey shrugged. "L.A. somewhere, I guess. I've got crews for the national stuff."

"But working," Gordie said. "Sure you don't want to come hiking? Good weather in the mountains. I get some time off next week."

"Good Lord," Harvey said. "I can't—"

"Why not? You really want to stick here for the end of the world?"

"It won't be the end of the world," Harvey said automatically. He caught the gleam in Vance's eye. "And anyway, if that Hammer *doesn't* fall and I haven't been busy covering it, it's the end of *my* world. No can do, Gordie. God, I'd like to get away, but no."

"Figures," Vance said. "Loan me your kid."

"What?"

"Makes sense, doesn't it?" Vance said. "Suppose that thing does hit. Andy'd have a much better chance up in the hills with me. And if it doesn't—well, you wouldn't want him to miss a good hike just to hang around in the L.A. smog, would you?"

"You make plenty of sense," Harvey said. "But . . . where'll you be? I mean, in case something does happen, how do I find you and Andy."

Vance's face took on a serious look. "You know damned

well what your chances of living through it are if it does hit and you're in L.A. . . ."

"Yeah. Slim and none," Harvey said.

". . . and besides, I'll be just about where you'd want to go. Out of Quaking Aspen. The old Silver Knapsack area. Low enough to get out of in bad weather, high enough to be safe no matter what happens. Unless we're under it, and that's a random chance, isn't it?"

"Sure. You ask Andy about this?"

"Yeah. He said he'd like to go, if it's okay with you."

"Who all's going?"

"Just me and seven boys," Gordie said. "Marie's got charity work to do, so she can't come. . . ."

Harvey envied Gordie Vance just one thing: Marie Vance went on hikes. On the other hand, she wasn't very easy to live with in town.

". . . which means under scout rules the girls can't come," Gordie was saying. "And some of the others—well, they're just not available. Hell, Harvey, you know the area. We'll be fine."

Harvey nodded. It was safe trail and a good area. "Right," he said. He drank most of the beer. "You all right, Gordie?" he asked suddenly.

Vance's face changed, subtly, and he was trying to hide the change. "Sure. Why wouldn't I be?"

"You just don't seem yourself lately."

"Work," Vance said. "Too much work lately. This hike will fix everything."

"Good," Harvey said.

The shower felt good. He let hot water pound on his neck, and he thought: Too late. The sensible, phlegmatic ones would stick it out, with the odds still hundreds, maybe thousands, to one in their favor. The panicky ones had already bought supplies and struck for the hills. There were also the sensible, cautious ones like Gordie Vance, who'd planned his hike months before, and who could say he wasn't letting a comet spoil his vacation—but who'd be in the hills anyway.

Then there were the ones in between. There must be tens of millions, and Harv Randall was one of them, and look at him now: scared too late, and nothing to do but wait it out. In five days the nucleus of Hamner-Brown would be past, on its way to that strange, cold region beyond the planets. . . .

Or it wouldn't be.

"There must be something." Harvey said, talking to himself in the privacy of a roaring shower. "Something I can do. What do I want out of this? If that damned dirty snowball ends the blessings of civilization and the advertising industry . . . okay, back to the basics. Eat, sleep, fight, drink and run. Not necessarily in that order. Right?"

Right.

Harvey Randall took Friday off. He called in sick, and by sheer bad luck Mark Czescu was in and took the call.

Mark got obvious pleasure out of asking it. "Hammer Fever, Harv?"

"Knock it off."

"Okay. Making a few plans myself. Meeting a couple of friends, getting to a nice safe place. Forgot to tell you. I won't be around on Hot Fudge Sundae, which falls on a Tuesdae next week. Want we should swing by your place after—if, as and when?"

He got no answer, because Harvey Randall had already hung up.

Randall went to a shopping center. He made his purchases carefully, and all on credit cards, or with checks.

At a supermarket he bought six big round roasts weighing twenty-eight pounds, and half their stock of vitamins, and half their stock of spices and considerable baking soda.

At a health-food store two doors down he bought more vitamins and more bottled spices. He bought a respectable amount of salt and pepper, and three pepper grinders.

Next door, a set of good carving knives. They'd needed new kitchen knives for a year. He also bought a sharpening stone and a hand-operated knife sharpener.

There was a tool kit he'd been wanting for years, and this was the time, he decided. While he was in the hardware store he picked up other odds and ends. Plastic plumbing parts, cheap stuff, that would thread onto iron pipe. There might be a use for it one day, if; and it would be handy around the house if not. There wasn't a camp stove to be had, but the clerk knew Harvey and obligingly fetched out four hand-pumped flashlights and two Coleman lanterns that had just come in, along with four gallons of Coleman fuel.

He also gave Harvey a knowing look that Randall was coming to recognize.

At the liquor store he bought a hundred and ninety-three dollars' worth of everything in sight: gallons of vodka and bourbon and scotch; fifths of Grand Marnier, Drambuie and other esoteric and expensive liqueurs. He loaded everything into the wagon and then went back for bottles of Perrier water. He paid by credit card—and got another knowing look from the clerk.

"I'm ready to throw one hell of a party," he told Kipling. The dog thumped his tail on the seat. He liked to go places with Harvey, although he didn't get the chance as often as he wanted. He watched as his master went from store to store; to drugstores for sleeping pills and more vitamins, iodine, first-aid cream, the last box of bandages; back to the grocery for dog food; back to the drugstore for soap, shampoo, toothpaste, new toothbrushes, skin cream, calamine lotion, suntan lotion . . .

"Where do we *stop?*" Harvey asked. The dog licked his face. "We have to stop somewhere. Good Lord, I never thought much about the blessings of civilization before, but there are just a *lot* of things I wouldn't want to live without."

Harvey took his purchases home, then went back down the hill to collect the TravelAll from the mechanic who usually worked on it. If Harvey hadn't been a very old and valued customer, he'd never have got squeezed in for tune-up, oil change, grease job, and general before-trip checkup; the garage wasn't taking on new jobs for a week, and there were dozens of cars waiting for rush jobs.

But he got the TravelAll, and filled both tanks with gas. He filled the strap-on tanks for good measure, but he had to go to three service stations to do it; there was unofficial gas rationing in the L.A. basin.

After lunch it was bloody work. Twenty-eight pounds of beef had to be sliced into thin strips—*thin!* The new knives helped, but his arms were cramped by dinner time, and the job still wasn't done. "I'll need the bottom oven for the next three days," he told Loretta.

"It *is* going to hit us," Loretta said firmly. "I knew it."

"No. Odds are hundreds, thousands, to one against it."

"Then why that?" she asked. It was a good question. "My kitchen is just *covered* with little slices of raw meat."

"Just in case," Harvey said. "And it keeps. Andy can use it for hikes, if we don't." He got back to work.

The easy way to make beef jerky is not the way the Indians used. They employed a slow fire, or a summer sun, and their quality control was poor. Far better to set a modern oven at 100° to 120° and leave the thin strips of beef in for twenty-four hours. The meat isn't supposed to cook; it's supposed to dry. A good strip of beef jerky is bone-dry, and hard enough to kill you if you file the end to a point. It will also keep practically forever.

Beef jerky is too limited a diet to keep a human being alive forever. The time can be greatly extended with vitamin supplements, but it's still dull. So? If the Hammer fell, boredom would not be the major cause of death. . . .

For bulk and carbohydrates, Harvey had grits. Nobody else in Beverly Hills, it seemed, had thought of them; and yet several of the stores carried them. He'd also found a sack of cornmeal, although there'd been no wheat or rye flour.

The fat from the beef he pounded into pemmican, mixing it with the little sugar they had around the house, with salt, with pepper, and some Worcestershire sauce for a bit of flavor. That he'd partly cook, keeping the fat that melted out for more pemmican, and to store bacon in. Bacon covered with fat and kept protected from air will keep a long time before going rancid.

So much for food, he decided. Now for water. He went out to the swimming pool. He'd started emptying it last night. It had almost drained, and he began filling it again. This time it wouldn't get chlorine. When it was filling well he put the cover over it to keep leaves and dirt out.

Take a long time to drink all that, he thought. And there's the contents of the hot-water heater at any given time. And, . . . He rooted around in the garage until he found a number of old plastic bottles. Several had held bleach and still smelled of it. Perfect. He filled them without rinsing. The others he washed out carefully. Now, even if the pool went, there'd be *some* water.

Eat, drink. What's next? Sleep. That one was easy. Harvey Randall never threw anything away, and he had, in addition to his regular backpacking bag, a U.S. Army Arctic sleeping bag, a summer-weight bag, bag liners, Andy's discarded bag, and even the one he'd bought that only time Loretta had tried a hike. He took them all out and hung them on the back clothesline. Solar heat. The simplest and most efficient

175

solar power system known to man: Hang your clothes out to dry, rather than use an electric or gas dryer. Of course not many "conservationists" did it; they were too busy preaching conservation. And I'm being unfair, and why?

Because I've got Hammer Fever, and my wife knows it. Loretta thinks I've gone crazy—and I'm scaring her, too. She's convinced I think it's going to hit.

And the more he did to prepare for Hammerfall, the more real it became. I'm even scaring myself, he thought. Have to remember that for the book. *Hammer Fever*. "Hey, hon . . ."

"Yes, darling?"

"Don't look so worried. I'm doing research."

"On what?" She brought him a beer.

"Hammer Fever. I'm going to write a book on it, once the comet's gone past. I've done all the work. It might even be a best seller."

"Oh. I'd love it if you had a book. People look up to an author."

Which, Harv thought, they do. Sometimes. Okay. Now we can eat, drink and sleep. That leaves fight and run.

Fight. Not so good. He had no faith in his skill with guns; either the shotgun or the target pistol. No gun would have given him real confidence. There was no limit to how good a weapon the other guy might have, or how skillful he might be with it, and Harvey Randall had spent the war as a correspondent, not as a soldier.

But there's also bribe. The liquor and spices might buy my way out of trouble. And if I can hang on to them, in a few years they'll be literally priceless, providing there's any surplus food left for luxuries, and there usually is, for someone. For centuries the price of black pepper was fixed, all across Europe, at its own weight in gold, ounce for ounce, and not everybody's going to have thought of hoarding pepper.

Harvey was proud of that idea.

So. That leaves running, and the TravelAll's in as good a shape as I can get it. Bicycles will fit on top, if, as and when. And there's Sunday to go for things I haven't thought of.

Harvey went in, exhausted, but with a feeling of satisfaction. He wasn't exactly ready, but at least he could pretend to be prepared. And a lot better than most. Loretta had waited up for him, and she had the Ben-Gay out. She didn't bug him with a lot of questions; she just rubbed him down good, decided he wasn't interested in anything more intimate and let him get to sleep.

As he dropped off he thought about how much he loved her.

June: Four

The Earth is just too small and fragile a basket for the human race to keep all its eggs in.
                                        Robert A. Heinlein

It was night below on Earth. Every ninety minutes Hammer-lab passed through day and night; time aboard was kept by a clock, not by light and dark outside.

Cities glowed across Europe at the world's edge, but the black face of the Atlantic covered half the sky, hiding nucleus and coma of Hamner-Brown. In the other direction stars blazed through thin mist. The comet's tail streamed up from the horizon on all sides, doming the black Earth with luminous blues and oranges and greens streaming upward to the dome's star-pierced dark apex. Far off to the side the half-moon floated in a matrix of shock waves, like diamond patterns in a still photograph of rocket flame. It was a sight that no one could tire of.

They had broken off work for dinner. Rick Delanty ate steadily, his attention on the glory beyond the windows. They had all lost weight—they always did—but Rick was already nine pounds light, and was trying to make up for it. (Considerable ingenuity had gone into devising a gadget to find a human's weight in null-gravity.)

"So long as you've got your health," Rick said, "you've got *everything*. Wow, it's good not to vomit."

He got puzzled looks from the *kosmonauts*, who had never watched American TV commercials. Baker ignored him.

The Sun exploded over the world's edge. Rick closed his eyes for a few moments, then opened them to watch dawn's blue-and-white arc roll toward them. Yesterday's hurricane pattern still squatted on the Indian Ocean like a sea monster on an ancient map. Typhoon Hilda. Far to the left was Everest and the Himalaya massif. "That's a sight I'm never going to get tired of."

"Yes." Leonilla joined him at the viewport. "But it seems so very fragile. As if I could reach out and . . . run my thumb across the land, leaving a path of destruction hundreds of kilometers wide. That is an uneasy feeling."

Johnny Baker said, "Hold that thought. The Earth *is* fragile."

"You are worried about the comet?" Her expression was hard to read. Russian face and body language is not quite the same as American.

"Forget the comet. The more you know, the more fragile we are," said Johnny. "A nearby nova could sterilize everything on Earth except the bacteria. Or the Sun might flare up. Or cool off a lot. Our galaxy could become a Seyfert galaxy, exploding and killing everything."

Leonilla was amused. "We need not worry for thirty-three thousand years. Speed of light, you know."

Johnny shrugged. "So it happened thirty-two thousand, nine hundred years ago. Or we could do it to ourselves. Chemical garbage killing the ocean, or heat pollution—"

Rick said, "Not so fast. Heat pollution could be the only thing saving us from the glaciers. Some people think the next Ice Age started a few centuries back. And we're running out of coal and oil."

"Sheesh! You can't win."

"Atomic wars. Giant meteor impacts. Supersonic aircraft destroying the ozone layers," said Pieter Jakov. "Why are we doing this?"

"Because we aren't safe down there," Baker said.

"The Earth is large, and probably not as delicate as it looks,' Leonilla said. "'But man's ingenuity . . . sometimes that is what I fear."

"Only one answer," Baker said. He was very serious now. "We've got to get off. Colonize the planets. Not just here, planets in other systems. Build really big spacecraft, more mobile than planets. Get our eggs into a lot of baskets, and it's less likely that some damn fool accident—or fanatic— will wipe us out just as the human race is becoming something we can admire."

"What is admirable?" Jakov said. "I think you and I would not agree. But if you are running for President of the United States, you have my support. I will make speeches for you, but they will not let me vote."

"That's a pity," said Johnny Baker, and thought for a moment of John Glenn, who *had* run for office, and won. "Back to the salt mines. Who's going out for samples this morning?"

The nucleus of Hamner-Brown was thirty hours away. In the telescopes it showed as a swarm of particles, with a lot of space in between. The scientists at JPL were excited at the discovery, but for Baker and the others it was a pain in the ass. It wasn't easy to get Doppler shift on the solid masses, because everything was immersed in the tail, and the gas and dust was streaming away at horrendous speeds, riding the pressure of raw sunlight. The masses were approaching Earth at around fifty miles per second. Finding a sideways drift was even more difficult.

"Still coming straight at us," Baker reported.

"Surely there is some lateral motion," Dan Forrester's voice said.

"Yeah, but it's not measurable," Rick Delanty told him. "Look, Doc, we're giving you the best we've got. It'll have to do."

Forrester was instantly apologetic. "I'm sorry. I know you're doing all you can. It's just that it's hard to make the projection without better data."

And then they had to spend five minutes soothing Forrester's ruffled feathers and assuring him they weren't mad at him.

"There are times when geniuses drive me crazy," Johnny Baker said.

"Easy way to fix that," Delanty said. "Just give him what he wants. You don't hear no complaints about *my* observations."

"Shove it," Baker said.

Delanty rolled his eyes. "Where?" He drifted over to Baker. "Here, I'll punch in the numbers. Just read 'em off."

When they finished the morning observations and had a few moments to relax, Pieter Jakov coughed apologetically. "There is a question," he said. "I have wanted to ask it for a long time. Please do not take it wrong."

It struck Johnny that Pieter had waited until Leonilla

had gone into the *Soyuz* and closed the hatchway. "Go ahead."

Pieter's eyes tracked back and forth between the two Americans. "Our newspapers tell us that in America the blacks serve the whites, the whites rule the blacks. Yet you seem to work together very well. So, bluntly: Are you equal?"

Rick snorted. "Hell no. He outranks me."

"But otherwise?" Pieter suggested.

Rick's face would have looked serious enough, except to another American. "General Baker, can I be your equal?"

"Eh? Oh, *sure,* Rick, you can be my equal. Why didn't you say something before?"

"Well, you know, it's a delicate subject."

Pieter Jakov's expression wasn't cryptic at all. Before he could explode, Johnny asked, "Do you really want a serious lecture on race relations?"

"Please yourself."

"How does Leonilla pee in free fall?"

"Hm. I . . . see."

"See what?" Leonilla came wriggling back through the double hatch.

"A minor discussion," Johnny said. "No state secrets involved."

Leonilla clung to a handhold and studied the three men. John Baker was tapping numbers into a programable hand computer, Pieter Jakov grinned broadly, watching in apparent admiration . . . but they *all* wore that broad, irritating, I've-got-a-secret grin. "They give you good equipment," said the *kosmonaut.* "There are not many things that we do better in space than you do."

Delanty seemed to have trouble with his breathing. Baker said quickly, "Oh, this pocket computer isn't NASA issue. It's mine."

"Ah. Are they expensive?"

"Couple of hundred bucks," Baker said. "Um, that's a lot in rubles, not so much in terms of what people make. Maybe a week's pay for the average guy. Less for somebody who'd actually have a use for it."

"If I had the money, how long would it take to get one?" Leonilla asked.

"About five minutes," Baker said. "Down there, in a store. Up here it might be a while."

She giggled. "I meant down there. They have . . . those . . . in stores, to buy?"

"If you've got the money. Or good credit. Or even not-so-good credit," Baker said. "Why? You want one? Hell, we'll find a way to get you one. You too, Pieter?"

"Could that be arranged?"

"Sure. No problem," Baker said. "I'll call the PR man at Texas Instruments. They'll give you a pair of them for the publicity. Help 'em sell more. Or would you rather have a Hewlett-Packard? Those use a different kind of notation, but they're fast—"

"That is what is confusing," Pieter said. "Two companies, two different rivals making such fine equipment. Wasteful."

"Maybe wasteful," Rick Delanty said, "but I can take you into any damn electronics store in the country and buy one."

"No politics," Johnny Baker warned.

"This ain't politics."

There was an awkward silence. Pieter Jakov drifted over to the UV camera with its digital readouts. He ran a hand lovingly over it. "So precise. So intricately machined, and the complex electronics. It is a real pleasure to work with your American machinery." He gestured around Hammerlab, at the containers of growing crystal, at the cameras and radars and recorders. "It is amazing how much we have learned on this short mission, thanks to your excellent equipment. As much, I think, as on any of our previous *Soyuz* flights."

"As much?" Leonilla Malik's voice was sarcastic. "More." Her voice held a bitterness that snapped three heads around in surprise. "Our *kosmonauts* go along for the ride. As passengers, to prove that we can send men into space and sometimes bring them down alive. For this mission we had nothing to contribute but food and water and oxygen—and one launch to your two."

"Somebody had to bring the lunch," Rick Delanty said. "Pretty good, too."

"Yes, but it is all we brought. Once we had a space program—"

Jakov interrupted in rapid-fire Russian. He spoke too rapidly for Johnny or Rick to follow, but what he was saying was obvious.

She answered with a short, sharp syllable and then continued. "The basis of Marxism is objectivity, is it not? It is time to be objective. We had a space program once. Sergei Korolev was as great a genius as anyone who ever lived! He could have made our space arm the greatest instrument for knowledge in the world, but those madmen in the Kremlin wanted spectaculars! Khrushchev ordered circuses to shame the Americans, and instead of developing our capabilities we

183

gave the world stunts! The first to have three men in orbit—by taking out all the scientific instruments and jamming a third man, a very *small* man, into a capsule built for two, for one orbit! Circuses! We might have been the first to the Moon, but now we have yet to go there."

"Comrade Malik!"

She shrugged. "Is any of this news? No. I thought not. So we had our spectaculars, and we used up our opportunities to gain headlines, and today the best pilot in the Soviet Union cannot dock his spacecraft with a target the size of a comfortable *daschal* And you offer to give us, *give* us as a promotion, something that the best engineers in the Soviet Union cannot build or buy for themselves."

"Hey, didn't mean to get you upset," Johnny Baker said.

Jakov made a final remark in Russian and turned away in disgust. Rick Delanty shook his head in sympathy. What had got into her?

They were quiet and formally polite until she went into the *Soyuz*. Baker and Delanty exchanged looks. They didn't need to say more. Johnny Baker went to the corner where Jakov had busied himself. "Need to get something straight," Johnny said.

"Yes?"

"You're not going to get her in trouble, are you? I mean, there's no need to report everything that gets said up here."

"Of course not," Jakov agreed. He shrugged. "We are all men of the world. We know that every twenty-eight days women become irrational. What married man does not know?"

"Yeah, that must be it," Johnny Baker said, and exchanged another glance with Delanty.

"And of course the State has been her parent," Jakov said. "Her father and mother died when she was young. It is not surprising that she would like to see our country more advanced than it is."

"Sure." Sure, Rick Delanty thought. Bullshit. If she had problems with her period she'd have told the Russian ground-control people and somebody else would have been sent up. Wouldn't she? I'd have told them about space sickness if I'd known I was going to get it. I'm sure I would have. . . .

Whatever her problem, it would be wise to treat Leonilla Malik diffidently during the next day or so. Hell. And Hamner-Brown was so close!

Barry Price laid down the telephone and looked up with excitement. Dolores had just come in with coffee. "Guess what happens next Tuesday!" he shouted in glee.

"A comet hits the Earth."

"Huh? No, no, this is serious. We go on line! I've got all the permissions, the last court suit was dismissed—San Joaquin Nuclear Plant becomes a fully operational facility."

She didn't look as happy as he'd thought she would. "I suppose there'll be some kind of ceremony?" she asked.

"No, we keep a low profile—why?"

"Because I won't be here. Not unless you absolutely need me."

He frowned. "I always absolutely need you—"

"Better get used to it," she said. She patted her stomach. There was no sign of a bulge, but he knew. "Anyway, I'm going to see Dr. Stone in Los Angeles. Thought I'd stay over and visit Mother, and come back Tuesday night."

"Sure. Dee?"

"Yes?"

"You want to keep this baby, don't you?"

"Yes. I'm going to."

"Then marry me."

"No, thanks. We've both tried that before."

"Not with each other," he said. He tried to sound convincing, but secretly was relieved. And yet . . . "Is it fair to the kid? Not having a father . . ."

She giggled. "Not being parthenogenetic, I'm relatively certain he has one. And I've a good idea who he is."

"Oh, dammit, you know what I mean."

"Sure." She put his coffee down on the desk and opened his calendar. "You have lunch with the Lieutenant Governor. Don't forget."

"That moron. If there was anything that would get me out of my euphoric mood, you've just said it. But I'll be nice. You can't believe how nice I'll be."

"Good." She turned to leave.

"Hey," he called, stopping her. "Look, let's talk about it. When you get back from Los Angeles. I mean, it's my kid too. . . ."

"Sure." Then she was gone.

"Hey, baby, that Hammer's gonna *waste* this town."

"Bull-fucking-shit," Alim Nassor said, and he smiled. "We're gonna do the wasting." He'd heard all the talk about what the comet was going to do. The preachers in their storefronts were getting big crowds, pulling in lots of bread. End of the world coming, make your peace with Sweet Jesus, and give money. . . .

More power to them. One thing that comet was doing— it was sucking the honkies right out of their houses. Alim's cruises through Brentwood and Bel Air turned up lots of houses with milk bottles and old newspapers on the porches. He went through in an old pickup truck, lawn mowers and garden tools piled in back. Who'd look twice at black gardeners? So when they stopped to collect the papers and milk cartons nobody noticed. And now he had the addresses, and they'd cleaned up so nobody else would come try a rip-off. . . .

They'd go through Bel Air and Brentwood like a mowing machine. Alim Nassor had set it up with half a dozen burglary outfits, with men who weren't so good at taking orders, but knew a good thing when they saw it. A Hammer of God didn't come twice in a man's lifetime.

Some of these places had to be setups. Pigs on stakeout. There were ways to take care of that little problem, too. It only took planning. They even mowed some yards. Did good work, and that way they could watch the whole block, see people piling stuff into trailers and taking off. Bel Air was half deserted. It was going to be easy pickings tonight! And afterward . . . maybe the political game could be played again. A lot of brothers would have bread, for awhile.

Still . . . there were so *many* honkies moving out. Rich honkies, people who knew things. Down at City Hall everybody was nervous, too. Maybe that thing could really hit?

Alim had gone through the newspapers and magazines. He could read pretty well. A little slow, but he could puzzle it out, and some of the drawings made it all clear. You didn't want to be on low ground. Waves a thousand feet high! The cat who drew them had some imagination. He showed the L.A. City Hall part underwater, the tower rising out of the flood, and the County Administration and the Courthouse with their roofs just sticking up. All them pigs dead, wouldn't that be something? But he sure didn't want to be here when that happened.

Maybe it wouldn't, and all the honkies would come home. "Won't they be surprised," Alim murmured.

"Huh?"

"The honkies. Won't they be surprised when they get home?"

"Yeah. Why just these places? If we hit just the richest houses in a lot bigger territory, we—"

"Shut up."

"Sure."

"I want us close to each other. If one of these places turns out to be full of pigs, we can call for help on the CB."

"Okay, sure."

Hammer of God. What if it was real? Where could they go? Not south, that was for sure. Politicians could talk about black-brown unity, but that was jive. Chicanos didn't like blacks, blacks hated chicanos. There were clubs where you had to kill a black to join down there in chicano turf, and they were tough mothers, and the further south you went the more there were.

"We take guns tonight," he said. "We take all the guns."

Harold flinched, and the truck swerved a little. "You think we'll get trouble?"

"I just want to be ready," Alim said. And if that fucking comet . . . Better to have guns and bullets, tonight and tomorrow. And take some food. He'd stash it himself, so as not to upset the brothers.

At least they'd be high up, if it came.

∎

Patrolman Eric Larsen had come to Los Angeles from Topeka with a university degree in English and an urgent impulse to write for television and the movies. The need to support himself and a chance opportunity led him to the Burbank Police Department. He told himself it would be valuable experience. Look what Joseph Wambaugh had managed from a police career! And Eric could write; at least, he had a degree that said he could.

Three years later he still hadn't sold a script, but he had confidence, strange tales to tell and a considerably better understanding of both human nature and the entertainment industry. He'd also done a lot of growing up. He'd lived with a woman, been engaged twice and got over his inability to have casual friendships with girls, even though he hadn't lost a strong tendency to idealize women. It hurt Eric to see young runaways exploited by the street people. He kept thinking of what they might have become.

He'd also learned the police view of the world: All humanity is divided into three parts—cops, scumbags and civilians. He hadn't yet adopted an attitude of contempt toward civilians. They were the people he was supposed to protect, and perhaps because he was not a career policeman (although Burbank didn't know that) he could take his job seriously. The civilians paid him. One day he would be one of them.

He'd learned to curse the judicial system, while keeping enough literary objectivity to admit that he didn't know what to replace it with. There *were* people who could be "rehabilitated." Not many. Most scumbags were just that, and the best thing to do with them would be to take them out to San Nicholas Island and put them ashore. Let them victimize each other. The trouble was, you couldn't always tell which ones should be put away forever and which could fit back into the real world. He often got into arguments with his partners over that. His buddies on the force called him "Professor" and kidded his literary ambitions, and the diary he kept; but Eric got along with nearly everyone, and his sergeant had recommended him for promotion to Investigator.

The comet fascinated Eric, and he'd read all he could about it. Now it dominated the skies above. Tomorrow it would be past. Eric drove with his partner through strangely active Burbank streets. People were moving about, piling goods into trailers, doing things inside their houses. There was a lot of traffic.

"Be glad when that thing's past," his partner said. Investigator Harris was all cop. The brilliant light show in the skies above was only another problem to him. If it was a pretty show, he'd look at films of it after it was past. Right now it was a pain in the arse.

"Car forty-six. See the woman at eight-nine-seven-six Alamont. Reports screaming in the apartment above her. Handle Code Three."

"Ten-four," Eric told the microphone. Harris had already sent the cruiser around a tight curve.

"That's not a family-fight house," Harris said. "Singles apartments. Probably some guy can't take no for an answer."

The cruiser pulled up in front of the apartment building. It was a large, fancy place, swimming pool and sauna. Rubber trees grew on both sides of the entrance. The girl standing behind the glass lobby doors wore a thin robe over a blue silk nightgown. She seemed scared. "It's in three-fourteen," she said. "It was horrible! She was screaming for help. . . ."

Investigator Harris stopped just long enough to look on the mailbox for 314. "Colleen Darcy." He led the way up the stairs, his nightstick drawn.

The even-numbered apartments on the third floor faced onto an interior hallway. Eric thought he remembered seeing the building from the other side. It had little private balconies, screened from the street. Probably good places for girls to sunbathe. The hall was freshly painted, and the impression was of a nice building, a good place to live for young singles. Of course the best apartments would be on the other side, overlooking the pool.

The hall was quiet. They couldn't hear anything through the door of 314. "Now what?" Eric asked.

Harris shrugged, then knocked loudly on the door. There was no answer. He knocked again. "Police," he said. "Miz Darcy?"

There was no answer. The lady who'd called them was coming up the stairs behind them. "You sure she's in there?" Eric asked.

"Yes! She was screaming."

"Where's the manager?"

"Not here. I called him, but there wasn't anyone there."

Eric and his partner exchanged glances.

"She was screaming for help!" the lady said indignantly.

"We'll probably catch hell for this," Harris muttered. He stood to one side and gestured to Eric. Then he drew his service revolver.

Eric stepped back, raised his foot and smashed it at the locked door. Once. Then again. The door burst open and Eric darted inside, moving quickly to one side the way he'd been taught.

There was only one room. There was something on the bed. Later Eric remembered thinking just that: "Something." It looked so little like a girl in her twenties. . . .

There was blood on the bed and on the floor beside it. The room smelled of bright copper and expensive perfume.

The girl was nude. Eric saw long blonde hair, arranged carefully on the pillow. The hair was spattered with blood. One of her teats was gone. Blood oozed from punctures below the missing breast. Someone had drawn figures in the blood, tracing an arrow down to point to her dark pubic hair. There was more blood there.

Eric doubled over, struggling with himself, holding his breath. His partner came in.

Harris took one look at the bed, then looked away. He sent his eyes searching the room, saw no one, then looked for doors. There was a door across the room, and Harris moved toward it. As he did, the closet door opened behind him and a man darted out, breaking for the opening to the hallway. He was past Joe Harris, running toward the screaming lady who'd called the police.

Eric breathed deeply, got control of himself and moved to intercept the man. The man had a knife. A bloody knife. He raised it high, point toward Eric. Eric brought up his pistol and leveled it at the man's chest. His finger tightened on the trigger.

The man threw up his arms. The knife dropped from his hand. Then he fell to his knees. He still said nothing.

Eric's pistol followed the man. His finger tightened again. A half-ounce more . . . No! I am a police officer, not a judge and jury.

The man held his hands in supplication, almost as if in prayer. When Eric moved closer, he saw the man's eyes. They did not hold terror, or even hatred. The man had a curious expression, of both resignation and satisfaction. It did not change when he looked past Eric Larsen at the dead girl.

Later, after the detectives and the coroner had come, Eric Larsen and Joe Harris took their prisoner to the Burbank City Jail.

"You'll get him there alive." The voice was a whine. It belonged to a lawyer who lived in the apartment building. He'd come while they were still questioning the suspect, and shouted that the police had no right to keep after the man. He advised the man to keep silent. The man had laughed.

Eric and Harris took their prisoner to the patrol car and put him inside. He would be turned over to the L.A. County Jail the next day.

During the whole time the man had said nothing. They knew his name from his wallet: Fred Lauren. They'd also heard his record from R & I. Three previous sex offenses, two with violence. Probation, probation, then parole after psychiatric treatment.

When they reached the station, Eric hauled Lauren roughly out of the car.

"That hurts," the man said.

"That hurts. You son of a bitch!" Harris moved close to Lauren. His arm jerked, sending his elbow into the pit of the
190

prisoner's stomach. He did it again. "Nothing that ever happens to you will hurt the way you . . ." Harris couldn't say anything else.

"Joe." Eric moved between his partner and the prisoner. "He's not worth it."

"I'll report you!" Lauren screamed. Then he giggled. "No. What's the point? No."

"Now he's scared," Eric said. "Not when he was arrested." And not now, Eric saw: As soon as Harris moved away and they began walking Lauren into the station, the fear vanished, replaced by the look of resignation. "Okay, tell me," Eric said. "You think the judge will give you probation again? You'll be on the street in a week?"

The man giggled. "There won't be any streets in a week. There won't be anything!"

"Hammer Fever," Eric muttered. He'd seen it before: Why not commit a crime? The end of the world was coming. The papers had a lot of stories about that. But none like this, and none in Burbank before.

"I'll be glad when that goddam thing's past," Harris said. He didn't mention the body on the bed. You lived with that, or you quit; but you worked it out on your own.

"It's going to be a long night," Eric said.

"Yeah, and we've got morning watch tomorrow." Harris looked up at the glowing sky. "Be damned glad when that thing's past."

◼

They camped at Soda Springs. It was a good campground, surprisingly uncrowded; Gordie Vance had expected a dozen other scout troops to be there. Instead, there was only Gordie and the six scouts he'd brought with him. Hammer Fever, Gordie thought. Nobody wants to be *this* far from roads and civilization.

They dropped their packs with relief. The boys went dashing off to the spring. There were two springs: One bubbled with clear mountain water, pure and cold; the other was rusty in color, and tasted awful, although the boys pretended they liked it. The water was naturally carbonated, and they made Wyler's root beer in their canteens. Gordie didn't bother telling them not to drink too much. Nobody ever did.

They cooked supper over the Svea gasoline backpacker stoves. Gordie let Andy Randall choose the dinner; Andy would have to get used to leading the group. It wouldn't be long before . . .

"But my teacher said it might," one of the younger boys was saying.

"Nuts," Andy Randall told him. "Dad's been out to JPL *dozens* of times, and their computer says it won't. Besides, Mr. Hamner told me—"

"You know *him?*" the younger scout asked.

"Sure."

"But he *invented* the Hammer." Involuntarily they looked upward, to the huge glowing smear in the evening sky. "It sure *looks* close," the younger scout said.

The long mountain twilight ended, and the stars came out. The Hammer glowed fiercely in the night sky before it sank behind the Sierra. Gordie got the boys into their sleeping bags. They wanted to stay up and watch; there were bright aurora displays across the sky, with the stars showing through jagged lines of green and red.

Gordie climbed into his own sack. As usual he dropped straight off to sleep, programed to wake in a couple of hours so that he could walk around and see that the boys were all right. I'm a conscientious bastard, he thought, just before he dozed off. It was funny, but Gordie wasn't laughing.

He woke at midnight—and that was all the sleep he got that night.

The sky was frantic. It streamed overhead like luminescent milk in black water. Stars winked in Hamner-Brown's tail, then sank into the background as blazes of color flashed across from horizon to horizon. Somewhere in the far distance there were brighter flashes, and after a long time, thunder. Gordie made his rounds in a trance.

Andy Randall was awake. He hadn't bothered to set up a tube tent, although it often rains in the Sierra in June. Andy lay in the open, his head propped on his pack, his long arms under his neck. "Quite a show," he whispered.

"That it is," Gordie said. He was careful to keep his voice cheerful and under control. When they asked later, Andy would have to say that Gordon Vance had shown no signs of depression. "Get *some* sleep," Gordie said. "We don't have far to go tomorrow, but the trail's tricky in places."

"I know."

"Right," Gordie said. He walked a little way uphill, to be alone, and sank down in the long grass.

Tomorrow it won't matter, he thought. I don't need any sleep.

He had the cliff all picked out. A fatal fall . . . it would have to be fatal. A mistake would leave him injured but alive, the kids frantic, while a rescue team moved in to get him to a hospital. He'd be in a hospital bed when the bank examiners found the shortages. Crippled, maybe. Not even able to run.

Not that he would run. He'd had that chance, and it was no good, no good at all. Where would he go? The money was gone, and there was nothing for an American exile without money. Besides, children ought to grow up in their own country. Gordie glanced over to where his own son, age twelve, lay huddled in his sleeping bag. It was going to be rough on Bert, but there wasn't any help for it.

Funny about that cliff. Gordie could remember it perfectly. The trail wasn't all that narrow there, but the edge was crumbly, and if you stood too close . . . he'd seen that two years ago, when they passed by it. He'd had different thoughts then.

I sure wish Bert wasn't along.

A red velvet curtain rippled across the sky. Magnificent show for my last night, Gordie thought. He tried to watch the sky, but he kept seeing the cliff.

One moment. One carefully careless moment and he'd be at the bottom with a broken neck, and worse. There was a path down, easy enough for the kids. Andy would see that they went down properly. Then Andy Randall would be in charge, and that would be okay. Gordie had been training Andy for two years. Not for this—well, yes, for this, just in case of a genuine accident. Funny how things work out.

The crescent moon rose over the hills, washing out some of the stars and blending its own eerie colors into the light show. Gordie imagined he could see shock waves in the comet tail— but that was probably imagination. The astronauts up there would be seeing it, though, with instruments if not with their eyes. Wonder what it's like to be up there? Gordie had been a flyer, for a short time, until he'd been low scorer in his class and washed out of flight school to become a navigator for the Air Force. Should have stayed in, he thought. But I had to be a banker. . . .

Too damn bad to ruin the boys' trip. No choice. None at all, and an accident solves all problems. Half a million in insurance, enough to cover all the bank shortages and leave Marie and Bert in pretty good shape. Call it three hundred thousand left, at seven percent. It's not magnificent wealth, but it's sure as hell better than having your father in prison and nothing to live on. . . .

Toward dawn the frantic sky became even more frantic. There was a bright spot in there. If it was the head, it was hard to see, looking down through the luminous tunnel of the tail. Cold light and shifting shadows, faint color splashes of aurora even in daytime. Then the land was afire with dawn, but the light was still funny. Elfin. Gordie shivered.

He went back to his sleeping bag and slid in. No point in catching a nap. It won't be long. . . .

The Svea was laid out with the fuel bottle, pan of water next to it. Gordie reached out with one arm and primed the tiny stove. His sleeping-bag breakfasts were a standard joke with everyone who'd been camping with him. He didn't really feel like eating, but it would be dangerous to change the routine. He brought a pan of water to a boil and made hot chocolate. It was surprisingly good, and then he was ready for oatmeal, and a big cup of Sherpa tea, strong tea with brown sugar and a lump of butter. . . .

One by one the boys woke. Gordie chortled to hear Andy Randall tell Bert, "You mean you slept through it? *All night?*"

No campfire. Not enough wood. Every year there were fewer and fewer places you could build a real fire. Not very many of the kids knew how to cook over a wood fire. Be bad if they really had to be out on their own, but that didn't happen anymore. Nowadays, if you get lost, you clear an area fifty feet in diameter and light a match in the middle of it. Pretty soon a fire patrol will be out to give you a citation. There aren't any deep woods anymore, not like when I was a kid. . . .

I should have got some sleep, Gordie thought. My mind's wandering. It doesn't matter, though. It's not very far now. I think I'll have one more cup of chocolate.

He put the water on. "Let's get it together," he called. "Time to be finishing up. Stuff your bags and lace your boots. I want us on the trail in five minutes."

The comet's nucleus is bathed in light. The tail and coma trap sunlight throughout a tremendous volume and reflect it, some to Earth, some to space, some to the nucleus itself.

The comet has suffered. Explosions in the head have torn it into mountainous chunks. Megatons of volatile chemicals have boiled away. The large masses in the head are crusted with icy mud from which most of the water ice has boiled out.

Yet the crusts retard further evaporation. Other comets have survived many such passages through the maelstrom. Much mass has been lost, poured into the tail; but much of the coma could freeze again, and the rocky chunks could merge; and crystals of strange ices could plate themselves across a growing comet, out there in the dark and the cold, over the millions of years . . . if only Hamner-Brown could return to the cometary halo.

But there appears to be something in its path.

2

THE HAMMER

And I beheld when he had opened the sixth seal, and lo, there was a great earthquake; and the sun became black as a sackcloth of hair, and the moon became as blood; and the stars of heaven fell unto the earth.
The Revelation of Saint John the Divine

Hammerfall Morning

There is a place with four suns in the sky—red, white, blue, and yellow; two of them are so close together that they touch, and star-stuff flows between them.

I know of a world with a million moons.

I know of a sun the size of the Earth—and made of diamond.

Carl Sagan, *The Cosmic Connection: An Extraterrestrial Perspective*

Rick Delanty woke on a wonderful morning, with a rectangle of hot sunlight crawling across his arm. The wonderful mornings came every hour and a half aboard Hammerlab, and he hadn't tired of them yet. He used the tube and crawled out of the Apollo.

The larger windows in Hammerlab were filled with telescopes and cameras and other instruments. You had to crane around them, holding on to handholds on the bulkheads, swimming across open spaces.

Baker and Leonilla Malik were feeding data into the on-board computer. She looked up and said quickly, "Hello, Rick," but turned back to work too quickly to see his quick grin.

It was time for work, but Rick Delanty was still partly tourist, and his eagerness was for the dawning of the comet. He found an observation scope unused at the moment; it had a big sun shield built into the optics, so that he could look at the comet without going blind.

The view was something like a stylized sunburst done in Day-Glo, and something like falling down a deep well while high on LSD. The gay streamers of the tail flowed outward as sluggishly as a lunar eclipse. There at the heart of the beast was a hint of graininess.

"Roger, Houston. We do have sideways motion relative to us. It should be coming onto your telemetry right now," Baker was saying. "And there's still activity, although that's been dying out ever since the Hammer rounded the Sun. We got only one explosive event last watch, nothing big, not like the monster we observed yesterday."

"Hammerlab, there appears to be something wrong with the Doppler data. JPL requests you get optical tracking on the largest piece you can find. Can do?"

"Can try, Houston."

"I'll get it, Johnny," Rick said. He cranked up the resolution on the telescope and peered into the murk. "Leonilla, can you lend a hand? Slave the output onto the telemetry—"

"Right," she said.

"Mark, mark, I'm off, mark, mark . . ."

Baker continued his report. "Houston, that nucleus is pretty well spread out, and the coma is huge. I fed the angular diameter into the computer and I get a hundred and forty thousand kilometers. As big as Jupiter. It could envelope the Earth without noticing."

"Don't be silly," a familiar voice crackled. "Gravity . . . rip it to pieces . . ." Charlie Sharps's voice began to fade.

"Houston, we're losing you," Baker said.

"That's not Houston, that's Sharps at JPL," Rick said without looking up from the scope. "Mark, mark . . ."

"It comes through Houston. Damn. The comet stuff is playing pure hell with the ionosphere. We're going to have communications problems until that thing's past. Better record every observation we can get, just in case they're not going through."

"Rojj," Delanty said. He continued to stare into the telescope. Hamner-Brown's nucleus was spread out before him. He was having trouble keeping the cross hairs exactly centered on the mass he'd picked. There wasn't enough contrast to use an automatic tracking system; it had to be done by eye. Delanty smiled. Another blow for man-in-space. "Mark, mark . . ."

He saw thick, glowing dust in sluggish motion, and a handful of flying mountains, and many more smaller particles, all jumbled, without order, parts moving in random patterns as they responded to light pressure and continuing chemical activity. It was the primal stuff of chaos. His mouth watered with the need to take a spacecraft into that, land on one of the mountains and walk out for a look around. The fifty-mile-per-second velocity of those mountains was not evident.

But it would be decades before NASA could build manned ships *that* good. If anyone built them at all. And when it was done, Rick Delanty would be a tired old man.

But this won't be my last mission. We've got the Shuttle coming up, if those goddam congresscritters don't turn it into pork for their own districts. . . .

Pieter Jakov had been working with a spectroscope. He finished his observations and said, "They have set us a hectic schedule for this morning. I see that extravehicular activity for final check of external instruments is optional. Should we? There are two hours left."

"Crazy Russian. No, we're not going to EVA into that. A snowflake at that speed can't hole the Hammerlab, but it can sure as hell leave a hole in your suit the size of your fist." Baker frowned at the computer readouts. "Rick, that last optical. What did you pick?"

"A big mountain," Rick said. "About the center of the nucleus, just as they asked. Why?"

"Nothing." Baker thumbed the microphone. "Houston, Houston, did you get the optical readings?"

". . . squeal . . . negative, Hammerlab, send again . . ."

"What the hell is it, Johnny?" Rick demanded.

"Houston and JPL get a miss distance of nine thousand kilometers," Johnny said thoughtfully. "I don't. Feeding your data into the onboard I come up with about a quarter of that. They've got more computing power down there, but we've got better data."

"Hell, two thousand kilometers is two thousand kilometers," Delanty said. He didn't sound confident.

"I wish we didn't have a glitch in the main Doppler antenna," Baker said.

"I will go out and work on it," Jakov said.

"No." Baker's answer was abrupt; the commander speaking. "We haven't lost anyone in space yet, and why start now?"

"Shouldn't we ask ground control?" Leonilla asked.

"They put me in charge," Johnny Baker said. "And I've said no."

Pieter Jakov said nothing. Rick Delanty remembered that the Soviets *had* lost men in space: the three *Soyuz* pilots on reentry that the world knew about, and a number of others, known only by rumors and tales told at night over vodka. He wondered (not for the first time) if NASA had been too cautious. With fewer safety precautions the United States could have reached the Moon a little sooner, done a good deal more exploring, learned more—and, yes, created a martyr or two. The Moon had been too expensive in money, but too cheap in lives to gain the popularity it needed. By the time Apollo XI reached it, it was dull. Routine.

Maybe that's what we ought to do. The picture of Johnny Baker crawling out on the broken Spacelab wing, of a *man* out in that hostile environment risking the loneliest death ever—*that* had given the space program almost as big a boost as Neil Armstrong's giant leap.

There was a ping. Then another, and red warning lights flared on the monitor board.

Rick Delanty didn't think. He leaped for the nearest red-painted box. A square box, duplicate of others that were put at various places in Hammerlab. He opened it and took out several flat metal plates with goop on one side, then some larger, rubberlike patches. He looked to Baker for instructions.

"Not holed," Johnny was saying. "Sand. We're being sand-blasted." He frowned at the status board. "And we're losing efficiency in the solar cells. Pieter, cap all the optical instruments! We'll have to save 'em for closest approach."

"Rojj," Jakov said. He moved to the instruments.

Delanty stood by with the meteor patches. Just in case.

"It depends on just how large that nucleus is," Pieter Jakov called from the far end of the space capsule. "And we have yet to get firm estimates of how widely the solid matter extends. I think it highly likely that the Earth—and we—will be hit by high-velocity gravel if nothing worse."

"Yeah. That's what I was thinking," Johnny Baker said. "We've been looking for sideways drift. Well, we found it, but is it enough? Maybe we ought to terminate this mission."

There was a moment of silence.

"Please, no," Leonilla said.

"I second that," Rick added. "You don't want to either. Who does?"

"Not me," Jakov said.

"Unanimous. But it's hardly a democracy," Baker said. "We've lost a *lot* of power. It's going to get warm in here."

"You stood it in Spacelab until you got the wing fixed," Delanty said. "If you could take it before, you can take it now. And so can we."

"Right," Baker said. "But you will stand by those meteor patches."

"Yes, sir."

Minutes later Hamner-Brown's nucleus dropped behind the Earth. The Moon rose in its ghostly net of shock waves. Leonilla passed out breakfast.

Dawn found Harvey Randall in an easy chair on the lawn, with a table to hold his cigarettes and coffee and another to hold the portable television. Dawn washed out the once-in-a-lifetime sky show and left him a little depressed, a little drunk, and not really ready to start a working day. Loretta found him in the same state two hours later.

"I've gone to work in worse shape," he told her. "It was worth it."

"I'm glad. Are you sure you can drive?"

"Of course I can." That was an old argument.

"Where are you going to be today?"

He didn't notice the worry in her voice. "I had a hell of a time deciding that. I really want to be everywhere at once. But hell, the regular network science team will be at JPL, and they've got a good crew in Houston. I think I'll start at City Hall. Bentley Allen and staff calmly taking care of the city while half the populace runs for the hills."

"But that's all the way downtown."

Now he heard it. "So?"

"But what if it hits? You'll be miles away. How can you get back?"

"Loretta, it's not going to hit us. Listen——"

"You've got the swimming pool filled with fresh water and I couldn't use it yesterday and you covered it up!" Her voice rose. "You made a couple of hundred dollars' worth of dried beef and you sent our boy into the mountains and you filled the garage with expensive liquor and——"

"Loretta——"

"——and we don't drink that kind of thing, and nobody could eat that meat unless they were starving to death. So you think we'll be starving. Don't you?"

"No. Honey, it's hundreds to one against——"

"Harvey, please. Stay home today. Just this once. I never make a fuss about you being off somewhere all the time. I didn't complain when you volunteered for another tour in Vietnam. I didn't complain when you went to Peru. I didn't complain when you took three weeks extra in Alaska. I've never said anything about having to raise your boy, who's smarter than I am only he's seen less of his father than Ralph Harris ever saw of his. I know your job means more to you than I do, but please, Harvey, don't I mean *something* to you?"

"Of course you do." He grabbed her and pulled her to him. "Lord, is that how you feel? The job doesn't mean more than you do." It's just the money, he thought. And I can't say that. I can't say that *I* don't need the money, you do.

"Then you'll stay?"

"I can't. Really can't. Loretta, these documentaries have been good. Really good. Maybe I'll get an offer from ABC. They'll need a new science feature editor pretty soon, and that's real folding money. And there's a real chance of a book. . . ."

"You've been up all night, Harvey, you're in no shape to go anywhere. And I'm scared."

"Hey." He hugged her tightly and kissed her hard. And it's all my fault, he told himself. How could she not be scared, after all the stuff I bought? But I can't miss Hammer Day. . . . "Look. I'll send somebody else down to City Hall."

"Good!"

"And I'll have Charlie and Manuel meet me at UCLA."

"But why can't you stay here?"

"Got to do something, Loretta. Manly pride if nothing else. How can I tell people I sat at home in the root cellar after telling everybody else there wasn't any danger? Look, I'll get some interviews, and the Governor's in town for a charity thing at Los Angeles Country Club, I'll go over there just after the thing has gone by. And I won't ever be more than ten or fifteen minutes from here. If anything happens, I'll come home fast."

"All right. But you still haven't eaten your breakfast. It's getting cold. And I filled your Thermos, and put a beer in the TravelAll."

He ate quickly. She sat and watched him the whole time, not eating anything at all. She laughed when he made jokes, and she told him to be careful when he drove down the hill.

■

Communications were still bad. Mostly they spoke into recorders. It would be important to get their observations because the instruments weren't going to be much use. Too much sandblasting. They had preserved the big telescope that could be attached to the color TV, though, and they'd record the video as well as try to send it back to Earth.

"Solar power's down to about twenty-five percent," Rick Delanty reported.

"Save the batteries," Baker said.

"Rojj."

It was getting warm in the spacecraft, but they needed the power for the recorders and other instruments.

Leonilla Malik spoke rapid-fire Russian into a mike. Jakov played with the transmitter controls, trying to get some response from Baikunyar. No luck. Leonilla continued to record. She had moored herself oddly, twisting to watch the observation port and still see the instrument board. Rick tried to follow what she was saying, but she was using too many unfamiliar words. Waxing lyrical, Rick thought. Letting her poetic streak have its way. Why not? How else could you describe being inside a comet?

They now knew less about Hamner-Brown's path than Houston did. The last report from Houston was a miss by one thousand kilometers, but Rick wondered. Was that based on his visual observation? Because if it was, it meant only that that particular mountain would be that far off, and the cloud of solid gup was large. Not *that* large, though. Surely not that large.

"We are effectively inside the coma," Leonilla was saying. "This is not especially evident. The chemical activity is long past. But we see the shadow of the Earth like a long tunnel leading through the tail."

Rick caught that last phrase. Nice, he thought. If I get a chance to broadcast live to Earth, I'll use it.

They all had work, which they did while they chattered into recorders. Rick had a hand-held camera, a Canon, which he worked like a madman, changing lenses and film as rapidly as he could. He hoped the automatic features were in good order, and forced himself to take a few frames with widely different speeds and apertures, just in case.

The status board inexorably ticked off seconds.

The long lens gave a good view through the observation port. Rick saw: half a dozen large masses, many more small ones and a myriad of tiny glinting points, all enmeshed in pearly fog. He heard Baker's voice behind him. "Duck's-eye view of a shotgun blast."

"Good phrasing," Rick said.

"Yeah. Hope it's not *too* good."

"I have lost all signal from the radar," Pieter Jakov said.

"Roger. Give it up and make visuals," Baker said. "Houston, Houston, are you getting anything from the inside TV?"

". . . roger, Hammerlab . . . JPL . . . Sharps is in love, send more . . . higher-power transmission . . ."

"I'll put on higher power when the Hammer's closer," Baker said. He didn't know if they heard. "We're saving the batteries." He looked up at the status board. Ten minutes before the solid objects got to closest approach. Twenty minutes maybe for it all to pass. A half-hour. "I'll increase transmitter power in five minutes; say again, increase to full power transmission in five minutes."

CLANG!

"What the fuck was that?" Baker demanded.

"Pressure remains unchanged," Jakov said. "Pressure holding in all three capsules."

"Good," Rick muttered. They'd closed the airlocks to Apollo and *Soyuz;* it seemed a reasonable precaution. Rick stood by with the meteor patches anyway. Hammerlab was by far the largest target.

And just how did the engineers estimate the size that a meteor patch ought to be? Rick wondered. From their size— about the maximum-size hole it would be worth repairing? Anything bigger would finish them anyway? To hell with it. He went back to his photographs. Through the Canon lens he looked into a galaxy of foamy ice, a tremendous, slow shotgun blast that was visibly coming toward them, spreading *around* Hammerlab rather than sliding sideways. "Jesus, Johnny, it's coming *close.*"

"Rojj. Pieter, get the main telescope uncovered. I'm going to full power. We'll send transmissions from here on in. Houston, Houston, visual indicates Earth is in the path of outer edges of nucleus; I say again, Earth is in the path of outer nucleus. Impossible to estimate size of objects that may strike Earth."

"Make certain that message gets through," Leonilla Malik said. "Pieter, see that Moscow knows as well." There was urgency and fear in her voice.

"Eh?" Rick Delanty said.

"It is passing east of the Earth," Leonilla said. "The United States will be more exposed, but there will be more objects close to the Soviet Union. The opportunities for deliberate misinterpretation are too great. Some fanatic—"

"Why do you say this?" Jakov demanded.

"You know it is true," she shouted. "Fanatics. Like the madmen who had my father killed because Great Stalin was not immortal! Do not pretend they do not exist."

"Ridiculous," Jakov snorted, but he went to the communications console, and Rick Delanty thought he spoke urgently.

205

Hammerfall: One

> *In 1968 the close approach of an asteroid called Icarus set off a small but very definite end-of-the-world scare. There had already been rumors that a series of world-wide cataclysms was going to begin in 1968. When news that Icarus was heading toward earth and was going to make its closest approach on June 15, 1968, got around, it somehow became combined with the other end-of-the-world rumors. In California groups of hippies headed for the mountains of Colorado saying that they wanted to be safe on high ground before the asteroid hit and caused California to sink into the sea.*
>
> Daniel Cohen, *How the World Will End*

"O my people! Hear the words of Matthew! Does he not say that the sun shall be darkened, and the moon shall not give off her light, and the stars shall fall from heaven? And does this not come to pass even in this very hour?

"Repent, my people! Repent, and watch, for the Lord cometh, the Hammer will fall upon this wicked Earth. Hear the words of the Prophet Micah: 'For behold, the Lord cometh forth out of his place, and will come down, and tread upon the high places of the Earth. And the mountains shall be molten under him, and the valleys shall be cleft, as wax before the fire, and as the waters that are poured down a steep place.'

"For He cometh! For he cometh to judge the Earth, and with righteousness to judge the world, and the peoples with his truth!"

"You have heard the Reverend Henry Armitage on 'The Coming Hour.' This and all broadcasts of 'The Coming Hour' have been made possible by your donations, and we ask the Lord to bless those who have given so generously.

"No further donations will be needed. The hour comes and is now at hand."

It was a bright, cloudless summer day. A brisk wind blew in from the sea, and the Los Angeles basin was clear and lovely.

Bloody good thing, Tim Hamner thought.

He'd been faced with a terrible problem. The spectacular night skies could best be seen from the mountains, and Tim had stayed at his Angeles Forest observatory for most of the week before; but the best view of Hamner-Brown's closest approach would be from space. Since he couldn't be in space, Tim wanted the next best thing: to watch *all* of it on color television. It hadn't been hard to persuade Charlie Sharps to invite him out to JPL.

But he was supposed to be there by nine-thirty, and the clear skies with their bright velvet ribbons of light had kept him up until dawn. He'd stretched out on the couch, careful not to go to bed, but a few minutes' rest wouldn't hurt. . . .

Of course he'd overslept. Now, muzzy-headed and watery-eyed, Tim aimed rather than drove his Grand Prix down the Ventura Freeway toward Pasadena. Despite his late start he expected to be on time. There wasn't much traffic.

"Fools," Tim muttered. Hammer Fever. Thousands of Angelenos taking to the hills. Harvey Randall had told him that freeway traffic would be light all week, and he'd been right. Light traffic for—in Mark Czescu's brilliant phrasing—Hot Fudge Sundae (which fell on a Tuesdae this week).

There was a flare of red ahead, a ripple of red lights. Traffic slowed. Tim cursed. There was a truck just ahead of him, so he couldn't see what was fouling things up. Automatically he cut over into the right-hand lane, acing out a sweet little old lady in a green Ford. She cursed horribly as Tim cut in front of her.

"Probably wears her tennis shoes to bed," Tim muttered. Just what *was* happening ahead? The traffic seemed to have stopped entirely. He saw a parking lot that stretched away before him as far as he could see. All the way to the Golden State interchange, Tim thought. "Damn." He glanced over his shoulder. No highway patrolmen in sight. He cut onto the shoulder and drove forward, passing stopped cars, until he came to an off-ramp.

To his right was Forest Lawn Cemetery. Not the original one, fabled in song and story, but the Hollywood Hills colony. The streets were thick with traffic too. Tim turned left and went under the freeway. His face was a grim mask of worry and hate. Bad enough not to be in his observatory on Hot Fudge Sundae Tuesdae, but *this!* He was in beautiful downtown Burbank, and his comet was approaching perigee. "It's not fair!" Tim shouted. Pedestrians glanced at him, then looked away, but Tim didn't care. "Not fair!"

■

The air was electric with storm and disaster. Eileen Hancock felt it as ghostly fingers brushing her neck hairs. She saw it in more concrete form while driving to work. Despite the light traffic, people drove badly. They fought for dominance at the wrong times, and they reacted late, then overreacted. There were many U-Haul trailers piled high with household possessions, reminding Eileen of newsclips from the war: refugees, only no refugees in Asia or Africa ever carried birdcages, Beautyrest mattresses, and stereo sets.

One of the trailers had overturned on the eastbound Ventura, blocking all three lanes. A few cars squeezed past on the shoulder, but the others were immobile behind a tumbled mass of furniture. The light pickup that had pulled the trailer was angled across the fast lane with a VW embedded in its side.

Thank God I came up the Golden State, Eileen thought. She felt a moment of pity for anyone trying to get to Pasadena this morning, and she cursed the trailer and its owner. People on her side of the freeway slowed to gawk at it, and it took five minutes to get the hundred yards to her off-ramp into Burbank. She drove viciously on the surface streets and pulled into her parking space—with her name on it, Corrigan kept his word about that—with a feeling of relief that the Burbank police seemed to be elsewhere.

Corrigan's was a storefront office near a supermarket, deceptively small because the warehouses were across an alley behind. The entry room was finished in blue nylon, brown Naugahyde, and chrome, and the chrome needed polishing. It always did; Eileen believed that wholesale customers ought to get the impression of a sound business able to keep its commitments, but not of opulence which might tempt them to dicker too hard on prices. The front door was already unlocked. "What ho?" Eileen called.

"Me." Corrigan stumped out of his office. A smell of coffee followed him; Eileen had long ago installed an automatic Silex system with a timer, and she set it up last thing before she left in the evenings. It had improved Corrigan's morning disposition wonderfully; but not this morning. "What kept you?" he demanded.

"Traffic. Wreck on the eastbound Ventura."

"Umph."

"You feel it too, huh?" Eileen said.

Corrigan frowned, then grinned sheepishly. "Yeah. I guess so. I was afraid you wouldn't show up. There's nobody in the front office, and only three back in the warehouse. Radio says half the shops in the city are missing half their people."

"And the rest of us are scared." She went past Corrigan to her own office. The clean glass surface of her desk shone like a mirror. She put her tape recorder down on it and took out her keys, but she didn't open the desk yet. Instead she went back out into the reception area. "I'll take the front office," she said.

Corrigan shrugged. He was looking out through the big plate-glass window. "Nobody's coming in today."

"Sabrini's due at ten," Eileen said. "Forty bathrooms and kitchens, if we can get the décor he wants at the right price."

Corrigan nodded. He didn't seem to be listening. "What the hell's that?" He pointed out the window.

There was a line of people, all dressed in white robes, all singing hymns. They seemed to be marching in step. Eileen looked closer and saw why. They were chained together. She shrugged. The Disney Studios were a few blocks away, and NBC not much further; they often used Burbank for city location shots. "Probably contestants for 'Let's Make a Deal.' Group effort."

"Too early," Corrigan said.

"Then it's Disney. Silly way to make a living."

"Don't see any camera trucks," Corrigan said. He didn't sound very interested. He watched for a few moments longer. "Heard from that rich boy friend of yours? This is his big day."

For just a moment Eileen felt terribly lonely. "Not for awhile." Then she began pulling out folders of color pictures and arranged them to show attractive combinations of accessories: the bathroom your clients dream of.

∎

Alameda was fairly speedy. Tim Hamner tried to remember the connections to the arroyo north of Pasadena. There were high hills just in front of him, the Verdugo Hills that cut through the San Fernando Valley and divided the foothill cities from Burbank. He knew there was a new freeway in there somewhere, but he didn't know how to find it.

"Goddammit!" he shouted. Months to prepare, months waiting for *his* comet, and now it was approaching at fifty miles a second and he was driving past the Walt Disney Studios. Part of his mind told him that was funny, but Tim didn't appreciate the humor in the situation.

Take Alameda to the Golden State, Tim thought. If that's moving, I'll get on it and back onto the Ventura. If it isn't, I'll just go on surface streets all the way and the hell with tickets . . . and *what was that ahead?*

Not just cars jammed across an intersection, motionless under a string of green lights. This was more, cars jockeying for room, cars pulling into driveways and through them to the alley beyond. More cars, stopped, and people on foot moving among the swarm. There was just time to get over into the right-hand lane. Tim turned hard into a parking lot, hoping to follow the moving cars into an alley.

Dead end! He was in a large parking lot, and the way was completely blocked by a delivery truck. Tim braked viciously and slammed the shift lever into PARK. Carefully he turned the key off. Then he pounded the dash and swore, using words he hadn't remembered for years. There was no place to go; more cars had come in behind him. The lot was jammed.

I'm in trouble, Tim thought. He abandoned the car to walk toward Alameda. TV store, he thought. If they don't have the comet on, I'll buy a set on the spot.

Alameda was jammed with cars. Bumper-to-bumper, and none of them moving at all. And they were *screaming* up ahead, at the intersection where the focus of action seemed to be. Robbery? A sniper? Tim wanted no part of that. But no, those were screams of rage, not fear. And the intersection swarmed with blue-uniformed policemen. There was something else, too. White robes? Someone in a white robe was coming toward him now. Hamner tried to avoid him, but the man planted himself in Tim's path.

It wasn't much of a costume, that robe; probably a bed-sheet, and there was certainly conventional clothing under it. The fuzzy-bearded young man was smiling, but insistent. "Sir! Pray! Pray for the safe passage of Lucifer's Hammer! There is so little time!"

"I know that," Tim said. He tried to dodge past, but the man moved with him.

"Pray! The Wrath of God is upon us. Yea, the hour is approaching and is now here, but God will spare the city for ten just men. Repent and be saved, and save our city."

"How many of you are there?" Tim demanded.

"There are a hundred Wardens," the man said.

"That's more than ten. Now let me go."

"But you don't understand—we will save the city, we Wardens. We have been praying for months. We have promised God the repentance of thousands." The intense brown eyes stared into Hamner's. Then recognition came. "You're him! You're Timothy Hamner! I saw you on TV. Pray, brother. Join us in prayer, and the world will know!"

"It sure will. NBC is just down the road." Tim frowned. There were two Burbank policemen coming up behind the Comet Warden, and they weren't smiling at all.

"Is this man annoying you, sir?" the larger cop asked.

"Yes," Tim said.

The policeman smiled. "Gotcha!" He took the robed man by the arm. "You have the right to remain silent. If you give up—"

"I know all that crap," the Warden said. "Look at him! He's the man who invented the comet!"

"Nobody invents a comet, you idiot," Tim said. "Officer, do you know where there's a TV store? I want to see the comet pictures from space."

"Down that way. Could we have your name and address—"

Tim took out a card and thrust it at the policeman. Then he scurried toward the intersection beyond.

■

Eileen had an excellent view through the storefront window. She sat with Joe Corrigan and sipped coffee; it was obvious that their architect wasn't going to get through that traffic jam. They brought over big chrome chairs and the glass coffee table, making a picnic out of watching a lot of angry people.

The cause of it all was diagonally across from them. Twenty or thirty men and women in white robes—not all of them bedsheets—had chained themselves across Alameda from lamppost to telephone pole. They sang hymns. The quality of singing had been pretty good for awhile, but the police soon led away their white-bearded leader, and now they were discordant.

On either side of the human chain an infinite variety of cars were packed like sardines. Old Ford station wagons, for grocery shopping; chauffeured Mercedeses—stars or studio executives; campers, pickup trucks, new Japanese imports, Chevies and Plymouth Dusters, all packed together, and all immobile. A few drivers were still trying to get out, but most had given up. A horde of robed preachers moved through the matrix of cars. They stopped to speak with each driver, and they preached. Some of the drivers were screaming at them. A few listened. One or two even got out and knelt in prayer.

"Some show, eh?" Corrigan said. "Why the hell didn't they pick some place else?"

"With NBC practically next door? If the comet goes past without smashing anything, they'll take credit for saving the world. Haven't we seen a few of those nuts on TV for years?"

Corrigan nodded. "Looks like they hit the big time with this one. Here come the TV cameras."

The preachers redoubled their efforts when they saw the cameramen. The hymn stopped for a moment, then began again: "Nearer My God to Thee." The preachers had to talk fast, and sometimes they broke off in midspeech to avoid the police. Blue uniforms chased white robes through the honking cars and screaming drivers.

"A day to remember," Corrigan said.

"They may just have to pave the whole thing over."

"Yep." For a fact that traffic jam was going to be there a long time. Too many cars had been abandoned. He could see more civilians darting among the cars, flowered sports shirts and gray flannel suits among the white robes and blue uniforms. And coveralled drivers. Many were bent on murder. More had locked their cars and gone looking for a coffee shop. The supermarket next door was doing a land-office business in Coors beer. Even so, a fair number were clustered on the sidewalks, praying.

Two policemen came into the store. Eileen and Corrigan greeted them. Both had regular beats in the neighborhood, and the younger, Eric Larsen, often joined Eileen for coffee at the local Orange Julius. He reminded Eileen of her younger brother.

"Got any bolt cutters?" Investigator Harris was all business. "Big heavy jobs."

"Think so," Corrigan said. He lifted a phone and pushed a button. He waited. Nothing happened. "Goddam warehouse crew's out watching the show. I'll get them." He went back through the office.

"No keys?" Eileen asked.

"No." Larsen smiled at her. "They chucked them before they came here." Then he shook his head sadly. "If we don't get those crazies out of here pretty soon, there'll be a riot. No way to protect them."

The other cop snorted. "You can tell Joe to take his time for all I care," he said. "They're *stupid*. Sometimes I think the stupid will inherit the Earth."

"Sure." Eric Larsen stood at the window watching the Wardens. Idly he whistled "Onward Christian Soldiers" through his teeth.

Eileen giggled. "What are you thinking about, Eric?"

"Huh?" He looked sheepish.

"The Professor's writing a movie script," Harris said.

Eric shrugged. "TV. Imagine James Garner marooned out there. He's looking for a killer. One of the drivers is out to commit murder. He does it, pulls out a sheet and a chain, and we come take him away before Garner can find him. . . ."

"Jesus," Harris said.

"I thought it was pretty good," Eileen said. "Who does he kill?"

"Uh, actually, you."

"Oh."

"I saw enough pretty girls killed last night to last me twenty years," Harris muttered. For a moment Eric looked like he'd been rabbit-punched.

Joe Corrigan came back with four pairs of long-handled bolt cutters. The policemen thanked him. Harris scribbled his name and badge number on a receipt, and handed two pairs to Eric Larsen. They carried them out to distribute to the other policemen, and blue uniforms moved along the chain, cutting the white robes free, then chaining them again with handcuffs. They jostled the Wardens toward the sidewalk. Few of the robed ones fought, but a good many went limp.

Corrigan looked up in surprise. "What was . . . ?"

"Huh?" Eileen looked vaguely around the office.

"I don't know." He frowned, trying to remember, but it had been too vague. As if clouds had parted to reveal the sun for a few moments, then closed again. But there were no clouds. It was a bright, cloudless summer day.

It was a nice house, well laid out, with bedrooms sprawling out like an arm, away from the huge central living room. Alim Nassor had always wanted a fireplace. He could imagine parties here, brothers and sisters splashing in the swimming pool, roar of conversation, smell of pot thick enough to get you high all by itself, a van delivering a great cartwheel of a pizza . . . Someday he would own such a house. He was robbing this one.

Harold and Hannibal were scooping silverware into a sheet. Gay was searching for the safe, in his own peculiar fashion: Stand in the middle of a room, look slowly around . . . then look behind paintings, or pull up rug . . . move to another room, stand in the middle and look around, and open closets . . . until he found the safe sunk in concrete beneath the rug in a hall closet. He pulled the drill out of his case and said, "Plug this in."

Alim did it. Even *he* followed orders when the need came. "If we don't find nothing this time, no more safes," he ordered.

Gay nodded. They'd opened four safes in four houses and found nothing. It looked like everyone in Bel Air had stashed their jewels in banks or taken them along.

Alim returned to the living room to look through the gauze curtains. It was a bright, cloudless summer day, and dead quiet, with nobody in sight. Half the families had fled to the hills, and the rest of the men were doing whatever they did to have houses like this, and anyone who stayed home must be inside watching TV to see if they'd made a mistake. It was people like this who were afraid of the comet. People like Alim, or Alim's mother with her job scrubbing floors and her ruined knees, or even the storekeeper he'd shot—people with something real to be afraid of didn't worry about no damn light in the sky.

So: The street was empty. No sweat, and the pickings were good. Fuck the jewels. There was silver, paintings, TV sets from tiny to tremendous, two or three or four to a house. Under the tarps in the truck bed they had a home computer and a big telescope—strange things, hard to fence—and a dozen typewriters. Generally they'd pick up some guns, too, but not this trip. The guns had gone with the running honkies.

"Shit! Hey, brothers—"

Alim went, fast. He and Hannibal almost jammed in the doorway.

Gay had the safe open and was hauling out plastic sandwich bags. It was stuff that couldn't be stashed in no bank vault. Three bags of good golden weed; oh, Mr. White, do your neighbors know about this? Smaller amounts of heavier stuff: coke, and dark hashish, and a small bottle of what might be hash oil, but you'd be crazy to try it without seeing a label. Gay and Harold and Hannibal whooped and hollered. Gay fished around and found papers; he started to roll a joint.

"Fuck that!" Alim slapped at Gay's hands, scattering paper and weed. "You crazy? In the middle of a job and four houses to go? Give me that! All of it! You want a party, fine, we'll have a *fine* party when we're home free!"

They didn't like it, but they passed the bags to Alim and he stashed them in the pockets of his baggy combat jacket. He slapped their butts and they went, carrying heavy bedsheet sacks.

He hadn't gotten it all. It didn't matter. At least they wouldn't be blowing the tops of their heads off till this was *over.*

Alim picked up a radio and a Toast-R-Oven and followed them out. He blinked in the daylight. Gay was in the back, adjusting tarpaulins. Harold started the motor. Good. Alim stopped with the truck door open to look down the driveway.

He saw a tall tree on the lawn casting two sharp shadows. And that smaller tree: two shadows. He looked down and saw his own two shadows, one moving. Alim looked up and saw it, a second sun dropping down the sky, dropping below the hill. He blinked; he squeezed his eyes shut, hard. The violet afterimage blocked everything.

He climbed in. "Get going," he said. While the truck rolled down the drive he started the CB. "Come in, Jackie. Come in, Jackie. Jackie, you motherfucker, answer me!"

"Who's that? Alim Nassor?"

"Yeah. Did you see it?"

"See what?"

"The comet, the Hammer of God! I saw it fall! I watched it burn its way down the sky till it hit! Jackie, listen good, 'cause these CB things ain't gonna be any good in a minute. We've been hit. It's all gonna come true, and we got to link up."

"Alim, you must've found something real special. Coke, maybe?"

"Jackie, it's real, the whole world been hit. There's gonna be earthquakes and tidal waves. You call everyone you can and tell them we meet at . . . the cabin up near Grapevine.

216

We got to stick together. We won't drown because we're too high, but we got to meet."

"Alim, this is crazy. I got two houses to go, we got lots of stuff, and you come on like the end of the world?"

"Just call someone, Jackie! Someone's got to have seen it! Look, I got to call the others while we still got the CB." Alim switched off.

They were still in the driveway. Harold was the color of wet ashes. He said, "I saw it too. George . . . Alim, do you think we're too high to drown? I don't want to drown."

"We're about as high as we can get. We got to go down before we get to Grapevine. Get movin', Harold. We want to be across the low spots before it rains too much."

Harold took off, fast. Alim reached for the CB. Were they really too high to drown? Was anybody, anywhere?

Hot Fudge Tuesdae: One

I ran to the rock to hide my face,
but the rock cried out, NO HIDING PLACE!
No hiding place down here. . . .

The crest of the Santa Monica Mountains was a thoroughly inconvenient place to live. Shopping centers were far away. Roads were an adventure. Driveways tended to be nearly vertical in spots. Yet there were many houses up here, and it was only indirectly due to population pressure.

Population pressure produced the cities.

The view from the crest on Monday night was incredible; unique. Downslope on one side was Los Angeles; downslope on the other, the San Fernando Valley. At night the cities became carpets of multicolored light stretching away forever. Freeways were rivers of light moving through seas of light. It looked like the whole world had turned to city, and loved it!

Yet there were vacant patches on the crest. Mark and Frank and Joanna left Mulholland Drive at sunset, took their motorcycles up the side of a hill. They camped in a rocky area out of sight of wandering fuzzmobiles, a couple of blocks distant from the houses on both sides.

Frank Stoner walked around the crest of the hill, looked at the slopes on both sides, then nodded to himself. Undevelopable. Too much danger of mudslides. Not that it mattered a damn why no one had built a house here, but Frank Stoner didn't like unanswered questions. He came back to where Joanna and Mark were setting up the Svea backpacker stove.

219

"We may have nervous neighbors," Frank said. "Let's get dinner over while there's light. After dark, no flashlights and no fires."

"I don't see—" Mark began.

Joanna broke in impatiently. "Look, these houses are a long way from the nearest police station. People wandering up here would tend to make them nervous. We do *not* need to spend the night before Hot Fudge Sundae at Malibu Sheriff Station." She went back to reading the directions on the freeze-dried dinner they'd brought. She was not a good cook; but if she left it to Mark, he'd do it however he felt, which might turn out well and might not. Following the directions was sure to produce something edible, and she was hungry.

She looked at the two men. Frank Stoner towered over Mark. A big man, strong, physically attractive. Joanna had felt that before. He'd be damned good in bed.

She'd felt that before, but she hadn't found herself thinking she was teamed up with the wrong man before. The thought puzzled her. Living with Mark was a lot of fun. She didn't know if she was in love with Mark, because she wasn't sure what love was, but they were compatible in bed, and they didn't often get on each other's nerves. So why this sudden pash for Frank Stoner?

She emptied the beef Stroganoff into a cooking pot and grinned down at it so the others couldn't see. They'd want to know why she was grinning, and it wasn't something she wanted to explain. If *she* wondered why she was getting the hots for Frank Stoner . . .

But it bothered her. Joanna had a very good education, courtesy of her upper-middle-class parents. She didn't make much use of it, but it had left her with considerable curiosity, particularly about people—which included herself.

"This is just about perfect," Mark said.

Frank grunted disapproval.

"No? Why not? Where else?" Mark demanded. He'd picked this spot and was proud of it.

"Mojave is better," Frank said absently. He laid out his sleeping bag and sat on it. "But that's a long way to go for nothing. Still . . . we're on the wrong plate."

"Plate?" Joanna said.

"It's plate tectonics," Mark said. "You know, the continents float around on top of the melted rock inside the Earth."

Frank listened absently. No point in correcting Mark. But the Mojave was certainly a better place. It was on the North American plate. Los Angeles and Baja California were on another. The plates joined at the San Andreas Fault, and if the Hammer fell the San Andreas would sure as hell let go. It would shake both plates, but the North American would get it less.

It was just an exercise anyway. Frank had checked with JPL; the odds of the Hammer hitting Earth were low. You were in more danger on the freeway. This business of camping out was for drill, but it was Stoner's nature that if he did anything, he did it right. He'd made Joanna bring her own bike, although she preferred riding behind Mark on his. Take all three; we might lose one.

"All for drill," Frank said. "But maybe the drill's worth the effort."

"Eh?" Joanna had the stove going now. It roared in the late afternoon.

"Nothing silly about being ready for the collapse of civilization," Frank said. "Next time it won't be the Hammer, it'll be something else. But it'll be something. Read your newspapers."

That's it, Joanna thought. He's got me thinking that way. And that's why . . . it sure made more sense to be teamed up with Frank Stoner than Mark Czescu if civilization was coming to an end.

And Frank had wanted to go to the Mojave. Only Mark talked him out of it. Mark couldn't quite admit to Hammer Fever. It would look silly.

They ate earlier than they usually did. Frank insisted. When they finished, there was just enough light to boil out the cooking pots. Then they lay down on their sleeping bags in near darkness, watching the glow die out over the Pacific, until the night grew cool and they climbed in. Joanna had brought her own bag and hadn't zipped it together with Mark's, although they usually did on camp-outs.

The light died in the west. One by one the stars came out. At first there were only stars. Then the turning sky brought a luminous film up from the east. It blended with the glowing lights over Los Angeles, grew brighter, until by midnight it was brighter than L.A., as bright as a good northern aurora. Still it thickened and brightened until only a few stars showed through the Earth-enveloping tail of Hamner-Brown Comet.

To keep themselves awake, they talked. Crickets talked around them. They had slept that afternoon, though neither Frank nor Mark would tell that to the others. It would have been an admission that each was in his thirties and feeling it. Frank told stories about the ways the world might end. Mark

221

kept interrupting to make points of his own, adding details, or anticipating what Frank would say and saying it first.

Joanna listened with increasing impatience. She fell silent, brooding. Mark *always* did that. It never bothered her before. Why was she getting pissed off at him now? Part of the same pattern. Wow, Joanna thought. Female instincts? Glom on to the strongest guy around? That didn't make sense. It certainly wasn't part of her philosophy. She was Joanna, fully liberated, her own person, in control of her life. . . .

The conflict made her think of other things. She wasn't yet thirty, but she was getting there, and what had she done? What was she doing? She couldn't just go on, making a few bucks when Mark was out of work, bopping around the country on a motorcycle. That was a lot of fun, but dammit, she ought to do something serious, one permanent thing. . . .

"I bet I can get the packs set so nobody can see the stove," Mark was saying. "Jo, want to make coffee? Jo?"

Full dawn found Frank and Joanna asleep. Mark smiled as if he'd won a contest. He enjoyed watching dawn break. It didn't happen often enough these days. Today's dawn still carried an elfin light, sunlight faintly thinned and transmuted by gases and dust brought inward from interstellar space.

It occurred to Mark that if he started breakfast now, he could reach a telephone while Harv Randall could be expected to be still at home. Randall had invited him to join the news team on Hot Fudge Tuesdae, but Mark had dithered. He dithered now. He set up the stove and pans for breakfast, debated waking the others; then crawled back into his own bag.

Frying bacon woke him.

"Didn't call Harv, huh?" Joanna said.

Mark stretched elaborately. "Decided I'd rather be watching the news than making it. Know where the best view in the world is right now? Right in front of a television set."

Frank looked at him curiously. He turned his head to indicate the height of the Sun. When Mark didn't get it, he said, "Look at your watch."

It was nearly ten! Joanna laughed at Mark's expression.

"Hell, we'll miss it," Mark complained.

"No point in racing anywhere now," Frank chortled. "Don't worry, they'll be showing instant replays all day."

"We could knock at one of the houses," Mark suggested. But the others laughed at him, and Mark admitted he didn't

222

have the guts. They ate quickly, and Mark broke out a bottle of Strawberry Hill wine and passed it around. It tasted perfect, fruity flavor like morning juice, but with some authority.

"Best pack up and—" Frank stopped in midsentence.

There was a bright light over the Pacific. Far away, and very high, and moving downward *fast*. A very bright light.

The men didn't speak. They just stared. Joanna looked up in alarm when Frank fell silent. She had never seen him startled by *anything*, and she whirled around quickly, expecting to see Charles Manson running at them with a chain saw. She followed their stare.

A tiny blue-white dwarf sun sank rapidly in the South, setting far beyond the flat blue Pacific horizon. It left a burning trail behind it. In the moment after it was gone, something like a searchlight beam probed back along its path, rose higher, *above* the cloudless sky.

Then nothing for one, two, three heartbeats.

Mark said, "Hot—"

A white fireball peeked over the edge of the world.

"Fudge Tuesdae. It's real. It's all real." The edge of a giggle was in Mark's voice. "We've got to get moving—"

"Bullshit." Frank used just enough volume to get their attention. "We don't want to be moving when the quakes hit. Lie down. Get your sleeping bag around you. Stay out in the open. Joanna, lie down here. I'll tie you in. Mark, get over there. Further."

Then Frank ran to the bikes. He carefully laid the first one on its side, then rolled the next away from it and laid it down too. He moved quickly and decisively. He came back for the third bike and moved it away.

Three white points glared at them, then winked out, one, two . . . The third and brightest must have touched down, far to the southeast. Frank glanced at his watch, counting the ticking seconds. Joanna was safe. Mark was safe. Frank brought his own bag and lay near them. He took out dark glasses. So did the others. The bulky sleeping bag made Frank look very fat. The dark glasses made his face unreadable. He lay stretched out on his back with his thick forearms behind his head. "Great view."

"Yeah. The Comet Wardens will love this," Mark said. "I wonder where Harv went? I'm glad I decided not to get up and go join him. We ought to be safe here. If the mountains hold up."

"Shut up," Joanna said. "Shut up, shut up." But she didn't say it loud enough to hear. She whispered, and her whisper was drowned out by rumbling that rolled toward them, and then the mountains began to dance.

■

The communications center at JPL was jammed with people: newsmen with special passes; friends of the Director; and even some people, like Charles Sharps and Dan Forrester, who belonged there.

The TV screens were bright with pictures. Reception wasn't as good as they'd have liked; the ionized tail of the comet roiled the upper atmosphere, and live TV pictures were apt to dissolve into wavy lines. No matter, Sharps thought. They'll make onboard recordings in the Apollo, and we'll recover them later. And there'll be all those film pictures, taken through the telescope. We'll learn more about comets in the next hour than we have learned in the last hundred thousand years.

That was a sobering thought, but Sharps was used to it. It was the same for the planets, for the whole solar system. Until men went—or sent probes—into space, they were guessing about their universe. Now they *knew*. And no other generation could ever discover so much, because the next generation would read it from textbooks, not from the universe itself. They would grow up knowing. Not like when I was growing up and we didn't know anything, Sharps thought. God, what exciting times. I love it.

A digital clock ticked off the seconds. A glass panel with a world map showed the current position of the Apollo capsule.

Apollo-*Soyuz*, Sharps reminded himself, and he grinned, because if the one hadn't gone, the other wouldn't have either. U.S.-Soviet rivalry was still good for something. Sometimes. To force U.S.-Soviet cooperation, if nothing else.

Pity we're having communications problems. Power losses on Hammerlab. Didn't anticipate that. Should have. But we didn't think it would be *this* close when we threw Hammerlab together.

"How close?" Sharps said.

Forrester looked up from his computer console. "Hard to say." He played his fingers across the keys like E. Power Biggs at the Milan Cathedral organ. "If that last input hadn't been garbled, I'd *know*. Best estimate is still around a thousand kilometers. *If*. If that garbled reading was right. And if the one I threw out because it didn't fit the others is wrong. There are a lot of ifs."

"Yeah."

"Taking shots . . . number thirty-one filter . . . hand-held . . ." They could barely recognize Rick Delanty's voice.

"One of your accomplishments," Dan Forrester said.

"Mine? Which one is this?"

"Getting the first black astronaut a mission," Forrester said, but he said it absently, because he was studying squiggles on the oscilloscope above his console. He did something, and one of the TV pictures improved enormously.

Charlie Sharps looked at the approaching cloud. He saw it only as a batch of not very sharply focused grays, but one thing was evident—it wasn't moving sideways at all. The seconds ticked on relentlessly.

"Where the devil is Hamner?" Sharps asked suddenly.

Forrester, if he heard, didn't answer.

". . . path of outer edges of nucleus; say again, Earth . . . outer . . . impossible . . . may strike . . ." The voice faded.

"Hammerlab, this is Houston, we do not copy, use full power and say again; I say again, we do not copy."

More seconds ticked off. Then, suddenly, the TV pictures on the screens swam, blurred and became clearer, in color, as Apollo used the main telescope and full transmission power.

"Jesus, it's coming close!" Johnny Baker's voice shouted. "Like it's going to hit . . ."

The TV screens changed rapidly as Rick Delanty kept the main telescope trained on the comet head. The comet grew and grew, shapes appearing in the maelstrom of fog, larger shapes, *details*, lumps of rock, jets of streaming gas, all happening even as they watched. The picture swung on down, until the Earth itself was in view. . . .

And flaming spots appeared on the Earth. For just one long moment, a moment that seemed to stretch out forever, the pictures stayed there on the TV screen: Earth, with bright flashes, light so bright that the TV couldn't show it as more than bright smears and lapses of detail.

The picture stayed in Charlie Sharps's mind. Flashes in the Atlantic. Europe dotted with bright smears, all over, with a big one in the Mediterranean. A bright flash in the Gulf of Mexico. Any west of that wouldn't be visible to the Apollo, but Dan Forrester was playing with the computer. All the data they had, from any source, was supposed to go into it.

225

Speakers were screaming. Several of them, on different channels, different sources, riding over the sudden static.

"FIREBALL OVERHEAD!" someone's voice shouted.

"Where was that?" Forrester called. His voice was just loud enough to go over the babble in the room.

"Apollo recovery fleet," came the answer. "And we've lost communications with them. Last words we got were: 'Fireball southeast.' Then 'Fireball overhead.' Then nothing."

"Thank you," Forrester said.

"Houston, HOUSTON, THERE IS A LARGE STRIKE IN THE GULF OF MEXICO; I SAY AGAIN, LARGE STRIKE THREE HUNDRED MILES SOUTHEAST OF YOU. REQUEST YOU SEND A HELICOPTER FOR OUR FAMILIES."

"Jesus, how can Baker be so calm about it?" someone demanded.

What damn fool is that? Sharps wondered. New man. Never heard the astronauts when there's a real problem. He glanced over to Forrester.

Dan Forrester nodded. "The Hammer has fallen," he said.

Then all the TV screens went blank, and the loudspeakers hissed with static.

Two thousand miles northeast of Pasadena, in a concrete-lined hole fifty feet below ground, Major Bennet Rosten idly fingered the .38 on his hip. He caught himself and put his hands on the Minuteman missile-launch-control console. They strayed restlessly for a moment, then one went to the key on its chain around his neck. *Bloody hell,* Rosten thought. The Old Man's got me nervous.

He had justification. The night before, he'd got a call direct from General Thomas Bambridge, and the SAC Commander in Chief didn't often speak personally to missile squadron commanders. Bambridge's message had been short. "I want you in the hole tomorrow," he'd said. "And for your information, I'll be up in Looking Glass myself."

"Goddam," Major Rosten had answered. "Sir . . . is this the Big One?"

"Probably not," Bambridge had answered, and then he'd gone on to explain.

Which wasn't, Rosten thought, very reassuring. If the Russkis really thought the U.S. was blind and crippled . . .

He glanced to his left. His deputy, Captain Harold Luce, was at another console just like Rosten's. The consoles were deep underground, surrounded by concrete and steel, built to withstand a near miss by an atomic bomb. It took both men to launch their birds: Both had to turn keys and punch buttons, and the timing sequence was set so that one man couldn't do it alone.

Captain Luce was relaxed at his console. Books were spread out in front of him: a correspondence course in Oriental art history. Collecting correspondence degrees was the usual pastime for men on duty in the holes, but how could Luce do it, today, when they were unofficially on alert?

"Hey, Hal . . ." Rosten called.

"Yo, Skipper."

"You're supposed to be alert."

"I am alert. Nothing's going to happen. You watch."

"Christ, I hope not." Rosten thought about his wife and four children in Missoula. They'd hated the idea of moving to Montana, but now they loved it. Big country, open skies, no big-city problems. "I wish—"

He was interrupted by the impersonal voice from the wire-grill-covered speaker above him. "EWO, EWO," the voice said. "EMERGENCY WAR ORDERS, EMERGENCY WAR ORDERS. THIS IS NO DRILL. AUTHENTICA-TION 78–43–76854–87902–1735 ZULU. RED ALERT. RED ALERT. YOUR CONDITION IS RED."

Sirens screamed through the concrete bunker. Major Rosten hardly noticed as a sergeant came down the steel ladder to the entrance and slammed shut the big Mosler Safe Company bank-vault door. The sergeant closed it from the outside and twirled the combination dial. No one would get into the hole without blasting.

Then, as regulations required, the sergeant cocked his submachine gun and stood with his back to the big safe door. His face was hard, and he stood rigidly, swallowing the sharp knot of fear.

Inside, Rosten punched the authentication numbers into his console, and opened the seals on an envelope from his order book. Luce was doing the same thing at his console. "I certify that the authentication is genuine," Luce said.

"Right. Insert," Rosten ordered.

Simultaneously they took the keys from around their necks and put them into the red-painted locked switches on their consoles. Once inserted and turned to the first click, the keys couldn't be withdrawn without other keys neither Luce nor Rosten had. SAC procedure . . .

"On my count," said Rosten. "One. Two." They turned the keys two clicks. Then they waited. They did not turn them further. Yet.

It was mid-morning in California; it was evening in the Greek isles. The last of the sun's disk had vanished as two men reached the top of the granite knob. In the east a first star showed. Far below them, Greek peasants were driving overloaded donkeys through a maze of low stone walls and vineyards.

The town of Akrotira lay in twilight. Incongruities: white mudwalled houses that might have been created ten thousand years ago; the Venetian fortress at the top of its hill; the modern school near the ancient Byzantine church; and below that, the camp where Willis and MacDonald were uncovering Atlantis. The site was almost invisible from the hilltop. In the west a star switched on and instantly off, *blink*. Then another. "It's started," MacDonald said.

Wheezing, Alexander Willis settled himself on the rock. He was mildly irritated. The hour's climb had left him breathless, though he was twenty-four years old and considered himself in good shape. But MacDonald had led him all the way and helped him over the top, and MacDonald, whose dark red hair had receded to expose most of his darkly tanned scalp, was not even breathing hard. MacDonald had earned his strength; archeologists work harder than ditchdiggers.

The two sat crosslegged, looking west, watching the meteors.

They were twenty-eight hundred feet above sea level on the highest point of the strange island of Thera. The granite knob had been called many things by a dozen civilizations, and it had endured much. Now it was known as Mount Prophet Elias.

Dusk faded on the waters of the bay far below. The bay was circular, surrounded by cliffs a thousand feet high, the caldera of a volcanic explosion that destroyed two thirds of the island, destroyed the Minoan Empire, created the legends of Atlantis. Now a new black island, evil in appearance and barren, rose in the center of the bay. The Greeks called it the New Burnt Land, and the islanders knew that some day it too would explode, as Thera had exploded so many times before.

Fiery streaks reflected in the bay. Something burned blue-white overhead. In the west the golden glow faded, not to black, but to a strange curdled green-and-orange glow, a backdrop for the meteors. Once again Phaethon drove the chariot of the sun. . . .

The meteors came every few seconds! Ice chips struck atmosphere and burned in a flash. Snowballs streaked down, burning greenish-white. Earth was deep in the coma of Hamner-Brown.

"Funny hobby, for us," said Willis.

"Sky watching? I've always loved the sky," MacDonald said. "You don't see me digging in New York, do you? The desert places, where the air's clear, where men have watched the stars for ten thousand years, that's where you find old civilizations. But I've never seen the sky like this."

"I wonder what it looked like after you-know-what."

MacDonald shrugged in the near-dark. "Plato didn't describe it. But the Hittites said a stone god rose from the sea to challenge the sky. Maybe they saw the cloud. Or there are things in the Bible, you could take them as eyewitness accounts, but from a long way away. You wouldn't have wanted to be near when Thera went off."

Willis didn't answer, and small wonder. A great greenish light drew fire across the sky, moving up, lasting for seconds before it burst and died. Willis found himself looking east. His lips pursed in a soundless *Oh*. Then, "Mac! Turn around!"

MacDonald turned.

The curdled sky was rising like a curtain; you could see beneath the edge. The edge was perfectly straight, a few degrees above the horizon. Above was the green-and-orange glow of the comet's coma. Below, blackness in which stars glowed.

"The Earth's shadow," MacDonald said. "A shadow cast through the coma. I wish my wife had lived to see this. Just another year . . ."

A great light glared behind them. Willis turned. It sank slowly—too bright to see, blinding, drowning the background —Willis stared into it. God, what was it? Sinking . . . faded.

"I hope you hid your eyes," MacDonald said.

Willis saw only agony. He blinked; it made no difference. He said, "I think I'm blind." He reached out, patted rock, seeking the reassurance of a human hand.

Softly MacDonald said, "I don't think it matters."

Rage flared and died. That quickly, Willis knew what he meant. MacDonald's hands took his wrists and moved them around a rock. "Hug that tight. I'll tell you what I see."

"Right."

MacDonald's speech seemed hurried. "When the light went

229

out I opened my eyes. For a moment I think I saw something like a violet searchlight beam going up, then it was gone. But it came from behind the horizon. We'll have some time.".

"Thera's a bad luck island," Willis said. He could see nothing, not even darkness.

"Did you ever wonder why they still build here? Some of the houses are hundreds of years old. Eruptions every few centuries. But they always come back. For that matter, what're *we* doing—Alex, I can see the tidal wave. It gets taller every second. I don't know if it'll reach this high or not. Brace yourself for the air shock wave, though."

"Ground shock first. I guess this is the end of Greek civilization."

"I suppose so. And a new Atlantis legend, if anyone lives to tell it. The curtain's still rising. Streamlines from the nucleus in the west, Earth's black shadow in the east, meteors everywhere. . ." MacDonald's voice trailed off.

"What?"

"I closed my eyes. But it was northeast! and huge!"

"Greg, who named Mount Prophet Elias? It's too bloody appropriate."

The ground shock ripped through and beneath Thera, through the magma channel that the sea bed had covered thirty-five hundred years before. Willis felt the rock wrench at his arms. Then Thera exploded. A shock wave of live steam laced with lava tore him away and killed him instantly. Seconds later the tsunami rolled across the raw orange wound.

Nobody would live to tell of the second Thera explosion.

Mabel Hawker fanned her cards and smiled inwardly. Twenty points: Her hand was a good one. Her partner, unfortunately, wasn't. The way Bea Anderson was bidding, they'd be out a hundred dollars by the time the plane landed at JFK.

The 747 was high above New Jersey in its descent into New York. Mabel and Chet and the Andersons were seated around a table in the first-class section, too far from the windows to see anything. Mabel regretted the bridge game. She'd never seen New York from the air; but she didn't want the Andersons to know that.

The windows flashed again.

"Your bid, May," Chet said.

People in the window seats were craning out. First class

buzzed with voices, and Mabel heard the fear that lies buried in every passenger's mind. She said, "Sorry. Two diamonds."

"Four hearts," Bea Anderson said, and Mabel cringed.

There was a soft ping. The sign lit: "FASTEN SEAT BELTS."

"This is Captain Ferrar," said a friendly voice. "We don't know what that flash was, but we'll ask you to fasten your seat belts, just in case. Whatever it was, it was a long way behind us." The pilot's voice was very calm and reassuring.

Did Bea have a jump bid? Oh, Lord, did she even know what an opening "two diamonds" meant? Have to bull it through. . . .

There was a sound: like something very large being slowly torn in two. Suddenly the 747 was laboring, surging forward.

She'd read that experienced travelers kept their seats belts fastened loosely, so she had done that. Now Mabel deliberately unfastened the belt, laid her cards face-down, and lurched toward a pair of empty window seats.

"Mother, should you do that?" Chet asked.

Mabel winced. She hated being called "Mother." It sounded country hick. She sprawled across the seats and looked out.

The big plane nosed down, diving, as the pilots tried to compensate for a sudden tail wind moving nearly with the speed of the plane. The wings lost all lift. The 747 fell like a leaf, yawing, lurching, as the pilots fought to hold her.

Mabel saw New York City ahead in the distance. There was the Empire State Building, there the Statue of Liberty, there the World Trade Center, looking just as she'd imagined them, but poking out of a landscape tilted at forty-five degrees. Somewhere out there her daughter would be going to JFK to meet her parents and introduce the boy she was going to marry. . . .

Flaps were sliding from the wing's trailing edge. The plane lurched and shuddered, and Mabel's cards flew like startled butterflies. She felt the plane surging upward, pulling out of its dive.

Far above, black clouds ran like a curtain across the sky, faster than the plane, sparking with lightning as they moved. Lightning everywhere. An enormous bolt struck the Statue of Liberty and played along the grande dame's upraised torch. Then lightning struck the plane.

■

Beyond Ocean Boulevard there was a bluff. At the bottom of the bluff, the Pacific Coast Highway, and then the sea. At the edge of the bluff the bearded man watched the horizon with a look of surpassing joy.

The light had flashed only for a second or two, but blindingly. Its afterimage was a blue balloon in the bearded man's field of view. A red glow . . . strange lighting effects outlining a vertical pillar . . . He turned with a happy smile. "Pray!" he called. "The Day of Judgment is here!"

A dozen passersby had stopped to stare. Mostly they ignored him, though he was a most impressive figure, with his eyes glowing with happiness and his thick black beard marked with two snow-white tufts at the chin. But one turned and answered. "It's *your* Day of Judgment if you don't step back. Earthquake."

The bearded man turned away.

The black man in the expensive business suit called more urgently. "If you're on the cliff when it falls, you'll miss most of Judgment Day. Come on now!"

The bearded man nodded as if to himself. He turned and strolled back to join the other on the sidewalk. "Thank you, brother."

The earth shuddered and groaned.

The bearded man kept his feet. He saw that the man in the brown suit was kneeling, and now he knelt too. The earth shook, and parts of the bluff fell away. It would have carried the bearded man with it if he hadn't moved.

"For He cometh," the bearded man shouted. "For He cometh to judge the Earth . . ."

The businessman joined in the psalm ". . . and with righteousness to judge the world, and the peoples with His truth."

Others joined. The heaving earth buckled and rolled. "Glory be to the Father and—"

A sharp sudden shock threw them to the ground. They scrambled back to their knees. The shaking stopped, and some of the group hurried away, looking for cars, running inland. . . .

"Oh, ye Heavens, bless ye the Lord," the bearded man cried. Those who had stayed joined in the canticle. The responses were easy to learn, and the bearded man knew all the versicles.

There were surfers out in the water. They had floated through the violent unheavals. Now they were invisible in a blinding curtain of salt rain. Many of the bearded man's group ran away into the wet darkening. Still he prayed, and others from the apartments across the street joined him.

"Oh, ye Seas and Floods, bless ye the Lord: praise Him and magnify Him forever."

The rains came hard, but just in front of the bearded man and his flock a trick combination of winds drove a clear path that let them see down the bluff to the deserted beach. The waters were receding, boiling away to leave small things flopping on the rainy wet sands.

"Oh, ye Whales, and all that move in the waters, bless ye the Lord. . . ."

The canticle ended. They knelt in the driving rain and flashing lightning. The bearded man thought he saw, far away, through the rain and beyond the receding waters, beyond that to the horizon, the ocean was rising in a hump, a straight wall across the world. "Save us, Oh God: for the waters are come in, even unto my soul," the bearded man cried. The others did not know the psalm, but they listened quietly. An ominous rumble came from the ocean. "I stick fast in the deep mire, where no ground is; I am come into deep waters, so that the floods run over me."

But no, the bearded man thought. The rest of that psalm is not appropriate. Not at all. He began again. "The Lord is my shepherd. I shall not want."

The water rushed forward. They finished the psalm. One of the women stood.

"Pray now," the bearded man said.

The noise from the sea drowned out all other words, and a curtain of rain swept over them, warm rain to hide the sea and waves. It came in a rush, a towering wall of water higher than the highest buildings, an onrushing juggernaut of water foaming gray and white at the base, rising as a green curtain. The bearded man saw a tiny object moving across the face of the water. Then the wall swept over him and his flock.

Gil rested face-down on the board, thinking slow thoughts, waiting with the others for the one big wave. Water sloshed under his belly. Hot sunlight broiled his back. Other surf-boards bobbed in a line on either side of him.

Jeanine caught his eye and smiled a lazy smile full of promises and memories. Her husband would be out of town for three more days. Gil's answering grin said nothing. He was waiting for a wave. There wouldn't be very good waves here at Santa Monica's Muscle Beach, but Jeanine's apartment was near, and there'd be other waves on other days.

The houses and apartments on the bluff above bobbed up and down. They looked bright and new, not like the houses on Malibu Beach where the buildings always looked older than they were. Yet even here there were signs of age. Entropy ran fast at the line between sea and land. Gil was young, like all the young men bobbing on the water this fine morning. He was seventeen, burned brown, his longish hair bleached nearly white, belly muscles like the discrete plates of an armadillo. He was glad to look older than he was. He hadn't needed to pay for a place to stay or food to eat since his father threw him out of the house. There were always older women.

If he thought about Jeanine's husband, it was with friendly amusement. He was no threat to the man. He wanted nothing permanent. She could be making out with some guy who'd want her money on a permanent basis. . . .

He squinted against the brilliance. It flared and he closed his eyes. That was a reflex; wave reflections were a common thing out here. The flare died against his closed eyelids, and he looked out to sea. Wave coming?

He saw a fiery cloud lift beyond the horizon. He studied it, squinting, making himself believe . . .

"Big wave coming," he called, and rose to his knees.

Corey called, "Where?"

"You'll see it," Gil called confidently. He turned his board and paddled out to sea, bending almost until his cheek touched the board, using long, deep sweeps of his long arms. He was scared shitless, but nobody would ever know it.

"Wait for me!" Jeanine called.

Gil continued paddling. Others followed, but only the strongest could keep up. Corey pulled abreast of him.

"I saw the fireball!" he shouted. He panted with effort. "It's Lucifer's Hammer! Tidal wave!"

Gil said nothing. Talk was discouraged out here, but the others jabbered among themselves, and Gil paddled even faster, leaving them. A man ought to be alone during a thing like this. He was beginning to grasp the fact of death.

Rain came, and he paddled on. He glanced back to see the houses and bluff receding, going uphill, leaving an enormous stretch of new beach, gleaming wet. Lightning flared along the hills above Malibu.

The hills had changed. The orderly buildings of Santa Monica had tumbled into heaps.

The horizon went up.

Death. Inevitable. If death was inevitable, what was left? Style, only style. Gil went on paddling, riding the receding waters until motion was gone. He was a long way out now. He turned his board, and waited.

Others caught up and turned, spread across hundreds of yards in the rainy waters. If they spoke, Gil couldn't hear them. There was a terrifying rumble behind him. Gil waited a moment longer, then paddled like mad, sure deep strokes, doing it well and truly.

He was sliding downhill, down the big green wall, and the water was lifting hard beneath him, so that he rested on knees and elbows with the blood pouring into his face, bugging his eyes, starting a nosebleed. The pressure was enormous, unbearable, then it eased. With the speed he'd gained he turned the board, scooting down and sideways along the nearly vertical wall, balancing on knees . . .

He stood up. He needed *more* angle, *more*. If he could reach the peak of the wave he'd be out of it, he could actually live through this! Ride it out, ride it out, and do it well. . . .

Other boards had turned too. He saw them ahead of him, above and below on the green wall. Corey had turned the wrong way. He shot beneath Gil's feet, moving faster than hell and looking terrified.

They swept toward the bluff. They were higher than the bluff. The beach house and the Santa Monica pier with its carousel and all the yachts anchored nearby slid beneath the waters. Then they were looking down on streets and cars. Gil had a momentary glimpse of a bearded man kneeling with others; then the waters swept on past. The base of the wall was churning chaos, white foam and swirling debris and thrashing bodies and tumbling cars.

Below him now was Santa Monica Boulevard. The wave swept over the Mall, adding the wreckage of shops and shoppers and potted trees and bicycles to the crashing foam below. As the wave engulfed each low building he braced himself for the shock, squatting low. The board slammed against his feet, and he nearly lost it; he saw Tommy Schumacher engulfed, gone, his board bounding high and whirling crazily. Only two boards left now.

The wave's frothing peak was far, far above him; the churning base was much too close. His legs shrieked in the agony of exhaustion. One board left ahead of him, ahead and below. Who? It didn't matter; he saw it dip into chaos, gone. Gil risked a quick look back: nobody there. He was alone on the ultimate wave.

Oh, God, if he lived to tell this tale, what a movie it would make! Bigger than *The Endless Summer*, bigger than *The Towering Inferno:* a surfing movie with ten million in special effects! If only his legs would hold! He already had a world record, he must be at least a mile inland, no one had ever ridden a wave for a mile! But the frothing, purling peak was miles overhead and the Barrington Apartments, thirty stories tall, was coming at him like a flyswatter.

What was once a comet is a pitiful remnant, a double handful of flying hills and boulders of dirty ice. Earth's gravitational field has spread them across the sky. They may still reach the halo, but they can never rejoin.

Craters glow across the face of the Earth. The sea strikes glow as brightly as the land strikes; but the sea strikes are growing smaller. Walls of water hover around them, edging inward.

The water hovers two miles high around the Pacific strike. Its edges boil frantically. The pressure of expanding live steam holds back the walls of water.

And the hot vapor goes up in a column clear as glass, carrying salt from vaporized seawater, and silt from the sea bottom, and recondensed rock from the strike itself. At the limits of Earth's atmosphere it begins to spread in an expanding whirlpool.

Megatons of live steam begin to cool. Water condenses first around dust and larger particles. What falls out of the pattern are the heavier globules of mud. Some join as they fall. They are still hot. In the drier air below, some water evaporates.

Hammerfall: Two

O! Sinner man, where you going to run to?
O, sinner man, where you going to run to?
O, sinner man, where you going to run to?
All on that day.

The TV store was closed. It wouldn't open for an hour. Tim Hamner searched frantically—a bar, a barbershop, anyplace that might have TV—but he saw nothing.

He thought fleetingly of taxis, but that was silly. Los Angeles taxis didn't cruise. They'd come if you called them, but it might be forever. No. He wasn't going to get to JPL— and Hamner-Brown's nucleus must be passing right now! The astronauts would see it all, and send their films down to Earth, and Tim Hamner wouldn't see any of it.

The police had removed some of the Wardens, but that had no effect on the traffic jam. Too many abandoned cars. And now what? Tim thought. Maybe I can . . .

It was as if a flashbulb had gone off behind him: *blink* and gone. Tim blinked. What exactly had he seen? There was nothing to the south but the green-brown hills of Griffith Park, with two horseback riders trotting along the trail.

Tim frowned, then thoughtfully walked back toward his car. There was a telephone in it, and he might as well summon a taxi.

Two white-robed Wardens, one with red trim on a tailor-made robe, came toward him. Tim avoided them. They stopped another pedestrian. "Pray, ye people! It is even now the hour, but it is not yet too late . . ."

The horns and shouts of anger had reached a crescendo when he got to his car—

The earth moved. A sudden, sharp motion, then something more gentle. Buildings shook. A plate-glass window crashed somewhere nearby. There were more sounds of falling glass. Tim could hear them because the car horns were suddenly quiet. It was as if everyone were frozen in place. A few people came out of the supermarket. Others stood in doorways, ready to get outside if it continued.

Then nothing. The horns began. People were yelling and screaming. Tim unlocked the car and reached inside for the radiophone—

The earth moved again. There were more sounds of falling glass, and someone screamed. Then, once again, silence. A flight of crows came winging out of the wooded patch at the corner of the Disney lot. They screamed at the people below, but no one paid any attention. The seconds stretched on, and the horns were once again beginning to sound when Tim was thrown violently to the asphalt parking lot.

This time it didn't stop. The ground shook and rolled and shook again, and whenever Tim tried to get up he was thrown down again, and it seemed that it would never stop.

The chair was on its back under a pile of catalogs, and Eileen was in it. Her head hurt. Her skirt was around her hips.

She rolled out of the chair very slowly and carefully, because there was shattered glass all the hell over the place, and pulled her skirt down. Her nylons were in ruins. There was a long, thin smear of blood along her left calf, and she watched, afraid to touch the spot, until she was certain there was no more blood coming out of her leg.

The front office was a chaos of catalogs, broken glass coffee table, tumbled shelving and the remains of the big plate-glass window. She shook her head dizzily. Silly thoughts boiled in her head. How could one window have had so much glass? Then, as her head cleared, she realized that *each* of those heavy shelves and their books had missed her head as it fell. She sagged against the receptionist's desk, dizzy.

She saw Joe Corrigan.

The plate-glass window had fallen inward, and Corrigan had been sitting next to it. Pieces of glass lay all about him. Eileen staggered to him and knelt, cutting her knee on a glass sliver. A dagger-size glass lance had gouged his cheek and bitten deep into his throat. Blood pooled beneath the wound, but there was no more flowing out. His eyes and mouth were wide open.

Eileen pulled the glass splinter free. She covered the wound with her palm, surprised that it wasn't bleeding more. What do you do about a throat wound? There were police outside, one of them would know. She took a deep breath, made ready to scream. Then she listened.

There were plenty of people screaming. Others were shouting. The noises from outside were chaotic. People, and rumbling sounds, as if buildings were still falling. Automobile horns, at least two, jammed on, not quite steady, wavering in mechanical agony. Nobody was going to hear Eileen call for help.

She looked down at Corrigan. She couldn't feel a pulse. She probed at the other side of his neck. No pulse there. She found a tuft of fuzz from the rug and put it on his nostrils. It didn't even quiver. But that's crazy, she thought. The neck wound couldn't have killed him, not yet! He was dead, though. Heart attack?

She got up slowly. Salt tears rolled down her cheek. They had the taste of dust. Automatically she brushed at her hair and her skirt before going outside, and she felt an impulse to laugh. She choked it down. If she started that, she wouldn't stop.

There were more sounds from out there. Ugly sounds, but she had to get outside. There were police outside, and one was Eric Larsen. She started to call to him, then she saw what was happening and she stood quietly in the ruined doorway.

Patrolman Eric Larsen was from Kansas. To him the earthquake was completely disorienting, completely terrifying. His urge was to run in circles, flapping his arms and squawking. He couldn't even get to his feet. He tried, and was thrown down each time, and presently decided to stay there. He put his head in his arms and closed his eyes. He tried to think of the TV script he could write when this was over, but he couldn't concentrate.

There was noise. The Earth groaned like an angry bull. That's a poetic image, where did I hear it? But there was more, cars crashing, buildings crashing, concrete falling, and everywhere people screaming, some in fear, some in rage, some just screaming.

Eventually the ground stopped moving. Eric Larsen opened his eyes.

His world had come apart. Buildings were broken or tilted, cars wrecked, the street itself buckled and crumpled. The parking lot was a jigsaw of asphalt at crazy angles. The supermarket across the street had fallen in on itself, walls collapsing, roof tumbled. People dragged themselves out of it. Still Eric waited, willing to take his lead from the natives. Tornadoes in Kansas, earthquakes in California: The natives would know what to do.

But they didn't. They stood, those few remaining, blinking in the bright, cloudless summer day, or they lay on the ground in bloody heaps, or they screamed and ran in circles.

Eric looked for his partner. Regulation blue trousers and black shoes protruded from under a load of plumbing supplies fallen from a truck. A crate labeled "Silent Flush" stood where the head should have been. The crate was very flat on the ground. Eric shuddered and got to his feet. He couldn't go near that crate. Not just yet. He started toward the supermarket, wondering when the ambulances would come, looking for a senior officer to tell him what to do.

Three burly men in flannel shirts stood near a station wagon. One walked completely around it, inspecting for damage. The wagon was heavily loaded. A porch with a railing of ornamental iron scrollwork had dropped through the back end. The men cursed loudly. One dug into the back of the wagon. He took out shotguns and handed them to his friends. "We won't get out of here because of those motherfuckers." The man's voice was quiet and strangely calm. Eric could barely hear him.

The others nodded and began thrusting shells into their guns. They didn't look back at Eric Larsen. When the guns were loaded, the three raised them to their shoulders and aimed at a dozen Wardens. The white-robed preachers screamed and pulled at their chains. Then the shotguns went off in volley.

Eric put his hand to his pistol, then drew it away quickly. Hell! He walked toward the men, his knees unsteady. They were reloading.

"Don't do that," Eric said.

The men jumped at the voice. They turned to see police blue. They frowned, their eyes wide, their expressions uncertain. Eric stared back. He had already noticed the "SUPPORT YOUR LOCAL POLICE" bumper sticker on the station wagon.

The oldest of the three men snorted. "It's over! That was the end of civilization you just saw, don't you understand?"

And suddenly Eric did understand. There weren't going to be any ambulances to take the injured to hospitals. Startled, Eric looked back down Alameda, toward the place where St. Joseph's was. He saw nothing but buckled streets and collapsed houses. Had St. Joseph's been visible from here? Eric couldn't remember.

The spokesman for the men was still shouting. "Those motherfuckers kept us from getting up into the hills! What use are they?" He looked down at his empty shotgun. It lay open in his hand. His other hand held two shells, and kept straying toward the breech of the gun, not quite inserting them.

"I don't know," Eric said. "Are you going to be the first man to start shooting policemen?" He let his eyes go to the bumper sticker. The burly man's followed, then looked down at the street. "Are you?" Eric repeated.

"No."

"Good. Now give me the shotgun."

"I need it—"

"So do I," Eric said. "Your friends have others."

"Am I under arrest?"

"Where would I take you? I need your shotgun. That's all." The man nodded. "Okay."

"The shells, too," Eric said. His voice took on a note of urgency.

"All right."

"Now get out of here," Eric said. He held the shotgun without loading it. The Wardens, the few that survived, watched in silent horror. "Thank you," Eric said. He turned away, not caring where the burly men went.

I've just watched Murder One and done nothing about it, he told himself. He walked briskly away from the traffic jam. It was as if his mind were no longer connected to his body, and his body knew where it was going.

The sky to the southwest was strange. Clouds flew overhead, formed and vanished as in a speeded-up film. It was all familiar to Eric Larsen, as familiar as the way the air felt in his sinuses. Anyone from Topeka would know. Tornado weather. When the air feels like this, and the sky looks that way, you head for the nearest basement, taking a radio and a canteen of water.

It's a good mile to the Burbank City Jail, Eric thought. He studied the sky judiciously. I can make it.

He walked briskly toward the jail. Eric Larsen was still a civilized man.

Eileen watched the incident in horror. She hadn't heard the conversation, but what happened was plain enough. The police . . . weren't police any longer.

Two of the Wardens were messily dead, five more writhed in the agony of mortal wounds, and the rest were writhing to free themselves from the chains. One of the Wardens had a pair of bolt cutters. Eileen recognized them. Joe Corrigan had given them to the police only minutes, or lifetimes, before.

The scene outside was incomprehensible. People lay in heaps, or dragged themselves from ruined shops. One man had climbed on top of a wrecked truck. He sat on the cab, feet dangling over the windshield, and drank deeply from a bottle of whiskey. Every now and again he looked up and laughed.

Anyone wearing a white robe was in danger. For the Wardens in chains it was a nightmare. Hundreds of enraged drivers, more hundreds of passengers, many fleeing the city, not really expecting Hammerfall but heading out just in case —and the Wardens had stopped them. Most of the people in the street were still lying flat on their backs, or wandering aimlessly, but there were enough: men and women converging on the robed and chained Wardens, and each carrying something heavy—tire irons, tire chains, jack handles, a baseball bat . . .

Eileen stood in the doorway. She glanced back at Corrigan's body. Two vertical lines deepened between her eyes as she watched Patrolman Larsen's retreating back. A riot was starting out there, and the only cop was walking away, fast, after calmly watching murder. It wasn't a world Eileen understood.

World. What had happened to the world? Gingerly she picked her way back through the broken glass toward her office. Thank God for medium heels, she thought. Glass crunched underfoot. She moved as quickly as she could, without a glance at the smashed goods and broken shelves and sagging walls.

A length of pipe, torn loose from the ceiling, had half crushed her desk, smashing the glass top. The pipe was heavier than anything she had ever lifted before, and she grunted with the effort, but it moved. She pulled her purse from underneath, then scrambled about looking for the portable radio. It seemed undamaged.

Nothing but static. She thought she heard a few words in the static. Someone shouting "Hammerfall!" over and over again, or was that in her head? No matter. There was no useful information.

Or, rather, there was, in that fact itself. This wasn't a local disaster. The San Andreas had let go. Okay, but there were plenty of radio stations in southern California, and not *all* of them were near the fault. One or more should still be broadcasting, and Eileen knew of nothing an earthquake could do that would cause so much static.

Static. She went on through the back of the store. She found another body there, one of the warehousemen. She knew from the coveralls; there wouldn't have been any point in looking for a face. Or for an upper torso, either, not under that. . . . The door to the alley was jammed. She pulled and it moved, slightly, and she pulled again, bracing her cut knee against the wall and straining as hard as she could. It opened just far enough to let her squeeze through, and she went out and looked up at the sky.

Black clouds, roiling, and rain beginning to fall. Salt rain. Lightning flashed overhead.

The alley was blocked with rubble. Her car couldn't possibly get through. She stopped and used the mirror from her purse, found a Kleenex and wiped away the dirty tear streaks and blood; not that it mattered a damn how she looked, but it made her feel better.

More rain fell. Darkness and lightning overhead, and salt rain. What did that mean? A big ocean strike? Tim had tried to tell her, but she hadn't listened; it had so little to do with real life. She thought about Tim as she hurried down the alley, back toward Alameda because it was the only way she could go, and when she got to the street she couldn't believe what she was seeing. Tim was there, in the middle of a riot.

■

The earthquake rolled Tim Hamner under his car. He stayed there, waiting for the next shock, until he smelled gasoline. Then he came out, fast, crawling across the buckled pavement, staying on hands and knees.

He heard screams of terror and agony, and new sounds:

concrete smashing on street pavement, concrete punching through metal car bodies, an endless tinkle of falling glass. And still he couldn't believe. He got up, trembling.

People in white robes, blue uniforms, street clothes, lay sprawled on shattered street and sidewalks. Some moved. Some did not. Some were obviously dead, twisted or crushed. Cars had been overturned or smashed together or crushed by falling masonry. No building stood intact. The smell of gasoline was strong in his nostrils. He reached for a cigarette, jerked his hand violently away, then thoughtfully put his lighter in a back pocket, where he'd have to *think* before finding it.

A three-story building had lost its east face; the glass and brick had disintegrated, spilling outward across the parking lot and side street almost as far as where Tim Hamner had been lying. A chunk with part of a bay window in it had dropped through the passenger section of Hamner's car. Gasoline ran from it in a spreading pool.

From somewhere he heard screams. He tried to shut them out. He couldn't think of anything to do. Then the riot spilled around the corner.

It was led by three men in white robes. They were not screaming; they were panting, and saving all their breath for it. The screaming came from those behind them, and not from those in the lead.

One of the robed ones screamed at last. "Help! Please!" he screamed at Tim Hamner and ran toward him.

The mob pursued. They were looking at Tim Hamner, all those eyes at once, and he thought, *They'll believe I'm with them!* Then a worse thought: *I could be recognized. As the man who invented the Hammer. . . .*

Time was too short to consider the idea. Tim reached into the trunk and brought out the portable tape unit. The robed youth running toward him had a wispy blond beard and a lean face set in classic lines of terror. Tim shoved his microphone toward the Warden and said loudly, "One moment, please, sir. Just how—"

Insulted and betrayed, the man swiped at the microphone and ran past him. The other two fugitives, and most of the mob, had continued on down the street—toward the dead end, and of course that was a pity. Some burly types ran past Tim, chasing the robed man into the broken building. One stopped, panting, and looked at Tim.

Hamner lifted the microphone again. "Sir? Have you any idea how all this happened?"

"Hell, yes . . . buddy. Those sons of bitches . . . those Wardens blocked us off just as we . . . were taking off for Big Bear. They were . . . going to stop the comet by praying. Didn't . . . work, and they . . . trapped us here, and we've . . . already killed about . . . half of the motherfuckers."

It was working! Somehow nobody ever thinks of killing a newsman. Too vividly public, maybe: The whole world is watching. Other rioters had stopped, were crowding around, but not as if they were waiting their turn to kill Tim Hamner. They were waiting for a chance to speak.

"Who you with?" one demanded.

"KNBS," Tim said. He fumbled in his pockets for the press press-card Harvey Randall had given him. There it was. Tim flashed it, but kept his thumb over the name.

"Can you get a message out?" the man demanded. "Send for—"

Tim shook his head. "This is a recorder, not a remote unit. The rest of the crew will be here soon. I hope." He turned back to the first man. "How are you planning to get out now?"

"Don't know. Walk out, I guess." He seemed to have lost interest in the fleeing Wardens.

"Thank you, sir. Would you mind signing . . ." Tim brought out a stack of NBS release forms. The big man stepped back as if they'd been scorpions. He looked thoughtful for a second.

"Forget it, buddy." He turned and walked away. Others followed, and the whole crowd melted away, leaving Tim alone by the ruins of his car.

Hamner put the press card into his shirt pocket, adjusting it so that the big lettering, PRESS, was visible, but his name wasn't. Then he put the recorder's strap over his shoulder. He also carried the microphone and a stack of release forms. It was all heavy and awkward, but it was worth it. He did not laugh.

Alameda was filled with horrors. A woman dressed in an expensive pantsuit was jumping up and down on a lumpy white robe. Tim looked away. When he looked back, there were more people swarming around him. They carried bloody tire irons. A man swung toward him, swung an enormous handgun toward Tim's navel. Tim pointed the microphone at him. "Excuse me, sir. How did you manage to get trapped in this mess?" The man cried as he told his tale. . . .

There was someone at Tim's elbow. Hamner hesitated, not wanting to look away; the man with the gun was still talking, tears of rage running down his face, and his gun still pointed at Tim's navel. He looked earnestly into Hamner's eyes. Whatever he saw, he hadn't fired yet. . . .

Who the devil was that? Someone reaching for the release forms—

Eileen! Eileen Hancock? Tim held the microphone motionless as Eileen stepped briskly to his side. He let her take the release forms.

"Okay, Chief, I'm here," she said. "Bit of trouble back there. . . ."

Tim almost fainted. She wasn't going to blow his cover, thank *God* she had brains for that. Tim nodded, his eyes still fixed on his interview subject. "Glad you got here," Tim said from the corner of his mouth, speaking low as if worried about ruining the interview. He did not smile.

". . . and if I see another of the sons of bitches I'll kill him too!"

"Thank you, sir," Tim said gravely. "I don't suppose you'd care to sign—"

"Sign? Sign what?"

"A release form."

The gun swung up to point at Tim's face. "You bastard!" the man screamed.

"Anonymous subject," Eileen said. "Sir—you do know there's a newspersons' shield law in California, don't you?"

"What—"

"We can't be forced to reveal our sources," Eileen said. "You don't need to worry. It's the law."

"Oh." The man looked around. The other rioters had gone, somewhere, and it was raining. He looked at Tim, and at Eileen, and at the gun in his hand. There were more tears. Then he turned and walked away. After a few steps he ran.

Somewhere a woman screamed, short and sharp. The background noise was screams and moans and thunder, thunder always, and very near. A brisk wind had risen. Two men were atop an intact car with a shoulder-carried television camera. No way to tell how long they'd been there, but they were all alone on an island of privacy. And so were Tim and Eileen.

"Rioters are publicity-shy," Tim said. "Glad to see you. I'd forgotten you work around here."

"Worked," Eileen said. She pointed toward the ruins of Corrigan's. "I don't suppose anyone will be selling plumbing supplies . . ."

"Not from Burbank," Tim said. "I am glad to see you. You know that, don't you? What do we do now?"

"You're the expert."

Lightning crackled nearby. The hills of Griffith Park were aflame with blue flashes.

"High ground," Tim said. "And fast."

Eileen looked puzzled. She pointed at the lightning.

"That *might* hit us," he agreed. "But we've a better chance out of this river valley. Feel the rain? And there may be . . ."

"Yes?"

"Tidal wave," Tim said.

"Jesus. It's real, isn't it? This way, then. Up into the Verdugo Hills. We can hike across. How much time do we have?"

"I don't know. Depends on where it hit. *They* hit, probably," Tim was surprised at how calm his voice was.

Eileen began walking. East on Alameda. The route led toward the head of the traffic jam, where the huddled bodies of the Wardens lay. As they got near, a car roared off through the intersection, into a filling station beyond, then onto the sidewalk. It squeezed through between a wall and a telephone pole, scraping paint off the right side.

The car that had been behind it was now clear, and it was unlocked. Keys dangled in the ignition. Eileen waved Tim toward it. "How good a driver are you?" she demanded.

"Okay."

"I'll drive," she said firmly. "I'm *damned* good at it." She got into the driver's seat and started the car. It was an elderly Chrysler, once a luxury car. Now the rugs were worn and it had ugly stains on the seat covers. When the motor turned over with a steady purr, Tim thought it the most beautiful car he'd ever seen.

Eileen took the route of the previous car. They drove over a white robe, *bump;* she didn't slow. The space between the telephone pole and the wall was narrow, but she went through it at speed, twenty miles an hour anyway, without worrying about it. Tim held his breath until they were through.

The street curved gently ahead of them. There were cars jammed in both lanes of traffic, and Eileen kept on the sidewalk, veering off into yards when she had to to avoid more utility poles. She drove through rose beds and manicured lawns until they were past the traffic jam.

"Lord God, you *are* a good driver," Tim said.

Eileen didn't look up. She was busy avoiding obstructions. Some of the obstructions were people. "Should we warn them?" she asked.

247

"Would it do any good? But yes," Tim said. He opened the window on his side. The rain was coming down hard now, and the salt stung his eyes. "Get to high ground," he shouted. "Tidal waves. Flood! Get to high ground," he shouted into the rising wind. People stared at him as they went by. A few looked around wildly, and once Tim saw a man grab a woman and dash for a car in sudden decision.

They turned a corner, and there were red flames. A whole block of houses was burning out of control, burning despite the rain. The wind blew flaming chips into the air.

Another time they slowed to avoid rubble in the street. A woman ran toward them carrying a bundled blanket. Before Eileen could accelerate, the woman had reached the car. She thrust the blanket in the window. "His name is John!" she shouted.

"But—don't you want—"

Tim couldn't finish. The woman had turned away. "Two more back there!" she screamed. "John. John Mason. Remember his name!"

Eileen speeded up again. Tim opened the bundle. There was a baby in it. It didn't move. Tim felt for a heartbeat, and his hand came out covered with blood. It was bright red, copper blood, and the smell filled the car despite the warm salt smell of the rain.

"Dead," Tim said.

"Throw him out," Eileen said.

"But—"

"We aren't going to eat him. We won't be that hungry."

It shocked Tim, so much that he thrust the baby out the window and let go. "I—I felt like I was letting some of my life drop onto that pavement," he said.

"Do you think I like it?" Eileen's voice was pinched. Tim looked at her in alarm; there were tears streaming down her cheeks. "That woman thinks she saved her child. At least she thinks that. It's all we could have done for her."

"Yes," Tim said gently.

"If . . . *When*. When we've got to high ground, when we know what's happening, we can start thinking civilization again," Eileen said. "Until then, we survive."

"If we can."

"We will." She drove on, grimly. The rain was coming down so hard that she couldn't see, despite the windshield wipers speeding away, smearing grime and salt water across the windshield.

The Golden State Freeway had cracked. The underpass was

248

blocked with wreckage. A tangle of cars and a large gasoline tank truck lay in the midst of a spreading pool of fire.

"Jesus," Tim said. "That's . . . shouldn't we stop?"

"What for?" Eileen turned left and drove parallel to the freeway. "Anyone who's going to survive that has got out already."

They were driving through a residential area. The houses had mostly survived intact. They both felt relief; for a few moments there was no one hurt, broken or dying. They found another underpass, and Eileen drove toward it.

The way had been blocked by a traffic barrier. Someone had torn down the barrier. Eileen drove through it. As she did, another car came out of the rain ahead. It dashed past, horn screaming.

"Why would anyone be going *into* the valley?" Tim demanded.

"Wives. Sweethearts. Children," Eileen said. They were climbing now. When the way was blocked by twisted remains of buildings and cars, Eileen turned left, bearing north and east always. They passed the ruins of a hospital. Police in blue, nurses in rain-soaked white poked at the wreckage. One of the policemen stopped and looked at them. Tim leaned out the window and screamed at him. "Get to high ground! Flood! Tidal wave! High ground!"

The policeman waved, then turned back to the wreckage of the hospital.

Tim stared moodily at the swirling smears on the windshield. He blinked back tears of his own.

Eileen had a moment to glance at him. Her hand touched his before returning to the wheel. "We couldn't have helped. They've got cars, and enough people. . . ."

"I guess." He wondered if he meant it. The nightmare ride went on, as the car climbed toward the Verdugo Hills, past wrecked stucco houses, a fallen school, burning houses and intact houses. Whenever they saw anyone, Tim screamed warning. It made him feel a little better for not stopping.

He glanced at his watch. Incredibly, less than forty minutes had passed since he'd seen the bright flash. He muttered it: "Forty minutes. H plus forty minutes, and counting."

The wave rushes outward from the center of the Gulf of Mexico, moving at 760 miles an hour. When it reaches the shallows along the coast of Texas and Louisiana, the foot of the wave stumbles. More and more water rushes up behind, piling higher and higher until a towering monster half a kilometer high falls forward and flows up onto the land.

Galveston and Texas City vanish under the pounding waves. The water that flows westward through the swamps into El Lago, further west into Houston itself, is now filled with debris. The wave strikes all along the arc from Brownsville, Texas, to Pensacola, Florida, seeking lowlands, rivers, any path inland and away from the burning hell at the bottom of the Gulf of Mexico.

The waters pile high along the Florida west coast; then they break across, carrying with them the sandy soil. They leave behind channels scoured clean, a myriad of passages from the Gulf to the Atlantic Ocean. The Gulf Stream will be cooler and much smaller for centuries to come.

The waters crossing Florida are capricious. Here a reflected wave joins the main body of rushing water to build even higher; there a reflection cancels, leaving parts of the Okefenokee Swamp untouched. Havana and the Florida Keys vanish instantly. Miami enjoys an hour's respite until the waves from the Atlantic strikes rush down, meet the outrushing waves from the Gulf, overpower them, and crash into Florida's eastern cities.

Atlantic waters pour into the Gulf of Mexico through the newly formed cross-Florida channels. The saucer bowl of the Gulf cannot hold it all, and the waters once again flow west and north, across the already drowned lands. One wave rushes up the Mississippi. It is forty feet above flood level when it passes Memphis, Tennessee.

■

Fred Lauren had been at the window all night. The bars didn't hide the sky at all. They'd put him alone in a cell after they photographed and fingerprinted him, and they left him. At noon he'd be taken to the Los Angeles Jail.

Fred laughed. At noon there wouldn't be a Los Angeles Jail. There'd be no Los Angeles. They'd never get a chance to put him in with those other men. Memories of another prison came, and he swept them away with better thoughts.

He remembered Colleen. He'd gone to her door with presents. He only wanted to talk. She'd been afraid of him, but he was inside before she could bolt the door, and he'd brought very nice presents for her, nice enough that she'd let him stand by the door while she stood on the other side of the room and looked at the jewelry and the gloves and red shoes, and then she'd wondered how he knew her sizes, and he told her.

He'd talked and talked, and after awhile she was friendly and let him sit down. She'd offered him a drink and they'd talked some more, and she had two drinks for herself, and then another. She'd been pleased that he knew so much about her. He didn't tell her about the telescope, of course, but he'd told her how he knew where she worked, and where she shopped, and how beautiful she was. . . .

Fred didn't want to remember the rest of it. How she'd had one drink too many, and told him that even though they'd just met she felt she'd known him a long time and of course he really had known her even if she didn't know it, and she'd asked if he wanted to stay. . . .

Tramp. Like all of them. A tramp. No, she couldn't have been, she really loved him, he knew she did, but why had she laughed, and then screamed and told him to get out when—

NO!

Fred always stopped remembering then. He looked up at the sky. The comet was there. Its tail blazed across the sky just as he'd seen in the paintings in the astronomy magazines, and when the sky was blue with hidden dawn, brightening in that tiny patch of western sky that Fred could see, there were still the wisps of comet among the clouds, and people moved on the streets below, the fools, didn't they know?

They brought him breakfast in his cell. The jailers didn't want to talk to him. Even the trustees looked at him *that* way. . . .

They knew. They knew. The police doctors must have examined her, and they knew she hadn't been, that he couldn't, that he'd tried but he couldn't and she laughed and he knew how he could do it, but he didn't want to, and she laughed again, and he bit her until she screamed and then he'd be able to only she kept on screaming!

He had to stop thinking. He had to, before he remembered the shape on the bed. The cops had made him look at her. One had held his hand in a certain way and bent his fingers until he opened his eyes and looked and he didn't want to, didn't they understand that he loved her and he didn't want . . . ?

The sky glowed strangely through the cracks of the buildings across the street. Somewhere to the left, far south and west. The glow died before he'd seen anything at all, but Fred smiled. It had happened. It wouldn't be long now.

"Hey, Charlie," the drunk across the block called. "Charlie!"

"Yeah?" the trustee answered.

"What the fuck was that? They making movies out there?"

"Don't know what you're talking about. Ask the sex maniac, he's got western exposure."

"Hey, Sex Maniac—"

The walls and floor jerked suddenly, savagely. He was flying. . . . He threw out his arms to ward the wall from his head. The stone wave broke against his arms, and Fred howled. Agony screamed in his left elbow.

The floor seemed to stabilize. The jail was solidly built. There'd been nothing damaged. Fred moved his left arm and moaned. Other prisoners were shouting now. One screamed in agony. He must have fallen from an upper bunk. Fred ignored them all and moved again to the window. He felt real fear. *Was that all?*

One ordinary day, with . . . clouds. Jesus, they were moving fast! Churning, forming and vanishing, streaming north and west. A lower cloud bank, calmer and more stable, began moving south and west. This wasn't what Fred had expected. One wave of fire, that was what he had prepared for. Doomsday was taking its own sweet time.

The sky darkened. Now it was all black clouds, swirling, churning, flashing with continuous lightning. The wind and the thunder howled louder than the prisoners.

The end of the world came in blinding light and simultaneous thunderclap.

Fred's mind recondensed to find him on the floor. His elbow was shrieking agony. Lightning . . . lightning must have struck the jail itself. There were no lights in the corridor, and outside was dark, so that he could see only in surrealistic flashes like a strobe-lit go-go bar.

Charlie was moving along the cellblock. He carried keys. He was letting the prisoners out. One by one. He opened the cells and they came out and moved down the corridor—and he had already passed Fred's cell. The cells on either side were open. His was locked.

Fred screamed. Charlie didn't turn. He went on until he reached the end of the cellblock, then he went out and down the stairs.

Fred was alone.

Eric Larsen looked to neither the right nor the left. He walked in long strides. He stepped around the dead and the injured, and ignored pleas for help. He could have helped them, but he was driven by a terrible urgency. His cold eyes and the carelessly carried shotgun discouraged anyone from getting in his way.

He saw no other policemen. He barely noticed the people around him, that some were helping the injured, some were disconsolately staring at the ruins of their homes and shops and stores, some were running aimlessly. None of it mattered now. They were all doomed, as Eric Larsen was doomed.

He might have taken a car and driven away into the hills. He saw cars race past him. He saw Eileen Hancock in an old Chrysler. If she'd stopped he might have gone with her, but she didn't, and Eric was glad, because it was tough enough to keep his resolve.

But suppose he wasn't needed? Suppose it was a fool's errand? There was no way to know.

But I should have taken a car, he thought. I could have finished it and had a chance. Too late now. There was the station house, City Hall, and the jail. They seemed deserted. He went into the jail. There was a dead policewoman under the wreckage of a huge cabinet that had stood against the wall. He saw no one else, living or dead. He went through, behind the booking cage and up the stairs. The cellblocks were quiet.

It *was* a fool's errand. He was not needed. He was about to go back down the stairs, but he stopped himself. No point in coming this far without being sure.

There'd been talk of a tidal wave following Hammerfall. There were people in the Burbank Jail, people that Eric Larsen had put there. Drunks, petty thieves, young vagrants who said they were eighteen but looked much younger. They couldn't be left to drown like rats in forgotten jail cells. They didn't deserve that. And Eric had put them there—it was his responsibility.

The barred door at the top of the stairs stood open. Eric went through and used his big flash in the near darkness. The cell doors stood open. All but one.

All but one. Eric went to the cell. Fred Lauren stood with his back to the corridor. His left arm was cradled in his right. Lauren stared out the window, and he didn't turn when Eric flashed the light on him. Eric stood watching him for a moment.

No one deserved to drown like a rat in a cage. No human did. The thieves and drunks and runaways and . . .

"Turn around," Eric said. Lauren didn't move. "Turn around or I'll shoot your kneecaps out. That hurts a lot."

Fred whimpered and turned. He saw the shotgun leveled at him. The policeman was holding the light off to one side, almost behind himself, so that Fred could see.

"Do you know who I am?" the policeman asked.

"Yes. You kept the other policeman from beating me last night." Fred moved closer. He stared at the shotgun. "Is that for me?"

"I brought it for you," Eric said. "I came to turn the others loose. I couldn't let you loose. So I brought the shotgun."

"It's the end of the world," Fred Lauren said. "All of it. Nothing will be left. But . . ." Fred whimpered deep in his throat. "But when? Would . . . please, you've got to tell me. Wouldn't she be dead now? Already? She couldn't live through the end of the world. She'd have died and I'd never have talked to her—"

"*Talked* to her!" Eric brought the shotgun up in rage. He saw Fred Lauren standing calmly, waiting, and he saw the bed and the ruins of a young girl, and the closet with the pathetically small wardrobe. There was a smell of copper blood in his nostrils. His finger tightened on the trigger, then relaxed. He lowered the shotgun.

"Please," Fred Lauren said. "Please—"

The shotgun came up quickly. Eric hadn't known it would kick so hard.

Hot Fudge Tuesdae: Two

Oh, I run to the hills and the hills were a-fallin',
Run to the sea and the sea was a-boilin',
Run to the sky and the sky was a-burnin'!
ALL ON THAT DAY.

Static roared in the crowded room. Random blobs and colors filled the large TV, but twenty men and women stared at the screen where they had watched lights blaze and die above the Atlantic, above Europe, Northwest Africa, the Gulf of Mexico. Only Dan Forrester continued to work. The screen above his console held a computer-drawn world map, and Forrester laboriously called up all the data received at JPL, plotting the strikes and using their locations as input for more calculations.

Charles Sharps felt that he ought to be interested in Forrester's calculations, but he wasn't. Instead he watched the others. Open mouths, bulging eyes, feet thrusting them back into their chairs. They cringed back from their blinded consoles and screens, as if these were the danger. And still Forrester typed instructions, made precise movements, studied results and typed again. . . .

"Hammerfall," Sharps said to himself. And what the hell do we do about it? He couldn't think of anything, and the room depressed him. He left his station and went to the long table against one wall. There were coffee and Danish there, and Sharps poured himself a cup. He stared into it, then lifted it in a mock salute. "Doom," he said. He kept his voice low. The others began to rise from their stations.

"Doom," Sharps repeated. Ragnarok. And what use now was man's proud civilization? Ice Age, Fire Age, Ax Age, Wolf Age . . . he turned to see that Forrester had left his station and was moving toward the door. "What now?" Sharps asked.

"Earthquake." Forrester continued to walk rapidly toward the exit. "Earthquake." He said it loudly, so that everyone could hear, and there was a rush toward the door.

Dr. Charles Sharps poured his cup almost full. He took it to the tap and ran a splash of cold water into it. It was Mocha-Java made less than an hour ago with a Melitta filter and kept in a clean Thermos. A pity to water it; but now it was just cool enough to drink. How long would it be before ships crossed major oceans again? Years, decades, forever? He might never taste coffee again. Sharps drained the cup in four swallows and dropped it onto the floor. The heavy china bounced and rolled against a console. Sharps went outside at a run.

The others had passed Forrester in the hall; the glass doors at the entrance were just closing behind him. That urgent waddle: Dan Forrester had never been athletic, but surely he could move faster than that? Did they have time to spare, then? Sharps jogged to catch up.

"Parking lot," Dan puffed. "Watch it—"

Sharps stumbled, recovered. Dan was dancing on one leg. The ground had jerked, emphatically, once. Sharps thought: Why, that wasn't bad. The buildings aren't even harmed—

"Now," Forrester said. He continued toward the parking lot. It was at the top of a long flight of concrete stairs. Dan stopped near the top, blowing hard, and Sharps got a shoulder under his armpit and managed to half-carry him the rest of the way to the top. There Dan lay down and rolled over. Sharps watched him with concern.

Forrester puffed, tried to say something and failed. He was too winded. He lifted one arm and gestured with palm down. *Sit.*

Too late. The ground danced under his feet, and Sharps sat down too hard, then found himself rolling toward the stairs. This time there was the sound of breaking glass, but when Sharps looked over the JPL complex he didn't see any obvious damage. Down below, the reporters were beginning to stream out of the Von Karman Center, but many paused after the mild quake, and some went back inside.

"Tell them . . ." puff puff. "Tell them to get out," Forrester said. "The worst one is coming—"

Charles Sharps called to the reporters. "Big shock coming! Get everyone outside!" He recognized the *New York Times* man. "Get them out!" Sharps called.

He turned to see that Forrester was on his feet and moving rapidly toward the back of the parking lot, away from the cars. He was walking as fast as Sharps had ever seen him move. "Hurry!" Sharps called to the others.

Men and women were spilling out of all the JPL buildings. Some came toward Sharps and the parking lot. Others milled about in areas between buildings, wondering where to go. Sharps gestured viciously, then looked at Forrester. Dan had reached a clear area, and was sitting down. . . .

Sharps turned and ran toward Forrester. He reached him and sprawled onto the asphalt. Nothing happened for a moment.

"First shock . . . was the ground wave . . . from the Death Valley strike," Forrester huffed. "Then . . . the Pacific strike. Don't know how long until it triggers—"

The earth groaned. Birds flew into the air, and there was an electric feeling of impending doom. Down at the end of the parking lot a group had just come to the top of the stairs and were moving toward Forrester and Sharps.

The earth groaned again. Then it roared.

"San Andreas," Forrester said. "It will let go completely. Way overdue. Hundred megatons of energy. Maybe more."

Half a dozen people had cleared the stairwell. Two came toward Sharps and Forrester. The rest sought their own cars. "Get them out of there," Forrester huffed.

"Get into the clear!" Sharps screamed. "And clear off that stairwell! Get off!"

A TV camera appeared at the top of the stairs. A man was carrying it, followed by a woman. There was a knot of people behind them. The TV crew started across the parking lot—

And the earth moved. There was time for them to curl up hugging their knees in the two or three seconds it took the quake to build strength. The earth roared again, and again, and there were other sounds, of people screaming, of falling glass and crashing concrete, and then the sound lost all form and became the shapeless chaos of nightmare. Sharps tried to sit erect and look back toward JPL, but nothing was solid. The asphalt rippled and ripped. The hot pavement slid gratingly away, throwing Sharps into a double somersault, then heaved and bucked once more, and the world was filled with sound and roaring and screams.

Finally it was over. Sharps sat and tried to focus his eyes. The world had changed. He looked up toward the towering Angeles mountains, and their skyline was different, subtly, but different. He had no time to see more. There was sound behind him, and he turned to see that part of the parking lot was gone, the rest tilted at strange angles. Many of the cars were gone, tumbled over the precipice that had developed between him and the stairs—only there weren't any stairs. They, too, had tumbled onto the lower parking lot. The remaining cars butted each other like battling beasts. Everywhere was sound: cars, buildings, rocks, all grinding together.

A Volkswagen rolled ponderously toward Sharps, like a steel tumbleweed, growing huge. Sharps screamed and tried to run. His legs wouldn't hold him. He fell, crawled, and saw the VW tumble past his heels, a mountain of painted metal. It smashed itself half flat against a Lincoln . . . and now it was only Volkswagen-sized again.

Another small car was on its back, and someone was under it, thrashing. Oh, God, it was Charlene, and there wasn't a hope of anyone getting to her. Abruptly she stopped moving. The ground continued to tremble and groan, then thrashed. More of the parking lot separated, dipped, slid slowly downhill, carrying Charlene and her killer car. Now Sharps no longer heard the roar. He was deaf. He lay flat on the shuddering ground, waiting for it to end.

The tower, the large central building of JPL, was gone. In its place there was a crumpled mass of glass, concrete, twisted metal, broken computers. The Von Karman Center was similarly in ruins. One wall had fallen, and through it Sharps saw the first unmanned lunar lander, the metal spider that had gone to the Moon to scoop up its surface. The spacecraft was helpless under the falling roof. Then the walls collapsed as well, burying the spacecraft, and burying the science press corps.

"End! When will it end?" someone was screaming. Sharps could barely hear the words.

Finally the quake began to die. Sharps stayed down. He would not tempt the fates. What remained of the parking lot was tilted downslope and bulged in the middle. Now Sharps had time to wonder who had been on the stairway behind the cameramen. Not that it mattered; they were gone, the camera people were gone; everyone who had been within fifty feet of the stairwell had vanished into the mass below, covered by the hillside and the mangled remains of cars.

The day was darkening. Visibly darkening. Sharps looked up to see why.

A black curtain was rolling across the sky. Within churning black clouds the lightning flared as dozens, scores, hundreds of flashbulbs.

Lightning flared and split a tree to their right. The instantaneous thunder was deafening, and the air smelled of ozone. More lightning crashed in the hills ahead.

"Do you know where you're going?" Tim Hamner demanded.

"No." Eileen drove on, speeding through empty, rainwashed streets. "There's a road up into the hills here somewhere. I've been up it a couple of times."

To their left and behind them were more houses, mostly intact. To the right were the Verdugo Hills, with small side streets penetrating a couple of blocks into them, each street with its "Dead End" sign. Except for the rain and lightning, everything seemed normal here. The rain hid everything not close to them, and the houses, mostly older, stucco, Spanish-style, stood without visible damage.

"Aha!" Eileen cried. She turned hard right, onto a blacktop road that twisted its way along the base of a high bluff, a protruding spur of the lightning-washed mountains ahead. The road twisted ahead, and soon they saw nothing but the hill to the right, the brooding mountains looming above and a golf course to their left. There were neither cars nor people.

They turned, turned again, and Eileen jammed on the brakes. The car skidded to a halt. It stood face-to-face with a landslide. Ten feet and more of flint and mud blocked their way.

"Walk," Tim said. He looked out at the lightning ahead and shuddered.

"The road goes a lot further," Eileen said. "Over the top of the hills, I think." She pointed to her left, at the golf course protected by its chain link fence. "Tear a hole in the fence."

"With what?" Tim demanded, but he got out. Rain soaked him almost instantly. He stood helplessly. Eileen got out on the other side and brought the trunk keys.

There was a jack, and a few flares, and an old raincoat,

oil-soaked as if it had been used to wipe the engine. Eileen took out the jack handle. "Use that. Tim, we don't have much time—"

"I know." Hamner took the thin metal rod and went over to the fence. He stood helplessly, pounding the jack handle into his right hand. The task looked hopeless. He heard the trunk lid slam, then the car door. The starter whirred.

Tim looked around, startled, but the car wasn't moving. He couldn't see Eileen's face through the driving rain and wet glass. Would she leave him here?

Experimentally he put the jack handle between the wire and a fence post and twisted. Nothing happened. He strained, throwing his weight onto the handle, and something gave. He slipped and fell against the fence, and felt his wet clothing tear as a jagged point snagged him. It cut him, and the salt on his clothes was in the wound. He hunched his shoulders against the pain and hopelessness, and stood, helpless again.

"Tim! How are you doing?"

He wanted to turn and call to her. He wanted to tell her it was no use, and that he was miserable, and he'd torn his clothes, and . . .

Instead, he crouched and inserted the jack handle again, twisting and prying at the wire, until it broke free of the post. Then again, and again, and suddenly the whole length of fence was loose there. He went to the next post and began his work.

Eileen gunned the car. The horn sounded, and she called, "Stand aside!" The car left the road and came at the fence, rammed it, tore it loose from another post and flattened it onto the grass, and the car drove over it. The car motor raced. "Get in," she called.

Tim ran for it. She hadn't stopped completely, and now it seemed she wasn't going to stop at all. He ran to catch up and tugged open the door, threw himself onto the seat. She gunned the car across the fairway, leaving deep ruts, then came to a green. She drove across it. The car tore at the carefully manicured surface.

Tim laughed. There was a note of hysteria in it.

"What?" Eileen asked. She didn't take her eyes off the grassy fairway ahead.

"I remember when some lady stepped on the Los Angeles Country Club green with spiked heels," Tim said. "The steward nearly died! I thought I understood Hammerfall, and what it meant, but I didn't, not until you drove across the greens. . . ."

She didn't say anything, and Tim stared moodily ahead

again. How many man-hours had gone to produce that perfect grassy surface? Would anyone ever again bother? Tim had another wild impulse to laughter. If there were golf clubs in the car, he could get out and tee off on a green. . . .

Eileen went completely across the golf course and back to the blacktop road up into the hills. Now they were in wilderness, high hills on either side of them. They passed a picnic ground. There were Boy Scouts there. They had a tent set up, and they seemed to be arguing with the scoutmaster. Tim opened the car window. "Stay on high ground," he shouted.

"What's happened below?" the scoutmaster asked.

Eileen slowed to a stop.

"Fires. Floods. Traffic jams," Tim said. "Nothing you'll want to go into. Not for awhile." He motioned the adult closer. "Stay up here, at least for the night."

"Our families . . ." the man said.

"Where?"

"Studio City."

"You can't get there now," Tim said. "Traffic's not moving in the valley. Roads closed, freeways down, lot of fires. The best thing you can do for your families is to stay up here where you're safe."

The man nodded. He had big brown eyes in a square, honest face. There was a stubble of red beard on his chin. "I've been telling the kids that. Julie-Ann, you hear that? Your mother knows where we are. If things were *really* bad down there, they'd send the cops after us. Best we stay here." He lowered his voice. "Lot of rebuilding to do after that quake, I guess. Many hurt?"

"Yeah," Tim said. He turned away. He couldn't look into the scoutmaster's eyes.

"We'll stay another day, then," the scoutmaster said. "They ought to have things moving again by tomorrow. Kids aren't really prepared for this rain, though. Nobody expects rain in June. Maybe we ought to go down into Burbank and stay in a house. Or a church. They'd put us up—"

"Don't," Tim said. His voice was urgent. "Not yet. Does this road go on over the top?"

"Yes." The man brought his face close to Tim's. "Why do you want to go up into that?" He waved toward the lightning that flashed on the peaks above. "Why?"

"Have to," Tim said. "You stay here. For the night, anyway. Let's go, Eileen."

She drove off without saying anything. They rounded a

bend, leaving the scoutmaster standing in the road. "I couldn't tell him either," Eileen said. "Are they safe there?"

"I think so. We seem to be pretty high."

"The top is about three thousand feet," Eileen said.

"And we're no more than a thousand below it. We're safe," Tim said. "Maybe it would be better to wait here, until the lightning stops. If it ever does stop. Then we can go on or go back. Where do we get if we go over?"

"Tujunga," Eileen said. "It's a good eighteen hundred, two thousand feet elevation. If we're safe, Tujunga should be." She continued to drive, winding further into the hills.

Tim frowned. He had never had a good sense of direction, and there were no maps in the car. "My observatory is up Big Tujunga Canyon—at least, you can get to it by going up that road. I've done it. And the observatory has food, and emergency equipment and supplies."

"Hammer Fever?" Eileen teased. "You?"

"No. It's remote up there. I've been snowbound more than once, a week at a time, more. So I keep plenty of supplies. Where are we going? Why don't you stop?"

"I'm—I don't know." She drove on, more slowly, almost crawling along. The rain had slackened off. It was still pouring down, hard for Los Angeles, unheard of for summer, but just then it was only rain, not bathtubs of water pouring out of the sky. In compensation the wind rose, howling up the canyon, screaming at them so that they were shouting at each other, but the wind was such a constant companion that by now they didn't notice.

They came around another bend, and they were on a high shelf looking south and westward. Eileen stopped the car, despite the danger of slides from above them. She turned off the motor. The wind howled, and lightning played above and ahead. The rain beat down so that the San Fernando Valley was obscured, but sometimes the wind whipped the rain in a thinner pattern and they could see blurred shapes out there. There were bright orange flares down on the valley floor. Dozens of them.

"What are those?" Eileen wondered aloud.

"Houses. Filling stations. Power-plant oil storage. Cars, homes, overturned tank trucks—anything that can burn."

"Rain and fire." She shivered, despite the warmth inside the car. The wind howled again.

Tim reached for her. She held back a moment, then came to him, her head against his chest. They sat that way, listening to the wind, watching orange flames blur through driving rain.

"We'll make it," Tim said. "The observatory. We'll get there. We may have to walk, but it's not that far. Twenty, thirty miles, no more. Couple of days if we walk. Then we'll be safe."

"No," she said. "No one will ever be safe. Not again."

"Sure we will." He was silent a moment. "I'm . . . I'm really glad you found me," he said. "I'm not much of a hero, but—"

"You're doing fine."

They were quiet again. The wind continued to whistle, but gradually they became aware of another sound—low, rumbling, building in volume, like a jet plane, ten jets, a thousand jets roaring for takeoff. It came from the south; and as they watched, some of the orange flares ahead of them went out. They didn't flicker and die; they went out suddenly, snuffed from view in an instant. The noise grew, rushing closer.

"Tsunami," Tim said. His voice was low, wondering. "It really did come. A tidal wave, hundreds, maybe thousands of feet high—"

"Thousands?" Eileen said nervously.

"We'll be all right. The waves can't move far across land. It takes a lot of energy to move across land. A lot. Listen. It's coming up the old Los Angeles River bed. Not across the Hollywood Hills. Anyone up there is probably safe. God help the people in the valley. . . ."

And they sat, holding each other, while lightning played around and above them, and they heard the rolling thunder of lightning and above the thunder the roar of the tsunami, as one by one the bright orange fires went out in the San Fernando Valley.

■

Between Baja California and the west coast of Mexico is a narrow body of water whose shoreline is like the two prongs of a tuning fork. The Sea of Cortez is as warm as bathwater and as calm as a lake, a playground for swimmers and sailors.

But now the pieces of Hamner-Brown's nucleus sink through Earth's atmosphere like tiny blue-white stars. One drops toward the mouth of the Sea of Cortez until it touches water between the prongs.

Then water explodes away from a raw orange-white crater. The tsunami moves south in an expanding crescent; but, confined between two shorelines, the wave moves north like the wave front down a shotgun barrel. Some water spills east into Mexico; some west across Baja to the Pacific. Most of the water leaves the northern end of the Sea of Cortez as a moving white-peaked mountain range.

The Imperial Valley, California's second largest agricultural region, might as well have been located in the mouth of a shotgun.

The survivors crawled toward each other across the broken JPL parking lot. A dozen men, five women, all dazed, crawling together. There were more people below, in the wreckage of the buildings. They were screaming. Other survivors went to them. Sharps stood dazed. He wanted to go below and help, but his legs wouldn't respond.

The sky was boiling with clouds. They raced in strange patterns, and if there was daylight coming through the swirling ink, it was much dimmer than the continual flash of lightning everywhere.

Wonderingly, Sharps heard children crying. Then a voice calling his name.

"Dr. Sharps! Help!"

It was Al Masterson. The janitor in Sharps's building. He had gathered two other survivors. They stood beside a station wagon that rested against a big green Lincoln. The station wagon was tilted at a forty-five-degree angle, two wheels on the blacktop, two above it. The crying children were inside it. "Hurry, please, sir," Masterson called.

That broke the spell. Charlie Sharps ran across the parking lot to help. He and Masterson and two other men strained at the heavily loaded station wagon until it tilted back to vertical. Masterson threw open the door. There were two young faces, tearstained, and an older one, June Masterson. She wasn't crying.

"They're all right," she was saying. "I told you they were all right. . . ."

The station wagon was packed to the roof and beyond. Food, water, cans of gas lashed to its tailgate; clothing, shotgun and ammunition; the stuff of survival, with the children and their blankets fitted in somehow. Masterson was telling everyone who would listen, "I heard you say it, the Hammer might hit us, I heard . . ."

A corner of Sharps's mind giggled quietly to itself. Masterson the janitor. He'd heard just enough from the engineers, and of course he hadn't understood the odds against. So: He'd been ready. Geared to survive, with his family waiting in the parking lot, just in case. The rest of us knew too much. . . .

Family.

"What do we do, Dr. Sharps?" Masterson asked.

"I don't know." Sharps turned to Forrester. The pudgy astrophysicist hadn't been able to help right the car. He seemed to be lost in thought, and Sharps turned away again. "I guess we do what we can for survivors—only I've got to get home!"

"Me too." There was a chorus of voices.

"But we should stay together," Sharps said. "There won't be many people you can trust—"

"Caravan," Masterson said. "We take some cars, and we all go get our families. Where do you all live?"

It turned out there was too much variety. Sharps lived nearby, in La Cañada. So did two others. The rest had homes scattered as far as Burbank and Canoga Park in the San Fernando Valley. The valley people had haunted eyes.

"I wouldn't," Forrester said. "Wait. A couple of hours . . ."

They nodded. They all knew. "Four hundred miles an hour," Hal Crayne said. A few minutes ago he'd been a geologist.

"More," Forrester said. "The tsunami will arrive about fifty minutes after Hammerfall." He glanced at his watch. "Less than half an hour."

"We can't just stand here!" Crayne shouted. He was screaming. They all were. They couldn't hear their own voices.

Then the rain came. Rain? Mud! Sharps was startled to see pellets of mud splatter onto the blacktop. Pellets of mud, hard and dry on the outside, with soft centers! They hit the cars with loud clatters. A hail of mud. The survivors scrambled for shelter: inside cars, under cars, in the wrecks of cars.

"Mud?" Sharps screamed.

"Yes. Should have thought of it," Forrester said. "Salt mud. From the sea bottom, thrown up into space, and . . ."

The strange hail eased, and they left their shelters. Sharps felt better now. "All of you who live too far to get to your homes, go down and help the survivors in the building area. The rest of us will go get our families. In caravan. We'll come back here if we can. Dan, what's our best final destination?"

Forrester looked unhappy. "North. Not low ground. The rain . . . could last for months. All the old river valleys may be filled with water. There's no place in the Los Angeles basin that's safe. And there will be aftershocks from the earthquake. . . ."

"So where?" Sharps demanded.

"The Mojave, eventually," Forrester said. He wouldn't be hurried. "But not at first, because there's nothing growing there now. Eventually—"

"Yes, but *now!*" Sharps demanded.

"Foothills of the Sierras," Forrester said. "Above the San Joaquin Valley."

"Porterville area?" Sharps asked.

"I don't know where that is. . . ."

Masterson reached into his station wagon and fished in the glove compartment. The rain was falling heavily now, and he kept the map inside the car. They stood outside, looking in at June Masterson and her children. The children were quiet. They watched the adults with awed eyes.

"Right here," Masterson said.

Forrester studied the map. He'd never been there before, but it was easy to memorize the location. "Yes. I'd say that's a good place."

"Jellison's ranch," Sharps said. "It's there! He knows me, he'll take us in. We'll go there. If we get separated, we'll meet there." He pointed on the map. "Ask for Senator Jellison's place! Now, those that aren't coming with us immediately, get down and help survivors. Al, can you get any of these other cars started?"

"Yes, sir." Masterson looked relieved. So did the others. They'd been used to taking orders from Sharps for years; and it felt right to have him in command again. They wouldn't obey him like soldiers, but they needed to be told to do what they wanted to do anyway.

"Dan, you'll come on the caravan with us," Sharps said. "You wouldn't be much use down below—"

"No," Forrester said.

"What?" Sharps was certain he'd misunderstood. The thunder was continuous, and now there was the sound of rising wind.

"Can't," Forrester said. "Need insulin."

It was then that Sharps remembered that Dan Forrester was a diabetic. "We can come by your place—"

"No," Forrester screamed. "I've got other things to do. I'd delay you."

"You've got—"

"I'll be all right," Forrester said. He turned to walk off into the rain.

"The hell you will!" Sharps screamed at Dan's retreating back. "You can't even get your car started when the battery's dead!"

Forrester didn't turn. Sharps watched his friend, knowing he'd never see him again. The others pressed around. They all wanted advice, orders, some sense of purpose, and they expected Charles Sharps to provide it. "We'll see you at the ranch!" Sharps called.

Forrester turned slightly and waved.

"Let's move out," Sharps said. "Station wagon in the middle." He looked at his tiny command. "Preston, you'll be with me in the lead car. Get that shotgun and keep it loaded." They piled into their cars and started across the broken lot, moving carefully to avoid the huge cracks and holes.

Forrester's car had survived. He'd parked it at the very top of the lot, well away from any others, well away from trees and the edge of the bluff—and he'd parked it sideways to the tilt of the hill. Sharps could just make out Forrester's lights following them down to the street. He hoped Dan had changed his mind and was following them, but when they got to the highway, he saw that Dan Forrester had turned off toward Tujunga.

■

The fire road narrowed to a pair of ruts tilted at an extreme angle, with a sloping drop of fifty feet or more to their right. Eileen fought for control of the car, then brought it to a stop. "We walk from here." She made no move to get out. The rain wasn't quite so bad now, but it was colder, and there was still continuous lightning visible all around them. The smell of ozone was strong and sharp.

"Let's go, then," Tim said.

"What's the hurry?"

"I don't know, but let's do it." Tim couldn't have explained. He wasn't sure he understood it himself. To Hamner, life was civilized, and relatively simple. You stayed out of the parts of town where money and social position weren't important, and everywhere they were, you hired people to do things, or bought the tools to do them with.

Intellectually he knew that all this was ending as he sat. Emotionally . . . well, this *couldn't* be Ragnarok. Ragnarok was supposed to kill you! The world was still here, and Tim wanted help. He wanted courteous police, briskly polite shopkeepers, civil civil servants; in short, civilization.

■

A towering wall of water sweeps eastward through the South Atlantic Ocean. Its left-hand edge passes the Cape of Good Hope, scouring lands which have been owned in turn by Hottentots, Dutch, British and Afrikaaners, sweeping up to curl at the base of Table Mountain, foaming up the wide valley to Paarl and Stellenbosch.

The right-hand edge of the wave impacts against Antarctica, breaking off glaciers ten miles long and five wide. The wave bursts through between Africa and Antarctica. When it reaches the wider expanse of the Indian Ocean the wave has lost half its force: Now it is only four hundred feet high. At four hundred and fifty miles an hour it moves toward India, Australia and the Indonesian islands.

It sweeps across the lowlands of southern India, then, focused by the narrowing Bay of Bengal, regains much of its strength and height as it breaks into the swamplands of Bangladesh. It smashes northward through Calcutta and Dacca. The waters finally come to halt at the base of the Himalayas, where they are met by the floods pouring out of the Ganges Valley. As the waters recede, the Sacred Ganges is choked with bodies.

■

They trudged through the mud, climbing steadily. The fire road went over the top of the hill in a saddle, not far below the peaks, but far enough; the lightning stayed above them.

Their shoes picked up huge gobs of mud, and soon weighed three or four times what they should. They fell in the mud and got up again, helped each other when they could, and staggered up over the top and down the other side. The world condensed into a series of steps, one step at a time, no place to stop. Tim imagined the town ahead: undamaged, with motels and hot water and electric lights and a bar that sold Chivas Regal and Michelob . . .

They reached blacktop pavement, and the going was easier.

"What time is it?" Eileen asked.

Tim pressed the button on his digital watch. "Just about noon."

"It's so dark—" She slipped on wet leaves and tumbled onto the blacktop. She didn't get up.

"Eileen . . ." Tim went over to help her.

She was sitting on the pavement, and she didn't seem hurt, but she wasn't trying to get up. She was crying, quietly.

"You've got to get up."

"Why?"

"Because I can't carry you very far."

Almost she laughed; but then her face sank into her hands and she sat huddled in the rain.

"Come on," said Tim. "It's not that bad. Maybe everything's all right up here. The National Guard will be out. Red Cross. Emergency tents." He felt it evaporating as he named it: the stuff of dreams; but he went on, desperately. "And we'll buy a car. There are car lots ahead, we'll buy a four-wheel drive and take it to the observatory, with a big bucket from Colonel Chicken sitting between us. You buying all this?"

She shook her head and laughed in a funny way and didn't get up. He bent and took her shoulders. She didn't resist, but she didn't help. Tim lifted her, got his arms under her legs and began staggering down the blacktop road.

"This is silly," Eileen said.

"Damn betcha."

"I can walk."

"Good." He let her legs drop. She stood, but she clung to him, her head against his shoulder.

Finally she let go. "I'm glad I found you. Let's get moving."

∎

"Count off," Gordie called.

"One," Andy Randall answered. The others sang out in turn: "Two." "Three." "Four." "Five," Bert Vance said. He was a little late, and glanced up nervously, but his father didn't seem to have noticed. "Six."

"And me," Gordie said. "Okay, Andy, lead off. I'll play tail-end Charlie."

They started down the trail. The cliff was less than a mile away. Twenty minutes, no more. They rounded a bend and had a magnificent view stretching eastward across the tops of the pine trees. The morning air was crystal clear; the light was . . . funny.

Gordie glanced at his watch. They'd been hiking ten minutes. He was tempted to skip his compulsory halt for bootlace adjustments. What difference would it make? Nobody would have blisters, not in another half-mile, and walking along, trying to be natural, was harder than the decision had been.

There was a bright flash to the east. Brilliant, but small. Much too bright to be lightning, and out of a clear sky? It left an afterimage that blinking couldn't get rid of.

"What was that, Dad?" Bert asked.

"Don't know. Meteor? Hold up, up in front. Time for boot adjustments."

They dropped their packs and found rocks to sit on. The bright afterimage was still there, although it was fading. Gordie couldn't look directly at his bootlaces. Then he noticed that the wind had died. The forest was deathly still.

Bright flash. Sudden stillness. Like—

The shock wave rumbled across them with a thunder of sound. A dead tree crashed somewhere above them, thrashing in final agony among its brothers. The rumbling went on a long time, with rising wind.

Atom bomb at Frenchman's Flats? Gordie wondered. Couldn't be. They'd never test anything *that* big. So what was it?

The boys were chattering. Then the ground rumbled and heaved beneath them. More trees fell.

Gordie fell onto his pack. The other boys had been shaken off their rocks. One, Herbie Robinett, seemed to be hurt. Gordie crawled toward him. The boy wasn't bleeding, and nothing was broken. Just shaken up. "Stay down!" Gordie shouted. "And watch for falling limbs and trees!"

The wind continued to rise, but it was shifting, moving around to the south, no longer coming from the east, where they'd seen the bright flash. The earth shook again.

And out there, far beyond the horizon, rising high into the stratosphere, was an ugly cloud, mushroom-shaped. It climbed on and on, roiling horribly. It was just where the bright flash had been.

One of the boys had a radio. He had it to his ear. "Nothing

but static, Mr. Vance. I keep thinking I hear something else, but I can't make out what."

"Not surprising. We almost never get anything in the mountains in daytime," Gordie said.

But I don't like that wind. And what was that thing? A piece of the comet? Probably. Gordie laughed bitterly. All that fuss about the end of the world, and it was nothing. A bright flash out there in Death Valley—or maybe it wasn't the comet at all. Frenchman's Flat was that way, a hundred and fifty miles or so. . . .

The ground had stopped shaking. "Let's move on," Gordie said. "On your feet."

He pulled on his pack. Now what? he asked himself. Can I . . . will the boys be all right without me? What's happening out there?

Nothing. Nothing but a goddam meteor. Maybe a big one. Maybe as big as that thing in Arizona, the one that made a half-mile crater. An impressive thing, and the boys saw it fall. They'll talk about it for years.

But it doesn't solve my problem. The bank examiners will still be around next Friday, and—

"Funny clouds up there," Andy Randall said. There was worry in his voice.

"Yeah, sure," Gordie said absently. Then he noticed where Andy was pointing.

Southwest. Almost due south. It was as if a pool of black ink had been poured across the sky. Huge, towering black clouds, rising higher and higher, blotting out everything . . .

And the wind was howling through the trees. More clouds, and more, seeming to form from nothing, and racing toward them at terrific velocity, faster than jet planes . . .

Gordie looked frantically along the trail. No good place to hide. "Ponchos," he shouted.

They scrabbled their rain gear out. As Gordie flipped his poncho open, the rain came like a torrent of warm bathwater. Gordie tasted salt.

Salt!

"Hammerfall," he whispered.

And the end of civilization. The paper shortages at the bank: gone, washed away. They weren't important now.

Marie? The clouds were building above Los Angeles—and it was a long way to the nearest car. Nothing he could do for her. No way to help Marie. Maybe Harvey Randall would look out for her. Right now, Gordie's problem was the boys.

"Back to Soda Springs," he shouted. It was the best place, until they found out just what was going to happen. It was sheltered, and there was a clearing and a flat.

"I want to go home!" Herbie Robinett screamed.

"Get 'em moving, Andy," Gordie called. He waved them ahead of him, ready to shove them if he had to, but he didn't. They followed Andy. Bert went past. Gordie thought he saw tears in his son's eyes. Tears through the dirty rainwater that hammered at them.

The trails will all be flooded in no time. Washed out, Gordie thought. And this warm crap will melt all the snow. The Kern's going to be up over its banks, and all the roads will be gone.

Gordie Vance suddenly threw back his head and yelled in triumph. He was going to live.

Hot Fudge Tuesdae: Three

When Adam farmed and Eve span,
   Kyrie Eleison,
Who was then the gentleman?
   Kyrie Eleison.
>   Marching song of the Black Company during
>   the Peasant Revolt, Germany, 1525

Harvey Randall had been fifteen minutes from home . . .
until Hammerfall.

It was day turned night, and the night was alive with
pyrotechnics. If daylight still leaked through the black cloud
cover, the lightning was far brighter. Hills flashed in blue-
white light and vanished, now a white sky over jagged black
skyline, now a look into the canyon on his left, now blackness
lit only by the headlamps of cars, now a nearby blast that
clenched Randall's eyelids in pain. The wipers were going
like crazy, but the rain fell faster; it all came through in a
blur. Randall had rolled down both side windows. Wet was
better than blind.

To drive in such conditions was madness, yet the traffic
was still heavy. Perhaps they were all mad. Through the
thunder and the drum of rain on metal came the bleat of
myriad horns. Cars shifted lanes without warning; they drove
in the oncoming lanes, and butted their way back into line
when oncoming lights faced them down.

Randall's TravelAll was too big to challenge. Where a
landslide had blocked half the road and a coward had stopped
to let oncoming traffic through, Randall drove the TravelAll
over the slide—it tilted badly, but held—and in front of the

coward and straight at the traffic, and butted the lead car until it backed up.

He didn't see the people who blocked his way. He saw only barriers: mudslides, breaks in the road, cars. He kept wondering if the house had collapsed, with Loretta inside. Or if Loretta, in blind panic, was about to come looking for him in the car. She'd never survive alone, and they'd never link up. Hell, it was almost an hour since Hammerfall!

The looters would come sooner or later. Loretta knew where to find his gun, but would she use it? Randall turned onto Fox Lane in floodwater that was hubcap-deep, drove to the end, used the remote. All the houses were dark.

The garage door didn't open.

But the front door was wide open.

The looting couldn't have started this soon, Randall thought, and he made himself believe it. Just for drill, then, he took the flashlight and handgun with him, and he left the TravelAll in a roll and immediately rolled back under the car, and studied the situation from there.

The house looked dead. And rain was blowing in the door.

He rolled out and sprinted and pulled up alongside the door. He still hadn't used the flash. First person he saw, he'd flick the beam in her face. It would be Loretta, coming to close the door, and if she had his gun he was going to do a swan dive off the steps, because the way he was behaving she'd be scared enough to shoot.

He poked head and flash around the doorjamb. Lightning only made confusing shadows. Thunder drowned out other sounds.

He flicked on the flashlight.

It jumped at him; it hit him straight in the face. Loretta was lying on the floor, face-up. Her face and chest were a shapeless wet ruin, the kind left by a shotgun blast. Kipling, headless, was a mess of blood and fur beside her.

He walked inside, and he couldn't feel his legs. Walking on pillows, they call it, the last stage of exhaustion before collapse. He knelt, set the gun down—it never occurred to him that someone might be here—and reached for Loretta's throat. He drew his hand back, with a rippling shudder, and reached for her wrist instead. There was no pulse. Thank God. What would he have done?

They hadn't raped her. As if it mattered now. But they hadn't taken the jewelry off her wrists either. And though the drawers from the buffet had been pulled out and dumped, the good silver was still lying there.

Why? What could they have wanted?

Randall's thoughts were slow and confused; they took strange paths. A part of him believed none of this: not the body of his wife, flickering in lightning, in and out of existence; not the weird weather, nor the earthquakes, nor the translation of a great light show into the end of the world. When he got up and went into the bedroom for something to cover Loretta, it was because he had been staring at her until he couldn't stand it anymore.

The dresser drawers were all pulled out. Randall saw cuff links and a gold ring and Loretta's amethyst brooch and matching earrings in the wreckage. The closets had been rifled too. Where were . . . ? Yes, they'd taken both of his overcoats. He waded through the wreckage.

The bed was piled high with senseless things: panty hose, bottles of cosmetics, lipsticks. He swept it to the floor, pulled the bedclothes off the bed and dragged them behind him into the hall. Something echoed in his mind . . . but he shied from it. He covered Loretta. He sat down again.

At no time had he wondered if "they" were still here. But he tried to picture the people who had done this. He? She? All men, all women, a mixed group? What could they have *wanted*? They'd left silver and jewelry, but taken . . . overcoats.

Randall shambled into the kitchen.

They'd found and taken the beef jerky, and his stock of vitamins, and all of his canned soup. Now he saw it, and he kept looking. They'd taken his canned gasoline from the garage. They'd taken his guns. They'd been ready, they'd planned this! At the moment of Hammerfall they had already known what they would do. Had they picked his house at random? Or his street? They could have raided every house on the block.

He was back in the entrance hall, with Loretta. "You wanted me to stay," he told her. More words clogged in his throat; he shook his head and went into the bedroom.

He was tired to death. He stood beside the bed, staring at what had been on the bed. This was what didn't make sense. Panty hose still in the packages. Shampoo, hair conditioner, skin conditioner, nail polish, a couple of dozen large bottles. Lipsticks, eyebrow pencils, Chap Sticks, emery boards, new boxes of curlers . . . scores of items. If he could figure this out, maybe he'd know who. He could go after them. He still had the handgun.

Even in his stupor he didn't really believe it. They were

275

gone, and he was here with Loretta. He sat down on the bed and stared at Loretta's hairbrush and dark glasses.

. . . Oh.

Of course. The Hammer had fallen, and Loretta had started packing her survival kit. The things she couldn't live without. Then the killers had come. And killed her. And left behind as garbage the lipsticks and eyebrow pencils and panty hose Loretta couldn't face life without. But they'd taken the suitcase.

Harvey rolled over on his belly and hid his face in his arms. Thunder and rain roared in his ears, drowning thoughts he wanted drowned.

He was aware that there was someone looking at him. The thunder went on and on; he couldn't have heard a noise. But there were eyes on him, and he remembered not to move, and then he remembered why. When he moved, it would have to be suddenly, and—he'd left the gun sitting beside Loretta. Oh, the hell with it. He rolled over.

"Harv?"

He didn't answer.

"Harv, it's Mark. My God, man, what happened?"

"Don't know. Raiders."

He had almost dozed off when Mark spoke again. "You all right, Harv?"

"I wasn't here. I was interviewing a goddam professor at UCLA and I was in a traffic jam and I was . . . I wasn't here. Leave me alone."

Mark shifted from one foot to the other. He wandered around the bedroom, looking into closets. "Harv, we've got to get out of here. You and your damn hot fudge sundae. The whole L.A. basin is under the ocean, you know that?"

"She wanted me to stay. She was scared," said Harvey. He tried to think of some way to make Mark go away. "Get out and leave me alone."

"Can't, Harv. We have to bury your old lady. Got a shovel?"

"Oh." Harvey opened his eyes. The room was still lit by surrealistic strobe lighting. Funny he didn't notice the thunder anymore. He got up. "There's one out in the garage, I think. Thanks."

They dug in the backyard. Harvey wanted to do it all, but he ran out of energy quickly, and Mark took over. The shovel made squishing sounds; the hard adobe was soaking faster than Mark could dig. Squish. Plop. Squish. Plop. And rolling thunder.

"Time?" Mark called. He was standing in a waist-deep hole, his boots nearly underwater.

"Noon."

Harvey looked around, startled at the voice from behind him. Joanna was perched above them on the slope, rain running down her face. She held a shotgun, and she looked very alert.

"Deep enough," Mark said. "Stay here, Harv. Jo, let's go inside. Give Harv the shotgun."

"Right." She came down from the slope, a tiny figure with a big shotgun. She handed it to Harvey without a word.

He stood in the rain, standing guard by looking down into an empty grave. If someone had come up behind him, he wouldn't have noticed. Or cared. Except that he did notice Mark and Joanna.

Big Mark and tiny Joanna, carrying a blanketed bundle. Harvey went over to help her carry, but he was too late. They lowered her into the grave. Water flowed up and around the blanket. It was an electric blanket, Harvey saw. Loretta's electric blanket. She could never stay warm enough at night.

Mark took the shovel. Joanna took the shotgun. Mark shoveled steadily. Squish. Plop. Harvey tried to think of something to say, but there weren't any words. Finally, "Thanks."

"Yeah. You want to read any words?"

"I ought to," Harvey said. He started toward the house, but he couldn't go in.

"Here. This was in the bedroom," Joanna said. She took a small book out of her pocket.

It was Andy's confirmation prayer book; Loretta must have included that in her survival kit. She would have. Harvey opened it to the prayers for the dead. Rain soaked the page before he could read it, but he found a line, half read and half remembered. "Eternal rest grant her, O Lord, and let light perpetual shine upon her." He couldn't see any more. After a long time Mark and Joanna led Harvey into the house.

They sat at the kitchen table. "We don't have long," Mark said. "I think we saw your raiders."

"They killed Frank Stoner," Joanna added.

"Who?" Harvey demanded. "What did they look like? Can we track the bastards?"

"Tell you later," Mark said. "First we get packed up and moving."

"You'll tell me now."

"No."

Joanna had rested the shotgun against the table. Harvey picked it up, calmly, and checked the loads. He pulled one outside hammer back. His firearms training was excellent: He didn't point it at anyone. "I want to know," Harvey Randall said.

"They were bikers," Joanna said quickly. "Half a dozen of them riding escort with a big blue van. We saw them turn out of Fox Lane."

"Those bastards," Harvey said. "I know where they live. Short side street, half a mile from here. The street's half a block long. They repainted the sign to read 'Snow Mountain.'" He stood.

"They won't be there now," Mark said. "They went north, toward Mulholland."

"Frank and Mark and I," Joanna said. "We had our bikes."

"They were coming out of your street," Mark said. "I wanted to know what was happening in there. I stopped and held up my hand, you know, the way bikers stop each other for a friendly talk. And one of the sons of bitches blasted at me with a shotgun!"

"And they missed Mark and hit Frank," Joanna said. "Frank went right over the edge. If the shotgun didn't kill him, the fall did. The bikers kept on going. We didn't know what to do, so we came here as fast as we could."

"Jesus," Harvey said. "I got here half an hour before you. They were here, somewhere. Right near here, while I was . . . while . . ."

"Yeah," Joanna said. "We'll know them if we see them again. Big bikes. Chopped, but not much. And murals on the van. We'll know them."

"Never saw that gang before," Mark added. "No way we can catch up with them just now. Harv, we can't stay here. The L.A. basin's flooded, everybody down there is dead from the tsunami, but there must be a million people in the hills around here, and there sure ain't enough for a million people to eat. There's got to be a better place to go."

"Frank wanted to head for the Mojave," Joanna said. "But Mark thought we ought to look in on you. . . ."

Harvey said nothing. He put the shotgun down and stared

at the wall. They were right. He couldn't catch the bike crew, not now, and he was very tired.

"They leave anything at all?" Mark demanded.

Harvey didn't answer.

"We'll do a search anyway," Mark said. "Jo, you take the house. I'll go the rounds outside, garage, everything. Only, we can't leave the TravelAll by itself. Come on, Harv." He took Harvey's arm and pulled him to his feet. Mark was surprisingly strong. Harvey made no resistance. Mark led him to the TravelAll and put him in the passenger seat. He put the Olympic target pistol in Harvey's lap. Then he locked all the doors, leaving Harvey sitting inside, still staring at the rain.

"He going to be all right?" Joanna asked.

"Don't know. But he's ours," Mark said. "Come on, let's see what we can find."

Mark found Harvey's Chlorox bottles of water in the garage. There were other things. Sleeping bags, wet, but serviceable; evidently the bikers had their own and didn't bother. Stupid, Mark thought. Harv's Army Arctic was better than any the bikers would have.

After awhile he brought his salvage to the TravelAll and opened the back. Then he got the small dirt bikes he and Joanna had ridden and brought them around. He started to ask Harvey to help, but instead found a heavy two-by-eight and used it as a ramp. With Joanna's help he wrestled one of the bikes into the back, and piled stuff in on top of it.

"Harv, where's Andy?" Mark said finally.

"Safe. Up in the mountains. With Gordie Vance. . . . Marie!" Harvey shouted. He jumped out of the car and ran toward Gordie's house. Then he stopped. The front door was open. Harvey stood there, afraid to go in. What if . . . what if they'd been in Gordie's place while Harvey was mooning over Loretta? Jesus, what a goddam useless bastard I am. . . .

Mark went into the Vance house. He came out a few minutes later. "Looted. But nobody home. No blood. Nothing." He went to the garage and tried to open the door. It came open easily; the lock was broken. When it swung up, the garage was empty. "Harv, what kind of car did your buddy have?"

"Caddy," Harvey said.

"Then she left, 'cause there's no car here and no Caddy with the bikers. You get back and watch the TravelAll.

There's more of your stuff we'll need. Or come help carry."

"In a minute." Harvey went back to the car and stood, thinking. Where would Marie Vance go? She was his responsibility; Gordie was taking care of Harvey's boy, Gordie's wife would be Harvey's lookout. Only Harvey didn't have a clue as to where Marie might be—

Yes he did. Los Angeles Country Club. Governor's fund-raising thingy. Crippled children. Marie was on the board. She'd have been there for Hammerfall.

And if she hadn't got back here by now, she wasn't coming back. Marie wasn't Harvey's responsibility anymore.

Mark came out of the house, and Harvey was finally startled. Mark was carrying something . . . OhmyGod. Carrying five thousand dollars' worth of Steuben crystal whale, Loretta's wedding present from her family. A couple of years ago Loretta had thrown Mark out of the house for picking it up.

Mark got the whale to the van without dropping it. He wrapped it in sheets and pillowcases and spare blankets.

"What's all that for?" Harvey asked. He pointed to the whale, and the skin cream, and Kleenex, and the remains of Loretta's survival kit. And other things.

"Trade goods," Mark said. "Your paintings. Some luxury items. If we find something better, we dump the lot, but we might as well be carrying *something*. Jesus, Harv, I'm glad your head's working again. We're about loaded up. Want to get in, or do you want to take another look through the house?"

"I can't go back in there—"

"Right. Okay." He raised his voice. "Jo, let's move it."

"Right." She appeared from out of a hedge, soaking wet, still holding the shotgun.

"You up to driving, Harv?" Mark demanded. "It's a big car for Joanna to handle."

"I can drive."

"Fine. I'll be outrider with the bike. Give me the pistol, and Jo keeps the shotgun. One thing, Harv. Where are we going?"

"I don't know," Harvey said. "North. I'll think of something once we get started."

"Right."

The motorcycle could hardly be heard over the roar of the thunder. They drove out, north toward Mulholland, along the same route the bikers had taken, and Harvey kept hoping. . . .

It rained. Dan Forrester saw his path in split-second flashes when the frenetic wipers disturbed the flood of water across his windshield. The rain ate the light of his headlamps before the light could reach the road. Continuous lightning gave more light, but the rain scattered it into flashing white murk.

Rivers ran across the twisting mountain road. The car plowed through them.

In the valleys it must be . . . well, he would learn soon enough. There were preparations he must make first.

Charlie Sharps would know sooner.

Dan worried for Charlie. Charlie's chances weren't poor, but he should not have been traveling with that loaded station wagon. It was too obviously worth stealing. But Masterson might have packed guns, too.

Even if they reached the ranch, would Senator Jellison let them in? Ranch country, high above the floods. If they accepted everyone who came, their food would be gone in a day, their livestock the next. They might let Charlie Sharps in, alone. They probably would not require the services of Dan Forrester, Ph.D., ex-astrophysicist. Who would?

Dan was surprised to find that he'd driven home. He zapped the garage door and it opened. Huh! He still had electricity. That wouldn't last. He left the door open. Inside, he turned on some lights, then set out a great many candles. He lit two.

The house was small. There was one big room, and the walls of that room were bookshelves, floor to ceiling. Dan's dining table was piled high with his equipment. He had bought his fair share of freeze-dried foods while they existed, but Dan had thought further than that. He had carried home far more than his share of Ziploc Bags and salad-size Baggies, insect spray and mothballs. The table was full. He set to work on the floor.

He whistled as he worked. Spray a book with insect spray, drop it in a bag, add some mothballs and seal it. Put it in another bag and seal it. Another. The packages piled up on the floor, each a book sealed in four plastic envelopes. Presently he got up to put on some gloves. He came back with a fan and set it blowing past his ears from behind. That ought to keep the insecticide off his hands and out of his lungs.

When the pile on the floor got too big, he moved. And when the second pile was as high as the first, he stood up carefully. His joints were stiff. His feet hurt. He moved his legs to build circulation. He started coffee in the kitchen. The radio gave him nothing but static, so he started a stack of records going. There was now room at the kitchen table. He resumed work there.

The two piles merged into one.

The lights went out, the Beatles' voices deepened and slowed and stopped. Dan was suddenly immersed in darkness and sounds he'd been ignoring: rolling thunder, the scream of wind and the roar of rain attacking the house. Water had begun to drip from a corner of the ceiling.

He got coffee in the kitchen, then moved around the library lighting candles. Hours had passed. The forgotten coffee had already been heated too long. Four-fifths of the shelves were still full, but most of the right books were in bags.

Dan walked along the bookshelves. Weariness reinforced his deep melancholy. He had lived in this house for twelve years, but it was twice since that long since he'd read *Alice in Wonderland* and *The Water Babies* and *Gulliver's Travels*. These books would rot in an abandoned house: *Dune; Nova; Double Star; The Corridors of Time; Cat's Cradle; Half Past Human; Murder in Retrospect; Gideon's Day; The Red Right Hand; The Trojan Hearse; A Deadly Shade of Gold; Conjure Wife; Rosemary's Baby; Silverlock; King Conan.* He'd packed books not to entertain, nor even to illustrate philosophies of life, but to rebuild civilization. Even Dole's *Habitable Planets for Man* . . .

Dammit, no! Dan tossed *Habitable Planets for Man* on the table. Fat chance that the next incarnation of NASA would need it before it turned to dust, but so what? He added more: *Future Shock; Cults of Unreason;* Dante's *Inferno; Tau Zero* . . . stop. Fifteen minutes later he had finished. There were no more bags.

He drank coffee that was still warm, and forced himself to rest before he tackled the heavy work. His watch said it was ten at night. He couldn't tell.

He wheeled a wheelbarrow in from the garage. It was brand-new, the labels still on it. He resisted the temptation to overload it. He donned raincoat, boots, hat. He wheeled the books out through the garage.

Tujunga's modern sewage system was relatively new. The territory was dotted with abandoned septic tanks, and one of these was behind Dan Forrester's house. It was uphill. You can't have everything.

The wind screamed. The rain tasted both salty and gritty. The lightning guided him, but badly. Dan wrestled the wheelbarrow uphill, looking for the septic tank. He finally found it, full of rain because he'd removed the lid yesterday evening.

The books went in in handfuls. He pushed them into the aged sewage with a plumber's helper, gently. Before he left he broke open an emergency flare and left it on the upended lid.

He made his second trip in a bathing suit. The warm lashing rain was less unpleasant than soaked and sticky clothes. The third trip he wore the hat. He almost fainted coming back. That wouldn't do. He'd better have a rest. He took off the wet suit and stretched out on the couch, pulled a blanket over himself . . . and fell deeply asleep.

He woke in a pandemonium of thunder and wind and rain. He was horribly stiff. He got to his feet an inch at a time, and kept moving toward the kitchen, talking encouragement to himself. Breakfast first, then back to work. His watch had stopped. He didn't know if it was day or night.

Fill the wheelbarrow half full, no more. Wheel it through slippery mud, uphill. Next trip, remember to take another flare. Dump the books by armfuls, then push them down into the old sewage. Unlikely that anyone, moron or genius, would look for such a treasure here, even if he knew it existed. The smell hardly bothered him; but these hurricane winds couldn't last forever, and then the trove would be doubly safe. Back for another load . . .

Once he slipped, and slid a fair distance downhill through the mud with the empty wheelbarrow tugging him along. He crossed just enough sharp rocks to dissuade him from trying it again.

Then: last load. Finished. He wrestled with the lid, rested, tried again. He'd had a hell of a time getting it off, and he had a hell of a time getting it back on. Then downhill with the empty barrow. In a day his tracks would be flooded away. He thought of burying the last evidence of his project —the wheelbarrow—but just the thought of all that work made him hurt all over.

He dried himself with all the towels in the bathroom. Why not? He used the same towels to dry the rain gear. He got more from the linen closet. He stuffed hand towels into the boots before he put them in the car, with the rain-coat and the hat and more dry towels. The old house leaked now; he wondered if the old car would too. Ultimately it wouldn't matter. Ultimately he would have to abandon the car and set out on foot, in the rain, carrying a backpack for the first time in his life. He'd be safe, or dead, long before this rain began to think about stopping.

Into the car went the new backpack he'd packed day before yesterday, including a hypo and some insulin. There were two more such medical packages elsewhere in the car, because someone might steal the whole backpack. Or someone might steal the hypos . . . but surely they would leave him *one*.

The car was an ancient heap, and nothing in it would attract thieves. He'd included a few items to buy his life, if and when it could be bought. There was one really valuable item; it would look like trash to the average looter, but it might get him to safety.

Daniel Forrester, Ph.D., was a middle-aged man with no useful profession. His doctorate would never again be worth as much as a cup of coffee. His hands were soft, he weighed too much, he was a diabetic. Friends had told him that he often underestimated his own worth; well, that was bad too, because it restricted his bargaining ability. He knew how to make insulin. It took a laboratory and the killing of one sheep per month.

Yesterday Dan Forrester had become an expensive luxury.

What was in his backpack was something else again. It was a book, wrapped like the others: Volume Two of *The Way Things Work*. Volume One was in the septic tank.

■

Harvey Randall saw the white Cadillac coming toward him. For a moment it didn't register. Then he jammed on the brakes so hard that Joanna was thrown forward against the restraining belts. The shotgun clattered hard against the dash. "You gone crazy?" she yelled, but Harvey had already opened the door and was running out into the street.

He waved his arms frantically. God! She had to see him! "Marie!" he shouted.

The Cadillac slowed, halted. Harvey ran up to it.

Incredibly, Marie Vance was unruffled. She wore a Gernreich original, a simple low-cut summer dress of white linen with a golden thread woven into it. Gold earrings and a small diamond pendant on a gold chain set it off perfectly. Her dark hair was coming out of place from the damp, but it wasn't long hair and had never been fully curled; even now she looked as if she'd merely been at the Country Club all day and was going home to change into evening clothes.

Harvey looked at her in astonishment. She eyed him calmly. His dislike of her boiled up inside him. He wanted to scream at her, to ruffle her. Didn't she realize . . . ?

"How did you get here?" he demanded.

When she answered, he was ashamed of himself. Marie Vance spoke calmly; too calmly. There was an undertone of unnatural effort in her voice. "I came up the ridge. There were cars in the way, but some men moved them. I went— Why do you want to know how I got here, Harvey?"

He laughed, at himself, at the world, and she was frightened at his laughter. He could see the fear come into her eyes.

Mark drove up on the motorcycle. He looked at the Cadillac, then at Marie. He didn't whistle. "Your neighbor?" he asked.

"Yes. Marie, you'll have to come with us. You can't stay at your place—"

"I've no intention of staying at my place," she said. "I'm going to find my son. And Gordie," she added, after a tiny pause. She looked down at her gold-colored sandals. "When I get some clothes . . . Harvey, where is . . . ?" Before she could finish she saw the pain, then the numbness in Harvey's eyes. "Loretta?" she said, her voice low and wondering.

Harvey said nothing. Mark, behind him, shook his head slowly. His eyes met Marie's. She nodded.

Harvey Randall turned away. He stood in the rain, saying nothing, looking at nothing.

"Leave the Caddy and get in the TravelAll," Mark said.

"No." Marie tried to smile. "Please, can't you wait until I get some clothes? Harvey—"

"He's not making decisions just now," Mark said. "Look, there'll be clothes. Not much food, but plenty of clothes."

"I have perfectly good outdoor equipment at home." Marie was firm. She knew how to talk to employees, Gordie's or Harvey's. "And boots that fit. I am very hard to fit. You can't tell me that ten minutes will make that much difference."

"It'll take longer than ten minutes, and we don't have any time at all," Mark said.

"It certainly will take longer if we stand here talking about it." Marie started the car. She began moving forward, slowly. "Please wait for me," she said, and drove away, south.

"Jesus," Mark said. "Harv? What. . .?" He let his question stay unfinished. Harvey Randall wasn't making decisions just now. "Get in the goddam car, Harv!" Mark ordered.

The bark in Mark's voice moved Harvey toward the TravelAll. He started to get into the driver's seat. Mark growled, "Joanna, take the bike. I'll drive."

"Where . . . ?"

"Back to Harvey's place. I guess. Hell, I don't know what we ought to do. Maybe we ought to just go on."

"We can't leave her," Joanna said firmly. She got out and took the bike. Mark shrugged and climbed into the TravelAll. He managed to turn in a drive and started back the way they'd come, cursing all the way.

When they reached the cul-de-sac, Marie Vance was sitting on her front porch. She wore trousers of an expensive artificial fabric. They were cut in a rugged square pattern and looked very durable. She wore a cotton blouse and a wool Pendleton shirt over it. She was lacing medium-height hiking boots over wool socks. A blanket lay beside her. The blanket was lumpy.

Joanna braked the motorcycle on the lawn. Mark got out and joined her. He stared at Marie, then back at Joanna. "Goddam, that's the quickest change I've ever seen. She could be useful."

"Depends on for what," Marie said evenly. "Who are you two, and what's wrong with Harvey?" She went on lacing her boots.

"His wife was killed. Same outfit that broke into your place," Mark said. "Listen, where were you going in that Caddy? Is your husband with Andy Randall?"

"Yes, of course," Marie said. "Andy and Burt are up there. With Gordie." She tied the boot and stood. "Poor Loretta. She—oh, damn it. Will you tell me your names?"

"Mark. This is Joanna. I worked for Harv—"

"Yes," Marie said. She'd heard about Mark. "Hello. You're staying with Harvey, then?"

"Sure—"

"Then let's go. Please put this bundle in the car. I'll be right out."

Hard as fucking nails, Mark thought. Coldest bitch I ever

saw. He took the blanket. It was lumpy with clothing and other objects. Marie came out with a plastic travel bag, the kind used to hang clothes when carried on board an airplane. There wasn't a lot of room in the back of the TravelAll, but she was careful about how she laid it, smoothing out wrinkles.

"What's all that?" Mark demanded.

"Things I'll need. I'm ready now."

"Can you drive Harv's buggy?"

"On roads," Marie said. "I've never tried to drive except on roads. But I can handle a stick shift."

"Good. You drive. It's too big for Joanna."

"I can manage."

"Sure, Jo, but you don't have to," Mark said. "Let Miz—"

"Marie."

"Let Miz Marie—"

She laughed. Hard. "It's just Marie. And I'll drive. Do you have maps? I don't have a good map. I know the boys are up near the southern edge of Sequoia National Park, but I'm not sure how to get there." Dressed in trousers and wool shirt, thin nylon jacket she'd brought from the house, hiking boots, she looked smaller than Mark remembered, and somehow less competent. Mark had no time to wonder why.

She'll have to do, Mark thought. "I'll lead on the bike. Joanna will ride shotgun in the car. I think we ought to put Harv in the back seat. Maybe if he gets some sleep his brain will turn on again. Christ, I never saw a guy go to pieces like that before. It's like he killed her himself." Mark saw Marie's eyes widen slightly. To hell with that, he thought. He went to the bike and kicked it into life.

They went back out, turned north again. The road was deserted. Mark wondered where to go now. He could ask Harv, but would he get the right answer, and how would he know if he did? Why the hell is he so broke up about it, Mark wondered. She wasn't much wife anyway. Never went anywhere with Harv. Good-looker, but not much of a companion. Why get so broke up? If Mark had to bury Joanna he'd hate it, but it wouldn't break him apart. He'd still function, and he'd turn a glass over for her next time he had a drink—and Harv had always been tough.

Mark glanced at his watch. Getting late. Time to move fast, through what was left of Burbank and the San Fernando Valley. How? If the freeways weren't down they'd be packed with cars. No good. He thought of routes, and wished Harvey's head was working again, but it wasn't and it was up to Mark to lead. When he reached Mulholland he turned left.

The horn sounded behind him. Marie had stopped at the intersection. "This isn't the way!" she shouted.

"Sure it is. Come on!"

"No."

God damn it. Mark drove back to the TravelAll. Marie and Joanna sat tensely in the front seat. The shotgun was poised in Joanna's hands, pointing upward; Marie sat with one arm carelessly near the gun. She was a lot bigger than Joanna.

"What is this?" Mark demanded.

"The boys. We are going to find our boys," Marie said. "And they are east of us, not west."

"Hell, I know that," Mark shouted. "This is the best way. Stay on high ground. We get across the valley on Topanga, stay along the Santa Susanna hills and go up through the canyons. That keeps us off the freeways and out of the passes where everybody else will be."

Marie frowned, trying to imagine a map of the L.A. basin. Then she nodded. That route would take them to Sequoia. She started the car moving again.

Mark roared on ahead. As he drove he muttered to himself. Frank Stoner had said the Mojave was the place to be. Stoner knew everything. It was good enough for Mark. It was a place to go, and once there they could figure out what to do next. It was a destination.

But Harv would want to get his kid out. And that Vance woman wanted hers. Funny she barely mentioned her husband. Maybe they didn't get along. Mark remembered Marie as he'd first seen her. Class. Lots of it. That might be interesting stuff.

They drove on through the rain, across the backbone of Los Angeles, and the rain kept them from seeing the destruction in the valleys to either side. The roads were clear of traffic, and the TravelAll got over the rapidly building piles of mud wherever the road dipped below the ridgeline. They were making miles, and Mark was pleased.

Randall dozed and woke, dozed and woke. The car seat jolted and tilted and jerked. Thunder and rain roared in his ears. His own ghastly memories kept pulling him almost awake. When lightning flashed he saw it again, his strobe-lit living room, crystal and silver intact, dog and wife dead on the Kashdan rug. . . . When voices came he thought he was hearing his own thoughts:

"Yes, they were very close . . . she was completely dependent on him. . . ."

The voices faded in and out. Once he was aware that the car had stopped, and there were three voices speaking in a tangle, but they might have been inside his head too.

"Wife is dead . . . wasn't there . . . yes, she said she was going to ask him to stay home . . . lost his house and his job and everything he owned . . . not just his job, but whole profession. There won't be any more television documentaries for a thousand years. Jesus, Mark, you'd be a basket case too."

"I know, but . . . didn't expect . . . curl up and die."

Curl up and die, Randall thought. Yeah. He curled tighter in the car seat. The car began moving again and it jolted him. He whimpered.

Tuesday Afternoon

Unhappily where matters as basic as territorial defense are concerned, our higher brain centers are all too susceptible to the urgings of our lower ones. Intellectual control can help us just so far, but no further. In the last resort it is unreliable, and a single, unreasoned, emotional act can undo all the good it has achieved.

Desmond Morris, *The Naked Ape*

For two hours the Earth had turned, while Hammerlab made one circle and a fraction more. Europe and West Africa had moved from sunset to night.

Perhaps they were all afraid to speak. Rick knew he was. If he spoke, what would come out? Johnny's ex-wife and children had not been in Texas. Rick hated him for it: a shameful secret. He watched the turning Earth in silence.

It was hot in Hammerlab. Sweat didn't run in free fall; it stayed where it formed. When Rick remembered he mopped it away with the soggy cloth clutched in his left hand. When tears formed they covered the eyes like thickening lenses. Blinking only distorted the lenses. They had to be mopped away; and then he saw.

Orange holes glowed on the dark Earth, like cigarettes poked through the back of a map. Hard to tell where each glowing spot was. City lights had disappeared across Europe, covered by clouds, or simply gone. Sea looked like land. Rick had watched land become sea in places: down the American East Coast, and across Florida, and deep into Texas. Texas. Could an Army helicopter move faster than a wall of water? But the winds! No, she was dead. . . .

But he'd seen the strikes in daylight, and Rick remembered.

The glow in the Mediterranean had died away. The smaller Baltic strike had been quenched almost immediately.

Much bigger strikes in the mid-Atlantic still showed. You saw only a diffuse pearly glow until Hammerlab was right above one. Then you looked down into the clear center of the tremendous hurricane: down through a clear pillar of live steam, into an orange-white glare. Three of these, and they were much smaller now. The sea was returning.

Four small bright craters scattered across the Sudan, and three in Europe, and a much larger one near Moscow, still shed their orange-white light back to space.

Johnny Baker sighed and thrust himself back from the window. He cleared his throat and said, "All right. We have things to discuss."

They looked at him as if he had interrupted a eulogy. Johnny went doggedly on. "We can't use the Apollo. That big Pacific strike was practically on our recovery fleet. The Apollo's built for sea landings, and the sea . . . all the oceans . . . hell . . ."

"You must beg a ride home," Pieter Jakov said, nodding. "Yes. We have room. Accept our hospitality."

Leonilla Malik said, "We have no home. Where shall we go?"

"Moskva is not all of the Soviet Union," Pieter said gently, reprovingly.

"Isn't it?"

Rick was giving him no help. He was framed in the window, and Johnny saw only his back. "Glaciers," Johnny said. Yes, he had their attention. "There was a strike above Russia, in the . . . ?"

"Kara Sea. We did not see it. It would have been too far north. We only infer it from the way the clouds swept down."

"The clouds swept down, right. That had to be an ocean strike. The clouds will keep coming down across Russia till the crater on the seabed is quenched. They'll dump tens of millions of tons of snow all across the continent. White clouds and white snow. Any sunlight that falls will be reflected back to space for the next couple of hundred years. I . . ." Johnny's face twisted. "God knows I hate to ruin your day, but those glaciers are going to sweep right down to China. I really think we ought to head for some place warm."

Pieter Jakov's face was cold. He said, "Perhaps Texas?"

Rick's back flinched. Johnny said, "Thanks a whole lot."

"My family was in Moskva. They die by fire and the blast. Your family dies by water. You see, I know how you feel. But the Soviet Union has survived disasters before, and glaciers move slowly."

"Revolution moves quickly," Leonilla said.

"Eh?"

Leonilla spoke in rapid Russian. Pieter answered in kind.

Johnny spoke low-voiced to Rick. "Let them talk it over. Hell, it's their rocket ship. Listen, Rick, they *could* have got a helicopter there in time. Rick?" Rick wasn't listening. Finally Johnny looked where Rick was looking, down toward the dark mass of Asia. . . .

Presently Leonilla switched to English. Almost briskly, almost cheerfully, she said, "Glaciers move slowly, but revolutions move quickly. Most Party members, and everyone in the government, were Great Russians like me, like Pieter. Well, too much of Great Russia was under the strike. What will be happening now, as the Ukrainians, the Georgians, all the subject people, realize that Moscow no longer holds their lives? I have tried to convince Comrade General Jakov . . . What are you staring at?"

Rick Delanty turned to her, and she shied back. Facial expressions differ among races and cultures, but she knew murderous hate when she saw it. A moment later Rick moved; but only to give her room at the viewport.

There were dozens of tiny sparks above the black cloud cover of Hammerfall. More were coming through. A field of tiny rising sparks, fireflies in formation . . .

Leonilla lost her handhold. She drifted back across the width of Hammerlab, held by the hate in Rick's eyes, unable to look away. Pieter saw that look and braced himself, one hand gripping hard to moor himself, the other fist clenched and ready, braced himself to defend the woman from a threat he didn't understand.

And Johnny Baker dived in a clean arc across to the communications panel. He turned frequency dials in carefully controlled haste, pushed buttons, and spoke. "LOOKING GLASS, THIS IS WHITE BIRD; LOOKING GLASS, LOOKING GLASS, THIS IS WHITE BIRD. SOVIET UNION HAS LAUNCHED MASSIVE ICBM FORCE; I SAY AGAIN, SOVIET ROCKETS ARE RISING. CONFIRMED OBSERVATION. Goddammit, the bastards are launching everything they've got! Five hundred birds, maybe more!"

Pieter Jakov reached the console. He pulled frantically at circuit breakers. The indicator lights on the panel went out. Baker and Jakov faced each other.

"Delanty!"

"Sir." Rick launched himself toward Jakov. Even as his body moved across the capsule, Leonilla was shouting in Russian. Then Rick had Jakov—but the Russian had gone passive. His face was a mask of hatred to match Rick's.

"Send your warning," he said. "You will tell them nothing they do not know."

"What the hell do you mean?" Rick Delanty shouted.

"Look," Pieter said.

Leonilla's voice was strangely flat. "There is another flare above Moscow. A new one."

"Eh?" Johnny Baker looked from the Russian general to the woman, finally let himself drift toward the viewport. He knew already. He knew what it would look like, and he saw it at once. At the edge of the red-orange glare that marked Moscow, a tiny vivid mushroom bloomed in red and violet-white.

"Late strike." The lie was thick on his tongue, for Hamner-Brown was two hours past and his eyes were already searching for the others. He found two small mushroom-shaped clouds and a tiny sun that blossomed as he watched. "Jesus," he said, "the whole world's gone crazy."

"Gilding the lily," Rick Delanty said. "Not enough to get hit by a comet. Some son of a bitch pushed the button. Aw, shit."

All four now watched the scene below: the rising fireflies of Soviet rockets, and the sudden blue-white glares across what had been European Russia. Whatever industry might have survived the comet was . . .

Madness, Johnny Baker thought. Why, *why, WHY?*

"I don't think we'll be welcome down there," Rick Delanty said. His voice was strangely calm, and Johnny wondered if Rick had gone crazy too. He couldn't look at Leonilla.

Finally Rick snarled deep in his throat. Just a sound. It had no meaning and was directed at no one. Then he turned and kicked himself away from them all, down the length of Hammerlab. Jakov was at the other end, near the airlock to the *Soyuz*, and Johnny Baker had the insane thought that the Russian was going for a concealed weapon.

That's what we need. A pistol fight in orbit. Why not?

Madness and revenge were fine old traditions where Jakov came from.

"That's that," Johnny said quietly. "It would have been nice to stick together. The last of the astronauts. But I guess not. Rick?"

Rick was down at the Apollo airlock, and he was cursing, quietly, but loud enough that they could hear.

Johnny turned back to watch Jakov. The Russian made no move to open the airlock to the *Soyuz*. He hung in space, poised as if ready to do something, but he didn't move at all. He was staring down at the stricken Earth below.

Rick's bellow echoed the length of the cabin. *"Shit!"* Then, "Sir. The Apollo's in vacuum. Shall I close up my hat and go see if the heat shield's damaged?"

"Don't bother. Shit!" A hole anywhere in the Apollo would kill them during reentry. They were back to one spacecraft. Johnny turned back to Pieter Jakov, who was still watching through the viewport.

A blow to the back of General Jakov's neck, right now, before he expects it. Or go back to Russia. As prisoners of war? Hardly. Johnny Baker remembered scenes from the *Gulag Archipelago*. His hand arched to strike. Rick could handle Leonilla, and they'd have . . .

He thought it, but he did nothing. And Pieter Jakov turned toward them all and said, carefully, "They're moving east. East."

They stared at each other, Baker and Jakov, for a moment that stretched endlessly, then both dived frantically toward the communication panel.

"Roger, Looking Glass, White Bird out," Johnny Baker said.

"You got through?" Rick demanded.

"Yeah. At least somebody acknowledged." Johnny Baker looked down at the roiling mess below. "I think God hears us pretty well up here. I don't see any other way we could have got a message through that."

"Skip distances. Random ionization patterns," Jakov said.

Johnny Baker shrugged. He wasn't interested in arguing theology. The capsule fell silent as they watched the flight of the missiles. The sparks were going out now as they reached their trajectories. They would light again, but far more brightly. . . .

But before the flames died, it had been easy to see that the missiles were not rising to curve over the North Pole. A slim crescent of Earth showed, more than enough to let them orient themselves, and the missiles were plainly moving east, toward China.

And there had been the nuclear explosions over Russia. The Chinese had attacked first, and what the Hammer had spared was now radioactive hell.

Pieter's family was down there, Johnny Baker thought. And Leonilla's, if she has any. I don't think she does. Jesus, I'm lucky. Ann left Houston weeks ago.

Johnny laughed quietly to himself. Ann Baker had no reason to stay in Texas. She'd taken the kids to Las Vegas for a divorce that had probably saved her life. As for Maureen . . . Yeah. Maureen. If any woman could have survived Hammerfall on brains and determination, it was Maureen. She'd said she was going to California with her father.

"There is much to be done." Pieter Jakov was a study in professional detachment, except for the quiet edge in his voice. "We cannot survive here more than a few weeks at most. General, we have no onboard computer. You must use your equipment to compute our reentry."

"Sure," Johnny said.

"We will need both of you." Jakov tilted his head toward the other end of the capsule, where Rick Delanty seemed huddled in on himself.

"He'll help when we need him," Baker said. "He's got to take this pretty hard. Even if his wife and kids are still alive, even if they got them out, he'll never know it."

"Not knowing is better," said Pieter. "Much better."

Johnny remembered Moscow, doubly destroyed, and nodded.

"Perhaps Dr. Malik should administer a tranquilizer," Jakov was saying.

"I told you, Colonel Delanty will be all right," Johnny Baker said. "Rick, we need a conference."

"Sure."

"Why?" Jakov demanded. "Why did they do it?"

The sudden question did not surprise Baker. He'd been wondering when Jakov would say something.

"You know why," Leonilla Malik said. She left her place at the viewport. "Our government had already coveted China. With the threat of glaciers coming, Russians have only one place to go. Europe has been destroyed, and there

296

is very little to the south. If we can reach that conclusion, the Chinese can also."

"And so they attacked," Jakov said. "But not in time. We were able to launch our own strike."

"So where will we land?" Leonilla asked.

"You are very calm about this," Jakov said. "Do you not care that your country has been destroyed?"

"I care both less and more than you think," she said. "It was my homeland, but it was not my country. Stalin killed my country. In any event we cannot go there now. We would land in the middle of a war, if we could find a place to land at all."

"We are officers of the Soviet Union, and this war is not over," Jakov said.

"Balls." They all turned toward Rick Delanty. "Balls," he said again. "You know damn well there's nothing you can do down there. Where would you go? Into China to wait for the Red Army? Or down into the fallout to wait for glaciers? For Christ's sake, Pieter, that war's not your war, even if you're crazy enough to believe it's still going on. It's over for you."

"So where do we go?" Jakov demanded.

"Southern Hemisphere," Leonilla said. "Weather patterns do not usually cross the equator, and most of the strikes were in the Northern Hemisphere. I believe we will find that Australia and South Africa are undamaged industrial societies. Australia would be difficult to achieve from this orbit. We would have little control over where we landed, and we would starve if we came down in the outback. South Africa—"

Johnny's laugh was bitter. Rick said, "If it's all the same to you, I'd rather stay here."

They all laughed. Baker felt the tension easing slightly. "Look," he said, "we could probably manage South America, and we wouldn't find much damage there, but why bother? We'd be four strangers, and none of us speaks the language. I suggest we go home. Our home. We can set down pretty close to where we aim for, and you'll be two strangers with native guides. And you know English."

"Things are pretty bad," Delanty said.

"Sure."

"So where?"

"California. High farming country in California. There won't be glaciers there for a long time."

Leonilla said nothing. Pieter said, "Earthquakes."

297

"You *know* it, but they'll be over before we can land. The shock waves must have triggered every fault there is. There won't be another earthquake in California for a hundred years."

"Whatever we do, it must be quickly," Pieter said. He pointed to the status board. "We are losing air and we are losing power. If we do not act quickly we will be unable to act at all. You say California. Will two Communists be welcome there?"

Leonilla looked at him strangely, as if she were about to say something, but she didn't.

"Better there than other places," Baker said. "We wouldn't want the South or the Midwest—"

"Johnny, there's going to be people down there who think this was all a Russki plot," Rick Delanty said.

"Yes. Again, more in the Midwest and South than in California. And the East is gone. What else is left? Besides, look, we're *heroes,* all of us. The last men in space." If he was trying to convince himself, it wasn't working.

Leonilla and Pieter exchanged glances. They spoke softly in Russian. "Can you imagine what the KGB would do if we came down in an American space capsule?" Leonilla asked. "Are the Americans such fools as well?"

Rick Delanty's reply was a soft, sad chuckle. "We're not in quite the same boat," he said. "I wouldn't worry about the FBI. It's the righteous patriotic citizens . . ."

Leonilla frowned the question.

"Well," Rick said, "what's to worry? We're coming down in a Soviet spacecraft plainly marked with a hammer and sickle and that big CCCP. . . ."

"Better that than a Mars symbol," Johnny Baker said.

No one laughed.

"Hell," Rick said. "If we had any choice, that wouldn't *be* the world we'd land on. You'd think people would get together after this. But I doubt they will."

"Some will," Baker said.

"Sure. Look, Johnny, half the people are dead, and the rest will be fighting over what's left of the food. Strange weather ruins crops. *You* know that. A lot of the survivors won't get through another winter."

Leonilla shivered. She had known people who lived— barely—through the great famine in the Ukraine that followed Stalin's ascension to the throne of the czars.

"But if there's any civilization left down there, anybody

who cares about what we've done, it'll be in California," Rick Delanty said. "We've got the records from Hamner-Brown. Last space mission for—"

"For a long time," Pieter said.

"Yeah. And we've got to save the records. So it will mean something."

Pieter Jakov seemed relieved, now that there were no more difficult choices. "Very well. There are atomic power plants in California? Yes. Perhaps they will survive. Civilization will form around electrical power. That is where we should go."

■

SAC communications are designed to survive. They are intended to operate even after an atomic attack. They were not designed for planetwide disaster, but they contain so much redundancy and so many parallel systems that even under the impact of the Hammer, messages got through.

Major Bennet Rosten listened to the chatter on his speaker. Most of it was not intended for him, but he got it anyway; if communications ever stopped, Major Rosten would own his missiles, and, after the timers ran out, could launch them. It was better that he knew too much than too little.

"EWO EWO, EMERGENCY WAR ORDERS. ALL SAC COMMANDERS, THIS IS CINC SAC."

General Bambridge's voice came through heavy static. Rosten could barely understand him.

"THE PRESIDENT IS DEAD. HELICOPTER ACCIDENT; I SAY AGAIN, THE PRESIDENT IS DEAD IN A HELICOPTER ACCIDENT. WE HAVE NO EVIDENCE OF HOSTILE ATTACK ON THE UNITED STATES. WE HAVE NO COMMUNICATION WITH HIGHER AUTHORITY."

"Christ on a crutch," Captain Luce muttered. "Now what do we do?"

"What we're paid for," Rosten said.

Static overlay the speaker's voice. ". . . NO REPORT FROM B-MEWS . . . HURRICANE WINDS OVER . . . SAY AGAIN . . . TORNADOES . . ."

"Jesus," Luce muttered. He wondered about his family up at ground level. There were shelters at the base. Millie would have sense enough to get to them. Wouldn't she? She was an Air Force wife, but she was young, too young and—

299

". . . CONDITION REMAINS RED; SAY AGAIN, CONDITION REMAINS RED. SAC OUT."

"We will unlock the target cards," Rosten said.

Harold Luce nodded. "Guess that's best, Skipper." Then, as he'd been trained to do, Luce noted the time in the log: "On orders of the CO the targeting cards and interpretations were removed at 1841 ZULU." Luce used his keys, then turned the combination panel. He took out a deck of IBM cards and laid them on the console. They gave no indication of what they were, but there was a code book that could interpret them. Under normal circumstances neither Luce nor Rosten knew where their missiles were aimed. Now, though, with good prospects that they'd own the birds, it seemed better to know.

Time went by. The speaker blared again. "APOLLO REPORTS SOVIET MISSILE LAUNCH . . . SAY AGAIN . . . MASSIVE . . . FIVE HUNDRED . . . TYARA TAM . . ."

"The bastards!" Rosten shouted. "Lousy red sons of bitches!"

"Calm, Skipper." Captain Luce fingered the cards and code book. He looked up at his status board. Their missiles were still sealed; they couldn't launch anything if they wanted to, not without orders from Looking Glass.

"LOOKING GLASS, THIS IS DROPKICK. LOOKING GLASS, THIS IS DROPKICK. WE HAVE MESSAGES FROM SOVIET PREMIER. SOVIETS CLAIM CHINESE ATTACK ON SOVIET UNION HAS BEEN MET BY MISSILE LAUNCHES. SOVIETS REQUEST U.S. ASSISTANCE AGAINST CHINESE UNPROVOKED ATTACK."

"ALL UNITS, THIS IS SAC. APOLLO REPORTS SOVIET MISSILES HEADED EAST; REPEAT . . . NO . . . AS FAR AS WE KNOW . . ."

"SQUADRON COMMANDERS, THIS IS LOOKING GLASS. NO SOVIET ATTACK ON UNITED STATES; I SAY AGAIN, SOVIET ATTACK ON CHINA ONLY, NOT ON UNITED STATES. . . ."

The speakers went dead. Luce and Rosten looked at each other. Then they looked at their target cards.

Red flags dropped over lights on their status board, and a new digital timer began ticking off seconds.

In four hours they would own their birds.

A handful of glowing coals scattered across Mexico and the eastern United States: the land strikes of the Hammer. Columns of superheated air stream up into the stratosphere, carrying millions of tons of dust and vaporized soil. Winds rush inward toward the rising air; as they cross the turning world their paths are deflected into half a dozen counter-clockwise spirals. Eddies form in the spirals and are thrown off as hurricanes.

A mother hurricane forms over Mexico and moves eastward across the Gulf, gaining heat energy from the boiling seawater that covers the Gulf Strike. The hurricane moves north, from sea to land, and spawns tornadoes as it goes. Hurricane winds drive floodwaters further up the Mississippi valley.

As heated wet air rises above the oceans, cold winds pour down from the Arctic. An enormous front forms along the Ohio valley. Tornadoes bud and break free and scatter. When the front moves past, another forms, and another behind it, spewing out a hundred, then a thousand tornadoes to dance out their fury on the graves of the ruined cities. The fronts move east. More form in the Atlantic, above Europe, across Africa. Rain clouds cover the Earth.

THE QUICK AND THE DEAD

> Day of wrath, and doom impending,
>> David's word with Sibyl's blending:
> Heaven and earth in ashes ending.
> What shall I, frail man, be pleading?
>> Who for me be interceding,
>> When the just are mercy needing
>> ***Dies Irae***

Rich Man, Poor Man

The value of a thing is what that thing will bring.
Legal maxim

Tim led Eileen over the slippery crest. They stopped to gape down at Tujunga.

Tujunga still lived! There was electricity: yellow lights shining from houses that still stood; bright bluish-white fluorescent light from stores with unbroken glass in their windows.

Cars moved down Foothill Boulevard. They drove with their lights on in the afternoon gloom, through the windy, rainswept streets, across foot-thick mud that ran in rivulets across the road. Not many, but they were cars, and they moved. There were police cars in the supermarket parking lot across from Tim and Eileen.

There were also armed men, in uniform. When Tim and Eileen got closer they saw that the uniforms were of all styles and ages, and many didn't fit any longer. It was as if everyone who had a uniform had gone home and put it on. The weapons were random: pistols, shotguns, .22 rifles, Mauser hunting pieces, a few military rifles carried by men in National Guard fatigues.

"Food!" Tim shouted. He took Eileen's hand and they ran toward the shopping center with a new spring in their walk. "I told you," Tim cried. "Civilization!"

Two men in outdated Army uniforms blocked the supermarket door. They didn't stand aside as Tim and Eileen tried to go in. One of the men had sergeant's stripes. He said, "Yeah?"

"We need to buy something to eat," said Tim.

"Sorry," the sergeant said. "All confiscated."

"But we're hungry." Eileen sounded plaintive, even to herself. "We haven't eaten all day."

The other uniformed man spoke. He didn't talk like a soldier. He sounded like an insurance salesman. "There'll be ration cards issued at the old City Hall. You'll have to go there to register. I understand they'll be setting up a soup line too."

"But who's inside the store?" Eileen pointed an accusing finger at aisles bathed in electric light, where people were piling goods into shopping carts. Some wore uniforms, some didn't.

"Our officers. The supply crew," the sergeant said. He had been a clerk in a hardware store until that morning. "They'll tell you all about it at City Hall." He looked at their muddy clothes, and something dawned on him. "You come from over the hills?"

Tim said, "Yes."

"Jesus," the sergeant said.

"Many more make it out?" the other man asked.

"I don't know." Tim took Eileen's hand again, holding it as if she might vanish into smoke the way his dream of normal civilization had vanished. "We're about dead on our feet," he said. "Where can . . . what should we do?"

"Beats me," the sergeant said. "You want my advice, you figure on getting out of here. We're not turning out strangers. Not yet. But it stands to reason there's only so much to go around. At least until we can get back over the hills and see what's out in the valley. They tell me . . ." His voice trailed off.

"Did you see it happen?" the private asked.

"No. The water came pretty high, I guess," Tim said. "But we couldn't see. We just heard it."

"I'll hear it the rest of my life," Eileen said. "It. . . . There must be a lot of people alive, though. In Burbank, maybe. And the Hollywood Hills."

"Yeah," the private growled.

"Too many for us to take care of." The sergeant peered out into the rain as if trying to see through the Verdugo Hills beyond the parking lot. "Way too many. You better register at City Hall while they're still taking in strangers. Maybe we won't be, if too many come. Over that way." He pointed.

"Thanks." Tim turned away. They started across the parking lot.

"Hey." The sergeant came toward them. He held the rifle carelessly. Tim kept watching it. The sergeant reached into his pocket. "I guess I can spare this. You look like you can use it." He held out a cellophane-wrapped packet, very small, and turned away before Tim could thank him. As if he didn't want to be thanked.

"What did we get?" Eileen asked.

"Cheese and crackers. About one bite each." He opened the package and used the little plastic stick to dig out cheese from the plastic container. He spread half of it onto crackers. "Here's your share."

They munched on the way. "Never thought this stuff would taste so good," Eileen said. "And it's only been a few hours. Tim, I don't think we ought to stay here. We should get to your observatory if we can." She remembered what she had seen Patrolman Eric Larsen do. And she'd known him. She didn't know these men in their too-small uniforms. "But I don't think I can walk that far."

"Why walk?" Tim pointed to a lighted building. "We'll buy a car."

The lot held used pickup trucks. Inside the showroom there were three GMC Blazers, four-wheel-drive station wagons. They went in, and saw no one. Tim went over to one of the cars. "Perfect," he said. "Just what we want."

"Tim—"

He turned at the alarm in her voice. There was a man in the doorway to the shop area. He held a large shotgun. At first Tim Hamner saw only the gun, barrels pointed toward his head, each as large as a cave. Then he noticed the fat man behind it. Large, not really fat—yes he was. Fat. Also beefy, with red face. Expensive clothes. Western string tie with a silver device on it. And a big shotgun.

"You want one of those, do you?" the man said.

"I want to buy one," Tim said. "We're not robbers. I can pay." Tim's voice was filled with angry indignation.

The man stared for a moment. Then he lowered the shotgun. His head tilted back. Peal after peal of laughter came from his mouth. "Pay with what?" he demanded. He could hardly speak for laughing. "With what?"

Tim swallowed the automatic answer. He looked at Eileen, and fear came to him. Money wasn't any good—and he didn't have any money to begin with. He had checks, and plastic credit cards, and what were they? "I don't know," Tim said finally. "Yes I do. Maybe. I have a place up in the hills. Stocked with food, and supplies. Big enough for a lot of people. I'll take you, and your family, and let you stay there. . . ."

The man stopped laughing. "Nice offer. Don't need it, but nice. I'm Harry Stimms. I own this place."

"My name is—"

"Timothy Hamner," Stimms said. "I watch TV."

"And you're not interested in my offer?"

"No," Stimms said. "Actually, I don't suppose these cars belong to me anymore. Expect the National Guard johnnies will take them over pretty quick now. And I've got a place to go." He looked thoughtful. "You know, Mr. Hamner, maybe things aren't as bad as they say. You want one of these?"

"Yes."

"Fine. I'll sell you one. The price is two hundred and fifty thousand dollars."

Eileen's jaw dropped. Tim's eyes narrowed a second. Talk about being rolled . . . "Done. How do I pay?"

"You sign a note for it," Stimms said. "Doubt it'll be any good, ever. But just in case . . ." He picked up the shotgun and kept it cradled in his arms. "Come on into the office. I've got the note forms. Never made one out for quite that much before. . . ."

"I can write small."

They drove through inches-deep water on side streets. The wind howled. On either side the old houses, built long before the Long Beach quake and still standing, were islands of light in the drizzle. Tim's watch said 4 P.M., but outside it was dark, with only a dingy gray except in the headlights. There were no sidewalks, and mud as well as water flowed across the blacktop road. Eileen drove carefully, eyes ahead on the road. The radio gave nothing but static.

"Nice car," Eileen said. "Glad it has power steering."

"For a quarter of a million bucks it ought to have," Tim said. "Damn, that frosts me—"

Eileen giggled. "Best deal you ever made in your life." Or ever will make, she thought.

"It isn't the car." Tim's voice held hurt indignation. "It was the extra fifty thousand bucks he charged for gas and oil and a jack!" Then he laughed. "And the rope. Mustn't forget the rope. I'm glad he had extra. I wonder where he's going?"

Eileen didn't answer. They crested a hill and started down, around a bend. There were no more houses. Thick mud covered the road and she shifted into four-wheel drive. "I've never been in a car like this before."

"Me neither. Want me to drive?"

"No."

There was water at the bottom of the hill. It came up to the hubcaps, then up to the doors, and Eileen backed away. She drove carefully off the road and onto the embankment beside it. The car tilted dangerously toward the swirling dark water to their left. They went on, carefully and slowly. On their right were the ruins of new houses and condominiums, just far enough away so that they couldn't see any details. A few lights, flashlights and lanterns, moved among the wreckage. Tim wished he'd got a flashlight from the car dealer. They had a spotlight, but it needed to be mounted on the car, and wouldn't be any good until it was.

They went around the valley, staying just above the water, and eventually found the road again where it rose out of the flood. Eileen gratefully shifted gears.

The road twisted up into the mountains. They passed stopped cars. Someone darted out in front of the Blazer and gestured them to halt. He wasn't wearing a shirt, but he held a pistol in his hand. Eileen gunned the car toward him, making him dive off to the side; then she accelerated.

There were gunshots, and a crash of glass. Tim looked back in amazement at the neat round hole through the rear window, then above at the exit hole angling up through the roof. Rainwater ran in through the hole and dripped between them. Eileen floorboarded the car, roaring around the curve without braking, and the car had the feathery feeling of an imminent skid. She got around, braked for the next curve, then accelerated again.

Tim tried to laugh. "My new car."

"Shut up." She was leaning forward against the wheel.

"You all right?"

"No."

"Eileen!"

"I'm not hit. I'm scared. I've got the shakes."

"Me too," he said, but he felt waves of relief wash over

him. There had been that tiny moment, only an instant really, when he thought she'd been hit. It had been the most terrifying moment of his life. Now that struck him as strange; because he hadn't seen her since she turned down his proposal. Of course not. He had his pride—

"Tim, there are bridges ahead, and we're getting closer to the Fault! The road may be gone!" She was shouting.

"Not much we can do about it."

"No, we can't go back." She slowed for another curve, then accelerated again. She was still strangling the wheel. She was going to wreck them if she didn't calm down, and he couldn't think of a thing to do about it.

The road was often blocked by mudslides, and Eileen, finally, had slowed to a crawl. Once they took half an hour to get fifty feet. Now, whenever they came to a clear section of road, Tim wished that she would drive faster. But she didn't; she kept the car in first or second gear, and never drove faster than twenty miles an hour, even when the headlights showed long clear stretches.

They drove on interminably. Eventually Tim stuffed his handkerchief into the hole in the roof.

Tim's watch showed 8 P.M., twilight time for Los Angeles June, but it was as black as ink outside. Rain fell intermittently. The windshield wipers in the Blazer were very good, and Stimms had showed them how to fill the washers. Eileen used them often.

As they rounded a sharp curve, the headlights showed empty space in front of them. Eileen braked, hard, and brought the car to a stop. The headlights bored small holes in the rainy dark, but there was enough light to show a jagged end to the road.

Tim got out in the rain and went toward the edge. When he saw where he stood he gulped, hard, and went back to the driver's side. "Back up, slow," he commanded.

She started to ask why, but the urgent fear in his voice stopped her. Carefully she put the car into reverse and crawled back. "Get back there and guide me, damn you!" she shouted.

"Sorry." Tim walked back behind the car and guided her with gestures. Finally he made chopping motions.

She switched off the ignition and got out to see where

they'd been. The bridge had been a slender concrete arch spanning a deep gorge. The bridge had fallen in the center, and they'd been well onto it before she stopped. Now they were back on solid ground.

They could see nothing. To the left they felt the loom of a flint-and-granite cliff rising high above them. On the right, beyond a broad earth hump, was a steep drop into nothing. Ahead was the ruined bridge.

There were no lights anywhere, and no sounds except howling wind driving the rain, and far below, sounds of rushing water.

"End of the line?" Eileen said.

"I don't know. It's a cinch we can't do anything about it tonight. I guess we stay here until daylight."

"If there's ever any daylight again," she said. She frowned, and began walking up the road. Tim didn't follow. He stood, exhausted, wanting to get back into the car, but reluctant to do it until she came back. Somehow it would have been cowardly to sit in the car out of the rain while she tramped up the road, looking for . . . for what? Tim wondered. Finally she came back and got in. Tim went around and joined her.

She began backing up, slowly, this time without his help. She went on and on, and Tim wanted to ask what she was doing, but he was too tired. She had made a decision, and that was good, because he didn't have to. Eventually she came to a wide gravel patch to the left side of the road and carefully backed into it so that the car was off the pavement entirely. "I don't like it," she said. "There might be a mud-slide. But I'd rather be here than on the road. Suppose someone else comes."

"No one will."

"Probably. Anyway, we're here."

"Beer?" Tim asked.

"Sure."

He took two cans from the six-pack the car salesman had thrown in. He opened one and started to throw the pull tab away.

"Save that."

"Huh? Why?"

"Save everything," Eileen said. "We don't have much. I don't know what we can use those for, but we'll never get more of them. Save it. Cans, too. Don't crush them."

"Okay. Here."

The beer was lukewarm, like the rain outside. They had

nothing else. Nothing to eat, and the rain outside was mildly salty. Tim wondered if they could drink it safely. Pretty soon they'd have to.

"At least it's warm," Tim said. "We won't freeze, even at this altitude." His clothes were damp, and it wasn't really very warm. He wished they'd saved the old raincoat from the first car. For a moment Tim thought about the Chrysler's owner. Had they killed him by taking his car? That wasn't something to think about. What was?

"Do we save this or drink it up and be done with it?" Tim asked.

"Better save at least two," Eileen said. Her voice was wooden and emotionless, and Tim wondered if he sounded that way to her. Wordlessly he opened another pair of cans and they drank that.

Two cans of beer, on an empty stomach, after the day's excitement: Tim found that it had more effect than he could have believed. He almost felt human again. He knew it wouldn't last, but for the moment there was a warm feeling in his stomach and a lightness in his head. He looked toward Eileen. He couldn't see her in the dark. She was only a shape on the seat beside him. He listened to the rain for a few moments longer, then reached for her.

She sat stiffly, not moving, neither pushing him away nor responding. Tim moved against her on the seat. His hand went to her shoulder, then down to her breast. Her blouse was damp, but her flesh was warm when he put his hand under the blouse. She still hadn't moved. He moved closer, putting his head to her breasts.

"Is this appropriate?" Her voice might have been a stranger's. It was Eileen, but detached, from a long way away.

"What is?" Tim said. He felt vaguely ashamed of himself. "I'm sorry." The glow from the beer was gone now.

"Don't be. I'll sleep with you, if that's what you want. I'd rather not. Not now . . ."

"Yeah, there have to be better times."

"Not if that's what you really want," she said. "I've been thinking. Were we ever really in love?"

"I asked you to marry me. . . ."

"And I wanted to, only I didn't want to marry anybody. Well, we're married now."

Tim was silent in the darkness. He felt an insane urge to giggle. Mother will be pleased, he thought. Little Timmy's married now. He wondered where his mother was, and the rest of his family. Could I have done anything? Should I have tried? I didn't try. I didn't do anything but run for my life.

"Sure you want me?" he asked.

"Tim, when I came out of Corrigan's and saw you I was never so glad to see anyone in my life. Yes."

Was she putting him on? And what was the point of worrying about it?

"We'll learn to love each other," she was saying. "We've been learning it all day. So if"—she patted his hand that still lay passively on her breast—"this is what you want, I'm willing."

He sat up and moved away from her.

"Tim, please don't be angry."

"No, that's okay. You're right, it feels wrong. The whole car is wet, and our clothes stick to us, and if you're not tired half to death, I am. Jesus, we came close to driving off that bridge!"

She reached to squeeze his hand.

"Wrong time, wrong place. Hey, how about the Savoy Hotel?"

"Huh?"

"Savoy Hotel in London. Elegance. *Incredible* room service. Huge bathtubs. If this is the wrong place for a love affair, the right place is the Savoy Hotel. Only, it's probably underwater." He was babbling. "Sure, there's a right place somewhere, but what if we never reach it? Eileen, I damned near didn't get that fence down, and it had to be done. You don't need me, you need Conan the Barbarian! Him for brawn and you for brains."

"Will you stop that?"

"I can't. You're the one who kept us going. If you want manly strength, I don't think I have it. I don't have the skills either. I used to know how to hire skills."

"You carried me down the hill," she said, exaggerating for effect. "You knew where to go. You've done all right."

He couldn't see her in the dark. But he knew she wasn't laughing at him, because she had a death grip on his hand. He moved toward her again, and she came to him, holding him desperately. He had no sexual urge now, only a feeling of innate protectiveness. Part of his mind knew this was silly; knew that Tim Hamner, however much he might share the ages-old instincts of male *Homo sapiens*, had neither the training nor the muscles to give them reality. But it was very pleasant to hold Eileen and have her go quietly to sleep with her head in his lap, and after a while he slept too.

■

The sea is withdrawing from England.

Sluggish with debris, the water that has conquered London flows back toward the Channel. Glutted with human bodies, and the lighter cars, and the wooden walls of older buildings, and the sea-bottom debris that came inland in three monstrous tidal waves, the water must force its way between and around and through mountainous chunks that were tall buildings yesterday. Windows that survived the wave break now to let the water through. It sifts the interiors as it goes, and carries away furniture, bedding, whole department stores full of clothing.

Buildings along the Thames have been smashed to their foundations, and even those are being torn loose. Tremendous pressures pry the concrete away in pieces and send them, with megatons of mud from the banks, down into the river bed.

Tomorrow and forever after, there will be no way to tell where the Savoy Hotel once stood.

■

They woke with cramps, tingling limbs and the shivers.

"What time is it?" Eileen asked.

Tim pushed the button on his watch. "One-fifty." He shifted uncomfortably. "The stuff we read in Lit classes made it sound romantic, this business of sleeping in each other's arms, but it's damned uncomfortable."

She laughed in the dark. Lovely, Tim thought. It was Eileen again, her laugh, and he could imagine her sunburst smile although he couldn't see it. "Do these seats do anything?" she asked.

"Dunno."

The car had a divided bench seat. Tim reached down, feeling for controls. He found a lever and pulled. The seat back collapsed against the seat behind, not quite horizontal but a great deal more comfortable than it had been. He told her what he'd done and she flopped hers back as well.

Now they were not quite lying side by side. She moved against him. "I'm freezing."

"Me too."

They huddled together, seeking each other's warmth. They were not very comfortable. Arms got in the way. She put her arm over him, and they lay still for a moment. Then she drew him tightly against her body, pushing her legs against his. She felt warm along her whole length. Suddenly her mouth found his and she kissed him. That went on for a moment and she drew away, and laughed, very softly. "Still in the mood?" she asked.

"Back in the mood," Tim said, and he gave up on speaking.

They kept most of their clothes on, peeling back shirt and blouse and skirt and pants, giggling, reaching under cloth that was needed for warmth; and they coupled suddenly, with a fervor that left no room for laughter. It felt right, now. Even the flavor of insanity matched what was happening to the world around them. Afterward they rested in each other's arms, and Eileen said, "Shoes."

So they curled around each other, maintaining contact, to wrestle their shoes off; they caressed each other with their toes; they coupled again. Tim felt the wiry strength of Eileen's legs and arms, caging him. She relaxed slowly, and sighed, and was out like a light.

He pulled her skirt down as far as it would go. She slept soundly, stirring only slightly when he moved. Tim lay awake in the dark, wishing for dawn, wishing for sleep.

Why did we do that? he wondered. The night the world ended, and we screw like mad minks, here at the end of nowhere on the Big Tujunga Canyon Road, with a dead bridge in front of us and ten million dead behind. . . . In a car seat, yet, like a couple of teen-agers.

She moved slightly, and he put his arm across her, protectively, without volition. He realized he had done that. Reflex. Protective reflex, he thought.

Suddenly Tim Hamner grinned in the dark. "Why the hell not?" he said aloud, and went to sleep.

There was a gray tinge to the sky when they both woke. They sat up together, wrapped in thoughts and memories, wondering what had wakened them. Then they heard it over the drumming of rain on metal: a motor, a car or truck coming very fast up the highway. Presently there were lights behind them.

Tim felt a terrible sense of urgency. He ought to be doing something. Warning. He ought to warn that car. He shook his head violently, trying to shake himself awake. It must have worked. He reached past Eileen for the steering wheel. The horn shrieked in mechanical terror.

The car went past them like a bat out of hell, followed by the terror-sound. Tim released the horn and heard *real* mechanical terror: a long scream of brakes, and then nothing, no sound at all for crawling eons. Then metal smashed rock, and light flared ahead of them.

They got out and ran toward half of a bridge. Below the bridge's twisted end was fire. Fire crawled away from the greater blaze, stopped, convulsed, then fell still. The car burned, casting its bonfire light on the canyon and the stream at its bottom.

Tim felt Eileen's hand seeking his. He took her hand and held it tightly.

"Poor bastards," she muttered. She shivered in the dawn cold. The rain had eased, but the wind was cold. It blew the fire. They could feel warmth from the blazing car fighting the wind's chill.

Eileen let go of Tim's hand and moved out onto the ruined bridge. She looked back at the walls of the gorge on the side where Tim still stood. Then she pointed. "We can get across, I think," she said. "Come look." Her voice was calm and detached now.

Tim went out to her, walking gingerly, afraid the rest of the bridge would collapse. He looked where she was pointing. There was a gravel road, barely a car's width wide, carved out of the side of the gorge and switchbacking down into the canyon. "Must be the old road," Eileen said. "I thought there might be one."

It didn't look adequate at all. Not even to walk on, but Eileen went back and started the engine.

"Shouldn't we wait for more light?" Tim asked.

"Probably, but I don't want to," she said.

"Okay. But let me drive. You get out and walk."

There was just light enough to see her face. She leaned over and kissed him, lightly, on the cheek. "You're sweet. But I'm a better driver than you. And you'll walk, because somebody has to go ahead and be sure I can drive down the trail."

"No. We'll do it together." He knew he wasn't making much sense, and he wondered if he would have said that if he hadn't known she would make him get out and walk.

"We both have a better chance if you scout," she said. "Now get to it."

The old road was a nightmare. Sometimes it tilted horribly toward the canyon below. At least, Tim thought, we're out of sight of the burning car. He could still see some light from the dying blaze.

At the switchbacks she had to go around in short segments, backing up and turning, again and again, with the wheels only inches from the edge. Tim felt terror at every turn. She had only to make one mistake: The wrong gear, or too much pressure on the accelerator, and she would be down there, burning alive, and Tim would be alone. He was barely able to walk when they reached the bottom.

"How deep is it?" Eileen asked.

"I . . ." Tim came back to the car and got in. "I'll find out in a minute." He reached for her, desperately.

She pushed him away. "Sweetheart, look." She pointed to her left.

There was just enough light to see. Beyond the ruins of the burned car rose a massive concrete wall, rising high above them. A dam. Tim shuddered. Then he got out and waded into the stream, fighting the current. It was only up to his knees, and he staggered across, then beckoned for her to follow.

The Landlord

*Ownership is not only a right, it is a duty. Ownership
obligates. Use your property as if it had been en-
trusted to you by the people.*

Oswald Spengler, *Thoughts*

At noon Tim and Eileen reached the top of the gorge. When
they were a third of the way up, another car had come to
the other side and begun working its way down. It was an
ordinary car without four-wheel drive, and Tim did not
understand how they had got that far up the canyon. The
other car held two men, a woman and many children. It
was still clinging to the side of the gorge when Tim and
Eileen reached the top on the other side. They drove away,
leaving the others perched on the side of the cliff, wondering
if they should have spoken to them, but not knowing what
they could have done to help.

Tim felt more helpless than ever. He was prepared for the
end of civilization: to be nearly alone, to find human beings
few and far between. He was not prepared to watch it die,
and he wondered what he should do about that, but he could
think of nothing.

The next bridge was mercifully intact, and the one after
that. They were only a few miles from the observatory.

They rounded a bend, to find four cars in the road. There
were a lot of people standing there. These were the first
people Tim and Eileen had seen since they left the gorge.

The road ran through a tunnel here, and the tunnel had
collapsed. The cars were parked while men with shovels

worked to prepare a way over the top of the rocky spur the tunnel had pierced. They had dug out part of a road, and were taking turns, since there were more men than shovels.

Six women and many children were gathered around the cars. Eileen looked hesitantly at the group, then drove up to them.

The children stared with big eyes. One of the women came over to the car. She seemed ancient, although she couldn't have been more than forty. She looked at the Blazer, noting the starred bullet hole in the rear windshield. She didn't say anything.

"Hello," Tim said.

"Hi."

"Have you been here long?"

"Got here just after dawn," the woman said.

"Did you come from town?" Eileen asked.

"No. We were camped up here. Tried to get back to Glendale, but the road's blocked. How'd you get up here? Could we go back the way you came?" Once she had found her voice, the woman talked rapidly.

"We came up Big Tujunga," Tim said.

The woman looked surprised, and turned to the hill. "Hey, Freddie. They came up Big Tujunga."

"It's blocked," the man called. He handed the shovel to another man and started down the hill toward them. Tim saw that he wore a pistol on his belt.

Their cars were not very new. A battered pickup truck, loaded with camping goods; a station wagon on sagging springs; an ancient Dodge Dart.

"We tried to get out Big Tujunga," the man was saying as he came closer. He wore typical camping clothing, wool shirt and twill trousers. A Sierra cup dangled from one side of his belt. The pistol hung in its holster on the other. He didn't seem to be aware of the gun. "I'm Fred Haskins. Reckon you came across the gorge by the old switchbacks?"

"Yes," Eileen said.

"What's it like back in L.A.?" Haskins asked.

"Bad," Tim said.

"Yeah. Earthquake shook the place pretty good, huh?" Haskins looked at Tim carefully. He looked at the bullet hole too. "How'd you get that?"

"Someone tried to stop us—"

"Where?"

"Just as we started up into the mountains," Tim said.

"Sheriff's honor farm," Haskins muttered. "All them prisoners loose, then?"

"What did you mean, 'bad'?" the woman asked. "What did you mean?"

Suddenly Tim couldn't stand it any longer. "It's all gone. The San Fernando Valley, everything south of the Hollywood Hills, drowned in a tidal wave. What wasn't drowned is burned. Tujunga looked pretty good, but the rest of the L.A. basin is finished."

Fred Haskins stared uncomprehendingly. "Finished? All those people dead? *All* of them?"

"Just about," Tim said.

"There are probably a lot of people still alive in the hills," Eileen said. "But—if the road's blocked, then they can't come up here."

"Jeez," Haskins said. "That comet hit us, right? I knew it was going to hit. Martha, I told you we'd be better up here. How long . . . ? I guess they'll send the Army to get us, but we may as well dig our way over," Haskins said. "Road on the other side looks in good shape. Far as we can see, anyway. Martha, you got anything on the radio yet?"

"Nothing. Static. Sometimes I think I hear a few words, but they don't make sense."

"Yeah."

"You folks had anything to eat?" Martha Haskins asked.

"No."

"You look starved. Here, I'll get you something, Mister—"

"Tim."

"Tim. And you're—"

"Eileen. Thank you."

"Yeah. Tim, you go with Fred there and help dig while I get lunch together."

As they climbed up the steep trail, Fred said, "Glad you came along. Not sure we could have got all the cars over. With that rig you can pull 'em over for sure. Then we'll go look for the Army people."

■

The road heaved and shifted and moved out from under the lead truck.

Corporal Gillings, dozing in his seat, was jarred nastily awake. Swearing, he looked out through the canvas. The convoy was trapped. The earth heaved like a sea—

"Hammerfall," he said.

The troops were muttering. Johnson asked, "What's that?"

"The end of the fucking world, you dumb motherfucker. Don't you read *anything*?" Gillings had read it all: the *National Enquirer*, articles in *Time*, the interviews with Sharps and others. He had planned it all a thousand times, daydreaming in his bunk, adding loving details to the scenario. Gillings knew what would happen when Lucifer's Hammer fell. End of civilization. And the end of the goddam Army, too. It would be every man for himself, and the right man could be a fucking *king* if he played his cards right.

Johnson was staring, bewildered and lost, waiting to hear more. Gillings felt light-headed, disoriented. He was not used to seeing his daydreams turn real.

Captain Hora called, "Out of the trucks. Everybody out!"

Gillings's head cleared. Right, it was all falling into place, and that was the first problem: Fucking officers! Hora wasn't bad, as officers went, and the men liked him. Something had to be done about that, and quick. Otherwise the RA son of a bitch would have them out working like slaves, trying to save the civilians' arses until fire and tidal waves took them all.

"We're trapped good, Captain," Sergeant Hooker shouted. "Landslides in front and behind. Don't think we can get the trucks out of here."

"Saddle 'em up, Sarge," Captain Hora called. "We'll hike it. Plenty of people up in these hills. We'll go see what we can do."

"Sir," Hooker said. His voice lacked enthusiasm. "What do we eat, Captain?"

"Time enough to worry about that when we get hungry," Hora said. "Go have a look up ahead. Maybe we can get through the mud."

"Sir."

"Rest of you, out of the trucks," Hora called.

Gillings grinned. Damned lucky we didn't get back to camp before Hammerfall. He smiled again and fingered the hard objects in his pocket. The troops hadn't been given ammunition, but it wasn't hard to come by, and he had a dozen rounds. There was plenty more ammo in the trucks.

Would the men follow him? Maybe not. Not at first. Maybe it would be better to let Hooker live. The troops would follow Hooker, and Hooker wasn't smart, but he was smart enough to know there wasn't any point in arresting Gillings after the

Captain bought it. No more courts-martial. No more courts. Sure, Hooker was that smart.

Gillings slipped three rounds into his rifle.

■

It took most of the day. Tim had never worked so hard in his life. He'd *paid* for his lunch. They dug out the steep parts, then used the Blazer to break trail, used it again to pull the other cars up the muddy road they'd built. The rain continued, although it was now not much more than a heavy drizzle.

Every muscle in Tim's body ached before they were over the ridge. The temporary road didn't have to climb more than a hundred feet, but the road they built switchbacked five times that in length.

When they reached the pavement on the other side of the ruined tunnel, they went in caravan. Four miles beyond the ruined tunnel they came to a ranger station. There were hundreds of people there. A church group, with ninety children and a few college students as counselors and one elderly preacher. Campers and fishing parties had come out of the fire trails and backwoods areas. A bicycling party of French coeds, only one with any English at all, and nobody else spoke French. One large camper which held a writer, his wife and an unbelievable number of children.

The rangers had set up a temporary camp. When Tim's party drove up, they were directed off to one side. Tim wanted to go on, but a green Forest Service truck blocked the way. Eileen stopped and they got out. A uniformed ranger had been talking with Fred Haskins. Now he came over to Tim and Eileen.

The ranger was in his middle twenties, a lanky, well-muscled man. His uniform gave him a look of authority, but he didn't seem very confident. "They say you came up the Big Tujunga Road," he said. He stared at Tim. "You're Hamner."

"I'm not advertising it," Tim said.

"No. I don't suppose you are," the ranger said. "Can we get down the Big Tujunga Road?"

"Don't you know?" Tim asked.

"Look, mister, there are four of us here, and no more. We're trying to take care of these kids, we've got parties out getting people in from dangerous campsites, there are mudslides all over, and most of the bridges are out. We didn't try to get beyond the tunnel when we saw it was down."

"And there's nothing on the radio?" Eileen asked.

"Nothing from the Big Tujunga station," the ranger admitted. "Don't know why. We did get something on CB from some people over at Trail Canyon. They say the big bridge is out and some people are trapped in the canyon."

"The bridge is out," Eileen said. "We got across on the old road. There were some people behind us trying to do the same thing when we left."

"You didn't stay to help?" the ranger demanded.

"There were more of them than us," Tim said. "And what good could we do? You can't pull cars on that road. Too many turns. It's not really a road anyway."

"Yeah, I know. We keep it as a foot trail," the ranger said absently. "Look, you're an expert on comets. Just what has happened? What should we do with these people?"

Tim was ready to laugh at the question, but the ranger's face stopped him. The young man looked too strained, too close to panic, and much too glad to see Tim Hamner. He wanted an expert to give him instructions.

Some expert.

"You can't go back to Los Angeles," Tim said. "There's nothing there. Tidal waves took out most of the city—"

"Jesus, we got something from Mount Wilson on that, but I didn't believe it—"

"And a lot of the rest of it was on fire. Tujunga's got some kind of vigilante group organized. I don't know if they'd be glad to see you or not. The road back to Tujunga's not too bad, but I don't think ordinary cars can get over parts of it even if you get past the gorge."

"Yeah, but where's the Army?" the ranger demanded. "The National Guard. Somebody! You say we shouldn't go back to Tujunga, but what do we do with these kids? We'll run out of food in another day, and we've got a couple of hundred kids to take care of!"

Hell, Tim thought, I am the expert. The knowledge produced elation and depression, oddly mixed. "Okay. I didn't get out to JPL, so I don't know, but . . . I know the comet calved a number of times. It—"

"Calved?"

"Broke up. Came on like a swarm of flying mountains, you understand? It must have hit us in pieces. No telling how many, but . . . it was morning in California, and the comet came out of the sun, so the main target area was the Atlantic.

Probably. If the East Coast got tidal waves as big as the one we got, they wiped out everything east of the Catskills, and most of the Mississippi Valley. No more national government. Maybe no more Army."

"Jesus Christ! You mean the whole country's gone?"

"Maybe the whole world," Tim said.

It was too much. The ranger sat down on the ground next to Tim's car. He stared into space. "My girl lives in Long Beach. . . ."

Tim didn't say anything.

"And my mother. She was in Brooklyn. Visiting my sister. You say that's all gone."

"Probably," Tim said. "I wish I knew more. But probably."

"So what do I do with all the kids, and all the campers? With all these people? How do I feed them?"

You don't, Tim thought, but he didn't say that. "Food warehouses. Cattle ranches. Anyplace there's food, until you can plant more crops. It's June. Some of the crops should have survived."

"North," the ranger said to himself. "There are ranches in the hills above Grapevine. North." He looked up at Tim. "Where are you going?"

"I don't know. North, I guess."

"Can you take some of the kids?"

"I suppose so, but we don't have anything to eat—"

"Who does?" the ranger demanded. "Maybe you ought to stay with us. We can all move out together."

"There's probably a better chance for small groups than large ones. And we don't want to stay with you," Tim said. He didn't want to be bothered with kids, either, but there was no way to refuse.

Besides, it was the right thing to do. He'd read it somewhere: In any ethical situation, the thing you want least to do is probably the right action. Or something like that.

The ranger went off and came back a few minutes later with four young children, ages six and under. They were clean and well dressed, and very frightened. Eileen packed them into the back of the Blazer, then got in the back seat, where she'd be close to them.

The ranger gave Tim a page torn from his notebook. There were names and addresses on it. "This is who the kids are." His voice fell. "If you can find their parents . . ."

"Yeah," Tim said. He started the Blazer. It was the first time he'd ever driven it. The clutch was very stiff.

"My name's Eileen," she was saying in the back. "And that's Tim."

"Where are we going?" the girl asked. She seemed very small and helpless, but she wasn't crying. The boys were. "Are you taking us to my mommy?"

Tim glanced at the paper. Laurie Malcolm, sent to a church camp by her mother. No father mentioned. Mother's address: Long Beach. Lord, what could they tell her?

"Can we go home?" one of the boys asked before Eileen could say anything.

How do you tell a six-year-old that his home has been washed away? Or a little girl that her mommy is—

"We're going up that hill," Eileen said. She pointed toward the mountain nearby. "When we get there, we'll wait for your mommy—"

"But what happened?" the boy asked. "Everybody was so scared. Reverend Tilly didn't want us to know it, but he was."

"It was the comet," Laurie told him solemnly. "Did it hit Long Beach, Eileen? Can I call you Eileen? Reverend Tilly says you aren't supposed to call grown people by their first names. Ever."

Tim turned off onto the side road leading up to the observatory. Long ago he'd had the old dirt road improved with logs and gravel and concrete in the worst places. The mud was thick, but the Blazer had no trouble. It wouldn't be long now. Then they'd have food, and they could stop running. For a while, anyway. The food wouldn't last forever, but it would be time enough to worry about that when they got there. Just now the observatory was home, a haven, a familiar place, with heat and dry clothes and a shower. A safe place to hide while the world ended.

The Blazer was no longer new and shiny. It was scratched along the sides from rockslides, and there was mud everywhere. It took the muddy road like a freeway, climbing over fallen rock, wading through deep pools. Tim had never had a car like this. It made him feel he could go anywhere.

And it had taken them home. Around one more bend. One more bend and they'd be safe. . . .

The concrete building stood unharmed. So did the wooden garage outside it. The shed roof of the garage sagged, leaning at an angle, but not so much that anyone but Tim would notice. The telescope dome was closed, and the shutters were in place on all the windows of the main building.

"We're here!" Tim shouted. He had to shout. Eileen had the children singing in the back seat. "There's a hair on the wart on the . . ."

"There it is! Safe! At least for a while."

The song cut off raggedly. "It looks all right," Eileen said. There was wonder in her voice. She hadn't expected to see the place intact. Somewhere after Tujunga she'd given up hoping for anything at all.

"Sure, Marty's competent," Tim said. "He's got the shutters up, and the . . ." His voice trailed off.

Eileen followed Tim's look. There were two men coming out of the observatory. Older men, about fifty. They carried rifles. They watched as Tim brought the Blazer to a halt in front of the big concrete porch. The rifles were held cradled in their arms, not quite pointing at the Blazer, not pointed away either.

"Sorry, chum, no room," one of the men called. "Best move on. Sorry."

Tim stared at the strangers, letting his rage gather strength. He let them have it between the eyes. "I'm Tim Hamner. I own this place. Now who're you?"

They didn't react at all.

A younger man came out onto the porch.

"Marty!" Tim screamed. "Marty, tell them who I am!" And when I learn what these strangers are doing here (he didn't say) I'll have words with you, Marty.

Marty smiled broadly. "Larry, Fritz, this is Mr. Timothy Gardner Allington Hamner, playboy, millionaire—oh, yes, and amateur astronomer. He owns this place."

"Think of that," Fritz said. The rifle didn't waver.

One of the boys began to cry. Eileen pulled him toward herself and hugged him. The other children watched with big eyes.

Tim opened the door of the Blazer. The rifles moved fractionally. Tim ignored them and got out. He stood in the dusky twilight. Rain soaked his clothing and ran down the back of his neck. He walked toward the porch.

"Better not," one of the riflemen, the one called Larry, said.

"The hell with you," Tim said. He climbed the steps onto the porch. "I am not going to shout at you and scare the children."

The men did nothing, and for a moment Tim felt courage. Maybe . . . was it all a joke? He looked at Marty Robbins. "What's happening here?"

"Not here," Marty said. "Everywhere."

"I know about Hammerfall. What are these people doing at my place?" A mistake, Tim realized instantly. Too late.

"It's not your place," Marty Robbins said.

"You can't get away with this! There are rangers down there. They'll be here as soon as they can get—"

"No they won't," Robbins said. "No rangers, no Army, no National Guard, no police. You've got good radio equipment here, Mr. Hamner." He said the "Mister" contemptuously. "I heard the last Apollo messages, and the rest of it, too. I heard what the rangers told each other. You don't own this place, because nobody owns anything anymore. And we don't need you."

"But . . ." Tim examined the other two men. They didn't look like criminals. How the hell do you know what a criminal looks like? Tim wondered. But they didn't. Their hands were clean, rough, like workmen's hands, not like Marty Robbins's hands. Or Tim's. One of the men had broken a nail off close and it was just growing back.

They wore gray trousers, work clothes. There was a label on Fritz's pants. "Big Smith." "Why are you doing this?" Tim asked them. He ignored Robbins now.

"What else can we do?" Larry asked. There was pleading in his voice, but the rifle was held steady, pointing somewhere between Tim and the Blazer. "There's not a lot of food here, but some. Enough for awhile. We have families here, Mr. Hamner. What can we do?"

"You can stay. Just let us—"

"But don't you see, we can't let *you* stay," Larry said. "What can you do here, Mr. Hamner? What are you good for now?"

"How the hell do you know what I can—"

"We discussed this before," Fritz growled. "Didn't think you'd get here, but we talked about what to do if you did. And this is it. Get out. You're not needed."

Marty Robbins couldn't meet Tim's eye. Tim nodded bleakly. He understood. There wasn't a lot more to say, either. Any equipment—radios, even astronomical and meteorological gear—Robbins knew how to work as well as Tim did. Better. And Robbins had lived here for over a year. If there was anything special to know about these mountains, he'd know more of it than Tim.

"Who's the chick?" Robbins demanded. He took a large flashlight from his pocket and shined it toward the Blazer. It didn't help the visibility much. It showed raindrops falling, and the muddy car, and a glint of Eileen's hair. "One of your relatives? Rich bitch?"

You little bastard. Tim tried to remember his assistant as he'd known him. They'd quarreled when Marty lived in Bel Air with Tim, but it hadn't been serious, and Robbins was excellent at the observatory. Not a month ago, three weeks ago, Tim had written a letter recommending Robbins to the Lowell Observatory in Flagstaff. I guess I really never knew . . .

"She can stay," Robbins was saying. "We're a woman short. She can stay. Not you. I'll go tell her—"

"You'll ask her," Larry said. "*Ask*. She can stay if she *wants* to."

"And me?"

"We're going to watch you drive away," Larry said. "Don't come back."

"There *are* some rangers out there," Marty Robbins said. "Maybe it's not such a good idea. Maybe we shouldn't let him have the car. That's a good car. Better than anything we have here—"

"Don't talk like that." Larry's voice dropped and he glanced behind at the door into the observatory.

Tim frowned. Something was happening here, and he didn't understand it.

Eileen got out of the Blazer and came up onto the porch. Her voice was wooden, exhausted. "What's wrong, Tim?"

"They say this isn't my place anymore. They're sending us away."

"You can stay." Marty said.

"You can't do this!" Eileen screamed.

"Shut up!" Larry shouted.

An ample woman came out of the observatory. She looked at Larry with a frown. "What is this?"

"Keep out of this." Larry said.

"Larry Kelly, what are you doing?" the woman demanded. "Who are these people? I know him! He was on the 'Tonight Show.' Timothy Hamner. This was your place, wasn't it?"

"It *is* my place."

"No." Fritz said. "We agreed. No."

"Thieves. Thieves and murderers." Eileen said. "Why don't you just shoot us and be done with it?"

Tim wanted to shout to her, to tell her to shut up. Suppose they did it? Robbins would.

"There's no call to say things like that," the woman said.

"It's simple. There's not enough here for all of us. Not for long. More people there are, the less there is, and we don't need Mr. Hamner giving orders, and I don't reckon he's good for a lot else. Not anymore. You go find another place, Mr. Hamner. There's other places to go." She looked to Larry for confirmation. "We'll have to move on pretty soon ourselves. You'll just have a head start."

She sounded thoroughly sane and reasonable. It was a nightmare for Tim: She sounded calm and reasonable, and her tone indicated that she was sure Tim would agree.

"But the girl can stay," Robbins said again.

"Do you want to?" Tim asked.

Eileen laughed. It was a bitter laugh, full of contempt. She looked at Marty Robbins and laughed again.

"There are children in that car," the woman said.

"Mary Sue, they're no business of ours," Fritz said.

She ignored him. She looked to Larry. "Who are those children?"

"From the camp," Eileen said. "They lived in Los Angeles. The rangers didn't have anything to feed them. We brought them. We thought—"

The woman left the porch and went down to the Blazer.

"You tell her no," Fritz said. "You make her—"

"I haven't been able to make her do anything for fifteen years," Larry said. "You know that."

"Yeah."

"We don't need kids here!" Marty Robbins shouted.

"Don't reckon they'll eat as much between them as this lady would," Larry said. He turned to Tim and Eileen. "Look, Mr. Hamner, you see how it is? We got nothing against you, but—"

"But you're leaving," Marty Robbins said. There was satisfaction in his voice. He let it drop so that the woman couldn't hear. She had gotten into the car and was sitting in the back seat talking with the children. "I still say there are rangers out there. Hamner might find one. Tell you what, I'll go along with him when he leaves—"

"No." Larry was clearly disgusted.

"Maybe he should," Fritz said. "Way he thinks, I'm not sure we ever want to have him behind us. Maybe he should go and not come back. We could tough it out without him."

"We made a deal!" Marty cried. "When you came here! I let you in! We made a deal—"

"Sure we did," Fritz said. "But you better shut up about

murder or we may forget that deal. I see Mary Sue's bringing the kids. You want us to keep 'em, Mr. Hamner?"

So damned calm, Tim thought. Fritz and Larry. Two . . . two what? Carpenters? Landscape gardeners? Survivors now, convincing themselves they were still civilized people. "Since there's no gas left in the car, and Eileen and I aren't likely to get out of the mountains alive, it would be a good idea. Eileen, staying here might be your—"

"Not with that." She was looking at Robbins.

Fritz looked at Larry. They stared at each other for a moment. "I guess we've got a little gas," Fritz said. "Ten-gallon can, anyway. You can have that. Ten gallons of gas and a couple cans of soup. Now get back in that car before we change our minds about the gas."

Tim got back in the car, pulling Eileen along before she could make any more suggestions. The children were clustered around Mary Sue, but they were looking toward the car, and that scared look was going to be on their faces a lot from now on. Tim dredged up a reassuring smile and a wave. His fingers twitched with the need to get *going*, get away from those guns! But he waited.

Larry filled their tank.

Tim backed out of the drive and drove off into the rain.

The Mailman: One

Everything that is called duty, the prerequisite for all genuine law and the substance of every noble custom, can be traced back to honor. If one has to think about it, one is already without honor.

Oswald Spengler, *Thoughts*

Harry Newcombe saw nothing of Hammerfall, and it was Jason Gillcuddy's fault. Gillcuddy had imprisoned himself in the wilderness (he said) to diet and to write a novel. He had dropped twelve pounds in six months, but he could afford more. As for his isolation, it was certain that he would rather talk to a passing postman than write.

As the best coffee cup was to be found at the Silver Valley Ranch, so Gillcuddy, on the other side of the valley, made the best coffee. "But," Harry told him, smiling, "I'd slosh if I let everyone feed me two cups. I'm popular, I am."

"Kid, you'd better take it. My lease is up come Thursday, and *Ballad*'s finished. Next Trash Day I'll be gone."

"Finished. Hey, beautiful! Am I in it?"

"No, I'm sorry, Harry, but the damn thing was getting too big. You know how it is; what you like best is usually what has to go. But the coffee's Jamaica Blue Mountain. When I celebrate—"

"Yeah. Pour."

"Shot of brandy?"

"Have some respect for the uniform, *if* you . . . Well, hell, I can't pour it out, can I."

"To my publisher." Gillcuddy raised his cup, carefully. "He

331

said if I didn't fulfill his contract he'd put out a contract on *me*."

"Tough business."

"Well, but the money's good."

A distant thunderclap registered at the back of Harry's mind. Summer storm coming? He sipped at his coffee. It really was something special.

But there were no thunderclouds when he walked outside. Harry had been up before dawn; the valley farmers kept strange hours, and so did postmen. He had seen the pearly glow of the comet's tail wrapping the Earth. Some of that glory still clung, softening the direct sunlight and whiting the blue of the sky. Like smog, but clean. There was a strange stillness, as if the day were waiting for something.

So it was back to Chicago for Jason Gillcuddy, until the next time he had to imprison himself to diet and write a novel. Harry would miss him. Jason was the most literate man in the valley, possibly excepting the Senator—who was real. Harry had seen him from a distance yesterday, arriving in a vehicle the size of a bus. Maybe they'd meet today.

He was driving briskly along toward the Adams place when the truck began to shake. He braked. Flat tire? Damage to a wheel? The road shuddered and seemed to twist, the truck was trying to shake his brains out. He got it stopped. It was still shaking! He turned off the ignition. *Still* shaking?

"I should have looked at that brandy bottle. Huh. Earthquake?" The tremors died away. "There aren't any fault lines around here. I thought."

He drove on, more slowly. The Adams farm was a long jog on the new route he'd planned to get him there early. He didn't dare go up to the house . . . and that would save him a couple of minutes. There had been no new complaints from Mrs. Adams. But he hadn't seen Donna in weeks.

Harry took off his sunglasses. The day had darkened without his noticing. It was still darkening: clouds streaming across the sky like a speeded-up movie, lightning flashing in their dark bellies. Harry had never seen anything like it. Summer storm, right; it was going to rain.

The wind howled like demons breaking through from Hell. The sky had gone from ugly to hideous. Harry had never seen anything like these roiling black clouds sputtering with lightning. It would have served Mrs. Adams right, he thought vindictively, if he had left her mail in the box outside the gate.

But it might be Donna who would have to make the soggy trip. Harry drove up and parked under the porch overhang. As he got out the rain came, and the overhang was almost no protection; the wind whipped rain in all directions.

And it might have been Donna who answered the door, but it wasn't. Mrs. Adams showed no sign of pleasure at seeing him. Harry raised his voice above the storm—"Your mail, Mrs. Adams"—his voice as cold as her face.

"Thank you," she said, and closed the door firmly.

The rain poured from the sky like a thousand bathtubs emptying, and washed from the truck in filthy brown streams. It shamed Harry. He hadn't guessed that the truck was that dirty. He climbed in, half soaked already, and drove off.

Was weather like this common in the valley? Harry had been here just over a year, and he'd seen nothing remotely like this. Noah's Flood! He badly wanted to ask someone about it.

Anyone but Mrs. Adams.

This had been the dry season in the valley. Carper Creek had been way down, a mere ripple of water wetting the bottoms of the smooth white boulders that formed its bed, as late as this morning. But when Harry Newcombe drove across the wooden bridge, the creek was beating against the bottom and washing over the upstream edge. The rain still fell with frantic urgency.

Harry pulled way over to put two envelopes in Gentry's mailbox. The only time he had ever seen Gentry, the farmer had been pointing a shotgun at him. Gentry was a hermit, and his need for up-to-the-minute mail was not urgent, and Harry didn't like him.

His wheels spun disconcertingly before they caught and pulled him back on the road. Sooner or later he would get stuck. He had given up hope of finishing his route today. Maybe he could beg a meal and a couch from the Millers.

Now the road led steeply uphill. Harry drove in low gear, half blind in the rain and the lightning and the blackness between. Presently there was empty space on his left, a hillside on his right, trees covering both. Harry hugged the hillside. The cab was thoroughly wet, the air warm and 110 percent humid.

Harry braked sharply.

The hillside had slipped. It ran right across the road and on down, studded with broken and unbroken trees.

Briefly Harry considered going back. But it was back toward Gentry's and then the Adamses', and the hell with it: The rain had already washed part of the mudslide away; what was left wasn't all that steep. Harry drove up the mud lip. First gear and keep it moving. If he bogged down, it would be a wet walk home.

The truck lurched. Harry used wheel and accelerator, biting his lower lip. No use; the mud itself was sliding, he had to get off! He floored the accelerator. The wheels spun futilely, the truck tilted. Harry turned off the ignition and dove for the floorboards and covered his face with his arms.

The truck gently rocked and swung like a small boat at anchor; swung too far and turned on its side. Then it smashed into something massive, wheeled around and struck something else, and stopped moving.

Harry lifted his head.

A tree trunk had smashed the windshield. The frosted safety glass bowed inward before it. That tree and another now wedged the truck in place. It lay on the passenger side, and it wasn't coming out without a lot of help, at least a tow truck and men with chain saws.

Harry was hanging from the seat belt. Gingerly he unfastened it, decided he wasn't hurt.

And now what? He wasn't supposed to leave the mail unguarded, but he couldn't sit here all day! "How am I going to finish the route?" he asked himself, and giggled, because it was pretty obvious that he wasn't going to get that done today. He would have to let the mail pile up until tomorrow. The Wolf would be furious . . . and Harry couldn't help that.

He took the registered letter for Senator Jellison and slipped it into his pocket. There were a couple of small packets that Harry thought might be valuable, and he put them in another pocket. The big stuff, books, and the rest of the mail would just have to take care of itself.

He started out into the rain.

It drove into his face, blinding him, soaking him in an instant. The mud slipped beneath his feet, and in seconds he was clutching wildly at a small tree to keep from falling into the rapidly rising creek far below. He stood there a long moment.

No. He wasn't going to get to a telephone. Not through that. Better to wait it out. Luckily he was back on his charted route again; the Wolf would know where to look for him—

only Harry couldn't think of *any* vehicle that could reach him, not through *that*.

Lightning flared above him, a double flash, *blinkblink*. Thunder exploded instantly. He felt a distinct tingle in his wet feet. Close!

Painfully he made his way back to the truck and got inside. It wasn't insulated from the ground, but it seemed the safest place to wait out the lightning storm . . . and at least he hadn't left the mail unguarded. That had worried him. Better to deliver it late than let it be stolen.

Definitely better, he decided, and tried to make himself comfortable. The hours wore on and there was no sign of the storm letting up.

Harry slept badly. He made a nest back in the cargo compartment, sacrificing some shopping circulars and his morning newspaper. He woke often, always hearing the endless drumming of rain on metal. When earth and sky turned from lightning-lit black to dull gray with less lightning, Harry squirmed around and searched out yesterday's carton of milk. A premonition of need had made him leave it until now. It wasn't enough; he was famished. And he missed his morning coffee.

"Next place," he told himself, and imagined a big mug of hot steaming coffee, perhaps with a bit of brandy in it (although no one but Gillcuddy was going to offer him that).

The rain had slackened off a bit, and so had the howling wind. "Or else I'm going deaf," he said. "GOING DEAF! Well, maybe not." Cheerful by nature, he was quick to find the one bright point in a gloomy situation. "Good thing it isn't Trash Day," he told himself.

He took his feet out of the leather mailbag, where they'd stayed near-dry during the long night, and put his boots back on. Then he looked at the mail. There was barely enough light.

"First class only," he told himself. "Leave the books." He wondered about Senator Jellison's *Congressional Record*, and the magazines. He decided to take them. Eventually he had stuffed his bag with everything except the largest packages. He stood and wrestled the driver's door open, trapdoor fashion, and pushed the mailbag out onto the side—now the top—of the truck. Then he climbed out after it. The rain was still falling, and he spread a piece of plastic over the top of the mailbag.

The truck shifted uneasily.

Mud had piled along the high side of the truck, level with the wheels. Harry shouldered the bag and started uphill. He felt his footing shift, and he sprinted uphill.

Behind him the trees bowed before the weight of truck and shifting mud. Their roots pulled free, and the truck rolled, gathering speed.

Harry shook his head. This was probably his last circuit; Wolfe wouldn't like losing a truck. Harry started up the uneasy mud slope, looking about him as he went. He needed a walking stick. Presently he found a tilted sapling, five feet long and supple, that came out of the mud by its loosened roots.

Marching was easier after he reached the road. He was going downhill, back from the long detour to the Adamses'. The heavy mud washed off his boots and his feet grew lighter. The rain fell steadily. He kept looking upslope, alert for more mudslides.

"Five pounds of water in my hair alone," he groused. "Keeps my neck warm, though." The pack was heavy. A hip belt would have made carrying it easier.

Presently he began to sing.

> I went out to take a friggin' walk by the friggin' reservoir,
> a-wishin' for a friggin' quid to pay my friggin' score,
> my head it was a-achin' and my throat was parched and dry,
> and so I sent a little prayer, a-wingin' to the sky. . . .

He topped the slight rise and saw a blasted transmission tower. High-tension wires lay across the road. The steel tower had been struck by lightning, perhaps several times, and seemed twisted at the top.

How long ago? And why weren't the Edison people out to fix it? Harry shrugged. Then he noticed the telephone lines. They were down too. He wouldn't be calling in from his next stop.

> And there came a friggin' falcon and he walked upon the waves,
> and I said, "A friggin' miracle!" and sang a couple staves,
> of a friggin' churchy ballad I learned when I was young.

The friggin' bird took to the air, and spattered me
with dung.
 I fell upon my friggin' knees and bowed my friggin'
head,
and said three friggin' Aves for all my friggin' dead,
and then I got upon my feet and said another ten.
The friggin' bird burst into flame—and spattered me
again.

There was the Millers' gate. He couldn't see anyone. There
were no fresh ruts in their drive. Harry wondered if they'd
gone out last night. They certainly hadn't made it out today.
He sank into deep mud as he went up the long drive toward
the house. They wouldn't have a phone, but maybe he could
bum a cup of coffee, even a ride into town.

 The burnin' bird hung in the sky just like a friggin'
sun.
It seared my friggin' eyelids shut, and when the job
was done,
the friggin' bird flashed cross the sky just like a
shootin' star.
I ran to tell the friggin' priest—he bummed my last
cigar.
 I told him of the miracle, he told me of the Rose,
I showed him bird crap in my hair, the bastard held
his nose. I went to see the bishop but the friggin'
bishop said, "Go home and sleep it off, you sod—and
wash your friggin' head!"

No one answered his knock at the Millers' front door. The
door stood slightly ajar. Harry called in, loudly, and there
was still no answer. He smelled coffee.
He stood a moment, then fished out two letters and a copy
of *Ellery Queen's Mystery Magazine*, pushed the door open
and went inside, mail held like an ambassador's passport. He
sang loudly:

 Then I came upon a friggin' wake for a friggin'
rotten swine,
by the name of Jock O'Leary and I touched his head
with mine,
and old Jock sat up in his box and raised his friggin'
head.

His wife took out a forty-four, and shot the bastard
dead.
  Again I touched his head with mine and brought
him back to life.
His smiling face rolled on the floor, this time she used
a knife.
And then she fell upon her knees, and started in to
pray,
"It's forty years, O Lord," she said, "I've waited for
this day."

He left the mail on the front-room table where he usually
piled stuff on Trash Day, then wandered toward the kitchen,
led by the smell of coffee. He continued to sing loudly, lest
he be shot as an intruder.

  So I walked the friggin' city 'mongst the friggin'
  halt and lame, and every time I raised 'em up, they
  got knocked down again, 'cause the love of God comes
  down to man in a friggin' curious way, but when a man
  is marked for love, that love is here to stay.

There was coffee! The gas stove was working, and there was
a big pot of coffee on it, and three cups set out. Harry poured
one full. He sang in triumph:

  And this I know because I've got a friggin' curious
  sign; for every time I wash my head, the water turns
  to wine! And I gives it free to workin' blokes to
  brighten up their lives, so they don't kick no dogs
  around, nor beat up on their wives.

He found a bowl of oranges, resisted temptation for a full
ten seconds, then took one. He peeled it as he walked on
through the kitchen to the back door, out into the orange
groves behind. The Millers were natives. They'd know what
was happening. And they had to be around somewhere.

  'Cause there ain't no use to miracles like walkin'
  on the sea; They crucified the Son of God, but they
  don't muck with me! 'Cause I leave the friggin' blind
  alone, the dyin' and the dead, but every day at four
  o'clock, I wash my friggin' head!

"Ho, Harry!" a voice called. Somewhere to his right. Harry went through heavy mud and orange trees.

Jack Miller and his son Roy and daughter-in-law Cicelia were harvesting tomatoes in full panic. They'd spread a large tarp on the ground and were covering it with everything they could pick, ripe and half green. "They'll rot on the ground," Roy puffed. "Got to get them inside. Quick. Could sure use help."

Harry looked at his muddy boots, mailbag, sodden uniform. "You're not supposed to stay me," he said. "It's against government regulations. . . ."

"Yeah. Say, Harry, what's going on out there?" Roy demanded.

"You don't know?" Harry was appalled.

"How could we? Phone's been out since yesterday afternoon. Power out. No TV. Can't get a damned thing—sorry, Cissy. Get nothing but static on the transistor radio. What's it like in town?"

"Haven't been to town," Harry confessed. "Truck's dead, couple miles toward the Gentry place. Since yesterday. Spent the night in the truck."

"Hmm." Roy stopped his frantic picking for a moment. "Cissy, better get in and get to canning. Just the ripe ones. Harry, I'll make you a deal. Breakfast, lunch, a ride into town, and I don't tell nobody about what you were singing inside my house. You help us the rest of the day."

"Well . . ."

"I'll drive you and put in a good word," Cissy said.

The Millers carried some weight in the valley. The Wolf might not fire him for losing the truck if he had a good word. "I can't get in any quicker by walking," Harry said. "It's a deal." He set to work.

They didn't talk much, they needed their breath. Presently Cissy brought out sandwiches. The Millers hardly stopped long enough to eat. Then they went back to it.

When they did talk, it was about the weather. Jack Miller had seen nothing like it in his fifty-two years in the valley.

"Comet," Cissy said. "It did this."

"Nonsense," Roy said. "You heard the TV. It missed us by thousands of miles."

"It did? Good," Harry said.

"We didn't hear that it missed. Heard it was *going* to miss," Jack Miller said. He went back to harvesting tomatoes. When they got those picked, there were beans and squashes.

Harry had never worked so hard in his life. He realized

339

suddenly it was getting late afternoon. "Hey, I have *got* to get to town!" he insisted.

"Yeah. Okay, Cissy," Jack Miller called. "Take the pickup. Get by the feedstore, we're going to need lots of cattle and hog feed. Damned rain's battered down most of the fodder. Better get feed before everybody else thinks of it. Price'll be sky-high in a week."

"If there's anyplace to buy it in a week," Cissy said.

"What do you mean by that?" her husband demanded.

"Nothing." She went off to the barn, tight jeans bulging, water dripping from her hat. She came out with the Dodge pickup. Harry squeezed into the seat, mailbag on his lap to protect it from the rain. He'd left it in the barn while he worked.

The truck had no trouble with the muddy drive. When they got to the gate, Cissy got out; Harry couldn't move with the big mailbag. She laughed at him when she got back in.

They hadn't gone half a mile when the road ended in a gigantic crack. The road had pulled apart, and the hillside with it, and tons of sloppy mud had come off the hillside to cover the road beyond the crack.

Harry studied it carefully. Cicelia backed and twisted to turn the truck around. Harry started toward the ruined road.

"You're not going to walk!" she said.

"Mail must go through," Harry muttered. He laughed. "Didn't finish the route yesterday—"

"Harry, don't be silly! There will be a road crew out today, tomorrow for sure. Wait for that! You won't get to town before dark, maybe not at all in this rain. Come back to the house."

He thought about that. What she said made sense. Power lines down, roads out, telephone lines out; *somebody* would come through here. The mailbag seemed terribly heavy. "All right."

They put him back to work, of course. He'd expected that. They didn't eat until after dark, but it was an enormous meal, suitable for farmhand appetites. Harry couldn't stay awake, and collapsed on the couch. He didn't even notice when Jack and Roy took his uniform off him and covered him with a blanket.

Harry woke to find the house empty. His uniform, hung to dry, was still soggy. Rain pounded relentlessly at the farmhouse. He dressed and found coffee. While he was drinking it, the others came in.

Cicelia made a breakfast of ham and pancakes and more coffee. She was strong and tall, but she looked tired now. Roy kept eying her anxiously.

"I'm all right," she said. "Not used to doing men's work and my own too."

"We got most of it in," Jack Miller said. "Never saw rain like this, though." There was a softness, a wondering in Jack Miller's voice that might have been superstitious fear. "Those bastards at the Weather Bureau never gave us a minute's warning. What are they doing with all those shiny weather satellites?"

"Maybe the comet knocked them out," Harry said.

Jack Miller glared. "Comet. Humph. Comets are things in the sky! Live in the twentieth century, Harry!"

"I tried it once. I like it better here."

He got a soft smile from Cissy. He liked it. "I'd best be on my way," he said.

"In this?" Roy Miller was incredulous. "You can't be serious."

Harry shrugged. "Got my route to finish."

The others looked guilty. "Reckon we can run you down to where the road's out," Jack Miller said. "Maybe a work crew got in already."

"Thanks."

There wasn't any work crew. More mud had slid off the hillside during the night.

"Wish you'd stay," Jack said. "Can use the help."

"Thanks. I'll let people in town know how it is with you."

"Right. Thanks. Good luck."

"Yeah."

It was just possible to pick his way across the crack, over the mudslide. The heavy mailbag dragged at his shoulder. It was leather, waterproof, with the plastic over the top. Just as well, Harry thought. All that paper could soak up twenty or thirty pounds of water. It would make it much harder. "Make it hard to read the mail, too," Harry said aloud.

He trudged on down the road, slipping and sliding, until he found another sapling to replace the one he'd left at the Millers' place. It had too many roots at the bottom, but it kept him upright.

"This is the pits," Harry shouted into the rain-laden wind. Then he laughed and added, "But it's got to beat farm work."

The rain had stopped Harry's watch. He thought it was just past eleven when he reached the gate of the Shire. It was almost two.

He was back in flat country now, out of the hills. There had been no more breaks in the road. But there was always the water and the mud. He couldn't see the road anywhere; he had to infer it from the shape of the glistening mud-covered landscape. Soggy everywhere, dimly aware of the chafe spots developing beneath his clinging uniform, moving against the resistance of his uniform and the mud that clung to his boots, Harry thought he had made good time, considering.

He still hoped to finish his route in somebody's car. It wasn't likely he'd find a ride at the Shire, though.

He had seen nobody while he walked along the Shire's split-log fence. Nobody in the fields, nobody trying to save whatever crops the Shire was growing. Were they growing anything? Nothing Harry recognized; but Harry wasn't a farmer.

The gate was sturdy. The padlock on it was new and shiny and big. Harry found the mailbox bent back at forty-five degrees, as if a car had hit it. The box was full of water.

Harry was annoyed. He carried eight letters for the Shire, and a thick, lumpy manila envelope. He threw back his head and hollered, "Hey in there! *Mail call!*"

The house was dark. Power out here, too? Or had Hugo Beck and his score of strange guests all tired of country life and gone away?

The Shire was a commune. Everyone in the valley knew that, and few knew more. The Shire let the valley people alone. Harry, in his privileged occupation, had met Hugo Beck and a few of the others.

Hugo had inherited the spread from his aunt and uncle three years ago, when they racked up their car on a Mexico vacation. It had been called something else then: Inverted Fork Ranch, some such name, probably named after a branding iron. Hugo Beck had arrived for the funeral: a pudgy boy of eighteen who wore his straight black hair at shoulder length and a fringe of beard with the chin bared. He'd looked the place over, and stayed to sell the cattle and most of the horses, and left. A month later he'd returned, followed by (the number varied according to who was talking) a score of hippies. There was enough money, somehow, to keep them alive and fairly comfortable. Certainly the Shire was not a successful business. It exported nothing. But they must be growing some food; they didn't import enough from town.

Harry hollered again. The front door opened and a human shape strolled down to the gate.

It was Tony. Harry knew him. Scrawny and sun-darkened, grinning to show teeth that had been straightened in youth, Tony was dressed as usual: jeans, wool vest, no shirt, digger hat, sandals. He looked at Harry through the gate. "Hey, man, what's happenin'?" The rain affected him not at all.

"The picnic's been called off. I came to tell you."

Tony looked blank, then laughed. "The picnic! Hey, that's funny. I'll tell them. They're all huddling in the house. Maybe they think they'll melt."

"I'm half melted already. Here's your mail." Harry handed it over. "Your mailbox is wrecked."

"It won't matter." Tony seemed to be grinning at some private joke.

Harry skipped it. "Can you spare someone to run me into town? I wrecked my truck."

"Sorry. We want to save the gas for emergencies."

What did he think this was? Harry held his temper. "Such is life. Can you spare me a sandwich?"

"Nope. Famine coming. We got to think of ourselves."

"I don't get you." Harry was beginning to dislike Tony's grin.

"The Hammer has fallen," said Tony. "The Establishment is dead. No more draft. No more taxes. No more wars. No more going to jail for smoking pot. No more having to pick between a crook and an idiot for President." Tony grinned beneath the shapeless, soggy hat. "No more Trash Day either. I thought I'd flipped when I saw a mailman at the gate!"

Tony really had flipped, Harry realized. He tried to side-step the issue. "Can you get Hugo Beck down here?"

"Maybe."

Harry watched Tony reenter the farmhouse. Was there anyone alive in there? Tony had never struck him as danger-ous, but . . . if he stepped out with anything remotely like a rifle, Harry was going to run like a deer.

Half a dozen of them came out. One girl was in rain gear; the rest seemed to be dressed for swimming. Maybe that made a kind of sense. You couldn't hope to stay dry in this weather. Harry recognized Tony, and Hugo Beck, and the broad-shouldered, broad-hipped girl who called herself Galadriel, and a silent giant whose name he'd never learned. They clustered at the gate, hugely amused.

Harry asked, "What's it all about?"

Much of Hugo Beck's fat had turned to muscle in the past three years, but he still didn't look like a farmer. Maybe it was the expensive sandals and worn swim trunks; or maybe it was the way he lounged against the gate, exactly as Jason Gillcuddy the writer would lounge against his bar, leaving one hand free to gesture.

"Hammerfall," said Hugo. "You could be the last mailman we ever see. Consider the implications. No more ads to buy things you can't afford. No more friendly reminders from the collection agency. You should throw away that uniform, Harry. The Establishment's dead."

"The comet *hit* us?"

"Right."

"*Huh.*" Harry didn't know whether to believe it or not. There had been talk . . . but a comet was nothing. Dirty vacuum, lit by unfiltered sunlight, very pretty when seen from a hilltop with the right girl beside you. This rain, though. What about the rain?

"*Huh.* So I'm a member of the Establishment?"

"That's a uniform, isn't it?" said Beck, and the others laughed.

Harry looked down. "Somebody should have told me. All right, you can't feed me and you can't transport me—"

"No more gas, maybe forever. The rain is going to wipe out most of the crops. You can see that, Harry."

"Yeah. Can you loan me a hatchet for fifteen minutes?"

"Tony, get the hatchet."

Tony jogged up to the farmhouse. Hugo asked, "What are you going to do with it?"

"Trim the roots off my walking stick."

"What then?"

He didn't have to answer, because Tony was back with the hatchet. Harry went to work. The Shire people watched. Presently Hugo asked again. "What do you do now?"

"Deliver the mail," said Harry.

"Why?" A frail and pretty blonde girl cried, "It's all over, man. No more letters to your congressman. No more PLAYBOY. No more tax forms or . . . or voting instructions. You're free! Take off the uniform and dance!"

"I'm already cold. My feet hurt."

"Have a hit." The silent giant was handing a generously

fat homemade cigarette through the gate, shielding it with Tony's digger hat. Harry saw the others' disapproval, but they said nothing, so he took the toke. He held his own hat over it while he lit it and drew.

Were they growing the weed here? Harry didn't ask. But . . . "You'll have trouble getting papers."

They looked at each other. That hadn't occurred to them.

"Better save that last batch of letters. No more Trash Day." Harry passed the hatchet back through the bars. "Thanks. Thanks for the toke, too." He picked up the trimmed sapling. It felt lighter, better balanced. He got his arm through the mailbag strap.

"Anyway, it's the mail. 'Neither rain, nor sleet, nor heat of day, nor gloom of night,' et cetera."

"What does it say," Hugo Beck asked, "about the end of the world?"

"I think it's optional. I'm going to deliver the mail."

The Mailman: Two

> *Among the deficiencies common to the Italian and the U.S. postal systems are:*
> - *inefficiency, and delays in deliveries*
> - *old-fashioned organization*
> - *low efficiency and low salaries of personnel*
> - *high frequency of strikes*
> - *very high operational deficit*
>
>   Roberto Vacca, *The Coming Dark Age*

Carrie Roman was a middle-aged widow with two big sons who were Harry's age and twice Harry's size. Carrie was almost as big as they were. Three jovial giants, they formed one of Harry's coffee stops. Once before, they had given Harry a lift to town to report a breakdown of the mail truck.

Harry reached their gate in a mood of bright optimism.

The gate was padlocked, of course, but Jack Roman had rigged a buzzer to the house. Harry pushed it and waited.

The rain poured over him, gentle, inexorable. If it had started raining up from the ground, Harry doubted he would notice. It was all of his environment, the rain.

Where were the Romans? Hell, of course they had no electricity. Harry pushed the buzzer again, experimentally.

From the corner of his eye he saw someone crouched low, sprinting from behind a tree. The figure was only visible for an instant; then bushes hid it. But it carried something the shape of a shovel, or a rifle, and it was too small to be one of the Romans.

"Mail call!" Harry cried cheerily. What the hell was going on here?

The sound of a gunshot matched the gentle tugging at the edge of his mailbag. Harry threw himself flat. The bag was higher than he was as he crawled for cover, and it jerked

347

once, coinciding with another gunshot. A .22, he thought. Not much rifle. Certainly not much for the valley. He pulled himself behind a tree, his breath raspy and very loud in his own ears.

He wriggled the bag off his shoulder and set it down. He squatted and selected four envelopes tied with a rubber band. Crouched. Then, all in an instant, he sprinted for the Roman mailbox, slid the packet into it, and was running for cover again when the first shot came. He lay panting beside his mailbag, trying to think.

Harry wasn't a policeman, he wasn't armed, and there wasn't anything he could do to help the Romans. No way!

And he couldn't use the road. No cover.

The gully on the other side? It would be full of water, but it was the best he could do. Sprint across the road, then crawl on hands and knees . . .

But he'd have to leave the mailbag.

Why not? Who am I kidding? Hammerfall has come, and there's no need for mail carriers. None. What does that make me?

He didn't care much for the question.

"It makes me," he said aloud, "a turkey who got good grades in high school by working his arse off, flunked out of college, got fired from every job he ever had. . . ."

It makes me a mailman, goddammit! He lifted the heavy bag and crouched again. Things were quiet up there. Maybe they'd been shooting to keep him away? But what for?

He took in a deep breath. Do it now, he told himself. Before you're too scared to do it at all. He dashed into the road, across, and dived toward the gulley. There was another shot, but he didn't think the bullet had come anywhere close. Harry scuttled down the gulley, half crawling, half swimming, mailbag shoved around onto his back to keep it out of the water.

There were no more shots. Thank God! The Many Names Ranch was only half a mile down the road. Maybe they had guns, or a telephone that worked . . . Did any telephones work? The Shire wasn't precisely an official information source, but they'd been so sure.

"Never find a cop when you need one," Harry muttered.

He'd have to be careful showing himself at Many Names. The owners might be a bit nervous. And if they weren't, they damned well should be!

It was dusk when Harry reached Muchos Nombres Ranch. The rain had increased and was falling slantwise, and lightning played across the nearly black sky.

Muchos Nombres was thirty acres of hilly pastureland dotted with the usual great white boulders. Of the four families who jointly owned it, two would sometimes invite Harry in for coffee. The result was diffidence on Harry's part. He never knew whose turn it was. The families each owned one week in four, and they treated the ranch as a vacation spot. Sometimes they traded off; sometimes they brought guests. The oversupply of owners had been unable to agree on a name, and had finally settled for Muchos Nombres. The Spanish fooled nobody.

Today Harry was fresh out of diffidence. He yelled his "Mail call!" and waited, expecting no answer. Presently he opened the gate and went on in.

He reached the front door like something dragged from an old grave. He knocked.

The door opened.

"Mail," said Harry. "Hullo, Mr. Freehafer. Sorry to be so late, but there are some emergencies going."

Freehafer had an automatic pistol. He looked Harry over with some care. Behind him the living room danced with candlelight, and it looked crowded with wary people. Doris Lilly said, "Why, it's Harry! It's all right, Bill. It's Harry the mailman."

Freehafer lowered the gun. "All right, pleased to meet you, Harry. Come on in. What emergencies?"

Harry stepped inside, out of the rain. Now he saw the third man, stepping around a doorjamb, laying a shotgun aside. "Mail," said Harry, and he set down two magazines, the usual haul for Many Names. "Somebody shot at me from Carrie Roman's place. It wasn't anyone I know. I think the Romans are in trouble. Is your phone working?"

"No," said Freehafer. "We can't go out there tonight."

"Okay. And my mail truck went off a hill, and I don't know what the roads are like. Can you let me have a couch, or a stretch of rug, and something to eat?"

The hesitation was marked. "It's the rug, I'm afraid," Freehafer said. "Soup and a sandwich do you? We're a little short."

"I'd eat your old shoes," said Harry.

It was canned tomato soup and a grilled cheese sandwich, and it tasted like heaven. Between bites he got the story: how the Freehafers had started to leave on Tuesday, and seen the sky going crazy, and turned back. How the Lillys had arrived (it being their turn now) with the Rodenberries as guests, and their own two children. The end of the world had come and gone, the Rodenberries were on the couches, and nobody had yet tried to reach the supermarket in town.

"What is this with the end of the world?" Harry asked.

They told him. They showed him, in the magazines he'd brought. The magazines were damp but still readable. Harry read interviews with Sagan and Asimov and Sharps. He stared at artists' conceptions of major meteor impacts. "They all think it'll miss," he said.

"It didn't," said Norman Lilly. He was a football player turned insurance executive, a broad-shouldered wall of a man who should have kept up his exercises. "Now what? We brought some seeds and farm stuff, just in case, but we didn't bring any books. Do you know anything about farming, Harry?"

"No. People, I've had a rough day—"

"Right. No sense wasting candles," said Norman.

All of the beds, blankets and couches were in use. Harry spent the night on a thick rug, swathed in three of Norman Lilly's enormous bathrobes, his head on a chair pillow. He was comfortable enough, but he kept twitching himself awake.

Lucifer's Hammer? End of the world? Crawling through mud while bullets punched into his mailbag and the letters inside. He kept waking with the memory of a nightmare, and always the nightmare was real.

Harry woke and counted days. First night he slept in the truck. Second with the Millers. Last night was the third. Three days since he'd reported in.

It was definitely the end of the world. The Wolf should have come looking for him with blood in his eye. He hadn't. The power lines were still down. The phones weren't working. No county road crews. Ergo, Hammerfall. The end of the world. It had really happened.

"Rise and shine!" Doris Lilly's cheer was artificial. She tried to keep it up anyway. "Rise and shine! Come and get it or we throw it out."

Breakfast wasn't much. They shared with Harry, which was pretty damned generous of them. The Lilly children, eight and ten, stared at the adults. One of them complained that the TV wasn't working. No one paid any attention.

"Now what?" Freehafer asked.

350

"We get food," Doris Lilly said. "We have to find something to eat."

"Where do you suggest we look?" Bill Freehafer asked. He wasn't being sarcastic.

Doris shrugged. "In town? Maybe things aren't as bad as . . . maybe they're not so bad."

"I want to watch TV," Phil Lilly said.

"Not working," Doris said absently. "I vote we go to town and see how things are. We can give Harry a ride—"

"TV *now!*" Phil screamed.

"Shut up," his father said.

"Now!" the boy repeated.

Smack! Norman Lilly's huge hand swept against the boy's face.

"Norm!" his wife cried. The child screamed, more in surprise than pain. "You never hit the children before—"

"Phil," Lilly said. His voice was calm and determined. "It's all different now. You better understand that. When we tell you to be quiet, you'll be *quiet*. You and your sister both, you've got a lot of learning to do, and quick. Now go in the other room."

The children hesitated for a moment. Norman raised his hand. They looked at him, startled, then ran.

"Little drastic," Bill Freehafer said.

"Yeah," Norm said absently. "Bill, don't you think we better look in on our neighbors?"

"Let the police—" Bill Freehafer stopped himself. "Well, there might still be police."

"Yeah. Who'll they take orders from, now?" Lilly asked. He looked at Harry.

Harry shrugged. There was a local mayor. The Sheriff was out in the San Joaquin, and with this rain that could be under water. "Maybe the Senator?" Harry said.

"Hey, yeah, Jellison lives over the hill there," Freehafer said. "Maybe we should . . . Jesus, I don't know, Norm. What can we do?"

Lilly shrugged. "We can look, anyway. Harry, you know those people?"

"Yes . . ."

"We have two cars. Bill, you take everybody else into town. Harry and I'll have a look. Right?"

Harry looked dubious. "I've already left their mail—"

"Jesus," Bill Freehafer said.

Norman Lilly held up an immense hand. "He's right, you know. But look at it this way, Harry. You're a mailman."

"Yes—"

"Which can be damned valuable. Only there won't be any mail. Not letters and magazines, anyway. But there's still a need for message carriers. Somebody to keep communications going. Right?"

"Something like that," Harry agreed.

"Good. You'll be needed. More than ever. But here's your first post-comet message. To the Romans, from us. We're willing to help, if we can. They're our neighbors. But we don't know them, and they don't know us. If they've had trouble they'll be watching for strangers. Somebody's got to introduce us. That's a worthwhile message, isn't it?"

Harry thought it over. It made sense. "You'll give me a ride after—"

"Sure. Let's go." Norm Lilly went out. He came back with a deer rifle, and the automatic pistol. "Ever use one of these, Harry?"

"No. And I don't want one. Wrong image."

Lilly nodded and laid the pistol on the table.

Bill Freehafer started to say something, but Lilly's look cut it off. "Okay, Harry, let's go," Norm said. He didn't comment when Harry carried his mailbag to the car.

They got in. They'd gone halfway when Harry patted his bag and, half laughing himself, said, "You're not laughing at me."

"How can I laugh at a man who's got a purpose in life?"

They pulled up at the gate. The letters were gone from the mailbox. The padlock was still in place. "Now what?" Harry asked.

"Good questi—"

The shotgun caught Norm Lilly full in the chest. Lilly kicked once and died. Harry stood in shock, then dashed across the road for the ditch. He sprawled into it, headfirst into the muddy water, careless of the mailbag, of getting wet, of anything. He began to run toward Many Names again.

There were sounds ahead of him. Right around that bend— and there was someone coming behind, too. They weren't going to let him get away this time. In desperation he crawled up the bank, away from the road, and began scrambling up the steep hillside. The mailbag dragged at him. His boots dug into mud, slipping and sliding. He clawed at the ground and pulled himself upward.

SPANG! The shot sounded very loud. Much louder than the .22 yesterday. Maybe the shotgun? Harry kept on. He reached the top of the first rise and began to run.

He couldn't tell if they were still behind him. He didn't care. He wasn't going back down there. He kept remembering the look of surprise on Norman Lilly's face. The big man folding up, dying before he hit the ground. Who were these people who shot without warning?

The hill became steeper again, but the ground was harder, more rock than mud. The mailbag seemed heavy. Water in it? Probably. So why carry it?

Because it's the mail, you stupid SOB, Harry told himself.

The Chicken Ranch was owned by an elderly couple, re-tired L.A. business people. It was fully automated. The chickens stood in small pens not much bigger than an individual chicken. Eggs rolled out of the cage onto a conveyor belt. Food came around on another belt. Water was continuously supplied. It was not a ranch but a factory.

And it might have been heaven, for chickens. All problems were solved, all struggling ended. Chickens weren't very bright, and they got all they could eat, were protected from coyotes, had clean cages—another automated system—

But it had to be a damned dull existence.

The Chicken Ranch was over the next hill. Before Harry got there he saw chickens. Through the rain and the wet weeds they wandered, bewildered, pecking at the ground and the limbs of bushes and Harry's boots, squawking plaintively at Harry, demanding instructions.

Harry stopped walking. Something must be terribly wrong. The Sinanians would never have let the chickens run loose.

Here too? Those bastards, had they come here too? Harry stood on the hillside and dithered, and the chickens huddled around him.

He had to know what had happened. It was part of the job. Reporter, mailman, town crier, message carrier; if he wasn't that, he wasn't anything. He stood among the chickens, nerving himself, and eventually he went down.

All the chicken feed had been spilled out onto the floor of the barn. There was little left. Every cage was open. This was no accident. Harry waded through squawking chickens the full length of the building. Nothing there. He went out and down the path to the house.

The farmhouse door stood open. He called. No one answered. Finally he went inside. It was dimly lit; the shades and curtains were drawn and there was no artificial light. His way led him to the living room.

The Sinanians were there. They sat in big overstuffed chairs. Their eyes were open. They did not move.

Amos Sinanian had a bullet hole in his temple. His eyes bulged. There was a small pistol in his hand.

Mrs. Sinanian had not a mark on her. Heart attack? Whatever it was, it had been peaceful; her features were not contorted, and her clothing was carefully arranged. She stared at a blank TV screen. She looked to have been dead two days, possibly more. The blood on Amos's head was not quite dry. This morning at the latest.

There wasn't any note, no sign of explanation. There hadn't been anyone Amos had cared to explain it to. He'd released the chickens and shot himself.

It took Harry a long time to make up his mind. Finally he took the pistol from Amos's hand. It wasn't as hard to do as he'd thought it would be. He put the pistol in his pocket and searched until he found a box of bullets for it. He pocketed those, too.

"The mail goes through, dammit," he said. Then he found a cold roast in the refrigerator. It wouldn't keep anyway, so Harry ate it. The oven was working. Harry had no idea how much propane there might be in the tank, but it didn't matter. The Sinanians weren't going to be using it.

He took the mail out of his bag and put it carefully into the oven to dry. Circulars and shopping newspapers were a problem. Their information wasn't any use, but might people want them for paper? Harry compromised, throwing out the ones that were thin and flimsy and soaked, keeping the others.

He found a supply of Baggies in the kitchen and carefully enclosed each packet of mail in one. Last Baggies on Earth, a small voice told him. "Right," he said, and went on stuffing. "Have to keep the Baggies. You can have your mail, but the Baggies belong to the Service."

After that was done he thought about his next move. This house might be useful. It was a good house, stone and concrete, not wood. The barn was concrete too. The land wasn't much good—at least Amos had said it wasn't—but somebody might make use of the buildings. "Even me," Harry said to himself. He had to have some place to stay between rounds.

Which meant something had to be done about the bodies. Harry wasn't up to digging two graves. He sure as hell wasn't going to drag them out for the coyotes and buzzards. There wasn't enough dry wood to cremate a mouse.

Finally he went out again. He found an old pickup truck. The keys were in the ignition, and it started instantly. It sounded smooth, in good tune. There was a drum of gasoline in the shed, and Harry thoughtfully filled the tank of the truck, filled two gas cans, then stacked junk against the drum to hide it.

He went back into the house and got old bedclothes to wrap the bodies, then drove the truck around to the front of the house. The chickens swarmed around his feet, demanding attention, while he wrestled the corpses onto the truck bed. Finished, Harry stooped and quickly wrung six chickens' necks before the rest of the chickens got the idea. He tossed the birds into the truck with the Sinanians.

He went around carefully locking doors and windows, put Amos's keys in his pockets and drove away.

He still had his route to finish. But there were things he must do first, not the least of which was burying the Sinanians.

The Stronghold: One

> *It is certain that free societies would have no easy*
> *time in a future dark age. The rapid return to uni-*
> *versal penury will be accomplished by violence and*
> *cruelties of a kind now forgotten. The force of law*
> *will be scant or nil, either because of the collapse or*
> *disappearance of the machinery of state, or because*
> *of difficulties of communication and transport. It will*
> *be possible only to delegate authority to local powers*
> *who will maintain it by force alone. . . .*
>
> Roberto Vacca, *The Coming Dark Age*

Senator Arthur Jellison was in a foul mood on Hammerfall Morning. The only people he could get at JPL were PR flacks, who didn't know anything that wasn't being reported on radio and TV. There was no way to reach Charlie Sharps. It made sense, but Senator Jellison wasn't used to having people too busy to talk to him. Finally he settled for a phone patch into the space communications network, so he could hear what the astronauts were saying.

That didn't help much because of the static. The live TV shots were bad, too. Was the damned thing going to hit or not?

If it did hit, there were a lot of moves Jellison should have made but hadn't, because he couldn't afford to look like a fool to his constituents, not even here in the valley, where he routinely got eighty percent of the vote. He'd brought his family and a couple of assistants and as much gear as he could buy without attracting a lot of attention, and that was about all he could do. Now they were all gathered in the house, most of them sitting with him in the big living room.

The phone speaker squawked. Johnny Baker's voice, and Maureen came unnaturally alert. Jellison had known about that for a long time, but he didn't think Maureen knew he was aware. Now Baker had his divorce, and his Hammerlab mission. Maybe, when he got down . . . That would be a good thing. Maureen needed somebody.

So did Charlotte, but she thought she had him. Jellison didn't care for Jack Turner. His son-in-law was too handsome, too quick to talk about his tennis medals, and not quick at all to pay back the sizable "loans" he asked for when his investments didn't turn out so well—as they almost never did. But Charlotte seemed happy enough with him, and the kids were being well brought up, and Maureen was getting old enough that maybe Charlotte's would be the only grandchildren he'd ever have. Jellison rather hoped not.

"Crummy pictures," Jack Turner said.

"Grandpa will get us good ones," Jennifer Turner, nine, told her father. She'd found that her grandfather could get photographs and pins and things that made a big hit in her school classes, and she'd read all about comets.

"Hammerlab, this is Houston, we do not copy," the telephone speaker said.

"Grandpa—"

"Hush, Jenny," Maureen said. The tension in her voice quieted the room. The TV picture became a crazy pattern of blurs, then sharpened to show a myriad of rocks enveloped in vapor and fog rushing toward them out of the screen.

"Jesus, it's coming close!"

"That's Johnny—"

"Like it's going to hit—"

The TV image vanished. The phone line continued to chatter. "FIREBALL OVERHEAD!" "HOUSTON, HOUSTON, THERE IS A LARGE STRIKE IN THE GULF OF MEXICO. . . ."

"Good Lord!"

"Shut up, Jack," Jellison said quietly.

". . . REQUEST YOU SEND A HELICOPTER FOR OUR FAMILIES. . . . THE HAMMER HAS FALLEN."

"You shouldn't talk to Jack that way—"

Jellison ignored Charlotte. "Al!" he shouted.

"Yes, sir," Hardy answered from the next room. He came in quickly.

"Round up all the ranch-hands. Quick. Any that have trucks should bring them. And rifles. Get moving."

"Right." Hardy vanished.

The others seemed stunned. Jennifer asked, plaintively, "What happened, Grandpa?"

"Don't know," Jellison said. "Don't know how bad it was.

Damned phone's dead. Maureen, see if you can get anything, anybody, at JPL on that phone. Move."

"Right."

Then he looked at Jack Turner. Turner wasn't known in the valley. No one would take orders from him. And what use was he? "Jack, get one of the Scouts started. You'll drive me into town. I want to see the Chief of Police. And the Mayor."

Turner almost said something, but the look on Jellison's face stopped that.

"Can't get through to L.A. at all, Dad," Maureen said. "The phone's working but—"

She was interrupted by the earthquake. It wasn't very strong, this far from California's major faults, but it was enough to shake the house. The children looked afraid, and Charlotte gathered them to her and took them to a bedroom.

"I can get the local phone numbers," Maureen finished.

"Good. Get the local police and tell them I'm coming to town to talk to their Chief, and the Mayor. It's important, and tell them I'm already on the way. Let's go, Jack. Maureen, when Al gets the ranch-hands together, you and Al talk to them. What we'll need is every friend they've got, all their trucks, rifles, everything. There's a lot to do. Send about half the troops into town to find me, and have the rest secure for rainstorms, mudslides . . ." He thought for a moment. "And snow, if Charlie Sharps knows what he's talking about. Snow within a week."

"Snow? That's stupid," Jack Turner protested.

"Right," Maureen said. "Anything else, Dad?"

The City Hall doubled as library, jail and police station. The local Chief commanded two full-time patrolmen and several unpaid volunteer auxiliaries. The Mayor owned the local feedstore. Government in Silver Valley was not a large or important activity.

The rain started before Jellison arrived at City Hall. Sheet lightning played over the High Sierra to the east. Rain fell like the outpouring of a warm bathtub, filling the streets and running over the low bridges over the creeks. Mayor Gil Seitz looked worried. He seemed very glad to see Senator Jellison.

There were a dozen others in the large library room. Chief of Police Randy Hartman, a retired cop from one of the large eastern cities; three city councilmen; a couple of local store

359

owners. Jellison recognized the bullnecked man sitting toward the rear of the group, and waved. He didn't see his neighbor George Christopher very often.

Jellison introduced his son-in-law and shook hands around. The room fell silent.

"What's happened, Senator?" the Mayor asked. "Did . . . that thing really did hit us, didn't it?"

"Yes."

"I saw magazine articles about it," Mayor Seitz mused. "Glaciers. East Coast wiped out." There was a crash of thunder and Gil Seitz waved toward the windows. "Didn't believe it before. Now I guess I have to. How long does that rain go on?"

"Weeks," Jellison said.

That sobered them all. They were all farmers, or lived in a community where farming—and farming weather—was the most important topic of conversation. They all knew what weeks of pounding rain would do.

"Animals will starve," Seitz said. There was a momentary smile as he thought of the prices his feedstore inventory would bring; then a frown as he thought it through. "Just how much damage did that do? Will there be trucks left? Trains? Feed deliveries?"

Jellison didn't say anything for a moment. "The science people tell me it'll be raining like this all across the country," he said slowly.

"Jesus Christ," the Mayor said. "Nobody gets in a crop this year. *Nobody*. What's in the elevators and granaries is *it*."

"And I don't reckon anybody's going to send much to us," George Christopher observed. Everyone nodded agreement. "If it's that bad. . . . Is it?"

"Don't know," Jellison said. "Good chance it's worse."

Seitz turned to study the big contour map of Tulare and adjacent counties that hung on the library wall. "Jesus, Senator, what do we do? The San Joaquin's going to fill up, rain like this. Fill right up. And there's a lot of people out there. A *lot*."

"And they'll all head this way, looking for high ground," George Christopher added. "Where'll we put 'em? How can we feed them all? We can't."

Jellison sat on the edge of a library table. "Gil, George, I've always suspected you both had more sense than you let on. That's the problem, no doubt about it. Half a million, maybe more people in the San Joaquin, and they'll all be looking for high ground. More people up in the Sierra, went up to get away from the comet, and they'll be coming down here now. People from as far as L.A. will come here. What do we *do* with them all?"

"Let's get this straight," one of the councilmen said. "It's a disaster, but you're saying . . ." He broke down, unable to finish for a moment. "You're saying that the Army, the President, Sacramento, everybody's knocked out? We're on our own *forever?*"

"We may be," Jellison said. "Maybe not, too."

"It makes a difference," George Christopher said. "We can take care of all those people for a week. Maybe two. Not longer. Longer than that, *somebody's* got to starve. Who'll it be? All of us because we tried to keep a hundred times too many alive for a couple of weeks?"

"That's the problem, all right," Mayor Seitz agreed.

"I'm not feeding any of them," George Christopher said. His voice was like granite. "I have my own to take care of."

"You can't . . . you can't just abandon all your responsibilities," Jack Turner said.

"Don't think I have any to outsiders," Christopher said. "Not if they're going to die anyway."

"Some of them won't make it," Chief Hartman said. He pointed to the big map. "Porterville and Visalia are both in old river bottoms. Flood basins. Rain like this, I doubt those flood-control dams will hold very long."

They all looked at the maps. It was true. Lake Success hung over Porterville, billions of gallons of water poised to plunge down on the city. Visalia to the north was no better off.

"Not just the rain," Mayor Seitz said thoughtfully. "Warm rain, while there's still some snow in the high country. Expect that's all melted by now, sure by this afternoon—"

"We have to warn those people!" Jack Turner said.

"Do we?" asked a councilman.

"Sure we do," Chief Hartman said. "And then what do we feed them with when they all come here? The stock out of Granny Mason's store?"

There was a babble of talk in the room.

"How long will those dams last?" Jellison asked. "All day?"

No one knew for sure. The telephone wasn't working, so they couldn't call the county engineers.

"What did you have in mind, Senator?" Chief Hartman asked.

"Is there time to get trucks down in that area? Strip the

361

supermarkets, feedstores, hardware stores, whatever, before the dams go?"

There was a long silence. Then one of the councilmen got up. "I reckon that dam will hold the day out. If the water don't come too fast it can't stop my truck anyway. I got a big ten-wheeler. I'll go."

"Not alone," Jellison warned. "And not unarmed."

"I'll send my constables down with him," Hartman said.

"What happens to the stuff?" George Christopher demanded.

"We share," Jellison said.

"Share. If you share with me, it means you expect me to share with you," Christopher said. "Not sure I like that."

"Dammit, George, we're in this together," Mayor Seitz said.

"Are we? Who's we?" Christopher demanded.

"Us. Your neighbors. Your friends," one of the councilmen said.

"That I'll go along with," Christopher told them. "My neighbors. My friends. But I won't put myself out for a lot of flatlanders. Not if they're finished anyway." The big man seemed to have trouble expressing himself. "Look, I got as much Christian charity as anybody here, but I won't starve my own people to help *them*." He started to leave.

"Where are you going, George?" Chief Hartman demanded.

"Senator's got a good idea. I'm getting my brother and heading for the flats with my truck. Lots of stuff down there we're going to need. No sense in letting the dam break on it." He went out before anyone could say more to him.

"You're going to have trouble with him," Mayor Seitz said.

"*I* am?" Jellison said.

"Sure, who else? I'm a feedstore owner, Senator. I can call myself Mayor, but I'm not ready for *this*. I expect you're in charge here. Right?"

There was a chorus of agreement from the others. It surprised no one.

George Christopher and his brother Ray drove down the highway toward Porterville. Lake Success lay on their right, high banks rose to the top of the ridgeline on their left. Rain fell steadily. Already the lake had risen nearly to the bridge where the highway crossed. Chunks of mud washed down from the ridge above and covered the road. The big farm truck went through the mud patches without slowing.

"Not much traffic," Ray said.

"Not yet." George drove grimly, his mouth a set line, his bull neck arched toward the steering wheel. "But it won't be long. All those people. They'll come up the road looking for high ground—"

"Most'll stop in Porterville," Ray said. "It's a couple of hundred feet higher than the San Joaquin."

"Was," George said. "With those quakes you can't tell. Land shifts, raises up and down. Anyway, when the dam goes, Porterville goes. They won't stay there."

Ray didn't say anything. He never argued with George. George was the only one in the family who'd gone to college. GI Bill. He hadn't finished, but he'd learned something while he was there.

"Ray, what do they eat?" George asked suddenly.

"I don't know—"

"You ready to see your kids starve?" George demanded.

"It won't come to that."

"Won't it? People all over the place. Salt rain running out in the San Joaquin. Lower San Joaquin fills up. Porterville washes out when the dam goes. People headed for high ground, and that's us. We'll have 'em everywhere, camped on the roads, stuffed into the schoolhouse, in barns, everywhere. All hungry. Plenty of food at first. Enough for everybody for awhile. Ray, you can't look at a hungry kid and not feed him."

Ray didn't say anything.

"Think about it. While there's food, we'll feed people. Would you turn people away while you've still got livestock? Ready to stew your dogs to feed a bunch of Porterville hippies?"

"There aren't any hippies in Porterville."

"You know what I mean."

Ray thought it through. They would come through Porterville. To the north and south were cities of ten million each, and if only one in ten thousand of them lived long enough to reach Porterville and turn east . . .

Now Ray's mouth formed a grim line like his brother's. Muscles stood out of his neck like thick cords. They were both big; the whole family ran big. When they were younger, George and Ray sometimes went to the tough bars looking for fights. The only time they'd ever been beaten, they'd gone home and come back with their two younger brothers. After that it was almost impossible to find a fight.

And they thought alike, though Ray thought more slowly. Now he saw it: thousands of strangers spread across the land like a locust plague, in all sizes and shapes and ages—college professors, social workers, television actors and game-show moderators and writers, brain surgeons, architects of condominiums, fashion designers, and the teeming hordes of the forever unemployed . . . all landless people without jobs or skills or tools or homes. Like locusts, and locusts could be fought. But what about the children? Strangers could be turned away, but children?

"So what do we do?" Ray asked finally.

"If they don't get here, they can't cause problems," George said. He eyed the hills above the road. "If about a hundred tons of rock and mud came down on the road just up ahead, nobody'd get into the valley. Not easy, anyway."

"Maybe we should pray for a hard rain," Ray said. He looked out at the driving rain pouring from the sky.

George gripped the wheel tightly. He believed in prayer and he didn't like hearing his brother's mocking tone. Not that Ray meant anything. Ray went to church too, sometimes. About as often as George did. But you couldn't pray for something like that.

All those people. And they'd all die, and dying they'd take George's people with them. He pictured his little sister, thin, belly protruding, last stages of starvation, the way those kids had looked in 'Nam. A whole village of kids trapped in the combat zone, nobody to look out for them, no place to go until the ranger patrol came looking for Cong and found the kids. Suddenly he knew he couldn't see that again. He couldn't think about it.

"How long you reckon that dam will last?" Ray asked.

"Uh—why are you stopping?"

"I brought a couple of sticks of forty percent," George said. "Right up there." He pointed to a steep slope above the road. "Two sticks there, and nobody'll use this road for awhile."

Ray thought about it. There was another road up from the San Joaquin, but it didn't show on gas station maps. A lot of people wouldn't know about it. With the main highway out, maybe they'd go somewhere else.

The truck came to a complete stop and George opened the door. "Coming?"

"Yeah, I guess," Ray said. He usually went along with George. He had since their father had died. The other two brothers, and their cousins and nephews, usually did too. George had made a big success out of his ranch. He'd brought in a lot of new ideas and equipment from that agricultural college. George usually knew what he was doing.

Only I don't like this, Ray thought. Don't like it at all. Don't guess George does much either, but what can we do? Wait until we have to look 'em in the eye and turn them away?

They climbed the steep bank behind the truck. Rain poured onto them, finding its way inside their slickers, under the brims of their hats and down their necks. It was warm rain. It drove hard, and Ray thought about the hay crop. That timothy was ruined already. What the hell would they feed the stock, come winter?

"About here, I think," George said. He scrabbled at the base of a medium-size rock. "Bring this down, it ought to drop a lot of the mud above it onto the road."

"What about Chief Hartman? And Dink Latham's already gone down to Porterville. . . ."

"So they find the road's out when they come back," George said. "They know the other way." He reached into his pocket and took out a bulky styrofoam case. It held five detonators, each in its own fitted compartment. George took one out, put it onto the end of a fuse, crimped it with his teeth and used his penknife to poke a hole in a dynamite stick. He pushed the detonator into the stick and shoved it into the hole. "No primacord," he said. "Have to put both sticks in the same hole. I think this'll do it." He tamped wet mud down into the hole he'd scooped, covering the dynamite. Only the fuse end protruded.

Ray turned his back to the wind and hunched low over a cigarette. He flicked the wheel of his Zippo until it caught and got the cigarette burning. Then, carefully, shielding the burning tobacco with his hat brim, he brought it down to the fuse end. The fuse sputtered once, then caught. It hissed softly in the rain.

"Let's go," Ray said. He scrambled down the bank, George behind him. They had many minutes before the fuse burned down, but they ran as if pursued by furies.

They were around the bend when they heard the explosion. It wasn't very loud. The rain dulled all sounds. George carefully backed the truck around until they could see.

The road was covered with four feet of mud and boulders.

More had tumbled across the road and down into the river valley below.

"Man might get over that with a four-wheel," George said. "Nothing else."

"What the hell are you sitting here for? Let's go!" Ray's enraged bellow was too loud for the truck cab, but he knew his brother wouldn't say anything about it.

There was water standing in the streets when they reached Porterville. It wasn't more than hubcap deep. The dam still held.

■

The City Hall meeting room smelled of kerosene lamps and damp bodies. There was also the faint odor of books and library paste. There weren't many books in the library, and they took up space around the walls but not in the center of the room.

Senator Jellison looked at his electric watch and grimaced. It was good for another year, but then . . . Why the hell didn't he have an old-fashioned windup? The watch told him it was 10:38 and 35 seconds, and it wouldn't be off by more than a second until the battery ran out.

The room was nearly full. All the library tables had been moved to make room for more folding chairs. A few women, mostly men, mostly in farm clothes and rain gear, mostly unarmed. They smelled of sweat and they were soaked and tired. Three whiskey bottles moved rhythmically from hand to hand, and there were a lot of cans of beer. There wasn't much talk as they waited for the meeting to start.

There were three distinct groups in the room. Senator Jellison dominated one of them. He sat with Mayor Seitz, Chief Hartman and the constables. Maureen Jellison was part of the group, and in the front rows, right up front, were their close friends. A solid bloc of support for the Jellison party.

Beyond them was the largest group, neutrals waiting for the Senator and the Mayor to tell them what to do. They wouldn't have put it that way, and the Senator would never have dreamed of saying it flat out. They were farmers and merchants who needed help, and they weren't used to asking for advice. Jellison knew them all. Not well, but well enough to know that he could count on them, up to a point. Some of them had brought their wives.

At the back, off in one corner, were George Christopher

and his clan. "Clan" is the right word, Arthur Jellison thought. A dozen. All men, all armed. You'd know they were relatives just to look at them (although, Jellison knew, it wasn't strictly true: Two were brothers-in-law. But they looked like Christophers—heavyset, red of face and strong enough to lift jeeps in their spare time). The Christophers didn't precisely sit apart from everyone else; but they sat together, and they talked together, and they had few words for their neighbors.

Steve Cox came in with two of Jellison's ranch-hands. "Dam's still holding," he shouted above rain and thunder and muted conversation. "Don't know what's keeping it together. There's water higher than the spillway behind it. It's eating out the banks at the sides."

"Won't be long now," one of the farmers said. "Did we warn the people down in Porterville?"

"Yes," Chief Hartman said. "Constable Mosey told the Porterville police. They'll get people out of the flood area."

"What's the flood area?" Steve Cox asked. "Whole damn valley's filling up. And the highway's out, they can't come up here—"

"Some have," Mayor Seitz said. "Three hundred, more or less. Up the county road. Expect there'll be more tomorrow."

"Too damn many," Ray Christopher said.

There was a babble of voices, some agreeing, some arguing. Mayor Seitz pounded for order. "Let's find out what we're facing," Seitz said. "Senator, what have you learned?"

"Enough." Jellison got up from his seat at the table and went around in front of it. He perched his buttocks on the table in an informal pose that he knew was effective. "I've got pretty good shortwave radio gear. I know there are amateurs trying to communicate. And I get nothing but static. Not just on amateur bands, on CB, commercial, even military. That tells me the atmosphere is all fouled up. Electrical storms. I don't need to guess about those," he said with a grin. He waved expressively toward the windows, and as if on cue lightning flared. There wasn't quite so much thunder and lightning as there'd been earlier in the day, but there was so much that no one noticed unless they were thinking about it.

"And salt rain," Jellison said. "And the earthquake. The last words I heard out of JPL were 'The Hammer has fallen.' I'd like to talk to somebody who was in the hills above L.A. when it happened, but what I've got adds up. The Hammer hit us, and bad. We can be sure of it."

No one said anything. They'd all known it. They'd hoped to find out something different, but they knew better. They were farmers and businessmen, tied closely to the land and the weather, and they lived in the foothills of the High Sierra. They'd known disaster before, and they'd done their crying and cursing at home. Now they were worried about what to do next.

"We got five truckloads of feed and hardware and two of groceries out of Porterville today," Jellison said. "And there's the stock in our local stores. And what you have in your barns. I doubt there'll be much else that we don't make or grow ourselves."

There were murmurs. One of the farmers said, "Not ever, Senator?"

"Might as well be never," Jellison said. "Years, I think. We're on our own."

He paused to let that sink in. Most of these people prided themselves on being on their own. Of course that wasn't true, hadn't been true for generations, and they were smart enough to know it, but it would take them time to realize just how dependent they'd been on civilization.

Fertilizers. Breeding stock. Vitamins. Gasoline and propane. Electricity. Water—well, that wouldn't be much of a problem for awhile. Medicines, drugs, razor blades, weather forecasts, seeds, animal feed, clothes, ammunition . . . the list was endless. Even needles and pins and thread.

"We won't grow much this year," Stretch Tallifsen said. "My crops are in bad shape already."

Jellison nodded. Tallifsen had gone down the road to help his neighbors harvest tomatoes, and his wife was working to can as many as she could. Tallifsen grew barley, and it wouldn't last the summer.

"Question is, do we pull together?" Jellison said.

"What do you mean, 'pull together'?" Ray Christopher asked.

"Share. Pool what we've got," Jellison answered.

"You mean communism," Ray Christopher said. This time the hostility showed through in his voice.

"No, I mean cooperation. Charity, if you like. More than that. Intelligent management of what little we have, so we avoid waste."

"Sounds like communism—"

"Shut up, Ray." George Christopher stood. "Senator, I can see how that makes sense. No point in using the last of the gasoline to plant something that won't grow. Or feeding the last of the soybeans to cattle that won't last the winter anyway. Question is, who decides? You?"

"Somebody has to," Tallifsen said.

"Not alone," Jellison said. "We elect a council. I will point out that I'm probably in better shape than anybody else here, and I'm willing to share—"

"Sure," Christopher said. "But share with who, Senator? That's the big question. How far do we go? We try to feed Los Angeles?"

"That's absurd," Jack Turner said.

"Why? They'll all be here, all that can get here," Christopher shouted. "Los Angeles, and the San Joaquin, and what's left of San Francisco . . . not all of 'em, maybe, but plenty. Three hundred last night, and that's just for starters. How long can we keep it up, lettin' those people come here?"

"Be niggers too," someone shouted from the floor. He looked self-consciously at two black faces at the end of the room. "Okay, sorry—no. I'm not sorry. Lucius, you own land. You work it. But city niggers, whining about equality— you don't want 'em either!"

The black man said nothing. He seemed to shrink away from the group, and he sat very quietly with his son.

"Lucius Carter's all right," George Christopher said. "But Frank's right about the others. City people. Tourists. Hippies. Be here in droves pretty soon. We have to stop them."

I'm losing it, Jellison thought. Too much fear here, and Christopher's put his finger on it. He shuddered. A lot of people were going to die in the next months. A lot. How do you select the ones to live, the ones to die? How do you be the Chooser of the Slain? God knows I don't want the job.

"George, what do you suggest?" Jellison asked.

"Roadblock on the county road. We don't want to close it, we may need it. So we put up a roadblock and we turn people away."

"Not everyone," Mayor Seitz said. "Women and children—"

"Everybody," Christopher shouted. "Women? We have women. And kids. Plenty of our own to worry about. We start takin' in other people's kids and women, where do we stop? When our own are starving come winter?"

"Just who is going to man this roadblock?" Chief Hartman asked. "Who's tough enough to look at a car full of people and tell a man he can't even leave his kids with us? You're not, George. None of us are."

"The hell I'm not."

"And there are special skills," Senator Jellison said. "Engineers. We could use several good engineers. Doctors, veterinarians. Brewers. A good blacksmith, if there is any such thing in this modern world—"

"Used to be a fair hand at that," Ray Christopher said. "Shod horses for the county fair."

"All right," Jellison said. "But there are plenty of skills we don't have, and don't think we won't need them."

"Okay, okay," George Christopher said. "But dammit, we can't take in everybody—"

"And yet we must." The voice was very low, not really loud enough to carry through the babble and the thunder, but everyone heard it anyway. A professionally trained voice. "I was a stranger, and ye took me not in. I was hungry, and ye fed me not. Is that what you want to hear at Judgment?"

The room was still for a moment. Everyone turned to look at the Reverend Thomas Varley. Most of them attended his community church, had called him to their homes to sit with them when relatives died, sent their children with him on picnics and camping trips. Tom Varley was one of them, bred in the valley and lived there all his life except for the years at college in San Francisco. He stood tall, a bit thinner since his sixtieth birthday a year before, but strong enough to help get a neighbor's cow out of a ditch.

George Christopher faced him defiantly. "Brother Varley, we just can't do it! Some of *us* are likely to starve this winter. There's just not enough here."

"Then why don't you send some away?" Reverend Varley asked.

"It might come to that," George muttered. His voice rose. "I've seen it, I tell you. People with not enough to eat, not even enough strength to come get chow when it's offered. Brother Varley, you want us to wait until we got no more choices than the Donner party had? If we send people away now, they might find someplace they can make it. If we take them in, we'll all be looking next winter. It's that simple."

"Tell 'em, George," someone shouted from the far end of the meeting room.

George looked around at the sea of faces. They were not hostile. Most were filled with shame—fear and shame. George thought that would be the way he'd look to them, too. He went on doggedly. "We do something, and we do it right now, or I'll be damned if I'm going to cooperate! I'll take everything I have, all the stuff I brought up from Porterville today, too, and go home, and I can damned well shoot anybody who comes onto *my* place."

There were more murmurs. Reverend Varley tried to speak,

but he was shouted down. "Damned right!" "We're with you, George."

Jellison's voice cut through. "I didn't say we shouldn't try to put up a roadblock. We were discussing practical difficulties." Arthur Jellison couldn't look the clergyman in the face.

"Good. Then we do it," George Christopher said. "Ray, you stay here and tell me what happens in this meeting. Carl, Jake, rest of you, come with me. There'll be another thousand people here by morning if we don't stop them."

And besides, Jellison thought, it will be easier at night when you can't see their faces. Maybe by morning you'll be used to it.

And if you truly get used to sending people off to die, will anyone want to know you?

The worst of it was, George Christopher was right; but that didn't make it any easier. "I'll have some of my people come with you, George. And we'll have a relief crew out in the morning."

"Good." Christopher went to the door. On the way he stopped for a moment to smile at Maureen. "Good-night, Melisande," he said.

One kerosene lamp burned in the living room of the Jellison house. Arthur Jellison sprawled in an easy chair, shoes off, shirt partly unbuttoned. "Al, leave those lists until tomorrow."

"Yes, sir. Can I get you anything?" Al Hardy glanced at his watch: 2 A.M.

"No. Maureen can take care of me. Good-night."

Hardy pointedly looked at his watch again. "Getting late, Senator. And you're supposed to be up in the morning. . . ."

"I'll turn in shortly. Good-night." This time the dismissal was pointed. Jellison watched his assistant leave, noted Hardy's determined look. It confirmed a guess Arthur Jellison had made earlier. That damned doctor at Bethesda Naval Hospital had told Hardy about the abnormal electrocardiograms, and Hardy was making like a mother hen. Had Al told Maureen? It didn't matter.

"Want a drink, Dad?" Maureen asked.

"Water. We ought to save the bourbon," Jellison said. "Sit down, please." The tone was polite, but it wasn't exactly a request. Not really an order, either. A worried man.

"Yes?" she said. She took a chair near his.

"What did George Christopher mean? Who's 'Melisande' or whatever he said?"

371

"It's a long story—"

"I want to hear it. Anything about the Christophers I want to hear," Jellison said.

"Why?"

"Because they're the other power in this valley and we've got to work together and not against each other. I need to know just who's giving in to what," Jellison said. "Now tell me."

"Well, you know George and I practically grew up together," Maureen said. "We're the same age—"

"Sure."

"And before you went to Washington, when you were a state senator, George and I were in love. Well, we were only fourteen, but it felt like love." And, she didn't say, I haven't really felt like that about anybody since. "He wanted me to stay here. With him. I would have, too, if there'd been any way to do it. I didn't want to go to Washington."

Jellison looked older in the yellow kerosene light. "I didn't know that. I was busy just then—"

"It's all right, Dad," Maureen said.

"All right or not, it's done," Jellison said. "What's with Melisande?"

"Remember the play *The Rainmaker?* The confidence man plays up to the old-maid farm girl. Tells her to stop calling herself 'Lizzie,' to come with him and she'll be Melisande and they'll live a glamorous life. . . . Well, George and I saw it that summer, and it was a switch, that's all. Instead of going off to the glamorous life in Washington, I should stay here with him. I'd forgotten all about it."

"You had, huh? You remember it now, though."

"Dad . . ."

"What did he mean, calling you that?" Jellison asked.

"Well, I—" She stopped herself and didn't say anything else.

"Yeah. I figure it that way too," Jellison said. "He's telling you something, isn't he? How much have you seen of him since we went to Washington?"

"Not much."

"Have you slept with him?"

"That's none of your business," Maureen flared.

"The hell it's not. Anything and everything around this valley is my business just now. Especially if it's got Christophers mixed up in it. Did you?"

"No."

"Did he try?"

"Nothing serious," she said. "I think he's too religious. And

372

we didn't really have many opportunities, not after I'd moved to Washington."

"And he's never married," Jellison said.

"Dad, that's silly! He hasn't been pining away for me for sixteen years!"

"No, I don't suppose so. But that was a pretty definite message tonight. Okay, let's get to bed—"

"Dad."

"Yes?"

"Can we talk? I'm scared." She took the chair next to his. He thought she looked much younger just then, and remembered her when she was a little girl, when her mother was still alive. "It's bad, isn't it?" she asked.

"About as bad as it gets," Jellison said. He reached for the whiskey and poured himself two fingers. "May as well. We know how to make whiskey. If there's grain, we'll have booze. If there's grain."

"What's going to happen?" Maureen asked.

"I don't know. I can make some guesses." He stared at the empty fireplace. It was damp from rain coming down the chimney. "Hammerfall. By now the tidal waves have swept around the world. Seacoast cities are all gone. Washington's gone. I hope the Capitol survived—I like that old granite pile." He fell silent for a moment, and they listened to the steady pounding rain and rolling thunder.

"I forgot who said it," Jellison said. "It's true enough. No country is more than three meals away from a revolution. Hear that rain? It's all over the country. Lowlands, river bottoms, little creeks, any low places in the roads, they'll be underwater, just like the whole San Joaquin Valley's going to be underwater. Highways, railroads, river travel, it's all gone. There's no transportation and not much communication. Which means the United States has ceased to exist. So have most other countries."

"But . . ." She shivered, although it wasn't cold in the room. "There have to be places that aren't damaged. Cities not on the coast. Mountain areas that don't have earthquake faults. They'll still be organized—"

"Will they? How many places can you think of that have food enough to last for weeks?"

"I never thought about it—"

"Right. And it isn't weeks, it's months," Jellison said. "Kitten, what do people eat? The United States has about thirty days' food at any given time. That's everything—warehouses, supermarkets, grain elevators, ships in harbor. A lot of it was lost. A lot more is perishable. And there isn't going to be *diddly* for a crop this fall. Do you expect anybody who's got barely enough to eat to come out and help anybody else?"

"Oh—"

"And it's worse than that." His voice was brutal now, almost as if he were trying to frighten her. "Refugees everywhere. Anyplace there's enough to eat, there'll be people after food. Don't blame them. We could have a million refugees on the way here right now! Maybe here and there the police and local governments try to survive. How do they manage when the locusts come? Only they're not locusts, they're people."

"But . . . what do we do?" Maureen cried.

"We survive. We live through it. And we build a new civilization. Somebody's got to." His voice rose. "We can do it. How soon depends on how far we get knocked down. All the way to savagery? Bows and arrows and stone clubs? I'll be damned if we can't do better than that!"

"Yes, of course—"

"No 'of course' about it, Kitten." Jellison sounded very old, but his voice held determination and strength. "It depends on what we can keep. Keep right here. We don't know what's left anywhere else, but here we're in pretty good shape if we can just hang on. Here we've got a chance, and by God we're going to take it."

"You'll do it," Maureen said. "It's your job."

"Think of anybody else who can?"

"I wasn't asking a question, Dad."

"Then remember that, when I've got to do something I don't much like." He set his jaw hard. "We're going to make it, Kitten. I promise you, the people of this valley are going to live through this and come out civilized." Then he laughed. "I do go on. It's time for bed. Lot of work to do tomorrow."

"All right."

"You don't need to wait for me. I'll be along. Git."

She kissed him and left. Arthur Jellison drained the whiskey glass and set it down with a long look at the bottle. He sat staring into the empty fireplace.

He could see how a civilization could be built from the wreckage Lucifer's Hammer had left. Salvage work. Plenty to salvage in the old seacoast cities. The water hadn't destroyed everything. New oil wells could be drilled. The railroads could be repaired. These rains wouldn't last forever.

We can rebuild it, and this time we'll do it right. We'll

spread beyond this one damned little ball, get human civilization out all through the solar system, to other stars even, so no one thing can knock us out again.

Sure we can. But how do we live long enough to start rebuilding? First things first, and right now the problem is getting this valley organized. Nobody's going to help. We have to do it ourselves. The only law and order will be what we can make, and the only safety Maureen and Charlotte and Jennifer will have is what we can put together. I used to be responsible to the people of the United States, and particularly to the people of California. Not anymore. Now it's my family, and how can I protect them?

That boils down to how do I keep this ranch? and maybe I can't do that, not without help. Whose help? George Christopher for one. George has a lot of friends. Between us we can do all right.

Arthur Jellison got wearily to his feet and blew out the kerosene lamp. In the sudden dark the pounding rain and crashing thunder sounded even louder. He could see his way to the bedroom through lightning flashes.

There was a light under Al Hardy's door. It went out after Hardy heard the Senator get into bed.

Sanctuary

God gives all men all earth to love,
But, since man's heart is small,
Ordains for each one spot shall prove,
Beloved over all.

Rudyard Kipling

Harvey Randall woke to strident sounds. Someone was screaming at him.

"Harvey! Help!"

Loretta? He sat up suddenly, and banged his head on something. He'd been asleep in the TravelAll, and the voice wasn't Loretta's. For a moment he was bewildered. What was nightmare, what was real?

"Harvey!" The shouting voice was real. And, oh, God, Loretta was dead.

It was raining, but there was no rain around the TravelAll. He opened the door and blinked in the dim light. His watch said 6:00. Morning or evening?

The TravelAll was parked under a rickety shed, no more than a roof with posts to hold it up. Marie Vance stood at the far end. Joanna was holding the shotgun on her. Mark was shouting and Marie was screaming for Harvey.

None of it made sense. Half-light, driving rain and howling wind, lightning and thunder, the screaming woman and Mark shouting and Joanna with the shotgun—dream or real? He made himself move toward the others. "What is this, Mark?"

Mark turned and saw him. His face lighted with a smile. That faded too, like Harvey's dream that it was a dream, like—

"Harvey! Tell him!" Marie shouted.

He shook the cobwebs from his head. They wouldn't go. "Mark?" he said.

Marie jerked like a puppet. Harvey stared in astonishment as she did it again. She seemed to be fighting an invisible enemy. Then, suddenly, she relaxed and her voice was calm, or nearly so. "Harvey Randall, it's time you woke up," she said. "Or don't you care about your son? You've buried Loretta, now think about Andy."

He heard himself speak. "What is all this?"

They both talked at once. The need for understanding, rather than any other emotion, made Harvey speak sharply. "One at a time! Mark, please. Let her talk."

"This—man wants to abandon our boys," Marie said.

"I don't. I'm trying to tell you—"

She cut Mark off. "The boys are in Sequoia. I told him that. Sequoia. But he keeps taking us west, and that's not the right way."

"All of you shut up!" Joanna shouted. There was an edge of hysteria in her voice, and it stopped Mark before he could say anything else. He'd never heard Joanna shout before. Not like that.

And she had the shotgun.

"Where are we going, Mark?" Harvey asked.

"To Sequoia," Mark said. "That's a big place, and she doesn't know where—"

"I do," Harvey said. "Where are we?"

"Simi Valley," Mark said. "Will you listen to me?"

"Yes. Talk."

"Harvey, he's—"

"Shut up, Marie! Harvey made his voice deliberately brutal. It stopped her.

"Harv, there's people all over," Mark said. "Roads were gettin' jammed. So I cut off onto a fire trail I know about. Bikers use it. It'll lead us through the condor reservation. Sure, it goes west awhile, but we stay off the goddam freeways! You stop to think how many people are trying to get out of L.A. right now? Not many know about this road. And it stays on high ground. It wasn't much of a road to begin with, less to go wrong with it." He turned to Marie. "That's what I was trying to tell you. We have to get over the mountains, all the way over. Then we get to the San Joaquin and we're on level ground, and we can cut over to Sequoia—"

"Let's get a map," Harvey suggested.

378

"It doesn't show on a map," Mark protested. "If it did, everybody—"

"I believe your road," Harvey said. "I want to see what happens after that. I've got maps in the TravelAll." He started to turn, but Joanna went to the motorcycle. She reached into a saddlebag.

"Frank Stoner made us take three copies. One for each bike," she said. She held up a big aeronautical chart. It showed terrain features in colors. "There are Auto Club maps, too."

It was too dark to read the map properly. Mark went to the TravelAll and came back with a flashlight. Marie was standing stiffly aloof, silent, her eyes still accusing.

"See?" Mark said. "Right across here. The highway goes past lakes. With dams. That sit on top of the San Andreas. You really think the big highway's still usable?"

Harvey shook his head. It wouldn't matter. If the highway could be used, a million people would be trying to use it. If not . . . "So we come out through Frazier Park."

"Right! Then down in the valley and it's a straight shot north," Mark said. "I was thinking of getting to the Mojave 'cause that's where Frank said we should be, but it's no good. Can't get to Sequoia that way." He pointed. "All the east-side routes lead past Lake Isabella. Follow the Kern River. Harv, with all this rain, how many bridges will there be over the Kern?"

"None. Marie, he's right. If we went the direct route we'd never get there."

Mark looked pleased. Joanna leaned the shotgun against the bike and collapsed onto the seat, sidesaddle.

"If you had explained before . . ." Marie began.

"Jesus, I tried!" Mark shouted.

"Not you."

She meant me, Harvey thought. And she's right. I can't curl up and die, I've got a boy up in those hills and I've got to go get him, and thank God for Marie. "How's our gas?" Harvey asked.

"Pretty good. We've made about fifty miles—"

"No more than that," Harvey muttered. Of course it was true, he could see it on the map. It seemed like much further. They couldn't have been going very fast. "Mark, how sure are you of this fire trail? Won't it wash out?" '

"Probably," Mark said. He pointed silently to the dams poised above Interstate 5. "Rather risk that?"

"No. If we're going, we'd better do it. I'll drive," Harvey said.

"And I'll scout ahead. Joanna can ride shotgun with you." Mark didn't mention Marie. He wasn't speaking to her.

It felt good to be doing something. Anything. He had a throbbing headache, the beginning of a migraine, and his shoulders and neck were so tense he could feel knots in them, but it was better than curling up in the seat.

"Let's go," Harvey said.

The road ran along ridgelines, curled around hills, boring north and west. It stayed on high ground. Rock and mud-slides spilled across it, but being high, the debris wasn't deep; and being almost untraveled, the road wasn't cut away at the edges.

The mountains had shifted. The road might have ended anywhere. Like Mark Czescu's judgment, it was nothing you could count on absolutely; but neither had failed them this time. Eventually they came to paved road, and Harvey could increase his speed.

He liked driving. He drove with single-minded determination, with no room for other thoughts. Watch for rocks. Ease around curves. Keep going, rack up the miles, on and on and never look back and never think about what's behind you.

Down and down now, into the San Joaquin. Water standing everywhere. That was frightening. Harvey stopped and looked at the map. Their way ran directly to a dry lake bed. It wouldn't be dry now. So cross the Kern River on the freeway, then get off and cut northeast. . . .

Would their gas hold? They had plenty so far. Harvey thought of the extra gas he'd stored, and of thieves and killers in a blue van. Wherever they hid, someday he would track them down. But they hadn't taken this road. He'd have noticed. So far they'd had the road almost to themselves.

Dawn found them north and east of Bakersfield. They'd made effective progress. Thirty miles an hour, and now they were on high ground, skirting the eastern edge of the San Joaquin, with nothing to stop them.

Harvey realized where they were heading. Their route would take them right past the Jellison ranch.

The Tule River was too deep, way too deep. Nobody had

dared to use the road that ran alongside. By the time Harvey realized this, it was too late. He could see the dam ahead.

Water streamed around one side and all along the top. He could just tell where the spillway was: a surging current in the river that poured over the face of the dam. He sounded the horn and waved Mark ahead. He clenched his fist and moved it vigorously up and down, the Army signal for double time. He pointed at the dam.

Mark got the message; he gunned the bike. Harvey slammed down the accelerator and roared after him. They were almost to the dam, then—

A river of mud submerged the road. A dozen people and half that many cars were mired in the mud. They'd tried to get past the slide and got stuck.

Harvey levered the TravelAll into four-wheel drive and went on without stopping. One man stepped forth to bar their way with spread arms. Harvey came close enough to see wide eyes and bared teeth, a rictus of terror and determination . . . and *he* saw *Harvey's* face. The TravelAll's headlight ticked his heel as he leaped away.

The mud was sliding and the TravelAll slid with it. Harvey turned hard, gunned the engine and fought a frantic race between his traction on the mud and the mud's adherence to the road. Rocks in the road tipped the TravelAll sickeningly. Then there was road under them again. Harvey heard Marie's gasp of relief.

There was a bridge ahead. It crossed an arm of the lake . . . and it was under water. Harvey couldn't tell how deep. He slowed.

Suddenly there were other sounds embedded in the sounds of river and rain and thunder. Screams. Joanna looked back. "Jesus!" she shouted.

Harvey stopped the TravelAll.

The dam was going. One whole side of it crumbled, all in a moment, and the lake went forth in a wall of water. The screams were drowned in its thunder.

"Our timing was s-superb," Joanna said.

"All those people," Harvey muttered. All the travelers in cars not as good as the TravelAll. All the farmers who thought they'd wait it out. People on foot, people already marooned on roofs and high points in the new shallow lakes, would look up to see the wall of water marching toward them.

It would be worse when the other dams went. The whole valley would be flooded. No dam would hold against this relentless rain.

Harvey took a deep breath. "Okay, it's over. *We* made it. Quaking Aspen is only thirty miles from here. Gordie'll bring them out there." He summoned up a mental picture of the road north of Springville. It crossed many streams, and the map showed small power stations and dams on some of them. Dams above the road.

Had they failed? Would they fail? It would be foolish, even insane, to charge up the road just in time to be washed down again.

"Let's go," Marie said.

Harvey drove on. There was no water above the bridge now. That water was on its way into the San Joaquin Valley. He drove across the bridge, and was surprised to see a big truck coming toward him. It stopped just at the far end of the bridge. Two big men got out. They stared as Harvey drove past them. One started to shout something, then shrugged.

Up ahead there was another bridge out. That decided it: Harvey had to detour past the entrance to Senator Jellison's place.

And where better to learn what was happening in the mountains? For that matter, where would they go once they found the boys? Marie hadn't thought past the moment of finding Bert and Andy. Neither ' had Harvey until now, but . . .

But this was perfect. The scout troop would have to come past the Jellison place.

And Maureen would be there.

Harvey despised himself for thinking of her. Loretta's face swam in front of him, and the vision of a body wrapped in an electric blanket. He slowed to a stop.

"Why are we—" Before Marie could finish there was an explosion behind them, then another.

"What the hell" Harvey started the car again. Remorse was replaced by fear. Explosions? Had they wandered into a range war or something? He drove ahead, while Joanna and Marie craned to look back.

Mark whipped the bike into a U-turn and drove back the way they'd come. He waved as he went past.

"Damn fool curiosity will kill him yet," Joanna said.

Harvey shrugged. He could stand not knowing, but it would be nice to find out. Up ahead, a couple of miles, not far at all, was the turnoff. Then safety, refuge, rest.

He drove slowly, and he'd just reached the Senator's drive when he saw Mark coming up behind him. He pulled to a stop.

"That bridge," Mark said.

"Yeah?"

"The one we came over," Mark said. "Those two dudes just blew it. Dynamite, I think. They dropped it at both ends. Harvey, a half-hour later and we'd be stranded back there."

"Two minutes later," Joanna said, "and we'd have been looking up at a million tons of water. We—Harv, we can't keep lucking out like this."

"It takes luck," Harvey said. "In combat, here, luck's as important as brains. But we won't need any more for awhile. I'm going in there." He waved toward the Senator's drive.

"Why?" Marie demanded, ready for war.

"Road conditions. Information." Harvey drove on to the gate. It was only just coming to him—it had never occurred to him, not for an instant—that a master of television documentaries might not be welcome at a politician's home.

He got out to open the gate.

There was a car parked inside. A young man got out and wearily came to the TravelAll. "Your business?" he inquired. He eyed Joanna and the shotgun, showed his empty hands. "Me, I'm not armed. But my partner's where you can't see him, and he's got a scope-sighted rifle."

"We'll be no trouble," Harvey said. The man had seen the NBS markings on the TravelAll—and he hadn't been impressed. "Can you get a message up to the big house?"

"Depends on the message. Might."

Harvey had thought it through. "Tell Maureen Jellison that Harvey Randall is here with three dependents."

The man looked thoughtful. "Well, you got the names right. She expecting you?"

Harvey laughed. It struck him as insanely funny. He leaned against the fender and chortled; he put a hand on the man's arm and got control of his voice and said, "From *Los Angeles?*" and lost it again.

The man withdrew a little. His large red face blanked out. There were things he didn't want to know. But—the Senator had told the meeting he'd like to talk to someone who'd seen what happened to L.A. And this city man did know the Senator's name, and Maureen's as well.

As suddenly as it had been funny, suddenly it wasn't. Harvey stopped laughing. "Maureen must think I'm dead. She'll be glad to know different." Or will she? Shazam! "I know she'll want to talk to me. Tell her I want to . . . never mind." He'd been about to say he wanted to talk about galactic empires, and that wasn't the right thing to say at all.

The man looked thoughtful. Finally he nodded. "Okay, I guess I can do that. But you wait right here. I mean *right* here, understand? And don't get gay with that shotgun."

"We don't want to shoot anybody. I just want to talk to Maureen."

"Okay. *Right* there. I'll be a while." He went to the car, locked it and walked up the driveway.

Walked. Saving gasoline already. Yes, the Senator had his place organized. Harvey went back to the TravelAll. Marie tried to say something; he cut through her voice with practiced ease. "Spread the map."

She thought it over, then did it. Harvey let his forefinger do the talking. "The scouts are in this area. The only route out is right past here. They don't have to worry about these dams—here, and here—because they don't have to stay on the road. We do, or else we walk. We're not equipped to walk it."

Marie thought that over. She glanced at her boots and fingered her jacket. She *was* ready to walk, and so was Harvey, but it made sense. Certainly if they had to walk, a few hours wouldn't make any difference.

"So we wait here?" Joanna asked.

Mark stuck his head in at the window. "Sure, this is Senator Jellison's place. Thought I recognized it. Harv, that was smart, sending a message to the Senator's daughter instead of him."

"Wait," Marie said. "How long?"

"Christ, how the hell do I know?" Harvey exploded. "As long as they'll let us. This ranch is organized, have you noticed? And they've got food; that guard wasn't hungry. We'd like to feed the boys when they get here. Not to mention ourselves."

Marie nodded in submission.

"The trouble is," Harvey continued, "how do we get them to let us in? Blowing up that bridge might have been a subtle hint that they aren't welcoming refugees in this valley. We have to be useful, which means we promise to do whatever they want us to do, and no goddam arguments about it. Marie, don't blow this for us. We're beggars here."

He waited for that to sink in before turning to Joanna. "That applies to your shotgun. I don't know if you noticed the subtle hand motions of that guy who stopped us, but he was doing strange things with his hand. His left hand. I expect sticking him up wouldn't be a good idea."

"I knew that," Joanna said.

"Yes." Harvey turned to Mark. "Let me do the talking."

Mark looked hurt. Who'd got Harvey out of his bedroom and across the state, all the way up here? But he stood in the rain, water running off his jacket and into his boots, and waited in silence.

"Company coming," Mark said finally. He pointed up the drive.

Three men on horseback, wearing yellow slickers and rain hats. One didn't ride very well. He clung grimly to the horse. When he came closer, Harvey recognized Al Hardy, Jellison's administrative assistant and political hatchet man.

Hatchet man, Harvey thought. That might be more literally true here than it had been in Washington.

Hardy dismounted and handed the reins to one of the mounted men. He came over to the TravelAll and peered inside. "Hello, Mr. Randall," he said.

"Hello." Harvey waited tensely.

"Who are these people?" He looked closely at Marie, but didn't say anything.

Hardy had met Loretta only once, months ago, Harvey thought. When? A long time, anyway. And Marie Vance never, but he knew she wasn't Loretta. A good memory for names and faces goes with the job of political adviser. . . .

"A neighbor," Harvey said. "And two employees."

"I see. And you came from Los Angeles. Do you know conditions in L.A.?"

"They do," Harvey said. He indicated Mark and Joanna. "They saw the tidal wave come in."

"I can let two of you come up," Hardy said. "No more."

"Then it's none," Harvey said. He said it quickly, before he could say something else. "Thanks, and we'll be on our way—"

"Wait." Hardy looked thoughtful. "Okay. Hand me the shotgun. Slow, and don't point it at me." He took the weapon and handed it to the original guard, who'd also dismounted. "Any more firearms?"

"This pistol." Harvey showed the Olympic target gun.

"My, but that's pretty. Give it to me, too. You'll get them back if you're not staying." Hardy took the weapon and thrust it into his belt. "Now make room for me in the back seat."

He climbed into the back seat, leaned out to speak so the others could hear. "You follow on that bike," he told Mark. "Stay close. I'm taking them up, Gil. It's all right."

"If you say so," the original guard said.

"Let's go," Hardy told Randall. "Drive carefully."

The gate swung open and Harvey drove through, followed by Mark, then, further behind, by the third man on horseback leading the other two horses.

"Why not leave a horse for the guard?" Harvey asked.

"We have more cars than horses. Rather lose a car if some damn fool tries anything," Hardy explained.

Harvey nodded. And the car was there, if anything urgent had to get up the hill. Obviously his message hadn't been thought urgent enough to waste gasoline on.

The TravelAll walked through the thick mud, and Harvey wondered just how long this drive would last. He went past the foreman's home and toward the big house at the top of the hill. The orange groves looked pitiful, many of the trees down from the high winds—but there was no fruit on the ground. Harvey approved.

Maureen wasn't in the big front room. Senator Jellison was. He had maps spread across the big dining table, and lists and other papers covered card tables nearby. A bottle of bourbon stood on the table. It was nearly full.

They left their boots out on the porch and came into the big stone house. The Senator stood. He didn't offer his hand. "I'll give you a drink if you'll recognize in advance that it's not permanent," Jellison said. "Long time ago, if you offered a man food and drink, that said you'd keep him as a guest. That's not decided yet."

"I understand," Harvey said. "I could use a drink."

"Right. Al, take the women back to the kitchen stove. They'll appreciate a chance to dry off. Excuse my manners, ladies, I'm a bit rushed just now." He waited until the girls were gone, then waved Harvey into a seat. Mark stood uncertainly at the door. "You too," Jellison said. "Drink?"

"You *know* it," Mark said. When the bottle was given to him, he poured an enormous drink into his glass. Harvey grimaced and examined the Senator's face. There was no change of expression.

"Is Maureen all right?" Harvey asked.

"She's here," Jellison said. "Where's your wife?"

Harvey felt himself flushing. "Dead. Murdered. She was in the house when some people decided to rob it. If you get word of a blue van escorted by chopped motorcycles . . ."

"Not on my list of priorities. Sorry about Mrs. Randall, though. So who've you got with you?"

"The tall woman is Marie Vance, my neighbor. Gordie Vance is at Quaking Aspen with a scout troop. He's got my son, I've got his wife."

"Uh-huh. She's elegant. Can she hike, or are those boots for show?"

"She can hike. She can also cook. And I can't leave her."

"Cooks I have. The others?"

"They saved my ass. I was ready to lie down and die after I found Loretta." The whiskey warmed him, and Harvey felt the intensity of the Senator's questioning. The man was judge and jury, and he wasn't going to take long to make his decision. "Mark and Joanna found me and carried me along till I came back to life. They brought Marie, too. They're with me."

"Sure. Okay, what are you trading?"

Harvey shrugged. "A TravelAll I know how to use. Some . . . hell, a *lot* of experience surviving—backpacking, war correspondent, helicopter pilot . . ."

"You were in L.A. You saw it?"

"Mark and Joanna did. We have information, if that's useful."

"Information is worth a meal and a drink. You're telling me if I let you in, the others stay too."

"Yes. I'm afraid that's it. We'll do our share, assuming you can feed us."

Jellison looked thoughtful. "You've got one vote," he said. "Maureen's. But it's mine that counts."

"I figured that. I gather you aren't exactly welcoming refugees. The bridge and all—"

"Bridge?"

"The big one over an arm of the lake. Just after the dam went—"

"Dam's gone?" Jellison frowned. "Al!" he shouted.

"Yes, sir?" Hardy came in quickly. His hand was in his raincoat pocket. It bulged. He relaxed at the sight of the three men seated in chairs, drinking calmly.

"He says the dam's gone," Jellison said. "Any word brought in on that?"

"Not yet."

"Yeah." Jellison nodded significantly. Hardy seemed to understand what he meant. "Now tell me about the bridge," Jellison said.

"Two men blew it up, just after the dam went. Dynamite, both ends."

"I will be dipped in shit. Describe the men." Jellison

listened, then nodded. "Right. Christophers. We may have trouble with them." He turned toward Mark. "Army?" he asked.

"Navy," Mark said.

"Basic? Can you shoot?"

"Yes, sir." Mark began one of his tales about 'Nam. It might or might not have been true, but Jellison wasn't listening.

"Can he?" he asked Randall.

"Yes. I've seen him," Harvey said. He began to relax, to feel the knots unwind in his neck. It looked good, it looked as if the Senator might want him. . . .

"If you stay here, you're on my team," Jellison said. "Nobody else's. Your loyalty is to me."

"Understood," Harvey said.

Jellison nodded. "We'll give it a try."

■

As the Mediterranean waters recede from the drowned cities of Tel Aviv and Haifa, rainstorms lash the highlands of the Sudan and Ethiopia. Floodwaters cascade down the Nile to smash against the High Aswan Dam, already weakened by the earthquakes following Hammerfall. The dam bursts, joining 130 million acre-feet of water to the flooded river. The waters smash across the Nile Delta, through the ancient cities, across Cairo. The Great Pyramid is undermined and falls beneath the torrent.

Ten thousand years of civilization are scooped up and carried with the water. From the First Cataract to the Mediterranean Sea, nothing lives in the Delta of the Nile.

Beggar Man

O hear us when we cry to thee
for those in peril on the sea.
Mariner's Hymn

Eileen slept with her seat tilted back to horizontal, her seat belt loose about her. She rolled with the motion of the car. Once Tim heard the beginnings of a snore. He reached over and tightened her belt when they started on the long downgrade. Then he switched the motor off.

He remembered his driver had done that in Greece. Everyone coasted down hills in Greece. Even down the twisted narrow road from Delphi across Parnassus to Thermopylae. That had been terrifying, but the driver insisted. Greece had the most expensive gasoline in the world.

Where was Thermopylae now? Had the waters washed away the grave of the Three Hundred? The waves wouldn't have reached Delphi, or been as high as the Acropolis. Greece had lived through disasters before.

The road twisted and tilted and Tim eased the Blazer around the turn, using the brakes warily. A long straight stretch was ahead, down all the way, then more downhill on a wet and broken and twisting road, and riding with Eileen had made him realize just how good a driver he wasn't.

The mountains had shifted.

Here the road ended in space. Tim braked sharply and came to a stop. He walked forward through the soft rain. It tasted sweet. No more salt rain, anyway.

The road, and the steep bank of cut rock, and this part of the mountain itself had sheared and dropped twenty feet or more. Mud had piled up below, so that there were places where the drop was no more than four or five feet.

Cars went over longer drops than that in TV commercials. One pickup ad had shown clips from a movie with that truck jumping over ditches, flying over banks, and the announcer had said the truck wasn't even especially modified. . . .

Would the Blazer take it?

Was there any choice? The drop looked as if it ran for miles. Tim got back in and backed up fifty yards. He thought through the physics of the situation. If the car fell over the edge it would land on its nose, and they'd be dead. It had to go over horizontally, and that meant *speed*. Easing it over would kill them.

He set the brake and walked back to the edge again. Wake Eileen? She was dead out of it. Headlights behind him, dim in the rain, decided it for him. He didn't know who that would be and he didn't want to know. He walked back toward the Blazer. His mind worked the equation: Call the Blazer fifteen feet long; it would fall at one G. He got in and started the car. If the front end shouldn't fall more than two feet before the rear left the pavement and also began to fall, then the whole car should be over in about a third of a second, which meant fifteen feet in a third of a second or forty-five feet per second, and forty-four feet per second was thirty miles per hour, so about thirty miles per hour ought to do it and here we GO . . .

The car fell about six feet all told. His instinct was to hit the brake but he didn't.

They hit hard, landing on the mud, rolling down the mud ramp onto the road itself. Amazingly that was all. They were rolling down the road as if nothing had ever happened.

Eileen bounced and rolled hard against the seat belt. She shook herself, sat partly upright and looked out. The wet countryside flowed past. She blinked, and then, satisfied, went back to sleep.

Slept right through the best driving I'll ever do, Tim thought. He grinned at the rain and mud, then switched off the engine to coast downhill.

An hour later she was still asleep. He envied her. He'd heard of people who slept most of the time: shell-shocked, or bitterly disappointed in their waking lives. He could understand the temptation. But of course that wasn't Eileen. She *needed* sleep. She'd be all the more alert when she was needed.

Here the road had shattered to discrete plates. Tim switched on the engine and kept the speed up, moving as if from island to concrete island. He remembered a TV program about the Baja race. One driver said the way to take a bad road was fast—that way you didn't touch the bumps but flew over them. It hadn't seemed like a very good idea when he heard it, but now there didn't seem to be much else to do. The plates lurched under the car's weight and impact. Tim's knuckles were white on the wheel, but Eileen smiled in her sleep, as if rocked in a cradle.

Tim felt very lonely.

She had not deserted him. At the risk of her life she had stayed with him. But she was sleeping and he was driving, and the rain pounded constantly on metal an inch over his head, and the road kept doing strange things. Here it lifted in a graceful arc, like a futuristic bridge, and a new stream ran beneath it. The concrete ribbon hadn't shattered under its own weight, not yet, but it for damn sure wouldn't hold a car. Tim drove around it, through the flood. The wheels kept moving and the motor didn't die, and he pulled back onto the road where he could.

He had been deserted by everything and everyone *but* Eileen. He could understand, that money and credit cards were worthless; sure. A bullet through the windshield was something else. Driving across the green of a country club felt like vandalism! The observatory . . . but Tim didn't want to think about that. He'd been thrown off his own land, and his ears burned with the memory. Cowardice. It felt like cowardice.

The road curled out of the mountains, widened and became a smooth straight line leading away. Where? No compass. Nothing to do but drive on. And the rain became a furious lashing attack. Tim started the motor and dared to increase speed to twenty mph.

Eileen asked, "How are we doing?"

"Out of the mountains. It's a straightaway, no breaks visible. Go back to sleep."

"Good."

When he looked she was asleep again.

He saw a freeway ahead. A sign told him: HIGHWAY 99, NORTH. He went up the ramp. Now he could go forty. He passed cars stalled in the rain, both on and off the highway.

People, too. Tim hunched low whenever he saw anything that could be a gun. Once it was real: Two men stepped out from either side of the highway and raised a pair of shotguns. They gestured: *Stop.* Tim hunched low, stamped on the accelerator, aimed for one of the men. The man leaped unhesitatingly into the muddy darkness. Tim listened for the guns with every nerve, but they did not speak. Presently he straightened up.

Now, what was that about? Were they afraid to waste ammunition? Or were the guns too wet to fire? He said to himself, softly, "If you can't stand not knowing . . ." Harv Randall's words.

They still had gas, they were still moving. The highway was awash with water; it must have stopped lesser cars than this one. Tim grinned in the dark. Two hundred and fifty thou for a car? Well, it pays to buy the best.

The rain hurled a sea of water across the land in one ferocious blast, then stopped just as suddenly.

For a long moment Tim had an unbroken view ahead. He hit the brakes as the rain slashed down again. The car achieved a marvelous floating sensation before it coasted to a stop.

They had come to the end.

Eileen sat up. She pulled the seat back up behind her and smoothed her skirt with automatic gestures.

"We've hit an ocean," said Tim.

She rubbed her eyes. "Where are we?"

Tim turned on the roof light. He spread the map across their laps. "I kept working north and west and downhill," he said. "Until we got out of the mountains. There were a lot of them. After a while I couldn't tell directions anymore, so I just went downhill. Eventually I came to Highway Ninety-nine." Tim spoke proudly: With his lousy sense of direction they might have ended up anywhere. "Ninety-nine's been good. No more breaks. You missed a couple of guys with shotguns, and a lot of cars that weren't running anymore, but no real trouble. Of course there was a lot of water on the road, but . . ."

She had raked the map with her eyes, once. Now she was peering ahead through the rain, along the beam of the head-lamps, piecing out the view from subliminal cues and imagina-tion. For as far as they both could see in the gray twilight there was nothing but a silver-gray expanse of rain-spattered water. No lights anywhere. Nothing.

"See if you can back up," she said. She fell to studying the map. Tim inched backward, out of the water, until it was only hubcap-deep.

"We're in trouble," Eileen said. "Have we passed Bakersfield?"

"Yes." There had been freeway signs, and the ghosts of dark buildings, a mountain range done all in right angles. "Not long ago."

She frowned and squinted at tiny print. "It says Bakersfield is four hundred feet above sea level."

Tim remembered the fallen mountains. "I wouldn't rely on elevations any longer. I seem to remember the entire San Fernando Valley dropped thirty feet during the Sylmar quake. And that was a little one."

"Well, everything gets lower and lower from here on. We're in the lowlands." And we're sinking in the lowlands, lowlands, low . . . "Tim, no tidal wave could have gotten this far. Could it?"

"No. But it's raining."

"Raining. Ye gods, how it must have rained, and it's still coming! This wasn't all in the comet head, was it?" She shushed him when he started to explain. "Skip it. Let's rethink from scratch. Where do we want to go?"

Back to high ground. "Well," Tim said, "that's a problem too. I know where we want to be. The high farming country, say around Sequoia National Forest. What I don't know is why anyone would want us there." He didn't dare say anything else.

She didn't say anything at all. She was waiting.

Tim worked on his nerve. "I did have one idea . . ."

She waited.

Damn, it was evaporating even as he tried to speak it! Like the restaurants and good hotels that waited in Tujunga: Speak your wish and they were gone. He said it anyway, a little desperately. "Senator Jellison's ranch. I contributed a lot of money to his campaign. And I've been to his ranch. It's *perfect*. If he's there, he'll let us in. And he'll be there. He's that smart."

"And you contributed money to his campaign." She chuckled.

"Money was worth good money then. And, honey, it's all I've got."

"Okay. I can't think of a single farmer who owes me anything. And the farmers own it all now, don't they? Just like Thomas Jefferson wanted it. Where is this ranch?"

Tim tapped the map between Springville and Lake Success, just below the mountainous Sequoia National Park. "Here. We go underwater for a way, then we turn right and resume breathing."

"Maybe there's a better way. Look to your left. Do you see a railroad embankment?"

He turned off the roof light, then the headlights. A little time for his eyes to adjust, and . . . "No."

"Well, it's there." She was looking at the map. "Southern Pacific Railroad. Swing us around and point the headlights that way."

Tim maneuvered the car around. "What are you thinking of? Catching a train?"

"Not exactly."

The headlights didn't reach far through the rain. They showed nothing but rain-stippled sea in all directions.

"We'll have to take the embankment on faith," Eileen said. "Slide over." She climbed over him to reach the steering wheel. He couldn't guess what she had in mind, but he strapped down while she started the motor. Eileen turned south, back the way they had come.

"There are people back there," he said. "Two of them have shotguns. Also, I don't think we've got a siphon, so we shouldn't use up too much gas."

"Good news from all over."

"I'm just telling you," said Tim. He noticed that the water was no longer hubcap-deep. Off to the west, higher ground made black humps in the shallow sea. Here was a grove of almond trees, there a farmhouse; and Eileen turned sharp right where there was no road. The car settled as it left 99, then shouldered forward through water and mud.

Tim was afraid to speak, almost afraid to breathe. Eileen wove a path that crossed one and another of the black humps of rising ground, but they weren't continuous. It was an ocean with islands, and they drove through it in an endless rainstorm. Tim waited, with both hands braced on the dashboard, for the car to plunge into some two-foot dip and die.

"There," Eileen muttered. "There."

Was the horizon slightly higher ahead? Moments later Tim was sure: The land humped ahead of them. Five minutes later they were at the base of the railroad embankment.

The car wouldn't climb it.

Tim was sent out into the rain with the tow rope. He looped it under a rail and pulled back on it, leaning his weight above the embankment, while Eileen tried to drive up sloping mud. The car kept sliding back. Tim looped the rope again around the other rail. He took in slack, inches at a time. The car would surge upward and start to fall back, and Tim would take up the slack and *heave*. One wrong move would cost him one finger. He had stopped thinking. It was easier that way, in the dull misery of rain and exhaustion and the impossible task. His earlier triumphs were forgotten, useless. . . .

It came to him, slowly, that the car was up on the embankment, almost level, and Eileen was leaning on the horn. He detached the rope and coiled it and trudged back to the car.

"Well done," Eileen said. He nodded. And waited.

If Tim's energy and determination were burned out, she still had hers. "A lot of cops know this trick. Eric Larsen told me about it. I never tried it myself. . . ." The car lurched up onto a rail; backed and turned, tilting on the embankment; lurched forward again, and was suddenly doing a balancing act on both rails. "Of course it takes the right car," said Eileen, with less tension and more confidence now. "Off we go. . . ."

Off they went, balanced on the rails. The wheels were just the right width. A new sea gleamed silver on both sides. The car moved slowly, tottering and recovering, balancing like a dancer, the steering wheel moving constantly, minutely. Eileen was wire-tense.

"If you had told me, I wouldn't have believed it," Tim said.

"I didn't think you'd get us up."

Tim didn't answer. He saw very clearly that the tracks were dipping gradually toward the water; but whatever it was that he didn't believe now, he kept it to himself.

Gliding, gliding over the sea. Eileen had been driving for hours over the water. Her slight frown, wide eyes, rigidly upright posture made her a closed universe. Tim dared not speak to her.

There was nobody to call on them for help now, and nobody to point guns. The headlights and an occasional lightning bolt showed them only water and the rails. In places the rails actually dipped below the water, and then Eileen slowed to a crawl and drove by feel. Once the lightning illuminated the roof of a large house, and six human forms on the peaked roof, all glistening in rain gear; twelve glinting eyes watching a phantom car drive across the water. And again there was a house, but it floated on its side, and nobody was near it. Once they drove for miles past a rectangular array of bushes, a drowned orchard with only the tops of the trees showing.

"I'm afraid to stop," Eileen said.

"I gathered that. I'm afraid to distract you."

"No, talk to me. Don't let me get drowsy. Make me real, Tim. This is nightmarish."

"God, yes. I'd know the surface of Mars at a glance, but this isn't anyplace in the universe. Did you see those people watching us?"

"Where?"

Of course, she dared not take her eyes off the rails. He told her about the six people on the roof. "If they live," he said, "they'll start a legend about us. If anyone believes them."

"I'd like that."

"I don't know. A *Flying Dutchman* legend?" But that was tactless. "We won't be here forever, though. These tracks'll take us as far as Porterville, and there won't be anyone trying to stop us."

"You think Senator Jellison will let you in, do you?"

"Sure." Even if that hope failed them, they'd be in a safe area. What counted now was a magic trick: driving to Porterville on railroad tracks. He had to keep her mind on that.

He was not expecting her next remark.

"Will he let *me* in?"

"Are you crazy? You're a lot more valuable than I am. Remember the observatory?"

"Sure. After all, I'm such a damn good accountant."

"If they're as organized around Springville as they were in Tujunga, they'll need an accountant to take care of distributing goods. They may even have a barter system. That could get complicated, with money obsolete."

"Now you're the crazy one," Eileen said. "Anyone who does his own income tax can keep accounts. That's everyone but you, Tim. The accountants and the lawyers run this country, and they want everyone to be like them, and they've damn near succeeded."

"Not anymore."

"That's my point. Accountants are a drug on the market now."

"I don't go in without you," said Tim.

"Sure, I know that. The question is whether we go in or not. Are you hungry?"

"But of course I'm hungry, my child." Tim reached into the back seat. "Fritz gave us tomato bisque and chicken with rice. Both concentrated. I could put them in front of the heater. Can you drive with one hand?"

"I guess not, not on this."

"Oh, never mind. We don't have a can opener."

Our thanks God for small miracles; they're easier to grasp. One small miracle was a road humping out of the sea to cross the tracks. Suddenly the tracks were sunk in blacktop, and Eileen stamped on the brake pedal almost hard enough to send Tim through the windshield.

They flopped their seats back, rolled into each other's arms and slept.

Eileen's sleep wasn't calm. She jerked, she kicked, she cried out. Tim found that if he ran the palm of his hand down her spine, she would relax and fall back to sleep, and then he could sleep too, until next time.

He woke in black night to the scream of wind and the panicky pressure of Eileen's fingernails and the perilous rocking of the car. Eileen's eyes were wide, her mouth too firmly set. "Hurricanes," he said. "The big ocean strikes'll keep spinning them off. Be glad we found a safe place first." She didn't react. "We're safe here," he repeated. "We can sleep through it."

She laughed then. "I dare you. What happens if one of these hits us while we're on the tracks?"

"Then you'd better be as good as you think you are."

"Oh, Jesus," she said, and—incredibly—went back to sleep.

Tim lay beside her in the howling and the rocking. Did hurricanes overturn cars? You bet they did. When he tired of thinking about that, he thought about how hungry he was. Maybe he could use the bumper to pry open a soup can. After the hurricane passed.

He dozed . . . and woke in total silence. There wasn't even rain. He located a soup can and stepped outside. He managed to bend the bumper a little, but he also tore the soup can open. He swallowed some of the condensed tomato bisque, and that was how he happened to look up.

He looked up into a wide patch of clear stars.

"Beautiful," he said. But he entered the car in some haste. Eileen was sitting up. He gave her the soup can. "I think we're in the eye of the hurricane. If you want to see the stars, look quick and come back."

"No, thanks."

The soup was cold and gluey. It left them both thirsty. Eileen set the can on the roof to collect rainwater, and they lay down again to wait for morning.

The rain came again, in frantic violence. Tim reached through the window for the can, and found it gone. He found the abandoned beer can on the floor, pried it open, filled it twice in the rainwater streaming from the car roof.

Hours later, the rain settled down to a gentle drumming. By then it was full daylight: just enough dirty gray light to see that the sea around them was thick with floating things. There were corpses of dogs and rabbits and cattle, far outnumbered by the bodies of human beings. There was wood in all its forms, trees and furniture and the walls of houses. Tim got out and fielded some driftwood and set it in front of the car heater. "If we ever find shelter, we've still got that other can of soup," he said.

"Good," said Eileen. She sat bolt upright at the steering wheel, and the motor was going. Tim didn't urge her. He knew better than to volunteer for the job, and he knew what it would cost her.

She shifted into gear.

"Hold it," Tim said, and he put a hand on her shoulder and pointed. She nodded and put the car back in neutral.

A wave came toward them in a long thread of silver-gray. It wasn't high. When it reached the car it was no more than two feet tall. But the sea had risen in the night until it stood around the tires. The wave slapped against the car and lifted them and carried them and set them down almost immediately with the motor still going.

Eileen sounded exhausted. "What was that, another earthquake?"

"I'd say a dam collapsed somewhere."

"I see. Only that." She tried to laugh. "The dam has broken! Run for your lives!"

"The Cherokees is escaped from Fort Mudge!"

"What?"

"Pogo. Skip it," Tim said. "All that water out there . . . this won't be the first dam that went. All of them, probably. Maybe here and there the engineers got spillways open in time. Maybe. But most of the dams are gone." Which, he thought, means most of the electric power everywhere. Not even local pockets of electricity. He wondered if the powerhouses and generators had survived. Dams could be built again.

Eileen put the Blazer into gear and started forward, slowly.

The Southern Pacific tracks took them most of the way to Porterville. The tracks and embankment rose gradually, until what surrounded them was no longer sea, but land that looked as if it had recently risen from the depths: Atlantis returned. Still Eileen kept to the tracks, though her shoulders were shivering with the strain.

"No people on the tracks, and no stalled cars," she said.

"We're avoiding those, aren't we?" They hadn't, completely; sometimes forlorn groups of refugees, usually in families, trudged along the right-of-way.

"I hate to leave them," Eileen said. "But—which ones should we take? The first ones we see? Be selective? No matter what we do, we'd have the car filled and people on top and there'd still be more—"

"It's all right," Tim said. "We don't have anyplace to go either." But he sat brooding, feeling her mood. What right did they have to expect anyone to help them? They weren't helping anyone themselves. . . .

South and east of Porterville they rolled down a wet embankment to resume their trek on 190. Tim took over the driving, and Eileen lay in the reclined passenger seat, exhausted but unable to sleep.

The land looked recently drowned. Studying the broken buildings and fences and uprooted trees, Tim became certain that a flood had come from the direction they were traveling. There was mud everywhere, and Tim had many occasions to feel proud of his judgment. He didn't think any other car in the world could have got them over some places they passed.

"Lake Success," Eileen said. "There was a big lake up there, and the dam must have gone. The road goes right past it. . . ."

"Yeah?"

"I'm wondering if there's any road there," she said. They went on, until they reached the junction that should have taken them up into the hills.

The land was mud everywhere, studded with cars in every possible attitude. There were bodies, but no living human beings. They were glad for the rain. It kept them from seeing very far into the muddy ditch to their left. The road became worse, washed out in places, covered with mud in others.

Eileen took over driving again, guessing where the road had been and hoping it was still there under the mud. The Blazer kept moving, but more slowly. . . .

Then they saw the campfire. A half-dozen cars, some as good as the Blazer. Here were people of all sexes and ages, a gathering of the hopeless. Somehow they'd started a fire, and there was a pile of wood under a plastic shelter. The people stayed in the rain; wood was kept near the fire to dry.

Tim brought in the dry wood from the Blazer. No one spoke to him. The children stared at him with hopeless eyes. Finally one of the men said, "You won't make it."

Tim wordlessly eyed the mudslide ahead. There were tracks in it. If any car could get through . . .

"This isn't the problem," the man said. "We got past that. But up ahead there's a bridge out."

"So walk—"

"And a man with a rifle. They don't talk. First shot was between my wife and myself. I got the impression the second would finish the job. Never even saw the rifleman."

So that was it. End of the line. Tim sat beside the fire and began to laugh, softly at first, then in rising hysteria. Two days. Two? Yes. This was Friday, Drowned Muddy Fridae after Hot Fudge Tuesdae and the roads to high ground were gone and you couldn't get to the Senator's place. More men with guns. The world belonged to men with guns. Maybe the Senator was shooting. The image was funny, Senator Jellison in full formals, striped trousers and morning coat and rifle, what the successful leader will wear. . . .

"It works," Tim said. "Tell your dream and kill it. It works!" He laughed again.

"Here." Another man, big, with thick hairy forearms, used a handkerchief to snatch a tin can from the fire. He poured into a styrofoam cup, then looked regretful and took a flat pint bottle from his jacket pocket. He splashed in rum, then handed Tim the cup. "Drink that, and don't lose the cup. And stop it. You're scaring the kids."

So what? But it was natural for Tim to feel ashamed. "Don't make a scene." How often had his mother told him that? And told his father that, and told everyone else . . . ?

The laced coffee tasted good and warmed him. It didn't help much, though. Eileen brought their remaining can of soup and offered it. They sat in silence, sharing what there was: the soup, instant coffee, and a bit of drowned rabbit broiled on a stick.

There was very little talking. Finally the others got up. "We'll strike for north," one man said. He gathered his family. "Anybody with me?"

"Sure." Others joined. Tim felt relieved. They were going away, leaving him with Eileen. Should he go with them? For what? They hadn't anyplace to go either.

The others got up and went to their cars, all but the big man who'd offered the coffee. He sat with his wife and two children. "You too, Brad?" the new leader asked.

"Car's not working." He waved toward a Lincoln parked near the mudslide. "Broken axle, I think."

"Any gas in it?" the leader asked.

"Not much."

"We'll try anyway. If you don't mind."

The big man shrugged. The others siphoned no more than a pint of gasoline out of the Lincoln. Their cars were already crowded. There was absolutely no room for anyone else. The expedition leader paused. He looked at them as one looks at the dead. "That's your plastic tarp. And your instant coffee," he said. He said it wistfully, but when he got no answer, turned away. They drove off, downhill into the rain.

Now there were six by the fire. Tim and Eileen, and— "Name's Brad Wagoner," the big man said. "That's Rosa, and Eric, and Concepcion. Named the boy for my side of the family, girl for Rosa's. Thought we'd keep that up if we had any more." He seemed glad of someone to talk with.

"I'm Eileen, and that's Tim. We're—" She stopped herself. "Of course we're not really pleased to meet you. But I guess I should say it anyway. And we're very grateful for the coffee."

The children were very quiet. Rosa Wagoner hugged them and spoke to them in soft Spanish. They were very young, five or six, not more, and they clung to her. They had on yellow nylon windbreakers and tennis shoes.

"You're stranded," Tim said.

Wagoner nodded. He still didn't say anything.

He'd make two of me, Tim thought. And he's got a wife and two kids. We better get out of here before he breaks my neck and takes the Blazer. Tim felt afraid, and was ashamed because the Wagoners hadn't said or done anything to deserve suspicion. Just that they were here . . .

"No place to go anyway," Brad Wagoner said. "We're from Bakersfield. Not much left of Bakersfield. I guess we should have struck up into the hills right off, but we thought we'd try to find some supplies in town. We just missed getting washed away when the dam went." He eyed the steep hill above him. "If this rain would stop, maybe we could see some place to walk to. You got any plans?" He couldn't disguise the plea in his voice.

"Not really." Tim stared into the dying fire. "I thought I knew somebody up there. Politician I gave a lot of money to. Senator Jellison." There. That finished it for sure. And now what would they do?

"Jellison," Wagoner mused. "I voted for him. Think that would count? Are you still going to try to get up there?"

"It's all I can think of." Tim's voice held no hope at all.

"What will you do?" Eileen asked. Her eyes kept straying to the children.

Wagoner shrugged. "Find some place and start over, I guess." He laughed. "I built high-rise apartments. Made a lot of money at it, but—I didn't get as good a car as yours."

"You'd be surprised what that one cost me," Tim said.

The fire died away. It was time. Eileen went to the Blazer. Tim followed. Brad Wagoner sat with his wife and children.

"I can't stand it," Tim said.

"Me either." Eileen took his hand and squeezed. "Mr. Wagoner. Brad . . ."

"Yeah?"

"Come on. Pile in." Eileen waited until the Wagoners had got into the Blazer, adults in the back seat, children on the floor behind that. She turned and drove down the hill. "I wish we had a good map."

"Maps I have," Wagoner said. He took out a soggy paper from an inner pocket. "Careful, it tears easy when it's wet." It was an Auto Club map of Tulare County. Much better than the Chevron map they'd been using.

Eileen eased the Blazer to a stop and examined the map. "That bridge there, is that the one that's out?"

"Yeah."

"Look, Tim, if we backtrack and go south, there's a road up into the hills—"

"Which beats hell out of spending more time on the Southern Pacific," Tim said.

"Southern Pacific?" Rosa Wagoner asked.

Tim didn't explain. They drove south until they found a sheltered place on the road, partway up a hill, and they

402

pulled off to sleep. They took turns letting the Wagoners use the seats while they huddled under the plastic tarp.

"High ground," Tim said. "It goes north. And east. And that road's not on the map." He pointed. The road was gravel, but it looked in good condition—and it looked traveled. It ran in the right direction.

Eileen was running out of hope, and the Blazer was running out of gas, but she took the road. It wound upward into the hills. It was luck that they'd found it, and more luck that the rain and mud and hurricanes hadn't ruined it. But no luck could protect them from the roadblock.

There were four big men, big like football stars or TV-Mafia goons. Guns and size made them look unfriendly, and they weren't smiling. Tim got out alone, wonderingly. One of the men came down to meet him. The others stood aloof. One of the men looked elusively familiar. Someone he'd seen on the Senator's ranch? That wouldn't help; and it was another of the armed men who had come to the barrier.

Tim told them, crisply (while very aware of how like a wandering tramp he looked), "We're on our way to visit Senator Jellison." The imperious voice cost Tim most of his reserves of self-control.

It hadn't impressed. "Name?"

"Tim Hamner."

The man nodded. "Spelled how?"

Tim spelled it, and was somehow glad that the name was not known. The man called behind him, "Chuck, see if Hamner's on the Senator's list. H-A-M-N-E-R."

One of the guards reacted to that. He came down toward the barricade. Tim was sure he'd seen him before.

"We've got a list of people to let through," the first guard said. "And, buddy, it's a short list. We've got another list of professions. Are you a doctor?"

"No—"

"Blacksmith? Machinist? Mechanic? Tool-and-die maker?"

"What have you got for playboy, retired? Or astronomer?" Tim remembered Brad Wagoner. "Or building contractor?" He had a thought as he said it, but he was interrupted.

A voice came from a parked truck. "No Hamner."

"Sorry," the guard said. "We don't want you blocking the road, so we'd be obliged if you'd move that car to where we can't see it. And don't come back."

If you tell your dreams, they won't come true. Tim started to turn away. But—

But you don't go off to die without even *trying*. He saw Eileen and Rosa Wagoner staring out at him from the car. Their faces said it all. They knew.

Other roads in? Nuts. The car was almost out of gas, and suppose they found one? These people knew the country. If there was a good way in, they had it covered.

Walk? Senator Jellison's ranch ended at a great white monolith the size of an apartment building, and maybe they could get that far—and get shot—

And anyway, Tim thought, if I'm good for anything, it's talking. No use at all creeping around in the bushes. . . . He turned back to the barricade. The guard looked disappointed. His rifle wasn't quite pointed at Tim. "Your car works fine, and you're not hurt," the man said. "I'd leave it at that—"

"Chescu," Tim shouted. "Mark Chescu!"

"That's *Czescu*," one of the men answered. "Hello, Mr. Hamner."

"You were going to let me *leave*? Without even *talking* to me?"

Mark shrugged. "I'm not really in charge here."

"Fucking-A you're not," one of the big men said.

"But . . . Mark, can we talk?" Tim demanded. "I have an idea—". He thought fast. There was something Wagoner had said. He built apartments. But . . .

"We can talk," Mark told him. "It won't do a lot of good." He handed his rifle to one of the others and came around the barrier. "What's to talk about?"

Tim led him to the Blazer. "Brad, you said you built apartments. Contractor or architect?"

"Both."

"I thought so," Tim said. He spoke quickly, words in a rush. "So you know concrete. And construction work. You could build a dam!"

Wagoner frowned. "I suppose—"

"See!" Tim was triumphant. "Dams." He pointed to the Auto Club map. "See, there are powerhouses, dams, all along the road up from here, all the way up into the Sierra, and those dams will be gone, but some of the little powerhouses will still be there, and *I* know enough about electricity to get them running if somebody can build the dam. You have here a complete electrical contracting team. That ought to be worth something." Tim was lying through his teeth,

404

but he didn't think any of these people would know enough about electricity to trip him in an exam.

And he did know the theory, even if he was a bit hazy about the practical aspects of polyphase alternators.

Mark looked thoughtful.

"Goddammit," Tim shouted. "I gave Jellison fifty thousand dollars back when that was real money! You can at least tell him I'm here!"

"Yeah. Let me think about it," Mark said. The story made sense. And Tim Hamner had been a friend of Harvey Randall's. If Hamner had gone off without recognizing him, Mark could have forgotten that, but not now. Harv would find out, and Harv might not like it. And fifty big ones. Mark hadn't spent much time with the Senator, but Jellison had this old-fashioned air and he might think that was important. And besides, that bit about dams and powerhouses—it added up. Mark would have let them in. Only he couldn't. The Christophers wouldn't let him. But they still listened to Jellison.

Mark eyed the other man in the car. A big man. "Army?" he asked.

"Marine Corps," Wagoner said.

"Can you shoot?"

"All Marines are riflemen first. Yes."

"Okay. I'll give it a try." Mark went back to the roadblock. "This guy seems to be an old friend of the Senator's," Mark said. "I'll go tell him."

The big guard looked thoughtful. Tim held his breath. "He can wait," the man said finally. He raised his voice. "Pull off to the side. And stay in the car."

"Right." Tim got into the Blazer. They jockeyed it until it was almost in the ditch. "If somebody comes here in a fighting mood, we don't want to get hit by stray bullets," he said. He watched Mark kick a motorcycle to life and drive away.

"Is fighting likely?" Rosa Wagoner asked.

"I don't know," Tim said. He huddled in the seat. "Now we wait. And see."

Eileen laughed. She pictured Tim trying to rewind a huge generator. "Cross your fingers," she said.

■

"You knew him, I didn't," Senator Jellison said. "Any use?"

405

Harvey Randall looked thoughtful. "I honestly don't know. He got here. That's a lot in his favor. He's a survivor."

"Or lucky," Jellison said. "Hamner, as in Hamner-Brown. He wasn't lucky for the world. Yeah, I know, discovery isn't invention. Mark, you say the other guy's an ex-Marine?"

"Says he is. Looks it, Senator. That's all I know."

"Six more people. Two women and two kids." Jellison looked thoughtful. "Harvey, you put any stock in this scheme to get the power plants working again?"

"The idea sounds useful—"

"Sure, but can Hamner do it?"

Harvey shrugged. "I honestly don't know, Senator. He's a college man. He must know *something* besides astronomy."

"And I owe him," Jellison said. "Question is, do I owe him enough? It can get *hungry* here this winter." He looked thoughtful again. "The guy who discovered the comet. That tells me one thing. He's probably got *patience*. And we could sure as hell use a lookout up on top of the crag, somebody who'd really watch. Let Alice move around a bit instead of sticking in one place.

"And a Marine who may or may not be able to build dams. Officer or enlisted, Mark?"

"Don't know, Senator. I'd guess officer, but I just don't know."

"Yeah. Well, I always did like the Marines. Mark, go tell Mr. Hamner this is his lucky day."

Mark's face said it all. Tim knew when Mark came to the car.

They were safe. After all of it, they were safe. Sometimes dreams do come true, even if you tell them.

The Stronghold: Two

The importance of information is directly proportional to its improbability.
                    Fundamental theorem of information theory

Al Hardy didn't like guard duty. It didn't do him much good to dislike it. Somebody had to pull guard, and the ranch-hands were more useful elsewhere. Besides, Hardy could make decisions for the Senator.

He looked forward to giving up the whole thing. Not too long, he thought. Not too long until we won't need guards at the Senator's gate. The roadblock stopped most intruders now; but it didn't get them all. A few walked up from the flooded San Joaquin. Others came down from the High Sierra, and a lot of strangers had got into the valley before the Christophers began sealing it off. Most would be sent on their way, and they'd heard the Senator could let them stay on. It meant a lot, to be able to talk to the Senator.

And the Old Man didn't like sending people away, which was why Al didn't let many get up to see him. It was part of his job, and always had been: The Senator said yes to people, and Al Hardy said no.

There'd be a flood of them every hour if they weren't stopped, and the Senator had important work to do. And Maureen and Charlotte would stand guard if Al didn't, and to hell with that. The only good thing about Hammerfall, women's lib was dead milliseconds after Hammerstrike. . . .

Al had paper work to do. He made lists of items they

needed, jobs for people to do, worked out details of schemes the Senator thought up. He worked steadily at the clipboard in the car, pausing when anyone came to the drive.

You couldn't tell. You just couldn't tell. The refugees all looked alike: half-drowned and half-starved, and worse every day. Now it was Saturday, and they looked just awful. When he'd been Senator Jellison's aide, Al Hardy had judged himself a good judge of men. But now there was nothing to judge. He had to fall back on routine.

These wandering scarecrows who came on foot, leading two children and carrying a third; but the man and woman both claimed to be doctors and knew the lingo . . . specialists, but even the woman psychiatrist had had GP training; they all did. And that surly giant was a CBS executive; he had to be turned back to the road, and he didn't stop swearing until Hardy's partner wasted a round through the side window of his car.

And the man in the remains of a good suit, polite and speaking good English, who'd been a city councilman out in the valley there, and who'd got out of his car, got close to Al and showed the pistol hidden in his raincoat pocket.

"Put your hands up."

"Sure you want it this way?" Al had asked.

"Yes. You're taking me inside."

"Okay." Al raised his hands. And the shot went through the city councilman's head, neat and clean, because of course the signal was Al raising his right hand. Pity the councilman had never read his Kipling:

Twas only by favour of mine, quoth he, ye rode so long alive,
There was not a rock for twenty mile, there was not a clump of tree,
But covered a man of my own men with his rifle cocked on his knee.
If I had raised my bridle-hand, as I have held it low,
The little jackals that flee so fast were feasting all in a row.
If I had bowed my head on my breast, as I have held it high,
The Kite that whistles above us now were gorged till she could not fly. . . .

A truck came up to the drive. Small truck, thin hairy man with mustache drooping. Probably a local, Al thought. Everyone around here drove a small truck. By the same token he might have stolen it, but why drive to the Senator's home with it? Al got out of the car and splashed through muddy water to the gate.

To all of them Alvin Hardy was the same: "Show your hands. I'm not armed. But there's a man with a scope-sighted rifle and you can't see him."

"Can he drive a truck?"

Al Hardy stared at the bearded man. "What?"

"First things first." The bearded man reached into the bag on the seat beside him. "Mail. Only I've got a registered letter. Senator will have to sign for it. And there's a dead bear—"

"What?" Al's routine wasn't working so well. "What?"

"A dead bear. I killed him early this morning. I didn't have much choice. I was sleeping in the truck and this enormous black hairy arm smashed the window and reached inside. He was huge. I backed up as far as I could, but he kept coming in, so I took this Beretta I found at the Chicken Ranch and shot the bear through the eye. He dropped like so much meat. So—"

"Who are you?" Al asked.

"I'm the goddam mailman! Will you try to keep your mind on one thing at a time? There's five hundred to a thousand pounds of bear meat, not to mention the fur, just waiting for four big men with a truck, and it's starting to spoil right now! I couldn't move him myself, but if you get a team out there you can maybe stop some people from starving. And now I've got to get the Senator's signature for this registered letter, only you better send somebody for the bear right away."

It was too much for Al Hardy. Far too much. The one thing he knew was the Beretta. "You'll have to let me hold that weapon for you. And you drive me up the hill," Al said.

"Hold my gun? Why the hell should you hold my gun?" Harry demanded. "Oh, hell, all right if it makes you happy. Here."

He handed the pistol out. Al took it gingerly. Then he opened the gate.

"Good Lord, Senator, it's Harry!" Mrs. Cox shouted.

"Harry? Who's Harry?" Senator Jellison got up from the table with its maps and lists and diagrams and went to the windows. Sure enough, there was Al with somebody in a truck. A very bearded and mustachioed somebody, in gray clothes.

"Mail call!" Harry shouted as he came up onto the porch.

Mrs. Cox rushed to the door. "Harry, we never expected to see you again!"

"Hi," Harry said. "Registered letter for Senator Jellison."

Registered letter. Political secrets about a world dead and burying itself. Arthur Jellison went to the door. The mail carrier—yes, that was the remains of a Postal Service uniform—looked a bit worn. "Come in," Jellison said. What the devil was this guy doing—

"Senator, Harry shot a bear this morning. I better get some ranch-hands out to get it before the buzzards do," Al Hardy said.

"You don't go off with my pistol," Harry said indignantly.

"Oh." Hardy produced the weapon from a pocket. He looked at it uncertainly. "Senator, this is his," he said. Then he fled, leaving Jellison holding the weapon in still more confusion.

"I think you're the first chap to fluster Hardy," Jellison said. "Come in. Do you call on all the ranches?"

"Right," Harry said.

"And who do you expect to pay you, now that—"

"People I bring messages to," Harry said. "My customers."

That hint couldn't be ignored. "Mrs. Cox, see what you can find—"

"Coming up," she called from the kitchen. She came in with a cup of coffee. A very nice cup, Jellison saw. One of his best. And some of the last coffee in the world. Mrs. Cox thought well of Harry.

That at least told him one thing. He handed over the pistol. "Sorry. Hardy's got instructions—"

"Sure." The mailman pocketed the weapon. He sipped the coffee and sighed.

"Have a seat," Jellison said. "You've been all over the valley?"

"Most places."

"So tell me what things are like—"

"I thought you'd never ask."

Harry had been nearly everywhere. He told his story simply, no embellishments. He'd decided on that style. Just the facts. Mail truck overturned. Power lines down. Telephone lines gone. Breaks in the road, here, and here, and ways around on driveways through here and across there. Millers okay, Shire still operating. Muchos Nombres deserted when he'd gone back with the truck, and the bodies—oops, getting ahead of himself.

He told of the murder at the Roman place. Jellison frowned, and Harry went to the table to show him on the big county engineer's map.

"No sign of the owners, but somebody shot at you, and killed this other chap?" Jellison asked.

"Right."

Jellison nodded. Have to do something there. But—first tell the Christophers. Let them share the risks of a police action.

"And the people at Muchos Nombres were coming to find you," Harry said. "That was yesterday, before noon."

"Never got here," Jellison said. "Maybe they're in town. Good land there? Anything planted?"

"Not much. Weeds, mostly," Harry said. "But I have chickens. Got any chicken feed?"

"Chickens?" This guy was a gold mine of information!

Harry told him about the Sinanians and the Chicken Ranch. "Lots of chickens left there, and I guess they'll starve or the coyotes will get them, so you might as well help yourself," Harry said. "I want to keep a few. There was one rooster, and I hope he lives. If not, maybe I'll have to borrow one. . . ."

"You're taking up farming?" Jellison asked.

Harry shuddered. "Good God, no! But I thought it'd be nice to have a few chickens running around the place."

"So you'll go back there—"

"When I finish my route," Harry said. "I'll stop at other places on the way back."

"And then what?" Jellison asked, but he already knew.

"I'll start over again, of course. What else?"

That figures. "Mrs. Cox, who's available as a runner?"

"Mark," she said. Her voice was disapproving; she hadn't made up her mind about Mark.

"Send him to town to find out about these tourists from Muchos Nombres. They were supposed to have come looking for me."

"All right," she said. She went off muttering. They needed the telephones working again. Her daughter was talking about a telegraph line last night. There were plans in one of her books, and of course the wires were still around, the old telephone lines.

After she sent Mark off she made lunch. There was plenty of food just now: scraps from what they were canning,

411

gleanings from the garden patches. It wouldn't last long, though. . . .

Harry had even been out of the valley. He traced the road on the map. "Deke Wilson's on my route," Harry said. "He's organized about the way you are. About thirty miles southwest."

"So how did you get back in?" Jellison demanded.

"County road—"

"That's blocked."

"Oh, sure. Mr. Christopher was there."

"So how in hell did you get past him?" Jellison asked. Nothing would surprise him now.

"I waved at him, and he waved at me," Harry said. "Shouldn't he have let me by?"

"Of course he should have." But I didn't think he had that much sense. "Did you tell him all this?"

"Not yet," Harry said. "There were some other people trying to talk to him. And he had his rifle, and four other big guys with him. It didn't seem the proper time for a friendly chat."

There was more. The flood. Harry's story confirmed what Jellison already knew, the San Joaquin was a big inland sea, a hundred and more feet deep in places, water lapping to the edges of the hills. Almond groves torn to shreds by hurricanes. People dead and dying everywhere. There would be a typhoid epidemic for damned sure if something wasn't done, but what?

Mark Czescu came in. "Yes, sir, the people from Muchos Nombres came into town yesterday," he said. "Tried to buy food. Didn't get much. I guess they went back to their own place."

"Where they'll starve," Harry said.

"Invite them to the town meeting," Jellison said. "They've got land—"

"But they don't know anything about farming," Harry said. "I thought I'd mention that. Willing to work, but don't know what they're doing."

Arthur Jellison made another note. Harry's tales filled in a lot of missing information. "And you say Deke Wilson has things organized," he said. That was news, too, about an area outside the valley itself. Jellison decided to send Al Hardy down to see Wilson. Best to stay on good terms with neighbors. Hardy, and . . . well, Mark could take him on the motorcycle.

And there were four million other things to do; and deep down inside, Arthur Jellison was tired in a way that Washington had never tired him. Have to take it easier, he thought.

∎

Cubic miles of water have been vaporized, and the rain clouds encircle the Earth. Cold fronts form along the base of the Himalaya massif, and rainstorms sweep through northeastern India, northern Burma, and China's Yünan and Szechwan provinces. The great rivers of eastern Asia, the Brahmaputra, Irrawaddy, Salween, Mekong, Yang-tze and Yellow rivers, all begin along the Himalaya foothills. Floods pour down across the fertile valleys of Asia, and still the rains fall in the highlands. Dams burst and the waters move on until finally they meet the storm-lashed salt water driven inland by waves and typhoons.

As the rains fall across the Earth, more steam rises from the hot seas near Hammerstrikes; with the water go salt, soil, rock dust, vaporized elements of the Earth's crust. Volcanoes send more billions of tons of smoke and dust rising into the stratosphere.

As Hamner-Brown Comet retreats into deep space, Earth resembles a brilliant pearl with shimmering highlights. The Earth's albedo has changed. More of the Sun's heat and light are reflected back to space, away from the Earth. Hamner-Brown has passed, but the effects remain, some temporary like the tsunamis which still surge through the ocean basins, some on their third journey; hurricanes and typhoons that lash land and sea; the planetwide rainstorms that engulf the Earth.

Some effects are more permament. In the Arctic the water falls as snow that will not melt for hundreds of years.

4

AFTER DOOMSDAY

Behold a white horse: and he that sat on him had a bow; and a crown was given unto him; and he went forth conquering, and to conquer.

And there went out another horse that was red: and power was given to him that sat thereon to take peace from the earth, and that they should kill one another: and there was given unto him a great sword.

The Revelation of Saint John the Divine

First Week: The Princess

*To doubt everything or to believe everything are two
equally convenient solutions; both dispense with the
necessity of reflection.*

H. Poincaré

Maureen Jellison stood at the top of the ridge. Warm rain
poured over her. Lightning flared in the mountains above.
She stepped closer to the deep cleft in the granite knob.
The surface was slippery. She smiled slightly, thinking of
how her father had told her not to come up here alone even
before . . .

It was difficult to finish that thought. She could not put a
name to what had happened. The End of the World sounded
trite, and for a little while it wasn't even true. Not yet. The
world hadn't ended here at the ranch they now called the
Stronghold. She couldn't see into the valley below because
of the rain, but she knew what was there. A bustle of
activity; inventory of *everything*—gasoline, cartridges, needles
and pins, plastic bags, cooking oil, aspirin, firearms, baby
bottles, pots and pans, cement—anything that might help
keep them alive through the winter. Al Hardy was going
about it systematically, using Maureen and Eileen Hamner
and Marie Vance as agents to call on every house in the
valley.

"Snoopers. That's what we are," Maureen shouted to the
wind and the rain. Her voice fell. "And it's all so damned
useless."

The snooping didn't bother her. If anything was necessary,

if anything could save them, it would be Al Hardy's careful work. It wasn't the snooping, or those who tried to hide their possessions. They were fools, but that was a folly that did not disturb her. It was the others; the ones who welcomed her. They believed. They were utterly certain that Senator Jellison would keep them alive, and they were pathetically happy to see his daughter. They didn't care that she had come to pry and snoop and perhaps take their possessions. They were only too glad to offer everything they had, freely, in exchange for a protection that did not exist.

Some farmers and ranchers had pride and independence. They understood the need for organization, but they weren't servile about it. But the others—the pathetic refugees who had somehow got past the roadblocks; the city people who owned houses in the valley, who had fled here to avoid Hammerfall, who had no idea what to do next; even rural people whose life-styles depended on feed trucks and refrigerated railroad cars and California weather—for them the Jellisons were "the government" which would care for them, as it always had.

Maureen couldn't bear the responsibility. She told them lies. She told them they would live, and she knew better. There would be no crops this year, here or anywhere. How long could the loot from flooded stores keep them alive? How many more refugees were there in the San Joaquin basin, and what right did she have to live when the world was dying?

Lightning flared nearby. She did not move. She stood on the bare granite, near the edge. *I wanted goals. Now I have them. And it's too much.* Her life didn't revolve around Washington parties and who was speaking to whom. You couldn't say that surviving the end of the world was trivial. *But it is.* If there's not more to life than just existing, how is it different? It was more comfortable in Washington. It was easier to hide the suffering. *That's the only difference.*

She heard footsteps behind her. Someone was coming along the ridgetop. She had no weapons, and she was afraid. She could laugh at that. She stood at the edge of a cliff, on a bare granite knob as lightning flashed, and she was afraid; but it was the first time she had felt fear of an approaching stranger in this valley, and that made it more terrifying. The Hammer had destroyed everything. It had taken her place of refuge. She looked toward the edge and slightly shifted her weight. It would be so easy.

The man came closer. He wore a poncho and a wide-brimmed hat, and carried a rifle under the poncho. "Maureen?" he called.

Relief washed over her in waves. There was an edge of hysterical laughter in her voice as she said, "Harvey? What are you doing up here?"

Harvey Randall came to the edge of the rock. He stood uncertainly. She remembered that he was afraid of heights, and she stepped carefully toward him, away from the cleft.

"I'm *supposed* to be up here," he said. "What the devil are you doing here?"

"I don't know." She summoned up a reserve of strength she hadn't known she had. "Getting wet, I suppose." Now that she'd said it she realized it was true. Despite the raincoat, she was soaked. Her low boots were filled with water. The rain was just cool enough to feel clammy on her back where it had come down inside her jacket. "Why are you supposed to be here?"

"Guard duty. I have a shelter over there. Come on, let's get in out of the wet."

"All right." She followed him along the ridge. He didn't turn back to look at her, and she followed passively.

Fifty yards away were boulders leaning against each other. A crude framework of wood and polyethylene garbage bags had been built under their partial shelter. There was no source of light inside except the afternoon gloom. The furniture was an air mattress and sleeping bag on the floor, and a wooden box to sit on. A post had been driven into the ground and pegs stuck into it; from them hung a bugle, a plastic bag of paperback books, binoculars, a canteen and lunch.

"Welcome to the palace," Harvey said. "Here, get that jacket off and let yourself dry out a bit." He spoke calmly and naturally, as if there were nothing strange about finding her alone on a bare rock knob in a lightning storm.

The shelter was large; there was room to stand. Harvey shrugged himself out of the rainhat and poncho, then helped her with the jacket. He hung the wet clothes on pegs near the open entrance.

"What are you guarding?" Maureen asked.

"The back way in." He shrugged. "In this rain it's not likely that anyone will come or that I'd see them if they did, but we have to get the shelter built."

"Do you live here?"

"No. We take turns. Me, Tim Hamner, Brad Wagoner and Mark. Sometimes Joanna. We all live down below here. Didn't you know?"

"Yes."

"I haven't seen you since we got here," Harvey said. "I came looking a couple of times, but I got the impression you wouldn't ever be at home for me. And I wasn't all that welcome around the big house. Thanks for voting for me, anyway."

"Voting?"

"The Senator said you'd asked to have me let in."

"You're welcome." That had been easy enough to decide. I don't sleep with every man I meet. Even if you got terminal guilt and went off to another room, it was nice, and I don't really regret it. There's an honest thought. If I thought enough of you to sleep with you, I sure as hell had to save your life, didn't I?

"Have a seat." He waved toward the wooden box. "Eventually there'll be furniture. Nothing else to do up here but work on the place."

"I don't see what good you're doing here," Maureen said.

"Nor I. But try to explain that to Hardy. The maps show this as a good place for a guard post. When the visibility is more than fifty yards it will be, too, but right now it's a waste of manpower."

"We've got plenty of manpower," Maureen said. She sat gingerly on the box and leaned back against the hard boulder. The plastic liner between her back and the boulder was damp from water condensing on its inside surface. "You're going to have to insulate this," she said. She ran a finger along the wet plastic.

"All in good time." He stood nervously in the center of the shelter, finally went over to the air mattress and sat on top of his sleeping bag.

"You think Al's a fool," she said.

"No. No, I didn't say that." Harvey's voice was serious. "I suppose I could do some good up here. Even if a raiding party got past me, I'd be an armed man behind them. And any warning I could give would be worth something down there. No, I don't think Hardy's a fool. As you say, we've got plenty of manpower."

"Too much," Maureen said. "Too many people, not enough food." She didn't recognize this matter-of-fact man who sat on his sleeping bag and never smiled; who didn't talk about galactic empires, and didn't ask why she was up

419

here. This wasn't the man she'd slept with. She didn't know who he was. Almost he reminded her of George. He seemed confident. The rifle he'd brought in was leaning against the post, ready to his hand. There were cartridges sewn in loops on his jacket pocket.

In all this world there are two people I've slept with, and they're both strangers. And George doesn't really count. What you do at fifteen doesn't count. A hurried, frantic coupling on this hill, not very far from here, and both of us so afraid of what we'd done that we never talked about it again. Afterward we acted as if it had never happened. That doesn't count.

George, and this man, this stranger. Two strangers. The rest are dead. Johnny Baker must be dead. My ex-husband too. And . . . There weren't many more to inventory. People she'd cared for, for a year, for a week, for one night even. They were few, and they had been in Washington. All dead.

Some people are strong in a crisis. Harvey Randall is. I thought I was. Now I know better. "Harvey, I'm scared." Now why did I say that?

She'd expected him to say something comforting. To be reassuring, as George would be. It would be a lie, but—

She hadn't expected hysterical laughter. She stared as Harvey Randall giggled, bubbled, laughed insanely. "You're scared," he gasped. "Lord God above, you haven't seen anything to be scared of!" He was shouting at her. "Do you know what it's *like* out there? You can't know. You haven't been outside this valley." Visibly he fought for control of himself. She watched fascinated, as he slowly won the struggle for calm. The laughter died away. Then, amazingly, the stranger was sitting there again, as if he hadn't moved. "Sorry about that," he said. The phrase was flippantly conventional, but it didn't come out that way. It came out as a genuine apology.

She stared in horror. "You too? It's only a big act? All this masculine calm, this—"

"What do you expect?" Harvey asked. "What else can I do? And I really am sorry. Didn't mean to crack like that. . . ."

"It's all right."

"No, it isn't all right," Harvey said. "The only damned chance we've got, any of us has got, is to go on trying to act rationally. And when one of us cracks, it makes it that much harder for the rest. *That's* what I'm sorry about. Not that it gets to me, out of the blue sometimes, wham! I'm learning to live with that. But I shouldn't have let you see it. It can't make things easier for you—"

"But it does," she said. "Sometimes you've got to . . . to say confession." They sat silently for a moment, listening to the wind and rain, the crackle of thunder in the mountains. "We'll swap," Maureen said. "You tell me, I'll tell you."

"Is that wise?" he asked. "Look, I haven't forgotten the last time we met up here on this ridge."

"I haven't either." Her voice was small and thin. She thought he was about to move, to get up, and she spoke quickly. "I don't know what to do about that. Not yet."

He sat, unmoving, so that she wasn't sure that he'd been about to get up after all. "Tell me," he said.

"No." She couldn't quite make out his face. There was a stubble of beard, and the light was very bad in the shelter. Sometimes lightning struck near enough to throw a brilliant flash, eerily green from the color of the plastic bags, but that only blinded her for an instant and she still could not see his expression. "I can't," she said. "It's horrible to me, but it would sound trivial—"

"And what if it does?"

"They hope," she said. "They come to the house, or I go to theirs, and they believe we can save them. That I can save them. Some of them are crazy. There's a boy in town, Mayor Seitz's youngest boy. He's fifteen, and he wanders around naked in the rain unless his mother brings him in. There are five women whose husbands never came back from a hunting trip. There are old people and children and city people and they all expect us to come up with a miracle —and, Harvey, I just don't have any miracles, but I have to go on pretending that I do."

Almost she told him the rest: of her sister Charlotte, sitting alone in her room and staring at the walls with vacant eyes, but then she'd come alive and scream if she couldn't see the children; of Gina, the black woman from the post office, who'd broken a leg and lay in a ditch until somebody found her and then she died of gas gangrene and nobody could help her; of the three children with typhus that nobody could save; of the others who'd gone mad. They wouldn't sound trivial. But they were. She could face horror. "I can't go on giving people false hopes," she said at last.

"You have to," Harvey said. "It's the most important thing in the world."

"Why?"

He spread his hands in astonishment. "Because it is. Because there are so few of us left."

"If life wasn't important before, why should it be now?"

"It is."

"No. What's the difference between meaningless survival in Washington and meaningless survival here? None of that means anything."

"It means something to the others. To the ones who want your miracles."

"Miracles I don't have. Why is it important that other people depend on you? Why does that make my life worth living?"

"Sometimes it's all that does mean anything," Harvey said. He was very serious. "And then you find there's more. A lot more. But first you do a job, one that you didn't really take on, looking out for others. Then after awhile you see that it's important to live." He laughed, not with humor but with sadness. "I know, Maureen."

"Tell me."

"Do you really want to hear it?"

"I don't know. Yes. Yes, I do."

"All right." He told her. She listened to his story: of the preparations before Hammerfall; of his quarrel with Loretta; of his self-doubts and guilt about his brief affair with her, not so much that he had slept with her, but that he had thought about her afterward and compared her with his wife, and how that had made it harder to take Loretta seriously.

He went on, and she heard, but she didn't really comprehend. "And then finally we were here," he said. "Safe. Maureen, you can't know that feeling: to know, really know, that you'll live another hour; that there may be a whole hour when you won't see someone you love torn apart like a used rag doll. I wouldn't want you to understand, not really, but you have to know that much: What your father is building here in this valley is the most important thing in the world. It's priceless, and it's worth anything to keep it, to know . . . to know that somebody, somewhere, has hope. Can feel safe."

"No! That's the real horror. It's all false hope! The end of the world, Harvey! The whole goddam world's come apart, and we're promising something that doesn't exist, won't happen."

"Sure," he said. "Sometimes I think that too. Eileen is

down there in the big house, you know. We hear what's going on."

"Then what's the point if we won't live through the winter?"

He got up and came toward her. She sat very still, and he stood next to her, not touching her, but she knew he was there. "One," he said. "It's not hopeless. You must know that. Hardy and your father have done some damned good planning. It takes some luck, but we've got a chance. Come on, admit it."

"Maybe. If we're lucky. But what if our luck has all run out?"

"Two," he went on relentlessly. "Suppose it's all a scam. We'll all starve this winter. Suppose that. Maureen, it's still worth it. If we can put off for an hour, if for a lousy hour we can spare somebody feeling the way I did curled up in the back of my car . . . Maureen, it's worth dying just to keep one human being from feeling that way. It is. And you can do that. If it takes an act, put on an act. But do it."

He meant it. Maybe he was acting too, doing what he had told her to do; but he meant it too, or why would he bother? Maybe he was right. Oh, God. Let him be right. Only You aren't there, are You?

How much do you believe all this, Harvey Randall? How strong is this resolve of yours? Please don't lose it, because you make me feel it too. I can share it. She looked up at him and said, very gently, "Do you want to make love to me?"

"Yes." He didn't move.

"Why?"

"Because I've thought about you for months. Because I won't feel guilt. Because I want someone to be in love with."

"Those are good reasons." She stood, and reached for him. She felt his arms go to her shoulders. He held her, not tightly, looking at her. The wet spot on her back was cold now. Almost she drew away; this wasn't something casual, not like the last time. This would mean something. It had to.

His hands were warm on her back, and he smelled like sweat and work; an honest smell, not something from a spray can. When he bent to kiss her, it was like an electric shock, and she grasped him and held him, burrowing into him, hoping to lose herself.

Presently they lay on the air mattress, on the open sleeping bag. Gently he held her, and she knew it would be good, and after a long time it was.

Later she lay against him and watched the lightning make strange patterns through the green plastic; and she thought of what she'd done.

Do your job. That's what life is all about, doing one's job. Harvey hadn't really said that, that was Albert Camus, *The Plague,* but it was what Harvey meant. And doing my job includes a lot of things, but I'm not sure it includes Harvey Randall. There's a paradox. He tells me what I should be living for, and I know damned well I can't hold onto it by myself, but what would George do if he knew where I was now?

He'd put Harvey on the road.

"What's the matter?" Harvey asked. His voice came from a long way off.

She turned to him and tried to smile. "Nothing. Everything. I was just thinking."

"You shivered. Are you cold?"

"No. Harvey . . . what about your boy? And Marie's son?"

"They're up there, somewhere. And I have to go look for them. I've been trying to get Hardy to let me, but he's been too busy to talk to me. I'll go without permission if I have to, but I'll ask once more. I'll try again tomorrow. No. Not tomorrow. There's something else tomorrow."

"The Roman place."

"Yes."

"You're in that?"

"Mark and I seem to have drawn the lucky numbers. With Mr. Christopher and his brother. And Al Hardy. And a few others, I guess."

"Will there be shooting?" *Are you going to be killed?*

"Maybe. They shot at Harry. They killed that other man, the one from the dude ranch."

"Aren't you afraid?" she asked.

"Terrified. But it's got to be done. And when it is, I'll ask Hardy to let me take Mark up to the mountains."

She didn't ask him if he had to go. She knew better than that. "Will you come back?"

"Yes. Do you want me to?"

"Yes. But . . . but I'm not in love with you."

"That's all right," he said. He chuckled. "After all, we hardly know each other. Will you ever be in love with me?"

"I don't know." I don't dare let myself be. "I don't think I'll ever love anyone." There's no future in it. There's no future at all.

"You will," he said.

"Let's not talk about it."

There is rain in the Sahara. Lake Chad fills to overflowing, and engulfs the city of Nguigmi. The Niger and the Volta are in flood, drowning millions who have survived the tsunami. In eastern Nigeria the Ibo tribe rises in rebellion against the central government.

Further to the east the Palestinians and Israelis suddenly realize there are no great powers capable of intervening; this time the war will go to a conclusion. The remnants of Israel, Jordan, Syria and Saudi Arabia are on the march. There are no jet planes, and little fuel for tanks. There will be no ammunition resupply, and the war will not end until it is fought with knives.

Second Week: Mountain Men

Time, like an ever-rolling stream,
Bears all its sons away;
They fly, forgotten, as a dream
Dies at the opening day.
Isaac Watts, 1719; *Anglican Hymnal #289*

Water poured from the sky. Harvey Randall was almost past noticing, as he hardly noticed the places where the road was gone. It was automatic to avoid the deepest holes, to walk carefully across the mud that flowed in rivers across the blacktop. It felt good to be moving, to stride up the steep winding road into the High Sierra. There were no cars and no people; only the road. He had food, and a knife, and the target pistol. Not much food, and not much ammunition, but he was lucky to have anything at all.

"Hey, Harv, how about we take a break?" Mark called from behind him.

Harvey kept on walking. Mark shrugged and muttered something under his breath, and shifted the shotgun from his right shoulder to his left. He carried the weapon barrel down under his poncho. The weapon was kept dry, but Mark didn't believe *he* was dry anywhere. He'd sweated enough that he might as well not have the poncho. It felt like a steam bath inside the rain gear.

Harvey picked his way across a rivulet of water. So far he hadn't found anyplace that he couldn't have taken the TravelAll, and he cursed the Senator and his hardnosed assistant; but he did that silently. If he said anything, Mark would agree, and Mark was in enough trouble with Al

Hardy. One of these days Mark would get himself shot, or thrown out of the Senator's Stronghold, and Harvey Randall would have a decision to make.

Meanwhile he could put all his effort into walking uphill. Step. Pause for a tiny fraction of a second, rear knee locked to catch an instant of rest; weight on the forward foot, swing on another step, another instant of rest . . . Absently Harvey reached into a belt pouch and took out a chunk of dried meat. Bear. Harvey had never eaten bear before. Now he wondered if he'd ever eat anything else. Well, by evening they'd be a good nine miles from the Stronghold, and anything they shot they could keep and eat for themselves. The Senator's rules again: no hunting within five miles of his ranch.

It made sense. The game would be needed, later, and no point in scaring it away. All of the Senator's rules made sense, but they were rules, laid down without discussion, orders issued from the big house with nobody to say no except the Christophers, and they weren't arguing. Not yet, anyway.

It was George Christopher who'd let Harvey go; Hardy hadn't wanted to risk it. Not that he cared about Harvey, but the weapons and the food Harvey carried were valuable. But Maureen had talked to Hardy, and then George Christopher had come out and given Harvey the supplies and told him about road conditions.

Not a coincidence. Harvey was sure of that. Christopher had no reason at all to help Harvey Randall—and he'd got into the act the day Maureen talked to Al Hardy and her father about it; the day she'd shown any open friendship with Harvey Randall. That made too much sense to ignore.

It was easy to see what Maureen meant to George Christopher. What did he mean to her? For that matter, what does Harvey Randall mean to Maureen Jellison?

I think I'm falling in love, Harvey whistled to himself. Only . . . I don't know what it's like. Being a faithful— well, very nearly faithful—married man for eighteen years is not much preparation for romance.

Or maybe it is. He had always thought that any two people sufficiently determined to make a go of it would be able to. Now he wondered. What is this love business? He'd have been willing to die for Loretta—but he hadn't been willing to stay home because she was afraid. He could face that now, but he wasn't sure what it meant.

Finally it was afternoon, time to start making camp. He

let his eyes search the woods around him as he hiked. He felt very alone and vulnerable. Time was, when you went far from trailhead you could count on meeting good people; but that was before Hammerfall. Some would-be robbers had come down from these hills not two days before, and they or others like them could be waiting in ambush anywhere. So far, though, he hadn't seen anyone, and that was fine with Harvey.

The road led through pine forest, steep hillsides, and there was standing water anyplace level. It wouldn't be easy to find a good campsite in this rain. A boulder cave, like the one they'd made the sentry shelter out of, would be best. He'd have to be damned careful, though; something or somebody would be making use of any dry spot he could find. Bears, snakes, anything.

There was a skunk in the first place they looked. Harvey passed it by with regret. It would have been a good campsite, two boulders tilted against each other, actually dry ground in there; but the beady eyes and unmistakable odor were invincible. Skunks could carry rabies, too. A skunk bite could be the most dangerous thing up here. There weren't going to be any Pasteur treatments for rabies, not for a long time. . . .

The next cave held a fox, or perhaps a feral dog. They chased it away. The area under the boulders wasn't dry, and wasn't really large enough, but they were able to rig up their ponchos on cut branches so that at least they didn't have water pouring on their heads.

Now for a fire. Harvey spent the rest of the daylight gathering wood. There was standing deadwood, soaked, but if he split it there was some dry wood at the core. There wasn't enough for more than an hour of fire, maybe longer if they were careful. When it was completely dark Harvey used some of his precious lighter fluid.

"Wish I had a railroad flare," Harvey said. He poured lighter fluid carefully onto the base of his tiny stack of dry wood. "You can start a fire in a blizzard with a flare."

"Fucking Hardy wouldn't give you one," Mark said.

"You'd better be careful around him," Harvey said. He lit a match. The lighter fluid caught, and the fire blinded them for a moment. The wood caught, and even that tiny bit of heat was welcome. "He doesn't like you."

"I don't think he likes anybody," Mark said. He began to arrange larger pieces of wood near the fire so they'd dry out. "Always smiling, but he doesn't mean it."

Harvey nodded. Hardy's smile hadn't change from before Hammerfall. He was still the politician's assistant, the man who was friendly with everyone, but now his smile was a threat, not something warm and friendly.

"Jesus," Mark said.

"Eh?"

"Just thinking about those poor bastards," Mark said. "Harv, it gave me the willies."

"Don't think about it."

"I had to pull on the rope," Mark said. "I won't forget it."

"Yeah." There had been four frightened kids in the Roman place. Two boys and two girls, none of them more than twenty. Two were wounded in the fight, when Hardy and Christopher captured them. Then there'd been a shouting match between Hardy and Christopher. George Christopher wanted to shoot all four of them on the spot. Al Hardy argued they ought to be taken back to town. Harvey and Mark had sided with Hardy, and eventually Christopher gave in.

Only, when they got them to town, the Senator and the Mayor held a trial the same afternoon, and by evening all four were hanging in front of the City Hall. George Christopher's way would have been kinder.

"They killed the Romans and that other chap, the guy from Muchos Nombres," Harvey said. "What else could we have done with them?"

"Hell, they got what was coming," Mark said. "It was just all so fucking *quick*. And the way those girls screamed and cried . . ." Mark fed the fire again, brooding.

The executions had shocked a number of the townspeople, Harvey thought. But nobody said anything. The Romans had been their friends. Besides, it could be dangerous to argue. Behind Al Hardy's smiles and perpetual calm and easy manners was the ultimate threat. The road. There was always the road, for those who wouldn't cooperate, for those who caused too much trouble. The road.

■

They were almost at the top, the highest point the road would reach, when it was time to make camp on their third day. The rain hadn't let up, and the higher they climbed, the colder it got. They'd need a fire tonight, which meant that they'd have to take turns tending it.

Harvey was carefully laying out his sticks, and hadn't yet

430

reached into his pockets for the lighter fluid, when they smelled it.

"Smoke," Mark said. "A campfire."

"Yes. Well hidden," Harvey said.

"It's got to be close. We'd never smell it from far, not in this rain."

They probably wouldn't see it, either. Harvey sat absolutely still, motioning Mark for silence. There was a strong wind blowing from higher up. It had to be carrying the campfire smells. The rain was like a wet curtain, and in the dying light they couldn't see more than a few yards.

"Let's go look," Mark said.

"Yeah. We'll leave the ponchos. We can't get any wetter than we are already."

They moved cautiously uphill, up the road, peering into the gloom.

"Over there," Mark whispered. "I heard something. A voice."

Harvey thought he'd heard it too, but it was very faint. They moved in that direction. There wasn't any point in trying to be quiet. The wind and rain covered most sounds, and their feet squished in the wet leaves and mud of the forest floor.

"Just hold it."

They stopped dead still. The voice had been a girl's. Not very old, Harvey thought. She was very close, probably hidden in a thicket just ahead.

"Andy," she called. "Two visitors."

"Coming."

Harvey stood rigid for a moment. It was . . . "Andy!" he shouted. "Andy, is that you?"

"Yes, sir." His son came down the trail.

Harvey rushed forward to greet him. "Andy, thank God, you're all right—"

"Yes, sir. I'm fine. Is Mother . . . ?"

Harvey felt it clutch him, the memory lying across his soul, the pathetic bundle in the electric blanket. "Raiders," Harvey said. "Looters killed your mother."

"Oh." Andy moved away from his father. A girl came out of the thicket. She held a shotgun. Andy went to her and they stood together. Together.

The boy's grown up in two weeks, Harvey thought. He saw the way he stood with the girl. Protectively, and very naturally, and it reminded him of the words in the marriage ceremony: "One flesh." They stood that way, two halves of one person, but so very young. There were wisps of thin hair on Andy's chin. Not a real beard, just the stubble that Loretta had made him shave because it looked bad, although it was nearly invisible. . . .

"Is Mr. Vance here?" Harvey asked.

"Sure. Come on this way," Andy said. He turned, and the girl went back to her thicket. She hadn't said a word. Harvey wondered who she was. His son's . . . woman. And he didn't even know her name, and the boy hadn't told him. And there was something terribly wrong, but Harvey didn't know what to do about it.

Gordie Vance was glad to see him. Harvey was even happier to see Gordie. Gordie had built a large shelter, logs and thatched roof that shed rain, and he had dry wood, and there were fish and birds hanging under the shelter. A pot of stew bubbled on the fire.

"Harv! I knew you'd get here. Been waiting," Gordie said.

Harvey looked puzzled. "How did you expect me to find you?"

"Hell, this is the jump-off place, isn't it? Where we always parked."

There wasn't enough light to be sure, but the place didn't look any different from any other clearing near the road, and Harvey knew he'd never have recognized it. "I'd have gone right past—"

"You'd have come back when you got to the lodge," Gordie said. "What's left of the lodge."

There were a dozen under the shelter. They were mostly in pairs, sleeping bags zipped together.

Boys and girls. One of each, in pairs. Boy Scouts and . . .

"Girl Scouts?" Harvey asked.

Gordie nodded. "I'll tell you about it later. We had some trouble up here last week. It's okay now. You . . . you met Janie, didn't you?"

"The girl with Andy?" Harvey looked around. Andy wasn't there any longer. He'd led Harvey and Mark to the shelter, and he'd left without saying a word.

"Sure. Janie Somers. She and Andy . . ." Gordie shrugged.

"I see," Harvey said, but he didn't see. Andy was a boy, a child. . . .

At fourteen a Roman boy was given a sword and shield and enrolled in a legion, and could legally become head of a household, a property owner. But that was Rome and this is . . .

This is the world after Hammerfall. And Andy has a family and he's an adult.

The other children—weren't children. They were watching Harvey very closely. Not the way children watch an adult. Suspicion, maybe. But neither anger nor respect nor . . . They were children who'd grown up a lot.

And there was a girl in Gordie's sleeping bag. She couldn't have been more than sixteen.

It was dry and warm. Harvey's clothes hung near the fire, and he sat in Gordie's sleeping bag, the bag's luxurious dryness wrapped around him, his feet and legs dry for the first time in days.

The tea was bark, not real tea, but it tasted good, and so had the bowl of stew Gordie served earlier. Mark slept, a smile on his face, very near to the campfire. The others were asleep too, or acted as if they were. Andy and Janie, clinging to each other in their sleeping bag, nestled together; others, Gordie's boy Bert with another girl. And Stacey, the girl Gordie slept with, was curled against Gordie's knees, dozing a little.

Old home week in the deep woods.

"Yeah, it got rough at first," Gordie was saying. "I took the crew back to Soda Springs after we saw the Hammer fall. We rode out the rain and the hurricanes there. Fourth day we started back this way. Hiked four days. When we got here, there were some bikers. They'd found the girls camping up here. Took over."

"Took over. You mean—"

"Christ, Harvey, you know what I mean. They'd raped one of the kids to death, and the lady who'd brought the kids up got herself killed trying to fight them."

"Jesus," Harvey said. "Gordie, you didn't have any guns—"

"Had a twenty-two pistol," Gordie said. "Just in case. But it didn't figure in what happened."

This was a new Gordie. Harvey wasn't sure how, because he made the same jokes, and in some ways he was a lot like the Gordie Vance Harvey had known, but he wasn't, not really. He wasn't a man you could imagine as a banker, to begin with. He seemed to belong up here, with a two-week beard, and no gut but not hungry. Comfortable and dry and very much in charge and at ease . . .

"They were stupid," Gordie was saying. "Didn't want to be wet. They'd rigged some tents up, store-bought tents, along with their camper. We've still got their gear. Used some of it putting this shelter together." He waved to indicate the logs-and-boulder structure, a shed roof with walls and fire pit. "They were all inside, even the ones they thought were on guard. So we knocked them in the head."

"Just like that?"

"Just like that," Gordie said. "Then we cut their throats. Andy killed two."

Gordie let that sink in for awhile. Harvey sat, motionless, then deliberately looked across the fire to where his son lay sleeping with his . . . his woman. A woman he'd won by conquest, rescued . . .

"And after that the girls just hopped into bed with you?" Harvey demanded.

"Ask them. You see how it is," Gordie said. "We didn't rape anybody, if that's what you mean."

"Only technically," Harvey said. He wished he hadn't said it, but the words were out.

Gordie wasn't angry. He laughed. "Statutory rape. Who's to enforce that? Who cares, Harvey?"

"I don't know. The Senator might. Gordie, Marie came with me. She's at the Senator's ranch—"

"Marie? I figured she'd be dead," Gordie said. "She really came looking for Bert, of course. She wouldn't have cared about me."

Harvey didn't say anything. It was true enough.

"She doesn't really care about Bert either," Gordie was saying.

"Bullshit. She's like a tigress. It was all we could do to keep her from coming up with Mark and me."

"Yeah? Maybe. When she knows he's safe, she won't care." Gordie stared into the fire. "So what happens now?"

"We take you back with us—"

"So the Senator can look at me funny and maybe try enforcing statutory rape laws? So he can split Andy away from his girl?"

"It won't be that way."

"Yeah? Get some sleep, Harv. I'll go change the guard. My turn on watch."

"I'll take—"

"No."

"But—"

434

"Don't make me say it, Harvey. Just get some sleep."

Harvey nodded and stretched out in the sleeping bag. Don't make him say it. Don't make him say I'm not one of them, they wouldn't trust me to be on guard for them. . . .

■

Breakfast was fried fish and several vegetables that Harvey didn't recognize. It was good. Harvey was just finishing when Gordie came over and sat next to him.

"We've talked it over, Harv. We're not going back with you."

"None of you?" Harvey demanded.

"That's right. We're staying together."

"Gordie, you're crazy. It's going to get cold up here. It'll be snowing in a couple of weeks—"

"We'll make out," Gordie said.

"Andy!" Harvey called.

"Yes, sir?"

"You're coming with me."

"No, sir." Andy wasn't arguing. He wasn't demanding. He was just saying what would happen. He got up and walked out into the rain. Janie followed closely. She had still not spoken a word to Harvey Randall since she had challenged him on the trail.

"You could stay with us," Gordie said.

"I'd like that. I'd like it better if Andy asked me," Harvey said.

"What do you expect?" Gordie asked. "Look, you made your choice. You stayed in the city. You had a job, and you stayed for it and sent Andy up into the hills—"

"Where he'd be safe!"

"And alone."

"He wasn't alone," Harvey insisted. "He—"

"Don't tell *me*," Gordie said. "Argue with Andy. Look, we put it to a vote this morning. Nobody objected. You can stay with us."

"That's silly. What's up here?"

"What's down there?"

"Safety."

Gordie shrugged. "What's that worth? Look, man." Gordie wasn't quite pleading, because he had nothing to plead. He was straining to make Harvey understand, knowing that

435

Harvey never would. And Gordie didn't really care, except that he owed this much to his friend. "Look, Harv. If he goes with you, he's a kid again. Up here he's second in command—"

"Of what?"

"Of whatever we are. He's a man up here, Harv. He wouldn't be, down there. I saw the way you looked at him and Janie. They're still children to you. Down there you'd make them into children again. You'd make them feel like kids, useless. Well, up here Andy knows he's not useless. We all depend on him. Up here he's doing something important, he's not just a cog in a survival machine."

"Survival machine." Yeah, Harvey thought. That's what we've got at the Senator's Stronghold. A survival machine, and a damned good one. "At least it's a pretty good chance at survival."

"Sure," Gordie said. "Think about it, Harvey. The world ends. Hammerfall. Shouldn't things be different after that?"

"Things *are* different. Lord God, how different do you want? We just took four kids and strung them up in front of City Hall. We're busting our balls to stay alive through winter, and it's a chancy thing, but we'll make it—"

"And what would we do down there?" Gordie asked.

Harvey thought that one over. He wasn't sure. He didn't know if Hardy would let that many into the Stronghold. A troop of Boy Scouts, yes; but this warrior band? Maybe they belonged up here: a new breed of mountain dwellers. "Dammit, that's my son, and he's coming with me."

"No, he's not, Harv. He's not *your* anything. He's his own man, and you haven't got any way to make him come with you. We're not going back, Harv. None of us. But you can stay."

"Stay and be what?"

"Whatever you like."

The offer wasn't even tempting. What would he do up here? And who would he be? Harvey got up and lifted his pack. "No. Mark?"

"Yeah, Boss."

"You coming or staying?"

Mark had been unnaturally quiet since they arrived. "Going back, Harv. Joanna's down there, and I don't think she'd care much for this. Me neither. It can get pretty old, camping out all the time. You?"

"Let's go," Harvey said. He looked around sadly. There wasn't anything up here that belonged to Harvey Randall.

The tsunamis have done their work. Around the shores of the Atlantic there is no trace of the works of man. The very shorelines have been changed. The Gulf of Mexico is a third larger than before; Florida is a chain of islands, Chesapeake Bay has become a gulf. Deep bays indent the western coast of Africa.

On land the craters no longer glow visibly, but they continue to change the weather. Volcanoes pour out lava and smoke. Hurricanes lash the seas.

Rain falls everywhere. The work of the Hammer is not yet completed.

Fourth Week: The Wanderers

> *There is one fact that will bring notable relief to*
> *many survivors: the grim problems facing them will*
> *at least be completely different from those that have*
> *been tormenting them in past years. The problems of*
> *an advanced civilization will be replaced by those*
> *proper to a primitive civilization, and it is probable*
> *that a majority of survivors may be made up of peo-*
> *ple particularly adapted to passing quickly from a*
> *sophisticated to a primitive type of existence. . . .*
>
> Roberto Vacca, *The Coming Dark Age*

The woods were lovely, dark and deep, but they dripped.
Dan Forrester sighed for a warm, dry world now lost, and
he kept moving. His five layers of clothing ran water in
pulses as he moved. It was no drier under the trees. It was
no wetter, either, and not much darker; and here the infrequent snow flurries never got through. Dan did not really
expect to live long enough to see the Sun again.

As he walked he munched on a bit of not-quite-spoiled
fish. One of his books had told how to tease fish from deep
holes in streams, and to Dan's surprise it had worked. So
had the snares he painstakingly set for rabbits. He had never
had enough to eat since leaving Tujunga, but he hadn't
starved, and that, he reflected, was something to set him apart
from a lot of others.

Four weeks since Hammerfall. Four weeks of moving
steadily northward. He had lost his car hours after leaving
his home. Two men and their women and children had
simply taken it away from him. They had left him his backpack and much of his equipment, because in the first days
after Hammerfall people hadn't known just how bad things
were going to be, or maybe they were just decent people
whose need was greater than his. They'd said that, anyway.
It hardly mattered.

Now, leaner and—he had to admit to himself—healthier than he'd ever been (except for his feet, which had blisters that wouldn't heal; diabetes interferes with circulation, which was why he could only make a few miles a day), Dan Forrester, Ph.D., astronomer without sight of stars or employer or possibility of employment, hiked on because there wasn't anything else to do.

The winds were no longer ferocious, except during hurricanes, and those were less frequent. The rain had settled to a steady pattering, or a drizzle, or, sometimes, blessedly, no rain at all. The rain had also turned cool, and sometimes there were snow flurries. Snow in July at four thousand feet elevation. That was much sooner than Dan had expected. The cloud cover over Earth was reflecting back a *lot* of sunlight, and Earth was cooling. Dan could imagine the beginnings of glaciers in the north. Now they were no more than mountainsides and high valleys covered lightly with snow; but it was snow that would never melt in his lifetime.

After awhile he rested, leaning against a tree, backpack caught on the rough bark so that he was not quite sitting. It took weight off his feet, and it was easier than taking off his pack and lifting it onto his back again. Four weeks, and the beginnings of snow. It would be a very hard winter. . . .

"Don't move."

"Right," said Dan. Where had the voice come from? He moved only his eyes. Dan was used to thinking of himself as harmless, in appearance and in reality, but he was thinner now, and his beard was scraggly, and no one looked harmless in this world of fear. A man in an Army uniform stepped from behind a tree. The rifle in his hands looked light; the hole in the end looked as big as Death.

The man's eyes flickered left and right. "You alone? You armed? Got any food?"

"Yes, and no, and not much."

"Don't smart-mouth me. Spill your pack." Behind that gun was a very nervous fellow, a man who kept trying to see through the back of his head. His skin was very pale. Surprisingly, the man had almost no beard, only stubble. He had shaved in the past week. Why? Dan wondered.

Dan opened his hip belt and shrugged out of the pack. He upended it. The Army man watched as he opened zippered pockets. "Insulin," he said, laying out the medical packet. "I'm a diabetic. I carry two," and he set out the other, and the wrapped book beside them.

"Open it," the man said, meaning the book. Dan did.

"Where is your food?"

Dan opened a Ziploc plastic bag. The smell was terrible. He handed the fish to the man. "Nothing to preserve it with," Dan said. "I'm sorry. But I think it's edible, if you don't wait too long."

The man wolfed down the handful of stinking raw fish as if he hadn't eaten in a week. "What else?" he demanded.

"Chocolate," Dan said. His voice was full of resignation. It was the last chocolate in the world, and Dan had saved it for days, waiting for something to celebrate. He watched the uniformed man eat it—no ceremony, not savoring it, just eating.

"Open those." The man pointed to the cooking pots. Dan took the lid off the largest; there was another pot inside it, and a small stove inside that. "No gasoline for the stove," Dan said. "Don't know why I go on carrying it, but I do. The pots aren't much use without something to cook." Dan tried not to look at the pieces of thin copper wire that had spilled from the pack. Snare wire. Without it Dan Forrester would probably starve.

"I'll have one of your pots," the man said.

"Sure. Big or little?"

"Big."

"Here."

"Thanks." The man seemed more relaxed now, although his eyes still darted about and he jumped at slight noises. "Where were you when it all . . . ?" The man gestured vaguely.

"Jet Propulsion Laboratories. Pasadena. I saw it all. We had live TV pictures from the Hammerlab satellite."

"All. What does that mean?"

"There were a lot of strikes. Mostly east of here, Europe, the Atlantic, but some close, some south of us. So I drove north until I lost my car. Do you know if the San Joaquin Nuclear Plant is working?"

"No. There's an ocean where the San Joaquin Valley used to be."

"What about Sacramento?"

"Don't know." The man seemed indecisive, but his rifle still looked Dan steadily in the eye. An ounce of pressure and Dan Forrester would not exist. Dan was surprised to learn just how much he cared, just how much he wanted to live, even though he knew he had no real chance; if he lived until winter he'd die then. He estimated that many more than half those who lived until winter would not see the spring.

"We were on a training run," the man said. "Army. When the trucks went into a ditch, some of us shot the officer and went into business for ourselves. Way Gillings told it, that would be a good idea. I went along. I mean, it was all dead anyway, you know?" The man poured out words in a rush. He needed to justify himself before he killed Dan Forrester. "But then we had to walk and walk and walk and we couldn't find any food, and—" The words cut off, suddenly, with a dark shadow of hate that crossed the soldier's face. Then, "I wish you had more food. I'm taking your jacket."

"Just like that?"

"Take it off. We didn't have rain gear."

"You're too big. It won't fit," Dan said.

"I'll tough it out somehow." The bandit was shivering, and of course he was as wet as Dan himself. He wasn't carrying much fat for insulation, either.

"It's just a windbreaker. Not waterproof."

"A windbreaker is fine. I can take it off you, you know."

Sure, with a hole in it. Or maybe not. A head shot doesn't put holes in jackets. Dan took off the jacket. He was about to throw it to the bandit when he thought of something. "Watch," he said. He stuffed the hood into the narrow pocket in the collar and zipped it up. Then he turned the big pocket inside out and stuffed the entire jacket into it. The package was now the size of two fists. Dan zipped it closed and tossed it.

"Huh," said the bandit.

"Do you know what you're stealing?" Dan's bitter sense of loss went deeper than his common sense. "They can't make the materials anymore. They can't make the machines to shape it. There was a company in New Jersey, and it made that jacket in five sizes and sold it so cheap you could toss one in your car trunk and forget it for ten years. You didn't even have to go looking for it. The company hunted *you* down and sent you thick packets of advertisements. How long will it be before anyone can do that again?"

The man nodded. He began backing into the trees, but stopped. "Don't go west," he said. "We killed a man and a woman and ate them. We. I didn't want anyone else to see how I felt. Next chance I got, I went off on my own. So don't cry real tears over this jacket. Just be glad there ain't no dry wood around." The bandit laughed a funny, painful laugh, turned, and ran.

Dan shook his head. Cannibalism, so soon? But he still had the net undershirt and the T-shirt and a long-sleeved flannel shirt and the sweater. He'd been lucky, and he knew it. Presently he began putting the pack back together. He still had his snare wire, more precious than the jacket. A few feet of thin, strong wire, a spool of strong monofilament —life itself, for a little while. He put on his pack.

Don't go west. The San Joaquin Nuclear Project was west, but the San Joaquin was filled with water. The plant couldn't have survived that, and besides, it wasn't finished. That left Sacramento. Dan called up a mental picture of California. He was in the hills that formed the eastern boundary of the flooded central valley. He'd intended to work his way down to lower ground, where the going wouldn't be so rough.

But the low ground was to the west. The cannibals were between him and the spreading lake that the San Joaquin had become. Best to go north and stay in the foothills. Dan didn't expect to live, but he had a violent antipathy to helping the cannibals.

Sergeant Hooker watched the sky as he marched.

The wind acted like a horde of catnip-maddened kittens. It slashed playfully under helmet rims, plucked at sleeves and pant legs, died for an instant, then whipped dust in the eye from a wholly different direction. The clouds, black and pregnant in the underbelly, shifted uneasily, promising violence. It hadn't rained in hours. Even by post-Hammerfall standards, this weather could do *anything*.

The doctor marched in sullen silence, pushing himself to keep up. He didn't have strength left over to run. At least Hooker didn't have *that* worry. But he worried about the grumbling behind him. No words reached him, only the flavor of complaint and anger.

He thought: We wouldn't eat each other, of course. There are limits. We don't even eat our dead. Yet. Should I have pushed that? There were complaints. I may have to shoot Gillings.

He probably would have shot Gillings there at first, when he came back and found Captain Hora dead and Gillings in charge, but he hadn't had any ammunition then, and the way Gillings told it they'd set up in business for themselves, they'd be fucking kings now that the Hammer had finished civilization.

That was funny, but Sergeant Hooker wasn't laughing. In random anger he told the doctor, "If we have to stop again, they'll eat *you*." His own belly rumbled.

"I know. I told you why you get sick," said the doctor. He was short and harmless-looking, half chipmunk, the resemblance accented by a brush of mustache under his forward-thrusting nose. He was sticking close to Hooker, which was sensible.

"You eat steak rare," he said. "There aren't too many diseases you can catch from a steer. You eat pork well done, because pigs carry some diseases men catch too. Parasites and such." He paused for breath, and to see if Hooker would backhand him to shut up, but Hooker didn't. "But you can catch anything from a man, except maybe sickle-cell anemia. You've lost fifteen men since you turned cannibal—"

"Eight got shot. You saw it."

"They were too sick to run."

"Hell, they were the recruits. Didn't know what they were doing."

The doctor didn't say anything for awhile. They trudged on, no sound but panting as they climbed the damp hillside. Eight men shot, four of them recruits. But seven of the Army men had died too, and not from bullets. "We've all been sick," the doctor said. "We're sick now." His thoughts made him gag. "God, I wish I hadn't—"

"You was just as hungry as us. What if you was too weak to walk?" Hooker wondered why he bothered; the doctor's feelings were nothing to him. Vindictively he hugged his secret to him: When they found a place to settle, then they could lame the doctor, like the cavemen lamed their blacksmiths to keep them from running away. But the need hadn't come yet.

Somewhere. Somewhere there had to be a place, small enough to defend, big enough to support Hooker's company. A farm community, with enough people in it to work the land, and enough land to feed everybody. The company could set up there. Good troops had to be worth something. That goddam Gillings! The way he told it they could just walk in and take over. It hadn't worked out that way.

Too hungry. Too damn many miles coming out of the hills, and all the stores looted, all the people run off or barricaded up so even the bazookas and the recoilless wouldn't make it sure. . . .

444

Hooker wanted to think about something else. If they'd fought earlier it would have been all right; but no, he let himself get talked out of that, talked into moving on to look for a better place, and by the time they got to it . . .

"If you've got to eat human meat . . ." The doctor couldn't leave it alone. He had to talk about it. His face wrinkled and he fought nausea. Hooker hoped it was just in the doctor's head.

"If you've got to eat human meat, the ones you want are the healthy ones, the ones who run the fastest and shoot back the best. The ones you can catch are the sick ones. The meat makes you sick, too. Better you eat diseased cattle than sick men—"

"Shut up, pussy doctor. You know why they died. They died because you're not a real doctor at all, you're only a pussy doctor."

"Sure. First time you catch a real doctor, I'm for the pot."

"Stick close to me if you want to live *that* long."

Cowles had been a gynecologist before Hammerfall. He had left a commercial hunting lodge and driven downslope in the endless rain, and stopped at the border of the new sea that covered the San Joaquin Valley. Hooker's band had found him there, sitting on the fender of his car in the pouring rain, slack-jawed and fresh out of ideas. If Cowles had not had just enough sense to name his profession, he would have joined the stewpot then.

He had protested at being conscripted into the army, until Hooker told him the true situation.

He was docile enough now. There had been no more mumbling about the rights of the citizen. Hooker didn't doubt that he did the best he could to save lives. And he marched as fast as the slowest of them—with the stewpot following behind, carried by three men who were still healthy. Gillings was one of them. It gave Hooker an extra measure of safety: Gillings would have to drop the stewpot before he shot Hooker in the back.

Hooker didn't want to shoot anyone. They'd already lost too many men, to disease, to desertion, to the guns in the valley behind them. Who'd have thought those farmers could put up such a good fight? Against a military outfit with modern weapons?

Only it wasn't a very good military outfit, and they didn't have much ammunition, and they hadn't been very smart about anything. No time to train the recruits. No real discipline among the troops. Everybody edgy, wondering if a

445

real Army patrol was out looking for them, or even a bunch of civilian cops.

There wasn't any turning back, though, not now. And they couldn't march faster than the news. What they needed was more recruits, only they couldn't do much recruiting until they had plenty to eat. Economics could be a terrible enemy. To kill a man for the pot, and gather the fuel and water to make him meat, required a given amount of effort. If the company's numbers dropped too low, the meat would spoil before it could be eaten. Waste of effort, waste of . . . murder.

It was small wonder that Hooker felt he was pursued by furies. Nothing had worked right since Hammerfall Day, and that was weeks ago. He'd forgotten exactly how many days, but two troopers kept an independent record, crossing off days on pocket calendar cards; if Sergeant Hooker needed to know precisely he could find out.

He'd learned to delegate other responsibilities too. He had to. As a sergeant he'd done the detail work; now that he was effectively the commanding officer he couldn't. He didn't think too much about how good an officer he was. There wasn't anybody else to do it.

Left. Right. Away from that valley, back south again, where they might find some place to stop, new recruits, something to eat besides . . .

He studied the clouds and wondered if they were really moving in a counterclockwise whirlpool. The only cover in sight was a house ahead and downslope. He ought to send scouts now. Shelter might be needed. He hoped it was abandoned. And maybe there'd be some canned goods inside. Not bloody likely. "Bascomb! Flash! Cover that farmhouse. See if anybody's home. If there is, get 'em talking, not shooting."

"Right, Sarge." Two troopers, two of the healthy ones, broke from the formation and ran down the hill.

"Talk them to death?" the doctor asked.

"I need recruits, pussy doctor. And we have some stewed meat left, enough to last another day. . . ." Hooker spoke absently. He was still watching Bascomb and Flash as they moved toward the farmhouse, and that weather worried him. It was only just past noon, but the clouds did seem to be moving in a bathtub whirlpool pattern. . . .

Something bright showed in the clouds. It couldn't be sunlight breaking through. It was only a ruddy pinpoint, moving very fast, almost parallel to the clouds, dipping in and out of their dark underbellies. Hooker cried, "Noooo . . ."

Doctor Cowles edged away, suspecting madness.

"No," Hooker said softly, "no, no, no. We can't take it. Enough is enough, don't you understand? It has to stop now," Hooker explained, his eyes on the falling bright point. He couldn't take it, nobody could take it, if the Hammer should fall again.

His prayer was answered, weirdly, as a parachute bloomed behind the meteorite. Hooker stared, not understanding.

"It's a spacecraft," Cowles said. "I'll be damned. Hooker, it's a spacecraft. Must be from Hammerlab. Hooker, are you all right?"

"Shut up." Hooker watched the descending parachute.

Gillings bellowed from behind him. "Hey, Sergeant, what does an astronaut taste like? Like turkey?"

"We'll never know," Hooker called, and it was good that his voice was under control; good that only Cowles had seen his face. Cowles wouldn't talk. "They're coming down in the valley. Right where those farmers shot the shit out of us yesterday."

Falling east, blind. Clouds shone fiercely bright beneath the meteorite *Soyuz*. Here and there were whirlpool patterns, hurricane patterns. North of their path there had been a towering spike of cloud, a mother of hurricanes spinning off little ones, above the hot water that must still cover the Pacific strike. The small window shook with the *Soyuz*'s vibration, and Johnny Baker's eyes vibrated in a different pattern. The *Soyuz* dipped low, dipped in and out of the cloud deck, and in, and the view went from gray-white gradually to gray-dark.

"Could be anything down there," he reported.

Falling more steeply now. Out of the clouds, but it was still dark below. Land, sea, swamp? It didn't matter. They were committed. The *Soyuz* had no fuel, no power, no way to maneuver. They'd stayed up as long as they could, until they were down to their last few pounds of oxygen, the last of their rations; until Hammerlab, with its low electrical power because of the sandblasted solar cells, was almost intolerably hot; until they couldn't stay in orbit any longer, and had to return to a blasted Earth.

It had seemed appropriate to make mankind's last space

flight last as long as possible. Maybe they'd done some good. They'd been able to pinpoint the strikes and broadcast their locations. They'd seen the rockets rise and fall and the atomic blasts, and that was all over now. The Sino-Russian war went on and on and might last forever, but it wasn't fought with atomic weapons any longer. They'd seen it all and broadcast what they saw, and somebody heard them. There'd been an acknowledgment from Pretoria, and another from New Zealand, and almost five minutes of conversation with NORAD and Colorado Springs. Not a lot to show for four weeks in orbit past Hammerfall, but they'd have stayed if there'd been nothing. The last of the space travelers.

"Parachute opening," Pieter said from behind him. Innocuous words, but something in the tone made Johnny brace himself. It was just as well.

"Rough ride," Rick said from behind his other ear. "Maybe because we're overloaded."

"No, it's always like this," Leonilla said. "Are your Apollos more comfortable?"

"I never came down in one," Rick answered. "It must be easier on the nerves. We wear pressure suits."

"Here there is no room," Pieter said. "I have told you, we made the design different after that trouble that killed three *kosmonauts*. We have had no leaks, *da?*"

"*Da.*"

The view was clearing, and coming up fast. "I think we are too far south," Pieter said. "The winds were not predictable."

"So long as we get down," Johnny Baker said. He looked down at the solid sheet of water below. "Can we all swim?"

Leonilla chuckled. "Can we all wade? The water doesn't look deep. In fact . . ." She stared down at the scene below while the others waited. She was in the chair beside Johnny; Pieter and Rick were in the cramped space behind them. "In fact, we are moving inland. East. I see three—no, four people running from a house."

"Two hundred meters," Johnny Baker said. "Get set. We're coming in. One hundred . . . fifty . . . twenty-five . . ."

Splot! The overburdened *Soyuz* landed hard. That felt like land. Johnny sighed and let muscles go limp one by one. No more vibration, scream of air, fear of explosive decompression or death by drowning. They were down.

They were all soaked in sweat. It had been a hot ride. "Everybody okay?" Johnny asked.

"Rojj."

"Yes, thank you."

"Let's get the hell out," Rick said.

Johnny didn't see the hurry; but Rick and Pieter must be hellishly cramped back there. Rick had suggested the arrangement himself, but that wouldn't make it more comfortable. Johnny fumbled with the unfamiliar locks. They wouldn't work until he cursed them; then the latch popped open.

"Oops."

"What is it?" Rick asked. Leonilla craned to look past him.

"Curtain time," said Johnny. He stood in the hatch and smiled brilliantly into a crowd that bristled with shotguns and rifles. More than a dozen men faced him, and no women. He wasn't counting, but he saw half a dozen shotguns and a lot of rifles and revolvers, and Jesus!—two Army submachine guns.

He raised his hands. It wasn't easy to keep them high and still scramble out of the capsule. What were they all so damned nervous about? He moved, rotated, so they could see the U.S. flag on his shoulder. "Don't shoot, I'm a hero."

They were not a prepossessing lot. They were half-drowned rats in farm clothes much the worse for total disaster, and their faces were as grim as their guns. There were a couple of bloody bandages in evidence, too. Johnny had a sudden wild impulse to speak in pidgin talk: Me-fella big astronaut, come from same country belong you-fella. He controlled it.

One spoke from the semicircle. He was white-haired and stout—though not as stout as his coveralls; they had all shrunk within their clothes. But his arms were as thick as a wrestler's. The lightweight machine gun looked fragile in his big hands. "Tell us, Hero, how you come to be in a commie airplane."

"Spaceship. We're from Hammerlab. You know about Hammerlab?" (Head belong you-fella him savvy big rocket go up up up in sky long-time not come down?) "Hammerlab was the joint Apollo-*Soyuz* mission in space. We went up to study the comet."

"We know."

"Okay, the Apollo got a hole poked through it. We think it got hit by a snowflake moving at God's own speed. We had to beg a ride home with the Soviets. In their spaceship. I'm—"

"Johnny Baker! I know him, that's Johnny Baker." The voice belonged to a man: thin, limp black hair, slender fingers wrapped around an enormous shotgun. "Hey!"

"Pleased to meet you," said Johnny, and he was. "Would it hurt if I put my hands down?"

"Go ahead," said the white-haired spokesman. He was obviously the man in charge, partly by tradition, partly because of bull strength. The submachine gun didn't hurt his leadership credentials. It hadn't moved, aimed not quite at Johnny. "Who else is in there?"

"The other astronauts. Two Soviets and another American. It's crowded in there. They'd like to come out, if . . . well, if you people can stay calm about it."

"Nobody excited here," the spokesman said. "Bring out your friends. I got some questions for them. Like why did the commies come down here?"

"Where could we go? Only one spaceship for the four of us. Leonilla?"

She stepped out, smiling, her hands slightly raised. Johnny announced, "Leonilla Malik. The first woman in space." It wasn't strictly true, but it sounded good.

The hard stares softened. The white-haired man lowered his weapon. "I'm Deke Wilson," he said. "Come on out, miss. Or is it comrade?"

"Whatever you choose," she said. She scrambled down from the open hatchway and stood blinking at the reflected light off the sheet of water two hundred yards to the west. "My first visit to America. Or outside the Soviet Union. They wouldn't let me out before."

"Others coming," Johnny said. "Pieter . . ."

Brigadier General Jakov was not smiling. His hands were high and his back was straight, the hammer-and-sickle and CCCP prominent on his shoulder. The farmers were looking wary again. "General Pieter Jakov," Johnny announced, making the pronunciation very Russian in the hope that nobody would get smart-mouthed about the name. "There's one more. Rick . . ."

A couple of the farmers were giving their friends knowing looks.

Rick emerged, also smiling, making certain that the U.S. flag showed.

"Colonel Rick Delanty, U.S. Air Force," Johnny said.

The farmers were relaxing. A little.

"First black man in space," Rick said. "And the last, for about a thousand years." He paused. "We're all the last."

"For awhile. Maybe not that long," Deke Wilson said. He slipped the submachine gun back on its shoulder strap so that it pointed to the sky. There was a subtle change in the way the others held their weapons. Now they were a group of farmers who happened to be carrying guns.

One of the men flashed a mischievous grin. "They made you ride in back?"

"Well, it was the only bus out there," Rick said.

There were laughs. "Derek, take your boys and get back to the roadblock," Wilson said. He turned back to Baker. "We're a little nervous here," he said. "Some Army mutineers running around the area. Killed an Armenian chap down the road and ate him. Ate him. One of the kids got to us, we had some warning. Ambushed the sons of . . . we ambushed them. But there's still a lot of them left. And others, city people, people with rabies . . ."

"It is that bad?" Leonilla said. "That bad so quickly?"

"Maybe we shouldn't have come down," Rick said.

"There are vital records in the spacecraft." Pieter Jakov laid a hand possessively on the *Soyuz*. "They must be preserved. Is there anyplace they can be studied? Any scientists or universities near here?"

The farmers laughed. "Universities? General Baker, look around you. Take a good look," Deke Wilson said.

John Baker stared at the desolation surrounding him. To the east were rain-drenched hills, some green, most barren. All the low areas were filled with water. The highway that ran north and east looked more like a series of concrete islands than a road.

To the west was a vast inland sea, lapped with waves a foot high, dotted with small brown hills that had become islands. Treetops rose from the water in regular arrays where an orchard was not quite submerged. A few boats moved across this sea. The water was muddy, dark and dangerous, and it stank with dead things. Cattle, and . . .

The remains of a rag doll bobbed gently with the waves. It floated about thirty yards offshore. Not far from it, perhaps somehow attached to it, were wisps of blonde hair and checkered cloth, not recognizable as the remains of anything human. Deke Wilson followed Baker's look, then turned away toward the farmhouse standing on the hill above the sea. "Nothing we can do," he said. His voice was bitter. "We could spend all our time burying them. All of it. And we'd still not get it done."

It was then that the full horror of Hammerfall struck Johnny Baker. "It doesn't go clean," he said.

Wilson frowned a question.

"It isn't just *Bang!* and it's over, civilization's fallen and we have to rebuild it. There's the aftermath, and that's worse than the comet—"

"Damn right," Wilson said. "You're goddam lucky, Baker. You missed the worst of it."

"There is no central government?" Pieter Jakov asked.

"You're looking at it," Wilson said. "Bill Appleby there's a deputy sheriff, but it's nothing special. We haven't heard from Sacramento since Hammerfall."

"But surely someone is organizing, is trying," Leonilla said.

"Yeah. There's the Senator's people," Wilson said.

"Senator?" John Baker kept his face from showing emotion. He turned away from the terrible inland sea, toward the hills to the east.

"Senator Arthur Jellison," Deke Wilson said.

"You sound like you don't like him much," Rick Delanty said.

"Not exactly. Can't blame him, but I don't have to like him."

"What's he done?" Baker asked.

"He's organized," Wilson said. "That valley of his"— Wilson pointed north and east, toward the foothills of the High Sierra—"is ringed with hills. They've got patrols, border guards, and they don't let anybody in without their say-so. You want help, they'll send it, but the price is damned high. Feed their troops, and send back more food, oil, ammunition, fertilizer, all the things you can't get now."

"If you have oil, I'd think you'd be in good shape," Rick Delanty said.

Wilson waved expansively. "How do we hold onto this place? No borders. No rock piles to make into fortresses. No time to build. No way to keep refugees from coming in and looting what we haven't got to yet. You want to lock that thing up? I'd rather not have this many people standing around. There's work to do. Always work to do."

"Yes. The records should be safe." Pieter climbed onto the *Soyuz* and closed the hatch.

"No electricity," Johnny Baker said. "What about nuclear plants? The one near Sacramento?"

Wilson shrugged. "Sacto used to be about twenty-five feet above sea level. Things got shifted in the quakes. That plant could be underwater. Maybe not. I just don't know. There's better than two hundred and fifty miles of swamp and lake between here and there, and most of the valley's under deep water. Got that locked up? Let's go."

They walked up the hill toward the farmhouse. When they got closer, Baker saw the sandbags and foxholes dug in around the buildings. Women and children worked to add to the fortifications.

Wilson looked thoughtful. "General, you ought to be doing something better than digging foxholes, but I don't know what it would be."

Johnny Baker didn't say anything. He was overwhelmed by what he'd seen and learned. There was no civilization here at all, only desperate farmers trying to hold a few acres of ground.

"We can work," Rick Delanty said.

"You'll have to," Wilson said. "Look, in a few weeks we'll hear from the Senator. I'll give word that you're here. Maybe he'll want you. Maybe he'll want you bad enough to think he owes us for sending you. I could use him owing us."

Fourth Week: The Prophet

Of all states that is the worst whose rulers no longer enjoy an authority sufficiently extensive for everyone to obey them with good grace, but in which their authority over a part of their subjects is sufficiently large to enable them to constrain others.

Bertrand de Jouvenal, *Sovereignty*

There had been a crazy world. It was vivid in Alim Nassor's memory. Once the honkies had poured bread into the ghettos, bribes to stop riots, and Alim had taken his share. Not just money; there was power, and Alim was known in City Hall, was headed for something bigger.

Then a black Tom was Mayor, and the money stopped, the power vanished. Alim couldn't stand that. Without money and the symbols you could buy with it, you were *nothing*, less than the pimps and the pushers and the other garbage that made their living out of the ghettos. He'd lost his power and had to have it back, but then he was caught ripping off a store, and the only way to get off was to pay a bondsman and a lawyer, both honkies. They got him out on bail, and then to pay them he had to rip off another store. Crazy!

Then hundreds of the richest honkies had run for the hills. Doom was coming from the sky! Alim and his brothers had been set to make themselves rich forever. They'd been *rich*, they'd had *truckloads* of what the fences paid money for, and then . . .

Crazy, crazy. Alim Nassor remembered, but it was like a dope dream, the time before the Hammer. He'd done his best to protect the brothers who would listen to him. Four of the six burglary teams had made it through the rain and

455

the quakes and the refugees, all those people! But they'd made it to the cabin near Grapevine. The engine in one of the trucks had a death rattle. They'd stripped it and siphoned off the gas and ditched it. They'd dumped all that electrical stuff, too: TVs, hi-fi's, radios, the small computer. But they'd kept the telescope and binoculars.

And they'd been all right for awhile. There was a ranch not far from the cabin, and there'd been cattle and some other food, enough to last two dozen brothers a long time. They hadn't even had to fight for it. The rancher was dead under his collapsed roof, leg broken, and he'd starved or bled to death. But then a lot of honkies with guns came and took it away, and eighteen brothers in three trucks had to take off into a howling rain.

Then things really went to hell. Nothing to eat, no place to go. Nobody wanted blacks. What were they supposed to do, starve?

Alim Nassor sat cross-legged in the rain, half dozing, remembering. There had been a crazy world, with laws drawn up by gibbering idiots, and unbelievable luxuries: hot coffee, steak dinners, dry towels. Alim wore a coat that fit him perfectly: a woman's mink coat, as wet as any sponge. None of the brothers had anything to say about that. Once again, Alim Nassor had power.

There were feet in his field of view: stolen boots burst at the seams, the soles worn thin by walking. Alim looked up.

Swan was a lightweight who carried all manner of sharp things on his person. He'd looked lean as a dancer, cool and dangerous, when Alim went to him with the burglary proposition. Now he looked half starved and diffident. He said, "Jackie been messing with Cassie again. Cassie don't like it. I think she told Chick."

"Shit." Alim stood up.

"We should kill that Chick," Swan said.

"Now you listen good." Alim was dismayed at the lack of force in his voice. He was tired, tired. He leaned close to Swan and spoke low, letting the threat show. "We need Chick. I'd kill Jackie before I killed Chick. And I'd kill you."

Swan backed up. "Okay, Alim."

Alim savored that. Swan hadn't gone for a blade. He'd backed off. Alim still had power. "Chick's the biggest, strongest brother we got, but that isn't the reason," Alim said. "Chick's a farmer. A farmer, you got that? You want to do *this* the rest of your life? Man, we were on foot for ten days, did you *like* that? There's gotta be a place for us somewhere, but it don't matter if we can't farm—"

"Let somebody else do the fucking work," Swan said.

"And how do you know if they do it *right?*" Alim demanded. "We . . ." He was on the verge of letting desperation show. "Where's Chick?"

"By the fire. And Jackie isn't."

"Cassie?"

"With Chick."

"Good." Alim walked down toward the fire. It felt good, to know he could turn his back on Swan and nothing was going to happen. Swan *needed* him. They all needed him. None of the rest could have got them this far, and they all knew it.

The first week after Hammerfall it rained all the time. Then it dwindled off to a drizzle, and that went on and on until nobody could stand it and still it went on. Now, four weeks after the Hammer of God, it drizzled more often than not, and it always rained, hard, at least once every day.

Today it had rained three times, and the drizzle kept on. The rain was hard on everybody. It rasped nerves. It rotted feet in their boots. Everything was hopelessly wet, and people could be killed for a dry place. The drizzle stopped, almost, at midnight. Now everyone was huddled around the fire under a sheet-plastic lean-to. Tomorrow Alim might regret letting them use gas for a fire, but shit, they'd probably run out of road before the truck they'd ripped off in Oil City ran out of gas. Most roads ended at a low spot, underwater, and you had to backtrack for miles to find a way around a stretch only a few dozen yards across. Crazy.

Where the roads did get across low spots there was often a roadblock, farmers with guns.

And they *needed* a fire. The gasoline had dried out enough wood to make it burn, but it smoked horribly; twenty brothers and five sisters were all crouched in a crescent, upwind they hoped, under a billowing plastic sheet, while the smoke curled around and sometimes sought them out. Alim heard laughter and was glad.

It was bad to have women in a gang like this. Worse to have no women. Alim wondered if he'd made a mistake, but it was too late now. Shit. Alim Nassor's mistakes could kill them all, and *that*, if you liked, was power.

They'd come down into the valley with eighteen brothers, no women. The people they'd met had been mostly white, mostly starving, mostly unable to fight. Alim's band had looted for food and dry places, and killed where they had to. When they met blacks, they recruited. There were damn few blacks this far north, and most were farmers, and some didn't want to join. That was good for Alim—fewer mouths to feed—and bad for them. Blacks would not be popular where Alim's band had passed. And as always they moved on. They had found no place they could hold and defend. There were never enough brothers, and always behind them were farmers with guns, the remnants of police forces, survivors with nothing left to live for except killing Alim Nassor's people. . . .

And now there were five women and twenty men. Four men had died fighting over women. Three had been the husbands; one of the widows had killed herself that same day. Alim was grateful. It had cooled things for awhile.

But not for long. Mabe's husband had been knifed in his sleep, and now Mabe was sleeping around, but in a strange fashion. Where she went, there were fights. Maybe she was taking revenge. But what could Alim *do* about it? If he killed her it would have to look like an accident. You can't kill the only pussy the brothers were getting. Maybe at the right time? If there was another big fight and everybody knew she caused it?

Chick and Cassie were a different problem. They were farmers. Their farm was part of an ocean now, the ocean that had been the San Joaquin Valley. They talked like redneck honkies; they didn't understand the speech of the city blood. Cassie was willowy, dignified, strong and lovely. Chick was a burly giant who could lift the back end of a car, or pick up a brother like Swan by one ankle and throw him pinwheeling a dozen feet through the air, and he'd done that.

They'd lost two kids under the water.

If the kids had been saved . . . Alim shook his head. Kids were the last thing this gang needed now! But in another sense . . . If Cassie had come on as a mother with two kids, maybe the brothers would think more about protecting her, less about getting into her.

They looked up as Alim strode into their midst, and Alim saw smiles. Yeah, the fire had been a good idea. Chick and Cassie were sitting with their arms around one another, staring broodingly into the fire. Alim squatted down before them and said, "Do we want to talk about somethin'?"

Chick shook his big head. Cassie didn't move.

"You sure?"

Chick said, "Keep your thieves away from my woman."

"I'm tryin'. It's nobody's fault, it's just the way things are. Anyone special?"

"Jackie. You know that son of a bitch pulled a knife on her?"

"He just showed it to me," Cassie said, "but it scared me."

"You're not scared of guns," Alim said. She had a tremendous revolver, and half a dozen kinds of hand loads, from birdshot to a slug that would stop a bear. Alim had never dreamed a revolver could do so many things at once. "Why knives?"

She just shook her head, and Chick glared.

Alim stood up. "I'll try to fix it. Where is he?"

"Hiding out."

Alim nodded and went.

Now, should he just hang around, or try to track Jackie? Hang around. He moved among the brothers and sisters, making himself visible in the firelight. Tomorrow they'd remember.

But time wore on, and the brothers and sisters spilled into the truck in twos and threes. The drizzle was winning out over the fire, and Jackie still hadn't come in. Alim had already decided where he must be.

To one side was the shoreline they'd been following for a week. Alim had wondered if they ought to strike off into the hills . . . but for what? The world the honkies built was dead, and somehow they would have to start over. A patch of farm, and a few like Chick and Cassie to show them how to work it, that was what they needed. The farmland was all there, under the water. If the water ever withdrew. . . . But the drizzle went on and on, the fire was almost out, and the freshwater ocean was still there, too dark to see, but still there, with its floating garbage and drowned corpses of cattle and men.

And behind was a single hill, the only place from which Jackie could watch the fire. Alim went up the hill. He moved like a blind man, feeling for branches and pushing them aside, shuffling so as not to break an ankle. Presently he said, "Jackie?"

The voice was close. "Yeah, Alim."

Alim climbed the rest of the way. Jackie was right at the peak, a man of average size in a coat three sizes too big, with his back turned. Alim said, "Why can't you leave Cassie alone?"

"I tried."

"You tryin' to get me killed?"

"I tried, Alim. I even went to that Mabe. She's got nothin' but a cunt, that woman, but I went to her, thinkin' I could ease my mind. She turned me down. Set Swan on me. Said it was his turn. She sleeps with three a night, any prick that asks, but she pushes me off. Me!"

"She wants your head fucked up." Alim began to see the right way to go. "She likes fights. She don't know who stuck that knife in James, so she's gonna get us all to kill each other. She fucks with Elliot and tells Rob she was raped. She don't spread her legs for you so you'll fight Chick. If I say so, she's got six men want my blood. Jackie, what do I do?" *Get him to think with his brain now, instead of his dick.*

"What we need," Jackie said, "is somethin' to take the brothers' minds off women." He said that as if he thought it was funny and sad at the same time.

"That'd take some doin'."

"Alim, where we going? What happens to us?"

"Hard to say." He could talk with Jackie, but he couldn't tell anybody that he didn't know what they'd do, where they'd go. And Jackie was smart. Jackie had been big in the Panthers once, political like Alim. They'd worked together, Jackie to stir up the ghetto until Alim got what he wanted from City Hall, then quiet things so it looked like Alim's doing. *Get Jackie thinking, but don't tell him, don't tell anybody, that Alim Nassor was scared and wet and miserable and all fucked up and just about out of control. . . .*

"Black power's finished," Jackie was saying. "Not enough blacks, not enough power."

"Yeah, I'd got that figured out," Alim said.

"And there ain't enough of us," Jackie continued. "Not enough to hold on anywhere. Chick says it'll take a couple of acres each to live on. A hundred acres could keep us alive, but it won't. Not enough of us know farming. Need people to do some of the work. Two acres for each one of them, too. Takes a big spread, and we can't hold a big spread—"

"We can't hold a little one," Alim said.

"Right on. So what we have to do is link up, find a honky outfit we can work with. Politics, not blood." Jackie was staring off into the night, his voice quiet, but Alim could feel it, Jackie had been brooding about this a long time. "Damn system's been smashed," Jackie said. "What we always wanted, system's gone, got rid of the pigs and City Hall and the rich bastards . . . and it don't do us any good at all, 'cause there ain't enough of us."

"Shit. I brought out all I could," Alim said. "You sayin' I didn't?"

"Naw, you did all you could," Jackie said. "Not your fault it wasn't enough. Alim, step up here and look down."

Through the drizzle there was a blur of light. It had to be a campfire, somebody's campfire, glowing beside the shoreline to the north.

"I see better than you," Jackie said, "so maybe you don't see that it's two fires. Two. How many people does it take before it's worth making two fires?"

"A lot. Think they saw ours?"

"Naw. Nobody's come up this way. And they don't give a shit whether somebody sees them or not. Think about that."

Power. That group didn't have to hide. It had power. "A posse? After us? Naw, we haven't gone north of here, nobody up that way has any reason to be after us."

"Maybe this'll take Chick's mind off killin' me," Jackie said.

"How you gonna distract *me?* You saw those fires and didn't come tell me."

"I had to keep watch. And nobody's come up here. I watched."

He'd been scared of Chick. "All right. You stay here. You watch. I'll send Gay back with the binoculars."

■

In gray morning light Jackie came down the south side of the hill. Alim already had his people up and their gear stowed, and the brothers stood around waiting with guns uncomfortable in their hands.

Jackie went first to Chick and Cassie. Alim didn't hear what they said, but Chick had a shotgun in his hand, and he didn't use it. Then Jackie turned aside and came to report.

"They're up. And they're organized. Fifty, sixty, maybe more. Maybe a lot more, they don't all get to one place at once. There's women, and a honky that's half rabbit and he's wearing what's left of a business suit and a tie. The rest is Army."

Jackie waited for that to sink in.

"Army? Aw, shit," Alim Nassor said.

"Funny thing about them mothers," Jackie said. "They got Army uniforms and little mean-looking rifles, but they don't act Army. And there's others in civvies."

461

Alim frowned. Jackie went on: "They got more than the rifles, Alim. They got machine guns, and things like stovepipes—"

"Bazookas," Alim said.

"Yeah. And a thing about as big as a cannon except two men carry it. They can blow a house apart with those things, I think. I saw 'em on TV once. And I think they're headin' north."

Alim digested that. It meant this group had to have come from the east, since they'd never seen them before. They certainly hadn't come from the west, out of the lake that covered the San Joaquin.

"Maybe we better follow them," Swan said. He'd been listening. "They sound like tough mothers."

"And everything's picked clean before we get to it," Alim said. He didn't want to say much. He didn't know what to do; it would be better to hear what the others thought before he said anything at all. "I best go up there and have a look."

He left Swan in charge, with instructions on where to run if the Army outfit moved toward them, and let Jackie lead him up the hill. Shit, he thought he'd had troubles before! Just what he always wanted, to go up against Army guns with a dozen Saturday-night specials and some shotguns. "Now we know," he said. Jackie looked at him. "Why everybody been hidin'," Alim said.

No food anywhere. Two days ago they'd taken a raft out to a half-sunken supermarket, and it was already looted. All they could find was weird stuff like canned salmon and anchovies, and not much of that. That Army outfit must have picked it clean.

It was getting lighter when he reached the top of the hill. Jackie motioned and Alim went to his belly and crawled forward through the bushes until he found Gay. Alim's fur coat was covered with mud from crawling, but those Army guys had to have binoculars too, and they had to be keeping watch or they wouldn't have lived this long.

The stranger camp was more than a mile away, right down by the shore. There were foxholes and low fortifications around it. Organized. It looked organized. And there were a lot of people, and they sat around fires they didn't bother to hide, and they had food. Alim counted seven women.

"The women do most of the work," Gay said. "Them and the rabbit stud in the blue suit. And a lot of them are white, but I counted ten blood, and one's the sergeant."

"The sergeant." Alim digested this, too. "And they do what he tells 'em?"

"They jump when he waves his arms," Gay said.

"Officers?"

"None I saw. I think the sergeant's in charge."

"They done it. Alim, they made it," Jackie said. "Shit. They really did."

Alim didn't say anything. Jackie would explain. After a moment he did. "What we were talking about last night," Jackie said. His voice was full of excitement. "Not black power, just power. And there's a *lot* of 'em, Alim."

"Not all that many."

"Maybe they want recruits," Jackie said.

"You crazy?" Gay snorted. "Join the fuckin' Army?"

"Shut up." Alim continued to study the camp through the binoculars. There was orderly activity down there. Garbage carried outside the camp and dumped into holes. Sentries and outposts. Tubs of water over the fire, and everybody washed out their mess kits in hot water. That camp was run like an army, but there was something wrong. It wasn't all the same, something just wasn't the way it ought to be.

"Alim, they got what we want," Jackie said. "Power. Enough guns to do whatever they want. We could join up with them, we could hold anyplace we wanted. Shit, we could do better. That many people, we could take over this whole goddam valley, shit, keep growing, keep recruitin', we could own the whole fucking *state*."

"You been sniffing?" Gay asked.

"Shut up," Alim said again, and he said it so they knew he meant it. The quick silence was gratifying. Power. And that was the problem: How could Alim Nassor have power if they joined up with that army? "They don't have no wheels at all?"

"A bike. Big Honda. It went scouting north with two on it. One blood, one honky."

"In uniform?"

"The honky had on overalls," Gay said. His tone made it clear he didn't know what was going on, and didn't know why Alim wanted to know, either.

"No wheels. We got a truck, and we know where there's some wheels," Alim muttered. A farmhouse back down the road. Three trucks, guarded by ten to fifteen men with rifles. Alim had no chance to take it, but this outfit—he shushed the others as the sergeant came into view. Blood all right, a big mother, not all black. Light brown, with a beard. Beard? In the Army? The sergeant wore chevrons, though, and a big pistol on his belt, and he was pointing to people and when he did they got up and did things, brought wood for the fires, washed cooking pots. He wasn't shouting and he didn't have to wave his arms and scream. Power. That man had power, and he knew how to use it. Alim studied him closely. Then he looked up and grinned.

"That's the Hook."

Gay said, "Huh?" Jackie began to grin.

"It's the Hook." Alim treated himself to a whistling sigh of relief. "I know him. We can deal."

It would take setting up. Alim had to talk to the Hook as an equal, as a commander of men. They had to talk as two men with power. He couldn't let Hooker know just how bad things were. Alim left Jackie on the hill and went back down to camp. Time to do some shouting and screaming. Time to get those bastards to *work*.

By noon his camp was organized. It looked good, and it looked like there were more of them than they were. He took Jackie and his brother Harold and went toward the Army camp.

"Shit, I'm scared," Harold said as they walked toward the shoreline.

"Scared of the Hook?"

"He beat the shit out of me once," Harold said. "Back in ninth grade."

"Yeah, and you had it comin'," Alim said. "Okay, they've seen us. Harold, you go in. Leave the rifle here. Go in, hands up, and tell Sergeant Hooker I want to talk to him. And be *nice* to him, you know? Respectful."

"You can bet your ass on that," Harold said. He straightened and walked tall, hands out where they could see they were empty. He tried to whistle.

Alim was aware that there were movements to his right. Hooker had sent men out to flank him. Alim turned and shouted to purely imaginary followers. "Hold it up there, you bastards! This is a *peace* talk, dig? I'll skin the first dude that shoots, and you know I'll do it." Too much, Alim thought. Like I'm worried they won't do what I say. But the Army dudes heard me, and it stopped them. And Harold's in the camp and nobody's done any shootin' yet. . . .

And he's done it, Alim shouted to himself. He's talking to

Hooker, and by God he's done it. Hook's comin' out to meet me. We're all right, all-fucking-right.

For the first time since Hammerfall, Alim Nassor felt hope and pride.

■

Two heavy farm trucks ground across the mud flats, taking a tortuous path to the new island in the San Joaquin Sea. They stopped at a supermarket, still half flooded, glass windows scraped of mud by laborious effort. Armed men jumped out and took up positions nearby.

"Let's go," Cal White said. He carried Deke Wilson's submachine gun. White led the way into the drowned building, wading waist-deep in filthy water. The others followed.

Rick Delanty coughed and tried to breathe through his mouth. The smell of death was overpowering. He looked for someone to talk to, Pieter or Johnny Baker, but they were at the far end of the column. Although it was their second day at the store, none of the astronauts had got used to the smells.

"If it was up to me, I'd wait another week," Kevin Murray said. Murray was a short, burly man with long arms. He'd been a feedstore clerk, and was lucky enough to have married a farmer's sister.

"Wait a week and those Army bastards may be here," Cal White called from inside. "Hold up a second." White went on with another man and their only working flashlight, hand-pumped, and Deke's submachine gun.

The gun seemed an irrelevent obscenity to Rick. There was too much death all around them. He wasn't going to say that. Last night Deke had taken in a refugee, a man from southwards with information to trade for a meal: a gang of blacks had been terrorizing the south valley, and now they were linked up with the Army cannibals. It might not be long before they came to Deke Wilson's turf again.

Poor bastards, Rick thought. He could sympathize: blacks in this shattered world, no status, no place to go, wanted nowhere. Of course they'd join the cannibals. And of course the local survivors were looking strangely at Rick Delanty again. . . .

"Clear. Let's get at it," White called from inside. They waded in, a dozen men, three astronauts and nine survivors. A driver brought one of the trucks around so that the headlights shone into the wrecked store.

Rick wished they hadn't. Bodies bobbed in the filthy water. He choked hard and brought the cloth to his face; White had sprinkled a dozen drops of gasoline on it. The sweet sickening smell of gasoline was better than . . .

Kevin Murray went to a shelf of cans. He lifted a can of corn. It was eaten through with rust. "Gone," he said. "Damn."

"Sure wish we had a flashlight," another farmer said.

A flashlight would help, Rick knew, but some things are better done in gloomy darkness. He pushed rotten remains away from a shelf. Glass jars. Pickles. He called to the others, and they began carrying the pickles out.

"What's this stuff, Rick?" Kevin Murray asked. He brought another jar.

"Mushrooms."

Murray shrugged. "Better'n nothing. Thanks. Sure wish I had my glasses back. You ever wonder why I don't pack a gun? Can't see as far as the sights."

Rick tried to concentrate on glasses, but he didn't know anything about how you might grind lenses. He moved through the aisles, carrying things the others had discovered, searching for more, pushing aside the corpses until even that became routine, but you had to talk about something else. . . . "Cans don't last long, do they?" Rick said. He stared at rotten canned stew.

"Sardine cans last fine. God knows why. I think somebody's already been here, there ain't so much as the last store. We got most of what was here yesterday, anyway." He looked thoughtfully at old corpses bobbing about him. "Maybe *they* ate it all. Trapped here . . ."

Rick didn't answer. His toes had brushed glass.

They were all working in open-toed sandals taken from the shoe store up the road. They couldn't work barefoot for fear of broken glass, and why ruin good boots? Now his toes had brushed a cool, smooth curve of glass bottle.

Rick held his breath and submerged. Near floor level he found rows of bottles, lots of them, different shapes. Fifty-fifty it was bottled water, barely worth room aboard the truck; but he picked one up and surfaced.

"Apple juice, by God! Hey, gang, we need hands here!"

They waded down the aisles, Pieter and Johnny and the farmers, all dog-tired and dirty and wet, moving like zombies. Some had strength to smile. Rick and Kevin Murray dipped for the bottles and handed them up, because they were the ones who didn't carry guns.

White, the man in charge, turned slowly away with two bottles; turned back. "Good, Rick. You did good," he said, and smiled, and turned slowly away and waded toward the doorway. Rick followed.

Someone yelled.

Rick set his bottles on an empty shelf to give himself speed. That had to be Sohl on sentry duty. But Rick didn't have a gun!

Sohl yelled again. "No danger; I repeat, no danger, but you guys gotta see this!"

Go back for the bottles? Hell with it. Rick pushed past something he wouldn't look at (but the floating mass had the feel, the weight of a small dead man or a large dead woman) and waded out into the light.

The parking lot was almost half full of cars, forty or fifty cars abandoned when the rains came. The hot rain must have fallen so fast that car motors were drowned before the customers in the shopping center could decide to move. So the cars had stayed, and many of the customers. The water washed around and in and out of the cars.

Sohl was still at his post on the roof of the supermarket. It would have done him no good to come closer; he was far-sighted, and his glasses had been smashed, like Murray's. He pointed down at what was washing against the side of a Volkswagen bus and called, "Will someone tell me what that is? It ain't no cow!"

They formed a semicircle around it, their feet braced against the water's gentle westward current, this same flow that held the strange body against the bus.

It was smaller than a man. It was all the colors of decay; the big, drastically bent legs were almost falling off. What was it? It had *arms*. For a mad moment Rick pictured Hammer-fall as the first step in an interstellar invasion, or as part of a program for tourists from other worlds. Those tiny arms, the long mouth gaping in death, the Chianti-bottle torso . . .

"I'll be damned," he said. "It's a kangaroo."

"Well, I never saw a kangaroo like that," White said with fine contempt.

"It's a kangaroo."

"But—"

Rick snapped, "Does your newspaper run pictures of animals two weeks dead? Mine never did. It's a *dead* kangaroo, that's why it looks funny."

Jacob Vinge had crowded close to the beast. "No pouch," he said. "Kangaroos have pouches."

The breeze shifted; the crescent of men opened at one end. "Maybe it's a male," Deke Wilson said. "I don't see balls either. Did kangaroos have . . . ah, overt genitalia? Oh, this is stupid. Where would it come from? There ain't any zoo closer than . . . where?"

Johnny Baker nodded. "Griffith Park Zoo. The quake must have ripped some of the cages apart. No telling how the poor beast got this far north before he drowned or starved. Look close, gentlemen, you'll never see another . . ."

Rick stopped listening. He backed out of the arc and looked around him. He wanted to scream.

They had come at dawn yesterday. They had worked all of yesterday and today, and it must be near sunset. None of them had even discussed what must have happened here, yet it was obvious enough. Scores of customers must have been trapped here when the first flash rain drowned their cars. They had waited in the supermarket for the rain to stop; they had waited for rescue; they had waited while the water rose and rose. At the end the electric doors hadn't worked. Some must have left through the back, to drown in the open.

In the supermarket there were half-empty shelves, and the water floated with corncobs and empty bottles and orange rinds and half-used loaves of bagged bread. They had not died hungry . . . but they had died, for their corpses floated everywhere in the supermarket and in the flooded parking lot. Scores of bodies. Most were women, but there were men and children, too, bobbing gently among the submerged cars.

"Are you . . ." Rick whispered. He bowed his head and cleared his throat and shrieked, "Are you all crazy?" They turned, shocked and angry. "If you want to see corpses, look around you! Here," his hand brushed a stained and rotting flowered dress, "and there," pointing to a child close enough for Deke to touch, "and there," to a slack face behind the windshield of the Volks bus itself. "Can you look anywhere without seeing somebody *dead*? Why are you crowding like jackals around a dead kangaroo?"

"You shut up! Shut up!" Kevin Murray's fists were balled at his sides, the knuckles white; but he didn't move, and presently he looked away, and so did the others.

All but Jacob Vinge. His voice held a tremor. "We got used to it. We just got used to it. We had to, goddamm it!"

The current shifted slightly. The kangaroo, if that was what it was, washed around the edge of the bus and began to move away.

The Jeep Wagoneer had once been bright orange with white trim, a luxury station wagon that only incidentally had four-wheel drive and off-road tires. Now it was splashed with brown and green paint in a camouflage pattern. Two men in Army uniform sat in the front seat, rifles held erect between their knees.

Alim Nassor and Sergeant Hooker sat in back. There was little conversation as the car wound through muddy fields and ruined almond groves. When it reached the encampment, sentries saluted, and as the Wagoneer came to a stop the driver and guards jumped out to open the rear doors. Alim nodded thanks to the driver. Hooker did not seem to notice the men. Nassor and Hooker went to a tent at one side of the camp. It was a new tent from a sporting-goods store, green nylon stretched over aluminum poles, and it did not leak. A charcoal hibachi inside kept it warm and dry. A kettle bubbled over the charcoal, and a white girl waited inside to pour hot tea as the two men sat on folding chairs. Hooker nodded dismissal when the tea was poured. The girl left, and the guards took up posts outside well out of earshot.

When the girl was gone, Sergeant Hooker grinned broadly. "Pretty good life, Peanut."

Nassor's grin faded at the name. "For God's sake don't call me that, man!"

Hooker grinned again. "Okay. Nobody to hear us in here."

"Yeah, but you might forget." Alim shuddered. He hadn't been called "Peanut" since eighth grade, when they studied the life of George Washington Carver, and inevitably the name was settled on George Washington Carver Davis until he obliterated it with fists and a razor blade embedded in a cake of soap. . . .

"Not much out there," Hooker said. He sipped tea, grateful for the warmth.

"No." Their scouting expedition had told them nothing they hadn't expected, except that once there was a break in the rain and they saw snow on the tops of the High Sierra. Snow in August! It had frightened Nassor, although Hooker said it had sometimes snowed in the Sierra before That Day.

They sat uncomfortably despite the hot tea and the warmth of the tent, despite the luxury of being dry, because they had too much to talk about, and neither wanted to begin. They both knew they would have to make choices soon enough. Their camp was too close to the ruins that had been Bakersfield. In the ashes and wreckage of the city there were a lot of people who might get it together, more than enough to come out and finish Nassor and Hooker. They hadn't got their shit together yet. The survivors lived in small groups, distrustful of each other, fighting over the scraps of food left in supermarkets and warehouses—the scraps that Hooker and Nassor had left.

It came down to this: In combination, Alim and Hooker had enough men and ammunition to fight one good battle. If they won it, they'd have enough for another. If they lost, they were finished. And they'd stripped the country around them. They had to move. But where?

"Goddam rain," Hooker muttered.

Alim sipped tea and nodded. If only the rain would stop. If Bakersfield dried out there'd be no problem. Wait for a good day with strong winds—there were always strong winds—and burn out the whole goddam city. A hundred fires started a block apart would do it. Fire storm. It would sweep across and leave nothing behind. Bakersfield would no longer be a threat.

And the rains were wearing down. There had been an hour of sunshine the day before. Today the sun was almost breaking through and it wasn't noon yet, and there was only misty rain.

"We got six days," Hooker said. "Then we start gettin' hungry. We get hungry enough, we'll find somethin' to eat, but . . ."

He didn't finish the sentence. He didn't have to. Alim shuddered. Sergeant Hooker saw Alim's expression, and his mouth twisted into a curl of evil contempt. "You'll join in," Hooker said.

"I know." He shuddered again at the memory. Of the farmer Hooker had shot, and the smells of the stew, and the sharing out of portions of the man, everyone in the camp taking a bowl and Hooker damned well seeing that they ate it. The ghastly ritual was what held the group together. Alim had to shoot one of the brothers who wouldn't eat. And Mabe. At least it did that. Their ritual feast let him shoot Mabe and get rid of that troublemakin' cunt. She wouldn't eat.

"Funny you never did before," Hooker said.

Nassor said nothing, his expression not changing. The truth was they'd never even thought of eating people. Not one of them. It was a source of secret pride for Alim. *His* people

470

weren't cannibals. Only, of course, they were, because that was the only way Hooker would let them join up . . .

"Lucky you had that beef jerky." Hooker couldn't let it alone, not now, not ever. "You never got hungry enough. Lucky."

"Lucky? *Lucky?*" Alim's explosion startled Hooker. "Lucky my ass!" Alim shouted. "There was a ton of the stuff in that van, and we got maybe two pounds because of that mother-fucker!" He looked out through the open doorway of the tent, toward a slim black who stood guard near the fire. "That one. That motherfuckin' Hannibal."

Hooker frowned. "That why you make him do all the work? He lose you some food?"

Alim was wild with remembered rage and pain. "Food. And liquor. Listen, we could *smell* it, it just about drove us crazy. You see the burns on Gay? We thought he was gonna die, and all of us got burned trying to—"

"What the fuck are you talkin' about?"

"Yeah, you don't know." Alim reached behind him to a footlocker and took out a bottle. Cheap whiskey from a drugstore. Thank God California had *everything* in drugstores. "We got together," Alim said. "Me and my people and some others. Back then, back when we didn't think . . ." He couldn't finish that sentence. "Before. All the honkies—"

Sergeant Hooker calmly leaned across the table and slapped Alim's face. Hard. Alim's hand went to his holster, but stopped. "Thanks," he said.

Hooker nodded. "Tell the story."

"The white people, the rich ones in Bel Air, about half of 'em took off. Left their places. Left 'em empty. We took in trucks, and we went through those houses. . . ." He paused, a delighted smile playing on his lips as he thought of it. "And we were rich. That watch I gave you. And this ring." He held the cat's-eye to catch the light. "TVs, hi-fi, Persian rugs, *real* Persian, the kind the fences pay twenty big ones for. All kinds of fuckin' shit, Hook. We were rich."

Hooker nodded. Okay, he'd done worse. It still made him uncomfortable. Hooker had been a soldier. He could have been sent to Bel Air to shoot motherfucking looters. Crazy world.

"And we found a stash," Alim said. "Coke, hash oil, weed, nothing but the *best*. I took it away before my dudes could start lighting up right there."

Hooker drank whiskey. "Get it all?"

"Don't be so fuckin' smart. No, I did not get it all. I wasn't

471

even tryin', Hook, I just wanted to make the point, if they used on the spot I'd take it off them. Hell, that was *then,* you know, there were cops on patrol all over—"

"Yeah."

"So it happened. The goddam Hammer. We got out, fire trails, roads, anything, we got out, headin' for Grapevine, and the truck starts wheezin'. We were out on one of the trails, tryin' to stay off the freeways, you know? So we come up on top of a rise and see this van coming behind us. Bright blue van, with four bikes, everybody with shotguns and rifles, like a stagecoach in the movies with the army ridin' escort—"

"Sure," Hooker said. He poured more whiskey. In a few minutes they'd have to talk for real, but it was nice to be dry, have a drink, not think about where they'd have to go now.

"We set it up real good," Alim said. "Got ahead of the van far enough, used a chain saw to drop a tree just as the van comes through a narrow place, and man, you should have seen it! Those bikes stopped and my studs wasn't more than five feet from 'em. Come out from the trees shootin'. Used a lot of bullets, but shit, with those pistols we had . . . Anyway, it was perfect. Knocked the bikes over, never touched one of the bikes at all. There's the van stopped, and the driver's got his hands on the wheel where we can see, nice and easy, and the van's not even *touched,* Hook, not even a scratch on that pretty blue paint.

"And did I get all that coke we found in Bel Air? No I did not. That motherfuckin' Hannibal was sniffing all along, and it was *good* stuff, you know, real, not the shit he used to get, but he sniffs two, three lines at a time. And those dudes are just openin' up that van, comin' out nice and easy, and Hannibal decides he's the last of the Mau Mau. He comes whooping up to the van with a Molotov cocktail! Shit, he threw that gasoline bomb right in the van, right inside."

"Aw, shit." Hooker shook his head, thinking about it. "Good stuff in the van?"

"Good? *Good?* Hook, you won't *believe* what was in that fuckin' van! That motherfucker went up like . . . like . . ."

"Gasoline."

"Yeah, a lot like that." Alim tried to laugh, but he couldn't. "The guys inside the van caught on fire and come out screamin', and a couple of the bastards have guns. I got to give 'em credit, clothes all burnin' up they're still shootin' at us, and we shoot back, and by the time *that* was over the whole van's on fire, can't get near it.

"Bottles start exploding in the truck. Oh, man, Hook, the

smells were enough to drive you out of your gourd! Here we're starvin', nothin' to eat, and out comes cookin' meat smells. And more. Scotch, brandy, fruity smells like those lick-kewers that nobody ever has the bread for, chocolate, raisins, apples—shit, Hook, that van was just stuffed with food and liquor! Food. Meat, not somebody in the truck, beef—"

Alim stopped suddenly. He looked sideways at Hooker. Hooker didn't have to say anything.

"Yeah. Anyway, something blew then, and out comes this package of beef jerky, still wrapped up in tinfoil and plastic bags, not burned, no gasoline on it, couple of pounds of beef jerky. Gay runs into the truck and comes out with two bottles, only we had to let him drink one of 'em to kill the pain, and when he *really* started feelin' it we'd drunk the other. Shit.

"But a couple of the studs on the bikes were still alive, and they told us what they had in that truck. Everything. Guns. food, every kind of liquor ever made, European stuff, can you *imagine* what it must be worth now? Europe can be on the fuckin' Moon for all we'll ever see from there again. There was a ton of beef jerky, and fatty stuff that tasted even worse only who cares when you're starving? And soup, and potatoes, and freeze-dried mountain food—shit, those dudes had waited until the Hammer came and looted all the places where they'd seen people gettin' ready."

"Smarter than you were," Hooker said.

Alim shrugged. "Maybe. I didn't think that fuckin' comet would hit. Did you?"

"No." If I had, Hooker thought. If I had, I'd never have been out in that truck, we'd have had a lot more ammo . . . shit, why did I go off and leave the captain alone back there? Shit.

". . . and bottles of gasoline," Alim was saying. "Big help, right? We could smell it, all of it, food burning, gasoline exploding, clothes burning, those motherfuckers must have really thought the glaciers were coming, and if they were right," Nassor screamed, "then that motherfuckin' Hannibal is going across them bare-ass, because I'll be wearing his clothes over mine!"

"What happened to the bikes?" Hooker asked. He didn't bother asking about their riders.

"Got burned up. Fuckin' truck kept blowing, more gasoline in there. Spread all over. Shit, Hooker, that fire was so fuckin' hot that it got the trees burning! In the middle of that rain, water comin' down like a bathtub of warm shit, and even the trees get to burning! We saved their shotguns, though."

"That's good. Too bad about the other stuff."

"Yeah."

They were safe, for a while, and just about everybody, even the slaves, was dry and warm and had almost enough to eat. They didn't want to think about leaving, or where they'd go, and they'd put off talking about it before, and they put it off now, but they wouldn't be able to put it off much longer.

"Alim! Sergeant!"

It was Jackie. There were others yelling too. Alim and Hooker ran out of the tent. "What is it?"

"Corporal of the guard, post number four!" someone yelled.

"Let's go!" Hooker waved troops to their perimeter positions, then went off toward the yelling sentry.

"Be not afraid, my brothers!" someone called from out in the misty rain. "I bring you peace and blessing."

"Shit fire," Sergeant Hooker said. He peered out into the mist.

An apparition materialized. A man with long white hair and long white beard, and a raincoat that looked something like a gown or a ghost's winding sheet. There were other figures in the gloom behind the man.

"Hold it right there or we shoot!" Hooker yelled.

"Peace be with you, brothers," the man called. He turned back toward those who were following him. "Be not afraid. Stay here, and I will talk with these angels of the Lord."

"A crazy," Hooker said. "Lot of crazies." He'd seen plenty of them before. He cocked the submachine gun. No point in letting the old goon get too close.

But the man walked in steadily, not afraid at all, facing Hooker's gun and not afraid of it, and certainly there wasn't any threat in his eyes. "You need not fear me," the man said.

"What do you want?" Hooker demanded.

"To talk with you. To bring you the message of the Lord God of Hosts."

"Aw, fuck that shit," Hooker said. His finger tightened on the trigger, but now the old man was too close. Two of Hooker's own people were near enough to the line of fire that Hooker didn't want to risk it. And the man looked harmless enough. Maybe there'd be some fun in this. And what could it hurt to let him come in? "The rest of you stay out there," Hooker yelled. "Gillings, get a squad and check them out."

"Right," Gillings called.

The white-haired man strode to the campfire as if he owned it. He looked into the stewpot and at the others around the fire. "Rejoice," he said. "Your sins are forgiven."

"Now just what do you want?" Hooker demanded. "And don't give me crap about angels and the Lord. *Angels*." Hooker snorted.

"But you can be angels," the man said. "You were saved from the holocaust. The Hammer of God has fallen upon this wicked world, and you have been spared. Don't you want to know why?"

"Who are you?" Alim Nassor demanded.

"I am the Reverend Henry Armitage," the man said. "A prophet. I know, I know. At the moment I do not look much like a prophet of God. But I am, just the same."

Alim thought Armitage looked very much like a prophet, with his beard and white hair, and that long flowing raincoat, and glittering eyes.

"I know who you are, my brothers," Armitage said. "I know what you have done, and I know it is not easy in your hearts. You have done all manner of sins. You have eaten forbidden foods. But the Lord of Hosts will forgive you, for He has spared you to work His will. You are to be His angels, and to you nothing shall be forbidden!"

"You're crazy," Hooker said.

"Am I?" Armitage chuckled. "Am I? Then you can listen for amusement. Surely a madman cannot harm you, and perhaps I will say something funny."

Alim felt Jackie come up alongside him. "He's good, that one," Jackie said. "Notice how he's got the sisters listening? And us, too."

Alim shrugged. There was a compelling quality about the man's voice, and the way he kept shifting, from that preachy jive to just talk, that was good. Just when you thought he was nuts, he'd talk like anybody else.

"What is this mission God has for us?" Jackie called.

"The Hammer of God has fallen to destroy an evil world," Armitage said. "An evil world. God gave us this Earth, and the fruits thereof, and we filled it with corruption. We divided mankind into nations, and within nations we divided men into rich and poor, black and white, and created ghettos for our brothers. 'And if any man has this world's goods and sees his brother in want, and shares not with his brother, that man hath no life.' The Lord gave this world's goods and those who had them knew Him not. They piled bricks upon bricks, they built their fancy houses and palaces, they covered the

Earth with the belch and stink of their factories, until the Earth itself was a stench in the nostrils of God!"

"Amen," someone shouted.

"And so His Hammer came to punish the wicked," Armitage said. "It fell, and the wicked died."

"We're not dead," Alim Nassor said.

"And yet you were wicked," Armitage answered. "But we were all wicked, all of us! The Lord God Jehovah held us in the hollow of His hand. He judged us and found us wanting. And yet we live. Why? Why has He spared us?"

Alim was silent now. He wanted to laugh, but he couldn't. This crazy old bastard! Nuts, truly cracked, but yet—

"He has spared us to do His work," Armitage said. "To complete His work. I did not understand! In my pride I believed that I knew. In my pride I believed that I saw the Day of Judgment coming in the morning of the Hammer. And so it was, but not as I believed. The scripture says no man knoweth the day and the hour of Judgment! And yet we have been judged, I thought upon this, after the Hammer fell. I had thought to see the angels of the Lord come to this Earth, to see the King himself come in glory. Vain! Vain pride! But now I know the truth. He has spared me, He has spared you, to work His will, to *complete* His work, and only when that work is done shall He come in glory.

"Join me! Become angels of the Lord and do His work! For the pride of man knoweth no end. Even now, my brothers, even now there are those who would bring back the evils the Lord God has destroyed. There are those who will build those stinking factories again, yea, who will restore Babylon. But it shall not be, for the Lord has His angels, and you shall be among them! Join me."

Alim poured whiskey into Hooker's cup. "You believe any of that jive?" he asked. Outside the tent Henry Armitage was still preaching.

"He sure do have a voice," Hooker said. "Two hours, and he ain't slowin' yet."

"You believe?" Alim asked again.

Hooker shrugged. "Look, if I was a religious man—which I ain't—I'd say he talkin' sense. He do know his Bible."

"Yeah." Alim sipped whiskey. Angels of the Lord! He was no goddam angel, and he knew it. But the old son of a bitch kept twitching memories. Of storefront churches and prayer meetings, phrases that Alim heard when he was a kid. And it bothered him. Why the hell *were* they still alive? He leaned out the tent flap. "Jackie," he called.

"Right." Jackie came in and took a seat.

Jackie was all right. Jackie hadn't had any problems with Chick for a long time. He'd found a white girl, and she seemed to like Jackie a lot, and Jackie was pretty sharp now.

"What about that preacher man?" Alim asked.

Jackie waved both hands. "He makin' more sense than you think."

"How's that?" Hooker asked.

"Well, some ways he's right," Jackie said. "Cities. Rich people. Way they treated us. He's not sayin' anything the Panthers didn't say. And dammit, that Hammer did end all that shit. We got the revolution, handed right to us, and what are we doin'? We sittin' around doin' nothin', goin' nowhere."

"Shee-it, Jackie," Alim said. "You lettin' that hon—" He bit the word off before Sergeant Hooker could react. "—that white preacher get to you?"

"He is white," Jackie said. "And I wouldn't be the onliest one. You remember Jerry Owen?"

Alim frowned. "Yeah."

"He out there. With the others that come with the preacher man."

Sergeant Hooker grunted. "You mean that SLA cat?"

"Wasn't SLA," Jackie said. "Another outfit."

"New Brotherhood Liberation Army," Alim Nassor said.

"Yeah, all right," Hooker said. "Called hisself a general." Hooker snorted contempt. He didn't like people who gave themselves military titles they hadn't earned. He was, by God, Sergeant Hooker, and he'd been a real sergeant in a real army.

"Where the hell he been?" Alim demanded. "FBI, every pig outfit in the country wanted him."

Jackie shrugged. "Hidin' out, not far from here, valley up near Porterville. Hid out with a hippie commune."

"And now he's with the preacher man?" Hooker demanded. "He believe that stuff?"

Jackie shrugged again. "He say he do. Course, he always was into environmentalism. Maybe he just thinks he's found a good thing, 'cause the Reverend Henry Armitage has got hisself a big followin' that *do* believe. A big followin'. And— he's a white man, and he preaches that blood don't matter, and those believers of his, they believe that too. You think about that, Sergeant Hooker. You think about that real good. I don't know if Henry Armitage is the prophet of God or crazy as a hoot owl, but I tell you this, there ain't going to be many big outfits left that'll let *us* be leaders."

"And Armitage—"

"Says you are the chief angel of the Lord," Jackie said. "He say your sins are forgiven, you and all of us, we're forgiven and we got to do God's work, with you as Chief Angel."

Sergeant Hooker stared at them, wondering if they were falling under the spell of that ranting preacher, wondering if the preacher meant what he was saying. Hooker had never been a superstitious man, but he knew Captain Hora used to take the chaplains seriously. So did some of the other officers, ones that Hooker had admired. And . . . dammit, Hooker thought, dammit, I *don't* know where we're going, and I *don't* know what we ought to do, and I *do* wonder if there's any reason for anything, if there's a reason we stayed alive.

He thought of the people they'd killed and eaten, and thought there had to be a purpose to it all. There had to be a *reason*. Armitage said there was a reason, that it was all right, all the things they'd done to stay alive. . . .

That was attractive. To think there'd been a purpose to it all.

"And he say I'm his chief angel?" Hooker demanded.

"Yeah, Sarge," Jackie said. "Didn't you listen to him?"

"Not really." Hooker stood. "But I'm sure as hell going to listen to him now."

Sixth Week: The High Justice

No proposition is likelier to scandalise our contemporaries than this one: it is impossible to establish a just social order.

Bertrand de Jouvenal, *Sovereignty*

Alvin Hardy made a final check. Everything was ready. The library, the great book-lined room where the Senator held court, had been arranged and everything was in its place. Al went to tell the Senator.

Jellison was in the front room. He didn't look well. There was nothing Al could put his finger on, but the boss looked tired, overworked. Of course he was. Everyone worked too hard. But the Senator had kept long hours in Washington, and he'd never looked this bad.

"All set," Hardy said.

"Right. Start," Jellison ordered.

Al went outside. It wasn't raining. There was bright sunshine. Sometimes there were two hours of sunshine a day. The air was clear, and Hardy could see the snow on the peaks of the High Sierra. Snow in August. It seemed to be down to the six-thousand-foot level yesterday; today it was lower, after last night's storm. The snow was inexorably creeping toward the Stronghold.

But we're getting ready for it, Hardy thought. From the porch of the big house he could see a dozen greenhouses, wood frames covered with plastic drop cloths found in a hardware store, each greenhouse covered with a web of nylon cord to keep the thin plastic from billowing in the wind. They wouldn't last more than one season, Al thought, but it's one season we're worried about.

The area around the house was a beehive of activity. Men pushed wheelbarrows of manure which was shoveled into pits in the greenhouses. As it rotted it would give off heat, keeping the greenhouses warm in winter—they hoped. People would sleep in them, too, adding their own body heat to the rotting manure and grass clippings, anything to keep the growing plants warm enough, which seemed silly today, in bright August sunshine—except that already there was a tinge of cold to the air, as breezes came down from the mountains.

And a lot of it was going to be wasted effort. They weren't used to hurricanes and tornadoes here in the valley, and no matter how hard they tried to place the greenhouses where they'd be sheltered from high winds, yet get enough sunshine, some of them would be blown down. "We're doing all we can," Hardy muttered. There was always more to do, and there were always things they hadn't thought of until too late, but it might be enough. It would be close, but they were going to live.

"That's the good news," Hardy said to himself. "Now for the bad."

A ragged group stood near the porch. Farmers with petitions. Refugees who'd managed to get inside the Stronghold and wanted to plead for permanent status and had managed to talk Al—or Maureen, or Charlotte—into getting them an appointment with the Senator. Another group stood well apart from the petitioners. Armed farmhands, guarding prisoners. Only two prisoners today.

Al Hardy waved them all inside. They took their places in chairs set well away from the Senator's desk. They left their weapons outside the room, all but Al Hardy and the ranchers Al knew were trustworthy. Al would have liked to search everyone who came to see the Senator, and one day he'd do that. It would cause too much trouble just now. Which meant that two men with rifles, men Al completely trusted, stood in the next room and stared through small holes hidden among the bookshelves, rifles ready. Waste of good manpower, Al thought. And for what? Who cared what the others thought? Anybody in his right mind would know it was important to protect the Senator.

When they were all seated, Al went back to the living room. "Okay," he said. Then he went quickly to the kitchen.

It was George Christopher himself today. One of the Christopher clan always attended. The others would go in and take

480

the seat reserved for the Christopher representative, and stand when the Senator came into the room, but not George. George went in with the Senator. Not quite as an equal, but not as someone who'd stand up when the Senator came in. . . .

Al Hardy didn't speak to George. He didn't have to. The ritual was well established now. George followed Al out into the hall, his bull neck flaming red . . . well, not really, Al admitted, but it *ought* to have been. George fell in with the Senator and they walked in together, just after Al. Everyone stood; Al didn't have to say anything, which pleased him. He liked things to run the way they ought to, precisely, smoothly, without it seeming that Al Hardy had to do anything at all.

Al went to his own desk. The papers were spread there. Across from Al's desk was an empty seat. It was reserved for the Mayor, but he never came anymore. Got tired of the farce, Al thought. Hardy couldn't blame the man. At first these trials were held in City Hall, which lent credibility to the pretense that the Mayor and the Chief of Police were important, but now that the Senator had given up wasting time going into town . . .

"You may begin," Jellison said.

The first part was easy. Rewards first. Two of Stretch Tallifsen's kids had devised a new kind of rat trap and caught three dozen of the little marauders, as well as a dozen ground squirrels. There were weekly prizes for the best rat catchers: some of the last candy bars in the world.

Hardy looked at his papers. Then he grimaced. The next case was going to be tougher. "Peter Bonar. Hoarding," Al said.

Bonar stood. He was about thirty, maybe a little older. Thin blond beard. Bonar's eyes were dulled. Hunger, probably.

"Hoarding, eh?" Senator Jellison said. "Hoarding what?"

"All kinds of stuff, Senator. Four hundred pounds of chicken feed. Twenty bushels of seed corn. Batteries. Two cases of rifle cartridges. Probably other stuff that I don't know about."

Jellison looked grim. "You do it?" he demanded.

Bonar didn't answer.

"Did he?" Jellison asked Hardy.

"Yes, sir."

"Any point in a trial?" Jellison asked. He looked directly at Bonar. "Well?"

"Hell, he's got no call to come out and search my place! He had no warrant!"

Jellison laughed.

"What beats me is how the hell they found out."

Al Hardy knew that. He had agents everywhere. Hardy spent a lot of time talking to people, and it wasn't hard. You catch someone and don't turn him in, send him out looking, and pretty soon you get more information.

"That all you're worried about?" Jellison demanded. "How we found out?"

"It's my feed," Bonar said. "All that stuff is mine. We found it, my wife and I. Found it and carried it in, in my truck, and what the hell right do you have to it? My stuff on my land."

"Got any chickens?" Jellison asked.

"Yeah."

"How many?" When Bonar didn't answer, Jellison looked to the others in the room. "Well?"

"Maybe a few, Senator," one of those waiting said. She was a forty-year-old woman who looked sixty. "Four or five hens and a rooster."

"You don't need any four hundred pounds of feed," Jellison said reasonably.

"It's my feed," Bonar insisted.

"And seed corn. Here we'll have people starve so we can keep enough seed corn to get in a crop next year, and you've got twenty bushels hidden away. That's murder, Bonar. Murder."

"Hey—"

"You know the rules. You make a find, you report it. Hell, we won't take it all. We don't discourage enterprise. But you sure as hell report it so we can plan."

"And you grab half. Or more."

"Sure. Hell, there's no point in talk," Jellison said. "Anybody want to speak for him?" There was silence. "Al?"

Hardy shrugged. "He's got a wife and two kids, ages eleven and thirteen."

"That complicates things," Jellison said. "Anybody want to speak up for *them?* . . . No?" There was an edge to his voice now.

"Hey, you can't . . . what the hell, Betty don't figure in this!"

"She knew it was there," Jellison said.

"Well, the kids—"

"Yeah. The kids."

482

"Second offense, Senator," Hardy said. "Gasoline last time."

"My gasoline on my land—"

"You talk a lot," Jellison said. "Too damned much. Hoarding. Last time we let you off easy. Goddammit, there's only one way to convince people I mean what I say! George, you got anything to say?"

"No," Christopher said.

"The road," Jellison said. "By noon today. I'll leave it to Hardy to decide what you can take with you. Peter Bonar, you're for the road."

"Jesus, you got no right to throw me off my own land!" Bonar shouted. "You leave me alone, we'll leave you alone! We don't need anything from you—"

"The hell you say," George Christopher shouted. "You already took our help! Food, greenhouses, we even gave you gasoline while you were holding out on us. The gasoline we gave you ran the truck that got that stuff for you!"

"I think Brother Varley will look after the kids," one of the women said. "Mrs. Bonar too, if she can stay."

"She'll come with me!" Bonar shouted. "And the kids too! You got no right to take my kids away from me!"

Jellison sighed. Bonar was trying for sympathy, gambling that they wouldn't send his wife and kids out on the road, and since they couldn't take the kids away from Bonar . . . Could he? Jellison wondered. And leave a festering sore inside the Stronghold? The kids would hate everyone here. And besides, family responsibility was important. "As you will," Jellison said. "Let them go with him, Al."

"Jesus, have mercy," Bonar yelled. "Please! For God's sake—"

Jellison sounded very tired when he said, "See to it, Al. Please. And we'll discuss who can be settled on that farm."

"Yes, sir." The boss hates this, Hardy thought. But what can he do? We can't jail people. We can't even feed what we have.

"You rotten bastard!" Peter Bonar shouted. "You fat son of a bitch, I'll see you in hell!"

"Take him out," Al Hardy ordered. Two of the armed ranch-hands pushed Bonar out. The farmer was still cursing when he left. Hardy thought he heard blows when they got to the hall. He wasn't sure, but the curses stopped abruptly. "I'll see to the sentence, sir," Hardy said.

"Thank you. Next?"

"Mrs. Darden. Her son arrived. From Los Angeles. Wants to stay."

Senator Jellison saw the tight line that formed where George Christopher's mouth had been. The Senator sat straight in his high-backed chair and he looked alert. Inside he felt tired, and defeated, but he couldn't give up. Not until next fall, he thought. Next fall I can rest. There'll be a good harvest next fall. There has to be. One more year, it's all I ask. Please, Lord.

At least this next one is simple. Old lady, no one to look after her, relative arrives. Her son is one of us, and George can't say different. That's in the rules.

I wonder if we can feed him through the winter?

The Senator looked at the old lady, and he knew that whatever happened to her son, she would not survive until spring, and Arthur Jellison hated her for what she would eat before she died.

Ninth Week: The Organization Man

One must point out, however, that many who now deplore the oppression, injustice, and intrinsic ugliness of life in a technically advanced and congested society will decide that things were better when they were worse; and they will discover that to do without the functions proper to the great systems—without telephone, electric light, car, letters, telegrams—is all very well for a week or so, but that it is not amusing as a way of life.

Roberto Vacca, *The Coming Dark Age*

Harvey Randall had never worked so hard in his life. The field was filled with rocks, and they had to be moved. Some could be picked up and carried by one, or two, or a dozen men. Others had to be split apart with sledges. Then the pieces were carried away to be built into low stone walls.

The crisscross pattern of low walls in New England and Southern Europe had always seemed charming and handsome. Until now Harvey Randall hadn't realized just how much human misery each of those walls represented. They weren't built to be pretty, or to mark boundaries, or even to keep cattle and swine out of the fields. They were there because it was too much work to haul those stones completely out of the fields, and the fields had to be cleared.

Most of the pastureland would be plowed for crops. Any crops, anything they had to plant. Barley, onions, wild grains that grew in ditches along the sides of the roads, anything at all. Seeds were scarce—and worse, there was the decision to be made: plant for later, or eat it now?

"Like a goddam prison," Mark grumbled.

Harvey swung the sledge. It rang against the steel wedge, and the rock split nicely. That felt good, and Harvey almost forgot the rumbling in his stomach. Heavy work, and not enough to eat; how long could they keep it up? The Senator's people had worked out diet schedules, so many calories for so many hours of heavy work, and all the books said they had figured correctly, but Harvey's stomach didn't think so.

"Making little ones out of big ones," Mark said. "A hell of a job for an associate producer." He grabbed an end of the piece they'd split off the rock as Harvey lifted the other end. They worked well together, no need for talk. They carried the rock to the wall. Harvey ran a practiced eye along the wall and pointed. The rock fit perfectly into the place he'd selected. Then they went for another.

They stood idle for a few seconds, and Harvey looked across the field where a dozen others were splitting and carrying rocks to the low wall. It could have been a scene from hundreds of years before. "John Adams," Harvey said.

"Eh?" Mark made encouraging noises. Stories made the work go easier.

"Our second President of the United States." Harvey forced the wedge into a tiny crack in the rock. "He went to Harvard. His father sold a field they called 'The Stony Acres' to get up the tuition. Adams would rather be a lawyer than clear the stones out."

"Smart man," Mark said. He held the wedge in place as Harvey lifted the sledge. "Not much left of Harvard now."

"No." Harvard was gone, and Braintree, Massachusetts, was gone, and the United States of America was gone, along with most of England. Would kids learn history now? But they have to, Harvey thought. One day we'll dig out of this, and there'll be a time when it's important whether we have a king or a president, and we'll have to do it right this time so we can get off this goddam planet before another Hammer falls. Someday we'll be able to afford history. Until then we'll think of England the way they used to think of Atlantis. . . .

"Hey," Mark said. "Look at that."

Harvey turned in time to see Alice Cox jump the big stallion over one of the low walls. She moved with the horse as a part of him, and again the impression of a centaur was very strong. It reminded Harvey of the first time he'd come to this ranch, a lifetime ago, a time when he could stand at the top of the big snailhead rock and at night talk about interstellar empires.

That had been a long time ago, in another world. But this one wasn't so bad. They were clearing the fields, and they controlled their boundaries. No one was raped or murdered here, and if there wasn't as much to eat as Harvey would have liked, there was enough. Breaking rocks and building walls was hard work, but it was honest work. There weren't endless conferences on unimportant matters. There weren't deliberate frustrations, traffic jams, newspapers full of crime stories. This new and simpler world had its compensations.

Alice Cox trotted up to them. "Senator wants to see you up at the big house, Mr. Randall."

"Good." Harvey gratefully carried the sledge over to the wall and left it for someone else to use. He squinted up at the sun to estimate how much daylight was left, then called to Mark. "You may as well go on back," he said. "You can put in the rest of the day on the cabin."

"Right." Mark waved cheerfully and started up the hill toward the small house where Harvey, the Hamners, Mark and Joanna, and all four Wagoners lived. It was crowded, and they were building on extra rooms, but it was shelter, and there was enough to eat. It was survival.

Harvey went the other way, downhill toward the Senator's stone ranch house. It had additions built onto it, too. In one of them Jellison kept the Stronghold's armory: spare rifles, cartridges, two field-artillery pieces (but no ammunition) that had been part of a National Guard training center before it was flooded out, hand-loading equipment to reload shotgun shells and rifle cartridges, loot recovered from a gunsmith's shop in Porterville. The dies had been underwater and were rusty, but they still worked. Powder and primers had been sealed in tins that hadn't yet rusted through when they were recovered, although that had been a near thing too.

In another annex the Senator's son-in-law sat with a telegraph and radio. The telegraph at present ran only to the roadblock on the county road, and there was nothing coming in on the radio, but they had hopes of extending the telegraph lines. Besides, it gave Jack Turner something to do. He wasn't good for a lot else, and he did know Morse code. He might as well be a telephone orderly, Harvey thought. Turner's only attempt to supervise a ranch project had been a disaster, with the men finally going to the Senator and demanding Turner's replacement. . . .

Turner hailed him as he went past. "Hey, Randall!"

"Hello, Jack. What's new?"

"We've got another President. A Hector Shorey of Colorado Springs. He proclaims martial law."

Jack Turner seemed to think that was funny, and so did Harvey. He said, "Everybody always proclaims martial law."

"Littman didn't."

"Yeah, I liked Emperor Pro Tem Charles Avery Littman. Even if he *was* getting most of his material out of 'Monty Python's Flying Circus.' The others were too damn serious."

"Shorey's group sounds serious enough. I got some good recordings through the static."

"Hold the fort, Jack," Harvey said, and he went on. Four Presidents now, he thought. Littman was just a ham radio operator, and half mad. But Colorado Springs . . . that was near Denver, a mile above sea level. That could be for real.

The big front room was crowded. This was no ordinary meeting. The Senator sat near the fireplace in the big leather armchair that reminded Harvey of a throne—and was probably meant to. Maureen sat on one side, and Al Hardy on the other, heiress and chief of staff.

Mayor Seitz and the police chief were there; and Steve Cox, Jellison's ranch foreman, the man now responsible for most of the agriculture in the valley; and half a dozen others who spoke for the valley people. And of course George Christopher, alone in one corner, with only one vote, though it counted for as much as the rest together except for Maureen's.

Harvey smiled at Maureen. He got a quick impersonal smile and nod, nobody home, and he pulled his eyes away fast.

Bloody hell! She wore two faces, and so did he. Maureen had been up to see him in the hut at the top of the ridge several times when Harvey had night guard duty. She'd met him at other times and places, too, but always very privately. It was always the same. They talked of the future, but never of *their* future, because she wouldn't. They made love with care and tenderness, as if they might never meet again; they made love, but never promises. She seemed to draw strength from him, as he knew he did from her; but never in public. It was as if Maureen had an armed, jealous, invisible husband. In public she barely knew him.

But in public she treated George Christopher no differently. She was a bit more friendly, but still cold. *He* wasn't her invisible husband . . . was he? Was she different with him when they were alone? Harvey couldn't know.

These thoughts ran through his head before an old reflex pushed them down below conscious thought. He didn't have time for them. Harvey Randall wanted something, and these were the men who could refuse him. It was a familiar situation.

"Come in, Harvey." Senator Jellison had not lost the warm

smile that had won him elections. "We can start now. Thank you all for coming. I thought it might be wise to get a full report on how things are here."

"Any reason for doing it now?" George Christopher asked.

Jellison's smile didn't falter. "Yes, George. Several. We have word from the telegraph that Deke Wilson's coming in for a visit. Brought some visitors, too."

"There's news from Outside?" Mayor Seitz asked.

"Some," Jellison said. "Al, would you begin, please?"

Hardy took papers from his briefcase and began to read. How many acres cleared of rocks, and how much they'd be able to plant in winter wheat. Livestock inventory. Weapons, and equipment. Most of the people in the room looked bored before Hardy finished. "The upshot is," Hardy said, "that we'll make it through the winter. With luck."

That got their interest.

"It'll be close," Hardy warned. "We'll get damned hungry before spring. But we've got a chance. We've even got medical supplies—not enough, but some—and Doc Valdemar's clinic is set up and running." Hardy paused for a moment. "Now for the bad news. Harvey Randall's people have been looking over the dams and powerhouses above here. They can't get them working again. Too much washed out. And out of the lists of stuff the engineering people have asked for, we don't have a quarter of the supplies. It'll be a while before we re-build much of a civilization here."

"Hell, we're civilized," Police Chief Hartman said. "Almost no crime, and we'll have enough to eat, and we've got a doctor and a clinic and most of us have plumbing. What more do we need?"

"Electricity would be nice," Harvey Randall said.

"Sure, but we can live without it," Chief Hartman said. "Goddam. We can live till spring."

And Harvey felt his joy. The journey to the Stronghold had been a terrible time: the end of the world passing in endless agony . . . and goddam! Listen to us now, talking like it isn't enough just to be alive! I could have been turned away, sent down the road. . . .

"I think I would express thanks in a more positive way," Reverend Varley said. "We should be singing hosannas." The minister's expression was grim, in contrast to his words. "Of course the cost has been high. Perhaps, Chief, you have said it correctly after all—"

Senator Jellison cleared his throat to get their attention. The room fell silent.

"There's a bit more news," Jellison said. "We have a new claimant to the office of President of the United States. Hector Shorey."

"Who the devil is Hector Shorey?" George Christopher demanded.

"Speaker of the House. Newly selected by the party caucus. I don't even remember the House taking a formal vote. Still, his claim is the best we've heard, and the Colorado Springs government at least talks like it's still in charge of the country."

"I could do that myself," Christopher said.

The Senator laughed. "No, George, you couldn't. I could."

"Who cares?" George Christopher was belligerent. "They can't help us and they can't jail us. They'd have to fight their way through all the other United States Governments, and even then they can't get to us. Why do we give a damn what they say?"

Al Hardy said, "I point out that Colorado Springs probably has the largest military detachment surviving in this part of the world. The cadets at the Academy. The NORAD—North American Air Defense—command under Cheyenne Mountain. Ent Air Force Base. And at least a regiment of mountain troops."

"They still can't get to us," Christopher insisted. "Understand, I've nothing against getting the United States going again. But I want to know the cost. Will they tell us to pay taxes?"

Jellison nodded. "Good question." He looked around him. "Whatever happens, it can wait till spring, can't it? Either we'll be out of the woods by then, or we'll be dead. Al says we won't be dead."

There were nods and murmurs of agreement.

"Now," Jellison said. "I asked Harvey to come to this meeting because he has a proposal. Harvey has asked for another expedition Outside, to get more equipment that we'll need for next spring." He held up a paper that Harvey recognized as a list he and Brad Wagoner and Tim Hamner had prepared. "Mostly things we won't need before spring."

"But perishable, Senator," Harvey said. "Electrical tools, transistors, components, electric motors . . . a lot of things that might still be useful even though they've been underwater. By spring they won't be."

"We lost four good men the last time we went Outside," George Christopher said. "It's bad out there."

"Because we didn't take enough men," Harvey answered.

"We need to go in force. A big column won't be attacked." He was proud of his control: He didn't think anyone would guess from his voice how the thought of going out of this valley terrified him. He glanced at Maureen. She knew. She wasn't looking at him, but she knew.

"And will use a lot of gasoline," Al Hardy said. "As well as throw work schedules off. And you still might have to fight."

"Well, we take enough men, it might not be so bad," George Christopher said. "But I'm not going out with just a couple of trucks anymore. Harvey's right. If we go, we go with a lot of people. Ten trucks, fifty to a hundred men."

"I suppose we have to think of these things," Reverend Varley said. His voice was wistful and sad.

"Yes, sir." Christopher was determined. "Reverend, I want peace as much as you do, but I don't know how to get it. Don't forget Deke's neighbors. The ones that got eaten."

Reverend Varley shuddered. "I hadn't," he said.

There was a pause, and Harvey jumped in. "Tim's worked with the phone book and maps," he said. "We've located a scuba shop. It shouldn't be under more than ten feet of water. We could dive in there and get the scuba gear—"

"What are you going to use for air?" Steve Cox demanded.

"We can build a compressor," Harvey said. "That's not hard to design."

"Might not be hard to design, but without electricity it's going to be hard to build," Joe Henderson said. He had owned the filling station in town, and was now helping Ray Christopher set up a blacksmith and mechanic shop.

"Let me name some other things we need," Harvey said. "Machine tools. Lathes, drill presses, all kinds of tools, and we've located most of them—on the map, that is. And we'll need them, one day."

Henderson smiled wistfully. "I could sure use some good tools," he said.

"Generator wire," Harvey continued. "Bearings. Spare parts for our transport vehicles. Electrical wire."

"Stop," Henderson said. "I give up. Let's go out."

"Al, could we spare fifty men for a week?" Jellison asked.

Hardy looked unhappy. "Eileen?" he called. She came in from another room. "Get me those manpower trade-offs, please."

"Right." She flashed Harvey one of her sunburst smiles before she left. Eileen Hancock Hamner had been wrong: Good administrators were needed even after Hammerfall. Al Hardy often told the Senator that she was the most useful person

491

in the Stronghold. Strong backs, farmers, riflemen, even mechanics and engineers weren't so hard to find; but someone who could coordinate all that effort was worth her weight in gold.

Or in black pepper. Hardy scowled. He didn't like this expedition; it was an unnecessary risk. If Randall had his way . . . Was Randall still chasing the blue van and the men who had murdered his wife? At least he'd stopped talking about it. . . .

"While she's getting that," Chief Hartman said, "let me put in a nickel's worth. We can spare fifty men for a week if nobody comes after us while they're gone. Fifty men and rifles is a big part of our strength, Senator. I'd like to be sure nobody's going to attack us before I go along with sending that many out at once."

"I can go along with that," Mayor Seitz said. "And maybe we send a patrol out through Trouble Pass before we go. Just to see if anybody's coming that way."

"Harry's due back from a sweep in a day or so," Senator Jellison said. "And Deke's coming within the hour. We'll find out what things are like Outside before we make any final decisions. George, you got anything to say about this?"

Christopher shook his head. "Either way suits me. If things aren't too bad out there, if there's nobody just waiting for us to send out a big party so they can jump us, then sure, we can go." He fell silent and stared at the wall, and they all knew what he was thinking. George Christopher didn't want to know what went on Outside. No one else did either. It just made things harder, to know of the chaos and death and starvation a few miles away while they were safe in their valley.

Eileen came back with papers. Hardy studied them for awhile. "It all depends on what you find," he said. "We need more fields cleared. We haven't got enough land cleared to plant all the winter seed. On the other hand, if you can find more materials to make greenhouses out of, we won't need so much land planted for the winter. Same for fertilizer and animal feed, if you can get those. Then there's the gasoline. . . ."

It was gasoline and man-hours against a return that could only be guessed at. So they guessed, and they talked it around, and presently Senator Jellison said, "Harvey, you're proposing that we take a risk. Granted it's a risk with a high payoff, and we don't lose much, but it's still a risk—and at the moment we don't *need* risks to stay alive."

"Yes, that's about the size of it," Harvey said. "I think it's worth it, but I can't guarantee it." He stopped for a moment and looked around the room. He liked these people. Even George Christopher was an honest man and a good one to have on your side if there was trouble. "Look, if it was left to me I'd stay here forever. You can't imagine how good it felt to get into this valley, to feel *safe* after what we saw in Los Angeles. If I had my druthers I'd never leave this valley again. But—we do have to look ahead. Hardy says we'll get through the winter, and if he says so, we will. But after winter there's spring, and the winter after that, and more years—years and years—and maybe it's worth some effort right now to make those future years easier."

"Sure, provided it don't cost so much there *aren't* any more years," Mayor Seitz said. He laughed. "You know, I was talking to that lady head doctor. Doc Ruth says it's a 'survivor syndrome.' Everybody who lives through Hammerfall gets changed by it. Some go completely nuts, and life isn't worth a damn to them, they'll do anything. But most get like us, so cautious we jump at our shadows. I know I'm that way. I don't want to take any chances at all. Still, Harvey's got a point. There *is* a lot of stuff out there we could use. Maybe we'll even find Harv's—"

"Blue van!" cried at least four men, and Hardy winced. Randall might have stopped talking about the blue van, but nobody else had. Black pepper, spices, beef jerky, pemmican, canned soup and canned ham, coffee, liquor and liqueurs and a partridge in a pear tree, everything you could dream of and all measured in ton lots. Machine tools, hah! If Hardy could read the minds of fifty men as they set out on this fool expedition, he knew what he would find: fifty images of a blue van, just behind their eyes.

Presently Senator Jellison ended the meeting. "It's obvious we can't decide anything until Deke gets here to tell us what things are like out there. Let's wait for him."

"I'll see if Mrs. Cox has the tea," Al Hardy said. "Harvey, would you help me a minute, please?"

"Sure." Harvey went out to the kitchen. Al Hardy was waiting for him.

"Actually," Hardy said, "Mrs. Cox knows what to do. I wanted a word with you. In the library, please." He turned and led the way.

Now what? Harvey wondered. It was obvious Hardy didn't care for the salvage expedition, but wasn't this something more? When Al Hardy ushered him into the big room and then closed the door, Harvey felt a familiar fear.

Al Hardy liked things neat.

There was an admiral Harvey had interviewed, years ago. Harvey had been struck by the man's desk. It was absolutely symmetrical: the blotter precisely centered, the identical IN and OUT baskets on either side, inkwell in the middle with a pen on either side . . . everything but the pencil the admiral was using to gesture. Harvey looked it over; and then he aimed the camera exactly down the middle of the desk, and he put the pencil right in front of him, in line with his tie tack.

And the admiral loved it!

"Sit down, please," Hardy said. The assistant reached into a drawer of the Senator's big desk and took out a bottle of bourbon. "Drink?"

"Thanks." Now Harvey was definitely worried. Al Hardy held almost as much power as the Senator; he executed the Senator's commands. And Hardy liked things neat. He precisely matched the network executives who would order Randall to cut the man-in-the-street crap and use motivational research; who would have found their jobs much easier if all men had been created not just equal but identical.

Could it be a problem with Mark? And if so, could Harvey save him again? Mark had almost got himself thrown out of the Stronghold: Hardy hadn't appreciated Mark's sign proclaiming the Stronghold "Senator Jellison's Trading Post and Provisional Government"; neither had George Christopher. They hadn't cared for the wasted paint, either.

Maybe it wasn't Mark. If Al Hardy decided that Harvey Randall was upsetting his neat patterns . . . the Stronghold couldn't survive without Hardy's mania for organization. The road was always there, and nobody ever forgot it. Harvey shifted nervously in the hard chair.

Al Hardy sat across from him, pointedly not taking the big chair behind the desk. No one but the Senator would ever sit there if Al Hardy had any choice in the matter. He waved toward the big desk with its litter of paper. Maps, with penciled lines showing the current shore of the San Joaquin Sea; manpower assignments; inventories of food and equipment, anything they could locate, and another list of needed items they didn't have; planting schedules; work details; all the paper work associated with keeping too many people alive in a world suddenly turned hostile. "Think all that's worth anything?" Al asked.

"It's worth a lot," Harvey said. "Organization. That's all that keeps us alive."

"Glad you think so." Hardy raised his glass. "What shall we drink to?"

Harvey waved toward the empty chair behind the desk. "To the duke of Silver Valley."

Al Hardy nodded. "I'll drink to that. *Skoal*."

"*Prosit*."

"He is a duke, you know," Hardy said. "With the high, middle and low justice."

That knot of fear in Harvey's stomach began to grow.

"Tell me, Harvey, if he dies tomorrow, what becomes of us?" Hardy asked.

"Jesus. I don't even want to think about it." The question had startled Harvey Randall. "But there's not much chance of that—"

"There's every chance," Hardy said. "I'm telling you a secret, of course. If you let it get out, or let him know I've told you, it won't be pleasant."

"So why tell me? And what's wrong with him?"

"Heart," Al said. "Bethesda people told him to take it easy. He was going to retire after this term, if he lived that long."

"That bad?"

"Bad enough. He could last two years, or he could die in an hour. More likely a year than an hour, but there's a chance of either."

"Jesus . . . but why tell me?"

Hardy didn't answer, not directly. "You said it yourself, organization is the key to survival. Without the Senator there'd have been no organization. Can you think of anyone who could govern here if he died tomorrow?"

"No. Not now. . . ."

"How about Colorado?" Hardy asked.

Harvey Randall laughed. "You heard them in there. Colorado can't keep us alive. But I know who *would* take over."

"Who?"

"You."

Hardy shook his head. "It wouldn't work. Two reasons. One, I'm not a local. They don't know me, and they take my orders only because they're *his* orders. Okay, in time I could get around that. But there's a better reason. I'm not the right man."

"You seem to do all right."

"No. I wanted his seat in the Senate, and he'd have

arranged that for me when he retired. I would have been a good Senator, I think. But not a good President. Harvey, a couple of weeks ago I had to go up to the Bonar place and evict his wife and two children. They cried and screamed and told me I was as much as killing them, and they were right, but I did it. Was that the right thing to do? I don't know, and yet I do know. I know because he ordered it, and what he orders is right."

"That's a strange—"

"Character deficiency," Hardy said. "I could go into my childhood in the Catholic orphanage, but you don't want to hear my life story. Take it from me. I do best when I've got someone else to lean on, somebody else to be the final authority. The Old Man knows that. There's not a chance in the world that he'd designate me as his successor."

"So what will you do, when . . ."

"I'll be chief of staff to whomever Senator Jellison designates. If he hasn't designated anyone, then to whoever I think will be able to carry on his work. This valley is his life work, you know. He's saved us all. Without him it would be like Outside here."

Harvey nodded. "I expect you're right." And I like it here, he thought. It's safe, and I want to be safe. "What has all this got to do with me?"

"You're ruining things," Hardy said. "You know how."

Harvey Randall's teeth clenched.

"If he dies tomorrow . . ." Hardy said. "If he does, the only person who could take over would be George Christopher. No, before you ask. I will not like being his chief of staff. But I'll do it, because nobody else could hold this valley. And I'll see that everyone knows that George is the Senator's chosen heir. The wedding won't trail the funeral by more than a day."

"She wouldn't marry George Christopher!"

"Yes, she will. If it means the difference between success and ruining everything the Senator has tried to build, she'll do it."

"You're saying that whoever marries Maureen ends up in charge of the Stronghold . . . ?"

"No," Hardy said. He shook his head sadly. "Not anybody. You couldn't, for example. You aren't local. Nobody would take orders from you. Oh, some would, if you were the Senator's heir. But not enough. You haven't been here long enough." Al paused for a moment. "It wouldn't work for me, either."

Harvey turned to stare at the younger man. "*You're* in love with her," he said musingly.

Hardy shrugged. "I think enough of her that I don't want to kill her. Which is what I would be doing if I married her. Anything that disorganizes this valley, that splits it into factions, will kill everyone here. We'll be a pushover for the first group that wants to come in—and, Harvey, there are enemies Outside. Worse ones than you think."

"You've heard something that wasn't told at the meeting?"

"You'll find out from Deke when he comes," Al said. He reached for the bottle and poured more bourbon into both their glasses. "Stay away from her, Harvey. I know she's lonely, and I know how you feel about her, but stay away from her. All you can do is kill her, and ruin everything her father has built."

"Now damn you, I—"

"It does no good to shout at me or be angry with me." Hardy's voice was calm and determined. "You know I'm right. She must marry whoever will be the new duke. Otherwise, Jack Turner will try to assert his rights, and I will have to kill him. Otherwise, there will be factions who will try to take power because they will believe they have as much right as anyone does. The only possible chance for a peaceful transfer of power is to appeal to loyalty to the Senator's memory. Maureen can do that. No one else can. But she cannot control everyone. Together, Maureen and George will be able to."

Finally Hardy's icy calm broke, just slightly. His hand trembled. "Do you think you are making things any easier for her? She knows what she must do. Why do you think she will see you secretly, but will not marry you?" Hardy got up. "We've been long enough. We should join the others."

Harvey drained his glass, but did not get up yet.

"I have tried to be friendly," Hardy said. "The Senator thinks highly of you. He likes the work you have done, and he likes your ideas. I think if he had a free choice he might . . . That doesn't matter. He does not have a free choice, and now I've told you." Hardy went out before Randall could say anything.

Harvey sat staring at the empty glass. Finally he stood and threw it to the carpet. "Shit!" he said. "Goddammit to hell."

When the meeting adjourned, Maureen went outside. There was a fine mist, so fine that she hardly noticed. No one bothered with mist. Visibility was good, several miles, and she could see the snow in the High Sierra, and lower. There was snow on Cow Mountain to the south, and that wasn't quite five thousand feet high. There would be snow in the valley soon.

She shivered slightly in the cold wind, but she wasn't tempted to go inside and get warmer clothing. Inside she'd have to see Harvey Randall again, and look away. She didn't want to see anyone or speak to anyone, but she smiled pleasantly as Alice Cox rode by on her big stallion. Then she felt, rather than heard, someone come up behind her. She turned, slowly, afraid of whom she'd see.

"Cold," Reverend Varley said. "You should get a jacket."

"I'm all right." She turned to walk away from him, and saw the Sierra again. Harvey's boy was up in those mountains. Travelers said the scouts were doing well there. She turned back again. "They tell me you can be trusted," she said.

"I hope so." When she didn't say anything else, he added, "Listening to people's troubles is my main business here."

"I thought you were in the praying business." She said it cynically, not knowing why she wanted to hurt him.

"I am, but it's not a business."

"No." It wasn't. Tom Varley pulled his own weight. He could claim a larger share than what he took from his own dairy herd; and many of the valley people gave him part of their own rations, which he distributed. He never said how. George thought he was feeding outsiders, but George wouldn't say anything to Tom Varley. George was afraid of him. Priests and magicians are feared in primitive societies. . . . "I wish this were really the Day of Judgment," she blurted.

"Why?"

"Because then it would mean something. There's no meaning to any of this. And don't tell me about God's will and His unfathomable reasons."

"I won't if you say you don't want to hear it. But are you sure?"

"Yes. I tried that. It doesn't work. I can't believe in a God who did this! And there's just no purpose, no reason for anything." She pointed to the snow in the mountains. "Winter will be here. Soon. And we'll live through it, some of us. And another after that. And another. Why bother?" She couldn't stand looking at him. His collie-dog eyes were filled with concern and sympathy, and she knew that was what she had wanted from him, but now it was unbearable. She turned and walked away quickly.

He followed. "Maureen." She went on, toward the driveway, but he kept pace with her. "Please."

"What?" She turned to face him. "What can you say? What can I say? It's all true."

"Most of us want to live," he said.

"Yes. I wish I knew why."

"You do know. You want to live too."

"Not like this."

"Things aren't so bad—"

"You don't understand. I thought I'd found something. Life consists of doing one's job. I could believe that. I really could. But I don't have a job. I am thoroughly and utterly useless."

"That's not true."

"It is true. It always was true. Even before . . . before. I was just existing. Sometimes I could be happy being a part of someone else's life. I could fool myself, but that wasn't any good either, not really. I was just drifting along, and I didn't see much point in it, but it wasn't too bad. Not then. But the Hammer came and took even that way. It took everything away."

"But you're needed here," Varley said. "Many of these people depend on you. They need you—"

She laughed. "For what? Al Hardy and Eileen do the work. Dad makes the decisions. And Maureen?" She laughed again. "Maureen makes people unhappy, Maureen has fits of black depression that spread like the plague. Maureen sneaks around to see her lover and then destroys the poor son of a bitch by not speaking to him in public because she's afraid she'll get him killed, but Maureen doesn't even have the guts to stop fucking. How's that for worse than useless?"

There was no reaction to her language, and she was ashamed of herself for trying to . . . to what? It didn't matter.

"Isn't it true that you do care for something?" Varley asked. "This lover. He is someone whose life you want to share."

Her smile was bitter. "Don't you understand? I don't know! And I'm afraid to find out. I want to be in love, but I don't think I can be, and I'm afraid even that's gone. And I can't find out because my job is to be the crown princess. Maybe I ought to marry George and be done with it."

This time he did react. He seemed surprised. "George Christopher is your lover?"

499

"Good God, no! He's the one who'll do the killing."

"I doubt that. George is a pretty good man."

"I wish . . . I'd like to be sure of that. Then I could find out. I could find out if I can still love anyone. And I want to know, I want to know if the Hammer took that, too. I'm sorry. I shouldn't have spoken to you. There's nothing you can do."

"I can listen. And I can tell you that I see a purpose to life. This vast universe wasn't created for nothing. And it *was* created. It didn't just happen."

"Did the Hammer just happen?"

"I don't believe so."

"Then why?"

Varley shook his head. "I don't know. Perhaps to shock a Washington socialite enough to make her take a strong look at her life. Maybe only that. For you."

"That's crazy. You don't believe that."

"I believe it has a purpose, but that purpose will be different for each of us."

"We'd better go in. I'm freezing." She turned and walked rapidly past him to the stone ranch house. I'll see Harvey tonight, she thought. And I'll tell him. Everything. I have to. I can't stand this any longer.

Journey's End

In the imminent dark age people will endure hardship, and for the greater part of their time they will be laboring to satisfy primitive needs. A few will have positions of privilege, and their work will not consist in . . . cultivating the soil or in building shelters with their own hands. It will consist in schemes and intrigues, grimmer and more violent than anything we know today, in order to maintain their personal privileges. . . .

Roberto Vacca, *The Coming Dark Age*

Ding!

The kitchen timer went off, and Tim Hamner put down his book and picked up the binoculars. He had two sets of binoculars in the guard shack: the very powerful day glasses he now carried, and a much larger night glass that didn't magnify so much, but gathered a lot of light. They'd have been perfect field-viewing astronomical glasses, except that there were always clouds and Tim rarely saw the stars.

The hut had been vastly improved. Now there was insulation, and more wood frame; it could even be heated. It contained a bed, a chair, a table and some bookshelves—and a rifle rack at the door. Tim slung the Winchester 30/06 over his shoulder on the way out, and only momentarily felt amusement at the thought: Tim Hamner, playboy and amateur astronomer, armed to the teeth as he ventured forth to search out the ungodly!

He climbed up onto the boulder. A tree grew next to it. From any distance away he'd be invisible in the foliage. When he reached the top he braced himself against the tree and began his careful scan of the terrain below him.

Trouble Pass appeared on no maps. It was Harvey Randall's name for the low spot in the ridges surrounding the Stronghold. Trouble Pass was the most likely route for any-

501

one invading on foot, and Tim scanned it first. He'd looked into it no more than fifteen minutes before; the timer was set for fifteen-minute intervals on the theory that nobody, on foot or horseback, could get over the pass and out of sight in less than fifteen minutes.

There was nobody there. There never was, these days. In the first weeks, walkers had tried to come in that way, and they'd be spotted, and Tim would use the bugle to sound an alarm; ranchers on horseback would go out to meet the intruders and turn them away. Now the pass was always clear. Still, it had to be watched.

Tim spotted two deer and a coyote, five jackrabbits and a lot of birds. Meat, if hunters could be spared. Nothing else in the pass. He swept the glasses on around, over the tops of the skylines and along the barren hillsides. It wasn't too different from looking for comets: You remember what things ought to look like, and search for anything different. Tim knew every rock on the hillsides by now. There was one shaped like a miniature Easter Island statue, and another that looked like a Cadillac. Nothing was on the hillsides that shouldn't be there.

He turned and looked down into the valley behind, and grinned again at his good fortune: better to be a guard on top of the ridge than down there breaking up rocks. "I expect the guards at San Quentin thought that, too," Tim said aloud. He'd taken to talking to himself lately.

The Stronghold looked good. Secure, safe, with greenhouses, and grazing herds and flocks; and there was going to be enough to eat. "I am one lucky son of a bitch," Tim said.

It came to him, as it often did, that he was far luckier than he deserved. He had Eileen, and he had friends. He had a secure place to sleep, and enough to eat. He had work to do, although his first scheme, to rebuild the dams above the Stronghold, hadn't worked out—no fault of his. He and Brad Wagoner had worked out new ways to generate electricity—always assuming they could get Outside and find the wire and bearings and other tools and equipment they'd need.

And books. Tim had a whole list of books that he wished for. He'd owned nearly all of them, back in a time that he barely remembered, a time when all he had to do if he wanted anything was to let someone know it, and let money do the rest. When he thought about books and how easy it had been to get them, his thoughts sometimes strayed further, to hot towels and the sauna and swimming pool, Tanqueray gin and Irish coffee and clean clothes whenever he wanted them. . . . But those times were hard to remember. They were times before Eileen, and she was worth a lot. If it took the end of the world to bring them together, then maybe it was worth it.

Tim was sad only when he thought of life Outside, when he remembered the dead baby and the police and nurses working at the Burbank hospital. Those memories of driving past helpless people sometimes rose to haunt him, and he couldn't help wondering why he'd survived—more than survived; lived to find security and a lot more happiness than he'd ever expected. . . .

Movement caught his eye. A truck was coming up the road. It was full of men, and Tim almost leaped down into the hut to call a warning. The air was clear of lightning except for the constant flashes up in the High Sierra; the little CB radio would work, but he wasn't supposed to use it more than necessary. It was damned tough hauling batteries up and down this hill, and it took precious gasoline to recharge them. He let the impulse pass. The truck had a way to go; there was time to examine it through the binoculars.

He didn't doubt that it was Deke Wilson's truck. He looked anyway. A single truck could carry considerable firepower, and a single such mistake could cost a score of lives and put the poor stuttering sentry back on the road without his balls.

It looked like Deke's truck, more crowded than usual; the truck bed was jammed with standing men. You wouldn't crowd an attack force together like that. One was a woman. . . .

Those four: Why did they leap to the eye like that? One was a woman, and one was black, and two were white men. But the four seemed clumped together as if . . . as if in mutual distaste for the mortals around them. No, they didn't look like mortals. Tim shifted his elbows on the rock and studied elusively familiar faces through the binoculars. . . .

But the truck was coming too close. Tim sprinted for the hut. He was picking up the microphone when he remembered.

"Yeah?"

"Deke Wilson's here, three minutes," said Tim, "and he's got the astronauts with him, the astronauts from Hammerlab! All four! Chet, you won't believe them. They look like gods. They look like they never went through the end of the world at all."

Faces. Dozens of faces, all white, all staring up at them in the truck. They were all talking at once, and Rick Delanty heard only snatches of conversation. "Russians." "Astronauts, it's really them." When he got down from the truck they crowded around, hanging back a bit to avoid crushing the men from space, staring, smiling. Men and women, and they weren't starving. Their eyes did not have the haunted look that Rick had got used to at Deke Wilson's place. These people had seen only a part of Hell.

They were mostly middle-aged, and their clothes showed signs of hard work and not much washing. The men tended to be large, the women plain, or was it only that they were dressed for work? At Deke Wilson's farm the women had dressed like men and worked like men. Here there was a difference. In this valley women were different from men. It wasn't like the world before Hammerfall. It wasn't that obvious, and if Rick hadn't been weeks with Deke Wilson he would have reflected on how things had changed since the Hammer; now, he noticed the similarities. This valley was as different from Wilson's fortified camp as . . .

Rick had no more time to reflect on it. There were introductions, and they were ushered up onto the big porch of the stone ranch house. Rick would have known who was in charge even if he hadn't recognized Senator Jellison: The Senator was not as large as the big, burly men, but everyone made room for him, waited for him to speak first; and his smile made them all feel welcome, even Pieter and Leonilla, who had been dreading this meeting.

More people were coming, some downhill from the fields, others up the drive. The word must have spread fast. Rick looked for Johnny Baker, and saw him, but Baker wasn't noticing Rick Delanty or anyone else. He was standing in front of a slim girl, tall, red hair, flannel shirt and work trousers. He gripped both her hands, and they devoured each other with their eyes.

"I was sure you were dead," Baker said. "I just . . . I never even asked Deke. I was afraid to. I'm glad you lived."

"I'm glad you lived, too," she said. Odd, Rick thought: From the sorrow on their faces, you would have thought they were attending each other's funeral. It was obvious to Rick, and to everyone else: They had been lovers.

And some of the men didn't like that at all! Trouble

building there. . . . Rick again had no time to reflect on it. The crowd was pressing around, everyone speaking at once. One of the big men turned from watching Johnny and his woman and spoke to Rick. "Are we at war with the Russians?" he demanded.

"No," Rick said. "What's left of Russia and what's left of the United States are allies. Against China. But you can forget about all that, the war's long over. Between the Hammer and the Soviet missiles, and we think maybe some of our own, there won't be anything left of China that can fight back."

"Allies." The big man was bewildered. "Okay. I guess."

Rick grinned at him. "The thing is, if we ever get to Russia we'll find nothing but glaciers. But if we go to China we'll find Russians, and they'll remember us as allies. See?"

The man scowled and walked away, exactly as if Rick had been putting him on.

Rick Delanty fell into the old routine. He was used to speaking at gatherings, keeping the words simple and the imagery vivid, explaining without condescending. There were plenty of questions. They wanted to know what it was like in space. How long did it take to get used to free fall? Rick was surprised at how many had watched their TV broadcasts from Hammerlab and remembered Rick's impromptu zero-G ballet performance. How did they move? Eat? Drink? Patch a meteor strike? Couldn't that raw sunlight burn your eyes out? Did they wear dark glasses all the time?

He learned the names. The young girl was Alice Cox, the woman with the tray of hot coffee—real coffee!—was her mother, the burly men with the challenging stance were both Christophers, and so was the one who'd wanted to know about the war, only that one had gone inside with Deke Wilson and Johnny Baker, leaving Mrs. Cox to be hostess. There was a man introduced as "Mayor" and another whom everyone called "Chief," but there was something subtle Rick didn't understand, because the Christophers, with no title, seemed to have higher status. All the men seemed big, and they were all armed. Was he already so used to the half-starved look of Deke Wilson's band?

"The Senator says we can spare some light," Mrs. Cox announced after one of her trips inside. "You can talk to the astronauts after it's too dark to work. And maybe we'll have a party Sunday."

There were murmurs of agreement, and goodbyes, and the crowd melted away. Mrs. Cox took them inside, and brought more coffee into the living room. The perfect hostess, and Rick found himself relaxing for the first time since they had landed. At Deke Wilson's there had been coffee, but not much, and it was consumed hurriedly by men about to go on guard duty. No one sat relaxed in a parlor, and the coffee certainly wasn't served in china cups.

"I'm sorry there's nobody around to keep you company," Mrs. Cox said. "Everyone's got work to do. They'll be back tonight, and then they'll talk your head off."

"It is not important," Pieter said. "We thank you for the welcome." He and Leonilla sat together, apart from Rick. "I hope we are not keeping you from your duties."

"Well, I've got dinner to cook," Mrs. Cox said. "If you want anything, just call me." She left them alone, pointedly setting down the coffeepot. "Better drink that before it gets cold," she said. "I can't promise there'll be any more for awhile."

"Thank you," Leonilla said. "You are all so kind to us. . . ."

"No more than you deserve, I'm sure," Mrs. Cox answered, and then she was gone.

"So. We have found a government," Pieter said. "Where is General Baker?"

Rick shrugged. "Back there somewhere with Deke and the Senator and some of the others. Big conference."

"To which we were not invited," Jakov said. "I understand why Leonilla and I are not needed, but why are you out here?"

"I thought about that," Rick said. "But they all left pretty quick. You know what Deke's got to tell them. And somebody had to stay out there and talk to the crowd. I took it as a compliment."

"I hope you are right," Jakov said.

Leonilla nodded agreement. "This is the first time I have felt safe since we landed. I think they like us. Surely they do not care that Rick is black?"

"I can usually tell," Rick said. "No. But there was something strange. Did you notice? After they found out about the war, all they wanted to know about was space. Nobody, nobody at all, asked about what was happening to the Earth."

"Yes. But soon we will have to tell them," Pieter said.

"I wish we could avoid that," Leonilla said. "But yes, we will have to."

They fell silent. Rick got up and poured the last of the coffee. From back in the kitchen there were sounds of activity, and outside they could see men carrying rocks, others plowing fields. Hard work, and it was certain that there'd be plenty for all of them, even Leonilla. Rick hoped so. He realized that he had been silently praying that there would be work, something to do, something to make him feel useful again, and to forget Houston and El Lago and the tsunami. . . .

But for the moment he'd been given a hero's welcome, and so had Leonilla and Pieter, and they were safe, surrounded by armed men who didn't want to kill them.

He heard a low buzz of voices from somewhere at the back of the house. That would be the Senator and Johnny Baker and Deke Wilson and the Senator's trusted staff, planning . . . what? Our lives, Rick thought. Was the Senator's daughter there, too? Rick remembered how she and Johnny had looked at each other, their voices inaudible, their noses almost touching, no thought of anyone around them. How would that affect the Senator's decisions?

It struck Rick that the Senator might like it fine. Johnny Baker was an Air Force general. If Colorado Springs had the power they claimed, that could be important.

"How many men here?" Pieter said. The question startled Rick from his reverie. "I estimate several hundred," Pieter was saying. "And many weapons. Do you think that is enough?"

Rick shrugged. He'd been thinking of the far future, weeks, months ahead, and had almost managed to forget why they had come to the Senator's Stronghold just now. "It's got to be," Rick said, and now he felt it too, the tension that Pieter and Leonilla had brought with them. It had never occurred to Rick that the Senator wouldn't have enough strength. He'd been so sure that somewhere there were civilized men and women, real safety and civilization and order. . . .

And maybe there wasn't any. Anywhere. Rick shuddered slightly, but he kept his smile in place, and the three of them sat in the paneled room, waiting and hoping.

"They call themselves the New Brotherhood Army," said Deke. He looked around him—at Harvey Randall and Al Hardy and General Johnny Baker, George Christopher, who sat far to one side of the room, and Senator Jellison in his judge's chair—and his eyes were haunted. He drank from his glass, and waited a minute while the whiskey worked its ancient magic, and said in a firmer voice, "They also claim to be the legal government of California."

"By what authority?" Al Hardy demanded.

"Well, their proclamation was signed by the Lieutenant Governor. 'Acting Governor,' he calls himself now."

Hardy frowned. "The Honorable James Wade Montross?"

"That's the name," Deke said. "Could I have some more of that whiskey?"

Hardy looked to the Senator, got a nod and refilled Deke's glass. "Montross," Al said musingly. "So The Screwball survived." He looked to the others and added quickly, "An insider's joke. In politics we usually have nicknames for people. The Loser. Grin and Bear It. Montross got tagged as The Screwball."

"Screwball or not, he's given me seven days to join his government," Deke said. "Otherwise his New Brotherhood Army will take the whole place by force." The farmer opened his Army-surplus field jacket and took a paper from an inner pocket. The paper was mimeographed, but the lettering was hand-drawn, in fine calligraphy. He handed it to Al Hardy, who glanced at it, then gave it to Senator Jellison.

"That's Montross's signature," Hardy said. "I'm sure of it."

Jellison nodded. "We can treat the signature as genuine." He looked up to include everyone in the conversation. "The Lieutenant Governor proclaims a state of emergency and asserts what amounts to supreme authority within California," he said.

George Christopher growled, a harsh grating sound. "Over us, too?"

"Everyone," Jellison said. "He mentions the Colorado Springs announcement, too. Do you know anything about that, General Baker?"

Johnny Baker nodded. He sat next to Harvey Randall, but he didn't seem to be part of the group in the room. The old gods have returned, Harvey thought. For the moment, anyway. How long will they be gods? Harvey had seen Baker with Maureen, and hated it.

"We caught a broadcast out of Colorado Springs," Baker

said. "I'm sure it was genuine. It was in the name of the Speaker of the House—"

"A senile idiot," Al Hardy said.

"—who is acting as President," the astronaut continued. "His chief of staff seems to be a brevet lieutenant general named Fox. I think that's Byron Fox, and if it is, I know him. One of the professors at the Academy. Good man."

George Christopher had been quietly fuming. Now he spoke, his voice low and full of anger. "Montross. That son of a bitch. He was around here a couple of years ago trying to organize the pickers. Came right onto my land! I couldn't even throw the trespassing bastard off. He had fifty state cops with him."

"I'd say Jimmy Montross has quite a lot of legal power," Senator Jellison said. "He is the highest-ranking civil officer in California. Assuming the Governor's dead, and he probably is."

"Sacramento's gone, then?" Johnny Baker asked.

Al Hardy nodded. "As far as we can tell, that area's all underwater. Harry took a sweep north and west a couple of weeks ago and met somebody who'd talked to people who tried to get to Sacramento. All they found was more of the San Joaquin Sea."

"Damn," Baker said. "Then the nuclear power plant's gone."

"Yes. Sorry," Hardy said.

"Deke, you're not going to knuckle under to this goddam Montross, are you?" George Christopher demanded.

"I came here to ask for help," Wilson said. "They can whip us. That army of his is big."

"How big?" Al Hardy asked.

"Big."

"Something puzzles me," Senator Jellison said. "Deke, are you certain that the cannibal band you fought is part of this outfit that Montross is associated with?"

"I said so, didn't I?"

"Now don't get upset." The Senator's famous charm was suddenly evident. "It just surprised me, that's all. Montross was a screwball, but he wasn't crazy. Or stupid, for that matter. He championed the underdog—"

There was a growl from Christopher.

"—or so he claimed," Jellison continued smoothly. "But I wouldn't have thought he'd be friendly with *cannibals*."

"Maybe they're holding him prisoner," Al Hardy suggested.

Jellison nodded. "The point I was about to make. In which case he has no legal authority at all."

"Legal, shmegal, what do I do?" Deke Wilson asked. "I can't fight him. Will you people help me? I don't want to give in to them—"

"Don't blame you," Christopher said.

"It's not just the cannibals," Deke said. "They may give that up if they can get . . . other food. But some of those messengers!"

"How big a party did they send?" Hardy asked.

"About two hundred camped down the road from us," Deke said. "They sent in a dozen. All armed. General Baker saw them. A captain of state police—"

"No shit?" Christopher exclaimed. "State cops with the cannibals?"

"Well, he wore the uniform," Deke said. "And some guy who'd been an official in Los Angeles, a black man. And others. Most of them were okay, but two were . . . hell, they were weird!" He looked to Baker and got a nod of agreement.

"Really weird," Deke continued. "Acted like they were on dope. The eyes looked like that, wide, you know, and they wouldn't look straight at you. And they talked about the angels of the Lord. 'The angels have sent us to deliver this message.' "

"How did the others react to that?" Harvey Randall asked.

"Like nothing happened. Like it was normal to talk about the angels sending them. And when I asked what the hell that meant, they just turned and left. 'You have the message.' That's all they'd say."

"And you said there were two hundred camped near you?" Al Hardy asked. "How near? Where?"

"Not far. South, down the road," Deke said. "Why?"

"Harry went out your way," Hardy said. "He not overdue, he doesn't keep any exact schedule, but we've been expecting him."

"He never got to my place," Deke said.

"Do you think this outfit has done anything to Harry?" Jellison asked.

Deke shrugged. "Senator, I don't know what to make of those people. They claim to have a lot more troops than the ones they let us see, and I believe it. We don't see traders anymore. No refugees. It's like there's nobody out there except you and the New Brotherhood."

"Angels," Al Hardy said. "It doesn't make much sense."

Not neat, Harvey Randall thought. Not neat at all, and it disturbs Al. "I met Montross a few times," Harvey said. "He didn't seem crazy to me. He was hyped up on the subject of environmentalism. Spray cans destroying the ozone, that kind of thing. Maybe the Hammer drove him over the edge."

"He may be crazy, he may be a prisoner, anything could be," Deke Wilson said. "But there's two hundred men camped down the road, I'd bet they've got five hundred more, and I don't know what the hell to do."

"No. I don't suppose you do," the Senator said. He paused for thought, and no one interrupted him. Presently he said, "Well. Six more days. Deke, I was going to make you an offer. You could bring your women and children and injured here, and your part would be to salvage things for us. Tools, electronics, that sort of thing, starting with scuba gear you could use to dive for—"

"Where does that leave us time to fight the New Brotherhood Army, Senator?"

Jellison sighed. "It doesn't, of course. And I don't suppose that Governor Montross—or whoever is controlling him—will be interested in sharing your salvage with us. It sounds as if he intends to take control of the whole state."

"Including our valley," George Christopher said.

"Yes, I expect so," Jellison said. "Well. Two governments we've discovered today. Colorado Springs, and the New Brotherhood Army. Plus the possibility of angels."

"So what the hell do I do?" Deke demanded.

"Be patient. We don't know enough," Jellison said. "Let's get some more data. General Baker, what can you tell us about the rest of the United States? The rest of the world, for that matter?"

Johnny Baker nodded and leaned back to organize his thoughts. "We never did have much for communications," he said. "We lost Houston right after Hammerfall. Colonel Delanty's family was killed in that, by the way. I'd go easy on asking him about Texas."

Baker was pleased to see that the others still had enough sensitivity to show sympathy for Rick. From what he had seen out there, most of the world couldn't find tears to shed for a few individuals. There was too much death. "My Russian friends also lost their families," Johnny said. "The war started less than an hour after the Hammer struck. China hit Russia. Russia hit China. A few of our missile bases launched at China, too."

"Jesus," Al Hardy said. "Harvey, have you got anything that would measure radiation?"

"No."

They all looked alarmed. Harvey nodded agreement. "We're right in the fallout pattern," he said. "But I don't know what we should do about it."

"Is there anything we *can* do about it?" Hardy asked.

"I think it's safe," Johnny Baker said. "Rain settles fallout. And there's plenty of rain. The whole world looks like a big ball of cotton. We hardly ever saw the ground after the Hammer fell."

"You mentioned communications," Jellison prompted.

"Yes. Sorry. Well, we talked to Colorado Springs, but it was very short, not much more than exchanging IDs. We got a SAC base, once. In Montana. They hadn't any communications with anyone. And that's all in the U.S." He paused to let that sink in.

"As for the rest of the world, South Africa and Australia are probably in good shape. We don't know about Latin America. None of us knew enough Spanish, and when we did get contact with somebody down there, it didn't last long. We got some commercial radio broadcasts, though, and as near as we can make out they're having a revolution a week in Venezuela, and the rest of the continent's got political problems too."

Jellison nodded. "Hardly surprising. And of course their most important cities were on the coasts. I don't suppose you know how high the tsunamis got in the Southern Hemisphere?"

"No, sir, but I'd guess they were big," Johnny Baker said. "The one that hit North Africa was over five hundred meters high. We saw that, just before the clouds covered everything. Five hundred meters of water sweeping across Morocco . . ." He shuddered. "Europe's gone. Completely. Oh, and all the volcanoes in Central and South America let go. The smoke came right up through the clouds. The whole Ring of Fire has let go. You've got volcanoes east of you, somewhere out in Nevada, I think, and up north of here Mount Lassen and Mount Hood and maybe Rainier, a lot of them in northern California and Oregon and Washington."

He went on, and as he spoke they realized just how alone they were. The Imperial Valley of California: gone, with a Hammerstrike in the Sea of Cortez that sent, *had* to have sent, waves washing clear up to the Joshua Tree National Monument in the mountains west of Los Angeles. Scratch

Palm Springs and Palm Desert and Indio and Twentynine Palms, forget about the valley of the Colorado River.

"And something must have hit in Lake Huron," Baker said. "We saw the usual spiral pattern of cloud with a hole in the center, just before everything turned white."

"Is there anything left of this country outside Colorado?" Al Hardy asked.

"Don't know again," Baker said. "With all that rain, I'd think the Midwest is drowned out—no crops, no transportation, lots of people starving—"

"And killing each other for what's left," Al Hardy said. He looked at each of the others in turn, and they all nodded agreement: The Stronghold was lucky. More than luck, because they had the Senator, and they had order, a tiny island of safety in a world that had very nearly been killed.

Why us? Harvey Randall wondered. Johnny Baker's report hadn't surprised him, not really. He had thought it out long before. There was the matter of no radio communications. True, the constant static made it unlikely they'd receive messages, but there ought to be something, once in awhile, and there almost never was, which had to mean that nobody was broadcasting, not with any real power, not constantly.

But it was different to *know* they were one of the few pockets of survivors.

What had happened to the world? A revolution a week in Latin America. Maybe that was the answer everywhere. What the Hammer and the Sino-Soviet war hadn't done, people were busily doing to themselves.

Al Hardy broke the silence. "It doesn't look as if the U.S. Cavalry will come charging over the hill to rescue us."

Deke Wilson's laugh was bitter. "The Army's turned cannibal. What we saw of it, anyway."

"We'll have to fight," George Christopher said. "That goddam Montross—"

"George, you can't be sure he's in charge," Al Hardy said.

"Who cares? If he's not, it's worse, it's the fucking cannibals. We'll have to fight sooner or later, we may as well do it while we've got Deke's people on our side."

"I'll go for that," Deke Wilson said. "Unless . . ."

"Unless what?" Christopher asked, his voice suddenly suspicious.

Wilson spread his hands. Harvey couldn't help noticing: Wilson had been a big man, who was now two sizes too small for his body and clothes. And he was scared.

"Unless you'll let us in," Wilson said. "We can hold that

gang off. You've got hills to defend. I don't. All I've got is what I can build, no ridgelines, no natural boundaries, nothing. But in here we can hold the bastards off until they starve to death. Maybe we can help that along. Go on raids and burn out what they've stored up."

"That's obscene," Harvey Randall said. "Aren't there enough people starving without burning crops and food? Jesus! All over the world, what the Hammer didn't get, we're doing to ourselves! Does it have to happen here, too?"

"We couldn't feed all of your people for the winter, Deke," Al Hardy said. "Sorry, but I *know*. The margin's just too thin. We can't do it."

"We don't know enough, not yet," Jellison said. "Maybe it's possible to come to terms with the New Brotherhood."

"Bullshit," George Christopher said.

"It is not bullshit," Harvey Randall said. "I knew Montross, and dammit, he is not crazy, he is not a cannibal, and he is not an evil man even if he did come onto your land and try to help the farmworkers organize a union—"

"That will do," Jellison said. He was very firm about it. "George, I suggest that we wait for Harry. We have to know more about conditions out there. I gather that Deke knows almost nothing he hasn't told us. Harvey, have you time to help, or do you have other work?" Jellison's tone made it plain that Harvey Randall wouldn't be needed in the library just now.

"If you can spare me, there are a few things. . . ." Harvey got up and went to the door. He almost chuckled when he heard George Christopher coming behind him.

"I'll see the maps when they're done," Christopher was saying. "I have some work too. Nice to meet you, General Baker." He followed Harvey out. "Just a minute."

Harvey walked slowly, wondering what would happen now. The Senator had obviously been unhappy about Harvey's outburst. As well he might have been, Harvey thought. And he tried to separate us, and it didn't work. . . .

"So what do we do now?" Christopher was saying.

Harvey shrugged. "We just don't know enough. Besides, we do have a few days. Maybe if we went out with Deke we could come up with enough fertilizer and greenhouse materials to keep all of Deke's people going through the winter—"

"That wasn't what I was talking about," Christopher said. "We're going to have to fight those damned cannibals, and we may as well do it before they get any stronger. Take every gun and every man big enough to carry one and go out there and get it the hell *over* with. I don't want to spend the winter looking over my shoulder. When somebody scares you there's only one thing to do, knock him down and stomp on him until he can't hurt you anymore."

Or run like hell. Or talk a lot, Harvey thought, but he didn't say anything.

"I used to get nervous about you and Maureen," George said.

"I want her too," Harv said. He stopped short of the closed kitchen door and stood facing Christopher in the narrow hallway. "If you knock me down and stomp on me a lot, we're all going to be terribly embarrassed. Your move."

"Not yet. When you get me mad enough, you'll be for the road. Right now we've both got a problem."

"Yah. I noticed that too," said Harvey. "Are you going to put *him* on the road?"

"Don't be stupid. He's a hero. Come on outside." Christopher led the way through the kitchen. There was no one there at the moment. They went out into the dusk.

"Look, Randall," Christopher said. "You don't like me much."

"No. I expect it's mutual."

Christopher shrugged. "I got nothing against you. I don't think you'll shoot me in the back or slug me when I'm not looking—"

"Thanks."

"And unless you do, you can't lick me. Question is, suppose she decides to marry General Baker. What'll you do about that?"

"Cry a lot."

"Look, I'm trying to be polite," Christopher said.

"Well, what do you want me to say?" Harvey asked. "If she marries Baker, she marries Baker, that's all."

"And you'll leave her alone? Not sneak around seeing her?"

"Why the hell would I do that?" Harvey demanded.

"Look, you think I'm some kind of bumpkin fool, don't you?" Christopher said. "And maybe I am, the way you see things. I lived out here before I had to. Went to church. Minded my own business. No swinging parties, no girl friend in every city to go see on expense accounts . . ."

Harvey laughed. "I didn't live that way," he said. "You've been reading too many playboys."

"Yeah? Look, Randall, I'm a cornball, I guess, but I happen to think that if a man's married, he stays at home. Now I never got married. Engaged once, but it didn't work, and then I found out Maureen got her divorce, and while I wasn't exactly just waiting for her—I knew better than to think she'd want to come live in this valley again or that I could live in Washington—I never found anybody. Then this happened. Now she has to live here. Maybe she could live with me. We would have married, once, only it didn't quite work, we were too young. . . ."

"Why are you telling me all this?"

"Because I've got something to say. Dammit, Randall, if I ever do get married, I'll *stay* married. Yeah, and I'll be faithful to my wife, too. Maybe Baker will be. You sure as hell wouldn't."

"Now what the hell . . . ?"

"I know what goes on in this valley, Randall. I knew before the goddam comet hit us and I know now. So you just leave Maureen alone. You're not the kind of man she needs."

"Why not? And who appointed you the guardian of public morals?"

"I did. And you're not good enough for her. You sleep around. All right, it was with her. I don't like that, but I had no claim on her. Not then. But you were a married man, Randall. What the hell was Maureen to you? Another one to add to your scorecard? Look, I'm getting myself upset, and I didn't want that. But you leave her alone. I'm telling you, leave her be." He turned and walked away before Harvey could say anything else.

Harvey Randall stood in shock, and barely restrained himself from running after the big rancher. I ought to be mad, he thought. I ought to hate the bastard. . . .

But he didn't. Instead he felt a wild impulse to run and catch up and explain that it hadn't been that way at all, that Harvey Randall thought about marriage the same way George Christopher did, and all right, so he and Maureen had . . .

Had what? Harvey wondered. Maybe Christopher was right. But Loretta never knew, and she wasn't harmed, and neither was Maureen, and it's all a pile of excuses because you knew damned well what you were doing.

Instead he went into the living room to talk with the other astronauts.

Exile's Story

When the Sun shall be folded up and when the stars shall fall,
And when the wild beasts shall be gathered together . . .
And when the leaves of the Book shall be unrolled
  And when Hell shall be made to blaze and Paradise brought
    near,
    Every soul shall know what it hath produced.
And by the Night when it cometh darkening on,
And by the Dawn when it brighteneth . . .
  WHITHER THEN ARE YE GOING?

The Holy Koran

"Hot water to soak your feet in," said Harry. "Cooked food. A change of clothes. And, man, they *need* you, and they'll *know* it."

"I'll make it," Dan Forrester puffed. "I feel light . . . as a feather without . . . that pack. And they've got sheep?" He'd been afraid to look at his feet, these last few days, but in a while he wouldn't need them. They'd served him well. As for his insulin stock, well, he'd had to increase the dosage; it must be deteriorating. "Have they got a working refrigerator?"

"Refrigerator, no. Sheep, yes. We'll have to deal with that right away. Won't be long now, that's the roadblock ahead."

Their companion, striding ahead of them on the deserted road with Dan Forrester's backpack riding lightly on his hips, stopped suddenly and glanced back.

"You're with me," Harry said. "It'll be all right." Hugo Beck nodded, but he waited for Dan and Harry to catch up. He was afraid, and it showed.

There was a sign fifty yards from the log barricade. It said:

DANGER!
YOU ARE ENTERING GUARDED LAND. GO
NO FURTHER. IF YOU HAVE BUSINESS

HERE, WALK SLOWLY TO THE BARRICADE
AND STAND STILL. THERE WILL BE NO
WARNING SHOTS FIRED. KEEP YOUR
HANDS IN PLAIN SIGHT AT ALL TIMES.

Under it was another, in Spanish, and beyond that a
large death's head with the universal traffic symbol for "Do
not enter."

"Strange welcome mat," Dan Forrester said.

Rotation of work: Mark Czescu was enjoying his day of
guard duty while someone else made little rocks out of big
ones. It wasn't always fun, though. Earlier there had been a
family on bicycles who had won their way through the San
Joaquin and had tales of cannibals and worse, and Mark
hadn't much enjoyed turning them away. He'd shown them
the road north, where there was a fishing camp that was
just hanging on to life.

Four people. The Stronghold could feed four more—but
which four? If these, why not more? The decision was right,
take in no one without special reasons, but it didn't make it
any easier to look a man in the eye and send him up the road.

Mark sat behind a screen of logs and brush where he
could watch without being seen. His partners watched *him*.
One of these days Bart Christopher was going to be slow,
and they'd lose the front man at the gate. . . .

There were three figures coming up the road, and Mark
came out when he recognized the remnants of a gray U.S.
Postal Service uniform. He hailed Harry joyfully, but his
smile had vanished when the three trudged up to the barrier.
He was looking at Hugo Beck when he said, "Happy Trash
Day, Harry."

"I brought him," Harry said. He said it belligerently. "You
know the rules, he's got my safe conduct. And this is Dr.
Dan Forrester—"

"Hi, Doc," Mark said. "You and your damned Hot
Fudge Sundae."

Forrester managed the ghost of a smile.

"He's got a book," Harry said. "He's got a lot of books,
but this one he brought with him. Show him, Dan."

It was drizzling lightly. Dan didn't open the tape seals.
Mark read the title through four layers of Baggies: *The Way
Things Work*, Volume II.

"Volume One is in a safe place," Dan said. "With four thousand other books on how to put a civilization together."

Mark shrugged. He was pretty sure they'd want Dan Forrester up at the Stronghold anyway. But it would be nice to know what other gifts Forrester had available. "What kind of books?"

"The 1911 *Britannica*," Forrester said. "An 1894 book of formulae for such things as soap, with a whole section on how to brew beer starting with barley grains. *The Bee-keeper's Manual*. Veterinary handbooks. Instructor's lab manuals starting with basic inorganic chemistry and running up through organic synthesis. I've got those for 1930 equipment as well as modern. *The Amateur Radio Handbook*. *Farmer's Almanac*. *The Rubber Handbook*. Peters's *Pour Yourself a House*, and two books on how to make Portland cement. *The Compleat Gunsmith* and a set of Army field manuals on infantry-weapon maintenance. The maintenance manuals for most cars and trucks. Wheeler's *Home Repairs*. Three books on hydroponic gardening. A complete set of—"

"Whoa!" Mark cried. "Enter, O Prince. Welcome back, Harry, they're getting worried about you up at the big house. Put your hands on the rail, Hugo. Spread your legs. You carrying heat?"

"You saw me unload the pistol," Hugo said. "It's in the waistband. And the kitchen knife. I need that for eating."

"We'll just put those in the bag," Mark said. "You probably won't be eating here. I won't say goodbye, Hugo. I'll see you on the way out."

"Up your nose."

Mark shrugged. "What happened to your truck, Harry?"

"They took it."

"Somebody took *your truck*? Did you tell them who you were?" Mark was incredulous. "Hell, this means war. They were wondering whether to take a big force Outside. Now they'll have to."

"Maybe." Harry didn't seem as pleased as Mark thought he would.

Dan Forrester cleared his throat. "Mark, did Charlie Sharps get here all right? There would have been a couple of dozen people with him."

"Was he coming here?"

"Yes. Senator Jellison's ranch."

"We never saw him." Mark looked embarrassed. So did Harry. It must be common enough to them, Dan thought

519

sadly: Someone never got somewhere, and the only question was, would the survivor make a scene?

Harry broke an uncomfortable silence.

"I've got a message for the Senator, and Dr. Forrester isn't walking so good. Have you got transportation?"

Mark looked thoughtful. "Guess we'd better telegraph that request in," he said. "Wait here. Watch the road for me, Harry, I'll be right back." Mark spread both hands wide and waved from his waist, making it look casual like a shrug so that Hugo Beck wouldn't figure out that he was signaling, then went off into the bushes.

Dan Forrester watched with interest. He'd read his Kipling. He wondered if Hugo Beck had.

The sun was falling behind the mountains; golden light and violent reds showed beneath the edges of the cloud cover. Sunrises and sunsets had been spectacular since Hammerfall, and, Dan Forrester knew, they would be for a long time. When Tamboura blew up in 1814, the dust it sent into the sky kept sunsets brilliant for two years; and that was only one volcano.

Dan Forrester sat in the cab of the truck with the taciturn driver. Harry and Hugo Beck were in back under a tarpaulin. There was no other traffic on the road, and Forrester appreciated the compliment they'd paid him. Or was it for Harry? Perhaps both together were worth the gasoline when neither alone would have been. They drove through a light drizzle, and the truck heater felt good on Dan's feet and legs.

There were no dead bodies. It was the first thing Dan noticed: nothing dead to be seen. The houses looked like houses, with someone living in every one of them. A few had sandbagged defenses, but there were many that had no signs of defenses at all. Strange, almost weird, that there should be a place where people felt safe enough to have glass windows without shutters.

And he saw two flocks of sheep, as well as horses and cattle. He saw signs of organized activity everywhere—newly cleared fields, some being plowed with teams of horses (no tractors that he could see), others still in process of clearing with men working to carry boulders and pile them into stone walls. The men generally had weapons on their belts, but not *all* of them were armed. By the time they came to the large driveway up to the big stone house, it had sunk in: For a few minutes, possibly for as much as a whole day,

Dan Forrester was safe. He could count on living until dawn.
It was a strange feeling.

There were men waiting for them on the porch. They waved Dan Forrester on into the house without speaking to him. George Christopher jerked his thumb at Harry. "They need you inside," he said.

"In a minute." Harry helped Hugo Beck get down from the truck, then lifted off Forrester's backpack. When he turned, George had his shotgun pointed at Hugo's midsection.

"I brought him," Harry said. "You must have heard that on the telegraph."

"We heard about Dr. Forrester. Not this creep. Beck, you were put on the road. I sent you out myself. Didn't I remember to say 'Don't come back'? I'm sure I did."

"He's with me," Harry repeated.

"Harry, have you lost your mind? This scummy little thief isn't worth—"

"George, if I have to start going around Christopher territory, the Senator will no doubt tell you any news he thinks you should hear."

"Don't push it," George said; but the shotgun moved slightly, so it wasn't pointed at anyone. "Why?"

"You can put him back on the road if you like," Harry said. "But I think you should listen to him first."

Christopher thought about it for a moment. Then he shrugged. "They're waiting inside. Let's go."

Hugo Beck stood before his judges. "I came bringing information," he said, too softly.

His judges were few. Deke Wilson, Al Hardy, George Christopher. And the others. It struck Harry as it had the rest: The astronauts looked like gods. Harry recognized Baker from his photograph on the cover of *Time*, and it wasn't hard to know who the others were. The lovely woman who didn't speak must be the Soviet *kosmonaut*. Harry burned to talk to her. Meanwhile, there were other things to be said.

"Do you know what you're doing, Harry?" Al Hardy asked. His tone made it a sincere question, as if he were half certain that Harry had lost his mind. "You're the information service. Not Beck."

"I know," Harry said. "I thought you should have this firsthand. It's a little hard to believe."

"And that I can believe," George Christopher said.

"Don't I get a seat?" Harry asked. Hardy waved him toward a chair and Harry settled back, wishing that Hugo would show more backbone. His behavior reflected on Harry. This reception wasn't what Harry was used to, and it was Beck that caused it. No china cups and coffee. No shot of whiskey.

The balance of power was life and death at the Stronghold. One played the game well or stayed out of it. Harry tried to stay out of it, enjoy his utility without getting involved in local politics. This time he'd had to play. Had he seriously offended Christopher? And did he give a damn? It was strange, how Harry's macho instincts had kicked in after Hammerfall.

"We put him on the road," George Christopher was saying. "Him and that Jerry Owen, on my orders. Hell, even the Shire threw them out, and those scummy jerks tried to live by stealing off the rest of us, and Owen tried teaching *communism* to *my ranch-hands!* Beck comes back in over my dead body."

There was a chuckle from the back of the room, from either Leonilla Malik or Pieter Jakov. No one paid any attention. There was nothing humorous in the situation, and Harry wondered if he'd gone too far. "While you're discussing Hugo Beck, Dr. Forrester is about dead on his feet," Harry said. "Can you do something for him, or does it depend on getting Beck settled first?"

Al Hardy didn't look away from the center of the room, where Christopher was glaring at Beck. "Eileen," he called. "Take Dr. Forrester out to the kitchen and take care of him."

"Right." Eileen came in; she must have been standing in the hall. She led Dan Forrester out. The astrophysicist followed woodenly, clearly about to pass out from exhaustion.

Hugo Beck licked his thick lips. "I'll settle for a meal," Hugo said, sweating. "H-hell, I'd settle for a stale soda cracker. I just want to know you're still here."

That earned him puzzled looks. "We're here," said Al Hardy. "Have you got information or not? I haven't wakened the Senator yet, and he wants to talk to Harry."

Hugo gulped. "I've been with the bandits. The New Brotherhood Army."

"Son of a bitch," Deke Wilson said.

"How long?" Al Hardy demanded. He was suddenly alert. "Did you learn anything?"

"Or," Christopher asked, "did you just run the first chance you got?"

"I learned enough to want my damn brain wiped clean," Hugo said, and Harry nodded; it was the strict truth.

"Maybe you'd better tell us," Hardy said. He turned toward the kitchen. "Alice, get us a glass of water."

He's got their attention, Harry thought. Now, goddammit, talk like a man!

"There are over a thousand of them," Hugo said. He watched Deke Wilson flinch at that. "Maybe ten percent are women, maybe more. It doesn't matter much. Most of the women are armed. I couldn't tell who was really in charge. It seems to be a committee. Other than that, they're pretty well organized, but God, they're madder than hatters! This crazy preacher is one of the leaders—"

Deke Wilson broke in. "Preacher? Did they give up cannibalism, then?"

Hugo swallowed and shook his head. "No. The Angels of the Lord have not given up cannibalism."

"I'd better get the Senator." Al Hardy left the room. Alice Cox came in with a glass of water, and looked around uncertainly.

"Just put it down on the table," George Christopher said. "Hugo, you may as well wait to tell your story."

Hugo said, "I told you why I left the Shire. My own land. Mine, dammit! They were giving me twice the work of anyone else. After Hammerfall they said their claim on the land was as good as anybody's, right? All of us equals, just the way I set it up. Well, every damned one of them had to prove he was my equal some way, now they all had the chance."

Nobody answered.

"All I want is work and a place to sleep," Hugo said. He looked around the room. What he saw was not good: Christopher's contempt for a man who couldn't handle his own hands; Deke Wilson afraid to listen, afraid not to; Eileen standing at the door, the spacewoman in her chair, both taking it all in and giving nothing back; Harry looking sour and wondering if he should have brought Hugo after all; Mayor Seitz . . .

The Mayor stood up suddenly and swung a chair into place. Hugo dropped into it, hard. "Thanks," he whispered.

The Mayor silently handed Hugo the glass of water and went back to his own place.

Leonilla spoke softly to Pieter. The room was still and everyone heard the fluid syllables. They looked at her, and she translated. "A meeting of the Presidium," she said. "At least it is as I imagine such meetings must have been. Excuse me."

George Christopher frowned, then took a chair. They waited a few moments longer, and Al Hardy came in leading the Senator. He stopped in the doorway and spoke down the hall. "Alice, could you ride up for Randall? And Mr. Hamner, I think. Better take horses for them."

Senator Jellison wore carpet slippers and a dressing gown over slacks and white shirt, his gray-white hair only partially combed. He came into the room and nodded to everyone, then looked at Harry. "Welcome back," he said. "We were getting worried about you. Al, why hasn't anyone brought Harry a cup of tea?"

"I'll see to it," Hardy said.

"Thank you." Jellison went to his high-backed chair and sat. "Sorry to keep you waiting. They like me to take a nap in the afternoon. Mr. Beck, has anyone made you any promises?"

"Just Harry." The gift of a chair had restored some of Hugo's composure. "I get to leave here alive. That's all."

"All right. Tell your story."

Hugo nodded. "You put Jerry Owen and me on the road, remember? Jerry was mad enough to kill. He talked about . . . well, revenge, about the seeds of rebellion he'd planted in *your* men, Mr. Christopher."

George smiled broadly. "They damn near kicked him to death."

"Right, Jerry couldn't move very fast, and I didn't want to go on alone. It was spooky out there. Somebody shot at us once, no warning, just zing! and we ran like hell. We went south because that's the way the road faced, and Jerry wasn't in shape to climb up into the Sierra. Neither was I. We walked all day and most of the night, and I don't know how far we got because all we had was an old Union Oil map, and everything's changed now. Jerry found some grain growing by the side of the road. It looked like weeds, but he said we could eat it, and the next day we managed a fire and cooked it. It's good."

"Okay, we don't need the story of every meal you scrounged," Christopher growled.

"Sorry. The next part's important, though. Jerry was telling me weird things. Did you know he was wanted by the FBI and everyone else too? He was a general—in the"—Hugo paused—"New Brotherhood Liberation Army." Hugo paused to let it sink in.

"New Brotherhood," Al Hardy mused. "I guess that does fit."

"I think so," Hugo said. "Anyway, he was using the Shire as a hideout. He kept his mouth shut and we never knew, until after Hammerfall. We were probably in Mr. Wilson's territory, and I was thinking about ditching Jerry. Being slowed down didn't bother me, but how was I going to join Mr. Wilson's crew if Jerry wanted to start a people's revolution? If I'd seen so much as a lighted window I'd have been gone, and Jerry'd never have known where.

"But we didn't see anything much. A truck once, but it didn't stop. And barricaded farmhouses, where they set the dogs on us if we tried to get close. So we kept going south and getting hungrier, and about the third or fourth day we saw this scraggly-looking bunch of people. Every one of them looked like he'd lost his last chance, but there were at least fifty of them, and they didn't look like they were starving.

"I was thinking about running, but Jerry walked right up to them. He called to me to come on with him, but they didn't look like any outfit I wanted to join. I thought it might be the cannibals Harry told us about, but they didn't look dangerous, they just looked finished."

"No Army uniforms? No guns?" Deke Wilson asked.

"I didn't get close enough to see what weapons they had, but there sure as hell weren't any Army uniforms," Hugo Beck said.

"Then that wasn't the New Brotherhood Army—"

"Just *listen*," Harry interrupted. "He's not finished yet."

Eileen came in with a tray. "Here's your tea, Harry." She poured a cup and set it on the table next to the mailman. "And yours, Senator."

Beck looked at Harry's tea, 'then sipped at his glass of water. "Well, Jerry went in with that outfit, and I split. I figured I'd seen the last of him, and I could get back up to Mr. Wilson's turf again. Instead I ran into an old lady and her daughter. They lived in a little house in the middle of an almond grove, and they didn't have any guns. Nobody'd bothered them because they lived way off the road, and they hadn't been out since Hammerfall. The girl was seventeen,

525

and she wasn't in good shape. She had fever, bad, probably from the water. I took care of them." Hugo Beck said it defiantly. "And I earned my keep, too."

"What did you live on?" Mayor Seitz asked.

"Almonds, mostly. Some canned stuff the old lady had put up. And a couple of bushels of potatoes."

"What happened to them?" George Christopher demanded.

"I'm coming to that." Hugo Beck shuddered. "I stayed there three weeks. Cheryl was pretty sick, but I made them boil all the water, and she came out of it. She was looking pretty good, when—" Beck broke off, and visibly fought for self-control. There were tears in his eyes. "I really got to like her." He broke off again. Everyone waited.

"We couldn't go anywhere because of Mrs. Horne. Cheryl's grandmother. Mrs. Horne kept telling us to light out, leave before somebody found us, but we couldn't do that." Beck shrugged. "So they found us. First a jeep went by. It didn't stop, but the people in it looked tough. We thought we'd make a run for it, but we hadn't got a mile when a truck came up to the house, and people got out of it looking for us. I guess they tracked us, because it wasn't long after that about ten people with guns came and grabbed us. They didn't talk to us at all. They just threw Cheryl and me in the truck and drove. I think some of the others moved into the house with Mrs. Horne. From what happened afterwards I'm sure of it. They wouldn't waste a place like that. And I'm sure now they killed her, but we didn't know that.

"They took us a few miles in the truck. It was dark by the time we got there. They had campfires. Three or four anyway. I kept asking what was going to happen to us, and they kept telling me to shut up. Finally one of them told me with his fist, and I didn't say anything else. When we got to the camp they threw us in with a couple of dozen other people. There were others with guns all around.

"Some of the people in with us were hurt, covered with blood. Gunshot wounds, stab wounds, broken bones . . ." Hugo shuddered again. "We were glad we didn't resist. Two of the hurt ones died while we were waiting. There was barbed wire all around us, and three guys with machine guns watching, and all these other people with guns were running around."

"Uniforms?" Deke Wilson asked.

"Some. One of the guys with a machine gun. A black man with corporal's stripes." Hugo seemed reluctant to talk now. The words came slowly, with effort.

Al Hardy looked a question at the Senator. He got a nod and turned to Eileen, who stood in the doorway. He tilted his head toward the study, and she left, walking quickly so she wouldn't miss the story.

"Cheryl and I got the prisoners to talking," Hugo Beck said. "There'd been a war, and these lost. They were farmers, they had a setup like Mr. Wilson's, I think, a bunch of neighbors trying to be left alone."

"Where was this?" Deke Wilson asked.

"I don't know. It doesn't matter. They're not there anymore," Hugo said.

Eileen came in with a half-full glass. She took it to Hugo Beck. "Here."

He drank, looked startled, and drank again, downing half of it. "Thank you. Oh, God, thank you." The whiskey helped his voice, but it didn't change the haunted look he gave them. "Then the preacher came," Hugo said. "He came up to the barbed wire and started in. Listen, I was so scared I don't remember everything he said. His name was Henry Armitage, and we were in the hands of the Angels of the Lord. He kept talking, sometimes just talk like anybody, sometimes in a singsong voice with a lot of 'my brethren' and 'ye people of God, hear and believe.' We'd all been spared, he said. We'd lived through the end of the world, and we had a purpose in this life. We had to complete the Lord's work. The Hammer of God had fallen, and the people of God had a holy mission. The part I really listened to was when he told us we could join up or we could die. If we joined we'd get to shoot the ones who didn't join, and then—"

"Just a minute." George Christopher's voice was a mixture of interest and incredulity. "Henry Armitage was a preacher on the radio. I used to listen to him. He was a good man. Now you say he's crazy?"

Hugo had trouble looking Christopher in the eye, but his voice was firm enough. "Mr. Christopher, he's so far around the bend that he can't see the bend from there. Listen, people, you *know* there were people driven nuts by Hammerfall. Armitage had more reason than most."

"He made sense. He always made sense. All right, go on. What drove him nuts, and why would he tell *you* about it?"

"Why, it was part of his speech! He told us how he knew the Hammer of God was bringing an end to the world. He warned the world as best he could—radio, television, newspaper—"

"That part's straight," George said.

"And on the last day he took fifty good friends, not just members of his congregation, but *friends*, and his family, up to the top of a mountain to watch. They saw three of the strikes. They went through that weird rain that started with pellets of hot mud and ended like Noah's Flood, and Armitage waited for the angels.

"None of us laughed when he said that. But then it wasn't just the prisoners listening, a lot of the . . . Angels of the Lord, they call themselves, were circled around listening. Every so often they'd shout, 'Amen!' and wave their guns at us. We didn't dare laugh.

"Armitage waited for the angels to come for his flock. They never came. By and by they went downhill again, looking for safety.

"They went along the shore of the San Joaquin Sea, and everywhere they saw corpses. Some of Armitage's friends lost hope and died. He was in despair. They found all kinds of horrors, places where the cannibals had been. Some of them got sick, a couple got shot when they tried to go up to a half-submerged school—"

"Get on with it," said the Senator.

"Yessir, I'm trying. The next part's hazy. All this time Armitage was trying to figure out where the hell all the angels had gone—so to speak. Somewhere in his wanderings he got it. Also, Jerry Owen fits in somehow."

"Owen?"

"Yes. This was the group he'd joined. According to Jerry, it was him who put new life into Armitage. I don't know if any of that's true. I do know that just after Jerry hooked up with him, Armitage ran into the cannibal band, and now it's calling itself the New Brotherhood Army, and it's led by the Angels of the Lord."

"And Jerry Owen is their general?" George Christopher said. He seemed to think that was funny.

"No, sir. I don't know what he is. He's some kind of leader, but I don't think he's all that important. Let me tell this please. I have to tell somebody." He lifted the whiskey glass and stared at it. "This is what Armitage told the cannibals, and this is what he told us."

Hugo gave himself time to think by finishing the whiskey. Hugo was doing fine, Harry thought; he was not going to disgrace Harry.

" 'The work of Hammerfall is not finished,' " said Hugo. " 'God never intended to make an end of mankind. It is God's intent that civilization be destroyed, so that man can

528

live again as God intended. In the sweat of his brow he shall eat his bread. No longer shall he pollute the earth and the sea and the air with the garbage of an industrial civilization that leads him further and further from God's way. Certain of us were spared to finish the work done by the Hammer of God.'

"And these who were spared for that work are the Angels of the Lord. They can do no wrong. Murder and cannibalism are something they do when they must, and it doesn't stain their souls. Armitage urged us to join the Angels.

"Now a couple of hundred people were waving machine guns and shotguns and cleavers and butcher knives, and this one girl was waving a fork, I swear it, the kind of two-pronged fork that comes with a carving set—and all that was pretty convincing. But *Armitage* was convincing. Mr. Christopher, you've heard him, he can be *damned* convincing." Christopher was silent.

"And the others were shouting 'Hallelujah' and 'Amen,' and by God there was Jerry out there, waving a hatchet and shouting with the rest of them! Jerry had bought it, all of it, I could see it in his eyes. He looked at me like he'd never met me before, like I hadn't let him live on my place for months."

The Senator looked up from his thronelike chair. He'd been listening with half-closed eyes. Now he said, "Just a minute, Hugo. Didn't you found the Shire with just this in mind? Natural living, everything organic and self-sufficient, no dominance games and no pollution. Wasn't that just what you were after? Because it sounds like this Armitage wants the same things."

The suggestion startled Hugo Beck. "Oh, no, sir. No. I just about had enough of that before Hammerfall, and *afterward* . . . Senator, we'd never realized just how much modern stuff we had. Hey, we had two microwave ovens! And that goddam windmill never made enough electricity to keep batteries charged, much less run the microwaves, and after the Hamner hit, it blew over in the hurricane! We tried growing the garden with no sprays, just organic fertilizer, and it wasn't humans that ate most of that crop, it was bugs! After that I wanted to spray, but we didn't, and every damned day somebody had to sit there in the dirt picking bugs off the lettuces. And we had the truck, and a rototiller, and a power mower. We had a hi-fi and Galadriel's record collection and strobe lights and electric guitars. We had a dishwasher and a clothes dryer, and we hung the clothes out to dry because it saved gas. Oh, sure, we washed clothes by hand sometimes, too, but there was always some special occasion when we didn't want to bother.

"And aspirin, and needles and pins, and a sewing machine, and a big cast-iron stove made in *Maine* for God's sake. . . ."

"I take it you did not agree with Armitage, then," Senator Jellison said.

"No. But I kept my mouth shut and watched Jerry. He seemed important, and I figured if he could join up and get his own hatchet, so could I. Cheryl and I talked about it, in whispers, because they didn't put up with any of us interrupting Armitage, and we agreed, we'd join up. I mean, what choice did we have? So we joined. As a matter of fact, all of us joined. That time. Two backed down later, at the last—"

It seemed that Hugo's throat closed on him. His haunted gaze roamed about the room and found no sympathy. All in a rush he said, "First we have to kill the ones who won't join. We'd have been given knives for that, I think, but I don't know because everybody joined. Then we'd stew them. That we did, because four prisoners were dead from gunshot wounds. A rabbity little guy told us we couldn't use two of them because they didn't look healthy enough. Only the healthy ones! I talked to him later, and . . ." Hugo blinked.

"Never mind. There were two big stewpots. We had to do the butchering. Cheryl kept getting sick. I had to help her. They gave us knives, and we cut those people up, and this rabbity doctor inspected everything before it went into the pot. I saw one woman pick up a butcher knife and stand there looking at this . . . bottom half of a dead man, and then she threw up, and then she ran at a guard and they shot her and the rabbity man looked her over and then we butchered her, too.

"And all the time the the . . . stew . . . was cooking, Armitage kept preaching. He could go for hours without stopping. All the Angels said that was a miraculous sign, that a man his age could preach without getting tired. He kept shouting that nothing was forbidden to the Angels of the Lord, that our sins were forgiven, and then it was time, and we ate, and one guy got through the butchering all right, but he couldn't eat, and they made us hold him down and cut his throat."

Hugo ran out of breath, and the room was silent.

"And you ate," Senator Jellison said.

"I ate."

"You didn't really think you could stay here after that?" George Christopher spoke almost in kindness.

Harry was looking at the women. Eileen was composed, but Harry had not seen her eyes meet Hugo's, not once. But the Soviet *kosmonaut* was staring at him in naked horror. Harry remembered the way his sister had stared at an enormous spider crawling in the bathtub she had been about to fill. The woman's eyes were wide, and she seemed to be forcing herself back in her chair. She couldn't turn away.

Now, notice! The typical capitalist shows certain predictable tendencies under stress, of which murder and cannibalism . . .

Harry hoped to God nobody looked his way. Nobody else was fighting an urge to laugh. And if it had been Harry up there in front of the table, Harry would have been under the table.

"No. Not really," said Hugo, "not here, not anywhere. That's their power. Once you've eaten human meat, where can you go? You're one of them then, with the crazy preacher to tell you it's all right. You're an Angel of the Lord. You can do no wrong, except if you run, and then you're an apostate." His voice dropped and became toneless. "It's their power, and it works. Cheryl wouldn't leave with me. She was going to turn me in. She was, she really was. So I killed her. It was the only way I could get out, and I killed her, and . . . and I wish I hadn't had to, but what could I do?"

"How long were you with them?" Al Hardy said.

"About three weeks. We had another war, and we got more prisoners. It went the same as before, only now I was outside the wire carrying a pistol and shouting hallelujah. We moved north again, toward Mr. Wilson's place, and when I saw Harry I didn't dare speak to him. But when they let him go—"

"They let you go?" Senator Jellison said.

"Yes, sir. But they took my truck," Harry said. "I have a message for you, from the Angels of the Lord. That's why they let me go. When they caught me I told them I was your mailman, that I was under your protection, and I showed them that letter you wrote. They laughed, but then Jerry Owen said—"

"Owen again," Christopher said. "I knew we should have killed him."

"No, sir, I don't think you should have," Harry said. "If it hadn't been for him, I wouldn't be here."

"So Owen is one of the leaders," Al Hardy said.

Harry shrugged. "They listen to him. But he doesn't give any orders, or at least I never saw him give any. But he said I'd be the perfect one to bring you a message, and I've got it here. I'd got a couple of miles along the road when Hugo caught up to me, and after he told me what it was like back there I thought you ought to hear that before you read the letter they sent."

"Yes. You've done well, Harry," Jellison said. "Well, George? It was on your orders that Beck was expelled."

Christopher looked stunned by all that he'd heard. "Twenty-four hours? Let him stay overnight, and give him three meals fit for a man to eat."

"I think we ought to read that message before we decide anything," Al Hardy said. "And there's a lot more information we need. Hugo, what's their strength? You said a thousand. How good is that estimate?"

"It's what Jerry Owen said Sergeant Hooker had told him. I think it's about right. But they've got more. They've got Bakersfield. It isn't organized yet, but they own it, and their people are sifting through what's left of the city, looking for weapons. And recruits."

"So there's more than a thousand?"

"Yes, I think so, but maybe not all armed. And maybe not recruited all the way. They will be."

"So they could possibly double that strength after they have an . . . initiation ceremony," Hardy said. "We're in trouble. You mentioned Sergeant Hooker. Who is he?"

Beck shrugged. "He's as close to a leader as anyone they have. A big black Army man, Army uniform anyway. There are generals and like that, but Sergeant Hooker outranks them all. I didn't see him much. He has his own tent, and when he goes anywhere they drive him in a car with plenty of bodyguards. And Armitage always talks polite to him, as polite as he ever is to anybody."

"A black man," George Christopher said. He looked around at Rick Delanty, who had sat silently during Beck's story. Then he looked hurriedly away.

"There are other black leaders," Beck said. "They spend a lot of time with Hooker. And you never say anything bad about blacks, or chicanos, or anybody else. First couple of days they just slap you for it, like if a black man says

532

'honky' or a white dude says 'nigger,' but if you don't learn fast they figure you're not really converted. . . ."

"Don't mind me," Rick Delanty said. "I've got all the equality I ever wanted."

Harvey Randall and Tim Hamner came into the room. They brought folding chairs from the library. Eileen went to Tim and whispered hurriedly, and everyone tried to ignore the growing horror on Hamner's face. Alice Cox brought in lighted kerosene lamps. Their cheery yellow glow seemed out of place. "Shall I light a fire, Senator?" Alice asked.

"Please. Hugo, did you see their arsenal?"

"Yes, sir. There were a lot of guns. Machine guns, and some cannon, and mortars—"

"I need details," Al Hardy said. "We all do, and things are getting busy around here. It might take more than one day to get all the useful information he has. Mr. Christopher, could you reconsider?"

Christopher looked as if he were going to be ill. "I don't want him here. He can't stay here."

Hardy shrugged. "And the Governor? Hugo, what do you know about Lieutenant Governor Montross?"

"Nothing, except he's there," Hugo said. "He stays in officer country, and when he goes anywhere there's a lot of bodyguards. Like Sergeant Hooker. The Governor never did talk to us, but we got messages in his name sometimes."

"But who's in control of this group?" Hardy demanded.

"I don't know! I think it's a committee. I never got to talk to the top bosses—mine was a black woman named Cassie, and she was big, and she was mean, and did she ever *believe!* The real bosses were Armitage, and Sergeant Hooker. The Governor, maybe. A black city man named Alim Nassor—"

"Alim Nassor? I know him," Randall said. "We did an interview with him once. A natural leader. Very powerful in the Watts area."

Eileen left Tim and went to kneel next to Randall. As she whispered, Harry watched with curiosity. Could a TV reporter be shocked? Yes. Definitely. And scared shitless, if Harry was any judge. He wasn't the only one. Deke Wilson had been looking sicker and sicker. It wasn't surprising that Deke's territory had been smaller every time Harry went down there. And now the New Brotherhood was at Deke's main area.

George looked disgusted. Finally he said, "I want to throw

up every time I look at him. Senator, how much whiskey do you have left? I'll trade you a pint of my cheap stuff for one stiff drink right now."

"The trade isn't needed," Jellison said. "Eileen, would you bring a bottle, please? I think we could all use a drink. And I gather there's more news. Harry, you mentioned a letter."

"Yes, sir."

"Perhaps I should read it while we all have a drink."

Harry got up and went to the Senator's chair. He took an envelope from an inner pocket and gave it to Jellison. The Senator opened it carefully and took out several sheets of paper. They were handwritten by someone who'd used a broad-nib pen, someone with excellent handwriting. Harry wanted very badly to see what that letter said, but he went back to his seat.

Eileen brought in a full bottle of Old Fedcal and poured for everyone. No one refused. She filled Hugo Beck's glass and he gulped it eagerly.

And he'll stay drunk the rest of his life if he can find booze, Harry thought.

"Are they starving or just hungry?" Christopher asked.

"Not even hungry," Hugo said. "Their doctor—the rabbity guy—says they find enough vitamin pills, and I ate well myself." He saw their faces close up and cried, "No! I only ate human meat twice! At the rituals! Most of what they fed us came from supermarkets, but there were some animals, too. They don't need cannibalism. They only do it when there's new recruits. It's a ritual."

"A damn useful ritual," said Harvey Randall. Heads turned toward him. "Look at Hugo. They've circumcised his soul. It's a mark on him that anyone can recognize. That's what it feels like, doesn't it, Hugo?"

Hugo nodded.

"Suppose I told you it isn't visible at all?" Hugo looked puzzled. Harvey said, "Right. *You* know it's there."

"Some of them like the taste," Hugo whispered, but they heard him.

Deke Wilson spoke in a voice filled with terror. "And I'm next! They're coming for me in four days!"

"Perhaps we can stall them." Jellison looked up from the letter. "This is an interesting document. There is a proclamation of authority by Acting Governor Montross. Then there is a letter to me, inviting me to discuss the terms under which my organization can be integrated into his own. It's

534

politely worded, but quite peremptory, and although he doesn't threaten us directly, there is discussion of unfortunate incidents in which various groups refused to recognize his authority, and had to be treated as rebels." Jellison shrugged. "But there's no mention of cannibals or Angels of the Lord."

"You don't mean . . . don't you believe me, Senator?" Hugo Beck asked in despair.

"I believe you," Jellison said. "We all do." He looked around the room and got nods from the others. "Incidentally, this gives us two weeks, and mentions Deke's White River area as well as our own. That may be simply to get Deke off his guard, but it may also mean they've delayed their attack—"

"I think they won't fight you just yet," Hugo Beck said. "They'd just found out about . . . another place. I think they'll go there first."

"Where?" Hardy demanded.

Visibly, Hugo considered trying to bargain, and decided against it. "The San Joaquin Nuclear Project. They just found out the plant's still operating. It set them crazy."

Johnny Baker spoke for the first time. "I didn't know there was a nuclear plant in the San Joaquin Valley."

"It wasn't on line yet," Harvey Randall said. "It's still under construction. I think they got it to the testing stage before Hammerfall. There wasn't much publicity, because of the environmentalists."

The *kosmonauts* spoke in excited Russian. Baker and Delanty joined in, speaking much more slowly. Then Baker said, "We were looking for an operating power plant. We thought Sacramento might have survived. Where is this San Joaquin plant? We've got to save it."

"Save it?" George Christopher's face was gray. "Can we save ourselves? Dammit, I don't believe it! How could that cannibal army grow so fast?"

"Mohammed," Harvey Randall said.

"What?"

"When Mohammed began he had five followers. In four months he controlled Arabia. In a couple of years he controlled half the world. And the New Brotherhood has the same kind of growth incentive."

Mayor Seitz shook his head. "Senator . . . I just don't know. Can we stop that outfit? Maybe we ought to head for the High Sierra while we've got the chance."

There was a long silence.

The Magician

Any sufficiently advanced technology is indistinguishable from magic.

Arthur C. Clarke

Dan Forrester dozed in front of the woodburning kitchen stove. His feet had been washed and bandaged. He'd taken a shot of insulin, hoping that it was still good, fearing that it wasn't. It was very hard to stay awake.

Maureen Jellison and Mrs. Cox fussed over him, bringing him clean clothes—dry clothes!—and pouring him hot tea. It was very pleasant to sit and feel safe. He could hear voices from the other room. Dan tried to follow the conversation, but he kept falling asleep, then jerking himself awake.

Dan Forrester had spent his life working out the rules of the universe. He had never tried to personalize it. Yet when the Hammer fell, a small bright core of anger had burned in Dan Forrester.

He had forgotten that anger, the anger he felt when he first learned what it meant to be a diabetic. The rules of the universe had never favored diabetics. Dan had long since accepted that. Methodically he set out to survive anyway.

Every day he was still alive. Tired to death, hiding from cannibals, hungrier every day, fully aware of what was happening to his insulin and to his feet, he had kept moving. The steady warmth of anger had never relaxed . . . but something within him had relaxed now. Physical comfort and the comfort of friendship let him remember that he was tired, and ill, and his feet had turned to broken wood. He fought it because of what he could hear from the next room:

Cannibals. New Brotherhood Army. An ultimatum for the Senator. Thousand men . . . they've taken Bakersfield, could double their numbers. . . . Dan Forrester sighed deeply. He looked up at Maureen. "It sounds like a war is coming. Is there a paint store here?"

She frowned down at him. Others had gone mad after less than Dan Forrester had faced. "Paint store?"

"Yes."

"I think so. There was a Standard Brands at the edge of Porterville. It was flooded, I think."

Dan tried to discipline his thoughts. "Perhaps they kept things in plastic bags. What about fertilizer? You have that? Ammonia, for instance. They use it for—"

"I know what they use it for," Maureen said. "Yes, we have some. Not enough for the crops."

Forrester sighed again. "It may not get to the crops. Or maybe we can use it where we'll be able to grow crops later. Were there many swimming pools? A swimming-pool supply store?"

"Yes, there was one of those. It's underwater now—"

"How deep?"

She looked at him sharply. He looked terrible, but his eyes were quite sane. He knew what he was asking. "I don't know. It will be on Al Hardy's maps. Is it important?"

"I think so—" He stopped abruptly. He was listening. In the other room they were talking about a nuclear power plant. Forrester stood up. He had to hold onto the chair. "Would you help me go in there, please?" His voice was apologetic, but somehow there was no way to refuse him. "Oh—one more thing. A filling station. I'll need some drums of grease solvent."

Maureen, mystified, helped Forrester down the hall toward the living room. "I don't know. We have a filling station here, but it was very small. There were bigger ones in Porterville, of course, but they were under the dam and were flooded pretty badly. Why? What can you make with all that?"

Forrester had reached the living room and went in hanging on Maureen's arm. Johnny Baker stopped talking and stared at him. So did the others. "Sorry to interrupt," Forrester said. He looked around helplessly for a chair.

Mayor Seitz was nearest to him and got up from the couch. He went back to the library for a folding chair while

Forrester took the Mayor's place on the couch. Forrester blinked rapidly at the others. "I'm sorry," he said again. "Did someone ask where the San Joaquin Nuclear Plant is?"

"Yes," Al Hardy said. "I know it was out there somewhere, but hell, it has to be underwater. It was right in the middle of the valley. It can't be working—"

"It was on Buttonwillow Ridge," Forrester said. "I looked on a map, and that's about forty feet higher than the land around it. But I thought it would be flooded too, and I wasn't able to get down to the edge of the San Joaquin Sea because of the cannibals."

Hardy looked thoughtful. Eileen Hamner hurried out and came back with a map. She spread it out on the floor in front of the Senator and he and Hardy stared at it.

Maureen Jellison went across the room and sat on the floor near Johnny Baker. Their hands sought each other and clasped involuntarily.

"We have that area about fifty feet underwater," Al Hardy announced. "Hugo, are you *sure* the plant's operating?"

"The Angels think so. As I said, it set them wild."

"Why?" Christopher asked.

"It's a Holy War," Hugo Beck said. "The Angels of the Lord exist only to destroy the forbidden works of man. What's left of industry. I watched them tear into what was left of a coal-powered station. They didn't use guns or dynamite. They swarmed over it with axes and clubs and hands. It was already wrecked, you understand. It had been flooded. But when they got through, you couldn't tell what it had been. And all the time Armitage was shouting at them to do the work of the Lord!

"He preaches every night, same theme. Destroy the works of man. Then three days ago—I think it was three days . . ." Hugo counted on his fingers. "Yeah. Three days ago they heard that nuclear plant was still going. I thought Armitage would burst a blood vessel! From that moment on it was constant: Destroy that Citadel of Satan. Look, *nuclear* power! Kind of the epitome of everything the Angels hate, you know? It even had Jerry Owen excited. He used to talk about how they might save a few things. Hydroelectric plants, maybe, if they could be rebuilt without hurting the Earth. But he hated nuclear power plants *before* Hammerfall."

"Do they destroy all technology?" Al Hardy asked.

Hugo Beck shook his head. "Sergeant Hooker and his people kept anything they think they can use, anything that might have military value. But they were all agreed, they didn't want that nuclear plant in the valley. Jerry Owen talked about how he knew ways to wreck it."

"We can't let them do that," Dan Forrester said. He leaned forward and spoke intently. He had forgotten where he was, the long tramp northward, possibly even Hammerfall itself. "We have to save the power plant. We can rebuild a civilization if we have electricity."

"He's right," Rick Delanty said. "It's important—"

"It's important that we stay alive, too," Senator Jellison said. "But we have heard that the New Brotherhood has over a thousand troops, possibly many more. We can put five hundred in the field, and many of them will not be well armed. Few have any training. We will be lucky to save this valley."

"Dad," Maureen said. "I think Dr. Forrester has some ideas about that. He asked me about . . . Dan, why did you want to know about grease solvents and swimming-pool supply shops? What were you thinking about?"

Dan Forrester sighed again. "Maybe I shouldn't suggest it. I had an idea, but you may not like it."

"For God's sake, man," Al Hardy said. "If you know something that can help us, say it! What?"

"Well, you've probably already thought of it," Forrester said.

"Goddamm—" Christopher began.

Senator Jellison held up his hand. "Dr. Forrester, believe me, you won't offend us. Please, what did you have in mind?"

Forrester shrugged. "Mustard gas. Thermite bombs. Napalm. And I think we can make nerve gas, but I'm not sure."

There was a long silence, then Senator Jellison said, low and under his breath but everybody heard, "I will be dipped in shit."

The Expedition

Tim Hamner ate his dinner while Eileen packed clothing into a makeshift backpack. There was a strong chill wind coming down from the slopes of the Sierra. It blew wispy sleet past the cabin, but failed to find any chinks. Eileen's tiny kerosene lamp gave off a warm glow, and the stove kept the kitchen warm and dry. Tim was relaxed for the moment. He stared into the vent opening of the stove, watching the tiny blue flames curl and rise. "Trouble rather the tiger in his lair," he said.

Eileen looked up. "What?"

"From the introduction of a science fiction story by Gordon Dickson. I don't know if it's a real quote or something Dickson made up. It went, 'Trouble rather the tiger in his lair than the sage among his books. For to you Kingdoms and their armies are things mighty and enduring, but to him they are but toys of the moment, to be overturned with the flick of a finger.' "

"Can he really do it?" Eileen asked.

"Forrester? He's a magician. If Forrester says he can make napalm and bombs and mustard gas, he can do it." Tim sighed. "I wish we didn't have to. I was brought up to hate poison gas. Of course, I don't suppose it matters whether it's

541

gas or a bullet; dead is dead." He reached for his rifle, then took an oily rag from a bag on the table and began wiping the barrel.

"Do you have to go?" Eileen demanded.

"We agreed not to talk about it," Tim said.

"I don't care what we agreed. I don't want you to go. I . . ."

"I don't like the idea much myself," Tim said. "But what can we do? Forrester insisted. He'll stay here and make terrible weapons to defend the Stronghold if we send reinforcements to the power plant." Tim shook his head in admiration. "He's the only man in the world who could blackmail both the Senator and George Christopher. You wouldn't think he'd have the nerve, with all those apologies and eye blinking and everything, but he sure as hell wasn't going to say one word more about weapons until they promised."

"But why you?" Eileen demanded. She packed a newly knitted pair of socks. The wool had been carded from dog fur.

"What else am I good for?" Hamner asked. "You know better than me. You helped Hardy work up the schedules. I can't farm, I'm not as good an engineer as Brad, I don't ride horses well so I can't go with Christopher's Paul Revere troop . . . I may as well be part of the suicide squad."

"For God's sake don't talk like that." She left off the packing and came over to stand beside him.

He patted her belly. "Don't worry, I'll be back if I have to swim." He laughed. "Or pull our famous Flying Dutchman act and drive over the water again. I intend to see our son or possibly daughter. Or twins? You already look somewhat like an inverted question mark." Dammit, he was babbling, the fear was showing through.

"Tim . . ."

"Don't make it harder, Eileen."

"No. Well, you're all packed."

Tim punched the button on his watch. "We have an hour before we leave," he said. He stood and grabbed her. "Gotcha."

"Tim . . ."

"Ye-ess?"

Whatever she had been about to say, she said instead, "Did you get our reservations at the Savoy?"

"They were all booked up. I found someplace closer."

"Goody."

There were a dozen of them, led by Johnny Baker. Three of Deke Wilson's ranchers. Jack Ross, a Christopher brother-in-law. Tim wasn't surprised to see Mark Czescu and Hugo Beck among the volunteers. He recognized most of the others as valley ranchers, but one man, middle-aged and far too small for his clothes, was a stranger. Tim went over to him and introduced himself.

"Jason Gillcuddy," the man said. "I saw your TV programs. Glad to meet you."

"Gillcuddy. I've heard that name. Where?"

Jason smiled. "From my books, maybe? More likely you heard it here. Harry and I are both married to Donna, used to be Donna Adams. Her mother raised pluperfect hell about that."

"Oh." Tim followed Gillcuddy's look to Harry and a slim girl, blonde, not more than nineteen, standing near Eileen. He pitched his backpack into the truck. The rifle was slung over his shoulder. "How long?" he asked.

"They're waiting for something," Jason said. "I don't know what. No point in standing here. See you." Jason went over to Harry and the girl. She embraced Gillcuddy while Harry stood watching.

Wonder what Hardy thinks of that? Tim thought. He likes everything neat. And what does it make Jason and Harry? Brothers-in-law? Husbands-in-law? The arrangement made sense, with Harry out on his rounds for weeks at a time. Someone had to work the Chicken Ranch while Harry was out. Tim found Eileen with Maureen Jellison. "My comet sure plays games with cultural patterns," he said. He inclined his head toward Harry and Jason and Donna.

Eileen took his hand and held tightly.

"Hi, Maureen," Tim said. "Where's General Baker?"

"He'll be out in a moment."

Eileen and Maureen and Donna, they all had the same look. Tim had an impulse to laugh, but he didn't. They looked exactly like the women in the old John Wayne movies, when the cavalry troop was about to ride out through the gates. Had they seen the movies, or had John Ford captured a truth?

A light truck drove up, and two ranch-hands jumped down. Chief Hartman got out of the cab. "Easy with that," Hartman said. He looked around, then came over to Tim and Maureen. "Where's the General?" he asked.

"Inside."

"Okay. Best more than one knows anyway. Mr. Hamner, come look. We brought your radio gear." He pointed to the boxes that the ranchers were loading in with the expedition baggage. "The set runs off a car battery. That other box contains a beam antenna. You get that to the highest place you can find, and point it at us. From the power plant that's twenty degrees magnetic. Maybe, just maybe, we'll be able to hear you. We'll listen from five minutes to until five minutes after each hour. Channel thirteen. And assume the New Brotherhood's listening in. You got all that?"

"Yes." Tim repeated the instructions.

Johnny Baker came out of the house. He carried a rifle and wore a pistol on his belt. Maureen went to him and held him possessively.

There certainly were a lot of grim faces showing tonight. Tim decided that looking nonchalant was a waste of effort. Mark Czescu looked indecently cheerful; but that fit. Tim had heard him asking Harry the Mailman, in all innocence, "What are we calling this, the War of Harry's Truck?" Mark didn't know why they were fighting, and didn't care.

Hugo Beck was grimmer than the rest. If the Angels got their hands on the apostate, he'd have reason . . . but maybe he had reason now. Nobody was going near him. Poor bastard.

"What the hell are we waiting on?" Jack Ross demanded. He was built like a Christopher, a massive, choleric man. There were three fingers missing from his left hand and a scar that ran clear to his elbow, the result of an argument with a harvesting machine. His fine blond mustache was nearly invisible, a mere token.

"The scouts," Baker said. "It shouldn't be long."

"Yeah, sure."

Rick Delanty seemed in a foul mood. He went to Baker, ignoring the others standing by. "Johnny, I want to go with you."

"No."

"Dammit—"

"I've explained before," Baker said. He took Delanty off to one side. Tim could barely hear their voices. He strained to catch it, eavesdropping or no. "We can't risk all of the last astronauts," Baker said. "We can't leave one Russian here alone, and Russians wouldn't be any use anyway. This is a diplomatic mission. They might not be welcome."

"Fine. Leave them here and take me."

"And who watches out for them, Rick? They're our friends, and we promised. 'Visit our home,' we said. 'You'll have a native guide,' we said. You saw the way some of these farmers reacted. Russians are not popular just now."

"Neither are blacks."

"But you are. You're a space hero here! Rick, we promised them, and *we* came down in *their* capsule."

"Fine. You stay. I'll go. Dammit, Johnny, that power plant is important."

"I know that. Now, just remember where we're going, and tell me what anyone will think if he sees a black man's face from a distance. You can't play ambassador. Shut up and soldier, Colonel Delanty."

Rick was silent for a moment. Finally: "Yes, sir. I'd file a protest, but I don't know the Inspector General's address."

Baker clapped Delanty on the shoulder, then came back to Tim. If he'd caught him eavesdropping, he didn't mention it. "They want you inside," he said.

Hamner blinked. "Right." He went up to the ranch house, still holding Eileen's hand. The swelling of her pregnancy was just beginning to show, but it threw her balance off, so that she stumbled and had to brace herself against his arm.

Jellison, Hardy and Dan Forrester were in the living room. Forrester thrust papers encased in a Ziploc Bag into Tim's hands. "These are some more ideas I had. General Baker has copies too, but . . ."

"Right," Tim said.

"If you get a chance, scout out the west shore," Al Hardy said. "We'd like to know what's going on over there. And there's a list of stuff you might be able to use."

Tim looked at the papers in his hands. Through the plastic he could see only the top sheet. It was a list: iron oxide (found in paint stores, called red pigment, red spall; also found in the rust pile in automobile wrecking yards; or can be scraped from any rusty iron and ground finely); powdered aluminum (found in paint stores as a pigment); plaster of paris . . .

The list was long, and most of the items seemed useless. Tim knew better. He knew that on the other sheets in the stack were the means for turning those common items into deadly weapons. He looked at Forrester. "I'd hate to have you mad at me."

Forrester looked embarrassed. "I remember everything I read, and I read a lot."

"Have you ever done any skin diving?" Al Hardy asked. Strange question. "Yes."

"Thought so," Hardy said. "Turns out you and Randall weren't the only ones to think of that idea. The fishing camp down by Porterville salvaged some scuba gear. They're selling it to us along with the boats." Hardy looked darkly at Forrester. "This expedition is expensive. You wouldn't believe how expensive. We had to trade for the boats, and they'll use gasoline we don't have enough of. And all those sacks of stuff you're taking with you. Good fertilizer . . ."

"I'm sorry," Forrester said.

"Sure," Hardy said. "Hamner, there are towns out in the valley. Under water. We're hoping either you or Baker will have a chance to do some salvage work. Both of you have scuba experience, but the only wet suit we could buy turns out to be small. I don't know if Baker can get into it, which means you may have to do the diving. There's another list in that packet of papers Forrester gave you. Stuff we need. But give his first priority."

"And we want information," Senator Jellison said. He sounded tired, and Tim thought he looked gray, but perhaps it was only the pale yellow kerosene light. "We've had short radio contact with people on the other side of the San Joaquin Sea," Jellison said. "There were oil fields out there, lots of them, and there seem to be survivors. They were friendly enough on the radio, but you never can tell. Anyway, find out what you can. Maybe the power-plant people know. We can use allies. Baker has authority to make deals. You don't, but you know conditions here better than Johnny does. He'll need your advice."

Tim looked thoughtful. "Everybody has assumed the people at the power plant will be friendly," he said. "What if they're not? I thought my observatory . . . anyway, what if they're not?"

"Baker has instructions on that," Jellison said. "Warn them about the cannibals and leave them alone."

"And see what you can salvage out in the valley," Hardy said. "We can't let all this manpower and gasoline go to waste."

A rancher put his head in the door. "Scouts are back," he said. "It's okay. We have the boats."

Hardy nodded. "All right. Hamner, get your goodbyes said. Now I'll go find out exactly what all this cost us," he said, with distaste. He went.

Under the black beard Dan Forrester's lips were a hard,

thin line. Forrester didn't always show his anger. It showed now only in the way he fumbled for words before saying, "Giving up the power plant would not turn out to be an optimum solution."

"We'll save it. You guard the home front." Tim went back out into the cold night. Four hours until dawn.

Maureen blinked back tears as the truck drove away. She watched the taillight dwindle and vanish on the highway south, and stood in the cold wind long after she couldn't see it any longer.

It all made sense. If they had to send off an expedition, Johnny Baker was the logical man to lead it. People knew who he was. They'd recognize him, or at least know of him, and nobody else in the Stronghold qualified that way. George Christopher and the others on horses could move down the east side of the valley, staying up in the hills, looking for ranchers, organized valleys, anyone to recruit for the attack on the cannibals; but no one across the Sea would have heard of the Christophers, and everyone knew Johnny Baker. Johnny was a hero.

She didn't want to go inside. In there Al Hardy and Harvey Randall would be working with Dr. Forrester, planning tomorrow's work, locating supplies and chemicals that Forrester could use. Her father might be there, too. She didn't want to see Harv just then, and she didn't want to see her father.

"I'm a goddam prize in a goddam contest," she said aloud, "in a goddam fairy tale. Why doesn't anyone ever speak for the princess?" She could hardly blame her father for the symmetry of it all, though she was tempted. But it was all so pat, it made so much sense.

The Stronghold had to have allies. People who might join to fight the cannibals were in the hills, where men could go only on foot or horseback. They would be locals, most of them. It made good sense to send twenty locals into the hills on horseback, led by a local, a farmer, a fine horseman: George Christopher.

And the power plant had to be saved, thanks to Forrester's gentle extortion. But, cut off from events by the sea around them, how were the defenders to know their friends from their enemies? Best to send a man with some military authority, a man any adult American would recognize in a fog on a moonless night: General Johnny Baker.

Which left Harvey Randall free to work with Dr. Forrester, whom he had known in a previous life, on the weapons to defend the Stronghold.

So the knights were riding off in three directions, and he who came back with the prize—his life—would inherit the princess and half the kingdom. They could all come back. It could happen. But when did the princess ever get her choice?

"Hello."

She didn't turn to look. "He's so damn visible."

"Yeah," Harv said. He wondered, but in silence, how the Angels who hated the atomic plant so much would feel about the space program. Someone like Jerry Owen would recognize Baker as fast as any power-plant operator would. "That's why he's there," he said. When she didn't answer, didn't even turn, he went back inside.

There were four boats for twenty men. Two were cabin cruisers, small fiberglass boats used in inland lakes, powered by outboards. There was a twenty-foot open dory, also with an outboard; and there was the *Cindy Lu*. She was a bomb. Twenty feet long, and only wide enough for two people to sit in the tiny cockpit. The rest of the boat was an enormous inboard engine covered with bright chrome.

Cindy Lu had lost most of her bright tangerine metallic-flake paint. The chrome didn't glow when Johnny Baker played a flashlight across her. She was a nautical drag-racer, but she wouldn't go very fast with an oil-drum barge hooked behind her and loaded with supplies.

"This was quite a find," said Horrie Jackson. "We can use her to—"

"She's gorgeous! Who cares what she's for?"

The fishing-camp leader chortled. "Isn't she just? But the Senator wanted something that could tow a load. And since I'm comin' along I'd as soon have something fast. Just in case we have to run away from anything."

"We're not going there to run away," Baker told him.

Jackson's grin was wide. He was missing a tooth. "General, I'm going because they hired me. Some of my boys are going because the Senator's man said he'd take their women

548

up into that valley and keep 'em there for the winter. I don't know what the last astronaut is doing here."

"Don't you care?" Baker demanded. "Isn't it worth saving? It could be the last nuclear power plant on Earth!"

Jackson shook his head. "General, after what I've seen I can't think more than a day ahead, and right now all I know is you're going to feed me awhile. I remember . . ." His brow furrowed. "Seems so long ago. The papers were screaming about how the gov'mint was putting an atomic plant right next to us and if a melt-down happened . . . I don't remember. But I can't get excited about saving an atomic plant."

"Or anything else," Jason Gillcuddy said. "Disaster syndrome."

"Let's board," Horrie Jackson said coldly.

Tim Hammer made his choice: One of the boats had an awning, protection from the drizzle. He sat next to Hugo Beck. The man must have had enough of being avoided. Mark and Gillcuddy boarded the same boat. Horrie Jackson took the pilot's chair, then looked around to find that Johnny Baker was in command of *Cindy Lu*.

"I don't suppose she'll be too fast for an astronaut," he called, "but you won't get so wet under the awning."

Baker laughed. "What's a little rain to a man in love?" He activated *Cindy Lu* with a marrow-freezing, mind-numbing roar.

The small fleet moved cautiously out from shore, out into the inland sea. The water was dangerous with treetops, floating debris, telephone poles. Horrie Jackson led the way in the cabin boat, going very slowly. The top of a silo marked where a submerged barn must be; he steered wide. He seemed to know exactly where to turn to find the channel among the islands and obstructions.

The night was not quite pitch black. A dull glow beyond the drizzle marked where the moon was hidden by the constant cloud cover.

Mark fished out corn dodgers and passed them around. They had bags of cornmeal with them, and enough of the round cornmeal cakes to feed them while they crossed the water. Enough, until Hugo Beck put one in Horrie Jackson's hand.

"Hey!" Horrie cried. He bit it, then stuffed it whole in his mouth and tried to talk around it. "Dried fish just by my foot. Pass it around. It's all yours. I want as much of these things as you can spare, and all for me."

Mark was stunned. "Just what is so extra special about corn dodgers?"

Horrie got his mouth clear. "They aren't fish, that's what! Look, for all of me the whole world is starving except us. We aren't starving. For a couple of months we were, then all of a sudden there was fish everywhere, but only two kinds. Catfish and goldfish. The only problem is cooking them. We—"

"Hold up!" That was Mark. "You didn't really say goldfish, did you?"

"They look like goldfish, but big. That's what you're eating now. Gary Fisher says goldfish can grow to any size. The catfish were always there, in the streams. You want me to shut up? Pass me that bag of corn dodgers."

They passed Horrie the bag. Tim ate with enthusiasm. He hadn't tasted fish in a long time, and it was good, even dried. He wondered why there were suddenly so many fish, then considered how their food supply had exploded. All those dead things floating in the water. It only bothered him for a moment.

"But why goldfish?" Mark Czescu wondered.

Gillcuddy laughed at him. "Easy to picture. Here's a rising freshwater sea, and here's a living room with a goldfish bowl in it. The water rises, breaks through the picture window, and suddenly the most docile of household pets is whirled out of his cage into the great wide world. 'Free at last!' he cries." Gillcuddy bit into a filet of goldfish and added, "Freedom has its price, of course."

Horrie ate corn dodgers in single-minded silence.

Mark rummaged through his pockets and came up with a tiny scrap of cigar. He popped it into his mouth and chewed. "I would kill for a Lucky Strike," he said.

"You may well have the opportunity," Jason Gillcuddy said.

Mark grinned in the dark. "I can hope. That's why I volunteered."

"Really?" said Tim.

"Not really. Anything beats breaking rocks."

Jason Gillcuddy laughed at a private thought. "Let's see," he said. "You'd kill for a Lucky Strike. I suppose you'd maim for a Tareyton?"

"Right!" Mark roared approval.

"And shout insults for a Carlton," Hugo Beck said. They all laughed, but it died quickly; they were still nervous around Hugo Beck.

"Now you know why I'm here," Mark said. "But why you, Tim?"

Tim shook his head. "It seemed like a good idea at the time. No, forget I said that. It feels like I owe somebody something . . ." The people he'd driven past. The cops working to unearth a hospital while a tidal wave marched toward them. ". . . and Eileen's pregnant."

When he didn't go on, Horrie Jackson called without looking back. "So?"

"So I'll have children. Don't you see?"

"I'm here," Hugo Beck said without being asked, "because nobody at the Stronghold would look at me."

"I'm glad you're here," Tim said. "If anyone wants to surrender, you tell 'em what it means."

Beck chewed that. "They don't *have* to know about me, do they?"

A look passed among them. "Not till they have to," Tim said quickly, and he turned to Jason. "You're the one I don't understand. You're Harry's friend. They couldn't possibly make you volunteer."

Jason chuckled. "No, I'm a genuine volunteer, all right. Had to. You ever read my books?" He went on before any of them could answer. "Full of the marvels of civilization, what great things science does for us. Now how could I not volunteer for this crazy mission?" Gillcuddy looked out at the dark night and darker water. "But there's places I'd rather be."

"Sure," Tim said. "The Savoy Hotel in London. With Eileen. That's what I want."

"And Hugo wants the Shire back," Mark said.

"No." Hugo Beck's voice was firm. "No, I want civilization." When nobody stopped him he went on, eagerly. "I want a hot car and some practice talking a cop out of giving me a ticket. I want *Gone With The Wind* on a noncommercial channel, no interruptions. I want dinner at Mon Grenier restaurant with a woman who can't spell 'ecology' but she's read the *Kama Sutra*."

"And spotted the mistakes," Mark said.

"You knew Mon Grenier?" Gillcuddy demanded.

"Sure. I lived in Tarzana. You've been there?"

"Mushroom salad," said Gillcuddy.

"Bouillabaisse. With a chilled Moselle," Tim said. They talked of meals they'd never eaten and now never would.

"And I missed most of my chances," Hugo Beck said. "I had to start a goddam commune. Fellows, let me tell you, it doesn't work."

"I'd never have guessed," Jason said. Hugo Beck retreated from the irony in Gillcuddy's voice, and the writer said quickly, "Anyway, we carry miracles. I think." He kicked a large sack that lay in the bottom of the boat. "Will this stuff work?"

"Forrester says it will," Mark said, "especially if you give it a good kick. But we don't have much with us. Hardy bargains hard."

Horrie Jackson looked back from his place at the wheel. "Jesus, I'll say he does. *I'm* here."

The drizzle turned gray and lighter gray. Ninety-three million miles eastward, the Sun must be placidly unaffected by the greatest disaster in written history. The boats floated on an endless sea dotted with debris. The corpses of men and animals were gone now. Horrie Jackson increased speed, but not by a lot. There were logs and bits of houses, inflated tires, the jetsam of civilization. Treetops showed like rectangular arrays of puffy bushes; but there were single trees, and some were just submerged. Any of that could tear the bottom out of their boat.

Hugo Beck called across the boat, "Hey, Mark. What would you do for a Silva Thin?"

"Get your hand off my knee and I'll tell you."

Jackson steered by compass through the gloomy dawn. There was no one else on the lake, only the small flotilla. *Cindy Lu* labored in the rear, a big motor with a tiny boat molded around her, roaring her frustration at the weight she must pull. Horrie bellowed above the sound of his own motor, "I'll come back with a boatload of fish, enough to feed everyone in that power plant. What I want in return is enough of those corn things to fill that gunnysack the fish was in. Now, it's not that big a sack. . . ."

Tim Hamner peered ahead into the rain. Something ahead? At first he saw an island with rectangular shapes jutting upward. Not unusual . . . but as they got closer he saw that some of the shapes were cylinders, and *big*. He looked for motion, human shapes. They had to have heard *Cindy Lu*'s roar.

■

Alim Nassor found Hooker and Jerry Owen in the command post. Maps were spread across the table, and Hooker was moving small cardboard units on them. A voice cut through the fabric wall to thunder in Alim's ear.

"For their pride is the pride of the magicians of old, who thought to force all Nature to their bidding. But ours is the pride of those who trust in the Lord. Our need is not for the magicians' weapons, but only for the Lord's favor. . . ."

Hooker looked up in disgust. "Crazy bastard."

Alim shrugged.

They needed Armitage, and despite the cynical talk they used when Armitage wasn't around, most of them at least partly believed in the preacher's message. "Well, I got nothing against wrecking the damn power plant," Hooker said. "It's got to go, I can see that. But it's—"

"Sure! It takes a lot of industry to support something like that." Jerry Owen spoke with no idea that he was interrupting. "If we have that plant, we'll want to use the electricity. First because it's convenient, then because we *need* it, and then it's too late! Then we'll need all the other industry to keep the nuclear plant running. Industrial society all over again, and that's the end of freedom and brotherhood, because we'll need wage slavery to—"

"I *said* I believe you. Just for God's sake stop with the fucking speeches."

"Then what's the problem?" Owen asked.

"Well, the plant isn't going anywhere, is it? It'll wait till we're ready. The question is *when?*" Hooker said. "Look, when we started off all we wanted was a place to hide. Like the goddam Senator has, someplace we can defend. Someplace *ours*. Well, we can't do that."

"You gave that up the first time you stewed a man."

"Think I don't know that, motherfucker?" Hooker's voice had a tightly controlled edge to it. "So now we're on a roller coaster. We can't stop. We have to keep growing. Take the whole goddam state. Maybe more. But we sure as hell can't stop now."

He pointed to the map. "And the Senator's valley sits right here. We can't go north of that till we take his place. Hell, we can't even hold White River and those hills as long as the Senator's people can come raiding our territory anytime they want to. One thing we learned in 'Nam: You leave the enemy a place to retreat and get organized, what they call a sanctuary, and you *cannot* beat him. And you know what that Senator is doing?" Hooker ran his finger along the line of hills to the east of the San Joaquin Sea. "He's sent fifty men on horses up in there. They're recruiting. On our flanks. Now I don't know how many there are up in those hills, but if they all get together they can do us trouble. So. We don't give 'em a chance to do it. We hit the Senator, and we do it now, before he gets organized."

"I see," said Jerry Owen. He stroked his blond beard. "And the Prophet wants us to go after the power plant—"

"Right," Hooker said. "Pull the whole army south. You see what that *does* to us? But how the hell do I talk that crazy bastard into letting me finish off the Senator's place before we go after that power plant?"

Owen looked thoughtful. "Maybe you don't. You know, I don't think they'd have more than fifty, sixty people in that plant. Not fighting people. They could have a lot more women and kids, but they won't have much of an army. And they're on an island out there, they can't have much food. Not much ammunition. No real defenses . . ."

"You saying it will be easy to knock off?" Alim Nassor said.

"How easy?" Hooker asked. "How many?"

Jerry shrugged. "Give me a couple of hundred men. And some of the artillery. Mortars. Hit the turbines with mortars and that finishes the electricity. They can't operate the nuclear reactor without electricity. They need it for the pumps. Hit the turbines, and the whole thing melts down—"

"Will it blow up?" Alim asked. The idea excited him and scared him. "Big mushroom cloud? What about fallout? We'd have to get out from under that fast, wouldn't we?"

Jerry Owen looked at him with amusement. "Nope. No great white light. No big mushroom cloud. Sorry."

"I'm not sorry," Hooker said. "Once we get that place, can you make me some atom bombs?"

"No."

"You don't know how?" Hooker showed his disappointment. Owen had been talking like he knew it all.

And Owen was offended. "Nobody does. Look, you can't make atom bombs out of nuclear fuel. Wrong stuff. It wasn't designed for that. Wasn't designed to blow up, either. Hell, we probably won't get a real melt-down. They put safety precautions on their safety precautions."

Alim said, "You guys always said they weren't safe."

"No, of course they're not, but safe compared to *what?*" Jerry Owen waved north toward the ruined dam and the drowned city of Bakersfield: cubistic islands rising from a filthy sea. "That was a hydroelectric plant. Was that safe? People who wouldn't go near an atomic plant lived downstream from dams."

"So why do you hate that place?" Hooker asked. "Maybe . . . maybe we ought to save it."

"Goddammit, no," Jerry Owen said.

Alim shot Hooker a look. Now you've started him off again, it said.

"It's too much, don't you see that?" Owen demanded. "Atomic power makes people think you can solve problems with technology. Bigger and bigger. More quick fixes. You have the power so you use it and soon you need *more* and then you're ripping ten billion tons a year of coal out of the earth. Pollution. Cities so big they rot in the center. Ghettos. Don't you see? Atomic power makes it easy to live out of balance with nature. For awhile. Until finally you can't get back in balance. The Hammer gave us a chance to go back to living the way we were evolved to live, to be kind to the Earth. . . ."

"All right, dammit," Hooker said. "You take two hundred men and two mortars and go shuck that plant. Make sure the Prophet knows what you're doing. Maybe he'll shut up long enough to let me organize." Hooker stared at the map. "You go play, Owen. We got to go after the real enemy." He'll ask for volunteers, Hooker thought, and he smiled. The crazies would go with Owen and leave Hooker alone for awhile.

The room Adolf Weigley took Tim to was beautiful. Granted that it was crowded: A massive wave of cables surged through a wall, divided, subdivided, ran in metal raceways overhead. But there were lights, electric lights! Neatly enameled green panels lined two walls, busy with dials and lights and switches, and clean with the dust-filtered cleanliness of an operating room. Tim asked, "What is this, the main control room?"

Weigley laughed. He was chronically cheerful, free from the jumpiness of disaster syndrome, and elaborately casual about all the technology. A baby-smooth face made him look younger than he was; the Stronghold men generally wore beards. "No, it's a cable-spreading room," he said. "But it's the only place we've got that you can sleep in. Uh . . . it wouldn't be smart to push any buttons." His smile was sly and partly concealed.

Tim laughed. "Not me." He gazed euphorically at fire extinguishers and winking lights and massive cables, everything precisely in place, all glowing in indirect lighting. Power hummed softly in his ear.

Dolf said, "Drop your backpack over there. There'll be others sleeping in here, too. Mind you stay out of the way. Duty operators have to get in here. Sometimes they have to work *fast*." His grin faded. "And there's a lot of voltage in some of those lines. Stay out of the way."

"Sure," said Tim. "Tell me, Dolf, what's your job here?" Weigley seemed too young to be an engineer, but he wasn't built like one of the construction workers.

"Power system apprentice," Weigley said. "Which means we do everything. Got that stuff settled? Let's go. They told me to show you around and help you set up the radio."

"Right. . . . What does it mean, 'everything'?"

Weigley shrugged. "When I'm on duty I sit in the control room and drink coffee and play cards until the duty operator decides something needs working on. Then I go do it. That could be anything at all. Get a reading on a dial. Put out a fire. Throw a switch. Turn a valve. Repair a break in a cable. Anything."

"So you're a robot for the engineers."

"Engineers?"

"The duty operators."

"They aren't engineers. They got their job doing what I do. One day I'll be an operator, if there's anything left to operate. Hell, Hobie Latham started by walking on snowshoes in the Sierra, measuring the snow to find out how much spring runoff we could expect, and he's Operations Manager now."

They went outside into the muddy yard. The big earthen levees loomed high around them. Men worked on them, putting up forms while others poured in concrete to reinforce the cofferdam that kept SJNP safe. Others did incomprehensible things with forklifts. The yard was a bustle of activity, seemingly chaotic, but everyone seemed to know what he was doing.

It made Tim feel curiously vulnerable, to stand inside the Project grounds and know that the water outside was thirty feet above them. San Joaquin Nuclear Project was a sunken island, surrounded by levees thrown up by bulldozers. Pumps took care of seepage through the earthen walls. One break in the levees, or a day without power to the pumps, would drown them.

The Dutch had lived with that knowledge all their lives, and what they feared had come to pass; Holland couldn't conceivably have survived the tidal waves following Hammerfall.

"I think the best place for your radio is on one of the cooling towers," Dolf said. "But those are cut off from the plant." He climbed a board staircase to the top of the levee and pointed. Across a hundred feet of water the cooling towers loomed up, four of them set inside a smaller levee that had leaked badly. Their bases were partly flooded. A thick white plume rose from each of the towers, climbed into the sky, growing ghostly, finally vanishing.

"They won't have any trouble finding this place," Tim said.

"No."

"Hey, I thought nuclear plants were nonpolluting."

Dolf Weigley laughed. "That's no pollution. Steam, that's all it is. Water vapor. How could it be smoke? We're not burning anything." He pointed to a narrow planked footbridge leading from the levee to the nearest tower. "That's the only way over unless we get out a boat. But I still think it's the best place for the radio."

"So do I, but we can't carry the antenna on that plank."

"Sure we can. You ready? Let's get the stuff."

Tim gingerly climbed the slanting ladder that zigzagged up the side of the big redwood tower. Once again he was impressed with the organization at SJNP. Weigley had gone into the yard and come back with men to carry the radio, car batteries and antenna, and they'd skipped along the narrow plank bridge with all the stuff in one trip, then gone back to work. No questions, no arguments, no protests. Maybe Hammerfall had changed more than marriage patterns: Tim remembered from the papers that SJNP had been plagued with strikes and arguments over which union would represent whom, overtime pay, living conditions. . . . Labor troubles had delayed the station almost as long as the environmentalists who'd done their best to kill it.

He reached the top of the fifty-foot tower. He was about thirty feet above the level of the sea. The base of the tower was surrounded by a leaking dam, and pumps worked to keep its intakes clear. There was a strong wind into the tower at its bottom.

The thing was big, over two hundred feet in diameter. The deck where Tim stood was a large metal plate pierced by innumerable holes. Pumps brought water up and poured it onto the deck, where it stood a few inches high. It trickled down into the tower and vanished. Above him a dozen smaller cylindrical columns jutted twenty feet above the deck. Steam poured out of each one. The deck vibrated with the hum of pumps.

"This is a good place for the radio," Tim said. He looked doubtfully out across the San Joaquin Sea. "But it's a little exposed."

Weigley shrugged. "We can put some sandbags up. Build a shelter. And we can string a telephone line from here back to the plant. Question is, do you want the radio here?"

"Let's find out."

It took an hour to get the beam antenna set up and clamped onto one of the smaller rising venturi columns. Tim connected the CB set to the batteries. They carefully rotated the beam antenna to point twenty degrees magnetic, and Tim looked at his watch. "They won't be listening for a quarter-hour. Let's take a break. Tell me how things are going here. We were really surprised to find out you were here, that the plant was going."

Weigley found a perch on the rail. "It surprises *me*, sometimes," he said.

"Were you here when . . . ?"

"Yeah. None of us believed the comet would hit us, of course. As far as Mr. Price was concerned, it was just another working day. He was mad about absenteeism. A lot of the crew didn't show up. Then, when it *did* hit, that just made it worse. We didn't have all our people."

"I still don't see how you could do it," Tim said.

"Price is a genius," Weigley said. "As soon as we knew, even before the earthquake, he was getting things set for survival. He had those bulldozers out scraping up a levee before the rain hit us. He sent me and some others out into the valley to the railroad, to fill up the tank trucks. Diesel fuel, gasoline, we got all we could. And there was a boxcar on the siding, full of flour and beans, and Mr. Price made us get all of it. We're sure glad he did. There's not much variety, but we didn't starve. Why you laughing?"

"The fishermen feel the same way."

"Who doesn't? Can you *believe* you'll never taste a banana again? We could use some orange juice, for that matter. We're worried about scurvy."

"The orange tree is extinct in California. Sometimes we can dig some Tang out of a market." The longer Tim looked at that wall of earth between him and the San Joaquin Sea, the bigger it got. "Dolf, how could you have put that up while the valley was flooding?"

"We couldn't have. It's a crazy story. The original idea

was to put the plant over nearer to Wasco. Mr. Price wanted it up here, on the ridge, because the blowdown from the cooling towers would drain better, we wouldn't have to dig the ponds as deep. The Department's managers didn't like that. Made the plant more visible."

"Oh, but it's beautiful! It's like a 1930s *Amazing Stories* cover. The *future!*"

"That's what Mr. Price said. Anyway, they did put the plant up here on the ridge."

It wasn't much of a ridge, of course; no more than a low rolling hill. The plant wasn't more than twenty feet higher than the surrounding valley.

"And after they did the work, the Department got scared and they built the levees," Weigley said. "Not for any real reason. Just to *hide* the plant so the environmentalists wouldn't think about it when they drove along Interstate Five." Weigley's lips tightened. "And *then* some of the bastards who tried to kill the plant raised hell because we spent the extra money on the levee! But it came in handy. All we had to do was bulldoze up enough dirt to fill the gaps, the places where the roads and railway came in through the screening banks, and a good thing, too. That water rose *fast* after Hammerfall."

"I'll bet. I drove over that sea," Tim said.

"How's that?"

Tim explained. "Heard any stories about Flying Dutchmen?"

Weigley shook his head. "But we haven't had much contact with outsiders. Mayor Allen didn't think it would be a good idea."

"Allen. I saw him. How'd he get here?"

"Showed up just before the water got too deep. He was in City Hall when the tidal wave came through Los Angeles. Man, has he got a story to tell! Anyway, he showed up the next day with a dozen cops and City Hall people. You know, Los Angeles owned the plant, before Hammerfall—"

"So Mayor Allen is the boss here."

"No! Mr. Price is in charge. The mayor's a guest. Just like you. What does he know about power plants?"

Tim didn't point out that it was Weigley who'd told him the mayor was the one who discouraged outside contacts. "So you've ridden out the end of the world," Tim said. "By keeping the plant going. What are you planning to do with it?"

Weigley shrugged. "That's up to Mr. Price. And don't

think it's been any soft job keeping things running. *Everything's* got to work, *all* the time. We can put out a thousand megawatts."

"That sounds like a lot of—"

"Ten million light bulbs." Weigley grinned.

"A lot, yeah. How long can you keep that up?"

"At full capacity, about a year. But we're not running full, and we won't ever be. It takes about ten megawatts to operate the plant. Cooling pumps, control equipment, the lights . . . you know. That's one percent of capacity, so we could keep that up for a hundred years. But then we've got another set of fuel elements, over in Number Two."

Tim looked back at the plant. Two enormous concrete domes, which contained the nuclear reactors. Each had a series of rectangular buildings attached that contained the turbines and control equipment.

"Number Two's not operational," Weigley said. "Getting her up will be our first job once the water's gone down. And then we'll be able to put twenty megawatts on line for somebody else to use. We can keep that up for fifty years."

"Fifty years." Tim thought about that. In fifty years the United States had gone from a horse-and-buggy to an automobile civilization; had opened mines, built cities, built industries; discovered electronics and computers; taken space flight from comic books to the Moon. And this one plant could put out more power than the whole United States generated in the Twenties. . . . "That's exciting. My God, it was *worth* coming here! Forrester was right, letting anything happen to this plant wouldn't be an optimum solution."

"Uh?" Weigley gave Tim a puzzled look.

Tim grinned. "Nothing. Time to try the radio out."

■

To enter the conference room was like walking into the past, straight into a Board of Directors meeting. It was all there, the long table with comfortable chairs, pads of paper, blackboards, chalk and erasers, even wooden pointers. Tim was jolted. He wondered what Al Hardy would give for a well-equipped conference room, and bulletin boards to hang maps and lists on, file cabinets . . .

There was an argument in progress. Johnny Baker waved Tim to a seat on his left. Tim whispered rapidly: The radio gave mostly static, but it worked; they had communications with the Stronghold. No further news. Baker whispered thanks and turned back to listen.

They looked like human scarecrows, diversely dressed, most of them armed, pale as ghosts except for Mayor Allen and a black Detective-Investigator. Their clothes were old, their shoes were worn. A few months ago they would have looked wildly out of place here. Now it was the room that was strange. The people were normal, except that they were so *clean.*

Tim wriggled inside his clothes. His hand patted his smooth-shaven cheek. Clean! There was hot water for bathing, and working electric razors. The washer-dryer hadn't stopped since the Stronghold party arrived. His shirt and shorts and socks were clean and dry. Tim wriggled and tried to listen. He was hearing the same sentence over and over again: "I didn't know there was going to be a goddam *army* after us."

Barry Price wasn't as large as the construction crew chief who confronted him, but there was no question who was in charge. Price wore khaki field clothing, bush jacket and a shirt bulging with pens; a pocket calculator hung from his belt; an assistant with a clipboard hovered nearby. His brush haircut and precisely trimmed pencil mustache made him look almost finicky. He said, "So what's changed? We were never popular."

"No, dammit, but a *cannibal* army?" It wasn't heat that made the crew chief sweat inside his hard hat. "Barry, we got to get *out* of here."

"There's nowhere to go."

"Nuts. West side of the sea. Anyplace. But we can't stay here! We cannot fight a whole army."

"We have to," Price said. "How can we let all this go down the drain? Robin, you worked as hard as anybody! We've got allies now—"

"Some allies. A dozen men." Robin Laumer leaned across the table toward Barry Price. They might have been alone in the room; certainly nobody was interrupting. "Look. Everything's got to work or nothing does, right?"

"Right."

"So they get one hit on the turbines, the switchyard, the cable rooms, the control rooms, and that's it! We're underwater, and nothing ever works again!"

"I know all that," Price said. "So we don't let them get one hit."

"Bullshit. Barry, I'm pulling out. Any of my people want

to come with me, I'll take. We'll give 'em back, but we're borrowing your boats—"

"Not mine you don't," Johnny Baker said. He sat at Barry Price's left, just across the table from Mayor Allen. "I did not bring boats to help evacuate this plant."

Laumer seemed about to argue; then he shrugged. "So I take the boats that were already here. One of 'em's mine anyway, that one I keep. But we're leaving."

He stalked out of the room. As he passed Tim Hamner, Tim told him, "You'll never be clean again." Laumer broke stride, then kept going.

Baker asked, "Shouldn't we stop him?"

"How?" Price demanded.

Baker dropped it. None of them were ready to use the only way they had of stopping Laumer. "So how many will go with him?"

"I don't know. Maybe twenty or thirty of the construction crew. Maybe not so many. We worked like slaves to save this plant. I don't think any of my operating people will leave."

"So you can still run the plant."

"I'm sure of that much," said Price.

Johnny turned to the Mayor. "How about your people? Especially your cops?"

"I doubt any will go," Bentley Allen said. "We had too damned much trouble getting here."

"That's good," Baker said. He saw the look on the Mayor's face. "That they won't run. And of course you're staying, Barry. . . ."

The effect on Price was disturbing. He didn't look nonchalant, or proud; he looked like a man in agony. "I have to stay," he said. "That ticket's already been paid for. No, you wouldn't know. When that goddam Hammer hit, I could go look for somebody in Los Angeles, or stay here and try to save the plant. I stayed." His jaw clenched. "So what do we do now?"

"I can't give you orders," Johnny said.

Price shrugged. "By me you can." He looked to Mayor Allen and got a nod. "Far as I'm concerned, Senator Jellison is in charge of this state. Maybe he's President. Makes more sense than the others."

"You too?" Johnny asked. "How many Presidents have you heard about?"

"Five. Colorado Springs; Moose Jaw, Montana; Casper, Wyoming . . . anyway, I'll take the Senator. Give us all the orders you want."

Johnny Baker spoke carefully. "You didn't understand me. *I've* got orders not to give *you* orders. Suggestions only."

Price looked uncomfortable and confused. Mayor Allen and an assistant whispered together, then Allen said, "Doesn't want the obligation?"

"Precisely," Baker said. "Look, I'm on your side. We've got to keep this plant going. But I don't control the Stronghold."

Mayor Allen said, "You may be the highest-ranking—"

"Try to give the Senator orders? Me? Bullshit!"

"Just a thought, General. All right, feudal obligations work both ways," Mayor Allen said. "At least they do if the King is Senator Jellison. So he wants to limit his obligations to us. So what *suggestions* do you have for us, General Baker?"

"I've given you some. Ways to build exotic weapons . . ."

Price nodded. "We're working on them. Actually, it only took thinking of them. You know, we've worked on defenses here, not enough, I guess, but none of us ever thought of poison gas. Incendiaries we knew about, but we didn't make enough. Or enough muzzle-loader cannon, either. I've got a crew on that right now. What else?"

"Lay in supplies. No water shortage, and you've got the power to boil it. There's dried fish coming, and you can catch more. Get set for a siege. Our information is that the New Brotherhood is serious about taking over all of California, and very serious about wrecking this plant."

"If Alim Nassor is involved, they're serious," Mayor Allen said. "Brilliant man, and determined as hell. But I don't see his motive. He was never involved in any of the anti-industrial movements. Quite the opposite. 'We're just getting into the game, and now you say you're shutting it down'—that approach."

"You're forgetting Armitage," Baker said. "Nassor and Sergeant Hooker together probably couldn't hold this army together. Armitage can. It's Armitage who wants the plant destroyed."

The Mayor pondered. "The Los Angeles area used to be famous for funny religions. . . ."

Tim was still hoping they wouldn't have to bring Hugo in. He spoke for Hugo: "If Islam was a funny religion, go ahead and laugh, Mayor. They're expanding that way. Join or get eaten, they assimilate everybody, one way or the other."

"If the plant goes, they'll never have another one," Barry Price said. "They must be crazy." Was he talking about the New Brotherhood or the Stronghold? Nobody asked.

But Baker stood up suddenly. "All right. We're here, with

our guns and Dr. Forrester's notes. Tim, you go try on that wet suit. Maybe we can dig up some of what we need to fight with. I wish I knew how much time we've got."

The policeman went up the slanting ladder slowly, carefully, with a fat sandbag balanced on his shoulder. He was sandy-haired and square-jawed, and his uniform was wearing through. Mark followed him with another sandbag. They added the bags to the barricade atop the cooling tower. By now Tim's radio was nearly walled in.

The man turned to confront Mark. He was Mark's own size, and angry. "We did not desert our city," he said.

"That wasn't what I meant." Mark resisted the urge to back up. "I only said most of us—"

"We were on duty," the policeman said. "I know at least a couple of us were watching TV if we could get to one. The Mayor was. I wasn't. First I knew, one of the girls was yelling that the comet had hit us. I stayed at my post. Then the Mayor came through collecting us. He herded us all into elevators and down to the parking garage and packed the women and some of the men into half a dozen station wagons that were already loaded with stuff. He put us cops on motorcycles for an escort and we headed for Griffith Park."

"Did you have any—"

"I had *no* idea what was happening," Patrolman Wingate said. "We got up into the hills, and the Mayor told us the comet had done some damage and we could ride it out here and go clean up the mess afterward. Oh, boy."

"Did you see the tidal wave?"

"Oh, boy. Czescu, there just wasn't anything left to clean up. It was all foam and mist down there, and some of the buildings were still sticking up, and Johnny Kim and the Mayor were yelling at each other and I was almost next to them, but what with the thunder and lightning and the tidal wave I couldn't hear a word. Then they got us together and headed north."

The policeman stopped. Mark Czescu respected his silence. They watched four boats leaving with Robin Laumer and part of his construction crew. There had been a shouting match when Laumer tried to claim some of the supplies, but the men with guns—including Mark and the Mayor's police—had won their point.

"We went through the San Joaquin in four hours," the policeman said, "and let me tell you, that was tricky driving.

We had the sirens, but we spent as much time off the road as on. We had to leave one of the wagons. We got here and it was already over the hubcaps, and that dike was a solid wall. We packed stuff from the wagons on our backs over the levees in the rain. When we'd done that, Price put us to work on the levees. He worked us like donkeys. Next morning it was an ocean out there, and it was six hours more before I got a shower."

"Shower."

The policeman turned to look at Mark. "What?"

"You said it so casually. Shower. A hot shower. Do you know how long . . . ? Skip it. All I ever said was, most of us had to do some running."

The policeman's nose almost touched Mark's. It was narrow, prominently bridged, a classic Roman nose. "We did not run. We were in the right place to put the city back together again afterward. Goddammit, there wasn't anything left! There's nothing left but this power plant, which the Mayor says is officially part of Los Angeles. We're here now. Nobody's going to hurt it."

"All *right*."

The four boats were dwindling with distance. A few of the remaining construction men had climbed the levee to watch them go—wistfully, perhaps. "I expect they'll be fishermen now," Mark said.

"Try to imagine how little I care," the policeman said. "Let's get to work."

●

Horrie Jackson cut the motor and let the boat drift to a stop. "Far as I can tell, Wasco is just under us," he said. "If it's not, there ain't much I can do about it."

Tim looked at the cold water and shuddered. The wet suit fit him, but there were loose spots, and it was going to be damned cold out there. He tested the air system. It worked. The tanks were fully charged; and that had been impressive, too. When the mechanics at SJNP hadn't had valves and fittings in stock, they simply went into the machine shop and *made* them. It was a reminder of another world, a world when you didn't have to make do with what was around, when you had some control.

"I keep thinking," Tim said. "If people's pet goldfish got loose, what happened to the *piranhas*?"

"Too cold for them," Jason Gillcuddy said, and he laughed.

"Yeah. Well, here goes." Tim climbed to the gunwale, sat balanced for a moment, and rolled off backward into the water.

The cold was a shock, but it wasn't as bad as he expected. He waved at the boat crew, then tried an experimental dive. The water was as black as ink. He could barely see his wrist compass and depth gauge. The gauge was another of the SJNP crew's miracles, fabricated and calibrated in a couple of hours. Tim turned on the sealed lantern. The beam gave him no more than ten feet of milky visibility.

The sea in Emerald Bay off Catalina had been clear as glass. He had flown through seaweed jungles rich with darting fish . . . long ago.

He kicked down into the white murk, searching for the bottom, and found it at sixty feet. There was no sound but the bubbles from his regulator, the sound of his breathing. A shape loomed up in front of him, monstrous, humpbacked; a Volkswagen, he saw when he got closer. He didn't look inside.

He followed the road. He passed an Imperial with hordes of fish swarming in and out of the broken windows. No buildings. More cars . . . and finally a gas station, but it had burned before it was flooded. He kept going. He would be out of air soon.

Finally, civilization: rectangular shadings in the murk. Visibility was too poor to let him be selective. The doors he tried were locked. Locked against the sea . . . He swam on until he found a smashed plate-glass window. It was frighteningly dark in there, but he forced himself to enter.

He was in a large room; at least it *felt* large. A dense cloud of white fog to one side proved to be a rack of paperback books turned to mush and floating particles. The mist followed him as he swam away. He found counters and shelves, racks and goods toppled to the floor. He coasted above the floor, finding treasure everywhere—lamps, cameras, radios, tape recorders, Tensor lamps, television sets, nose drops, spray cans of paint, plastic models, tropical fish tanks, batteries, soap, scouring pads, light bulbs, canned salted peanuts . . .

So many *things,* and mostly ruined. His air supply cut off abruptly; in panic he looked behind for his diving partner, then realized that despite all his training he was diving without a buddy. That was almost funny. You had to have more than one scuba outfit in the world before you could use the buddy system. He calmed himself and reached back to the air tanks, arm contorting to grasp the regulator valve and turn it to reserve. Now he had only a few moments, and he used them to scoop up objects and stuff them into the goody bag tied to his weight belt.

He left the store and surfaced. He was a long way from the boat. He waved until he had their attention, and let them come to him. He was exhausted when they hauled him aboard.

"Did you find any food?" Horrie Jackson wanted to know. "We found some food with that scuba stuff before we ran out of air. We get back to Porterville I can show you lots of places where there's food. You dive for it and we'll split."

Tim shook his head. He felt an infinite sadness. "That was a general store," he said.

"Can you find it again?"

"I think so. It's right under us." Probably he could, and there would be much to salvage; but in his exhaustion he could not feel any excitement over his find. He felt only a terrible sense of loss. He turned to Jason Gillcuddy as probably the only man who could understand—if anyone could.

"*Anyone* could walk in there and buy," Tim said. "Razor blades, Kleenex, calculators. Books. Anyone could afford to buy those; and if we all work very hard for a long time, maybe a few of us will have them again."

"What did you bring up?" Horrie Jackson demanded.

"General store," Adolf Weigley said. "Did you get any of that stuff on Forrester's list? Solvent? Ammonia? Any of that?"

"No." Tim held up the bag. When they opened it they found a bottle of liquid soap and a Kalliroscope. They all looked at him strangely—all but Jason Gillcuddy, who put his hand on Tim's shoulders. "You're not in shape to dive again today," he said.

"Give me half an hour. I'll go down again," Tim said.

Horrie Jackson dug further into Tim's goody bag. Fishhooks and fishing line. A vacuum tin of pipe tobacco. The peanuts: Horrie opened the tin, passed it around. Tim took a handful. They tasted like . . . a cocktail party in progress.

"Diving can do funny things to your head," he said, and knew at once that that wasn't the explanation. All the world that he had lost was down there under the water, turning to garbage.

Gillcuddy said, "Here. One sip left." He handed Tim a bottle of Heublein Whiskey Sour that Tim didn't even remember stowing. One sip, a blast of nostalgia on the palate, and he threw the bottle far over the water. And there, sinister specks on the eastern horizon, were the boats of the New Brotherhood.

"Start the motor. Horrie, start the motor quick. They'll cut us off," he said. He strained forward for details, catching his balance when the motor started up, but all he could see was a lot of little boats and one much larger . . . a barge, with *things* on it. "They've got a gun platform, I think."

Expendables

It was not their fault that no one had told them that the real function of an army is to fight and that a soldier's destiny—which few escape—is to suffer, and if need be, to die.

T. R. Fehrenbach, *This Kind of War*

Dan Forrester looked exhausted. He sat in the wheelchair Mayor Seitz had brought up from the valley convalescent home, and he was plainly fighting off sleep. He was padded against the cold: a blanket, a windbreaker with hood, flannel shirt and two sweaters, one of which was three sizes too big; that one he wore backward. A .22 bullet would not have reached his skin.

The dairy barn was unheated. Outside, the wind howled at twenty-five miles an hour, with gusts at twice that. It blew thin flurries of snow and sleet. The swaying gasoline lantern threw out a bright ring of light, leaving shadows of lunar blackness in the contours of the concrete barn.

Three men and two women took turns rotating the cement mixer by hand, while others shoveled powders into it. Two of red, one of aluminum powder, while the dry cement mixer turned. When the powders were well mixed, others took them out and put them in cans and jars, then cast plaster of paris around them.

Maureen Jellison came in and shook the snow from her hair. She watched from the door for a moment, then went to Forrester's wheelchair. He didn't see her, and she shook his shoulder. "Dan. Dr. Forrester."

He looked up with glazed eyes. "Yes?"

569

"Do you need anything? Coffee? Tea?"

He thought that through, slowly. "No. I don't drink coffee or tea. Something with sugar in it? A Coke. Or just sugar water. Hot sugar water."

"Are you sure?"

"Yes, please." What I need, he thought, is fresh insulin. There's nobody here who knows how to prepare that. If they ever give me the time I can do it myself, but first . . . "First thing is to bring the benefits of civilization back to the Stronghold."

"What?"

"I might have known I'd walk into a war," he told Maureen. "I was looking for the haves. The have-nots were bound to be somewhere around."

"I'll bring tea," Maureen said. She went to the men turning the cement mixer. "Harvey, Dad wants you up at the house."

"Right," Harvey Randall said. "Brad, you stay with Dr. Forrester, and make sure—"

"I know," Brad Wagoner said. "I think he should get some sleep."

"I can't." Forrester was far enough away that they didn't think he could hear them . . . and he looked like death warmed over anyway. The dead don't hear. "I have to get to the other barn now." He started to get up.

"Dammit, stay in that chair," Wagoner shouted. "I'll wheel you over."

Harvey followed Maureen out of the barn. He zipped up all his clothes against the wind, and they walked on in silence for a moment. Presently he caught up to her. "I don't suppose there's anything to talk about," he said.

She shook her head.

"You're really in love with him?"

She turned and her expression was . . . strange. "I don't know. I think Dad wants me to be. Wouldn't that turn you off? Breeding for politics! It's Johnny's rank Dad wants. I think he believes in Colorado Springs."

"Oddly phrased. Well, it certainly would be convenient."

"It would, wouldn't it? Harv, Johnny and I were sleeping together before you ever met me, and not because I was ordered to, either."

"Yeah?" He smiled suddenly, and she saw and wondered; but he wasn't going to mention George Christopher's tirade. No. "Have I got a chance?"

"Don't ask me now. Wait till Johnny gets back. Wait till it's all over."

Over? When is that? He pushed the thought away. Despair would be too easy. First Hammerfall and Loretta dead. The drive through nightmare, with Harv Randall curled around his wounded ego, a dead weight in the passenger seat. The fight to be ready for winter, for *Fimbulwinter*. The glaciers had been here once; every damn boulder in that damn wall was a reminder. Harv tasted the urge to howl at the heavens: Isn't that enough? Wasn't it enough without cannibals, war gases, thermite?

"You didn't say no," he said. "I'll hang onto that."

She didn't answer, and that was encouraging, too. "I know how you must feel," he said.

"Do you?" She was bitter. "I'm the prize in a contest. I always thought it was a joke, poor little rich girl. Suddenly nothing is funny anymore."

They reached the house and went in. Senator Jellison and Al Hardy had maps spread out on the living-room floor. Eileen Hamner held more papers, Hardy's eternal lists.

"You look frozen," Jellison said. "There's something hot in the Thermos. I won't call it tea."

"Thanks." Harvey poured a cup. It smelled like root beer, and tasted much like that, but it was hot and it warmed him.

"Progress?" Hardy asked.

"Some. The thermit bombs are coming along, but the fuses have to be made. Over in Hal's barn they're cooking up a god-awful brew that Forrester says will be mustard gas, but he's not sure how long it takes to finish the reaction. He's cooking it slow so as not to take chances."

"We may need it quicker than we think," Jellison said.

Harvey looked up quickly. "Sir?"

"Deke's people sent us a message on the CB an hour ago," Jellison said. "Couldn't make it out. Alice took another CB out to get on top of Turtle Mountain."

"Alice? Turtle Mountain?" Harvey was incredulous.

"It's in line of sight to us and Deke," Al Hardy said. "And communications are better lately. It should work."

"But Alice? A twelve-year-old girl?"

Hardy looked at him strangely. "Do you know anyone else who'd have a better chance of getting a horse up that mountain at night in the snow?"

Harvey started to say that of course he did, but then he thought better of it. If a horse and rider could climb that mountain in the dark, Alice and her stallion could. But it didn't seem right, to send young girls out into the snow and dark. Wasn't that what civilization was all about, to protect Alice Cox?

"Meanwhile," Hardy continued, "we called in some reserves. Just in case. They're loading up your TravelAll."

"But . . . what do you think Deke was saying?" Harvey asked.

"Hard to say." Jellison sounded tired. He looked as exhausted as Forrester, and had the same gray color. His voice was grim. "You know the New Brotherhood tried an attack on the power plant this afternoon."

"No." Harvey felt relief. The power plant was over fifty miles away. The New Brotherhood was there, not here. They'd be fighting Baker. Relief, then guilt, and he shrugged off the guilt because it was the last thing he needed now. "What's happening?"

"They were in boats," Al Hardy said. "They sent in a surrender demand, and when Mayor Allen told them to go to hell—"

"What? Wait! Mayor Allen?"

Hardy showed his irritation at the interruption. "Mayor Bentley Allen is in charge at the San Joaquin Nuclear Plant, and no, I don't know the details. The point is, Randall, that the New Brotherhood only had about two hundred people for the attack on the power plant. It was not much of an attack, and it did not succeed, and they did not renew it."

Harvey looked over at Maureen. She was gathering up the Thermos and some honey and brown sugar in a briefcase. She'd known about the fight at the power plant, and she didn't look as if she'd lost anyone there. He asked, "Casualties?"

"Light. One killed, of the Mayor's police. Three wounded, don't know how bad. None of them were from our relief force," Hardy said.

"Hm. Good news from all over. I knew Bentley Allen," Harvey said. "I know he was on duty in central L.A. at Hammerfall. He's some kind of man, to get out of *that!* Funny, though, how we always assume anyone who isn't at the Stronghold must be dead."

Al, Maureen, the Senator: They watched him thoughtfully, seriously. "Not so funny as all that," he said. "All right, so two hundred New Brotherhood attacked the power plant. That means . . . What *does* it mean?" Harvey followed the thought to a conclusion he didn't like. "They thought the power plant would be easy. They sent their main strength somewhere else. Here? Sure, here. Before we can get ready."

Hardy nodded. His lips pulled tight in a thin line, not a grin, a gesture of self-disgust. "Dammit, we did the best we could."

"I was in charge," Jellison said.

"Yes, sir, but I should have thought of it. But we were so busy trying to organize for the winter. We never had time to think about defense."

"Hell, we've *got* defenses," Harvey said. "You couldn't expect a whole damned army to show up in the San Joaquin Valley."

"Why couldn't I?" Hardy demanded. "I should have. The point is, I didn't, and now we all have to pay for my mistakes."

"Look," Harvey said. "If you hadn't got us all working on food, there'd be nothing here to fight *for*. You don't have to—"

The CB set beside Eileen came alive. Alice Cox's voice came through clearly, high-pitched, young and afraid, but every word intelligible. "Senator, this is Alice."

"Go ahead, Alice," Eileen said into the mike.

"Mr. Wilson reports they are under heavy attack," Alice Cox said. "There are a lot of them. Hundreds. Mr. Wilson says over five hundred. Mr. Wilson says he can't hold them. He's sending his people out now, and he wants instructions."

"Holy shit," Harvey Randall said.

"Tell her we'll have orders for them in five minutes," Senator Jellison said.

Eileen nodded. "Alice, can they wait five minutes?"

"I think so. I'll tell Mr. Wilson."

"You don't sound surprised," Harvey said. "You knew already."

Al Hardy turned away. Senator Jellison spoke carefully. "Surprised? No. I had hoped the New Brotherhood would wait until their deadline ran out, but I am not surprised that they did not."

"So what do we do now?" Harvey asked.

Al Hardy bent down to the maps. "We've been doing it since we got their ultimatum. I've had everybody we could spare from Forrester's work digging in up on these ridges." He pointed to penciled lines on the map. "Chief Hartman and his people have been working up there two days straight. George Christopher isn't due back for three days. We hope he'll have reinforcements, but we can't count on it. Hartman's people are exhausted and they are nowhere near through digging in. I gather that Forrester's superweapons are not complete."

"No. He expected another week," Harvey said.

"Which we don't have," Jellison muttered.

Al Hardy nodded. "Harvey, you've been working all day, but not outside digging the way Hartman's people have been. And someone must go buy us some time."

Harvey had been expecting that. "You mean me." He saw that Maureen had paused, briefcase full of sassafras and honey in her hand. She closed the door without going out and stood at the door looking back into the room. "It's time I earned my keep," Harvey said.

"That's about the size of it," Jellison said. He glanced at Maureen. "Was that stuff important?"

She nodded.

"You'll get to talk to him before he goes. He's got an hour or so," Jellison said.

"Thank you." She opened the door. "Be careful, Harvey. Please." Then she was gone.

"I've got some troops for you," Al Hardy said crisply. Now that the decision was made, he was all business again. Harvey thought he'd liked him better when he was sounding worried. "Not the best people we have. Kids, I'm afraid."

"Expendables," Harvey Randall said. He kept his voice flat.

"If need be," Al Hardy said.

The worst of it, Harvey thought, is that it makes sense. You don't put your best people out to buy time. You keep your best troops to dig in, and you send out what you can spare. Hardy can spare me! So can the Stronghold. . . .

"We don't expect miracles," Senator Jellison said. "But it's important."

"Sure," Harvey said.

"We want you to take the TravelAll," Hardy said. "We put your CB back into it. Take the TravelAll and a truckload of gear and go buy us some time. Days if you can, but hours anyway. As the Senator said, we don't expect miracles. Deke's people will make a fighting withdrawal. They'll blow bridges and burn what they can on the way out. You go meet them. Take chain saws and dynamite and the winch on that Travel-All and make a mess out of the road."

"Put them on foot," Jellison said. "Get the New Brotherhood on foot. Ruin those roads. That buys us a day, maybe more, right there."

"And how long do I stay out?" Harvey asked. He was having trouble with his breathing, and hiding it. You need time to psych yourself up, he thought; that, or zero time to get scared.

574

Jellison laughed. "I can't order you to go sit there until they kill you. Maybe I would if I thought you'd do it. . . . Never mind. Just let Deke's people get past you, then come home—and take as long getting here as you can. Unless you've got a better idea?"

Harvey shook his head. He'd already tried to think of a better idea.

"You'll do it?" Hardy barked the question, as if trying to catch Harvey in a lie.

It was irritating as hell, and Harvey barked back. "Yah."

"Good man," Hardy said. "Eileen, have the message relayed to Deke. Operation Scorched Earth is on."

Task Force Randall, a dozen boys, the oldest seventeen; two teen-age girls; Harvey Randall; and Marie Vance.

"What the hell are you doing here?" Harvey demanded.

She shrugged. "They don't need a cook just now." She was dressed for hiking: boots, hat with earmuffs, and several layers of clothing topped by a jacket that was all pockets. She carried a scope-sighted rifle. "I've done some varmint hunting. I can drive. You know that."

Harvey looked at the rest of his command and tried not to show dismay. He knew only a few of them. Tommy Tallifsen, seventeen, would be his other leader. He couldn't imagine what Marie's status would be. "Tommy, you drive the pickup."

"Okay, Mr. Randall. Barbara Ann will come with me. If that's all right." He indicated a girl who didn't look more than fifteen.

"It's all right," Harvey said. "Okay, everybody get in." He went back up onto the porch. "Jesus, Al, they're just kids."

Hardy looked at him, mildly disappointed, mildly disgusted. *You're messing up my patterns.* Or, *Don't make waves.* "They're what we've got. Look, they're farm kids. They know how to shoot, and most of them have worked with dynamite before. They know these hills pretty well, too. Don't put them down."

Harvey shook his head.

"And," said Hardy, "they'll die just as dead if the New Brotherhood breaks through. Marie too. You too. Me too. Hell, you're not going out to fight!"

"Not with just four guns, we're not."

"These are the guns we can spare. These are the people we can spare. Just get out there and work. You're wasting time."

Harvey nodded and turned away. Maybe farm kids were

575

different. It would be nice to believe . . . because he had seen too many city boys, older than these, in Vietnam; kids just out of training camp, who didn't know how to fight, and they were scared all the time. Harvey had done a series on them, but it had never been cleared by the Army.

He told himself: We aren't going out to fight. Maybe it will be all right. Maybe.

They stopped in town and loaded supplies into the truck, and onto the carrier on top of the TravelAll. Dynamite. Chain saws. Gasoline. Picks and shovels. Fifty gallons of used crankcase oil, a bitch to move. When it was all loaded, Harvey let Marie drive. He sat in the second seat to let one of the local boys sit up front with the map. They drove down the highway, out of the valley.

Harvey tried to get the boys talking, to get to know them, but they didn't volunteer much. They'd answer questions, politely, but they sat wrapped in their own thoughts. After a time Harvey leaned back in his seat and tried to rest. But that reminded him gruesomely of the last time Marie had driven the TravelAll, and he jerked upright.

They were leaving the valley. It made Harvey feel naked, vulnerable. He and Mark and Joanna and Marie had gone through too much getting there. He wondered what the boys thought. And the girl, Marylou, he couldn't remember her last name. Her father was the town pharmacist, but she'd never been interested in the store. She seemed interested in the boy she sat with. Harvey remembered his name was Bill, and Bill and Marylou had both managed some kind of state scholarship to UC Santa Cruz. The others thought them odd, that they'd want to go so far away to college.

Marie drove up the ridge that led out of the valley. Harvey had never been here before. Up on top of the ridge were moving lights: Chief Hartman's people digging in, still working at midnight despite the cold blowing wind. The roadblock below the ridge had only one guard huddled in the small shelter. They passed it and were out of the valley.

He saw it and felt it: They had entered the universal chaos left by Hammerfall. It was scary out here. Harvey held himself very still, so that he wouldn't shout at Marie to turn the TravelAll and break for safety. He wondered if the others felt the same way. Better not to ask. Let us all feel that nobody else is scared, and that way nobody will run. They drove on in unnatural silence.

The road was washed out in places, but vehicles had made paths around the broken pavement. Harvey noted places where the road could easily be blocked; he pointed them out to the others in the car. He couldn't see much through the intermittent sleet and the thick dark out there. The map showed they were in another valley, with a series of ridges to the south much lower than those surrounding the Stronghold.

This would be the battleground. Below lay a branch of the Tule River, the main line of defense for the Stronghold. Beyond was territory Hardy wouldn't even attempt to hold. In a few days, perhaps only hours, the valley they were now driving through would be a killing ground, a place of battle.

Harvey tried to imagine it. Noise, incessant noise: the stutter of machine guns, a crackle of rifle fire, dynamite bombs, mortars; and through it all the screams of the wounded and dying. There wouldn't be any helicopters and field hospitals here. In Vietnam the wounded were often in hospitals faster than they'd have been if they'd been civilians at home in an auto accident. Here they'd have to take their chances.

They? Not they. *Me,* Harvey thought. Who was it that said "A rational army *would* run away"? Somebody. But run to where?

The Sierra. Run to Gordie and Andy. Go find your son. A man's duty is to his children. . . . Stop it! Act like a man, he told himself.

Does acting like a man mean to sit calmly while they drive you where you'll be killed?

Yes. Sometimes. This time. Think about something else. Maureen. Have I got a chance? That wasn't a satisfying line of thought either. He wondered why he was so concerned about Maureen. He hardly knew her. They'd spent an afternoon together here, a lifetime ago, and then they'd made love; and three times since, furtively. Not much to build a life around. Was he interested in her because she was a promise of safety, power, influence? He didn't think so, he was certain there was more, but objectively he couldn't find reasons. Fidelity? Fidelity to the woman he'd had an adulterous relationship with; in a way a kind of fidelity to Loretta. That wasn't getting him anywhere.

There were a few lights visible through the gloom; farmhouses in the battleground, places not abandoned yet. They weren't Harvey's concern. Their occupants were supposed to know already. They drove on in silence until they came to the south fork of the Tule River. They crossed it, and now there was no turning back. They were beyond the Stronghold's de-

577

fenses, beyond any help. Harvey felt the tension in the car and felt strangely comforted by it. Everyone was afraid, bu they weren't saying it.

They turned south and went over a ridge to the valley be yond. The ground seemed even and smooth on both sides o the road. Harvey stopped and planted homemade mines: jar of nails and broken glass over dynamite and percussion caps shotgun shells pointed upward and buried just above a board pierced by a nail.

Marie watched, puzzled. "How will you get them to walk out here?" she asked.

"That's what the oil is for." They wrestled the drum of crankcase oil to the side of the road. "We shoot holes in that when we get past. When the oil's on the road, nobody can walk on it, drive on it, anything."

The route beyond was ridge, valley, ridge, valley, with the road curving to cross low spots in the ridges. It was rippling landscape, a land with waves in it. Ten miles beyond the Stronghold they passed the first of Deke Wilson's trucks. It was filled with women and children and wounded men, household possessions and supplies. There were baskets tied to the top and sides of the truck bed, filled with goods—pots and pans, useless furniture, precious food and fertilizer, priceless ammunition. The truck bed was covered by a tarpaulin, and more people were huddled under it, along with more goods. Bedding and blankets. A birdcage but no bird. Pathetic possessions, but everything these people had.

A few miles on there were more trucks, then two cars. The driver of the last didn't know whether any others would get out. They crossed a broad stream and Harvey stopped and planted dynamite, leaving the fuses marked with rocks so that any of his party could find them to blow the bridge.

There was a faint tinge of gray-red in the east when they reached the top of the last ridge before the low rolling hills where Deke Wilson's farm band lived. They approached it carefully, concerned that the New Brotherhood might have got past Deke's people and come to secure the road, but no one challenged them. They stopped the TravelAll to listen. The infrequent popping of gunshots came from far away. "All right," Harvey said. "Let's get to work."

They cut trees and built a maze on the road: a system of fallen trees that a truck could get through, but only slowly, by stopping to back up and turn carefully. They made dynamite bombs and put them at convenient places to throw down onto the road, then Harvey sent half his troops out to the sides, the others down the hill. They cut trees partway through so that they would fall easily. The others ranged out to both sides, and Harvey could hear the growl of the chain saws, and sometimes the sharp *whump* of half a stick of dynamite.

The gray became a red smear behind the High Sierra when the work parties returned. "A couple more trees cut and one charge set off, and that road's blocked for hours," Bill reported. "This won't be so hard."

"I think we should do it now," someone said.

Bill looked around, then back at Randall. "Shouldn't we wait for Mr. Wilson's truck?"

"Yes, wait," Marie said. "It would be awful if we stopped our own people from getting through."

"Sure," Harvey said. "The maze will stop the Brotherhood if they get here first. Let's take a break."

"The shooting is getting closer," one of the boys said.

Harvey nodded. "I think so. Hard to tell."

"It's officially dawn," Marie said. "Muslim definition. When you can tell a white thread from a black one. It's in the Koran." She listened for a moment. "There's something coming. I hear a truck."

Harvey took out a whistle and sounded it. He shouted to the boys nearest him to spread out and get off the road. They waited while the truck noises got louder and louder. It came around the bend and there was a screech of brakes as it stopped just short of the first tree. It was a large truck, still only an indistinct object in the gray light. "Who's there?" Harvey shouted.

"Who are you?"

"Get out of the truck. Show yourself."

Someone leaped out of the truck bed and stood on the road. "We're Deke Wilson's people," he shouted. "Who's there?"

"We're from the Stronghold." Harvey started toward the truck. One of the boys was much closer. He stepped up to the cab and looked in. Then he backed up fast.

"It's not—"

He never finished. There were pistol shots, and the boy was down. Something smashed Harvey in the left shoulder, a hard blow that knocked him backward. There was more shooting. People were jumping out of the truck.

Marie Vance fired first. Then there was more shooting from the sides of the road and the rocks above it. Harvey struggled to find his rifle. He'd dropped it, and he scrabbled around for it.

"Stay down!" someone yelled. A sputtering object landed

579

just in front of the truck and rolled underneath. Nothing happened for an eternity, and there were more gunshots; then the dynamite exploded. The truck lifted slightly, and there was a gasoline smell; then it blew up in a column of fire. Fire danced in the air near Harvey's face as the gasoline was flung around. He could see human shapes in the fire: Men and women screamed and moved in dancing flame. There were more shots.

"Stop. Stop shooting. You're wasting ammunition." Marie Vance ran down toward the burning truck. "Stop it!" The gunfire died and there were no sounds but the burning fire.

Harvey found his rifle at last. His left shoulder was throbbing and he was afraid to look, but he forced himself, expecting to see a bloody hole. There was nothing at all. He felt it, and it was sore, and when he opened his coat he found a large bruise. Ricochet, he thought. I must have been hit by a ricochet. The heavy coat stopped it. He got up and went down to the road.

The girl, Marylou, was trying to get closer to the fire, and two boys held her back. She wasn't saying anything, just struggling with them, staring at the burning truck and the bodies near it.

"He was dead when he hit the ground," one of the boys shouted. "Dead, dammit, you can't do anything." They seemed dazed now as they stared at the bodies and the fire.

"Who?" Harvey asked. He pointed at the dead boy near the truck cab. The boy lay on his face. His back was on fire.

"Bill Dummery," Tommy Tallifsen said. "Shouldn't we . . . what do we do, Mr. Randall?"

"Do you know where Bill planted the charges downhill?"

"Yes."

"Show me. Let's go light them." They moved down the hill. Visibility was increasing fast. A hundred yards, two hundred. They found a rock that overhung the road. Tommy pointed. As Harvey bent down to light the fuse, Tommy grabbed his shoulder. "Another truck coming," he said.

"Aw, shit." Harvey reached for the fuse again. Tommy said nothing. Finally Harvey stood. "It'll be light before they get up here. You go on back up the hill and alert the troops. They can't get past that burning truck anyway. Don't get close to it until you *know* who it is."

"All right."

Harvey waited, cursing himself, Deke Wilson, the New Brotherhood. Bill Dummery, with a scholarship to Santa Cruz and a girl named Marylou. My fault.

The truck came on up the hill. It was loaded with people. No household goods at all. In a cartop carrier on top of the cab, two children in bulky raincoats hunkered down against the wind. As the truck got closer Harvey recognized the man standing in the bed next to the cab. He was one of the farmers who had come with Wilson to the Stronghold. Something Vinge?

The people in the truck were all women and children and men patched with bloody bandages. Some lay in the truck bed, not moving as the overloaded vehicle ground its gears and crawled uphill. Harvey let it pass him, then lit the fuse. He followed behind it. He could walk almost as fast as it could go. The dynamite went off behind him, but the boulder didn't roll onto the road.

The truck stopped at the log maze. There was no question about who was in this truck. The boys came out of cover. Vinge jumped down. He looked exhausted, but showed no obvious wounds or bandages. "You weren't supposed to block the goddam road until we got through!" he shouted.

"Fuck yourself!" Harvey screamed in rage. He fought for self-control. The truck was filled with wounded and with women and children, and all of them looked half dead from exhaustion. Harvey shook his head in pity and resentment, then called to Marie Vance. "Get the TravelAll! We'll have to use the winch to clear a way for them."

It took half an hour to saw through two logs and snake them out of the way so the truck could get through. While they worked, Harvey sent Tommy Tallifsen down to try again with the boulder. At the rate they were using the stuff, they'd run out of dynamite right here, with miles of road still to block. This time the boulder rolled. It formed a formidable obstacle, with no easy way around it. Others with chain saws dropped more trees on the road.

"All clear," one of the boys called. "You can roll."

Vinge went up to the truck cab. There were four people crammed into it. The driver was a teen-age boy, fourteen or so, barely big enough to reach the controls. "Take care of your mother," the farmer shouted.

"Yes, sir," the boy answered.

"Get moving," the farmer said. "And . . ." He shook his head. "Get moving."

"Goodbye, Dad." The truck crawled away.

The farmer came back to Harvey Randall. "Name's Jacob

Vinge," he said. "Let's get to work. There won't be any more coming out of our area."

The fighting sounded much closer. Harvey could see across the hills and out to the San Joaquin Sea. There were columns of smoke to mark the burning farmhouses, and a continuous popcorn crackle of small-arms fire. It was strange to know that men and women were fighting and dying not a mile away, and yet see nothing. Then one of the boys called, "There's somebody running."

They spilled over the top of the hill half a mile off. They ran haltingly, not in any order, and few carried weapons or anything else. Running in terror, Harvey thought. Not a fighting withdrawal. Run away! They flowed down into the valley, and on toward the hill held by Task Force Randall.

A pickup truck came over the top of the next ridge. It stopped and men jumped out. Harvey was startled to see more men on foot to each side; they'd come over so carefully that he hadn't noticed them. They gestured to the people in the pickup, and someone in the back of the truck stood up and leaned on the cab. He held binoculars to his eyes. They swept over the men fleeing uphill toward Harvey, paused only a moment there, then swept up along the road, examining each of Harvey's roadblocks with care. The enemy had a face now; and the enemy knew Harvey Randall's face. So be it.

In less than five minutes the valley and ridge beyond swarmed with armed men. They walked carefully; they were spread out half a mile to each side. They advanced toward Harvey.

The fugitives staggered uphill, to Harvey's men and trucks and past them. They breathed like terminal pneumonia cases. They held no weapons, and their eyes were blind with terror.

"Stop!" Harvey shouted. "Stand and fight! Help us!" They staggered on without seeming to hear. One of Harvey's boys stood up, looked back at the grimly advancing skirmish line below, then ran to join the fugitives. Harvey screamed at him, but the boy kept running.

"Lucky the others stayed," Jacob Vinge said. "I . . . hell, I'd like to run, too."

"So would I." This wasn't going according to plan. The New Brotherhood wasn't coming up the ridge to clear the road. Instead they were fanning out to each side, and Harvey didn't have nearly enough troops to hold the ridgeline. He'd hoped to delay them longer, but there was no chance. If they didn't get out fast they'd be cut off. "And we're going to." He lifted his whistle and blew loudly. The advance below broke into a run even as he did.

Harvey waved his command into their truck and the Travel-All. Jacob Vinge took Bill's place. Harvey sent the truck out, then hesitated. "We ought to try. Come on, a few rounds . . ."

"It won't do any good," Marie Vance said. "There's too much cover and they aren't showing themselves enough. We'd be trapped and we wouldn't have hurt any of them."

"How do you know so much about strategy?" Harvey demanded.

"I watch war movies. Let's get out of here!"

"All right." Harvey turned the TravelAll and drove away, down off the ridge and into the next valley. The truck stopped and let the running men get aboard.

"Poor bastards," Marie said.

"We fought them for a day," Vinge said, "but we couldn't hold them. Like the ridge back there. They spread out and get around you, behind you, and then you're dead. So you have to keep running. After awhile it can get to be a habit."

"Sure." Habit or not, Harvey thought, they had run like rabbits, not like men.

The road led down to a stream swollen with the rain of Hammerfall. The low parts of the valley were deep mud. Harvey stopped at the far side of the small bridge, and got out to light dynamite sticks already in place.

"There they are!" one of the boys shouted.

Harvey looked up on the ridge. A hundred and more armed enemies boiled over the top and came down the hill at a dead run. There was a staccato chatter, and a rustle in the grass not far from Harvey.

"Get it done!" Jacob Vinge shouted. "They're shooting at us!"

It was nearly a mile up to the ridge, but that sound was familiar from Vietnam: a heavy machine gun. It wouldn't take long to walk its fire over to Harvey and the TravelAll and then they'd be finished. He flicked his Zippo and blessed it when it caught the first time, even though it was filled with gasoline rather than regular lighter fluid. The fuse sputtered, and Harvey ran for the TravelAll. Marie had slid over into the driver's seat and was already rolling. Harvey caught on and hands grabbed him and pulled him inside. There was more of the chatter, *brup-brup-brup*, and something roared past his ear.

"Holy shit!" he yelled.

"They shoot pretty good," Vinge said.

The dynamite went off, and the bridge was in ruins. But not completely, Harvey saw. There was still a full span, wide enough to walk across. It wasn't going to take long to repair, but he sure wasn't going back. They drove up to the top of the next ridge, and got out, looking for more trees to drop, boulders to dynamite into the road, anything.

The New Brotherhood troops came on into the valley, some on foot, a dozen on motorcycles. They reached the ruined bridge and stopped, then a few swam and waded across and came on. Others spread along the banks and found new crossings. In five minutes a hundred had crossed and they walked on steadily toward Harvey's work crews.

"Jesus, it's like watching the tide come in," Harvey said.

Jacob Vinge didn't say anything. He kept on digging under a boulder to make a hole for the dynamite. Just above them a tree crashed across the road, and the boys moved to another.

There were motors in the valley ahead. Two motorcycles gingerly drove across the narrow remains of the bridge. Extra riders got on and the bikes gunned forward toward Harvey's position.

Marie Vance unslung her rifle and worked the sling around her left arm. "Go on digging," she called. She took a sitting position and rested the rifle on a large rock, then squinted through the telescopic sights. She waited until the bikes were about a quarter of a mile away before she fired. Nothing happened. She worked the bolt and aimed again, fired. At the third shot the lead motorcycle wobbled and swerved into the ditch at the side of the road. One of the riders got up. Marie aimed again, but the other bike moved off the road and the riders scrambled for cover. They waited for the advancing skirmish line. That came steadily closer, and Marie changed her aim point, firing to slow the advance.

Again the center of the line slowed, while more attackers spread to each side, fanning out well beyond any point Harvey could defend. "Get finished," Harvey shouted. "We have to get out of here!"

No one argued with that. Vinge put two sticks of dynamite into the hole beneath the boulder and tamped mud in on top of it.

"Look!" Barbara Ann, Tommy Tallifsen's partner, shouted in horror. She pointed at the opposite ridge, where they'd spent the dawn hours putting barriers on the road.

A truck appeared at the top of the ridge. It went over and

came down the road, and another followed, then another. When the trucks reached the downed bridge, men jumped out with timbers and steel plates. More trucks came over the ridge.

Harvey looked at his watch. They had delayed the enemy trucks by precisely thirty-eight minutes.

Valley of Death

The pattern was always the same. No matter what obstructions Harvey's group put into the road, the New Brotherhood Army was delayed for no longer than it took to put them up. If Task Force Randall could have actively defended its roadblocks, they might have stopped the advancing enemy for much longer, but there was no chance of that. The New Brotherhood used its trucks to bring troops as far forward as possible; their skirmishers then spread out to both flanks and advanced, threatening to cut Harvey off; and once again Harvey had to retreat.

The enemy developed a new tactic as well: They mounted heavy machine guns in one of their trucks, and brought that forward to fire on Harvey's workers from well out of rifle range. It kept Harvey from doing a proper job of ruining the road, and he couldn't even shoot back. The enemy were faceless ghosts who couldn't be harmed, and Harvey couldn't stop them. Their infantry continued to advance, avoiding Harvey's defenders, trying always to get around and behind. It was battle at long range, with few casualties; but the New Brotherhood's advance was relentless. By midafternoon they had come a dozen miles toward the Stronghold.

Work and run; and running was becoming a habit. A dozen times Harvey wanted to keep going, to drive for the Stronghold, and the devil with the roadblocks. His mind found a dozen excuses for running.

"It's like nothing can stop them," Tommy Tallifsen screamed. They had halted at another ridgeline. The maps said the valley below—where the New Brotherhood was busily removing trees, filling in holes, repairing the road quicker than Harvey had been able to destroy it—was called "Hungry Hollow." The name seemed appropriate.

"We've got to try," said Harvey.

Tallifsen looked doubtful. Harvey knew what he was thinking. They were all exhausted, they'd lost five of Task Force Randall: one shot dead as he worked with a chain saw, the other four vanished—run away, captured, wounded and lying back in the hills, they didn't know. They hadn't got aboard when it was time to bug out, and the New Brotherhood had been too close to let them look for them; and running had become a habit. What could eight exhausted people do to stop a horde that flowed forward like the tide?

"It will be dark in a couple of hours," Harvey said. "Then we can rest."

"Can we?" Tallifsen asked. But he went back to work, digging out under another boulder above the road. Others stretched the cable from the TravelAll's winch around the rock. There wasn't enough dynamite to use on every rock they found.

An hour before dark they were forced out of Hungry Hollow and over the ridge beyond. They fled across Deer Creek, pausing only long enough to light the fuse on the dynamite they'd placed there. When they climbed onto the next ridge, they found men already there.

It took Harvey a moment to realize they were friends. Steve Cox and almost a hundred troops had been sent from the ranch to hold the ridge. The Stronghold forces were through running away; now they would stand and fight. Cox had spread his forces along the ridge and they'd dug in. Harvey and Task Force Randall—what was left of it—could rest. There was even cold supper and a Thermos of hot tea.

"We're all dead on our feet," Harvey told Steve Cox. "We won't be much help."

Cox shrugged. "That's all right. Get a good night's sleep. We'll hold them."

You're a fool, Harvey wanted to say. There are a thousand of them and a hundred of you, and they come like death, like

army ants, and nothing can stop them. "Have you brought
. . . how is Forrester's work? Have you got any of his superweapons?"

"Thermit grenades." Cox showed Harvey a box of what
looked like lumps of baked clay with fuses stuck out of the
top. Each was about six inches in diameter, and each had two
feet of parachute cord attached to it. "You light the fuse and
whirl it around," Cox said. "Then throw it."

"Do they work?"

"They sure do." Cox was enthusiastic. "Some explode like
bombs. Others just break open, but even then they throw
fire ten or twelve feet. They'll scare the hell out of those cannibal bastards."

"But what about the other weapons? Mustard gas?"

Cox shrugged. "They're working on it. Hardy says it will
take time. That's why we're out here."

In the valley below, the lead elements of the New Brotherhood force had reached the ruined bridge. Deer Creek was
high and swift, and the bridge was entirely gone; the few men
who tried to wade it gave up quickly. The Brotherhood army
stopped, then began to spread along the banks. Elements went
upstream until they vanished. Others turned downstream toward the sea a few miles to the west.

"They'll get around us," Harvey said nervously.

"Nope." Cox grinned. He pointed upstream, toward the
towering Sierra. "We've got allies up there. About fifty Tule
Indians, some of Christopher's reinforcements. Tough bastards. Get some sleep, Randall. They won't get through here,
not tonight and not tomorrow. We've got a good position.
We'll hold them."

"I think Cox is crazy," Harvey told Marie. "I've . . .
we've seen the New Brotherhood fight. He hasn't."

"They have our radio reports," Marie said. She stretched
in the back seat of the TravelAll. "Feels good to relax. I
could sleep for a week."

"So could I," Harvey said; but he didn't. The TravelAll
was parked on the far side of the ridge from Deer Creek.
He had sent the others back further, to a farmhouse where
they could get proper rest, and he knew he should join them,
but he was worried. Harvey had learned to respect whoever
was in charge of the New Brotherhood. The enemy general
hadn't wasted a man, had never exposed his people recklessly,

589

yet he had swept through eighteen miles and more in less than a day.

And he was using gasoline and ammunition recklessly. This was an all-out war; the New Brotherhood must have stripped their territory, must be gambling on taking the Stronghold for new supplies.

Dusk brought a chill wind, but no more sleet. A few stars showed through the overcast, blinking points of light too far apart to recognize as constellations. Harvey remembered a hot sauna followed by a cold swimming pool in hot sunlight; he remembered driving the TravelAll south through the blazing desert beauty of Baja California, finally to swim in an ocean warm as a bathtub; bellysurfing the bigger, more exciting waves of Hermosa Beach, and spreading a towel over sand too hot to walk on.

Down in the valley they could hear the sounds of Brotherhood trucks and men moving heavy objects. There was no way to know what the enemy was doing. Cox had patrols alert for infiltrators, but instead the enemy commander had his men fire weapons at irregular intervals, raise shouts, throw grenades and rocks across the creek; and often the ranchers responded, shooting wildly into the night, wasting ammunition, losing sleep.

Harvey knew that was what the Brotherhood wanted, but the knowledge didn't help. He slept fitfully, awakened too often. Marie stirred in the seat behind him. "You awake?" she whispered.

"Yes."

"Who was it? In the truck, with the binoculars. Do you know?"

"Probably the sergeant. Hooker. Why?"

"Put a name on him and he's less frightening. Do you think we can win? Is Hardy smart enough?"

"Sure," Harvey said.

"They keep coming. Like a machine, a huge grinding machine."

Harvey sat up. Somewhere a grenade went off, and Cox shouted not to waste ammunition.

"That's a frightening image. Fortunately it's not the right one," Harvey said. "It's not a meat grinder. It's one of those kinetic structures where the artist invites a horde of newsmen to stand around and drink and watch while the machine tears itself to pieces."

Her laugh sounded forced. "Nice imagery, Harv."

"Hell, I made a living off imagery, before I took up breaking rocks. And ruining roads. I used to think of battles as a chess game, but they're not. It's like those sculptures. The commander puts together this huge sculpture, knowing that the pieces will grind each other up, and he doesn't control them all. Half of them are controlled by an art critic who hates him. And each one tries to see that he has pieces left when it's over, but there won't be enough, so it has to be done over and over."

"And we're some of the pieces," Marie said. "I hope Hardy knows what he's doing."

In the morning there was new excitement in the Stronghold camp. During the night Stephen Tallman, Vice-President of the Tule Council, had come in to tell how his warriors were dug in to the east, and more were coming. The rumors grew. George Christopher was coming back, and he had a hundred, two hundred, a thousand armed ranchers he'd recruited from the hill country. Anyone who doubted it was shouted down.

But certainly there were fifty Indians to the east, and all the ranchers talked about how tough the Indians were, and what great allies they'd be. There were other stories, of an attempt in the night by the New Brotherhood to force passage of Deer Creek five miles upstream, and how Tallman's Indians had beaten them back and killed dozens; how the New Brotherhood had run away. When Harvey talked to the others, he could find nobody who had seen the battle. He found a few who claimed to have spoken to someone who was in it. Everyone had a friend who'd talked to Tallman himself, or to Stretch Tallifsen, who was with the ranch force sent upstream to hold the western end of the line.

It was always like this. The new guys were demons incarnate; they would go through the enemy like so many mincing machines. The new guys always thought so too. But it could be true . . . sometimes it was true . . . maybe they would win this after all. The New Brotherhood could be stopped, and it wouldn't even take the full strength of the Stronghold to do it.

Clouds parted in the east; the sun shone shockingly bright. Full daylight, and still nothing happened. The ranchers and the forward skirmish line of the Brotherhood exchanged sniping shots, with little effect. Then—

Over the opposite ridge trucks appeared. They didn't look like trucks. They looked strange, for they had large wooden structures attached in front of them. They came down the hill, not too fast, because with all that weight in front they were hard to drive and unstable, but they came on toward the swollen creek.

At the same time, hundreds of the enemy came out from behind rocks and folds of ground where they'd been hidden. They began firing at anything that moved. The trucks with their strange towers advanced to the stream edge, and some drove across meadows that should have been too swampy, except that during the night the Brotherhood had laid down tracks of fencing wire and planks to get them across the mud.

They went to the stream edge and the towers fell, making bridges across the stream. Brotherhood troops rushed toward the bridges, began swarming across. Other Brotherhood units concentrated fire on any Stronghold defenders who dared show themselves. Harvey heard the sharp *whump!* which he recognized from Vietnam: mortars. The mortar bombs fell among the rocks where Cox's ranchers hid, and each time they fell more accurately. Someone across the river was directing them, and he had good control: Wherever Cox's men tried to oppose the crossing, the mortars soon found them.

And more of the Brotherhood troops poured across the river. They fanned out and moved forward, along a line almost a mile wide, and Cox's forward troops either fell back or were overrun. Suddenly—it had taken no more than half an hour—the river line was gone, and Cox held only the ridge; and even there the relentless mortars and machine guns, far out of range of effective rifle fire, sought them out, pinned them down, while more Brotherhood troops advanced up the hills, hiding behind boulders, dodging and leapfrogging and always moving on. . . .

"Ants!" Harvey screamed. "Army ants!" Now he knew. The cannibals couldn't be stopped. They'd been fools to think they could do it. And at the rate they advanced, Cox would lose most of his force. Already groups of men had begun to break and run, some throwing down their weapons, others grimly hanging on to them and stopping to shoot back at the enemy. But there was no organization to the defense any longer, and more and more saw it and thought only of saving themselves. There was no place to make a stand: Every posiion was threatened by a breakthrough at some other point, and these men had not fought together, lived together; they didn't have confidence that the man down the line wouldn't run and leave an opening for the yelling cannibals to pour through and cut them off forever.

A dozen men clung to the TravelAll, piled into it, hung on top or lay on fenders as Harvey drove away. Deer Creek, which Cox had expected to hold all day, perhaps even to break the Brotherhood and stop them permanently, had fallen in less than an hour and a half.

The rest of the morning was nightmare. Harvey could not find his truck; the only equipment he had left was in the TravelAll, and only a few of Cox's ranchers were willing to help. Reinforcements from the Stronghold came finally, twenty men and women with more dynamite and gasoline and the chain saws from the truck, but they could never get far enough away from the advancing Brotherhood forces to do any useful work.

The Brotherhood tactics had changed: Now instead of fanning out and outflanking the defenses, they flooded forward trying to close; they wanted to keep the Stronghold force running, and now their general was willing to spend men to do it.

If Marie had not been with him, Harvey would have run with the rest; but she wouldn't let him. She insisted they keep on with their mission, at least that they stop and light the fuses of the charges they'd set two nights before when they went forward. Once they delayed too long, and there was a crash; shattered glass from the rear window sprayed over them and the front windshield was smashed out as well. A .50 slug had passed all the way through the TravelAll, passed between them, missing them by inches. The next time they stopped, the ranchers who'd stayed with them abandoned the car.

Harvey yelled to Marie, "Why the hell are you so—" He didn't finish the sentence. He'd wanted to say "brave," but if he did, it meant he wasn't, that he was a coward. "—determined?" he finally said.

She looked up from where she was digging. They had one last stick of dynamite and she wanted to plant it. She pointed up toward the Sierra. "My boy is up there," she said. "If we don't stop them, who will? This is good enough. Give me the dynamite."

Harvey had already crimped fuse onto the cap. He handed her the stick and she thrust it into the hole, then shoveled dirt and rock onto it.

"That's enough!" Harvey screamed. "Let's get out of here!" They were on the far side of a low hill and couldn't see the advancing enemy, but Harvey didn't think they would be far behind.

"Not yet," Marie said. "Something I have to do first." She walked toward the hilltop.

"Come back here! I swear, I'll leave you! Hey!"

She didn't look back. After a moment he cursed, then followed her uphill. She was adjusting her rifle, setting the strap on her left arm. She braced herself against a rock. "Down there is where you put the oil. And the mines," she said. "We drove right past it."

"We had to! They were right behind us!" And it's all so damned futile anyway. Motorcycles were coming up the road. They'd reach the ridge in a minute or two.

Marie took careful aim. Fired. "Good," she muttered to herself. She fired again. "I'd be done quicker if you'd do some shooting too," she said.

Harvey knew he wasn't about to hit the oil drum set three hundred yards away. He braced his rifle on a rock and aimed at the first of the oncoming motorcycles. He fired again and again, and missed each time. But the cyclists slowed, then stopped and took cover in the ditch to wait for the infantry. Marie continued to fire, slowly, carefully. Finally she said, "That ought to do it. Let's go. . . . Actually, what's the hurry? They're stopped." She took up her position again and waited.

Harvey clenched his fists and took a deep breath. She was right. There was no immediate danger. The oil was spilling across the road now, and the two motorcycles were going nowhere.

Another motorcycle reached the oil slick. It skidded into the ditch and the biker screamed. Marie smiled faintly. "Good idea, those pungie sticks of yours."

Harvey looked at her in horror. Marie Vance: on the board of governors of half a dozen charities; banker's wife, socialite, country club member; and she was grinning at the thought of a man impaled on a stick smeared with human shit to make the wounds fester. . . .

A truck came to the oil slick and stopped; then it started forward, slowly. Marie put a bullet through its windshield. I

594

slid forward and skidded, turning slightly sideways. The motor gunned and the wheels spun, but it did not move.

Another truck came up behind it and started around; one of the dynamite mines went off, loudly, and the truck went up in flames. Harvey felt it now: the urgent impulse to shout in triumph. Something had worked. Those weren't people down there, scrambling to get away from the burning truck, some themselves burning; they were army ants, and the trick had worked—

They heard the *plop!* from in front of them, then a faint whistle. Something exploded twenty yards to their left. Another *plop!*

"The car! *Now*, dammit!" Harvey shouted.

"Yes, I think it's time." Marie followed. The second mortar round went off somewhere behind them. They leaped into the TravelAll and drove off laughing and shouting like children.

"Son of a bitch, it worked!" Harvey shouted. He looked over at Marie and her eyes shone with triumph to match his own. We make a great team, he thought.

" 'Run away!' " cried Harvey.

Marie looked at him strangely.

"Monty Python and the Holy Grail," Harvey said. "Didn't you see it?"

"No."

They drove on, still laughing with excitement. Inside, Harvey knew it wasn't really much of a victory, but it was better than the rest of the day. There was no question of stopping now, not until they reached the next large barrier, which was a fork of the Tule River. That would be a formidable barrier once its bridge was blown; surely it would stop the New Brotherhood. It had to; beyond was the ridgeline that marked the entrance to the Stronghold itself. The Tule was their most important defense line.

They came around a curve and started down into the Tule Valley—and there was no bridge. It had already been blown.

Harvey drove up to the wrecked bridge and stared at the swollen river. A hundred feet wide, and deep, and swiftly flowing. "Hey!" he shouted.

Across the river, one of Hartman's constables rose from hiding behind a log bunker. "They said you'd had it," he called.

"What do I do now?" Harvey shouted.

"Whatever it is, do it quick," Marie said. "They won't be far behind us—"

"Go upstream," the constable yelled. "We've got troops up there. Make sure you radio ahead that you're coming."

"All right." Harvey turned the TravelAll and started up the county road toward the Tule Indian Reservation. "Get on that CB," he told Marie. "Tell 'em the reports of our death have been greatly exaggerated."

A mile and a half upstream the road crossed the Tule. A dozen men were working with shovels at the bridge foundations. Harvey drove up warily, but they waved him on. He drove across and stopped.

They looked like ranchers, but they were darker and did not show the effects of months without sunlight. Harvey wondered if lack of vitamin D would affect them; pale faces were evolved for life in a cold, cloudy environment.

One of the work crew left off digging and came over to the TravelAll. "Randall?"

"Yes. Look, the New Brotherhood must be right behind us—"

"We know where they are," the man said. "Alice can see them, and we've got a radio. You're supposed to go on up there onto Turtle Mountain and help her observe. Find a place where you can see the valley and still get her on the CB."

"All right. Thanks. And we're glad to have you on our side."

The Indian grinned. "I see it that you're on *our* side. Good luck."

Their earlier mood of elation had vanished now. They drove on along an increasingly difficult road: mud, fallen rocks, deep ruts. Harvey put the TravelAll into four-wheel drive. As they climbed higher the entire valley came into view. To the southwest was the south fork of the Tule, and the road junction and bridge they'd just left. The fork ran northwest to the remains of Lake Success, where it joined the Tule itself.

A ridge separated the forks of the Tule; the ridge that guarded the Stronghold. From their vantage point Harvey and Marie could see the defense line of Police Chief Hartman's troops—trenches and foxholes and log bunkers. There were less elaborate defenses thrown forward into the south fork valley; they didn't look adequate to hold. Only the high ridgelines seemed well defended. A classic crust defense, Harvey thought; the enemy need only punch through, and there was nothing to stop them from overrunning the entire Stronghold.

At dusk it was clear what the enemy's plan was. He brought up his trucks, dug in his troops and lit large campfires in plain sight of the Stronghold. They looked relaxed, confident, and Harvey knew they'd be working on bridges during the night. Finally dark came, and the hills were silent.

"Well, we can't see anything more," Harvey said. "Now we really don't have anything to do."

Marie moved restlessly beside him. In the dark she was only a presence, her very shape indeterminate; but Harvey grew itchingly aware that Marie Vance was only inches away, and that they were cut off from the universe until sunrise. His memory played him a dirty trick. It showed him Marie Vance some weeks before Hammerfall, as she met Harvey and Loretta at her front door. She wore emeralds and a vividly green evening gown cut nearly to the navel; her hair was set in fantastic convolutions; she smiled graciously and hugged him and welcomed them in. His mind superimposed that image on the dark blur next to him, and the silence grew really uncomfortable.

"I can think of something," she said softly.

Harvey found his voice. "If it isn't sex, you'd better tell me now."

She said nothing. He slid toward her and pulled her against him. Things crunched and crackled; not one of the dozen pockets in that jacket was empty. She chuckled and took it off while he doffed his own jacket with its own lumpy pockets.

Then the terror of the day and the danger of tomorrow, the slow, agonizing death of a world and the coming end of the Stronghold, could be forgotten in the frantic importance of each other. The passenger foot-well grew cluttered with clothing until Harvey broke off and dumped the whole armful behind the steering wheel. The passenger seat wasn't shaped for this, but they coupled with care and ingenuity, and maintained the position afterward: he half reclining in the passenger seat, she kneeling before him, her face above his. Their breath fell each on the other's cheek.

"I'm glad you thought of something," he said presently. (He couldn't say he loved her.)

"Ever screwed in a car before?"

He thought back. "Sure. I was more limber then."

"I never did."

"Well, generally you use the back seat, but . . ."

"The back seat's covered with broken glass," Marie finished, and they felt each other's tension as they remembered: a .50-caliber bullet, glass showering everywhere, Marie brushing the tiny splinters off him while he drove. But there was a way to forget.

And again, later, there was a way to forget, the same way repeated, with the same frantic urgency. They were not drawn to each other, he thought; they were thrust against each other in their fear of what was outside them. They made love with their ears cocked for gunfire; but they made love. Even when it's bad, it's good.

Harvey woke before dawn. He was covered with the blanket from the back seat, but he couldn't remember getting it. He lay awake, not moving, his thoughts confused.

"Hi," Marie said softly.

"Hi yourself. I thought you'd be asleep."

"Not for a while. You get some rest."

Harvey tried. But there were twinges from muscles he'd overused last night, and twinges from his conscience, which apparently hadn't been informed that he was a widower whose new girl had dropped him for an astronaut. To hell with that. But he still wasn't sleeping. "Oh, well," he said, and sat up. "We seem to have survived the night."

"I didn't work you that hard."

There might have been something false in his own laugh, or . . . she'd known him a long time. She turned toward him in the dark. "You're not worried about Gordie, are you? That's all over. He's got his new girl, and it doesn't need a judge to say a marriage is over. We didn't really need one before."

Harvey hadn't been thinking of Gordie. "What will you do now?" he asked. "When this is over? If?"

She laughed. "I won't stay a cook. But thank you for bringing me to this valley. It's been much better than anything I could have found for myself." She was quiet for a moment, and they heard a sound outside: an owl, and the squeal of the rabbit it had caught. "It's a man's world now," Marie said. "So I guess I'll just have to marry an important one. I've always been a status-conscious bitch, and I don't see any reason to change now. In fact, there's more reason than ever. Muscle counts. I'll find me a leader and marry him."

"And who would that be?"

She giggled. "After yesterday you're a leader. You're an important man." She slid across to him and put her arm around him. Then she laughed aloud. "What's got you so tense? Am I that terrifying?"

"Certainly." She was.

She laughed again. "Poor Harvey. I know exactly what you're thinking. Obligation. You've seduced the girl, and you ought to marry her, and you know damn well you can't resist if I really work at it . . . see?" Her hands moved to intimate places.

Living with Loretta hadn't readied him for this kind of warfare. He kissed her hard (she couldn't bluff Harvey Randall!) and maintained the kiss (because it felt so good, and hell, Maureen had her winged man) until she drew back.

"That wasn't very nice of me," she said. "Don't worry, Harv, I'm really not after you. It wouldn't work. You know me too well. No matter what we did, even if we really did learn to love each other, you'd always wonder about it. You'd wonder if it was all an act, wonder when I'd decide to drop it. And we'd fight, and play head games, and dominance games. . . ."

"I was thinking something like that."

"Don't talk yourself into anything," Marie said. "I don't need that. I would like to be your friend."

"Sure. I'd like that. Who's your real target?"

"Oh, I'm going to marry George Christopher."

Harvey was startled. "What? Does he know?"

"Of course not. He still thinks he's got a chance with Maureen. He tells me about her every chance he gets. And I listen, too."

"I just bet you do. What makes you think he won't get Maureen?"

"Don't be silly. With you and Johnny Baker to choose between? She'll never marry George. If they hadn't known each other forever, if he weren't her first, she wouldn't even consider him."

"And me?"

"You got a chance. Baker has a better one."

"Yeah. I suppose it would be silly to ask if you're in love with George," Harvey said.

Marie shrugged. He could feel that in the dark. "He'll be sure I am," she said. "And it won't be anybody else's business. There won't be any repetitions of tonight, Harvey. This was . . . something special. The right man at the right time.

I've always . . . Tell me, all those years we lived next door, weren't you ever tempted to come over some afternoon when Loretta was out and Gordie was at the bank?"

"Yes. But I didn't."

"Good. Nothing would have happened, but it always worried me that you didn't try. Good. Now let's get some sleep." She turned away and curled up in the blanket.

Poor George, Harvey thought. No. That's not right. Lucky George. If I didn't know her so damned well . . . Dammit, I'm still tempted. George, you don't know it, but you're about to be a happy man.

If you live long enough.

If Marie lives!

Dawn: a red smear in the Sierra. The winds blew fitfully, light airs. Mist rose from the San Joaquin Sea.

When the sun was high, they saw them: A hundred or more of the New Brotherhood had crossed during the night. They were concentrated near the old Lake Success bed, and they moved back toward the ruined bridge, sweeping aside the screen of Stronghold defenders. The Brotherhood's mortars began to fire, forcing the defenders back up the valley and onto the ridges.

The withdrawal was orderly, but steady. "By noon they'll have cleared the valley," Harvey told Marie. "I thought—I *hoped*—they'd hold longer. At least they aren't running like rabbits."

She nodded, but went on reporting the enemy positions on the CB. There wasn't anything else to do.

Alice sounded terrified whenever she spoke, but she demanded their reports anyway.

Useless, Harvey thought. It's no good. He looked at the map, wondering if he could find a way into the Sierra that didn't go back down and through the enemy—or where the New Brotherhood would be soon.

"They're repairing the bridge," Marie reported. "They've got big trees, and hundreds to carry them."

"How long until they can get trucks across?" Alice asked.

"No more than an hour."

"Stand by, I have to report that to Mr. Hardy," Alice said. The radio went silent.

"It's no good," Harvey said. He tried to smile. "Looks like it's you and me after all. Maybe we can get up there and find the boys. I don't suppose I'll have to fight Gordie for you—"

"Shut up and watch," Marie said. She sounded scared, and Harvey couldn't blame her.

The bridge took a little more than an hour; then a stream of trucks, led by the pickups with the machine guns, moved over them. They swept on up the valley roads. Other trucks brought the New Brotherhood mortars forward, while crews dug in emplacements for them. The Brotherhood army swarmed into the valley below, probed toward the ridges, fell back wherever opposed. They had plenty of time—and night would be on their side now. They could infiltrate men through the rocks, over the ridges, into the Stronghold itself.

The day became warmer, but not for Harvey and Marie. The rising air from the San Joaquin Sea drew a cold wind down from the Sierra. The enemy moved on forward in the cloudy bright day. Noon came, and they had reached the far end, were beginning to climb the ridges toward the last defenses.

"Stand by," Alice said. She sounded excited now. Not afraid.

"Stand by for what?" Harvey demanded.

"To watch, and report," Alice said. "That's why you're there. I can't see. . . ."

Something was happening on the ridge far below. Men had pushed something big, it looked like a wagon, to the brow of the ridge. They shoved, and it went over, tumbling down the ridge, rolling down until it came to rest a hundred yards from the repaired bridge. It sat, did nothing for thirty seconds . . . and exploded. A huge cloud burst from it and was carried downwind toward the bridge, across it, through the traffic jam at the bridgehead.

And everywhere along the ridge, objects came lobbing over, falling slowly. Men pushed heavy framework forward, boxes with long arms that spewed tiny black dots in an arcing trajectory.

"Catapults!" Harvey yelled.

They were. He didn't know what powered them. Nylon cords, probably. Carthaginian women donated their hair; maybe . . .

The catapults didn't have much range, but they didn't need it. They threw jars that burst into yellow fog on impact. The wind carried the fog down through the valley, across the advancing enemy . . .

The New Brotherhood screamed in panic. They threw away

601

weapons, ran in pain, tearing at their clothes, threw themselves into the river to be carried away by the rushing water. They fought to get across the bridge, and from the ridges rifles fired again and again, cutting the running men down as they fled. The catapults poured a continuous rain of bursting jars, renewing the deadly yellow fog.

Harvey's voice broke as he screamed into the microphone. "They're running! They're dying! Good Lord, there must be five hundred of them down out there."

"What is happening to those who didn't cross the river?" The voice was Alice Cox, but the question had to be Al Hardy.

"They're loading up the trucks."

"What about their weapons? Are they getting those out?"

Harvey scanned with the binoculars. "Yes. They hadn't brought all the mortars across . . . there goes one of their trucks." Harvey shuddered. The pickup, with a load of men gasping in horror, drove down the road at high speed and didn't slow when it reached the bridge. It flung a dozen off the bridge into the water and kept going, leaving behind those it had run down in its flight.

"There were two of their machine guns on that truck," Harvey reported. "Looks like they got away."

The gas didn't cover the entire valley, and some of the New Brotherhood were able to escape. Many ran screaming without weapons, but Harvey saw others pause, look for a route, and leave carrying heavy weapons. Two of the mortars were carried away before the catapults closed off that escape route. Harvey grimly reported clear areas, and watched as minutes later the gas canisters dropped into them.

"Something's happening upstream," Harvey shouted. "I can't see—"

"Don't worry about it. Is the road down from the reservation clear of gas?" Alice demanded.

"Hold on a second. . . . Yes."

"Stand by."

Moments later trucks came down that road. They carried Tallman's Indian troops, and more ranchers. Harvey thought he recognized George Christopher in one of the trucks. They roared on in pursuit of the fleeing enemy, but were stopped at the top of the ridge beyond the road junction. Now it was the Stronghold's turn to deploy and probe, search for weak spots, clear the roads. . . .

While behind them the valley had become an alien world. Its unusual atmosphere was yellow-tinged, deadly to men without pressure-suits. Its native life was eerie to look upon: slow-moving quadrupeds and belly-crawlers, some armed with metallic stings, growing ever more torpid until most seemed to hibernate and only a few still moved. Like snails they crawled on their bellies, leaving trails of red slime, and they moved at snail's pace downhill toward the river. River life thrashed about, incredibly active, then suddenly stopped moving, to float motionless with clumsy blunt fins wavering in the current.

When dark came, the silence was that of a dead, deserted world.

Aftermath

From the Far East I send you one single thought, one sole idea—written in red on every beachhead from Australia to Tokyo—"There is no substitute for victory."

General of the Army Douglas MacArthur

It was too dark to see. A cold wind blew down from the Sierra. Harvey turned to Marie. "Victory."

"Yes! We did it! My God, Harvey, we're safe!" It was too dark to see her face, but Harvey knew she must be grinning like an idiot.

He started the TravelAll. Alice had told him to stay out of the valley, away from the main road. They'd have to drive to the Stronghold on the dirt cowpath. He put the car in gear and moved gingerly ahead. The headlamps showed the road ahead, smooth, untraveled, but the drop to the left was steep, and Harvey knew they were sinking deep into the mud surface. It would be easy to go over the edge. That was frightening—that they could be killed after the battle was over—but it was only a bad road, and he'd been on a lot of those; it wasn't malevolent.

A wave of exhilaration swept over him. He had to fight an urge to gun the car. He had never been so aware of being alive. They rounded the mountain and crossed the ridge leading down to Senator Jellison's house, and then he did let himself go, gunning the car forward and driving through the mud at high speed, dangerously fast over the ruts and potholes. The TravelAll leaped as if to share their joy.

He drove as if running away from something. He knew

604

that, and knew that if he let himself think about it, about what he'd seen, he would not feel joy but an infinite sadness. Back in that valley of battle were hundreds, all ages, men, girls, women, boys, crawling with ruined lungs, leaving trails of blood that had been visible through binoculars until the merciful dark fell across the land: the dying, who had survived the end of the world.

"Harvey, you can't think about them as people."

"You too?"

"Yes. A little. But we're alive! We've won!"

The TravelAll leaped upward at the top of a small hillock, all four wheels briefly leaving the ground. It was stupid driving at this speed, but Harvey didn't care. "We've fought our last battle," he shouted. "Ain't gonna study war no more." Euphoria again: The world was a lovely place for the living. Let the dead bury the dead. Harvey Randall was alive, and the enemy was defeated. "Hail the conquering heroes come. Wish I could remember the tune. Silly language. Hero. Hell, you're more of a hero—heroine?—than I am. I'd have run like hell if you'd let me. But I couldn't. Sexism—men can't run while women are watching. Why am I babbling? Why aren't you?"

"I'm not because you won't give me a chance!" Marie shouted. There was laughter in her voice. "And you didn't run, and neither did I, and it would have been so easy. . . ." She laughed again, this time with a peculiar note in it. "And now, my friend, we go collect the traditional reward for heroes. Find Maureen. You've earned it."

"Strange to say, I thought of that. But of course George will be coming back—"

"You leave George to me," Marie said primly. "After all, I've got a reward coming, too. You leave George to me."

"I think I'm jealous of him."

"Too bad."

The mood lasted only until they reached the Senator's stone ranch house and went inside. There were many others there. Al Hardy, drunk but not with liquor, grinning like a fool while others pounded him on the back. Dan Forrester, exhausted, introspective and unhappy, and no one caring; they praised him and thanked him and let him have his mood, to enjoy or hate, be glad or sad. Magicians may do as they please.

Many were absent. They might be among the dead, they might have joined the pursuit; they might have fled, and be fleeing still, unaware that nobody was hunting them. The victors were too tired to think about them. Harvey searched until he found Maureen, and he went to her. There was no lust between them, only an infinite tenderness, concern; they touched each other like children.

There was no party, no celebration. Within minutes the gathering was finished. Some dropped into chairs and slept; some went to their own houses. Harvey felt nothing now; only the need to rest, to sleep, to forget everything that had happened that day. He had seen this before, in men returned from patrol in Vietnam, but he had not felt it himself: drained of energy, drained of emotion, not unhappy, able to rouse himself to brief moments of excitement only to have them slip away and leave him more exhausted than ever.

He woke remembering that they'd won. The details were gone; there had been dreams, vivid and mixed with memories of the past few days, and as the dreams faded so did the memories, leaving him only the word. Victory!

He was lying on the floor of the front room, on a rug and covered with a blanket; he had no idea how he had come there. Perhaps he had been talking with Maureen and simply fallen to the floor. Anything was possible.

There were sounds in the house, people moving, smells of cooking food. He savored them all, the sounds and smells and sensations of life: The gray clouds outside the window seemed infinitely detailed, vivid and brilliant as sunlight; the bronze trophies on the walls were a marvel that needed investigation. He treasured each moment of life and what it might bring.

Gradually the mood faded. It left him desperately hungry. He got up, and saw that the living-room rug itself looked like a battlefield. They lay where fatigue had dropped them. Someone had lasted long enough to spread blankets . . . and had run short. Harvey spread his own blanket over Steve Cox, who was coiled into a ball against the cold, and followed his nose toward breakfast.

■

There was bright sunlight in the room. Maureen Jellison stared in disbelief. She was afraid to get out of bed; the bright sun might be a dream, and it was a dream she wanted to savor. Finally she convinced herself that she was awake. It was no illusion. The sun came in the window, warm and yellow and bright. It was over an hour high. She could feel its warmth on her arms when she threw back the covers.

Gradually she came to full wakefulness. Terror and blood and a fatigue like death itself; the memories of yesterday ran together like a too-fast movie film. There had been the horror of the morning, when the Stronghold forces had to hold fast, retreating slowly, letting the Brotherhood into the valley but never on the ridges; the gradual retreat that could not seem too obvious, with troops who couldn't be told the battle plan for fear that they would be captured; finally the general panic, when they had all run.

"When you run they bunch up and follow," Al Hardy had said. "Randall's reports make that pretty clear. Their commander goes by the book. So will we, up to a point."

The problem had been to hold along the high ground, so that the Brotherhood would stay down in the valley; to give way along the valley floor until enough of the Brotherhood had crossed the bridge. How could they get the ranchers to fight and not run until the signal? Hardy had chosen the simplest solution to that. "If you're out there," he'd said, "if you stand, some of them will stay with you. They're men."

She had resented that, but it had been no time to give Al Hardy a lecture; and he'd been right. All she'd had to do was hold on to her own courage. For someone who wasn't sure she wanted to live, that had seemed a simple job. It wasn't until she was actually under fire that she began to have doubts.

Something unseen had ripped Roy Miller's side. He tried to block the wound with his forearm. His forearm nestled neatly in the great gap of torn ribs. Maureen's breakfast rose in her throat . . . and in his last moment Roy looked around and caught her expression.

A mortar shell had exploded behind Deke Wilson and two of his men. The others rolled over and over and lay sprawled in positions that would have been hideously uncomfortable if they hadn't been dead; but Deke flew forward and upward, his arms flapping frantically, and fluttered downhill like a fledgling just learning to fly, down into the yellow murk.

Joanna MacPherson turned to yell at Maureen. A bullet whispered through her hair, through the space where her skull had been only a moment before, and Joanna's message became frantically obscene.

A fragment of metal from a mortar blast shattered Jack Turner's mustard bomb as he was winding up for the throw. His friends ran from him, and his sister-in-law ran too, and

Jack Turner staggered and thrashed within the yellow cloud, drowning.

Pudgy Galadriel from the Shire swung her sling round and round, stepped forward and sent a bottle of nerve gas flying far down the hill. A moment too long on the follow-through, and Galadriel stood poised like Winged Victory, with her head gone. Maureen saw black spots before her eyes. She leaned against a boulder and managed to stay upright.

It was one thing to stand on a clifftop and contemplate (at her leisure) jumping off (but would she have had the nerve? or was it all an act? Now she'd never know). It was quite another to watch poor, homely Galadriel crumple with the stump of her neck spitting blood, and then, without looking to see if anyone was actually watching her, to pick up her sling and a bottle of nerve gas and swing the deadly, evil thing round and round her head and, remembering at the last second that the damn thing would fly at a *tangent* and *not* in the direction the sling was pointing when she let go, sling it down into the cannibal horde that was still coming up at them. Suddenly Maureen Jellison had found quite a lot to live for. The gray skies, cold winds, brief snow flurries; the prospect of hunger in winter; all of that faded away. First there was a simple realization: If you could feel terror, you wanted to live. Strange that she'd never understood that before.

She dressed quickly and went outside. The bright sun was gone. She could not see the sun at all, but the sky overhead was bright, and the clouds seemed much thinner than usual. Had the sunlight been a final dream? It didn't matter. The air was warm, and there was no rain. The small creek below the house was very high, and the water gurgled happily. It would be cold water, just right for trout. Birds dipped low into the stream and cried loudly. She walked down the drive to the highway.

There was no traffic. There had been, earlier, when the Stronghold's wounded had been taken to the former county convalescent home that served as the valley's hospital, and later there would be more when the less critically injured were brought in horse-drawn wagons, but for now the road was clear. She walked steadily on, aware of every sight and sound: the ring of an ax in the hills above; the flash of red as a red-winged blackbird darted into the brush nearby; the shouts of children herding the Stronghold's pigs through the woods.

The children had adjusted quickly to the new conditions.

One elderly adult as teacher, a dozen or more children, two working dogs and a herd of swine: school and work. A different sort of school with different lessons. Reading and arithmetic, certainly, but also other knowledge: to lead the pigs to dog droppings (the dogs in turn are part of the human sewage); and always to carry a bucket to collect the pig manure, which must be brought back at night. Other lessons: how to trap rats and squirrels. Rats were important to the new ecology. They had to be kept out of the Stronghold's barns (cats did most of that), but the rats were themselves useful: They found their own food, they could be eaten, their fur made clothing and shoes, and their small bones made needles. There were prizes for the children who caught the most rats.

Closer to town was the sewage works, where the animal and human wastes were shoveled into boilers with wood chips and sawdust. The heat of fermentation sterilized everything, and the hot gases were led out through pipes that ran under City Hall and the hospital to form part of the heating system, then condensed. The resulting methanol, wood alcohol, ran the trucks that collected the wastes, with some left over for other work. The system wasn't complete—they needed more boilers, and more pipes and condensers, and the work absorbed too much skilled labor—but Hardy could be deservedly proud of the start they had made. By spring they'd have a lot of high-nitrogen fertilizer from the residue in the boilers, all sterilized and ready for the crops they'd plant—and there should be enough methanol to run tractors for the initial heavy work of plowing.

We've done well, she thought. There's a lot more to do, all kinds of work. Windmills to build. Waterwheels. Crops to plant. A forge to set up. Hardy had found an old book on working bronze and methods of casting it in sand, but they hadn't had time to do much about it yet. Now they'd have the time, now that there was no threat of war hanging over them. Harvey Randall had been singing when he came into the ranch house after the battle. "Ain't gonna study war no more!"

It wasn't going to be easy. She looked up at the clouds; they were turning dark. She wished the sunlight would break through, not because she wanted to see the sun again, although she certainly did, but because it would be so appropriate: a symbol of their eventual success. Instead there were only the darkening clouds, but she refused to let them depress her. It would be so easy to fall back into her black mood of despair.

Harvey Randall had been right about that: It was worth almost anything to spare people that feeling of helplessness and doom. But first you had to conquer it in yourself. You had to look squarely at this new and terrible world, know what it could and would do to you—and shout defiance. *Then* you could get to work.

The thought of Harvey reminded her of Johnny Baker, and she wondered what had happened to the expedition to the power plant. They should be all right now. With the New Brotherhood defeated, the power plant should be all right, now that they'd repelled that first, tentative attack. But . . .

Their last message had come three days ago.

Maybe there had been a second attack. Certainly the radio was out. Maureen shivered. Maybe a damn transistor had given up the ghost, or maybe everybody was dead. There was just no way to tell. Johnny would have been in the thick of things . . . he was too damn visible. . . .

So let it be a transistor, she told herself, and keep busy. She turned downhill toward the hospital.

■

Alim Nassor gasped for breath and couldn't find it. He sat propped up in the truck bed; if he lay down, he would drown. His lungs were filling anyway, and it wouldn't be long. They had failed. The Brotherhood was defeated, and Alim Nassor was a dead man.

Swan was dead. Jackie was dead. Most of his band, dead in the valley of the Tule River, killed by choking clouds of yellow gas that stung like fire. He felt Erika's hands moving a cloth over his face, but he couldn't focus his eyes on her. She was a good woman. White woman, but she stayed with Alim, got him out when the others ran away. He wanted to tell her so. If he could speak . . .

He felt the truck slow, and heard someone call a challenge. They had reached the new camp, and somebody had organized sentries. Hooker? Alim thought the Hook had lived. He hadn't crossed the river; he was directing the mortars, and that should have been safe unless he was caught by the pursuit. Alim wondered if he wanted Hooker to have lived. Nothing really mattered anymore. The Hammer had killed Alim Nassor.

The truck stopped near a campfire, and he felt himself being lifted out. They put him near the fire, and that felt good.

Erika stayed by him, and someone brought him a cup of hot soup. It was too much trouble to tell them they were wasting good broth; that he wouldn't live past the next time he fell asleep. He'd drown in his own phlegm. He coughed, hard, to try to clear his lungs so he could talk, but that hurt too bad, and he stopped.

Gradually he heard a voice.

"And ye have defied the Lord God of Hosts! Ye placed your faith in armies, ye Angels of the Lord. Strategy! What do the Angels need of strategy! Place your trust in the Lord God Jehovah! Do His work! Work His will, o my people. Destroy the Citadel of Satan as God wills it, and then can ye conquer!"

The voice of the prophet lashed over him. "Weep not for the fallen, for they have fallen in the service of the Lord! Great shall be their reward. O ye Angels and Archangels, hear me! This is no time for sorrow! This is a time to go forth in the Name of the Lord!"

"No," Alim gasped, but no one heard.

"We can do it," a voice said nearby. It took Alim a moment to recognize it. Jerry Owen. "They don't have any poison gas in the power plant. Even if they do, it won't matter. We take all the mortars and recoilless rifles out on the barge and blow up the turbines. That'll end that power plant."

"Strike in the Name of God!" Armitage was shouting. There were some answers now. "Hallelujah!" someone called. "Amen!" another said. Tentative at first, but as Armitage continued, the responses became more enthusiastic.

"Shee-it." That had to be Sergeant Hooker. Alim couldn't turn his head to look at him. "Alim, you hear me?"

Alim nodded slightly.

"He says he hears," Erika said. "Leave him alone. He's got to rest. I wish he'd get some sleep."

Sleep! That would kill him for sure. Every breath was a fight, something to struggle for, an effort of will. If he relaxed for a moment he'd stop breathing.

"What the hell do I do now?" Hooker was asking. "You the only brother left I can rap with."

Words formed on Alim's lips. Erika translated. "He asks how many brothers are left."

"Ten," Hooker said.

Ten blacks. Were they the last blacks in the world? Of course not. Africa was still there. Wasn't it? They hadn't seen any black faces among their enemies, though. Maybe there weren't any more in California. He whispered again. "He says ten is not enough," Erika said.

"Yeah." Hooker bent low, to speak into Alim's ear. No one else could hear. "I got to stay with this preacher," he said. "Alim, is he crazy? Is he right? I can't think no more."

Alim shook his ?ead. He didn't want to talk about that. Armitage was speaking again, of the paradise that waited for the fallen. The words blended into the vague, slow thoughts that crept into Alim's consciousness. Paradise. Maybe it was true. Maybe that crazy preacher was right. It was better to think so. "He knows the truth," Alim gasped.

The fire's warmth was almost pleasant. Darkness gathered in his head despite the glimpses of morning sunshine he thought he'd seen earlier. The preacher's words sank through the dark. "Strike now, ye Angels! This very day, this very hour! It is the will of God!"

The last thing Alim heard was Sergeant Hooker shouting "Amen!"

When Maureen reached the hospital, Leonilla Malik took her and led her firmly into a front room.

"I came to help," Maureen said. "But I wanted to talk to the wounded. One of the Tallifsen boys was in my group, and he—"

"He's dead," Leonilla said. There was no emotion in her voice. "I could use some help. Did you ever use a microscope?"

"Not since college biology class."

"You don't forget how," Leonilla said. "First I want a blood sample. Please sit down here." She took a hypodermic needle from a pressure cooker. "My autoclave," she said. "Not very pretty, but it works."

Maureen had wondered what happened to the pressure cookers from the ranch house. She winced as the needle went into her arm. It was dull. Leonilla drew out the blood sample and carefully squirted it into a test tube that had come from a child's chemistry set.

The tube went into a sock; a piece of parachute cord was attached to the sock, and Leonilla used that to whirl the test tube around and around her head. "Centrifuging," she said. "I show you how to do this, and then you can do some of the work. We need more help in the lab." She continued to swing the test tube.

"There," she said. "We have separated the cells from the fluid. Now we draw off the fluid, so, and wash the cells with saline." She worked rapidly. "Here on the shelf we have cells and fluid from the patients who need blood. I will test yours against theirs."

"Don't you want to know my blood type?" Maureen asked.

"Yes. In a moment. But I must make the tests anyway. I do not know the patient blood types and I have no way to find out, and this is more certain. It is merely very inconvenient."

The room had been an office. The walls had been painted not long ago and were well scrubbed. The office table where Leonilla worked was Formica, and very clean. "Now," Leonilla said, "I put samples of your cells into a sample of the patient's serum, and the patient's cells in yours, so, and we look in the microscope."

The microscope had also come from a child's collection. Someone had burned the local high school before Hardy had thought to send an expedition for its science equipment.

"This is very difficult to work with," Leonilla said. "But it will work. You must be very careful with the focus." She peered into the microscope. "Ah. Rouleaux cells. You cannot be a donor for this patient. Look, so that you will know."

Maureen looked into the microscope. At first she saw nothing, but she worked the focus, the feel of it coming back to her fingers. . . . Leonilla was right, she thought. You don't really forget how. She remembered that you weren't supposed to close the other eye, but she did anyway. When the instrument was properly focused she saw blood cells. "You mean the little stacks like poker chips?" she asked.

"Poker chips?"

"Like saucers—"

"Yes. Those are rouleaux formations. They indicate clumping. Now, what was your blood type?"

"A," Maureen said.

"Good. I will mark that down. We must use these file cards, one for every person. I note on your card that your blood clumps that of Jacob Vinge, and note the same on his card. Now we try yours with others." She went through the procedure again, and once more. "Ah. You can be a donor for Bill Darden. I will note that on your card and his. Now. You know the procedure. Here are the samples, clearly labeled. Each must be tested against the others, donors against patients. When that is done we must test donors against each other, although this is not so critical; then we will know, in case we must someday give one of you a transfusion—"

"Shouldn't you be drawing blood for Darden?" Maureen tried to remember him; he'd come to the Stronghold late, and was let in because his mother lived here. He'd been in Chief Hartman's group in the battle.

"I gave him a pint already," Leonilla said. "Rick Delanty. We have no way to store whole blood, except as now—in the donor. When Darden requires more, I will send for you. Now I must go back to the ward. If you truly wish to help, you may continue with the cross matching."

Maureen spoiled the first test, but when she was careful she found it wasn't difficult, merely tedious. The work wasn't made easier by the smells from the sewage works nearby, but there wasn't much choice about that. They needed the heat from the fermenting boilers; by running the extraction through City Hall and the hospital they got that heat free, but at the cost of the ripe smells. . . .

Once Leonilla came in and removed a patient sample and card. She didn't explain; it wasn't needed. Maureen reached for the card and looked at the name. One of the Aramson girls, age sixteen, wounded while throwing a dynamite bomb.

"With penicillin I might have saved her," Leonilla said. "But there is none, and there will never be any."

"We can't make it?" Maureen demanded.

Leonilla shook her head. "Sulfa, perhaps. But not the other antibiotics. That would require more equipment than we will have for years. Precise temperature regulation. High-speed centrifuges. No, we must learn to live without penicillin." She grimaced. "Which means that a simple cut untreated can be a death sentence. People must be made to understand that. We cannot ignore hygiene and first aid. Wash all cuts. And we will soon be out of tetanus vaccine, although perhaps that can be made. Perhaps."

The crossbow was large, and wound with a wheel. Harvey Randall turned it with effort, then laid the long, thin shaft into the weapon. He looked up at Brad Wagoner. "I feel like I ought to have on a black mask."

Wagoner shuddered. "Get it over," he said.

Harvey took careful aim. The crossbow was set on a large tripod, and the sights were good. He stood on the ridge above

Battle Valley. That name would stick, he thought. He aimed the crossbow at a still figure down below. The figure moved slightly. Harvey checked the sights again, then stood aside. "Okay," he said. He gently pulled the lanyard.

The steel springs of the bow gave a humming sound, and the traveler block clattered. The shaft flew out, over a yard long, a thin steel rod with metal feathering at the end; it went in a flat trajectory and imbedded itself in the figure below. The hands jerked convulsively, then were still. They hadn't seen the face. At least this one hadn't screamed.

"There's another. About forty yards to the left," Wagoner said. "I'll take that one."

"Thanks." Harvey turned away. It was too damned personal. Rifles would be better. Or machine guns. A machine gun was very impersonal. If you shot someone with a machine gun, you could persuade yourself that the gun had done it. But the crossbow had to be wound with your own muscle-power. Personal.

There was nothing else to do. The valley was death to enter. In the cold night the mustard had condensed, and now small streamers of the yellow gas were sometimes visible. No one could enter that valley. They could leave the enemy—thank God all the Stronghold wounded had been taken out before the gas attack, although Harvey knew that Al Hardy would have ordered the attack even if they hadn't been—they could leave the enemy wounded, or they could kill them. And they couldn't spare rifle or machine-gun ammunition for the purpose. The crossbow bolts were recoverable. After the first good rain, or after a few days of warmth, the gas would be dispersed.

It made good fertilizer. So would the dead. Battle Valley would be good cropland next spring. Now it was a slaughter-house.

We won. Victory. Harvey tried to recall the elation he'd felt the night before, the sense of life he'd had when he woke in the morning, and he knew he'd be able to. This was horrible work, but it was needed. They couldn't leave the Brotherhood's wounded to suffer. They'd die soon enough anyway; better to kill them cleanly.

And it was the last. No more wars. Now they could build a civilization. The Brotherhood had done the Stronghold's work: They had cleared out much of the area near the Stronghold. It wouldn't take a big expedition to go looking for salvage. Harvey kept his thoughts on that: on what they could find, on the wonders out there that they could search for and bring home.

When he heard the bow, Harvey turned back. His turn. Let Brad be alone for a moment.

■

The blood typing was done, and she'd visited the wounded. That had been tough, but not as bad as she'd thought. She knew why, but she didn't think about it.

It wasn't too bad in the hospital, because the worst cases had already died. Maureen wondered if they'd been . . . helped. Leonilla and Doc Valdemar and his psychiatrist wife, Ruth, knew their limits, knew that many who had inhaled mustard or taken gut shots were finished because they didn't have the drugs and equipment it would take to save them, and the mustard cases would end up blind anyway, most of them. Had the doctors been more than choosers of the slain? Maureen didn't want to ask.

She left the hospital.

In City Hall they were preparing for a party. A victory celebration. And we damned well deserve it, Maureen thought. We can mourn the dead, but we have to go on living, and these people have worked and bled and died for this moment: for the celebration that said the fighting was over, that the Hammer had done its worst and now it was time to rebuild.

Joanna and Rosa Wagoner were shouting with joy. They'd got a lamp burning. "It works!" Joanna said. "Hi, Maureen. We've got the lamp burning on methanol."

It didn't give off much light, but it would do. At the end of the big central book-lined room some of the children were setting up punch bowls. Mulberry wine, really quite good (well, not too bad); a case of Cokes someone had saved. And there would be food, mostly stew, and you didn't want to know what was in it. Rats and squirrels weren't really very different kinds of animals, nor did cat taste much different from rabbit. There wouldn't be many vegetables in the stew. Potatoes were scarce and terribly valuable. There were oats, though. Two of Gordie Vance's scouts had come down with oats, carefully separated: the scrawny ones for eating, and the best separated out to be kept as seed. The Sierra was full of wild oats.

And Scotland had built a national cuisine on oats. Tonight they'd find out what haggis tasted like. . . .

She went through the main hall, where women and children were putting up decorations, bright-colored drapes now used as wall hangings, whatever might add a festive air. The Mayor's office was through a door at the far end.

Her father, Al Hardy, Mayor Seitz and George Christopher were in there with Eileen Hamner. Their conversation stopped abruptly as she entered. Maureen greeted George and got an answer, but he seemed slightly nervous, somehow made to feel guilty in her presence. Or was she imagining it? She wasn't imagining the silence in the room.

"Go on with what you were doing," she said.

"We were just talking about . . . things," Al Hardy said. "I don't know if you'd be interested. . . ."

Maureen laughed. "Don't worry about it. Go on." Because if you're going to treat me like a goddam princess, she thought, I can sure as hell learn what's going on.

"Yes. Well, it's a bit of an ugly subject," Al Hardy said.

"So?" She took a seat next to her father. He didn't look good. He didn't look good at all, and Maureen knew he wouldn't live through the winter. The doctors at Bethesda had told her he would have to take things a lot easier—and there was no way he could do that. She put her hand on his arm and smiled, and he returned it. "Tell Al I'll be all right," she said.

His smile broadened. "Sure about that, Kitten?"

"Yes. I can do my part."

"Al," Jellison said.

"Yes, sir. It's about the prisoners. What do we do with them?"

"There weren't many of their wounded in the hospital," Maureen said. "I'd have thought there would be more—oh."

Hardy nodded. "The rest are being . . . taken care of. It's the forty-one men and six women who surrendered that we've got to worry about." He held up his hand and ticked off points on his fingers. "I see the following alternatives. One. We can take them in as citizens—"

"Never," George Christopher growled.

"Two. We can take them in as slaves. Three, we can let them go. Four, we can kill them."

"We don't let them go, either," George said. "Let them go, they'll rejoin the Brotherhood. Where else would they go? And the Brotherhood is still bigger than we are. Don't forget

617

that. They put up a good fight after the first ten or fifteen miles. They've still got leaders, some trucks, mortars. . . . Sure, we captured a lot of their weapons, but they're still out there." He grinned wolfishly. "But I bet they don't ever stick their noses *our* way again." Then he looked thoughtful. "Slaves. I can think of a lot we could do with slaves."

"Yes." Hardy nodded agreement. "So can I. Brute labor. Turning compressor pumps so we can have refrigeration. Musclepower for hand lathes. Grinding lenses. Even pulling plows. There's a lot of work nobody wants to do—"

"But slavery?" Maureen protested. "That's horrible."

"Is it? Would you like it better if we call it imprisonment at hard labor?" Hardy asked. "Would their lives be so much worse than they were as part of the Brotherhood? Or worse than convicts in prisons before the Hammer?"

"No," Maureen said. "It's not *them* I'm thinking of. It's *us*. Do we want to be the kind of people who keep slaves?"

"Then let's kill 'em and get it over with," George Christopher said. "Because we're sure as hell not going to just turn them loose. Inside or outside."

"Why can't we just let them go?" Maureen demanded.

"I already told you," George said. "They'll go back to the cannibals—"

"Is the Brotherhood all that dangerous now?" Maureen asked.

"Not to us," Christopher said. "They won't come *here* again."

"And by spring there won't be many of them left, I suspect," Al Hardy added. "They don't have much organization for winter. Or if they do, the ones we captured don't know about it."

Maureen fought the feeling that threatened her. "It's all pretty horrible," she said.

"What can we afford?" Senator Jellison asked. His voice was low; conserving energy. "Civilizations have the morality and ethics they can afford. Right now we don't have much, so we can't afford much. We can't take care of our own wounded, much less theirs, so all we can afford to do for theirs is put them out of their misery. Now what can we afford to do with the other prisoners? Maureen's right, we can't let ourselves become barbarians, but our abilities may not be up to our intentions."

Maureen patted her father's arm. "That's what I figured out, somewhere in the last week. But—if we can't afford much, then we have to build so that we can! What we don't dare do is get *used* to evil. We have to *hate* it, even if we can't do anything else."

"Which doesn't settle what we do with the prisoners," George Christopher said. "I vote for killing them. I'll do it myself."

And he hadn't brought any back from his pursuit, Maureen knew. And he'd never understand. Yet in his way he was a good man. He'd shared everything he had. He worked longer than anyone else, and harder, and not just for himself.

"No," Maureen said. "All right. We can't let them go. And we can't keep them as citizens. If all we can afford is slavery, then keep them as slaves. And put them to work so we can afford something more. Only we don't call them slaves, either, because that makes it too easy to think like a slavemaster. We can put them to work, but we call them prisoners of war and we treat them as prisoners of war."

Hardy looked confused. He'd never seen Maureen so assertive. He looked from her to the Senator, but all he got from the Senator was the look of a man tired unto death.

"All right," Al said. "Eileen, we'll have to organize a POW camp."

The Final Decision

> *The peasant is eternal man, independent of all Cultures. The piety of the real peasant is older than Christianity, his gods are older than those of any of the higher religions.*
> Oswald Spengler, *The Decline of the West*

The van had not been new when the comet fell. In these past few months it had aged many years. It had bulled its paths across roadless land and through fresh sea bottom. It stank of fish. Maintenance had been impossible, and continual rain had caused years of corrosion. Half blinded with one headlamp working, it seemed to know that its era was dead. It groaned, it limped; and with every jolt of its dying shock absorbers, Tim Hamner felt a needle of pain stab his hip.

Shifting gears was worse. His right leg wouldn't reach the clutch pedal. He used his left, and it was like an ice pick being wiggled in the bone. Still he drove fast across the potholed road, balancing the jouncing against the need for speed.

Cal Christopher was on guard at the barricade. His weapon was an Army submachine gun. He carried a bottle of Old Fedcal in the other hand, and he beamed, he swaggered, he wanted to talk. "Hamner! Good to see you." He thrust the bottle through the truck window. "Have a drink—hey! What happened to your face?"

"Sand," said Tim. "Look, I've got three wounded in the truck bed. Can somebody drive for me?"

"Gee, there are only two of us here. Rest are celebrating.

You guys won, huh? We heard you'd had a fight and beat them off—"

"The wounded," Tim said. "Is there somebody at the hospital?"

"You better believe it. We had wounded here, too. But we won! They weren't expecting it, Tim, it was beautiful! Forrester's brew really clobbered them. They won't stop running until—"

"They did stop. And I can't take time to talk, Cal."

"Yeah, right. Well, everybody's celebrating at City Hall, and the hospital's right next door, so you'll get plenty of help. They may not be sober, but—"

"The barricade, Cal. I can't help you with it. I got hit myself."

"Oh. Too bad." Cal moved the log aside, and Tim drove on. The road was dark, and none of the houses were lit. He saw no one along the way, but the going was easier here; the potholes had all been filled in. He rounded a bend and saw the town.

City Hall glowed softly through the dark. Candlelight and lanterns in every window: not an impressive sight after the brilliant glare of the atomic plant, but still a sign of celebration. The crowd was too big for the building. It had spilled onto the street despite the tiny flurries of snow. People formed tight clumps against the chill and the wind, but their laughter reached him for all that. Tim parked next door, in front of the county convalescent home.

People moved toward him from outside City Hall as he climbed from the cab. One was running—off-balance. Eileen, her sunburst smile wide and familiar. "Easy!" he cried, but too late. She crashed into him and hugged him tight, laughing, while he tried to maintain balance for both. Agony twisted and grated in the bone. "Easy. Jesus Christ. There's a piece of metal in my hip."

She jumped back as if scalded. "What *happened?*" And saw his face. Her smile faded. "What *happened?*"

"Mortar shell. It went off just in front of us. We were up on the cooling tower with the radio. It blasted the radio to bits, and it shredded the cop, uh, Wingate, his name was, and I was standing right between them, Eileen. Right between them. All I got was a blast of sand from the sandbags and this thing in my hip. Are you okay?"

"Oh, sure. And you're all right, aren't you? You can walk. You're safe. Thank God." Before Tim could interrupt she went on. "Tim, we won! We must have killed half of the cannibals, and the rest are still running. George Christopher chased them for fifty miles!"

"They'll never try *us* again," someone boasted, and Tim realized he was surrounded. The man who spoke was a stranger, an Indian, by his looks. He handed Tim a bottle. "Last Irish whiskey in the world," he said.

"Should save it for Irish coffee," someone laughed, "but there ain't no more coffee."

The bottle was nearly empty. Tim didn't drink. He shouted, "There are wounded in the back! I need stretcher bearers!" He called again, "Stretcher bearers. And stretchers, come to that." Some of the merrymakers moved toward the hospital. Good.

Eileen was frowning, more in puzzlement than sadness. She kept looking at Tim to be sure he was still there, that he was all right. "We heard about the attack on the plant," she said. "But you beat them. None of our people hurt—"

"That was the first attack," Tim said. "They hit us again. This afternoon."

"This afternoon?" The Indian was incredulous. "But they were running. We chased them."

"They stopped running," Tim said.

Eileen put her mouth close to his ear. "Maureen will want to know about Johnny Baker."

"He's dead."

She looked at him, shocked.

Men came with stretchers. The wounded were in the back of the van, wrapped in cocoons of blankets. One was Jack Ross. The men carrying the stretchers stopped in surprise at seeing the others: Both were black. "Mayor Allen's police," Tim told them. He wanted to help carry, but he was lucky to carry himself. He found the stick Horrie Jackson's fishermen had given him and used it for a cane as he limped into the hospital.

Leonilla Malik directed them into a heated front room. It had a large office table set up as a surgery. They put the stretchers on the floor and she examined the men quickly and carefully. First Jack Ross; she used her stethoscope, frowned, moved the instrument, then lifted a hand and pressed hard on the thumbnail. It went white and stayed that way. Silently she pulled the blanket over his head and went to the next.

The policeman was conscious. "Can you understand me?" she asked.

"Yeah. Are you the Russian spacewoman?"

"Yes. How many times were you hit?"

"Six. Shrapnel. Guts are on fire," he said.

As she felt for the pulse, Tim limped out of the room. Eileen followed, hugging at his arm. "You've been hit! Stay here," she said.

"I'm not bleeding. I can come back. Somebody's got to tell George about his brother-in-law. And there's something else I have to do. We've got to have reinforcements. Fast."

He saw it in her face. Nobody here wanted that kind of news. They'd fought and won, and they didn't want to hear that there was more fighting to do. "We don't have a doctor at the plant," Tim said. "Nobody wanted to dig that steel out of me."

"Get back in that hospital!" Eileen commanded.

"I will. But the cops come first, they're hurt worse than me. The plant nurse squeezed sulfa in the hole and covered it with sterile gauze. I'll be okay for awhile. I've got to talk to Hardy." It was hard to keep his thoughts in order; his hip felt like fire, and the pain kept him confused.

He let Eileen help support his weight as they crossed the narrow way toward City Hall. Damn, they were surrounded again. Steve Cox, Jellison's foreman, asked, "Hamner, what happened?" Someone else bellowed, "Let him alone, let him tell all of us at once." And another: "Hamner, are you going to drink that?"

Tim discovered the near-empty bottle still in his hand. He surrendered it.

"Hey," Steve Cox yelled. "Give that back to him. Come on, man, have a drink with us. We won!"

"Can't. Have to talk to the Senator. And Hardy. We've got to have help." He felt Eileen stiffen. The others looked as she had: They hated him for his bad news. "We can't take another attack," Tim said. "They did us too much damage."

"No. It's got to be over," Eileen whispered. Tim heard.

"You thought it was all over," Tim said.

"Everybody does." Eileen's face showed unbearable grief. It should have melted Tim Hamner, but it didn't. "Nobody wants to fight again," Eileen said.

"We won't have to!" Joanna MacPherson's high, clear voice cried, "We slaughtered the sons of bitches, Tim!" She edged up to him and put her shoulder under his other armpit. "There aren't enough of them left to fight. They'll split up and pretend they never heard of the Brotherhood. And that won't work either. We'll know them." Joanna had tasted blood. Suddenly she said, "Is Mark all right?"

"Mark's fine." Tim was just beginning to realize what he

was up against. A hopeless task. But it had to be done, they had to understand. He added, "Healthy and happy and cleaner than you are. They've got hot showers and washing machines at the power plant."

It could help.

In a room off the meeting hall at City Hall, Rick Delanty argued for his honor against Ginger Dow, who seemed determined to take him home with her. She was also indecently amused by the whole thing. "You don't have to marry me, you know."

When he didn't answer, she laughed. She was a sturdy matron in her mid-thirties whose long brown hair had been brushed to a soft glow, possibly for the first time since Hammerfall. "Although if you like everything, you could move in. And if you don't, leave in the morning. Nobody will care. This isn't Mississippi, you know. There's probably not another black woman other than the cannibals for a thousand miles."

"Well, I admit it makes me nervous," Rick said. "The whole situation. But it isn't just that. I'm in mourning."

He would have been less nervous if he and Ginger hadn't been trying to raise their voices against the singing in the big room next door. The tune seemed to be optional, but at least they were loud.

> He never shaved a whisker
> From off his horny hide;
> He hammered in the bristles,
> And bit them off inside!

Ginger lost some of her smile. "We're all in mourning for someone, Rick. We don't let it get to us. The last I ever saw of Gil, my husband, he was off to Porterville for lunch with his lawyer. Then bang! I think the dam must have got them both."

> I saw my logger lover
> Go shoulderin' through the snow,
> Goin' gaily homeward,
> At forty-eight below!

"It's not mourning time," she told him. "It's time to celebrate." Her mouth puckered into a pout. "There are a lot of men. Lots more than women. And nobody's ever told me I was ugly."

"Ugly you're not," Rick said. Was it the astronaut's scalp she wanted to collect, or the black man's? Or was she husband hunting? Rick found he was flattered; but the memories of the house in El Lago were too vivid. He opened the connecting door.

> The wind it tried to freeze him,
> It tried its level best,
> At a hundred degrees below zero,
> He buttoned up his vest.

The City Hall was also the town library, police station and jail. The large book-lined meeting room had been decorated with paintings and drapes. They absorbed some of the sound, but it was still a damned noisy party. Rick found Brad Wagoner at the end of the big room. Wagoner was staring at something in a glass display case.

"Where did that come from?" Rick asked. "Somebody up here collect Steuben glass?"

Wagoner shrugged. "Don't know. Right classy whale, isn't it?" Wagoner had a large bandage around his forehead. It looked impressive, like a scene from *The Red Badge of Courage*. He didn't tell people about it though: that he'd slung a thermit grenade with too much vigor and fallen onto a rock and rolled downhill until he thought he was going to be gassed, but he wasn't. He was pretty well gassed now, on bourbon and water. He told Rick, "At least we won't ever have to do that again." He'd been saying that a lot.

Happiness was contagious. Rick wanted to join in. If only he could quit worrying about that damned power plant, and about Johnny. And forget El Lago. He decided to go over to the hospital and do some honest work. He wouldn't be spoiling anybody's party at the hospital. As he made his way toward the door, Tim Hamner came in, a girl at each arm and a crowd around him all trying to talk at once.

Rick shoved toward Hamner. The noise level doubled. Hamner kept moving toward the back of the hall, toward the Mayor's office, and Rick followed. A number of people shouted for silence, adding to the general noise level. Eileen Hamner saw Rick, slipped from under Tim's arm and came toward him. "There's something I have to tell you," she said.

Rick knew at once. It turned him cold with the chill of a man about to faint. "How did Johnny buy it?" he asked.

"Tim says saving their asses. That's all I know."

He felt his knees weaken, but he stayed stiffly upright. "I should have made him let me go," he said to nobody. Now there are three astronauts left in the world. "Does Maureen know?"

"Not yet. Where is she?"

"Last I saw, in the Mayor's office with her father." The Senator wasn't going to like this much either. "I'll come with you." He pushed through, making a way for both of them.

So Johnny was dead. Now everybody he loved was dead. The Hammer had got them all. He felt a crazy impulse to laugh: America's record was still perfect. Not one astronaut lost on space duty. "Saving their asses from what?" he demanded, but Eileen was too far away and the noise was too great.

Someone passed Tim a bottle. Scotch. This time he drank, and carried the bottle into the Mayor's office. The leaders were there: the Senator, sitting behind the Mayor's desk; Al Hardy, hovering over him; Maureen, Chief Hartman, the Mayor. They looked happy, triumphant. Tim resented that. He knew he was irrational, that they deserved their celebration, but his grief was too great. He limped on into the office, pleased to see their grins fade as they saw the way he walked, the expression on his face. He felt Eileen and Rick Delanty crowd in behind him, then the door was closed.

"You were attacked again?" Al Hardy asked.

"Yes." Tim looked at Maureen. She knew. She knew from his face. No point in being gentle about it. "General Baker is dead. We stopped their attack, but just barely. And the rest of it I want to say to everybody." He kept his attention on the Senator. He didn't want to see Maureen's face.

Hardy turned to the Senator. "All right with me," he said. Jellison nodded, and Hardy went past Tim to the door. "Get it quiet out there," he said.

Steve Cox went to the podium and rapped for attention, while Hardy led Tim over and a dozen hands helped him up on the platform. Someone moved the Senator's chair to the doorway so that he could hear. The Mayor and Chief Hartman stood behind him, leaning forward. Tim couldn't see Maureen.

He braced himself on the lectern, facing hundreds of eyes, and drank more scotch. It warmed him. The room was almost quiet: no talking, except for newcomers crowding in by the door, and shushing noises from those already inside. He had never spoken before a live audience in real life . . . before the comet fell. They were too close, too real; he could smell them. He saw George Christopher making his way through the crowd like an icebreaker, moving triumphantly, like Beowulf displaying the arm of the monster Grendel, and hell, they all looked like that. Triumphant. And waiting expectantly.

"Good news first," he said. "The power plant's still running. We were attacked. This afternoon. We beat them, but it was close. Some of us are dead and some of us are wounded and more will die of the wounds. You already know that most of the Brotherhood wasn't even there—"

Applause and triumphant laughter erupted. Tim should have expected that, from the warriors who'd decimated the New Brotherhood's main force, but he hadn't. He was jolted. Where did these yahoos get off, drinking and dancing and bragging while the men and women Tim Hamner had left behind waited to die? When quiet came he spoke in anger.

"General Baker is dead. The New Brotherhood isn't," Tim said. He watched the reaction. Anger. Incredulity.

"They won't come here again," someone shouted. There were more cheers.

"Let him talk. What happened?" George Christopher demanded. The room was silent again.

"The Brotherhood came at us with boats, the first time," Tim said. "It wasn't hard to drive them off. Then we heard on the radio that you were fighting them, and we figured that would be the end of it, when you said you'd won." He gripped the lectern, remembering the shouting celebration they'd held in the San Joaquin plant after news of the Stronghold victory.

"But they did come back. Today. They had a big raft. Sandbags around it. Mortars. They stayed out of range of anything we had, and they were blowing us apart. One of the shells got a steam line, live steam, and Price's people had a hell of a time putting it back together. Another shell got Jack Ross."

Tim watched George Christopher lose his triumphant grin.

"Jack was alive when we took him off the boat and put him in the van. But he was dead when we got here," Tim said. "Another mortar went off just in front of me. It hit the sandbags we'd put on top of the cooling tower, where we had the radio. It killed the guy next to me and blew the

627

radio apart, and it punched a piece of shrapnel into m
hipbone. It's still there.

"They kept that up. Standing off where we couldn't shoo
back. Price's people had made some cannon. Muzzle-loader
made out of pipe, powered by compressed air. They weren
accurate enough. We couldn't hit the barge. And the damne
mortar shells kept dropping on us. Baker took some troop
out in boats. That didn't do any good either. The Brother
hood had machine guns and the boats couldn't get clos
enough—they had those sandbags anyway. Finally Bake
brought the boats back. He put everybody off."

In the corner of his eye Tim saw Maureen in the doorwa
of the Mayor's office. She stood behind her father, her han
on his shoulder. Eileen was near her.

"We had a racing boat we used as a tug," Tim said. *"Cindy
Lu.* Johnny told Barry Price, 'I used to be a fighter pilot
They always taught us there was one way not to miss.' The
he took *Cindy Lu* out at top speed and rammed her right int
the barge. Covered the raft with burning gasoline. He'
carried some extra gasoline and thermit on the deck. Afte
that the Brotherhood came on with their other boats, but the
had to come in range of our stuff, and we did some damage
Finally they left."

"Ran away," George Christopher said. "They always run.

"They didn't run," Tim said. "They retreated. There wa
some crazy white-haired guy standing in plain sight on on
of the boats. We kept shooting at him, but we never hit him
He was shouting at them to kill us. Last I heard, he still wa
They'll be back."

Tim paused to see what effect he'd had. Not enough. He'
killed the gay mood of the party, but all he saw was resent
ment and sorrow. Nothing else.

"They killed fourteen of us, counting Jack. Hit mayb
three times that many, and a lot of them will die. There's
nurse and some medicines, but no doctor. We need one. W
need another radio." Their looks: anger, sorrow, resentment
They knew what he'd say next. He went doggedly on. "Wha
we need most is reinforcements. We can't take anothe
attack like that one. I don't think gas bombs will do it
either. We need guns. Machine guns you took from the New
Brotherhood would help. But mostly we need men, becaus
it takes just about all the power-plant staff on standby jus
to keep the place going in case there's a hit on the plant
Price's people are . . ." He fumbled for words. Hell, i
would sound corny. So what? "They're magnificent. I saw

guy wade into a cloud of live steam. *Live steam.* He walked right into it to turn a valve, to turn the steam off. He was still alive when I left, but there wasn't any point in bringing him here.

"Another of the power workers spliced live wires. Thousands of volts, and he worked on it hot while mortar bombs fell around him. Baker's dead. They're still alive. And they need help. We need help. I'm going back." He couldn't look at Eileen as he said that.

He felt someone behind him. Al Hardy had climbed onto the podium. He came to the left side of the lectern and stood there with his hand held up for attention. When he spoke, it was with an orator's voice that rolled about the large room. "Thank you, Tim," he said. "You are persuasive. Of course you want to go back. But the question is, have we anything to gain? How many people are there at the nuclear plant? Because we have boats, and now we have food, and we can bring all of them here. It will not be hard to evacuate that plant, and I'm sure we will have no trouble getting volunteers for the job."

Harvey Randall came in from the hospital in time to hear Tim's report begin. He'd come in the back way, through the Mayor's office, and he found himself next to Maureen. When Tim told of what had happened to Baker, he was there, with his hand on her arm, but lightly. She wasn't going to faint or scream; she may have been crying, but even that wasn't obvious. And Harvey didn't want to be obtrusively present, not now.

He was thinking: Son of a bitch! Maureen was taking it better than Delanty. The black astronaut seemed ready to murder. Well, that figured. Baker's other two companions weren't in the room. Leonilla was operating on the gut-shot policeman, with Comrade helping her.

(They called him Comrade now. Brigadier Pieter Jakov was the last Communist, and proud of it, and it avoided the difficulty of his name.)

The Senator's face was ashen gray and his hands were clasped tightly in his lap. There went one of his plans, Harvey thought. It struck him, then: One prince was dead, and one was enthralled by a witch.

George Christopher wasn't alone. Marie stood with him: Marie, the only woman in the room in stockings and heels as well as skirt and sweater and simple jewelry; and she and

George stood as a couple, not as two single people. Whenever anyone got too close to Marie or ogled her too suggestively, George's face clouded.

Three princes. One was killed by ogres. One was spellbound by a witch. The third was standing beside the princess, and the enemy had been defeated. The need for fighting men was not over, but it was no longer critical. Now the Stronghold needed builders—and *that* Harvey Randall could do. I'm crown prince now, he thought. Son of a bitch.

But Tim Hamner was calling for a new battle!

Harvey, fresh from his work with the crossbow, was thinking helplessly: Shut up, shut up! When Al Hardy came up to offer the power-plant personnel refuge at the Stronghold, Harvey wanted to cheer, and some of Hardy's audience did cheer. But Rick Delanty still looked like murder, and Tim Hamner . . .

"We won't leave," Tim said. "Use your boats to bring us men and guns and ammunition! Not for us to run away. We're not leaving."

"Be reasonable," Al Hardy said. His voice projected; it reached all corners of the hall. It projected warmth, friendliness, understanding: a politician's basic skill, and Al Hardy was well trained. Tim was outclassed. "We can feed everyone. We can use engineers and technical people. We lost people to the New Brotherhood, but we lost none of our food; we even captured some of their stores. We not only have enough to eat, we have enough to be well fed during the winter! We can feed everyone, including Deke Wilson's women and children and the few survivors from his area. The New Brotherhood has been hurt, badly hurt"—he paused for the cheers again, and went on just as they died, his timing perfect—"and is now far too weak to attack us again. By spring the few surviving cannibals will be starving—"

"Or eating each other," someone shouted.

"Exactly," Hardy said. "And by spring we'll be able to take their land. Tim, not only do we not need to turn any of our friends away, we need new people to work the lands we have taken or will have in spring. I don't mean for your friends to run. I mean to welcome them as our guests, friends, as new citizens here. Does everyone agree?"

There were shouts. "Hell yeah!" "Glad to have them."

Tim Hamner spread his hands, palms outward, pleading. He wobbled on his damaged hip. There were the beginnings of tears in his eyes. "Don't you understand? The power plant!

We can't leave it, and without help the New Brotherhood will destroy it!"

"No, dammit," Harvey muttered. He felt Maureen stiffen. "No more wars," Harvey said. "We've had enough. Hardy's right." He looked for approval from Maureen, but only got a blank stare.

George Christopher was laughing. It carried, like Al Hardy's voice. "They're too damned weak to attack anything," he shouted. "First we crunched them. Then you did. They won't stop running until they're back to Los Angeles. Who needs to worry about them? We chased the bastards fifty miles ourselves."

More laughter in the room. Then Maureen broke away from Harvey and moved past her father. When she spoke her voice did not carry the way Hardy's did, but it commanded silence, and the crowd listened to her. "They still have their weapons," she said. "And, Tim, you said their leaders are still alive. . . ."

"Well, one of them is," Hamner said. "The crazy preacher."

"Then some of them will try to destroy the power plant again," Maureen said. "As long as he's alive, he'll keep trying." She turned to Hardy. "Al, you know that. You heard Hugo Beck. You know."

"Yes," Hardy said. "We can't protect the plant. But again I invite everyone there to come live here. With us."

"Damn right, the Brotherhood's no threat to *us*," George Christopher said. "They won't be back."

"But they—" Whatever Al Hardy had been about to say, he cut himself off at a wave from Senator Jellison. "Yes, sir," Hardy asked. "Do you want to come up here, Senator?"

"No." Jellison stood. "Let's cut this short," he said. His voice was thick with either drunkenness or exhaustion, and everyone knew he hadn't been drinking. "We are agreed, are we not? The Brotherhood is not strong enough to harm us here in our valley. But their leaders are still alive, and they have enough strength to destroy the power plant. It is not that they are strong, but that the plant is fragile."

Hamner jumped on that. He was interrupting the Senator, but he didn't care. He knew he should speak carefully, weighing every word, but he was too tired, the sense of urgency was too strong. "Yes! We're fragile. Like that whale!" He pointed to the glass case. "Like the last piece of Stueben crystal in the world. If the power stops for one day—"

631

"Beautiful and fragile," Al Hardy's voice cut in. "Senator, did you have something else to say?"

The massive head shook. "Only this. Think carefully. This may be the most important decision we have made since . . . that day." He sat, heavily. "Go on, please," he said.

Hardy looked worriedly at the Senator, then motioned to one of the women near him. He spoke to her, too low for Harvey to hear what he said, and the woman left. Then he stood at the lectern again. "Fragile and beautiful," he said. "But not much use to a farming community—"

"No use?" Tim exploded. "Power! Clean clothes! Light—"

"Luxuries," Al Hardy said. "Are they worth our lives? We're a farm community. The balance is delicate. Not many weeks ago we did not know if we would live through the winter. Now we know we can. A few days ago we did not know whether we could resist the cannibals. We did. We are safe, and we have work to do, and we cannot afford more people for a needless war." He looked to George Christopher. "You agree, George? Neither of us runs from a fight—but do we have to run *to* one?"

"Not me," Christopher said. "We won our war."

There were murmurs of agreement. Harvey stepped forward, intending to join in. Not another war. Not another afternoon with the crossbow . . .

He felt Maureen beside him. She looked up at him, pleading in her eyes. "Don't let them do this," she said. "Make them understand!" She dropped her hand from Harvey's arm and bent over the Senator. "Dad. Tell them. We have to . . . to fight. To save that power plant."

"Why?" Jellison asked. "Haven't we had enough war? It doesn't matter. I couldn't order it. They wouldn't go."

"They would. If you told them, they would."

He didn't answer. She turned back to Harvey.

Randall stared at her without comprehension. "Listen," he said. "Listen to Al."

"Reinforcements wouldn't be enough, Tim," Al Hardy was saying. "Chief Hartman and the Senator and the Mayor and I, we looked at the problem this afternoon. We hadn't forgotten you! And the cost is too high. You said it yourself, the plant is fragile. It's not enough to put a garrison in there, to keep it filled with troops. You have to keep the Brotherhood from dropping *one* mortar shell in the right place. Tell me, if that plant worker hadn't turned off the steam valve, wouldn't that have done it?"

"Yes," Tim snarled. "That would have finished us. So a

632

twenty-year-old kid parboiled himself to save the plant. And General Baker made *his* decision."

"Tim, Tim," Hardy pleaded. "You don't understand. It wouldn't do any good just to send reinforcements. Look, I'll send volunteers. As many as want to go, and with plenty of food and ammunition . . ."

Tim's face showed joy, but only for a moment.

". . . but it won't do any good, and you know it. To save that power plant we will have to send out all our strength, *everyone*, not to defend the plant, but to attack the New Brotherhood. Pursue them, fight them, wipe them out. Take all their weapons. Then set up patrols around the edges of the lake. Keep the enemy at least a mile from the plant. It would take all our strength, Tim, and the cost would be horrible."

"But—"

"Think about it," Hardy said. "Patrols. Spies. An army of occupation. All to stop *one* fanatic from getting *one* hit on *one* crucial piece of equipment and putting it out of commission for *one* day. That's the task. Isn't it?"

"For now," Tim said. "But given peace and quiet for a few weeks, Price will have Number Two on line. Then as long as either works, the other can be repaired."

The roomful of survivors was sobering now, most of them, because the last of the liquor was as dead as the coffee supply. They muttered to each other, spoke, argued, and they seemed to Harvey to be divided in opinion, but the strength was against Tim. As it should be, Harvey thought. Not more war.

But . . . he looked at Maureen. Now she was crying openly. Because of Baker? Baker had made his choice, and Maureen wouldn't let him be wasted? Her eyes met his. "Talk to them," she said. "Make them understand."

"I don't understand myself," Harvey said.

"What we can afford," she said. "A civilization has the ethics it can afford. We can't afford much. We can't afford to take care of our enemies—you know about that."

He shuddered. He knew about that.

Leonilla Malik came in the back way, through the Mayor's office. She bent over the Senator. "I am told that you need me," she said.

"Who told you that?" Jellison demanded.

"Mister Hardy."

"I'm all right. Get back to your hospital."

"Doctor Valdemar is on duty. I have a few minutes."

She stood slightly behind the Senator, and she watched him carefully, her expression professional—and concerned.

"We must count the costs," Al Hardy was saying. "You ask us to risk everything. We have assured survival. We are alive. We have fought the last battle. Tim, electric lights are not worth throwing that away."

Tim Hamner swayed from exhaustion and pain. "We won't leave," he said. "We'll fight. All of us." But his voice was not strong; he sounded beaten.

"Do something," Maureen said. "Tell them." She gripped Harvey's arm.

"You tell them."

"I can't. But you're a hero, now. Your force held them—"

"You stand pretty high yourself," Harvey said.

"Let's both tell them," Maureen said. "Come with me. We'll talk to them. Together."

And that's a hell of an offer, Harvey thought. For the power plant itself? For Johnny Baker's memory? Because she was jealous of Marie with George Christopher? Whatever her motive, she'd just offered him the leadership of the Stronghold—and her look made it plain that he wasn't going to get another such.

"We'd have to hold their territory," Al Hardy was saying. "Deke couldn't do it—"

"We could!" Tim cried. "You beat them! We could."

Hardy nodded gravely. "Yes, I suppose we could. But first we have to take it—and we can't do that with magic weapons. Grenades and gas bombs aren't much use in the attack. We'd lose people. A lot of people. How many lives are your electric lights worth?"

"Many," Leonilla Malik said. Her voice didn't carry very far. "If I had had proper lights for the operating theater last night, I could have saved ten more at least."

Maureen was moving toward the platform. Harvey hesitated, then went with her. What would he say? Men would charge machine guns for a cause. *Viva la republic!* For King and Country! Duty, Honor, Country! Remember the Alamo! *Liberté! Égalité! Fraternité!* But nobody had ever gone over the top shouting "A Higher Standard of Living!" or "Hot Showers and Electric Razors!"

And what about me? he thought. When I get up there, I'm committed. When the New Brotherhood comes over the water with their new raft and their mortars, I'd have to be first into the boats, first to attack, first to be blown apart.

And what could I possibly be yelling that would make me do it?

He remembered the battle: the noise, loneliness, fear; the shame of running, the terror when you didn't. Running was a decision of the moment, but *not* running went on and on. A rational army *would* run away. He caught her arm to hold her back.

She turned, and her look was . . . full of concern. Sympathy. She spoke, low, so no one else would hear. "We all have to do our jobs," she said. "And this is right. Don't you see that?"

The short delay had been too much; Al Hardy was retiring, having made his point. The crowd was turning away, talking among themselves. Harvey heard snatches of conversation:

"Hell, I don't know. I sure as hell don't want to fight anymore." "Dammit, Baker got killed for that place. Wasn't that worth something?" "I'm tired, Sue. Let's go home."

Before Hardy could leave the platform, Rick Delanty barred his way. "The Senator said this was an important decision," he said. "Let's talk about it. Now." Delanty was no longer planning murder, Harvey saw with relief. But he seemed determined. "Al, you say we'll live through the winter. Let's talk about that."

Hardy shrugged. "If you choose. I think it has all been said."

Delanty's grin was crafty, artificial. "Oh, hell, Al, we're all here and the liquor's gone, and tomorrow it's back to moving rocks. Let's talk it all out right now. We can survive the winter?"

"Yes."

"But without coffee. That's all gone."

Hardy frowned. "Yes."

"How are we fixed for clothing? There are glaciers coming, and the clothes are rotting off our backs. Can we dig anything out of underwater department stores?"

"Some plastics, maybe. It can wait, now that we don't have to worry about the New Brotherhood getting there first." Oddly, there was no cheering this time. "We'll have to make most of our clothing. Or shoot it." Hardy smiled.

"Transportation? The cars and trucks are dying like sterile beasts, aren't they? Will we have to eat the horses?"

Al Hardy ran his hands through his hair. "No. For awhile I thought . . . No. Horses don't breed fast, but we'll have the trucks for years yet."

"What else have we run out of? Penicillin?"

"Yes—"

"Aspirin? And the liquor. No anesthetics of any kind."

"We'll be able to ferment liquor!"

"So. We'll live. Through this winter, and the next one and the one after that." Rick paused, but before Hardy could say anything, he thundered, "As peasants! We had a ceremony here today. An award, to the kid who caught the most rats this week. And we can look forward to that for the rest of our lives. To our kids growing up as rat catchers and swineherds. Honorable work. Needed work. Nobody puts it down. But . . . don't we want to hope for something better?

"And we're going to keep slaves," Delanty said. "Not because we want to. Because we need them. *And we used to control the lightning!*"

The phrase struck Harvey Randall with a physical shock. He saw it hit the others, too. A lot of them. They stood, unable to turn away.

"Sure we can huddle here in our valley," Delanty shouted. "We can stay here and be safe and our kids can grow up herding pigs and shoveling sewage. There's a lot here to be proud of, because it's so much more than what might have been—but is it enough? Is it enough for *us* to be safe when we leave everybody else out in the cold? You all say how sorry you are to have to turn people away. To have to send people Outside. Well, we've got the chance now. We can make all of Outside, the whole damn San Joaquin Valley, as safe as we are.

"Or there's another way. We can stay here, safe as . . . as ground squirrels. But if we take the easy way this time, we'll take it next time. And the next, and the next, and in fifty years your kids will hide under the bed when they hear the thunder! The way everybody used to hide from the great thunder gods. Peasants always believe in thunder gods.

"And the comet. *We* know what it was. In ten more years we'd have been able to push the damned thing out of our way! I've been in space. I won't go there again, but your children could! Hell yes! Give us that electric plant and twenty years and we'll be in space again. We know how, and all it takes is power, and that power's right out there, not fifty miles from here, if we've just got guts enough to save it. Think about it. Those are the choices. Go on and be good peasants, safe peasants, superstitious peasants—or have worlds to conquer again. To control the lightning again."

He paused, but not long enough to let anyone else speak.

"I'm going," he said. "Leonilla?"

"Certainly." She moved toward the platform.

"And I," Comrade General Jakov shouted from the back of the room. "For the lightning."

"Now." Harvey slapped Maureen's butt and bounded ahead of her onto the platform, moving quickly before the moment died away. Decisions were simple, now that he knew what he'd be shouting. "Task Force Randall?"

"Sure," someone shouted. And then Maureen joined him, and another farmer came forward, and Tim Hamner, and Mayor Seitz. Marie Vance and George Christopher were arguing. Good! Marie belonged to Task Force Randall, unless there was a Task Force Christopher. Christopher would join them.

Al Hardy stood in confusion, wanting to speak but held by the command in Maureen's eyes.

He could stop them, Harvey Randall thought. It wouldn't take much to stop them. Once everyone's committed it will be hard to back down, but right now this bandwagon can be stopped, or it can be shoved forward so hard nothing can stop it, and Al Hardy has that power. . . .

Hardy was looking past Maureen now, at the Senator. The old man was half rising from his chair, and he gasped for breath before he fell back into it. Leonilla ran toward him, but he waved her away, beckoning to Hardy. "Al," he gasped.

Leonilla had her medical bag in the office. She threw it open and seized a hypodermic needle, fought away the Senator's feeble resistance as she ripped open his jacket and shirt. She swabbed his chest quickly and thrust the needle directly into his chest, near the heart.

Al Hardy tore through the crowd like a madman. He knelt beside the gasping man. Jellison thrashed and writhed in the chair, his hands reaching for his chest while Chief Hartman and others held them. His eyes focused on Al Hardy. "Al."

"Yes, sir." Hardy's voice was choked, almost inaudible. He bent closer.

"Al. Give my children the lightning again." The voice was clear, projecting through the hall, and for a moment Jellison's eyes were bright, but then he slumped into the chair, and they heard only a thin whisper that faded to nothing. "Give them the lightning again."

Epilogue

The Earth is just too small and fragile a basket for the human race to keep all its eggs in.

Robert A. Heinlein

Tim Hamner stood at the top of a low hill. Paper crackled in his breast pocket when he shifted weight.

The long slope behind him buzzed with activity. Animal teams dragged harrows through the hard soil, while methanol-powered tractors worked with deep plows in adjacent fields. Myriads of white flecks gleamed in the soil behind the harrows. Enriched by mustard gas and the defeat of the New Brotherhood Army, this land would produce in abundance.

Three electric carts hummed along the road below. Another stood beside Tim Hamner, ready for his use. It was time to get back down the hill and go to work, but he stood a few moments longer, enjoying bright sunshine and the clear blue sky of spring. It was a glorious day.

Before him was the San Joaquin Sea. Much of what had been underwater was now a vast swampland. Directly ahead was a low island in the sea: the prisoner colony, where those of the Brotherhood who hadn't wanted to go into permanent exile worked to grow crops. Jakov's preserve. They called him "Comrade" now . . . and Comrade hadn't given up communism. But Marxist theory said that history followed definite stages, slave society to feudal, feudal to capitalist—and the Valley was barely past the slave stage of

history. The earth would not be ready for communism for a long time. Meanwhile Comrade was willing to re-educate the prisoners.

Tim shrugged. Comrade and Hooker kept them organized, and they grew their own crops, and if they escaped nobody cared.

Further to his left, distant in the south, he saw the rising plumes of steam from the nuclear power plant. Closer, the work crews stringing power lines. In another two weeks they would have electricity in the Stronghold. Tim tried to imagine what that new life would be like, but it was difficult. The winter had been hard. Damned hard. Eileen's baby had almost died, and was still in the hospital. The infant mortality rate was above fifty percent, but it was slowly falling now; and Forrester's notes showed that when they recovered his books from Tujunga they would know how to make penicillin. Forrester's notes. That was Tim's job, to transcribe the reels and reels of tape Dan Forrester had dictated before he died. They could have made insulin, maybe, if they hadn't committed themselves to saving the power plant; and of course Forrester had known that. The winter had cost them the life of their magician, as it had so many other lives. To learn that a friend had survived, that was always good. Tim patted his pocket.

The past could hit you across the back of the head, no warning. Whap! Tim Hamner patted the telegram in his pocket. Half of a comet! Kitt's Peak had confirmed his sighting. He shook his head violently and laughed at himself. It was only the rain-wrinkled scrap of paper Harry the Mailman had brought yesterday, an IOU for $250,000.

Harry Stimms was alive! Now, what would he take for that IOU? A job at the power plant? Stimms must have mechanical skills, and the power plant boys owed Tim. Failing that . . . could he promote a pregnant cow? That'd be worth $250,000 easy. Tim gazed into the sky, enjoying himself.

A clear thin line crossed the sky, the tip of it moving forward even as he watched. For a second he still did not know what it was. Shout a warning! But what did we used to call that?

"C-contrail! Jet plane!"

They'd heard something from Colorado Springs: that some of the aircraft had survived. Harvey and Maureen would have to come to terms with Colorado Springs when they got back from visiting a septic tank in Tujunga. But though they'd

heard it on the radio, it was not the same as seeing that
clean white line across the sky. He'd forgotten how beautiful
that could be.

Tim waved solemnly at the plane. "You can fly," he said.
His voice rose. "You can fly. But we control the lightning."

*The asteroid was a child of the maelstrom: a rough nugget
of nickel-iron with some stony strata, three miles along its
long axis. No man had ever seen a mastodon when the passing of mighty Jupiter plucked the nugget from its orbit and
flung it out toward interstellar space.*

*It was on the second lap of its long, narrow elliptical
orbit. The iron surface was frosted with strange ices now, as
it passed the peak of the curve and began to coast back
toward the Sun.*

*And the black giant was there. Its ring of cometary snow-
balls glowed broad and beautiful in starlight. Infrared light
traced bands and whorls in its stormy surface. It was the
only major mass out here between the stars, and the
asteroid curved toward it and increased speed.*

*Infrared light bathed and thawed the frosted iron. The
ringed planet grew huge.*

*The asteroid plunged through the plane of the ring at
twelve miles per second. Battered and pocked with glowing
craters, it receded, carrying in its own small gravitational
field a spray of icy masses from the ring. They came like
attendants, ahead and behind, in a pattern like the curved
arms of a spiral galaxy.*

*The asteroid and a score of comets pulled free of the black
giant and began their long fall into the maelstrom.*